The Only Place to Be

THE ONLY PLACE TO BE

A Novel by

Joan Juliet Buck

Random House New York

 Published in the United States by Random House, Inc., New York and simultaneously in Canada by Random House of Canada Limited, Toronto.

Grateful acknowledgment is made to the following for permission to reprint previously published material:

Chappell Aznavour S.A.: Several lines from "Tu Veux" by Charles Aznavour. Paroles and musique Charles Aznavour © 1964 by Editions Musicales Charles Aznavour, Chappell Aznavour S.A.

Spectorious Music Corp.: Several lines from "From the Underworld" by Howard Blaikley. © 1967 by Lynn Music Ltd. for the United States & Canada Spectorious Music Corp. Used by permission. All rights reserved.

Library of Congress Cataloging in Publication Data
Buck, Joan Juliet.
The only place to be.
I. Title.
PS3552.U33305 813'.54 81-48291
ISBN 0-394-52300-8 AACR2

Manufactured in the United States of America
Typography and binding design by J. K. Lambert
98765432
First Edition

To John

Contents

PART III ||| REAL LIFE

Part I
FAMILY LIFE

1.

Manners

Iris Bromley was brought up in Paris, where seven is the age of reason. By the time she was six she had learned from watching her mother that the important things in life were famous people, fine houses and good manners. Iris's mother, Charlene, cultivated the first, arranged to be set up in the second, and made a fetish of the third.

Notions of ethics and grammar she left to Iris's school, le Cours Victor Hugo, an institution in the sixteenth arrondissement devoted to turning sour tots into haughty debutantes. Iris's little classmates were destined to be baronesses and marquises or at least *de* something-or-other one day, if they weren't already. Better still, the teachers seemed to appreciate Iris. They rewarded her good conduct with a cross, which Iris wore with modest pride. It hung on her chest from a taffeta ribbon, a large blue-and-white enamel Maltese cross flamboyant enough to have come from the Chanel Boutique. To Charlene's eye, the cross bursting across the flat surface of Iris's tailored gray cardigan had a definite *je ne sais quoi;* as Charlene operated on the principle that an unreported life was not worth living, she took Iris to lunch at Le Relais Plaza, which in the spring of 1956 was the best place in Paris to pretend to eat lunch while sniffing out the strength and direction of the prevailing social winds.

They sat at a table near the bar: Charlene, a small red-haired woman with the tiny proportions that only rich Americans or the seriously ill can achieve, and her small, dark daughter. Iris, of course, wore her cross; Charlene was dressed with a certain boldness in the latest style, and wore jewelry of the primitive design favored a quarter of a century ago: freshly mined hunks of mineral imprisoned in smudges of gold wire were skewered into the nubbly curry-colored tweed of her suit. At the other tables beautiful women in little hats giggled softly, pale mink coats spilling over the backs of their chairs to reveal satin linings embroidered with flowers and initials. A group of men in business suits, with the tanned faces of those whose business is conducted solely on polo fields or the decks of yachts, hugged the bar. At the end of the counter, long gladioli stretched from a high vase toward the ceiling. The sun shone through the tall windows by the door, but farther back, where the restaurant rose into a terrace of more tables, a sleek beige gloom prevailed, conducive to longer lunches and chilling gossip. The air palpitated with conflicting smells, the sharp green of Je Reviens, the sienna thrusts of Detchema, the unctuous false repose of Shalimar, the brittle spikes of Femme. The sounds of laughter merged and collided much as the smells did; here and there a conversation spilled over from its own table to silence its neighbors with the glamour of dropped names and privileged information.

They ate eggs Benedict, which reminded Charlene of home, or at least of the Beverly Hills Hotel. Just as she had hoped, French acquaintances came over to comment on the manifest excellence of such a child. *"C'est très bien, il faut continuer comme ça,"* said Yves Furet, with just enough stern paternalism to show that his standards were as high as those of the Cours Victor Hugo. Jenny Wright, a timid young woman who wrote the society pages of the New York *Herald Tribune* Paris edition, came over and assured Charlene that no French school had ever given a cross to an American child before.

"She's practically a native," said Charlene. "I have to get her to translate to the cook for me."

Iris was watching a tall black man dressed in a red outfit with ballooning pants and a little bolero; he had a red fez on his head—she didn't know the name for it, but she recognized it from the ads for Banania, the banana-flavored chocolate drink—and he was carrying a round glass jug of coffee from table to table. As he approached, Iris shrank away from him. Charlene motioned that he was to fill her cup and slapped Iris's wrist.

"You mustn't do that, it's not polite," she said.

"But I'm afraid of him," said Iris.

"You mustn't be," said Charlene. "He's very special. Everyone knows him and loves him. He's famous."

Famous. Iris understood at once. Famous people were not like the rest. There were special rules for them: they could dress as they pleased, burp, belch, stub out their cigarettes where they felt like it, arrive late, leave all their food on their plate. It didn't matter. Ordinary mortals, adults and children alike, were subjected to the laws of good behavior.

Iris watched as the heads of the men at the bar turned to follow the progress of a tall blond woman with sunglasses and a loose coat that she held at her throat with one nervous gloved hand. Ladies at other tables leaned forward and whispered to each other without taking their eyes off the blonde. Iris saw on Charlene's face a look that combined eagerness with ecstasy. "Why are you smiling like that?" she asked her mother.

"It's Sheila McCoy," said Charlene. "I didn't even know she was in town." She raised her arm, not far enough to make the imploring wave her instinct prompted, but high enough to indicate to anyone watching that there was something unusual about her table. Sheila McCoy's eyes caught the sudden asymmetry of the gesture and fixed on Charlene, who shouted, "Sheila! Sheila!" and then sat back.

Sheila McCoy hesitated: she counted among her acquaintance three redheads, and all of them were bigger than this one, who barely reached over the tablecloth. On the other hand, she had only come into the restaurant for a quick drink before she met her musical arranger in the lobby of the Plaza Athénée, and saw that she had already attracted too much attention to be able to sneak a brandy at the bar. She turned and started toward Charlene; the folds of her coat impeded the flow of her movement, sticking to the plush covers of the chairs, bunching up into thick obstacles as she tried to push forward between two tables; it was in a state of some irritation that she finally reached the table.

"Charlene O'Malley," said Charlene, holding out her hand and rising from the table. "The Magnolia Gardens, remember? You were still Gertie Tamlyn then."

"Why my God," said Sheila. "Yes. You look wonderful."

"So do you," said Charlene. "It's wonderful to see you. Do you want to join us?"

"Only for a second," said Sheila, feeling the eyes of the room on her back and furious at herself for her lack of grace in negotiating her arrival. "I need a drink, anyway." Charlene held out a chair for her, and Sheila sat down, putting a large white patent makeup case on her knees. Charlene registered how ugly it was before assuring Sheila that it was safe to leave it next to her on the floor. "I couldn't do that," said Sheila. "It's got my jewels in it."

"This is Iris," said Charlene. "Iris, curtsy to the lady." Iris slid out of her chair and, facing the famous guest, went into her little routine: point right foot forward, slide to the right, point harder, slide it behind, and dip. Sheila watched Iris and then gave her her hand; Iris took it and felt the bump of rings beneath the gummy beige suede. "*Bonjour, madame,*" she said.

"What's with the cross, she joined a religious order or something?" asked Sheila, who was not one to mince words.

Charlene touched Iris for the first time that day. She stroked her head. "She won it at school. What do you want to drink?"

"I'm on the wagon because of the show, so I'll just have a little brandy and soda to keep my energy up."

"Tell me about the show," said Charlene, and while she listened to Sheila she allowed herself a few little glances beyond her table, just to make sure that they were being observed. She basked in spilled limelight.

Maintaining one's position was no easy task, however.

"Who's doing your hair for the show?" she asked, watching Sheila's bleached split ends dance around her head.

"I brought the guy who always does me."

"You need your nails touched up?" continued Charlene. Sheila looked at her hands without removing her gloves: through the soft suede, the outline of sharp ovals could be seen at her fingertips. "They're okay," she said.

Charlene sought another weak spot. "I can show you where the safe is, to put your jewelry away. I used to live here when I first came to Paris. The hotel's like a second home to me."

"I just took it out of there," said Sheila. "I'm going to be photographed before the rehearsal, and I thought I'd wear some." Charlene was not to be defeated. She led with her only advantage. "Life in Paris is so exciting. Every day here is so enthralling that I don't have a minute to think."

"Your husband works here?" inquired Sheila, a touch automatically.

"Maybe you know him. Saul Hyott . . . ?"

"The guy with the dancers?"

"He doesn't have them anymore. He's an entrepreneur now."

"Ah."

"I must go for my fitting at Dior," said Charlene. "Iris, hurry up and finish."

"*Christian* Dior?" asked Sheila. Charlene smiled. Couture always got them interested. She had her hooked now, and could afford to attack. "Listen," she said, pointing to the white case, "I know a place where you can get a really good-looking bag instead of that." Sheila stared at it: she had taken in Charlene's suit, and although it was not her style—she preferred big prints, organzas and voluminous coats—she had to admit that Charlene had Parisian chic. "You do?" she said. "It's very handy."

"That's the problem with America," said Charlene. "Things are handy instead of being elegant. Come with me, I'll take you to Hermès for something that really is worthy of you."

"Hermès is a fortune," said Sheila, who had always been tight with her money.

"*Then,*" said Charlene, her voice rising in the excitement of revelation, "there's a place where they copy every single thing Hermès makes, at half price. It's wonderful."

"What's the address?" asked Sheila.

"Oh no," said Charlene. "You can't just walk in there off the street."

"Do I have to call first?" Sheila had taken a pen from her case and was ready to write on one of the paper napkins on the table.

"They have to know you," said Charlene, "before they'll let you in. But I'm a good customer there. I'll take you, whenever you want."

"Is it really cheaper?" asked Sheila, not to be won over so easily.

"Half the price! And the leather is just as good."

"I don't think I'll have the time," said Sheila, uncharmed by the idea of being Charlene's protégée. "I'm rehearsing every day."

"We'll be at your opening," said Charlene. "Saul always takes me to the openings. We'll probably be with Edith Piaf and Jojo Cléry, the boxer."

"Good, I'll see you then," said Sheila. Charlene realized these names meant nothing to an American. Quickly she continued: "And then I think we should give a party for you. There must be lots of people you'd like to see here. Huston's in town, and Zanuck, and Art Buchwald, of course, he's so funny, do you get to see his column in America? And then Aly Khan might be around unless he's gone to the country, although he usually goes later than this."

Sheila began to show some interest. She made no move to leave the table. Charlene's patter soared. "Of course, Burt Lancaster and Kirk are here, making that circus film, and Gina is here too, doing something about a church with Anthony Quinn. Oh, it would be such a nice party!" Charlene lit a cigarette.

"Well, maybe Saturday would be fun, after the last show, or right at the end of the run, it's only a week. Have you ever met Maurice Chevalier?"

"Maurice? He's one of Saul's best friends."

Suddenly Sheila felt more comfortable in Charlene's company. "I thought you'd married a guy who was some kind of farmer," she said.

"A farmer? You've got to be joking."

"No, it's coming back to me now. Soula told me you'd married a farmer. Remember Soula?"

"Oh, Soula!" said Charlene with scorn. "She's a big star now too, and she didn't have a quarter of your talent."

"She married a French director, and I think she lives in Paris. Maybe you could track her down, we could have a reunion!"

Soula, thought Charlene, I never liked her. "I'd love to do that," she answered. "She'll be so surprised."

"Why did she tell me you married a farmer?" asked Sheila.

"Well, Tyler, my husband, was in agriculture," she said. "He owned plantations. Groves, oranges."

"Huh," said Sheila, now bored. "I thought you were married to Saul Hyott."

"Sheila," Charlene answered, "I know I can tell you this because you're sophisticated. Paris isn't like the States"—she lowered her voice, in the pretense of keeping from Iris a fact of which the child was necessarily aware—"I'm . . . I'm not married to Saul. The servants and everybody think we are, but we're not."

Sheila, unfazed, looked at her watch. "I'd better get to the lobby, some poor guy's been waiting for me there for twenty minutes. Call me later. Room two twenty-seven."

"You don't mind that I'm not married to Saul?" asked Charlene, imputing to her friend standards of decency that were part of her memory of the States, and hoping, just a little, to shock.

"Honey," said Sheila, "why should I mind? I'm a dyke."

Iris, who had followed the conversation with great and silent application, watched Sheila leave the table, pushing the bulk of her coat before her, and asked, "Maman, what is a dyke?"

"You speak when you are spoken to," said Charlene, who then ordered *fraises*—big ordinary strawberries, not *fraises des bois,* which were too exotic for a child—for Iris and more coffee for herself. As she drank it she reflected that the mere fact of living in Paris—Paris, France, to the unsophisticated—imbued her life with a glamour that made someone like

Sheila McCoy seem, for all her loose talk, oddly provincial. Expatriatism offered the best of many worlds: with the privacy of distance, far from home, she could be who she wanted to be with no one watching but foreigners and other racy types like herself, brave people who had taken their destiny in hand. Those too dull or fearful to travel had been automatically eliminated. From the vantage point of her table at the Relais Plaza, Charlene felt that she owned the town, which for her was inhabited by people who stayed in good hotels or houses they rented for six months at a time. She had not read Henry James or Edith Wharton, and thought Proust was a peculiar version of the verb "to push." To her, the tall green portals in the long streets across the Seine concealed not generations of aristocrats but a smell of drains. Instead of the social citadels of the Faubourg Saint-Germain, she had chosen to storm the undefended bastions of luxury, the shops and couture houses. It was easy: the cash that Saul carried in huge quantities was always welcome, and so, in consequence, was she.

She spoke French, but her relationship with the language was a hostile one, limited to kidnapping certain expressions for use within English. In her first years she had learned restaurant French—*à point, bien cuit, pas de sel, vinaigrette, champagne sec*—and couture French, and shopping French—*c'est trop cher, c'est trop petit, c'est trop grand, avez vous une autre couleur?*—and just a touch of mood French. She was prone to such ills as *chagrin, ennui,* a touch of *mal du siècle.* Too much drinking gave her a *gueule de bois* rather more often than she would have liked to admit. Monthly she had a little *mal au ventre,* and took a *sieste tous les jours.* She no longer went to the movies but to the *cinéma,* although she preferred *projections privées.* Nothing sent her to sleep faster than a *suppositoire,* and she enjoyed shocking raw newcomers with references to her daily *douche,* by which she meant what happened in the shower rather than over the *bidet.* Her *savoir faire* was endless; although she generally described herself as *sans souci* and full of *joie de vivre,* she tolerated no trace of *sans gêne* from those around her.

She read the local paper, which by good luck was written in English and had the same name as the paper her friends took in New York. She read French dirty books, which by another stroke of luck were written and published in English by the Olympia Press. Sometimes, when an allergy to shellfish or something in the air caused her to seek a remedy from the corner *pharmacie,* she was forced to read the directions on a box of salve; and that was the extent of her effort to assimilate. Her doctor, thank God, was the English-speaking heart throb at the American Hospital in Neuilly.

She and Saul mingled with some locals, of course, but they were boxers, actors, singers, whose talent and good luck had freed them from the cloister of nationality. What she called Paris was no more than an idealized no-man's-land that had nothing to do with France.

They walked home (she had no fitting that day, it had been just a detail to flash at Sheila) through the city she thought she knew.

Iris led the way up the Rue Jean-Goujon, where the fishmonger's wife greeted them from her cavern of blue mosaics; past the Boucherie Chevaline, with its immense gold horse's head advertising, alas, horse steaks; past Le Petit Ange, where she lingered tediously at the window, sighing at a little blouse with puffed sleeves and cherries on its collar. They crossed the Avenue d'Iéna and walked up the Rue Dumont d'Urville, where the wide courtyards of the great houses were separated by little doors from which peered interested concierges. At number 127, they turned into their own *cour.*

A tall gate made of iron wrought into the scrolls and acanthus leaves popular under the Third Empire led into a wide cobbled courtyard graced with two chestnut trees. This functioned as a moat: before crossing, visitors had to submit to inspection by Madame Huron, the concierge who lived in the gatehouse. In the interest of symmetry, there was a second gatehouse tucked inside the railings, but it served no function and lacked authority. Its shutters were always closed. The Marquis d'Encient, who owned the courtyard and its contents, had installed an invalid relative of his upstairs, while below a local ragpicker squatted among towering piles of old magazines. Charlene's sense of grandeur was offended by the smells coming from the little lodges: the smoky odor of old and ill-cured ham from the Huron house, and from the other the unmistakable smell of urine and damp newspaper. Still, these inaesthetic assaults set off the magnificence of the trio of houses lining the back of the yard, each with its fan-shaped roof of frosted glass over the front door. Charlene's door was on the right.

The architecture was a testament to the values of the French ruling class in 1860. The ground floor contained three reception rooms and a study; on the floor above, a sumptuous bedroom was lodged between two boudoirs, and flanked by a bathroom dominated by a deep tub with arthritic clawed feet gripping flattened balls. Iris occupied one of the boudoirs, which also served as Saul's dressing room. On the two highest floors the ceilings were lower and the rooms grew barer as they neared the roof. It was here that the servants had lived in the old days. Charlene's cook went home at night and her cleaning lady only did half days, so the only occupant of the top floor was Iris's nanny, the timorous Julie, who awoke during the night to listen for rats.

The rats stayed for the most part in the basement; not in the kitchen —Céleste would never have stood for that. Nor in the laundry room, dank with old steam, nor in the sewing room, which looked out into the back garden. The rats kept to the long passage that led underneath the garden, past the niches housing boilers and pipes and valves, past locked storerooms where the marquis's ancestral trunks were locked away, down to a door beyond which lay the sewers of Paris. The basement provided the essentials for the house: heat, food, and, in case of another revolution, escape.

Julie opened the door for them, and Bijou and Toasty, the Yorkshire terriers, tumbled across the marble floor to Charlene and followed her into the *salon*. Iris automatically headed toward the backstairs, and descended cautiously to the kitchen, where a bag full of homework was waiting for her. "Hello," she said to Céleste, and amended it quickly to "*Bonsoir*." She wasn't always sure what language she should be using. She gave a little shrug, took a *langue de chat* from the cookie tin, and slid onto a chair at the kitchen table. Julie came into the kitchen and began emptying ice into a crystal bucket. "Pour Madame," she said, rolling her eyes. Iris took her history book and her *cahier* from her schoolbag, and licked the end of her ink pencil. "*Jeudi*" she wrote in her notebook, in careful script.

She had been thrown into the deep end of French before she was three, and since then, navigating between two languages, nothing had been simple. If Charlene's perception of French was that it was a necessary adjunct to the good life, Iris's response was more complex. Her knowledge of the language was so thorough that it was to lay syntactical traps for her throughout her life. It was more of a terrarium to her than a mother tongue: she was trapped inside it, looking out, and desperately trying to adjust herself to the actions that its multiple meanings demanded of her. This was not noticed immediately as an affliction: her many mistranslations into English afforded Saul and Charlene much mirth, as when Iris inquired politely if she was "déranging" them when she came into their room. She startled little American children by calling them dirty muzzles, an apt description of their candy-smeared mouths, which, unfortunately, did not carry the same weight as *sales mufles*.

The world about her, the suite of rooms at the Plaza Athénée, the Cours Victor Hugo, and now the apartment were minefields of misapprehension. The paneling in the drawing room was "woodery" to her; the drapes were dyed things; the lampshades, *abats-jours,* were "kill-the-days." The Venetian blinds at school, rattling parallels of ivory plastic, were "jealousies."

Life in the kitchen did nothing to ease Iris's semantic fears. As she sat doing her homework between Julie, who leafed through *Cinémonde, Paris Match* and *Elle* with equal interest, and Céleste, who was cutting things into tiny pieces on her chopping board, Iris that afternoon learned that only the poor paid, that Madame took herself for she didn't know who, that Monsieur seemed to have a lot to do with *la pègre,* whoever Peg was.

Upstairs in the *salon*, Charlene made herself a drink and watched Saul on the telephone. At fifty-two, Saul Hyott managed to be gray and suntanned at the same time, as if pewter ran under his skin. The tailoring of his suits left something to be desired, but he made up for his lack of sartorial finish with personalized jewelry: cuff links that were an S and an H joined by a gold chain, tiepins that made his monogram into a dollar sign (thus: $), a watch whose strap was a series of gold H's. He was not the sort of man one would have found immediately alluring, but he had an infectious laugh, he was generous, and he knew everyone. All Charlene's friends were people she had met through Saul. His connections with show business, and his deeper connection with the gambling worlds of Reno and Miami, gave him the contacts; his easy manner and instant intimacy shored them up, and Charlene, with her brisk attentions, her opening-night telegrams, her solicitous mailing of baby shoes, her devotion to the cause of the art of others, sealed the relationships.

Saul knew the black-market prices on everything, and his were lower. He was the man to get objects and services as diverse as Cadillacs, ringside boxing seats, caseloads of Zippo lighters, whores of all sizes and colors; he could also secure the disappearance of unwanted people, though he rarely went so far. Only his flashing cabochons and twinkling pinky rings gave any indication of his profession. On a Sunday at the races, a passing Rothschild might remark to himself that Saul's pearl-gray tie was a little wide and his shoes a little too new to be entirely respectable, but that was all.

Still fresh from her triumph of the afternoon, Charlene averted her eyes from him. When she was feeling glum, his unkempt bonhomie reassured her: when she was on an up, she sometimes found the physical presence of Saul almost too high a price to pay for the life she was leading. "Forty thousand dollars is nothing!" she heard him shout into the telephone. She hated it when he talked like that, and put on the original-cast album of *Damn Yankees* to drown out the sound of his wheeling deals. She was better than that, and the pictures around here confirmed it.

From every wall duchesses, marquises and ladies, all with bare lashless eyes and long, flabby oval faces, gazed down at her, framed by plaster moldings painted with gold leaf. They hugged little dogs, held baskets, laid long fingers on their skirts. They were the landlord's relatives, and therefore hers.

In the kitchen, Iris was hunched dutifully over her history book. She was puzzled: the picture in front of her showed a pair of strolling players. "Here are two troubadours," she read in French, "who are coming to entertain the lord of the castle and his family. Describe their costumes. Why do they each carry a musical instrument?" She figured them to be an early version of Sheila McCoy, with a musical arranger, on their way to a rehearsal. She looked across at the cabinet, where the blue-and-gold soup tureens were kept. If Sheila McCoy was a troubadour, surely that meant that Charlene was the Lady of the Castle. Then why did her mother act as if Sheila McCoy were more important than she was?

2.

Names

The circumstances that brought Charlene Bromley, née O'Malley, to Paris in the summer of 1953 were somewhat complicated, but their basic elements were to fuel her travels for the next twenty years: alimony, optimism and a new beau. The word "beau" in itself is interesting, as Charlene lacked any connection with the South, and her use of this term to designate the men who at various times in her life were to pay her rent indicated that she lived in a world of willful self-deception. If she said "beau" when she meant lover, protector, boyfriend, it was because she did not enjoy admitting to herself that her responsibility toward the man entailed anything more on her part than the sharing of a few jokes, a bit of hand holding, perhaps a stolen kiss.

Her mother, a strict Hungarian called Coquette, believed only in good deeds and their rewards. Coquette brought up her seven daughters in the Depression in New York's Yorkville section with scant help from her husband, Eddie, a dining-car head steward on the *Twentieth Century* and, later, the *Super Chief.* She had inculcated into her first five daughters a fear of hell that was second only to the fear of being thought a trollop. Her own mother, Ilse, had worked "standing up," as they say, in the dark violin bars of Budapest, and her noisy returns to the apartment in the middle of the night had seemed to the child Coquette to be the unleashing of a thousand devils.

Coquette had a phobic hatred of the smell of cheap perfume, the dust of face powder, the sight of dense red stumps of lipstick in tarnished gold cases. The sight of money lying on any surface—a dressing table, a chest of drawers, a chair—sent her into palpitations. These unreasonable symptoms abated after Ilse's death, when Coquette, pregnant with Charlene, her sixth, had sat vigil at her mother's bed and heard Ilse's last declaration to the effect that God was just. Reassured by these words, Coquette summoned up a feeling of tenderness toward the wayward Ilse, uncorked a bottle of Violette di Parma and inhaled the oily green scent as her mother breathed her last. Having closed Ilse's eyes and allowed the priest in to perform a belated last rite, she scooped up some dusty sticks of Rouge Baiser from the bedside table as a memento, and put them in her bag. Whether the ethos of these artifacts penetrated the amniotic sac where Charlene lay basking, or whether Coquette's softened emotions forced a change in her attitude toward carnal sin, cannot be said. The two youngest O'Malley daughters, Charlene and Josephine, were brought up with wonderful tales of their grandmother who had had regiments drinking out of her slippers solely because she kept her faith in God. Josephine was able to assimilate the contradictions in the myth without questioning them, but Charlene found the juxtaposition of sex appeal and religion confusing. She turned for guidance to *Movie Life, Photoplay, Movie Stars Parade* and any other publications she could find that were dedicated to examining sex appeal and how to get it. None of them mentioned God, but instead devoted a large proportion of their pages to movie stars. Somehow God and the movie stars became magically synonymous to Charlene.

She grew up with a respect for fame so total and exacting that people who were not famous felt inadequate in her presence. Her sisters left her alone; they didn't like the blank way she looked at them. When she was eighteen, she announced that the only place to be was Hollywood. Appalled, Coquette forbade her to leave the house, which caused her to be fired for absenteeism from her job modeling coats on Thirty-eighth Street for Koster's Model Balmacaans. Coquette consulted her priest, Father Ignatius of the Second Irish Church, about the wisdom of allowing her daughter to move to the Devil's playground. Father Ignatius inquired what line of work the girl was currently engaged in, and when Coquette informed him that she had been modeling, he replied, "Seventh Avenue is a temple of Mammon, run by Jews. At least in Hollywood those people are engaged in a form of teaching: Look at *The Bells of St. Mary's.*" Father Ignatius imagined he bore some resemblance to Bing Crosby. Eddie O'Malley, who had waited on many actors as they chugged to Chicago, hazarded that Charlene might care to try acting in a theater before becoming what he called a "fillum star."

Charlene would never have gotten to Hollywood had it not been that her sister Bridget, a nun since the age of sixteen, was transferred by her convent to a job as a cook at the College of the Holy Cross in Los Angeles. To Coquette, Los Angeles was a holier place than Hollywood, and she allowed Charlene to accompany Bridget on the train. From Chicago they were under the watchful eye of their father. Eddie took his lay daughter aside during the trip, and cautioned her never to Do It with a man, and, even more important, never to allow a man to tell other men he'd Done It with her. He did not want this advice to be overheard by Bridget; he thought he should not sully the ears of a nun with such filth. Charlene took her father's advice at face value; she would avoid men, and deal only with movie stars.

The sisters split up at the train station; Bridget was met by her sisters in religion, while Charlene found her way to an all-girl hotel called the Magnolia Gardens that she had read about in *Movie Life*. In her first week there she learned startling details about the sexual merits of various actors who until then had been no more to her than newsprint and fantasy; secondhand gossip brought them excitingly close. She registered with Central Casting as an extra—her professional ambition was limited, one had to say that for her—and waited for something to happen. Before she had the chance to mingle in her first crowd scene, she knew which stars screwed, and how. Whatever vestigial innocence she had brought West soon withered under the onslaught of gossip, and she deeply regretted having given her all to Mr. Koster, her boss on Thirty-eighth Street, when she could have saved herself for Clark Gable. She resolved to get herself a stock of stories as amazing as the ones she was hearing. Aiming for a little originality, she took to hanging around the Farmer's Market rather than Schwab's, and it was there that her first encounter took place over a box of pearl-sized grapes. The man, who was handsome, young, and built like a star, took her for a drive in his red convertible. In the fast breeze of the moment she forgot to inquire what he did; he was the best-looking man who had ever looked at her, and she assumed he could only be some star she hadn't caught up with yet. His name, he said, was Tyler Bromley.

When they stopped at a bar for a drink, he told her he had orange groves; she leaped to the conclusion that he owned Los Angeles. When

Tyler dropped her off at the Magnolia Gardens, Charlene was rewarded by the sight of two of the boarders gaping at her with what could only be envy.

"Must be a producer," muttered one Soula Tithe. "He's rumpled and seems in a hurry."

"Hi, girls," said Charlene as she proceeded past them on the porch.

"Producer, huh?" said Gertie Tamlyn. Charlene made no noises to correct her.

That night he took her to dinner at an Italian restaurant and then back to his hotel. As they necked behind a palm in the lobby of the Biltmore, she asked how come he lived in a downtown hotel if he owned orange groves, and he explained that the groves were in Florida. Charlene was a little disappointed; she hadn't come so far to go throwing herself away on someone who wasn't anybody, and she politely extricated herself from his arms. She sighed that she didn't know him well enough yet to be doing all this, and he drove her back to the Magnolia Gardens and promised to call.

It was Soula Tithe who caused her to drop him. She was going through what she called hell—to wit, no men, no work, and no money. Tyler kept calling for Charlene while Charlene was working as one of three hundred outraged Parisians in a film about the French Revolution. Soula, whose early popularity had convinced her that the good things in life all had her name on them, found the pile of messages for Charlene from Tyler irritating. She had a batch of nickels she had won in a slot machine, and she spent her days making anonymous calls, trying out various accents. The name Tyler Bromley intrigued her: it sounded aristocratic and powerful, and she decided to call the studios, find out which one he worked at, and propose herself for whatever was going.

That evening, as Charlene came through the door with Gertie Tamlyn, Soula greeted her with one word: "Liar."

Charlene stopped dead in the hallway, under the woven raffia ceiling fixture that threw a wan and insincere light over the walls, which were painted the same color as the inside of a slice of lime.

"You mean me?" she asked. Soula nodded her head; Gertie Tamlyn, relieved, moved away from Charlene, who put down her makeup case and crossed her arms, primed for a fight. She waited.

"He's no producer!"

Charlene looked blank.

"Your boyfriend."

Charlene blushed; her reaction was immediate. "He is so!"

"He isn't. There isn't a switchboard in this town that's heard of him."

"He's from out of town, dummy. That's why. He doesn't work in a studio."

"*At* a studio," corrected Gertie Tamlyn. Her interruption was not welcomed by Soula, who liked embarrassing people on a one-to-one basis.

"Well?" Soula asked Charlene, glaring at Gertie.

"He's from Florida."

At this, even Gertie burst out laughing: there were no producers in Florida, everyone knew that. Charlene made a dash for her room. Soula took out a Camel, and Gertie lit it for her. Soula inhaled deeply and sent twin funnels of smoke shooting out of her nostrils.

"I've always hated runts with red hair," she said.

The phone rang, and Soula reached out to pick it up. When she heard the voice, she opened her eyes wide and waved Gertie away.

"Who was it?" asked Gertie when she hung up.

"The Big One," said Soula. "He's taking me out tonight."

"I thought you said he couldn't get it up, and when he did you needed a magnifying glass to find it."

Soula raised her voice and continued, "He's taking me to Romanoff's. This may be it. The photographers will be there. I'd better get ready." As she proceeded toward her room she added, "He wants me to bring another girl. There's some guy with him needs a date." Gertie pushed her chest out, in a reflex she couldn't control. Soula eyed her plump breasts and shook her head. "I can't have competition like you around, honey," she said gravely, with infinite diplomacy. "Anyway, it's some fat old slob, I couldn't do that to you."

Gertie let out a sly giggle. "Take the runt," she said.

Soula thought about it for a second. The Big One hated redheads. It was perfect.

So it was that Charlene was rouged and curled and dressed in one of Gertie's double-flounced skirts, and Soula's off-the-shoulder Mexican blouse, which had been offered in the full knowledge that it bunched unflatteringly just below the armholes. A long black car arrived to pick them up. The Big One was inside, alone, and when Soula saw this, she marched Charlene back up the steps of the hotel, handed her two dollars and told her to call a cab. "He has some private things to discuss with me, and you'd feel in the way."

Charlene cried as she dialed the number for a taxi; being left out of an evening before it had even begun was not her idea of fun. When Charlene arrived at Romanoff's, she was seated between two rotund gentlemen of

Middle European extraction, one of whom would perform expert cunnilingus on her later that night without ever finding out that she was the granddaughter of the very woman between whose legs he had prematurely ejaculated on his first foray into sex one night in 1912.

Charlene's social life began to improve. She learned how to return favors with her mouth and her tongue, and Gertie took her to be fitted for a diaphragm. Every day there were phone messages for her from friends of friends of her original dinner partner who came to pick her up in their own long black cars. Charlene was grateful to Soula for having launched her into the world. "Don't thank me," said Soula. (The Big One had promised to get her a film test, and she was feeling generous.) "It's only natural that a girl like you should get a crack at the big time. I expect you to do the same for me one day. "Anyway," she added, "it gets you away from that creep impostor."

Charlene continued to work as an extra, gracing the backgrounds of various costume epics and even once appearing as an incongruously red-haired Mayan maiden in *The Treasure of the Golden Llama.* As she rocketed around the circuit of temporarily unattached Hollywood males she occasionally encountered a director who would place her in shot and in focus, at the midpoint between his two principals. Only twice did she manage to go to bed with an actor; the first was a singing cowboy whose career never quite recovered from the revelation that he had pledged half of his earnings to the Communist party, the second, a rather edgy British actor whose great talent at speaking verse, honed in provincial repertories, never found the scope it deserved in a series of roles where he portrayed every variety of domestic servant save gamekeeper. Charlene liked him a lot, but his wife was away for only ten days, so their affair was brief.

The actors impressed upon Charlene the fact that it was a cruel rotten world out there among the palms, while the old men told her everything was going to be just fine as they took greedy delight in her passive and virginally unwilling little body. She never returned Tyler Bromley's phone calls, and eventually he stopped calling. Soula Tithe moved out of the hotel; Gertie Tamlyn moved back East to understudy on Broadway and sold Charlene her car. Charlene moved into a small apartment on a courtyard where her neighbors spent as much time waiting for phone calls as the girls at the Magnolia Hotel; the only difference was that they had their own phones.

Twice a month Charlene would go down to the station to meet her father, and they would eat dinner at the Ambassador Hotel.

After three years she had still not said one line on screen, and although her miniature proportions were a big hit with the folks in the wardrobe departments (where a "Charlene special" was a child's dress with falsies sewn into it), no one else at the studio paid her much attention. This was true, too, of the directors with whom she had taken illicit naps. Although in a safe corner of her mind she considered them her boyfriends, they shrank away slightly when she attempted to cozy up to them on the sets, and sent word back via their acquaintances that they would prefer the little redhead to act a little more professional.

On the day she turned twenty-one, Charlene drank an entire bottle of Jack Daniel's that a visiting scriptwriter had given her that morning in his room at the Beverly Wilshire. She considered her life: she was doing it, and men were telling each other that she did it, but she wasn't accepting money for it, at least not directly. She told her father about the beaux, generous and sophisticated, who showered her with corsages. The truth was that the corsages consisted solely of twenty or, sometimes, fifty dollar bills "for the hairdresser," handed over by said beaux as they parted in the morning. The money came in handy, but it wasn't what she wanted. Becoming despondent about the future of her body and even slightly worried about her immortal soul, she suddenly remembered that there had once been a man who had treated her like a lady, and she tried to find him.

She called the Biltmore, which would not give an address for him; she called the Farmer's Market, figuring not unreasonably that the switchboard would know how to find orange-juice suppliers, but they told her that all the Farmer's Market sold was California orange juice. Finally, she was inspired to call Orange County, Florida, and ask the operator if there was a listing for a Tyler Bromley. The operator could not find anyone by that name; Charlene, by now desperate and convinced that Tyler was the answer, managed to remember something about "easy vitamins," and the operator found an Ezy Vite Juices company. She called Ezy Vite and asked for Tyler Bromley; "There's no one here by that name," she was told.

"The owner," she specified.

"The owner's name is Tevye Bronstein."

The evidence that Tyler was no more than an employee saddened her, and almost prompted her to hang up before she could be put through.

"Hello," said a man's voice.

She asked imperiously for Tyler Bromley.

"Speaking," said the man.

She couldn't believe it—what was *he* doing in Mr. Bronstein's office?

"Who's there?"

"Tyler, hi, it's Charlene."

A slight silence, which she broke rapidly.

"Charlene O'Malley. We met at Farmer's Market a while ago. I'm the *actress.* With red hair?"

The only actress with red hair he could think of was Maureen O'Sullivan; but the names were similar enough to convince him that Charlene and Maureen O'Sullivan were the same person. He was flattered to be called by a woman he couldn't recall meeting, pleased further by the call being person-to-person and not collect, and readily assured her that he couldn't wait to see her the next time he came West. When he did, a few weeks later, he took her to dinner at the Luau; as she reached his table he remembered the cute little redhead, and although he was forced to relinquish his daydream about Maureen O'Sullivan, he adjusted quickly. He told her over spareribs in honey that he was buying some groves in California, and was even thinking of moving there. Charlene took this as an omen and proceeded to tell him how often she had thought of him in the past three years. She was clever enough to say little about her work, and to refrain from referring to it as her career; he found this refreshing in an actress.

The combination of her ambition to settle down and his passivity in the face of it led to her helping him pick out a little pink-and-white house not far off Coldwater Canyon, and his picking out a one-carat diamond ring in a shop on Beverly Drive. Charlene felt rescued.

She spent her days selecting plates and rugs and curtains for the new house, and with Tyler she endlessly discussed the merits of various schools of interior décor; her interest had shifted from movie magazines to *House Beautiful* and *Good Housekeeping.* Unaware that this was a passing fancy, Tyler imagined he had domesticated her, much to his relief, as her obsessive allusions to her Hollywood pals and the movie stars she had known struck him as a little pathetic. He was not immune to the lure of celebrity, however; when they ran into Soula Tithe, now a rising young star, at the entrance of Chasen's, it was he who pushed Charlene forward to greet the actress. Soula's smile was not entirely benign, but she allowed herself to be hugged. Charlene, forgetting the incident at the Magnolia Gardens that had signaled the beginning of the life she was now so eagerly abandoning, shoved Tyler at Soula. "This is my fiancé, Tyler Bromley. We're going to be married next month."

Soula never forgot a name; she narrowed her eyes and tapped Tyler's lapel with her index finger. "Charlene, honey," she said, "I thought I'd taken you out of a rut, but it seems I forgot you can't take the rut out of the girl." Then she swept by with her date, a tall, dark stranger.

"What did that mean?" asked Tyler.

"Nothing," said Charlene. "She's a bitch."

"But pretty," said Tyler.

Thus reminded of the dangerous path she had chosen into obscurity, Charlene sought to ascertain how secure her social prospects were. She waited until dessert, and over coconut ice cream she broached the subject of Mr. Bronstein. "I'd love to meet your boss," she said. "He must come to the wedding."

"I haven't got a boss."

"Well then, who's that Terry Bronstein who owns your company?" she asked.

Tyler wiped his mouth carefully with his napkin and said, "This is something I maybe should have told you before." Charlene thought she was going to throw up; she let her spoon fall on the plush seat, leaving a hirsute trace of coconut chips. Tyler, normally a neat man, failed to notice.

"It's very simple," he said. "Folks in Orange County Florida don't mind Jews. They have enough problems with wetbacks. But Orange County, California—why, it's full of white Protestants. And I thought that I should change my name before I moved here. I'm, I mean my family is, Jewish." He slid a look over at Charlene.

"We have wetbacks here too," she said.

"I've been meaning to extend the business here since before the war. But with the war, things slowed down. And I've been kind of getting used to the name since '44. I am Teyve—not Terry, Teyve—Bronstein."

Charlene's relief was such that she burst into tears. "I thought you were going to tell me something awful," she sobbed. "That you were just a . . ." She censored herself before the word "nobody" came out. Tyler was relieved to find her so free of prejudice.

When she had patched up her makeup, she bombarded him with questions. "Why Tyler? I mean, Terry's a nice name."

"It's not Terry, it's Teyve; Terry's kinda Irish for my taste." Tyler was in such a state of grace that he was ready to discuss his name all night. He ordered two brandies, and was surprised to see how fast Charlene put hers away.

"Tell me about Bromley," she said. "It's an English name, isn't it?"

"Boy, you're bright," said Tyler approvingly. "I got it in England during the war."

Charlene had heard enough from him about the war: stories about spaghetti stolen from a factory outside Naples, about a cook taken on south of Monte Cassino who was running a fifth column devoted to poisoning the Allies and who used to stuff the ravioli with corpse meat, and about the great K-ration famine of the Moroccan campaign. Tyler had been a quartermaster.

"They had a stock of names and you just picked one out?" she asked, laughing at her own joke.

"You hit the nail right on the head. I was in charge of the store, see, and for some reason one week we get in all this good stuff; we were at a place called Ruislip, and for some reason, instead of army issue, all this great stuff comes in. Well, it wasn't all great, the toilet paper was shitty." Charlene trilled with delight. "It was called Bronco or something. I was noticing names like crazy around then, because— You know, I've never told anyone all this before."

"I'm going to be your wife, I have a right to know," she reproached him.

Tyler gazed at her thoughtfully. "I wish Pop could have met you," he said. "Okay, so I was looking at all these place names, because in Italy it was no good—I mean, I wasn't going to change my name to Salerno or Leone. I mean, that's the frying pan into the fire, sound like some dago, hell no! And Morocco was the same, El this, El that, forget it. But in England—boy! I tried 'em all. I'd lie in my bunk at night and roll them over in my mind, Ted London, Tom Pancras, Ted Churchill, Ted Leamington . . . Tony Ruislip, that was better, except I always hated the name Tony, sounded too goddamn fairy to me. So there I was in the store, watching the guys unpack, and I'm reading the labels, and I'm going Ted Yardley—I'm telling you, there was some good stuff there—Tad Taylor, that was my favorite until suddenly I have to count the soap and it's called Bromley. Well, that's a great name, isn't it? Sounds like a cross between a bomb and a nice place in the country, so that did it. Bromley."

Charlene sighed and repeated "Bromley" a few times, as if to get used to it. "What about Tyler?" she asked.

"My second favorite," he said. "It's Taylor, without the *a.* Makes it more mysterious."

Charlene insisted that he change his name officially before the wedding, and that he do it in Florida. She had no intention of telling Coquette she was marrying a Jew; she described him as a Southern landowner, which was more or less true. Coquette assumed the wedding was to be a religious one, and consulted every day with Father Ignatius, who only wanted to be sure that the young man had been confirmed. When Charlene got wind of her mother's plans through her father, she wired New York and told her mother that she was twenty-one years old, practically a married woman, and free to choose a civil ceremony, adding, "We will marry in New York," so that none of her family would get it into their heads to come out to Hollywood.

Bridget was detained in the kitchen at the Holy Cross school, and Caithleen, who had also become a nun, made an excuse about Holy Week keeping her in Philadelphia.

Mary, Annie, Eileen and Jo all wore pink, which clashed with their uniformly red hair. Coquette wore black, and Eddie wore pinstriped trousers and a cutaway coat.

There was a large boozy lunch for the family at a Hungarian restaurant; Coquette had insisted on no violins, but the owner took this as having been said in a spirit of economy and decided to have the string trio serenade the young couple at his own expense. The strains of the "Blue Danube" sent Coquette to the ladies' room in mid-meal, there to sob her heart out and give thanks to God that at least one of her daughters had found the middle path between whore and nun. Not that Mary, Annie, Eileen and Jo were whores, but they were unmarried, three were nearing thirty, and she was sure she could catch whiffs of the odor of sexual license in their sweat.

Tyler found the O'Malleys exotic and entertaining, this mixture of Hungarian and Irish blood that pumped under uniformly red thatches of bright hair. He and Eddie exchanged stories about the care and feeding of large numbers of people, Eddie with precise details about the menus on the *Twentieth Century* and *Super Chief,* Tyler with shocking details about the spaghetti stolen from the factory south of Naples. Tyler was fascinated by Coquette: his own father had once assured him that the Bronsteins had originated in Hungary, and Tyler plied her with questions about the old days in Budapest. "I can't remember a thing," said Coquette firmly. "And I never heard of any Hungarians called Bromley." Tyler explained that he was referring to his father's mother, and let the subject drop.

Charlene's doubts about marrying a man who lacked prominence in any field other than that of orange juice were put to rest for one year as she occupied herself with being a decorative housewife. A large black lady named Hannah took care of the house; Tyler went to his groves every day, where a thin blonde named Francine took care of his phone calls; Charlene went to the hairdresser's, went shopping in Beverly Hills, and sun-bathed. Her friends were the wives of other agricultural tycoons. Midge, whose husband was in grapefruit, and Sally, whose husband was in tomatoes. They shared her interest in movie magazines and silver-screen gossip, though not to the same obsessive extent.

Her craving for her old life surfaced around the time she found herself pregnant: the thicker her body grew, the more she found herself thinking about the men who had handled it and commented on its delicacy, its perfect tiny proportions. In her second month she was impelled to call the Magnolia Gardens to see if any of her old girlfriends were around, but in four years they had all moved on. In her third month she found herself needing to cross the lobby of the Beverly Wilshire Hotel several times a day; where other pregnant women craved pickles, she hungered for the places that had seen her dangerous days. On two occasions she caught sight of former romantic attachments, but in the interest of vanity, she resolutely kept her sunglasses on and changed direction.

In her fourth month she read in *Movie Stars Parade* that Soula Tithe was married to a European director and had a bouncing baby named Paula. She figured that her old benefactress would jump at the opportunity to give her some advice on mothering, and left a message for her at Metro-Goldwyn-Mayer. Soula did not return the call.

In her fifth month Charlene took to buying not only the fan magazines but every publication likely to print, however briefly, the names of the people she had once known. From the pages of *Variety* and the *Hollywood Reporter,* from the columns of Hedda and Louella, she gleaned what she could about the life that was still going on without her. She saw that the British actor had left his wife, after all. Her heart leaped; she read on to discover that he was "seeing" an actress twenty years older than he, and the column said they were having a hard time with the pronunciation of the words "hot tomato." She deduced from a photograph of Gertie Tamlyn captioned Sheila McCoy that Gertie was on her way to fame and fortune; learned that the scriptwriter was up for an Oscar; found out Shelley Winters' weight and the precise number of her boyfriends. She envied them all, and wondered why she had left the ring.

Gazing around the white wall-to-wall carpeting, the hide-covered sofas and the orange lamps in the shape of amphoras, she was struck by the realization that there was little joy to be derived from luxury if the money that had bought it came from oranges.

The last three months of her pregnancy were spent writing letters to the magazines, asking for recondite details about the lives of movie stars. She had to know what Errol Flynn's favorite food was, whether Tyrone

Power liked dogs, whether it was true that Rita Hayworth waxed her hairline. The letters were published, with answers, the very week that she gave birth to her daughter. Her one worry was that Tyler would forget to bring her the magazines in the hospital.

The baby, a girl, was named Iris after Tyler's mother. Had Charlene had her choice the child would have been a Janet, a Donna, a Lauren or an Alma, but on this point Tyler prevailed.

Iris was cute. She had tiny fingers that wriggled a lot, flat soft feet and black hair. She did not look at all like Charlene, which made Charlene feel a little funny about breast-feeding her. To her relief, the doctor advised against it and recommended a new wonder formula.

In time, the baby walked. It talked, it babbled and peed. It ate onions; it liked having its picture taken. It perceived that the walls of its room were pink, and that some of that pink could be picked off, to show a satisfying whiteness beneath. It got slapped for this by Hannah. Its mother did not deal with such matters.

The advent of motherhood increased Charlene's longing for her old life. She insisted that Tyler take her out on the town. Tyler complied, but with the naïve single-mindedness of a young tycoon, he sought to combine pleasure with duty, and their forays into restaurants were in the company of Sally, Midge and their husbands. Charlene wished, not for the first time, that Tyler were in the movies, or really big-money things like airplanes or stocks. Sitting in the Brown Derby, Romanoff's or Chasen's listening to the wife of a planter talk about schooling in the South, or the planter himself discussing diversification, crop failures, aphids and the possible effects of radiation fallout on the rate of mutation in double-centered navels, only exasperated her longing. Now and then she would see one of those men whose abuses she now counted as acts of great and desperate love with a young girl on his arm, and she would sigh.

Tyler at first thought her mooning was due to the postpartum blues that he had read about in Dr. Spock. He wondered if they lasted a whole year. Charlene granted him conjugal rights three nights a week, and on those nights she didn't wear face cream, a detail that he appreciated. She was beginning to bore him, but rather than mention this to her, he preferred to eliminate everything that distracted her attention from him, starting with the magazines, which he began to throw out before she had read them. She simply bought more. He suggested a trip to Florida; she declined. He proceeded to tear up her magazines and leave them lying there, in two pieces. One night he tore up the *Movie Life* she was reading, and when she returned from the wet bar with a Coke to find it lying on the couch like a parking ticket, she burst into tears.

"You never want me to have any fun," she said.

"What's fun about a magazine?"

"You hate me," she said with unusual insight. Tyler was about to answer that he loved her, when he realized he didn't. To cover his confusion he began hurling to the floor every knickknack in the living room, and stormed out of the house into the night. He slid behind the wheel of the Plymouth and found himself driving down the hill and turning in the direction of Orange County. He stopped on the street where his secretary, Francine, lived. She was someone he could talk to: a decent, honest girl who shared with him a fear of union action and a well-founded apprehension about what the guys in the freezer business were doing. She opened the door to her upper bungalow at the sound of his voice, though it was past midnight. "Is it a strike?" she asked at once, and he knew that this was a woman who would never put her own petty interests before his own.

She made him some instant coffee and sat him down in her kitchen. "Francine, what do you think about movie people?" he asked. "Goddamn Commies, all of them," she said, a true native of Pasadena. They spent the night in her kitchen talking about his childhood, his parents and his dogs when they weren't talking about oranges. In the morning he drove her to the plant with him; it had been a chaste night, but he felt closer to her than he ever had to Charlene. That day they shared a tuna-fish salad that she made herself at his desk. She ventured that he wasn't happy at home, a bold thing to do. "I married the wrong girl," said Tyler. "She's not in your league," said Francine.

The official reason for the divorce was incompatibility, and because, underneath it all, Tyler had a soft heart, he gave Charlene a large settlement on top of the alimony when she returned from Reno. After all, she hadn't been unfaithful to him. Once the divorce was final he felt pure enough to sleep with Francine, but the next day in a flush of guilt he went to his lawyer and put one hundred acres of the California groves in Iris's name. This made him feel more comfortable. Francine was soon cooking him dinner every night. Her cooking was so good, and her grasp of Ezy Vite problems so acute, that he soon proposed to her. Having done this, he bought Charlene a house on Mulholland Drive, but put it in his own name. He went to Brentano's and bought a *Photoplay* annual for 1951, which he presented to Charlene along with a giant poinsettia on the day she moved into the new house. She already had the *Photoplay* album, but was touched by the gesture. She would have tried to get him back if she had not come to the conclusion, during her six weeks in Reno, that she had been saved from a life of acute monotony by his sudden actions and was a very lucky girl.

Charlene liked the new house: she did not know that Tyler had gotten it at a good rate from a buddy of his in the construction business; if she had known, she would have hated it. While the habits of her youth had helped her cultivate a parsimonious streak, she respected only one thing in others, and that was extravagance.

She took a job at Jax; she did not need the money, but had found that reading magazines all day long with only the maid for company was nowhere near as fulfilling as it had been when Tyler was there to watch her. Also, she tended to cry a lot around six o'clock in the evening, and she didn't know who to see at night. It was her parsimonious streak that impelled her to go to Beverly Hills, for she had heard that if you worked at Jax you only paid half price for the clothes you bought there.

It was while working in a decorative and desultory way that one day she helped a middle-aged man pick out thirty-three identical shell sweaters. As he made out the check she could not resist asking whom they could be for. "After all," she said, batting her lashes, "no one could *possibly* have that many poodles." The man, who had just finished signing "Saul Hyott" on a check drawn on the First Bank of Las Vegas, let out a laugh that shook the hangers on all the dress rails. His work, in close association with hotels in Miami and Las Vegas, where stand-up comedians warmed up the audiences before the big shows, had taught him to laugh loud and long at anything even remotely funny, and he had developed a laugh that other people could not hear without echoing. Three salesladies began giggling at the other side of the shop, and an old man carrying a newspaper and just at that moment passing in front of the open door suddenly doubled over, gasping for breath, laughing his guts out.

Charlene found Saul attractive: here was a man with magnetism (the word "charisma" had not yet taken up its protected tenancy in the language), a man who led where others followed. Her eyes lit up.

"I have this troupe, and we're all going on a trip to Europe and I thought it would be cute if they all came off the plane wearing the same thing," he explained. Charlene nodded, but sought elucidation: "Troupe?"

"Dancers. Saul Hyott's Hi-Fliers. They'll all over five-nine, legs that just won't quit, trained in ballet but they move like firecrackers. They're going to the Lido in Paris, and we may do a show for the armed forces in Germany." He looked down at Charlene; her face had fallen at the mention of the girls' height, and fallen further with his reference to their legs. He was sensitive enough to notice that she looked a trifle bitter, and had been around enough girls of all sizes to realize that it might have to do with her own height. Bending down a little, he murmured confidentially in her ear, "The customers like 'em big, but to me they're just horses. I'm the china-doll type myself, can't handle all that yardage." Pleased with his sensitivity, he took the packages from her and proceeded toward the door.

Charlene wasn't having any of that. His words had tickled her ears with a soft breath the likes of which she hadn't felt in years: Tyler didn't know about ears, and she had never bothered to teach him, fearing it might betray too much about her experience. She rushed to the door and stood by it as Saul Hyott was about to cross the threshold. He smiled at her, and his features, which were etched in a substance the approximate color and texture of summer-weight flannel, took on a benevolent cast. Charlene smiled back. He paused. Considered. Acted: "How's about a drink? I'm just over the road at the Beverly Wilshire." Charlene almost swooned with nostalgia. "Meet you in the bar in half an hour, give me time to feed the poodles." Charlene laughed. Saul Hyott almost laughed, but stopped himself as he knew he should: never laugh at your own jokes, it betrays a loser.

Saul and Charlene turned out to be made for each other, at least at that particular moment. As they were sitting in the bar, Saul was approached by no fewer than three movie stars, two singers and the personal assistant to Harry Cohn. He introduced Charlene each time, and by her full name, a delicacy of manners with which none of her previous escorts had seen fit to indulge her. He did not make an immediate pass, but told her about the hotel in Vegas, the dancers, and the logistics of the projected trip to Europe. Charlene had never given Europe much thought before; she figured that it was full of people like her mother and her father, and battlefields littered with cans of chili con carne. But Saul waxed lyrical about the great, gray, tree-lined streets of Paris, about the beauty of places she had never heard of before, like Enghien-les-Bains and Le Touquet. Charlene looked at her cocktail watch and said she had to leave; as she got up from the table, Saul asked her if she was free for dinner that night.

Saul came to Los Angeles twice a week, except when he was on tour with the Hi-Fliers, and he began to see Charlene regularly. The impending trip to Europe served to add a dimension of haste to the progress of their affair. Saul found Charlene piquant in a way that few American women ever managed to be; he told her she would fit in well in Paris. She did not take this as an immediate hint, but when a few days later they were sitting on the deck at the back of the house on Mulholland, sipping champagne that Saul had picked up at the liquor store on the way in from the airport, he brought it up again. "Look at this desert!" he said, pointing to the scrub and brush that tumbled down the rocky canyon. A reservoir glittered in the distance; Charlene liked to think it was a lake, and told Saul so. He squinted, and told her real lakes didn't have concrete shores. They both looked out over the hills, where no sound could be heard except the steady hum of a bulldozer. "It's a desert," he repeated, taking in with his outstretched arm the very area that Tyler's friend the builder was at that moment describing to a potential investor as "verdant hills." Charlene stared out over the canyon. The sun was about to set. "Yes?" she asked.

"Well, it's a desert. What art does it have? What history? What literature?"

Charlene thought for a second. "There's the movies, you can't forget movies. Even my mother's father confessor thinks movies are art."

"That's not what I mean," said Saul gently, for he was embarked on what can only be termed a soft sell. "It's all new here. Don't you long for a past?"

Charlene shuddered. At this particular moment, with champagne on her tongue and Saul's affection and the alimony from Tyler and Hannah being a real angel and Iris enrolled in pre-nursery school, she was perfectly happy to let bygones be bygones. "The past is a closed book to me," she said with a little too much emphasis.

"I don't mean your past, honey," explained Saul. "I mean *the past,* history, that kind of past. People who've lived and died hundreds of years before you, who've accumulated beautiful things and built beautiful houses, and done—done great things. Conquests. Cathedrals. Revolutions. Wars."

Wars. That's all she ever heard about Europe, wars. They always had them there. It sounded like a terrible place.

"What I'm trying to say," continued Saul, his fervor undiminished, "is that I've been having some talks with the boys in Miami and there's a good chance I might be spending a lot of time there. In France. And . . . I wouldn't like to spend it without you." His choice of the word "spend" was felicitous; Charlene's mind had wandered slightly and she only came back to hear him say "spend it without you." This rang an alarm bell for her. Hastily she said, "Don't do that!"

"You mean you'll come?" Saul could not believe his luck. Charlene nodded. She thought he meant a trip.

As it happened, Charlene did not accompany Saul on tour with the dancers. But when he returned after three weeks away, he brought with him a petit-point evening bag, six embroidered sweaters—the man liked buying in bulk—and a small box from Boucheron in which was nestled a solid gold compact. Charlene received the presents with little cries of joy; the sweaters were in graduated shades of apricot—to match her hair, he said—and she had never received anything so profligate before. Saul also brought a doll for Iris, a wooden German doll with a sweet face hewn delicately out of stained pine and two long yellow braids made of cotton.

After the presents, it did not take much for Saul to persuade Charlene to move to Paris. He showed her photographs of himself with Maurice Chevalier and someone called Eddie Constantine taken in a nightclub, and explained that the five blondes in the picture were members of Saul Hyott's Hi-Fliers. Charlene was a little miffed that he should fraternize with his employees when she wasn't around, but to her relief, he explained that he would be handing over all thirty-three of the girls to one of his associates in Vegas, as he wouldn't have time to manage them and run the French business as well. Charlene's other doubts had to do with whether the alimony checks would continue coming if she did something that might look to her ex-husband as if she were skipping the country. A short meeting with her lawyer put her fears to rest, but the lawyer added that she could do what she wanted only as long as she neither remarried nor cohabited with a man. She took this information back to Saul, who reassured her: it was better for him if they lived in a hotel at first, and they could have adjoining rooms. Within a month she had rented out the house, found Hannah a job cooking for the manageress of the Jax Boutique, and booked her passage via New York. Saul was able to come with her as far as New York, but last-minute snags called him back to Vegas, and they decided she might as well go on alone. Charlene had trepidations about being all alone in an unknown city in a foreign country, but knowing that Saul considered her witty and world-wise, she decided not to voice them.

Her worry was whether she would see anyone she knew; her biggest fear was that by going to Paris she would drop out of sight permanently and be forgotten. And she doubted that they sold movie magazines in Europe.

3.

Arrivals

The journey was arduous and debilitating. Iris had thrown up twice on the Constellation that took them to New York. Coquette and Mary, Annie, Eileen and Jo had descended on Charlene at the Plaza. Charlene told them she was going to Paris to improve her mind now that she had the freedom and the money to do so. She did not mention the existence of Saul or anyone remotely like him: she wanted to be spared descriptions of the fires of hell. Her three older sisters were delighted that she had lost her husband so fast: each had found a man at last, and thought it was her turn now. Charlene's younger sister, Jo, asked her whether her heart was broken, which set Charlene off on a train of thought that made her unresponsive to Saul when he joined her later that night. He put it down to travel nerves. He was an understanding man.

Iris threw up four times on the Stratocruiser that took her and Charlene to Paris, despite the therapeutic comfort of the bunks, and once on the feet of a French cardinal while they were stretching their legs among the reeds and ducks of Shannon Airport. Charlene had never been in sole charge of her daughter before, and vowed that the first thing she would do in Paris was find a woman to take care of the child. In desperation, on the last leg of the journey—between Shannon and Paris—she crushed a tranquilizer in some sugared water and gave it to Iris to drink, so that by the time they drew up in a taxi in front of the Plaza Athénée, the girl was as immobile and soundless as a doll.

A three-room suite awaited them on the third floor, all gray and gold and cream, with fake Marie Laurencins on the paneled living-room walls. The bedroom had scalloped curtains rising to a crescendo of fringe restrained by thick silk knots above the bed, and the windows were veiled with two layers of fine net, overlaid with two sets of thick satin drapes. Charlene had never seen anything like it before. The chairs were covered in petit point, just like the evening bag that Saul had given her. The sofa in the living room looked like a small bed; its sides were made of cane painted white and gray, like the chests of drawers. The dank humidity that pervaded the afternoon and weighed down the curtains reminded Charlene of home, but the rooms themselves surpassed anything she could consider familiar. Now she knew what the hotels she had stayed in were hinting at; this was the real thing—grandiose, elaborate, yet somehow cozy. She took off the jacket of her suit and sat down on what she knew to be a Louis chair. She looked up: carved and flower-decked cornices on the ceilings beamed rosebuds down at her. For the first time she felt in touch with history.

Iris, who had been deposited by one of the porters on the small bed in the second bedroom, was beginning to stir. The afternoon light here was not screened by quite such a wealth of curtains and a powdery stripe of sunlight fell straight across that part of the bed where her head lay. It warmed her cheek until she woke up from the soft pressure of the heat. She opened her eyes and was unable to understand where she was, but instead of crying she rolled herself carefully off the bed.

Still under the slow spell of the pill Charlene had administered, she staggered toward the door; its handle was out of her reach, but the door was only flush with the jamb, not closed, and a simple pull on the edge opened it toward her. The dark cavern of the living room lay before her. Warily she stepped across the threshold, and then gazed up at the high ceiling with bumps arranged in patterns across it. She thought better of an incursion into the unprotected center of the room, and groped for the wall. Leaning her hand on the thick upper ridge of the dado, she slowly and carefully proceeded around the perimeter. Her hands, which were used to the clean hard surfaces of Formica, polished redwood and rawhide, encountered the chunky impasto of generations of oil-based paint; her fingers played along painted cane, woven like hairnets into adjoining straight-sided holes, and drew lines in fine beige dust. Where she knew nubby tweed and raw silk by touch, here her palms slid along shining satin, bumped across the serrated stripes of grosgrain, counted the dizzying dots of needlepoint. It was completely and absurdly foreign, incomprehensible to the touch, but her mother was there, in the middle of the room, and this was all probably some harmless invention of hers, like making Iris ride in the coachman seat of the supermarket cart. There was a knock on the door; Iris promptly ran to her mother's chair, although she felt sure it had to be Hannah outside.

Charlene called, "Come in!" A woman in a white starchy dress like a nurse's came through the door. Was this a doctor's office? was Iris's immediate reaction. She steeled herself. Whatever happened, she would keep her socks on. But something more alarming than any hypodermic needle issued forth from the woman: a stream of utterly strange, loud, alien, guttural, deep, abrasive, bellicose, staccato sounds. Iris hit the floor and covered her head with her hands, as she had been drilled to do in nursery school in the event, as the teacher knew but didn't say, of a nuclear attack. Charlene rose and faced the woman. "Say it in English, I can't understand," she ordered.

Iris was relieved: at least her mother couldn't be one of them, since she didn't know what the creature was saying. And then panic swept her: if her mother didn't know what the woman was saying, who did?

"Ze bed, ze bed, I make ze bed!" the woman said. Charlene waved her toward the bedroom. Iris tugged at her mother's leg, and Charlene looked down to see her in an agony of dumb fear. She picked her up and held her on her lap, soothing her with nervous fingers.

"Where are we? Who is *she?*" asked Iris, through sobs.

"We're in Paris, darling. Paris, France."

"Is that near home?" asked Iris.

Charlene laughed softly. "No, it's very far away."

"How far?"

"Well, we've been on two airplanes and we've been traveling for three days. That's how far."

Iris wriggled in her grasp; she felt she could hardly breathe. "Mommy, quick, I want to go home! I want to go home!" Maybe she could just shut her eyes and be home again, with the high chair she had outgrown and Hannah cutting wedges in the grapefruit, and the sun on the cactus by the kitchen door, and the pink paint, the wonderful pink paint yielding under her busy fingers . . . She twisted on her mother's lap. The convoluted gray walls of the room, so different, so strange, so ugly, so dark, so hideously foreign, held nameless threats. "Mommy, please, can we go home?" She was panting with distress.

Charlene shook her head. "It's all right, there's nothing to be scared of. It's very nice here, and next week Saul will be with us."

Iris liked Saul, but this information failed to calm her. "Hannah? Hannah, too?" Charlene felt that saying no would make matters worse, so she began to embroider a little. "Hannah's coming, and your high chair is coming."

"The dogs, too?" asked Iris.

"No, darling, your daddy's got the dogs. You haven't seen the dogs for over a year."

The gray walls seemed to be getting closer, encroaching on the minuscule territory that had been hewn out of the vastness of the room just by talking about Saul and Hannah. Iris's breathing stopped again as she caught sight of the view outside the window: an imponderable gray mass stood across the street, with a frieze of green beneath it. The notion of distance took hold of her again, tilted her out of her temporary calm. It was a feeling of such removal, of such enormous and terrible distance, from everything she knew that crying could only express the surface of what she felt. Her mother hugged her, tears forming in her own eyes.

"Now now, Iris, it's all right. Be a big girl now and face the world, come on. Give us a smile, a little smile." She tickled Iris's cheek lightly, and hastily brushed away her own tears as her daughter looked up. And smiled, if uncertainly. "That's better," said Charlene. Iris thought for a moment, and some instinct to bargain for her survival surfaced through the tears. "Mommy," she said, "if I'm good, can we go home tomorrow?"

Charlene resisted the impulse to grind another tranquilizer into another glass of sugared water; congratulating herself on her cheerful shouldering of the martyrdom of motherhood, she carried Iris into the bathroom, where she ran what she hoped would be a bath deep enough for the two of them to splash in, but which turned out to be only a few inches of tepid water. She remembered about the war, and came to the conclusion that shortages were probably still common in Europe. She coaxed Iris into taking a nap, and drew the curtains so that the energizing sunlight could not penetrate, and carefully closed the door.

Once outside in the living room again, she leaned against the wall and took a couple of deep breaths, followed by a sigh. Iris's mistrust of the surroundings had set off a complementary dizziness in her, but it was more diffuse and in another key. She walked rapidly to the window.

Across the street she saw gray buildings, but the gray was a pretty shade, like old silver. Fenced-in trees had gnarled arthritic knuckles from which shot myriads of tiny leaves bunched together as if in bouquets. A woman was walking a poodle; Charlene noted her dress, its full skirt, the cut of her hair. The sky was not the uniform blue she had expected: frothy cumuli stood in formal orchestration up over to the left, above what looked like a gigantic greenhouse. She realized that the clouds looked a little like the curtains over her bed; I bet that's where they got the idea, she said to herself. Encouraged by this first attempt at making artistic connections, she went over to the phone and extracted her address book from her handbag. Under *P* for Paris, Saul had neatly printed the names and numbers of the people who would steer her through the first difficult week until he got there.

ALZAGA, Pedro. My lawyer.
COLBURN, Mike. Army buddy. Knows everybody.
DEL CICCO, Monty. My right hand. He'll call you.
SZOS, Ferdinand. You'll love him.
PIERRET, Carole. A great girl. Secretary.

And that was it. No Maurice Chevalier, no Greta Garbo. Not even James Jones. Just plain people. Charlene ran through it again. The lawyer sounded dull and doubly foreign with his Spanish name. The army buddy she could do without; Tyler had shown her enough army buddies to last a lifetime. She figured it was incorrect to phone Del Cicco until he phoned her. She placed the book on the table and saw a long and lonely evening stretching ahead of her. A small booklet by the lamp advertised itself as *The Complete Guide to Paris,* and she flipped through it. Paris appeared to be full of discount perfume shops and nudie shows; she registered a slight shock at the sight of bare breasts, reproduced in slightly grimy smudged offset on every other page. Two pairs of nipples advertised the Lido; her heart made a little leap, and she wondered whether Saul Hyott's Hi-Fliers danced around with nothing on top. She dismissed the idea: nice clean girls who worked in Miami and Vegas couldn't possibly work without full costumes. She made herself a drink from the Scotch she had bought on the plane, took a sip, and asked for Pedro Alzaga's number.

"Mr. Alzaga? This is Charlene Bromley. I'm Saul Hyott's friend."

"Of course. He said you would call." The voice was deep, the English correct, with a slight accent.

"Mommy!" Iris was in the living room again.

Charlene ignored her. "I've just gotten in," she said into the phone, "and I was wondering—" A loud cry interrupted her. Iris gave all the signs of being about to throw a fit. "Darling, I'm busy! Go play . . ."

"You have a child," said Mr. Alzaga judiciously.

"That's one of the things that you could help me with. I need a nanny. Saul said you could tell me how . . ."

There was a moment's silence. Then: "Of course. Is there any nationality you prefer?"

"No, none at all." The thought had not occurred to Charlene that different nationalities were available.

"Some people prefer British governesses, and many of my friends have Fraüleins. German girls."

"Oh, I couldn't have a German, not after what they did in the war," said Charlene, proud of her principles.

"I will arrange a French nanny for you. Though perhaps, as I am not an expert in these matters"—he stressed the word *expert*—"you would do better with an agency in the morning."

"Oh no," said Charlene, "I need her as soon as possible."

"Is there anything else you need, Madame Bromley?" asked Alzaga, resigned to indulging this woman, whom he divined to be naïve, demanding and quite impossible.

"Well, what do you think I could do tonight? I mean, I'm so excited to be here and I feel a little strange all alone."

Alzaga got the hint; deliberated whether he felt like leaving his apartment on a Sunday afternoon with his children playing a noisy card game and his wife stabbing out a cushion cover on her embroidery frame, and found it was his dearest wish. And Saul was a good client. "Why don't you allow me to show you Paris?" he suggested. "We could look at Notre Dame, and then have a drink at Fouquet's. Watch the world go by."

"What about Iris?"

"You can get the chambermaid to sit with your child. I will meet you downstairs in an hour . . . You are at the Plaza, *non?*"

Alzaga was delighted to see how petite, pert and piquant Madame Bromley was. The little circles under her eyes gave her a nicely jaded look, and complemented the *fauve* shade of her hair. Charlene in turn was astounded by Pedro Alzaga: he looked like a cross between a dark Leslie Howard and George Brent. He picked her up in a Citröen with mudguards and runners, and drove her across the river to Notre Dame.

She was a little taken aback to find herself ushered into the presence of Jesus before she had been in Paris three hours. Inside the cathedral, a mass was just winding down into a sea of Amens. Charlene crossed herself, an act that Alzaga imputed to her having been convent-bred. He pointed out the stained-glass windows, miraculously spared by the war. She looked up at the immense central rosette where jewels of color glittered, lit by the sunset.

"What a scarf that would make," she said. It was her own form of blasphemy. Alzaga was captivated by the reflection of the colored glass on her hair; by the freckles on her forearm.

He suggested Fouquet's. I leave it to the reader's discretion to imagine what Charlene thought she heard, being unfamiliar with the café of that name. She stiffened. Alzaga interpreted this as a reluctance to dally on the Champs-Elysées, and asked if she might prefer having a drink downstairs in her own hotel. She wondered briefly at such a rapid change of heart, but assented.

They drank martinis. Their conversation was a little stilted; despite his appreciation of the way nature and Max Factor had assembled her components, he was stalking carefully through the signposted paths of small talk.

"What good English you speak."

"I studied at Harvard."

Charlene had never known anyone who had studied at Harvard. She didn't know how to follow that declaration. Alzaga helped out. "My father was ambassador." This was better: a diplomat's son.

"Have you ever been to Los Angeles?" she asked. Alzaga said that, unfortunately, he hadn't, and added, "You must be an actress."

Charlene looked at the glass surface of the little table between them. A card had been slipped beneath it, advertising the ladies' beauty salon in the *sous-sol.* "Yes, I am." The lie didn't feel too bad, so she added, "But none of my films has been shown in France, I'm afraid."

"I am sure they will, and I look forward to seeing them," said Alzaga. With what she calculated to be a beguiling modesty, Charlene changed the subject. "It's so hot here. Is it always hot here?"

"No," said Alzaga. "In the winter it is cold."

"Oh, I haven't had a cold winter since New York." They discussed the merits of New York. Pedro Alzaga peered surreptitiously at his watch and realized he had to abridge the conversation.

"The nanny will be here at nine, tomorrow," he said. "She is the sister of the maid of my aunt."

Charlene thanked him profusely. "It's so kind of you, I don't know what I would have done without your help."

Charlene wanted to linger in the lobby, flirt with him, inveigle him into seducing her; but she also felt very tired, so tired that the ground seemed to be pulling away from beneath her feet.

"You must rest," he said. "Have a half bottle of champagne in bed, and you'll fall asleep like a baby."

She wanted to tell him that was exactly what she always did, but the words didn't come out. She shook his hand and returned to her room, thinking to herself how good she was being. Iris was fast asleep, and the chambermaid was sitting on a stiff chair reading *Intimités,* an illustrated magazine. Charlene tipped her, and fell onto her sheets under the *baldaquin.*

The next morning she awoke with Iris curled against her. There was a sharp rap at the door; a bellboy entered bearing a massive bouquet of summer flowers—bright fat petals, grasses, leaves, round buds, in red and blue and a blazing orange.

The card said, "Many thanks for a charming company," and was signed "Pedro." On the back was written: *1 p.m. at Bagatelle.* Charlene ordered breakfast: orange juice and cereal for Iris, toast for herself.

The phone rang. "Charlene! It's Saul. Thought I'd give you time to recover. How're you doing?" At that moment Saul was the last person on Charlene's mind. The greeting she gave him erred toward the perfunctory, but once it had gone through the undersea cable and been transmitted across America to come out of the mauve receiver of the phone Saul was holding in his tanned paw, it sounded perfectly adequate: bright and affectionate. Saul, who was calling from an all-mauve bedroom somewhere in Las Vegas, said he was in his office, still hard at work. "It's one in the morning here, which makes it nine there." He was fond of handing out this kind of information, especially when it cost so much to impart. "I'm coming tomorrow. Everything okay? How's Baby?"

Baby, having peed in the bidet (which she found a remarkably intelligent piece of plumbing), was now eating a cigarette.

"She's fine. Loving every minute of it."

"Good. Now one more thing zipf cccdrllllefzdzdzdzdzd . . ." The connection turned into a demented radio and Charlene replaced the receiver with relief. Another knock on the door announced breakfast; Iris hoisted herself up into the armchair, and Charlene poured herself some coffee three shades darker than licorice. Iris sat staring at the silver dome in front of her until Charlene reached over and removed it. Iris looked down into a plate of porridge: hot, thick, steaming oats. She burst into tears. "Eat your cereal," said Charlene, putting down her cup in disgust after one sip. Iris wailed even louder. Charlene peered over the single Baccarat rose in its cut-glass vial to see what had caused this outburst.

"Goddamn idiots," she said. "I asked for cereal, not Quaker Oats." She called room service again, and inquired in strident New York tones whether they had ever heard of Kellogg's Cornflakes. They had not.

The door resounded with another knock. She yelled "Come in" twice, slammed down the phone and opened the door herself. A greasy-haired young woman in a starched blouse stood there, carrying a tote bag of absurd dimensions. *"Je suis Julie,"* she said. *"La garde-enfant."* Julie did not speak much English, but at least she had clean hands.

She took Iris to the park, where the child learned in the space of a day how to say "I'm thirsty," "Stop, I'm dizzy," "I'm hot," and "I want to pee-pee" in French. This last request was fulfilled, to her shame, in the street while Julie held her up by her armpits over the gutter and enjoined her: *"Vas-y, c'est comme ça qu'on fait en France."* For a long time afterwards, Iris thought *Vas-y* meant pee and was shocked on her first visit to the racecourse at Longchamp to hear the entire mob screaming *"Vas-y! vas-y! vas-y!"* at the horses.

Julie became a part of Iris's life. She came every day at nine, bathed her, dressed her, supervised her breakfast and took her to the park. She took her also to see the puppet shows at the Rond Point, and to the Jardin d'Acclimatation to ride on the small merry-go-round and pet the baby elephants. Every night she gave Iris her dinner, read her a fairy tale in French, and tucked her in at seven.

Saul was delayed in America for a month, and Pedro Alzaga became part of Charlene's life. Instead of accompanying his wife and children to Quiberon, where he kept a modest summer villa, he stayed in Paris and devoted himself, during the slow and dreary month of August, to teaching Charlene how to become a real *parisienne*. His international upbringing had left him with the kind of enthusiasm for historic sights that was usually found only in tour guides. He showed Charlene Versailles, La Tour d'Argent, Chartres Cathedral, the castle of Anet, the forest of Fontainebleau and every good restaurant in Paris that was not undergoing its *fermeture annuelle*. He made Carole Pierret, his personal secretary, get seats for Charlene at various couture shows. He showed Charlene the sunset through the roof of the Grand Palais and sunrise over the Place de la Concorde; he also, almost as an afterhought, showed her himself straining in bed above her, screaming "Resussssss!" as he came.

Charlene had not wanted to have an affair, but Pedro Alzaga had easily made her understand that he was simply introducing her to Paris under the best circumstances possible. In public he treated her with the polite solicitude of a family lawyer shepherding an innocent American around town; in private he was so thoroughly involved in the quest for his own pleasure that Charlene had little trouble telling herself that nothing was actually happening. At times she would excite herself with little phrases such as "hung like a horse," "randy as a stallion," or "big as a broomstick"; these little tricks helped her to attain some semblance of ecstasy while lying beneath him. It was convenient for her that she felt no particular attachment to Alzaga, either physically or emotionally. She reasoned that she was getting the kind of education that money couldn't buy, and applied herself diligently to learning as much about French culture was she could in a half-closed town overrun with tourists.

By the time Saul arrived she knew there were at least three different kinds of white wine, and that you didn't drink Sauternes with fish. With Iris she went to collect him in a car that Del Cicco had arranged. When she saw Saul joking with a stern customs officer, his kindness and his sense of humor—two qualities that Alzaga, for all his class and manners, lacked—came back to her and she began jumping up and down like an excited child, waving and shouting. The peculiar thought that she probably knew Pedro Alzaga better than the man across the barrier with whom she was about to share her life made her all the more agitated, and she screamed out his name several times. When Saul came through at last, he embraced her with the words: "I'll bet you're a true Parisian by now."

He had no idea, of course, of what he was talking about.

4.
The Flowering of Opportunity

A hundred and fifty people came to Charlene's party for Sheila McCoy, whose face was on every poster plastered on every billboard, on every wall around every construction site, and wrapped, illegibly, around every kiosk. Only four of the guests were business associates of Saul's; Charlene had roundly declared that she didn't think Sheila wanted to meet gangsters, and Saul was kind enough to see it her way. She had no objection, however, to the boxers, and Jojo Cléry was there, as was Charles Corday, whose prognathous jaw, wiry hair and legendary reputation made him a great favorite of women. Two managers brought their young stars of the ring, and on the arm of one of them came a respected French actress who helped set a more mature tone to the evening. Will Anderton, Gabby Firth, Yves and Annabelle Furet, Ferdinand Szos and Pedro Alzaga, with Madame, made up the party's hard core. Around them, and particularly around Sheila McCoy, who, despite the late hour, had chosen to wear a picture hat and sat on an armchair by the window to the garden, milled producers from Hollywood who had been caught on the wing in the lobbies of the Plaza, the George V, the Prince de Galles; a four-star general who had been tracked down by Charlene as he was leaving the Ritz and had deferred his return to Germany, such was his admiration for the Morristown nightingale; a conductor who was leading a symphony into battle that night at the Salle Pleyel and would have to leave early; and every single American Charlene could get her hands on, with the exception of the Buchwalds—and Soula Tithe. She had called the Lancaster Hotel several times and left messages, to no avail; as she continued calling, a strange feeling of déjà vu came over her. In her last message Charlene had specified that she was giving a party for Sheila McCoy, but even that had not moved Soula to return her call. It's her bad luck, thought Charlene, bemoaning her own. She would have liked to meet this husband of hers, who looked so dark and attractive in pictures.

It was a great party. Sheila, having received ovations every night and the keys to the city of Paris from the mayor, was relaxed and buoyant. The weather was warm, and the twilight descending through the well of back walls into the garden was exquisite. The pigeons gurgled but didn't shit on anyone. The guests, many of whom had never been there before, settled themselves into agreeable little groups and, for the lack of anything better to say, commented on the elegance of their surroundings. Saul's friend Ferdinand Szos, a theatrical agent with the face of a degenerate pixie, a Hungarian accent and a position of trust in the household, helped Charlene greet people. It was he who took Iris, dressed in a new nightgown and robe, from the hands of her nanny and brought her over to Sheila, who said, "Where's ya medal, kid?"

Charlene took Iris over to Darryl Zanuck, an elderly gentleman who sat with a cane by his side; he nodded a curt hello to Iris, and resumed listening to the quiet but intense words of his companion, a woman dressed entirely in black with hair cut in long bangs, who was huddled in her chair like an orphan. Charlene pulled Iris away from them. "Don't bother them now," she said. This confused Iris. "Why did you take me there?" she asked, but Charlene was steering her toward Jojo Cléry. The boxer sat on the end of a chaise longue with his legs apart and his fists resting on his knees. *"Salut, la petite,"* said Jojo Cléry. "That's it now," said Charlene. "Go to bed." Iris looked through the crowd of legs and skirts for her nanny and saw Julie hugging the doorjamb, autograph book in hand. Charlene was too busy to go over and tell Julie she was not to do that, *ever,* at a party; she resolved to talk to her about it in the morning.

"I have to go to bed now," said Iris, tugging at Julie's arm.

"Wait, Louis Jourdan is just coming over here," said Julie in a whisper. Louis Jourdan was indeed walking toward them, but, alas, he turned left and headed for the bar. Julie sighed, *"C'est la vie,"* and pulled Iris through the door and up the stairs.

Saul settled into an armchair next to Szos. He longed to get back into show business, and the collection of stars and singers in his house that evening had sharpened his nostalgia for the good days of the Hi-Fliers.

"I think Jojo Cléry could make a great singer," he said.

"You do?" Szos allowed himself a little sigh, but in the name of friendship he allowed Saul to continue. He had met Saul some ten years before, when the Hi-Fliers, in an early, chunkier incarnation, were entertaining troops stationed in Berlin, and Szos had been there with an American film director who was making what turned out to be a distressingly tasteless film about occupied Germany. Over the years Saul had never failed him, coming up with profitable deals and introductions to the right people at the right times. Szos liked the man for being somewhat racy, a bit of a character. His own resemblance to Peter Lorre—which he checked in the mirror every day in the morning, when it was at its most pronounced—had given him the idea that he belonged with underworld types. Saul's connections with the gambling worlds of Reno and Miami sufficed to make him emblematic of the dangerous circles that Szos dared not approach directly. Szos was what was described in those days as a confirmed bachelor; Iris had overheard this once, and thought that meant he was a Catholic bachelor who had taken certain special vows. He exorcised a little of his taste for low life by mingling among sailors and truck drivers, and Saul's occasional confidences about gangsters he had known fleshed out his dangerous fantasies. The only disadvantage to relying on Saul to furnish and cast his dream life was that Saul could not resist the temptation to turn boxers into actors, mistresses of tycoons into singers, and hookers—multitudes of hookers—into movie stars. He patted Saul's knee. "Forget it," he said. "He doesn't photograph well."

Saul looked grave, and nodded into his drink. "That could be a problem," he agreed.

The next day Charlene read in the *Herald Tribune* that cocktail parties were back, thanks to Charlene Hytt. The typographical error was more than made up for by the lengthy description of her dress, and the even lengthier one of the apartment, which was followed by a full list of the guests. She was a little peeved to read that both Burt Lancaster and Kirk Douglas had been there, when she hadn't seen either of them. Armed with the praise that the *Tribune*'s Jenny Wright had lavished on her talents as a hostess and social magnet, she phoned the Lancaster Hotel once more; Soula would no doubt be abject and apologetic after reading the paper. The concierge informed her that Miss Tithe—he pronounced it "Ties"—had just left for the airport, but Monsieur was still there, and did she care to speak to him? Charlene decided against it; she could have invited Soula's daughter to tea with Iris, but she was too hung over to start inventing children's parties.

Sheila McCoy sent her an immense bunch of pink dogwood and pussy willow, and a note inviting her to stay with her in Los Angeles anytime she wanted.

The summer passed in a haze of nervy conviviality, interrupted only by visits to Normandy and Monte Carlo with Saul. On returning from one of these, Charlene received a message from the offices of French *Vogue.* She phoned the magazine and spoke to a woman who said that Jenny Wright had suggested her for some pages they were doing. Charlene all but dropped the receiver. Later that week at the *Vogue* studios in the Place du Palais Bourbon she was made up, coiffed and gently placed on a large piece of white paper, then sent back into the *cabine* to have her makeup changed. She sat herself back in the canvas chair and closed her eyes for the *maquilleur* to go over them again.

"*Vous connaissez* Soula Tithe?" he asked.

Her eyes shot open. "*Oui, oui,* she's a friend," she said.

"*Quel dommage,*" he said.

"*Dommage?*" She wondered what the pity was.

"That film she was doing, it will never be shown," he said.

"I don't know what you're talking about," she said.

"Didn't you hear? She was drowned off the coast of Malta. They were making *Pirate's Permission,* and she drowned in a little boat."

Charlene looked down at the white makeup table, littered with pan stick and powder rouge, and thought there was some kind of justice in this dumb world, after all. When she returned to pose on the white paper, she allowed the photographer's assistant to place her arm on a high bench so that her hand was in front of her face: the photographer had to see the diamond-studded watch the editor had fastened on her wrist. "*L'heure américaine,*" explained the editor. Charlene smiled engagingly at the camera and reflected on the appropriate title: her time was coming, she just knew it.

Saul's business needed constant attention, and he was endlessly disappearing: when he wasn't off to Luxembourg, Andorra and San Marino, he was making forays to Divonne and Enghien-les-Bains. His main purpose was to make sure that certain casinos, technically under the management of the French government but linked to his associates, remained in a condition known as clean. Grime in this case took the form of bounced checks, unhappy deposed Egyptian potentates, curious winning streaks, and any native of Corsica who might chance his way through the revolving doors. Saul's associates considered Corsica a fresh little upstart of an island that had no business being there in the first place, and any move its prodigal sons might make toward other shores was viewed with strong distaste. Charlene's refusal to accompany him on these trips had at first struck Saul as capricious and ungrateful, but he later resigned himself to going to the country, as he called it, alone.

Ever since her day at *Vogue,* Charlene had decided that she should stay in Paris to make the best of any opportunity that came her way. The signs were clear, and she would be a fool to ignore them. The success of her party for Sheila McCoy had resulted in a deluge of invitations; the glitter in her drawing room at cocktail time was now at its highest, and she didn't see why she should give up her time to running around dingy little resorts with Saul; what did it matter that he always returned with bags full of fresh cash? She viewed these expeditions as sordid sorties down a mine. She wanted to talk about art.

Saul wanted to marry her, and she could feel it. Her obstinate preservation of her alimonious state seemed to him overly prudent, which was why he took care to wave the multicolored notes of many currencies at her whenever he was carrying takings. To him, her diffidence implied a lack of trust in his financial abilities, and in their future together. He was right, of course, but he let his instincts go unheeded. If Szos had said, "Watch it, she's after the big time," he would have said, "Hey, I'm the big time."

Charlene's beatitude faded slowly through the autumn, like a suntan. Nothing happened; she was left alone much of the time while Saul was on his trips, and she began to feel her age, as women do when they are without men for a few days. She was the extra girl at too many dinner tables, and wanted to be romanced. Charlene suspected that her dissatisfaction could have a sexual basis. After all, Saul was fifty-three; she was thirty—well, thirty-one. The affair with Alzaga, which she had imagined to be a wonderful harbinger of things to come, remained her only indiscretion. Indeed, save for certain innuendos when Saul was out of town, Alzaga behaved as if nothing had ever happened, and Charlene refrained from even thinking of him as a former beau.

The issue of *Vogue* came out in mid-November, as is the wont of Christmas issues, and try as she might, she could not find herself in its pages. An apologetic woman called, and explained that due to a mistake on the part of the fashion editor, they had had to drop the picture: she was meant to be *"l'heure américaine,"* but the wrong watch had been put on her. The vistas of triumphs before her faded.

In moments of deep reflection under the hair dryer or while submitting to her masseur's knowing hands, Charlene realized she had wasted her life. She could have been an actress. She was fluent in two languages, French and English. She could be witty; she had a flair for color that the couture houses recognized. She was the first name on the list for anyone going to Paris, and she received her guests like a mother. She was too young for that: she wanted some excitement, kicks—danger, even.

And there was no one to talk to: Szos, since the end of October, had concerned himself exclusively with what was happening in Hungary. He spent his days hanging around the telex machines in the offices of the *Herald Tribune,* phoning New York and occasionally Budapest, when he could get through. At the beginning of November he had begun weeping at odd moments, and could not be talked into having a normal conversation. One evening he came to the Rue Dumont d'Urville and asked wearily for a glass of water. Charlene, standing by the bar with ice tongs in her hand, said, "Perrier?"

"Just water, tap water."

"From the tap? I never touch it."

Szos said, "When I was a boy, the water had tadpoles in it. Right now, my countrymen are lying face down in the mud, dead. They are crossing bridges made of twigs to get to freedom. They have been crushed, there have been tanks in the street."

"You need a stiff drink," said Charlene.

"And I can't even get a drink of water."

Charlene gave a light laugh, assuming he was being his usual funny self, and brought a glass to him. "Sold any good talent lately?" she asked as she sat herself down.

"Charlene"—he pronounced it "Zharleen"—"what is a little talent compared to what is happening to my country?"

"Oh, Hungary!" Charlene exclaimed. She made an effort to catch up with his feelings and an obliging set of tears formed in her eyes. "My poor darling! Do you still have family there?"

"My brother. His wife. Their children."

"I thought your brother was the furrier in New York."

"No, the other brother, the one who converted in '34. I have been trying to reach them, but in the last weeks, *rien à faire.* I only pray they are safely in Austria."

Charlene resigned herself to hearing about Hungary, although she was furious. Normally, Szos could be relied on to offer lighthearted advice about life, to tell her she was gorgeous.

In the kitchen that evening, Iris listened with alarm to Céleste and Julie as they discussed her mother. The women were *au courant de la comptabilité de la maison,* they thought *Madame* was a little *deboussolée* and was showing signs of *inconduite,* which might lead her to *découcher avec le premier passant,* which wouldn't *reviver les choses* especially if she were to *afficher* herself with him. To Iris it meant they were in the running of the accountability of the house, they thought her mother had lost her compass and was inconducting herself in a way that might lead her to unsleep with the first passerby, which wouldn't give life again to things, especially if she turned herself and him into a poster. The next day she asked Charlene if she had ever had a compass; Charlene said, "Of course not, what would I do with a compass?"—which somewhat eased Iris's fears.

At the end of November, Saul went to Miami for a week. When he returned, he left at once for a circular visit of the establishments in the country. As Christmas approached, Charlene felt at loose ends. One evening when Iris was spending the night with a classmate, Szos arrived and announced, "We are going to the circus."

"Don't be ridiculous," said Charlene.

"It will cheer me up, and you, and it will cheer up a friend of mine, a client."

Charlene did not respond. "It's the gala," offered Szos. Charlene stirred a little. "I have six tickets; someone gave them to me. So it will be me, and you, and someone called Arto that you don't know, and the Baron de Chemin and his *bonne femme.* And Raoul. He's even more depressed than I am."

"Raoul?"

"Raoul Abime."

Charlene felt a surge of purpose. "The one who was married to poor darling Soula?" she asked. She used terms of endearment now that Soula was dead; who was to say that they hadn't been best friends?

Iris was helping her classmate Sabine Abramovitz pile dolls into a cardboard box while Madame Abramovitz watched with approval; she was sending the boxes to Hungary on a Red Cross plane, to try to make the children's Christmas there *"un peu plus gai."* Sabine had asked Iris to bring some toys for her mother's parcel, and Iris had arrived with a case full of dolls and most of her school uniform. Madame Abramovitz rescued the uniform and told Iris she could not give that away, but she wrapped up the dolls. Iris was proud to have given her best dolls; the first principle of Christian thought that she had grasped from the catechism at school was that of selflessness.

Madame Abramovitz fed them chicken soup, having sent her maid away for the holidays. Her husband, a journalist, was in Suez. Aline Abramovitz was a daunting-looking woman, a former Résistance fighter, a Communist and a Jew. She made the girls wash the dishes after dinner, much to Iris's outraged surprise, and then sat them down to give them her version of Christmas, something she did every year with Sabine. "*Alors,*" she asked, "What is *Noël* about?"

Iris leaped in. "The Jews killed Christ." Then she covered her mouth with her hand: that was Easter, how silly of her.

"Propaganda!" shouted Sabine.

"Bravo!" said Madame Abramovitz. "It's propaganda. And," she said, turning her fierce eyes on Iris, "the Jews did not kill Christ. Sabine, tell us."

"It was in Galilee—" she began. Her mother interrupted her: "Galilee was under a *régime d'oppression,* a *tyrannie,* it was being exploited by imperialist Rome, which did what, Sabine?"

"Killed people," said Sabine.

"What else?"

"Ate babies?" ventured Iris. Aline almost slapped her, but she had firm principles against bodily attack. She simply said, "Now listen. Nobody, nobody ate babies, not Jews, not Romans, nobody. Sabine, what did the Romans do?"

"Ask for taxes."

"Bravo! And take away land, livestock, houses."

Sabine was nodding happily. It was her yearly tale, and each year her mother added nice long words for her to learn. Iris was mystified, but she supposed if her mother taught her about curtsying, it was all right for Sabine's mother to tell her about Romans.

"*Noël* is about revolution," continued Madame Abramovitz. "A certain group of Jews decided that sharing was the principle by which men should live—sharing work, pleasure, and the honest fruits of their labors. They also believed there was—what, Sabine?"

"One god," said Sabine.

"Very good. One god, not a hundred of them, and that he stood for the communal good. But that the ordinary people wouldn't accept him unless they had a . . ."

"Representative!" shouted Sabine.

"So you know what they did? They formed a committee, and they pulled straws to see which one would be the representative. And he was called Jesus Christ. And the Romans killed Jesus Christ to stop the revolution, but his legend lives on. And do you know why?" But she didn't stop for an answer. "Because they wrote about it! Each man in the committee wrote about what he wanted to see, and they gave their friend Jesus Christ enormous publicity, and they disseminated the information everywhere. And finally, although nothing extraordinary happened, the committee made everyone believe in miracles, because they read about them! And what is the day of *Noël?*"

Proudly Sabine answered, "The day of the first committee meeting!"

On the day of the gala, Szos passed by the Boulevard Saint-Germain, where he picked up a male prostitute and performed actions of suction and insertion on him in his apartment on the Île Saint-Louis until six o'clock, when he sent him home with a generous Christmas *pourboire.* He then changed into his evening clothes, put ice in his ice bucket, which looked like a shimmering red apple, and emptied a jar of green olives stuffed with anchovies into a little Russian silver bowl. It would no more have occurred to him to ask the boy to stay than to dance naked on the balcony. He did not believe in mixing sex with pleasure. He caught sight of the enamel border on the Russian bowl, and quickly poured the olives into a decent French dish, and threw the bowl away.

The baron and his usherette mistress arrived first, at six-thirty. Szos served Polish wodka and handed the olives around. Charlene made an entrance worthy of the Folies Bergère, in a piece of gold cloth that she had picked up at the Marché Saint-Pierre and bound around her torso in the Balinese style. Szos introduced her to the baron and his friend, and to a squat gentleman with a face like an Indian, whom he described to her in the privacy of his kitchen as a failed snake charmer from Peru.

"Where's Raoul Abime?" asked Charlene, unable to mask her interest.

"I'll put you next to him at the circus, I promise," he said.

Raoul Abime made his entrance shuffling across the carpet with the air of a man who was so far beyond the end of his tether that he had lost it completely. He hugged Szos. Charlene, who had taken up a position next to the illuminated aquarium containing tropical fish, held herself upright in a pose of gracious expectancy, a glass of wodka in her hand. She took in dark hair, dark eyes, stormy good looks. He looked a little bad-tempered, she thought, and in the few seconds before he looked into her eyes and she surrendered herself to the idea of him, she noticed that he had a liverish yellow coloring and the hint of jowls.

Raoul had come because at this stage, six months after Soula's death, even a circus was better than staying at home listening to Frank Sinatra on the record player and looking at pictures of his wife. After Soula's death his friends had rallied around him, shocked at having to consider the feelings of a man who was legendary for stating that feelings were a luxury of the bourgeoisie. They had provided him with drink, and houses in the country to hide in, and cars. They had tried to provide him with women, but the only one he had accepted was Mauricette, the Swiss nursemaid for his daughter, Paula; the producer André Roth had found her for him, and she came with the use of a chalet in Klosters. The press had begun to treat him kindly, for there is nothing like grief to make a man respectable, and his latest film had been lauded beyond the limits of his own expectations. He had been called "a bold talent," "a fearless inventor," "*un poète de l'écran.*" These descriptions were part of his aura; he carried them with him wherever he went, and people responded more to what they had read about him than to anything he said these days, because he no longer said much.

When he first caught sight of Charlene, he saw a sort of human torch topped by the brightest red hair he had ever seen; the sharp turquoise light of the aquarium sent kingfisher reflections over her shoulders. She looked to him like something between a salamander and a water nymph, and he was charmed.

"He's so magnetic," Charlene whispered to Szos as they all pulled on their coats to leave. "It's not that I want to cheat on Saul, but I loved his last film."

But Raoul was not to be had so easily: he insisted on driving the snake charmer to the circus, in his new Sunbeam convertible. Charlene reluctantly got into a taxi with Szos and the others, wondering where she had failed. She could have spoken to him, of course, but somehow he had rendered her speechless.

Raoul went through three red lights; he was thinking about the redhead. The Peruvian, who had never been known for his courage, was unnerved. Being the last of a line of high-climbing Indians, he was the possessor of a thoracic expansion so pronounced that he had spent his childhood looking like a dwarf, and the rest of his life fearing he would be taken for one. His name, Arto, was short for Arturo. His reaction to Raoul's driving was to reach into his pocket for a small post office envelope containing some of the powder that he habitually sold to jazz musicians, the pure substance dear to his fellow South Americans.

When Raoul parked the car, Arto held up the envelope. "Have some," he offered. Raoul shook his head.

"It makes you feel like a tiger," enticed Arto. Raoul shook his head again.

"It makes you feel six feet tall," added Arto.

"I *am* six feet tall," said Raoul.

"Well, so am I," Arto snapped back defensively. Throwing an offended glance at Raoul, he dropped a spill of cocaine on the flat part of the dashboard and inhaled through a rolled-up banknote. "It makes you fuck like a demon," said Arto, sniffing the stuff back into his throat.

Raoul signaled that he would have some, after all.

"Vous êtes charmante," Raoul whispered to Charlene during a slow interlude where clowns were throwing silver spangles over one another. She turned slightly, exhibiting her pert three-quarter profile in which, she had been told by the *Vogue* photographer, the planes of her face formed a magic number of perfect triangles. *"Merci,"* she said. Her accent was good particularly when it did not have to extend over more than a pair of syllables.

"Vous êtes mariée?" inquired Raoul, leaning his elbows on the back of her chair.

"Oui," she said out of habit, and before she could correct herself, he asked her what one asks a married woman: *"Vous avez des enfants?"*

"Une fille." A warm, motherly smile spread over the triangles of her face, which did their best to adapt to it.

"Moi aussi," he said.

She nodded. *"Je sais."* Already, with words like *sais,* the accent faltered a little; the muscles of her mouth, although exquisite, were not up to holding the sharp, fast *ā* and produced an American *y* with a suspicion of a drawl.

"Vous devez l'aimer beaucoup," suggested Raoul.

She turned fully to him now, ignoring the elephant that had just lumbered into the ring wearing what appeared to be a red curtain. *"Oui . . . Je t'adore!"* The moment she said it she knew she had made a gaffe, because Raoul's instant reaction was to place his hand on the flesh that folded over so slightly above her tight bodice. As his long fingers began to caress that portion of her anatomy, Charlene's mind raced to remember every possible rule about verbs that Julie had imparted to her. *J'aime,* I love. *Tu aimes,* you love. *Il aime,* he loves . . . no no no, not that . . . Shit!

Where in hell was it? Oh—yeah: *Je m'aime,* I love myself. *Je t'aime,* I love you. *Je l'aime,* I love him or her.

"I meant I love her." She wanted to say that. That was what she was thinking about saying. She could say it now, before it was too late. Too late? She found herself looking into Raoul's liverish brown eyes. A question in her glance, a charming suspension of thought, were what he saw there. Just as the lights went out, he leaned forward and applied his lips to hers.

Raoul offered to drive Charlene home, as she had pretended a headache and refused to join the others at Le Boeuf sur le Toit. What he meant by home, of course, was his apartment on the Rue de Berri, a trio of rooms that he had kept since his bachelor days and which Soula had always disdained to visit. With Paula safely in Switzerland, he had moved back into the apartment and filled it with mementos of Soula: photographs, a painting of her as Venus emerging from the sea—the retrospective irony never failed to reinforce his distrust of life—and an almost complete collection of the magazines in which she had appeared. Raoul was not a man who paid much attention to publicity, but when Soula's agent had offered him her "archive," Raoul had accepted; he enjoyed reading interviews in which she talked of the great bliss she had found in her marriage to him.

The cocaine was still fueling his blood with a lambent energy. He offered Charlene a brandy as she hesitated at the door to his *salon*, contemplating the face of her enemy repeated in oil, paper, newsprint, and even in a small bronze head. She accepted the brandy; something told her that tonight was her night, and if she delayed she would find Saul back in her bed and this dark, soulful man gone forever. She lay on the sofa and allowed him to sit by her knees. He took her chin in his palm and turned her face a little to the left, a little to the right.

"The camera must be in love with you," he said. "Have you ever acted?"

"No," she said, feeling that this moment demanded truth. "I did some nonsense in Hollywood when I was very young, but that's all."

He breathed in sharply, then looked up at Soula's portrait. "Did you ever know . . . ?" he asked her.

Charlene shut her eyes and nodded a yes; she summoned up those emotions that enabled her to look overcome.

But Raoul was having none of that: for the first time in half a year, he was interested in life. He put his hand low down on her belly, and pressed gently. "Are you," he asked, "red down there as well?"

As questions go, it was both intimate and cruel. Charlene kept her eyes closed in the hope that he would think she was asleep. She heard no sound from Raoul, felt no change in the pressure of his hand. She briefly considered falling asleep, and rejected the idea: something had to happen. She opened her eyes. Raoul was looking at the gold bandage that enclosed her chest.

"Tu n'as pas mal?" he asked, and without waiting for an answer, he flicked the knot of lamé out of its tuck by her right armpit and pulled her forward. She prepared herself to kiss him, but his arms reached around her back and he began to unwind the fabric, rolling carefully like a field nurse undoing a bandage. In no time her breasts stood exposed. Charlene felt inadequate and her hands flew up to cover them. Slowly Raoul took her hands away and looked at the sharp nipples protruding from two small, soft bumps, each the size of half an apple. He looked with curiosity and delight. Charlene hated him for it. *"C'est trop petit pour toi,"* she said in remarkably good French, considering the moment. He smiled. "They are charming beestings," he said. "Like those of a girl of thirteen." And he set to work exploring their volume with his tongue. Charlene was so overcome with gratitude that even when she found her body lurching toward the wet, warm grainy surface of his tongue, she was flooded not so much with the sweat and hope of excitation, as with the sense of a social triumph. Raoul Abime.

The evening could have ended with cries of joy. Once Raoul had divested himself of his baggy whipcord trousers, allowing Charlene to observe that he was among the wild men of this world who do not bother with underwear, something failed him. The sight of a photograph, framed in brass on the desk, of Soula holding Paula forced him to call upon inner resources to complete the task he was engaged in, but, unfortunately, his resources, having consisted that evening of extract of coca leaf, had by then been used up. But Raoul was a strategist. He sat down on the sofa, next to Charlene, who was writhing in expectation, her eyes closed once again.

"Let us be serious," he said.

"Serious?"

"You are a *femme mariée.* You have your obligations. It is very well to behave like adolescents, but I cannot compromise you."

"You aren't compromising me," said Charlene, lowering the zipper on her long black skirt. "I'm not married."

"But I want you to stay here. You cannot do that, you must go home, or your absence will be noticed," he pleaded, with solemn good sense.

"I don't care," said Charlene, between gritted teeth.

"You are willing to take the responsibility for your action?" asked Raoul, little knowing that Charlene desired the responsibility as much as, if not more than, the action.

"Yes!" She almost screamed it. He took her hand and helped her off the couch. Slowly he led her to the door of the living room, turned her to the left and, with gentle pressure on the back of her bare shoulders, made her precede him down the hall. At the end was an unlit room; Charlene halted at the door. Two taps on her shoulder blades propelled her in. Raoul clicked the button on a lamp and she saw a large unmade bed, stark in the center of a long low-ceilinged room; there was nothing else there. Charlene moved toward the bed with speed and determination: she wanted to be compromised as fast as possible. Letting her skirt drop in a reckless attempt at being unselfconscious, she found that her girdle had stayed fast to her lower body and needed to be laboriously rolled down. She dispensed with disengaging her stockings from the rubber hooks, and wriggled herself into nudity, perched on the side of the bed. To her relief, Raoul was already lying on the bed, facing away from her. He had not taken off his shirt. She rose to her feet and crossed the room to turn off the single standing lamp, but could not find the switch. She returned to the bed, lay down, and put an arm out to Raoul. "*Chéri,*" she whispered, a trifle presumptuously, but he didn't hear: he was fast asleep.

She reasoned that she could leave at once, but that would be unfair both to her and to Raoul. He had evinced desire, he should be allowed to act on it in his own good time. It did not occur to her to be humiliated: in her mind, Raoul was too big a prize for her to encumber herself with such frills as self-esteem. She knew the qualities required of her: patience, a passive expectancy, mystery. Although mystery would have been best served by her getting dressed and going home, leaving perhaps no more than a piquant note scrawled in lipstick on his bathroom mirror, she rejected this course of action: she had no idea what she'd write. Opting for patience and passive expectancy, and hoping for a little beauty sleep, she laid her head down next to his and pretended to sleep. Her method for attaining most things in life was to pretend she had them until they materialized. Sleep turned up just as she hoped it would.

December dawns in Paris are notorious for not arriving until decent people are already hard at work. By the time the windows paled it was already ten o'clock. Charlene sat up in bed and looked around. To any other woman, the sight of a bare, dirty room in which she has failed to be seduced would look like the battlefield of defeat, but to Charlene the props were merely in place for the second act. She resisted the impulse to scratch herself, which she habitually gave in to when forced to sleep between unfamiliar sheets, and turned toward Raoul. Their bodies had miraculously not touched during the brief period they had slept. Charlene pressed her body against his in a facsimile of gratified desire. Raoul's arm reached behind him, and found her stomach; he gave a grunt, and opened his eyes. While he reassembled his recent memories his hand investigated the surface of the flesh it touched; the soft but somewhat wiry texture of the hair he found there rekindled an image of fire, of flame, and he heaved himself around to face Charlene.

His eyes went first to her breasts, which he touched lightly with his hand, and then down to his penis, which lay crouched in unsociable privacy beneath the sheets. Charlene crawled down into the dark linen cave and availed herself of every art to coax the cranky troglodyte out of its torpor; after half an hour of an exercise that would have enabled her to pronounce *"Je sais"* with impeccable sharpness for at least a month, the troglodyte arose and stretched. Raoul pulled Charlene up into the light, rolled her over on her back, and, levering himself with one arm, raised his body onto hers. She received him with open legs.

"La chair," he said as he kneaded her back, her arms, her hips, and ran his hands over her thighs, *"la chair."* This term for flesh was not familiar to her. She had encountered *viande* when dealing with the butcher, but *la chair* was quite beyond her. She understood *"ma chère"* because she wanted to, and Raoul's repetition of so touching a term of endearment rocked her into a greater and more total abandonment than she had ever known.

They collided and joined all too briefly; Raoul's sperm, which had not been anywhere near a dark, wet female recess for even longer than he had been a widower, became frenzied at the prospect of legitimate release and invaded Charlene before he would have wished; but Charlene, who had been experiencing a mild form of orgasm since the moment Raoul had opened his eyes, felt no need to reproach him.

Raoul subsided like a beached wave and, after a minute, asked, *"Tu as joui?"*

"Joui?"

"Did you have a ball?" he asked, incongruously.

Charlene tried not to laugh. "A ball? Sure, I had a ball. But that's not what I call it . . ." The magic of the situation was being spoiled by this expression out of her Hollywood days.

"Soula told me that was the word," said Raoul, sheepish.

"I know." The way she said this made Raoul speculate on the extent of Charlene's relationship with his late wife. The notion excited him. He gave Charlene a kiss—the first one they had exchanged since the circus. Charlene would have been content to stay in bed with him all day, reflecting on her good fortune, but Raoul had a better idea.

"Have you ever been to the South of France?" he asked. Charlene thought of Monte Carlo and Cannes, and said no; she wanted him to think he could show her things she had never seen before.

"My family is there, in Marseilles. It's where they arrived when we left Rumania. I cannot think of staying in Paris alone this Christmas. I will go there, and have my daughter brought down from Switzerland." Charlene listened patiently, her heart beating hard. "My mother will be there, my brother—he's a steelworker—his wife, their children . . . Would you like to come with me?"

It flashed through Charlene's mind that today must be the twenty-third; Saul would be returning tonight. She had to act quickly. "I'd love to go anywhere with you, anytime, anyplace," she said. Raoul was flattered—not by the words but by the mess she was going to get into by carrying them out; he liked to feel sacrifice around him. As he expected, she cautioned that she had a few things to attend to first, but transmitted this information in a light, brisk tone that betrayed none of its importance. "What time were you going to leave?" she asked.

"I am booked on the wagon-lit from the Gare de Lyon. Eight o'clock. Have you ever *baisé* in a train? It's very sexy." He reached for her buttocks and shook them; "Tchou-tchou, tchou-tchou," he said.

"Chug-chug, chug-chug," corrected Charlene, adding, "I must get up and go home. Do you have a sweater I can borrow?" Raoul gestured toward a cupboard, the doors of which stood wide open. "Take what you want," he said. Charlene chose a gray cashmere turtleneck sweater, and, delicately scooping up her skirt and her girdle by the side of the bed, went to wash her face. While she was in the bathroom Raoul lit a cigarette and considered: he was delighted at having found a woman so apparently willing to do whatever he wished. He did not worry about her becoming too attached to him: he had enough cunning to elude her if she became too clinging, and whatever happened after Christmas was up to him. He briefly pitied the poor fool who lived with her, knowing what was about to befall him, and stubbed out the cigarette on the inside curve of a metal shoe tree that lay handily near the bed.

Charlene came back and leaned over to kiss him. He offered to call her a taxi, but she refused: she would walk a little. She found a taxi on the

Champs-Elysées, where shoppers were already hurtling along the sidewalks. In a last-minute fit of discretion, she made him drop her off at the corner of her street, and closing her fur coat at the neck and hiding her evening bag under her arm, she strode into the courtyard as if she had just been on a little *promenade.* She didn't have her key, so she rang the doorbell. The yaps of the Yorkshire terriers preceded Julie's slow step; when the door opened, the dogs raced at her ankles, and Julie looked at her mistress with frank surprise: it was only eleven, and she had thought Madame was still in bed. Charlene smiled a little aggressively, and climbed the stairs to her bedroom without a word.

Iris came running up from the basement and found Charlene sitting on her bed, with her address book open in front of her. "My bath's going to run over, sweetheart—would you turn it off?" she asked.

When Iris came back she announced, "I have to go away."

"Now?" asked Iris.

"Tonight."

"Am I coming with you?" asked Iris.

"No, darling, you can't. But I'll be back soon with a really big surprise for you."

Iris had heard of these journeys before: her school friends had told her about them, and she knew what the surprise was. "A little sister!" she screamed.

"No!" answered Charlene. "Well, maybe. But not that little."

Iris began picking the stray pieces of silk off the places on the bedcover where it had separated from age. Her mother said, "Stop that, Iris," but Iris felt she had every right to do what she pleased, since her Christmas was ruined anyway. She said so. "You're going away and it's Christmas!"

"Now listen to me, sweetheart. We are going to have the most wonderful life very, very soon. But it's a secret. You mustn't tell a soul."

"Not even Julie?"

"Not Julie, not Céleste. Not anyone. Now here's"—she extracted a big new fifty-thousand-franc note from her bag and handed it to Iris—"some money to buy a tree. And all the decorations. You keep the money, and Julie will take you wherever you want to go to get the balls and things. Isn't that fun?"

"What about Saul? Is he going with you?" asked Iris, reaching for the money.

"Uncle Saul will be home tonight."

"Who's Uncle Saul?" asked Iris.

"Saul, Saul's Uncle Saul. Now go down to the kitchen and tell Julie to take you out shopping."

"But what time are you leaving?" asked Iris, on the verge of tears.

"You'll see me when you come back. Don't worry! I'm not going to abandon you!"

Iris decided that her mother had become so bizarre that it was safest not to cry in front of her, so she left the room and did her crying on the way down to the kitchen.

Charlene phoned Saul's lawyer at home. "Is Saul still away?" asked Pedro Alzaga, hope in his voice.

"This is important. Does Saul have any legal hold on me?"

"No, not strictly. He pays your rent. Why?"

"I'm leaving him and I don't want anything to happen to Iris."

"I'm sure it won't."

"And what about those thugs he's in business with? Can they hurt me?"

"But, Charlene, I'm not your lawyer. I'm Saul's—"

Charlene hung up. If the suspicion that she sounded like a B movie crossed her mind, it only served to sharpen her purpose; after all, the movies that Raoul made relied heavily on gangster dialogue and fell into that very category. She was not so sure about her chances of getting Saul out of her life; but having rejected murder, lies and denials as all being beneath her, she found that Raoul's invitation left her with only one choice, the most romantic one: flight.

She asked Szos to baby-sit. When he heard her voice on the phone, he hoped for a second that she was going to say a full night's sleep had cured her headache, but he soon realized he was deluding himself. "I'm leaving Saul," she said; the scenario that had unwound in his head over dinner the night before now proved to be correct. As he faced a world that was obviously falling apart a feeling of deep resignation was the only thing that prevented him from trying to dissuade her. Incautiously he told her that Raoul was one of the men he most admired in Paris; confronted by Charlene's folly, he felt it was incumbent on him to be honest about his feelings, and also to hedge his bets. Had he conferred the same praise on Saul he might have saved the situation; but the nicest thing he could summon up about Saul at that moment was the fact that he was a good friend, which weighed lightly in the balance against the most admirable man in Paris. He made up for this disloyalty by querulously demanding if she had informed Saul.

"I'm leaving a note," she said with finality.

"A note! That's terrible!" cried Szos. "I'm not going anywhere within five kilometers of your apartment if you're only leaving a note."

"Céleste will cook you roast goose if you come over."

"What do you think I am, a German? Roast goose! Goose! In Hungary we eat wild boar!"

"Céleste will cook you wild boar, then," retorted Charlene. She was preparing her flight, not planning menus, for God's sake.

"And where," asked Szos petulantly, "do you think she will get it on the twenty-third of December? No, Charlene, you do not know what you are talking about! I will not put my life in danger for something so trivial. There is a war going on."

"What about Iris? Don't you love her? She's going to be awfully lonely."

Szos thought this was something Charlene could have considered before she made travel plans with Raoul. He was about to tell her so when she changed tactics. "Szos, you know, it's you who introduced us in the first place."

"I can't be held responsible for all my actions."

"Well, Saul doesn't have to know. I'll tell him I met Raoul by chance, somewhere else, and you'll be safe."

"Just leave me out of it. As for your daughter, I'll come and see her. But I can't stay with her. I'll just drop in."

"You're a sugar. I'll call you from Marseilles. Merry Christmas."

Once Charlene hung up, Szos began to wonder what joy Charlene could possibly find in Marseilles. It seemed a terrible idea; she'd be home in no time, there might even be bloodshed. The phone rang again. It was Raoul.

"Congratulations," said Szos.

"On what?" asked Raoul, who was always dreaming of a better world.

"La conquête."

"She's adorable. I called for her phone number."

Szos gave it to him, his innocence falling away at each digit. "Listen, don't do anything crazy," he said, to absolve himself.

"Like what?" asked Raoul.

"She's a good friend of mine. She's very special. I don't want you to hurt her."

"She knows what she's doing. And I don't need any lectures from you."

"She's very sophisticated. Are you taking her to—" Szos interrupted himself, not wanting to let Raoul know about his conversation with Charlene. "—to Klosters?"

"To Marseilles."

"That's not possible."

"You're telling me how to handle a woman?"

"Look, Raoul, she doesn't speak French. Your family doesn't speak English. You never took Soula there; why Charlene?"

He had a point. "Where should I take her?" asked Raoul quickly, so that it wouldn't sound as if he needed any advice.

"Somewhere glamorous. She is a *femme du monde.* Take her to the Grand Hôtel du Cap. Treat her like a lady."

"Go have yourself buggered" is the translation of what Raoul said to Szos.

Charlene packed seven suitcases containing outfits for every occasion and the good-luck three meters of gold lamé. Iris and Julie came home at four with a pine tree ten feet tall, which they attempted with Céleste to raise in the living room against all odds, until at last Madame Huron's husband, a lineman on the Paris–Brest train, was called in to secure it in an upright position. Saying good-bye, Iris embraced her mother somewhat absently; she was counting the red balls, the blue balls, the green and the gold balls that were to go on the tree. A taxi arrived, and Charlene's bags were loaded on by Monsieur Huron, who looked a little surprised.

When Charlene arrived at Raoul's, he congratulated himself on having taken Szos's advice. The Hôtel du Cap had found two rooms, not a suite but good enough rooms with two balconies facing the gardens and the sea. He told Charlene of their change of destination and she secretly breathed a little sigh of relief. She had lunched at the Hôtel du Cap with Saul once on their way to Monte Carlo, and it had seemed just the right place for a passionate affair.

The note she left Saul was in the style that she fell back on when making emotional declarations. It said: "There comes a time when we have to put our chips on the table, and I've found my one true love. No words can express the distress that I feel towards you, but I know you wish for my happiness above all things." She had made one telephone call to a news agency that was to clarify the whole thing for him.

When they arrived at the station—Raoul's car closely followed by a taxi carrying six of the seven cases—they were met by some twenty press photographers. Raoul cursed; Charlene kept her mouth closed and looked surprised. Agence France-Presse had proved even more efficient than she had hoped. As he helped her out of the car he muttered imprecations. "Don't you want to be seen with me?" she asked sweetly. Raoul took her by the waist and gave her a kiss by way of an answer.

5.

Childhood at Last

"Szos?"

"Yes? Charlene? Is it over already?"

"Not at all. How . . . how's Saul?"

"He was drunk the first night back. He read about you and Raoul the next day in *France-Soir,* I don't know how they learned your name. He consulted his lawyer. What can I say? He's in a state. How's the weather?"

"Beautiful. Listen, have you seen Iris like you promised?"

"She's here with me. Saul went out yesterday and the servants haven't heard from him since. So I invited Iris to tea. It's Christmas Day, you know."

"I know. Are you busy?"

"Busy? Busy?" He looked at Iris, who was leaning against his knees, pressing his kneecaps with her fists; "I want to speak to Mommy!" she was saying fiercely. "Of course I'm busy."

"Do you have a lot of work in Paris?" asked Charlene.

"No, it's dead. Why?"

"Raoul and I were wondering if you felt like taking the Blue Train down to Nice. And bringing Iris with you."

Iris took the phone.

"Darling, Uncle Freddy is going to bring you down here."

"When?"

"Tonight, if he can. I can't wait to see you. And you have a little sister here. She wants to meet you really badly."

"A baby?"

"No, she's your age. She's so pretty and so nice and so sweet you'll just adore her. She's called Paula . . ."

Iris handed the phone back to Szos and sulked over to the bar, where she extracted a maraschino cherry from a bowl of congealed syrup. She heard Szos's protests softening to vague agreement. The little sister sounded like the worst idea anyone had yet come up with. Had her mother gone and adopted someone? Wasn't she good enough on her own? She heard the bell as Szos put down the receiver. "Let's not go," she said.

"We must," said Szos. "It's important. Anyway, you haven't had a very nice Christmas yet."

"I loved the perfume you gave me. And your jokes. Tell me the one about the four black women and one of them is a cannibal, again, please?"

Szos took Iris home and instructed Julie to pack a case. Céleste eyed him warily: both women were worried about their "situation" in the disintegrating household. Szos handed each of them a five-thousand-franc note, "*pour les étrennes.*" Julie curtsyed, but Céleste remained sullen. Szos remembered Charlene's rash promise about roast goose and wondered how anyone could persuade this old cow to produce any kind of meal, much less to cook goose. He phoned the station from the library and found out there were no berths available; he called a high *fonctionnaire d'état* in the country who pulled the correct strings to obtain a double-berth *couchette*. Since Szos wasn't paying the bill, he phoned his brother in New York as well.

Unused to playing the role of nanny, Szos filled what he supposed to be the lacunae in his experience with children with extravagance: he bought a copy of every comic book available at the station bookstall—even *Pif,* which he knew to be a Communist party organ—and refrained, out of deference to his charge, from buying himself any reading matter that might include photographs of unclothed males.

Iris was wildly excited at the prospect of joining her mother at the far end of a long train trip. She was not sorry to leave Julie behind; ever since her mother had left, Julie had taken to talking about how the Devil lived in looking glasses and couture dresses, and Iris was afraid to fall asleep at night in case the Devil leaped out of the mirror over her bed and took hold of her. The train, with its dark-blue sides, its twinkling yellow light bulbs, its paneled corridors, reminded her of her dollhouse: it felt safe. She was a little worried about traveling with a man, even if it was Szos: she was aware that there were certain things that she should not allow him to know, such as when she went to the toilet, and she dreaded having to change into her nightgown in front of him. They sat side by side on the hairy beige banquette, reading. The train lurched, set up a clatter of wheels on rails, and began to take on speed. "Well," said Szos, "what about dinner?"

Over the *services complets* Szos told her more jokes. He spoke to her in French, and some of the jokes had to do with the act of *dépucelage.* He told them with no fear of corrupting her mind; Szos was the only person who knew how she would interpret the word, despite her confident precocity, for he, too, straddled the barriers of several languages. *Dépucelage,* the act of deflowering, was to Iris no more than de-fleaing, which presented a cozy image of two baboons grooming themselves in the zoo. She laughed as various young men managed to rid various young ladies of their fleas, and thought it a little strange that the fathers should always mind so much. But then, Julie had once described Szos to Céleste as *"ce sale pédé"* within Iris's hearing, and Iris ever after looked on Szos as a man who was at peace with dirt.

But she would not eat. The *hors-d'oeuvre variés* were followed by little curls of sole, which were followed by slices of red meat in a brown sauce, and Iris did no more than pensively suck the gravy off a strand of watercress from the rim of her plate. Szos was not going to be a nursemaid: he offered her a glass of wine to sharpen her appetite, which she at first declined, and then accepted, watering it down with some Vittel from the half bottle she had ordered herself from the youngest of the white-coated waiters. Szos finished his meal, declined dessert, and took an oppressively long cigar from the breast pocket of his blazer. He called over a waiter, and asked for something light to be brought for the child. The waiter warned him that he would have to pay full price for both meals even if she had not eaten hers, and that a *yaourt*—the only light food the wagons-lits carried—would be *en supplément.* By way of an answer Szos waved the cigar at him and demanded a light. The waiter produced a Zippo lighter and flicked it open near the end of the cigar, which Szos pulled away quickly. *"Pour un havane,"* he said, *"il faut des allumettes."* The waiter understood that a man who smoked Havanas had no qualms about a few extra francs for a yogurt, and brought a plain glass pot, which he set before Iris, and a tiny box of Italian wax matches, which he put on the table just beyond Szos's reach.

Iris took a cube of sugar and carefully unwrapped it; then she placed it in the center of the skimmy surface of the yogurt, tested the texture with a spoon, and put the spoon back down.

"Eat something," said Szos. "Have some yogurt."

Iris shook her head. "When it's ready," she said.

"Eat," said Szos, again. Iris looked at the white-on-white effect of the sugar cube in the yogurt and gave a long sigh. "Eating," she said, "only makes you fat. And once you swallow what you eat, it comes out the other end, and then you pull the chain and it's gone."

"So what else is new?"

"And then you have to eat again. And then it happens again, it goes through you. And if it doesn't everybody makes a fuss and gives you things to take so it will. And then you have to eat again, and again, and again. What's the use of it?"

Szos repeated her question. *"A quoi ça sert?* I don't know. It keeps you alive. You have to eat to live."

Iris slowly turned her head from left to right, dismissing this notion. *"Tu ne vois pas?"* she asked. "It's just for *that* that I can't see the use. Because you die, anyway."

She waited, hands on the table, staring intently at Szos. Maybe, just maybe, there was a slim chance he would tell her that it was different. Give her an answer that would be the key to escaping the vicious circle she had worked out. Instead, he smiled at her, and said, "You know, you're right. That's probably why they have to pretend cooking is an art, because eating is useless." He sucked on his cigar and cocked his head at her; he wondered what sort of things Charlene had been teaching her. "You know," he said, "you're intelligent, but I don't think it will help you."

Iris excused herself, and would not allow Szos to tell her where the *toilettes* were. She asked the oldest of the waiters instead.

Szos finished his coffee and watched the cube of sugar slowly begin to sink through the yogurt's surface as he considered the enormity of his crime. Was he a kidnapper? he wondered, or an accessory to adultery? He wondered if Saul cared enough about Charlene to put cement overshoes on him and throw him in the Seine. He was saved from further brooding by the return of Iris, and suggested bedtime as the logical conclusion to their evening of urbane chat and self-abnegation. Iris sat down. "The yogurt is ready now," she said, and began to eat it in tiny spoonfuls taken from the inner edge of the rim of the glass pot.

"Tomorrow we will wake up in Cannes," said Szos.

Uncharacteristically, Iris said, "Pooh."

"Pooh?" inquired Szos. "I thought you were excited."

"Do you know this sister Mommy's bought me?" she asked.

"Ah," said Szos. In his musings he had pictured Charlene and Raoul in attitudes of raunchy felicity; he had forgotten about Paula. "A sister. How big?"

"My size, I think."

"Well, yes, I know her," he admitted. "She's called Paula. She's very nice—"

"I don't want to hear *about* her," specified Iris with care. "I just wanted to know if you knew her."

"I didn't know you were going to meet her," said Szos. He was a little annoyed at Charlene; he felt that she should have given him every detail of her escapade.

Iris was so afraid of bad news that she always took care to meet it halfway. Therefore she asked the question that was even more troubling to her than the matter of the ultimate destiny of food: "Is it true that she's prettier and nicer and more intelligent and more *sympathique* than me?"

Szos's experience as an agent determined his reply, which was automatically geared to dispel doubts in his clients. "No one is prettier or nicer or more intelligent or more *sympathique* than you," he said. It was something he had said so many times in answer to so many similar questions that it lacked the forceful sincerity that would have allowed Iris to believe him.

She put her spoon down. "I'm ready for bed," she said. "I'm not used to being up this late." Already, *déjà,* they're lying to me, she thought.

In the compartment, which had been turned into an elegant version of a Nissen hut by the magic hands of an invisible employee of the SNCF, Szos assigned Iris the upper bunk and delicately offered to wait outside while she changed. When he returned, she was in the bunk with a comic book in front of her face.

He washed his hands in the little sink, gargled with a mouthful of Botot, and took some fennel pills that his homeopathic doctor had prescribed for flatulence. Once he was in bed, clad in his boxer shorts and his cashmere robe, he opened *The Well of Loneliness*—not that he found much joy in lesbian literature, but it was a possible project for Raoul if one of the characters was turned into a man. Stephen, perhaps, or Mary. After all, someone else was playing around with *Les Liaisons Dangéreuses.*

Iris went to sleep listening to Szos's heavy breathing and watching the warm light cast by the lamp beneath her bunk. Szos awakened at his usual intervals, in the kind blue light of the *veilleuse,* and refrained from wanking himself back to sleep in case it disturbed Iris. The compartment grew hot from their breaths mingled with the enthusiastic heating, hot and heavy.

The train pulled into the Cannes station at a quarter past nine. Szos's face was puffy and green as he shook Iris awake, and she was covered with a film of sweat. A curious unease had sprung up between them: both had a certain dignity and disliked being seen in their respective conditions. It did not make for easy conversation. "Cannes," said Szos as he released the thick green plastic blind, which snapped up. Bright red tiles and pink walls glowed; the guards and the porters were shouting in thick rolling accents. Szos began rapping on the window to attract the attention of one of the porters.

"Why do we need a porter?" asked Iris. "We didn't have one in Paris."

"It's better to always have someone else carry your things," explained Szos. Seeing Raoul walking past the window, Szos pounded on the glass until he found the way to open the window and pulled it down. Raoul reached up for Szos's hand. *"Merci, mon vieux,"* he said.

"Who's that?" hissed Iris. "Why are you holding hands with a porter?"

Szos did not hear her; he was saying, "It was nothing, a pleasure." Raoul shaded his eyebrows with his hand and peered into the compartment to take a look at Charlene's daughter. Iris glared at him: she did not enjoy the scrutiny of strangers. Raoul clambered aboard and found their compartment; slapping Szos on the back, he scooped up Iris in his arms and carried her out of the train, Iris fighting him furiously. In the warm, surprising sun she found herself being conveyed down the platform in this stranger's arms. She yelled; she howled. She opened her eyes to see what their destination was and saw her mother, who was screaming *"Ici!"* Next to her was a little girl with dark hair in bangs and big green eyes. The man set her down at Charlene's feet. Iris reached up, indignant and wailing like a baby. *"Merci,"* said Charlene to the man before looking down at her. Iris knew he had to be some kind of servant, since her mother never spoke French to anyone but domestics. "Welcome to Cannes," said Charlene, hugging her.

"Who is that porter?" hissed Iris. Charlene ignored the question: her relief at recovering Iris was immeasurable. When Raoul had summoned his daughter—within one day, one miserable day, of their arrival at the Grand Hôtel du Cap—certain limits had been placed on their passion. Charlene figured he was trying to tell her something. She did what any other woman would have done and retaliated in kind. She blessed Szos for having been able to come down so fast, and looked at her child, who was staring at Raoul's child.

"Yes, darling," said Charlene, looking misty and motherly.

"Who *is* that?" asked Iris.

"That—" said Charlene, watching Raoul with his arms around Szos, "that is—" She found she needed his confirmation to help her say it. "Raoul!" she screamed. "*Viens ici.*" As Raoul let go of Szos she knelt and put her arms around both girls and looked up at him. "Iris," she said in tones of the utmost formality, "this is Raoul." She wondered what else she could say about him. "And this is Paula. This is the little sister I told you about."

The girls were the same height; their hair was similar. Paula's eyes were lighter, her fringe a little shorter.

"How old are you?" asked Iris.

"Eight," said Paula.

"I'm seven," said Iris. Looking up at Charlene, she asked, "Who did you buy her from?" Charlene, who felt that she had acted rashly in describing Paula as a sister when Raoul had not exactly popped anything like a question at her yet, ordered Iris to kiss Paula.

"They'll like each other," said Raoul, ignoring the tension between the children. "They both speak French and they've been brought up in hotels."

Szos came down the platform carrying Iris's little suitcase in one hand, while a porter carried his voluminous gladstone bag and two airline bags full of papers and books. Raoul nodded knowingly at Szos's luggage. "We figured you'd want to rest from your trip, so we booked you a room."

"What did you expect me to do, hand her over and take the next train back?" asked Szos a little sharply.

They climbed into a white *quarante chevaux*. The adults sat on the backseat, and the girls took the jump seats as their common birthright, like upper bunks or the first squares in a chocolate bar. But they each stared out a different window, Paula at the houses and Iris at the sea. "Can we go swimming?" she asked her mother.

"Not this time of year, it's too cold," said Charlene.

Raoul squeezed Charlene's arm and pointed his finger at the girls. From the back their dignified little heads looked identical. Charlene saw it at once; she said, "They're exactly alike," hoping this was a good omen. Paula and Iris shot sly looks at each other; neither of them was used to being around other children.

"She was charming company and kept me entertained in a most delightful way," said Szos. Iris sat up a little straighter and frowned studiously at the green water and the palm trees. Paula scratched her foot.

"She didn't drive you crazy? Did she eat?" asked Charlene. Iris's mouth slipped into a pout. Paula looked around at her father and beamed.

"She discoursed like Plato on the nature of existence," said Szos. "You'd better give her an education, she can take it." Iris breathed deeply and concentrated on the silver knob by the window of the car door. It was a beautiful knob. Paula was fiddling with the apron of her dress, a Tyrolean costume composed of a blouse, an embroidered pinafore and an apron edged in rickrack.

"I hope she didn't bore you," said Charlene; the intimation caused Iris to slump in her seat. Paula turned around and blew her father a kiss.

"Are we dropping him off first?" inquired Iris, as the car slowed on entering the narrow streets of Juan les Pins.

"Who?" asked her mother.

"The porter."

Charlene leaned forward and slapped Iris, who received the blow with an outraged yelp. Wagging her finger at Iris, she said: "Raoul Abime is a very important movie director and I want you to respect him. And Paula, who is his daughter, is a nice, kind, wonderful girl, not a little snob bitch like you." Having delivered her speech, she sank back against Raoul and took his hand.

Paula climbed through the little space between the jump seats and clambered onto Raoul's lap. "Daddy, I'm going to vomit, make the car stop," she said.

Szos told himself that if Saul didn't get to him first, it was entirely possible that Raoul would be the one to throw him in the Seine. Domestic quarrels had little to do with the kind of dangers he enjoyed. He looked out the window at a bar behind some trees across the square. LE TABOU, it said; he wondered if he could bail out when the car stopped at the lights. "We're almost there," Raoul told Paula, *"Contrôles-toi un peu."*

At the hotel Raoul told Paula to take Iris up to her room. Paula stared silently at Iris in the elevator as it rose in its golden cage in the middle of the lobby. A week before, she had been in Heidi-land in the Swiss Alps with Mauricette, her nanny. Now there were these two new people in her life. The only consolation was that Charlene was her father's guest, and this Iris was her guest; she knew one had little to fear from guests, for if they became difficult, one simply asked them to leave.

Iris looked around Paula's room. There were dolls and toys everywhere. Iris quickly counted them, classifying as she went. Stuffed animals: one comic spaniel, one bear, one giraffe. Dolls, blond: one tall eye-closer in a blue dress, one American doll with feet arched for high heels, one little girl. Dolls, brunette: one antique china-face in a rumpled linen nightgown, one little bride with her veil askew, one child in a checked dress —missing her shoes. She sat down on one of the beds, furious that, in an effort to be adult, she had left her dolls at home. "That's mine," said Paula. Iris stayed put. "I said that is my bed," repeated Paula. Iris kicked her legs up and brought them down on the center of the bed. *"Je suis tellement fatiguée,"* she moaned in a yawn. Under her back she felt something bumpy; she pulled down the stiff spread and uncovered a monster of a rag doll: it had red hair and huge red spots painted on its face. Its hair was the exact color of Charlene's. "It's not nice to make fun of people with red hair," she said. "You mustn't let my mother see it or she will be upset."

"She tucked me in last night, and the night before. She saw it. She wasn't upset," said Paula. The idea that Charlene had been tucking Paula in, when she had never tucked her in, made Iris feel more alone than she already did; she wanted to hit this other girl, this rival. She began to cry.

Feeling the dangerous thrust of Iris's anger, Paula threw herself on the second bed and began to howl. Iris stopped sobbing and glared at the figure on the other bed for a short indecisive minute, wavering between the need to express her dismay and curiosity as to why the other girl should be crying. Curiosity won out. She tiptoed to the other bed and paused.

"What is it?" No answer. "Why are you crying like that?" A grunt. More wails. "Please tell me." Iris sat down on the bed.

"My mother's dead!" screamed Paula. "She's dead, she can't tuck me in, she's dead! I haven't got a mother anymore!"

So Iris hugged her; it seemed the proper thing to do. Paula sobbed on, and after a while she looked up at Iris and said, "You can't mind if your mother loves me too, because I am an orphan. Don't be jealous. I have a right to be loved by a mother too, because I haven't got one anymore."

Iris saw that Paula was right.

Charlene, Szos and Raoul sat on the terrace having before-lunch drinks with sweaters wrapped around their shoulders against the idea of December, although the day was warm. Charlene told them both what a wonderful child Iris was, which Szos found endlessly tedious, even if he did like the girl. He longed to ask about the wisdom of suddenly creating this nuclear family out of nothing, but did not want to lose a client or a friend.

When Mauricette came out to the terrace in her starched uniform, holding the two girls by the hand, Charlene redoubled her superlatives. "Aren't they the best twins?" she asked. "Aren't they incredibly alike? It's just unbelievable how much they look like sisters, isn't it, Szos?" The girls went down the sloping walk to the sea, followed by Mauricette.

Szos gulped down his Campari and took another cigar from his breast pocket. "Do I dare to inquire what your plans are for the new year?" he asked.

"A quiet New Year's Eve," announced Raoul. That was not what Szos had meant. "I'll stay about two or three days," he said, "and then I was thinking of going over to Genoa for some fun."

"Fun?" asked Charlene. "In Genoa?"

"Sailors," said Szos, biting the end off his cigar; he gave a little sigh. "Then I'll go back to Paris. Any messages for anyone?"

"We'll tell you when you leave," said Charlene, her fingers crossed.

By dinner time the girls were inseparable. They had explored the garden together, giggling over the fat thick leaves of the succulent plants, daring each other to touch the needles on the cactus, venturing beyond Mauricette's vigilance to the boarded-up restaurant by the sea, closed for the winter, and, in its shuttered state, full of foreboding. Iris began to think of Paula protectively, as *l'orpheline,* a sacred animal that must be spared more pain. Paula found Iris likable, but a little dangerous. At dinner time—in the brightly lit restaurant, and early, because Charlene had insisted that they all eat together like a family—the girls exchanged knowing looks and giggles over the inclusion of a succulent stem among the flowers of the centerpiece, and Charlene thanked Jesus to see them so obviously bound by friendship. She had not addressed many words to Jesus in the past ten years, but she knew she needed grace to get Raoul to the *mairie* as soon as possible. She could not tolerate being anything less than his wife: for one thing, it wouldn't be clear enough to Saul that she had left him if she simply returned to Paris with Raoul. The thought of returning to Paris without Raoul did not so much as hover in the back of her mind. After all, the papers had shown them going away together, and together they would have to return. It would be too embarrassing otherwise. She had caught him; now all she had to do was somehow secure him.

Szos excused himself after dinner to go for a walk in Juan les Pins. Raoul took Charlene up to the girls' room. "*Bonsoir,*" said Raoul to Iris. "*Dors bien.*" She was a little in awe of him; Charlene had said in the car that he was very important, and Iris remembered that she was not supposed to impose herself on anyone Charlene called very important. She didn't answer him but essayed a little smile. When he ruffled her bangs she held her breath so that it would not disturb him while he did so.

"Sleep well, my little sweetheart," said Charlene to Paula.

"I like Iris," said Paula. Charlene felt her heart swell. Maybe everything would be easy.

"Paula loves Iris," she said to Raoul as they walked along the corridor.

"Iris is very timid," said Raoul.

They went out into the garden for a breath of air; it was chilly now. "I think—" Raoul began. Charlene ruined her chance by saying very quickly, "Yes? What do you think?"

"Nothing," said Raoul. He had to think about it some more before he said anything. He let her go back into the bar alone while he stayed in the garden. It would be absurd, of course, to marry her just because his daughter liked her. On the other hand, what wasn't absurd? If Paula hadn't liked her, if she had reacted badly to Charlene when she first arrived, he would, of course, have broken it off at once. Charlene was touchingly anxious to please him, but no matter how many times she sucked his cock, if his daughter didn't like her she had no chance. The problem was, his daughter did like her. Maybe, he thought, he had wanted Paula to hate Charlene on sight. It would have been an acceptable excuse to use on someone who had a daughter and was as full of maternal feelings as Charlene appeared to be, to say, "*Ma chère,* Paula is the most important thing to me, and she does not like you. I'm sorry, but that is the first thing I have to consider. *Au revoir. Adieu.*" It occurred to him that there was something a little weak in allowing his daughter to make decisions about his life. He should not delegate this thing, he thought; Charlene loved her daughter too much to use her the way he was using Paula. Feeling ashamed of his breach of loyalty to Soula—by asking her daughter to pronounce, even unconsciously, on the suitability of another woman as his wife, what an act of treason to her memory!—he went back into the hotel.

Charlene welcomed him with a nervous little pressure on his thigh. She had been pulling the petals off a daisy, for lack of a better oracle. "It's such a thrill for me to see Iris with a child her own age," she said. "She's always been alone, and I can't believe how well she adapts. But Paula's really the remarkable one." How generous, thought Raoul.

During his brief stay, Szos was able to observe that Raoul behaved with Paula exactly the way he had with Soula. When she came into a room, he stopped talking; he took every opportunity to touch her, feel her little arms, massage her little trapezius muscles, look for splinters in her little fingers, compare their thumbs. There was something a little obsessive about it; he had eyes only for her, and Charlene had to wait for his attention.

On New Year's Eve the girls stayed up until midnight; they ate foie gras in the hotel restaurant, took naps on the sofa in an alcove off the lobby, and sipped champagne in the bar with Raoul and Charlene. Raoul was still watching Paula for signs; it had crossed his mind that killing a pigeon in the park and delving through its entrails would be a more ethical though messier method of divination, but rejected it as impractical. Twice already, Paula had asked if Charlene was her new *maman;* it seemed inevitable that she would be. His heart sank as he saw Paula put an arm around Charlene's neck and play with her thick gold chains, and he took Iris on his knees in a concern for symmetry. At the stroke of midnight they all blew into curled paper whistles that unrolled to expose feathers at their tips. Raoul kissed Paula, and Charlene hugged Iris and covered her with kisses; Paula then went to Charlene and hugged her; Charlene responded by putting her arms around Paula and holding on to her as if her life depended on it, which at that point it more or less did. Iris patted Raoul timidly on the sleeve. Paula turned to look at him with an imploring expression. Plunging in, reckless, heedless, but anxious to allay the lonely little question he fancied he saw in Paula's eyes, he stood up and raised his champagne glass. "This is to the new year and to my new wife, Charlene."

Both little girls clapped their hands and hugged his legs. Charlene burst into tears; she had to use one of the little paper bar napkins to keep her mascara from running down her cheeks.

"I knew it," said Paula to Iris once they were tucked into bed.

"So did I," said Iris. "That's why they told us that we were sisters."

In their room, Raoul stroked Charlene's breasts with the tips of his fingers. "I'm so happy I could die," said Charlene. He found himself wishing she would, and then realized that this would be likely to upset Paula. "Don't do that," he said, feeling unexpectedly warm toward her.

"They'll look so pretty," said Charlene. "They'll carry little bouquets of yellow roses. Oh, Raoul, this is a wonderful night."

"Where will we live?" Paula asked Iris the next morning as they had breakfast with Mauricette, who had been told and couldn't stop sighing. It seemed a little hasty to her, and she asked herself whether it reflected on her ability that Monsieur was so ready to find a new wife. Didn't he like the way she had been taking care of Paula? Wasn't the good Grisons air wonderful for the child?

"At home, I suppose. We have a nice big apartment," said Iris. "It's more of a house, but my room is really small, and I have to share it with—with—" She didn't think it was right for Paula to know about Saul, but she had started the sentence and had to finish it. "—with some awful golf clubs."

"Golf clubs?" Paula thought about this. "Does Charlene play golf?" She wasn't dumb.

"No-o-o," said Iris. She tried to change the subject. "We have two Yorkshire terriers—they're very small, have you ever seen Yorkies?"

"I don't think so. Smaller than poodles?"

"Much smaller. They're called Bijou and Toasty."

"We used to live in a house too, all of us together, when my mother was alive." Paula hovered over the opportunity to cry, but decided against it. Whenever she cried, Mauricette gave her cod liver oil, and she was watching. Iris took her hand. "My mommy's your mommy now," she said. Paula smiled a thanks.

"We'll be sisters," she continued.

"Yes," said Paula. "I always wanted a sister."

"But a sister the same age, that's rare," said Iris.

"I'm a year older than you," said Paula.

On the train back to Paris, Raoul tried to find a way to make Paula detest Charlene as fully as she had approved of her, but nothing came to mind. Finally he hit on something. "Charlene," he said, "Charlene, Charlene, Charlene."

"Yes?" said his betrothed; she was leafing through a nice fat, shiny new *Vogue* she had bought at the station; it was the first magazine she had allowed herself since she had met Raoul. She could no longer resist.

"I'm not sure this is a name I like," he went on. Charlene stopped turning the pages, closed the magazine, and put it down on the seat beside her. Iris stared at Raoul.

"What does it mean, 'Charlene'?" he said. "Charles, yes. Charlotte, yes. Charlemagne, of course. Charlot, a genius. But Charlene?"

Iris decided to side with Raoul at once. "It's long," she said.

"Exactly," said Raoul. "To me, you are a short name. Charlie, for instance."

"Never," said Charlene, not knowing that eventually she would retract her words.

"Charlé," repeated Paula in French. *"C'est très joli."* She was saving Charlene.

"Charlé. Charlé Abime. Pas mal," said Raoul.

Charlene averred that she rather liked it; coupled with Abime, it sounded rather good. Charlene Abime had run through her mind like an old record for the past two weeks, and it sounded sometimes, when she found herself saying it out loud, like some peculiar Hindu greeting.

Mauricette was installed in a maid's room next to Julie, underneath the roof. There was a sealed note from Saul for Charlene, now Charlé. "I'm at the Prince de Galles," it said. "Don't call me. Alzaga will call you."

"I must call him," she said to Raoul, and repaired to the study to do so in privacy.

"I'm getting married," she told Saul.

"I wish you everything that's coming to you," he said; she could hear the sound of other people in his room and wondered who they were.

"That's mighty big of you," she said.

"I'm a big guy," said Saul. "In fact, I'd like to come to the wedding." Charlé found herself imagining Saul at her wedding, and was startled to hear his laugh. As always, she started to laugh upon hearing his chortles and had to pull herself together.

"Listen," he said, "the rent is paid up until March. After that, you can eat crow or suck cock or do whatever you need to get a roof over your head."

She took the insult with the equanimity of the truly happy. He could roast in hell for all she cared, and the wonderful thing was that she didn't need him anymore.

"Raoul has plenty of money," she said. "We don't need your apartment."

"No, I insist. Keep it. It's my wedding present to you."

"And he makes his money from art, not crime," she added, and hung up.

Saul's golf clubs were gone; they were the first thing Iris looked for; so were the bottles of Aqua Velva, his little leather chest of drawers, where he kept his cuff links and his collection of jewelry: the large fob watches, the tiepins, the waistcoat chains. The note he had left Iris had been thrown out by the maid. Had she read it, she would have seen that Saul had written: "It's not your fault, kid, and one day I'll see you again. Be a glamour girl and keep smiling."

He had left the original Broadway-cast albums but taken his autographed pictures of Sugar Ray Robinson and Al Brown and Max Schmeling, of Piaf and Chevalier. Charlé was a little miffed about the latter two; she had hoped that Raoul would feel at home when he saw them, in their silver frames, illegibly dedicated to Saul.

Céleste had gone. She didn't like *le divorce,* or *la publicité.* Madame had proved herself an *indigne adultère;* had Céleste known that Charlé was never married to Saul in the first place, she might have dropped the charge of adultery but replaced it with the even worse one of *concubinage.* Edwige, the maid, told Charlé that Céleste's wages were to be sent to the address that was left on the desk in the *salon*; she left out Céleste's added threat that if they were not, she would have the whole lot of them deported.

Iris returned to the Cours Victor Hugo and announced that she had received a new father and a new sister for Christmas. The other girls raised their eyebrows. "You get a sister or a brother, usually; not a father, too," said one. The *surveillante* who was in charge of the recreation period when this news was handed around marveled at the typical American mythomania of the little girl.

Paula stayed at home and took lessons from Mauricette, as she had in Switzerland, for it was difficult to enroll her in the school before Easter. Iris spent her time at school thinking about Paula, whom she imagined in the *salon,* sitting at one of the little gold-bordered tables and wearing a frilly dress, while Mauricette spun wool at a spinning wheel: an irrational image, made up of an illustration of Switzerland in a magazine and a postcard representing a princess and her governess. Iris was relieved in the afternoon to find Paula looking quite ordinary, waiting to have her *goûter* at the kitchen table, just like she was.

They shared the tiny dressing room, and played house within the space circumscribed by the mahogany panels and the fat-bellied chest of drawers. They tented the portion of floor between the two little beds with an old plaid traveling rug of Paula's mother, and made secret boundaries that were not to be crossed. They had a little trouble sleeping: late at night the cries issuing from Charlé's room were disturbing, and exciting. "It never used to happen," whispered Iris, awakened, like Paula, by a particularly fervent "Whnnnnnhuuuugh!"

6.

Marriage à la Mode

Raoul Abime and Charlene Bromley married on the seventh of February 1957 in the Mairie du Huitième Arrondissement. Charlé, who was in the curious elated state of not believing her own luck, had assuaged her fears by ordering from Madeleine de Rauch a new wardrobe, for which she had no possibility of paying. For the ceremony itself she had ordered a suit the color of warm urine with square topaz buttons. She carried a bouquet of yellow roses, as did Iris and Paula, who were dressed by La Grande Maison de Blanc in little English wool coats with yellow velvet collars. The Yorkies sported yellow leashes, from Le Chien Elégant.

Charlé insisted that Raoul sleep at his old apartment the night before the wedding. He had moved into the Rue Dumont d'Urville only to the extent that a crumpled black leather sponge bag now crouched in the upstairs bathroom, a territorial marker. Raoul had announced privately to Szos that he intended to get drunk and pay a small visit to one of his favorite *maisons.* This news reassured Szos, who feared most of all that Raoul would spend the evening staring at pictures of Soula and get himself into an impossibly maudlin state.

At eleven-thirty two long black Citröens arrived. Szos was in one of them, wearing his formal suit with an electric-blue shirt and a white-and-gray silk cravat. Charlé winced when she saw his color scheme but didn't say anything; she was already hoarse from screaming at the hairdresser, who had insisted on giving her what appeared to be marcel waves, a look he had never tried on her before. Hell of a time to get creative, she had thought, but being unable to translate the thought into accurate French, she had contented herself with hurling a bottle of Femme on the floor.

Szos checked himself in the hall mirror. He liked the cravat; it implied that he was a man unbowed by the exigencies of official behavior, and, better still, that he didn't give a damn about this wedding one way or another. Charlé stood in the doorway to the living room, yellow gloves in hand, breathing slowly and regularly. "You K.O.?" asked Szos. It was his little joke.

"You could say that."

He took her arm and swept her down the three small steps to the front door. Iris and Paula followed, holding on to Mauricette. Julie took up the rear, carrying the Yorkies. A yellow velvet ribbon held back her hair: she wanted to be *dans le ton.*

Szos and Charlé took the first car. The servants and the children sat in the second one. Raoul was waiting outside the *mairie,* leaning against the wall smoking a cigarette. Not far from them was a knot of photographers, conferring. They had big black boxes on the ground into which they were reaching for film and cigarettes. They had already taken pictures of Raoul arriving and Raoul waiting, and they were beginning to wonder whether they had a story at all. When the car stopped and Charlé got out, they rushed forward to photograph her, and then, as a man, stopped and waited until Raoul joined her; without him, after all, where was the picture? *"Drôle de petite rousse,"* said Eric Castiglione, from Magnum by way of Indochina.

The party crossed the courtyard. Jenny, from the *Herald Tribune,* was waiting by the steps, wearing a cloth coat and mittens. She waved at Charlé, who waved back and checked to see whether she was carrying her notebook. Jenny dug a small box of Uncle Ben's rice out of her pocket and brandished it at Charlé, who was no longer looking at her, for inside the glass doors of the *mairie* she had caught sight of Michèle Morgan, and Anatole and Sophie Litvak, and Louis Jourdan, and Christian Marquand and some fifteen other people who, for her, went by the collective term of Everybody. The photographers now surged forward to record her being embraced by the film stars. Julie dropped the Yorkies when she saw who was waiting for her mistress, causing internal injuries to Bijou that were to hasten his early demise. She pulled out her autograph book and waited, mouth hanging open, for Louis Jourdan's eyes to alight on her face. They skimmed past it once or twice, but just when she felt he was about to look at her, the tall double doors of the *salle des mariages* were thrown open and an usher announced, *"Par ici, mesdames, messieurs."*

Raoul searched for Paula. Taking her by a moist little palm, he marched her into the *salle des mariages* with confidence. Paula held on to him with a firm grip; she liked Charlé pretty well, but she wanted Raoul to know that she liked him better. Raoul squeezed her hand. It was his way of letting her know that he was doing this for her.

Throughout the ceremony Iris attempted to join Charlé and Raoul. First Mauricette restrained her, then Julie darted forward to catch her just as she reached Charlé's chair, and dragged her back to a seat two rows behind. Iris felt abandoned: her mother had not looked at her once all day. Paula was out of reach at Raoul's side. The ceremony was long, interrupted only by spasmodic clicks from the photographers massed behind the mayor. Julie wept, Michèle Morgan wept, as did three other actresses, for reasons of their own. Raoul wondered what he was doing there, why he was answering this fool in a tricolor sash in front of him, and who the woman at his left was, and tried to calm himself by reciting a few lines from good reviews he had garnered in the past. *"Un poète de l'écran,"* "a bold and virile talent from France," "a fearless inventor." These descriptions of himself and his work had the talismanic property of making him feel not only that he was absent from the proceedings, but also that he truly belonged in another realm, a classical place of high standards and mighty moral architecture to which he had gained entry through the exercise of his natural talent. What he was doing now was mere housekeeping, a necessary chore to insure the smooth running of his daily life.

Charlé, as aware of the tight fit of her yellow suit as she was of the clicks of the Hasselblads congregated to her left, was so happy that she would have been willing to die on the spot just to preserve the moment. At last, she felt, she was taking possession of her rightful place in society, in showbiz, in the world.

The newlyweds led the way out into the front hall, where the swift photographers had gathered once again. *"Un portrait!"* shouted one; then another added, *"Comme souvenir!"* Eric Castiglione, who had photographed Raoul before, found himself the recipient of a hug from the groom. Arto scurried about rounding up the various people who constituted Everyone and guided them out to the front porch. He tactfully placed the two maids at the very end of the back row, and just as gently managed to head off Szos's secretary, who was trying to place herself next to Raoul.

Iris attempted to stand in front of her mother, and found a bouquet of yellow roses being repeatedly shoved over her face. She tried to catch Charlé's hand, but all she got was "Later, sweetie," in a half whisper through Charlé's clenched smile. Mauricette, who had appointed herself guardian of Iris's welfare, clucked her teeth very loud and crossed in front of the triple row of movie stars to collect her and drag her to one side. Iris bawled: the photographers, who had stopped because of Mauricette ruining what they liked to term their fine *brochette* (any one of those faces got a good spread in any national paper, and Jourdan and Morgan even sold in America), urged Mauricette to one side. Iris pulled out of Mauricette's grasp and found herself in front of Szos, who extended two kind hands, which he placed on her shoulders. "Look at the camera, and smile," he said. She leaned back against his round belly and glared at her mother.

Raoul and Charlé went to Maxim's for lunch, followed by the wedding party. At lunch Paula and Iris sat together on a banquette, eating little pieces of the liver that Mauricette had instructed the waiters to bring. "I think everyone else is having lobster," Paula politely informed her, but Mauricette would not be overruled.

"I'm so happy," said Paula, "to have a new sister."

Iris just nodded. She was chewing her liver and then depositing the wads of masticated meat into her napkin. Three more mouthfuls, and it would look as if she had finished, but she had to be furtive about it, which required her entire concentration. Szos came over to the table. "The Misses Abime!" he said. Paula beamed up at him.

"Am I Abime now, too?" asked Iris.

"I think you are," said Szos.

"Do I have to be?"

Paula turned to her and nodded. "Of course you have to be."

At home the bags were packed: Charlé was taking Raoul to New York for two weeks. Rather, Raoul was taking Charlé away for two weeks, and she had insisted on New York. It was simpler and cheaper than flying the whole O'Malley family out to Paris, and she knew that Coquette would be delighted that she had at last married a Catholic.

Iris and Paula were left in the Rue Dumont d'Urville with Mauricette and Julie, who was amazed to find that she had not been dismissed. Iris and Paula shared the red baldaquin bed and counted the pleats in its silken ceiling. They tickled each other until they were hoarse with laughter. They tormented the dogs, tied ribbons around their legs, wrapped them in blankets, shoved them deep under the bedcovers and then yelled when the dogs' sharp little teeth nipped their legs as they made their way back up from the linen depths.

Iris showed Paula the caves behind the kitchen where the boiler lived, the storerooms that belonged to the marquis where huge old trunks, covered with mold, were piled one upon another. She showed her the grisly door to the sewers, and they ran all the way back up to the bedroom and lay on the red bed panting in a fit of horror-struck giggles. Finally Paula said, "This place is creepy. *We* never lived anywhere creepy."

"Are you scared?" asked Iris, feeling fear wind around her, although it was only three o'clock and the pigeons were billing away outside.

"No, I'm not scared, I just don't like it, that's all."

That night they were sent to bed early. They lay side by side talking about the future.

"When I grow up I'm going to have red hair," said Iris.

"When I grow up I'm going to be a movie star," said Paula, and then she worried whether that meant she would have to drown too. Iris failed to notice: she was carrying herself away. "I'm going to be a movie star too, and have photographers around me all the time," she said.

"Oh, I don't want the press!" said Paula, repeating her mother's favorite phrase. "They ruin everything! Never a moment's peace!"

"They'll be all around *me,* " said Iris. "I don't mind them at all. They're necessary."

"I'm going to live in the country and have children," said Paula.

"I'm going to wear silver dresses," said Iris, and a vision touched her and took her breath away: she saw herself in a silver gown, with red hair swept up and off her face, falling in little waves by her ears, on which were clipped huge earrings, clusters of diamonds; and the dress swept down her body, revealing ample curves on her chest, a vast bosom, a bosom that jutted out and was rounded on top and had a deep dark line separating the . . . she couldn't think the word, it was so strong . . . the breasts, the *seins,* separating two huge *seins* from each other, two huge white breasts with pale brown tips like Julie's, but bigger than hers and bigger than her mother's, so big . . . Paula nudged her. "Why aren't you talking?" she asked. Iris sighed; she didn't want to share this picture—it was too important and too personal as well. What Paula said prompted her: she was reading her mind: "I'm going to have long legs," she said, "long, long legs like a goddess." Iris felt encouraged to talk about it. Very quietly she said, "I'm going to have big . . . big bosoms."

"You *are?*" asked Paula with some disbelief. "Really?"

"Enormous," confirmed Iris. "Big and full and bulging so that my dresses are really tight . . ." They both held their breath at the image of a tight dress holding in round, big, generous, bulging flesh. It was too beautiful: the image set up a vibration on their skin that demanded immobility, concentration, quiet. Finally Paula, having contemplated the imaginary yet so real breasts hovering in the dark, let out a small "They're so beautiful . . ." in a wistful tone, which redoubled their trance. Iris felt herself slipping into a bliss so profound that she was paralyzed by it; and as she clenched her fists by her sides to increase it, she added to the burgeoning plenty of the image by adding more breasts to it; and adding women to the breasts—all sorts of women, young, old, fat, plump, middling, with huge globes on their chests. She forgot Paula; she watched as a line of women formed in a red light, their breasts at attention. Paula had her hands on her chest, trying to feel where her nipples were, trying to gauge by touch the change in the color of her skin from white to pale rose. She was absorbed in this exercise, but Iris was drifting down, down . . . the women assembled in a light that grew redder; she became scared and tried to stop them, to open her eyes and cancel them out, but still they kept gathering. Their breasts began to hang, to hang like the dugs she had seen on Gypsy women feeding their children, like sad bolsters and cushions where the feathers have settled, to hang like spaniels' ears, like hairless long dogs' ears, like cows' udders, down to their stomachs, down to their navels, down to their knees. And they were assembling in a line for hell, this red light was hell, there were devils, skinny tall black men with pitchforks calling out orders and poking at the women with their pitchforks, jabbing at their long white breasts with fierce black tridents.

She screamed. Paula screamed too, and dived under the quilt, scurried down to the bottom of the bed, and huddled there waiting for Iris to join her and tell her the bad news, whatever it was. Iris screamed again: she wanted the light on, the shadows banished, the white light of the bedside lamp to chase away the devils. She couldn't have moved her hand toward the lamp; there were devils there, shreds of breasts in the air and devils waiting for her hand. She screamed again; in the bottom of the bed, Paula began crying with fear.

Mauricette came in. She turned on the switch at the door that controlled the chandelier, and twenty fake candles burst upon the darkness. Iris opened her eyes. *"Qu'est-ce que tu as fait de Paula?"* asked Mauricette. Iris couldn't answer. Mauricette looked under the bed, and found one slipper and a comic book. When she straightened herself out, she found herself face-to-face with Paula, who had burrowed out from under the sheets on the side of the bed nearest the door. *"Ah! Te voilà!"* said Mauricette, and pulled her out of bed. Iris had stopped crying: she was lying perfectly still. Paula whispered to Mauricette, "I think she is *malade,*" and then checked herself; she did not want to betray her new sister to her nanny, but she thought something should be done. *"Un cachet,"* she said. Mauricette felt Iris's forehead; it was damp with sweat. *"Ce n'est rien,"* she said, but offered to make a tisane for them both. Iris and Paula grabbed her wrists and said no, thank you, could they hear a story instead? Neither of them wanted to see her go.

Further excursions into the underworld were halted by the return of Charlé and Raoul the next day. The girls were once more relegated to the dressing room, along with new American dresses in a size described as "Petite Pre-teen." It took exactly two days for Charlé and Raoul to realize that although he could amply afford the rent, they needed another place to live. Charlé was hell-bent on ostentation, but Raoul's arguments had a more sinister ring to them, which she would have noticed had she not been deafened, as well as blinded, by the image of her present success.

"I think each of us should have a room of our own," he said.

That sounded like a huge apartment. Charlé counted out loud: "A room each for Julie and Mauricette; a room for the girls—after all, they're sisters now so they should share—a room for you and a room for me, and our bedroom."

"No . . ." Raoul corrected, "a bedroom for you and a bedroom for me."

"Oh." Charlé was taken aback.

Raoul winked: "Much more sexy."

"Oh. Fine, then that's a room for Julie and a room for Mauricette, and a bedroom for you and a bedroom for me, and a bedroom for the girls and a study—you need a study—and a dining room, and a living room, and maybe a garden or something. And bathrooms for everyone. Raoul, we'll never find it."

It was Szos who found it. It was a palace. Among the more arcane literary estates that he managed was that of the Comte Florent de Saintlinger. A publisher who wanted to make an illustrated album of Saintlinger's life drove him out one afternoon to Saint-Germain-en-Laye, a proper suburb of Paris, to look at the house where the writer had installed Madame de Pompadour's bath as a pond in the garden, built secret inner stairways, and set an intaglio sun in the living-room floor to be lit from beneath by electric bulbs. The house, known as Château Rose, was in better condition than they had expected. It was occupied by the head of the Vietnamese legation and his family, who were happy to show the two men around. The ambassador, a small man with high, wide cheekbones and white hair, reported that he and his family were having to move out suddenly, due to certain political problems at home—which explained the packing cases that littered the floor of every room. Szos, who thought an album about Saintlinger was an idea that would sell three copies and do no one any appreciable good, began counting bedrooms. The place was built like Versailles, a long low façade facing a formal garden. The main floor had a *chambre d'apparat,* which would do for Charlé and Raoul, with a dark-green study attached to it that had a bathroom with a double sink, and, next to it, a blue bedroom, which was a little simpler. He asked to see the rest of the house and was shown the three sitting rooms and the *jardin d'hiver.* He insisted on going down to the lower floor, where he counted substantial servants' quarters. When he inquired about the rest of the accommodations, he was shown two bedrooms on the far side of a modest dining room, both of which gave onto the flower borders of a healthy-looking garden. While his publisher friend was testing the ice on the surface of Madame de Pompadour's fountain out in the front garden, Szos accepted a cup of tea from the ambassador's valet and, cupping it in his hands and remarking on the delicacy of the rice-pattern design, casually inquired who held the lease to the château—was it the government? Such a fine building. The ambassador startled him by proffering, from his crocodile wallet, a card giving the name and address of a Turkish restaurant; fearing he had been misunderstood, Szos handed it back with that foolish little laugh people use when they no longer know what is going on, but the ambassador pointed to it and said, "That is the owner. I believe he was the chauffeur of the Marchesa Assati who bought it from your writer. She left it to him. You should have seen the state it was in when we found it!" The butler coughed discreetly behind them, and the ambassador turned; the servant made the gesture of holding a receiver to his ear, and the ambassador excused himself. Great! thought Szos, you can't even hear the telephone ring.

"The fucking country?" said Charlé, and stubbed out her cigarette. She had taken to smoking often and with large gestures since she began living with Raoul, which at this point was all of eight weeks. Raoul had a different reaction: "It's good for the children, and there's nothing better than letting people come to you." Szos said, "It's a legendary place." Raoul said that wasn't important to him; it was the feeling of the place that counted. Szos turned to Charlé and told her about the Marchesa Assati: "One of the few genuine eccentrics to have been allowed to live as she pleased. Remember, it was fifty years ago. She had snakes that climbed up the curtains and hung from the rods; she had a cheetah that she took to balls. Van Dongen painted her; she bathed in asses' milk."

Paula and Iris, who were sitting side by side on an armchair, began to scream, "We want to live there!"

"You'll have to change schools," said Charlé to her daughter.

"And," added Szos, "the house is listed as a historic monument."

7.

Fairyland

Later, when people began to say that Raoul Abime had lost his grip on reality, they would point to his time as tenant of the Château Rose and blame the place itself, rather than him. One cannot credit mere architecture with the power to muddle a perfectly good mind, even if the exquisite façade, the enfilade of rooms, and the proportions of the doorways made visitors temporarily forget the twentieth century. The fact that the Château Rose was a late-nineteenth-century pastiche of Versailles in no way diminished its power: it was there that Raoul began to think of himself as an aristocrat. Perhaps it was the restless ghost of the Marchesa Assati, slipping into his soul in the middle of the night, who turned his head with the jangling of her golden bangles and the beating of her peacock-feather fan. But why then did she ignore Charlé, who would have been so grateful to meet her, even as a ghost, and who remained unhaunted, untouched by the Château Rose save in matters pertaining to the vocabulary of interior design? What is it about French windows that can turn an earthy and basic twentieth-century man into a weak and pallid, overrefined *fin-de-race* wraith? Perhaps no man should be allowed to live as he dreams, for nothing lasts forever save the bitter memory of a paradise found, and found wanting.

Until the Château Rose, Raoul had been comfortable in the context of messy rooms where scripts and cans of film vied for space with the remains of room service, or waxy paper squares from the local *charcuterie.* Once or twice he had felt impelled to claim a chair or a rug that had figured in a scene he had directed, but he had never lost sight of the difference between backdrops that serve to enhance a drama and furniture that is simply there to be sat on, or slept in, or eaten at. The grand style had little appeal for him until he married Charlé: his dreams as a child in Rumania had been about food, later about sex and then money. When he was directing his first films as a young man in Hollywood, married to Soula and earning three thousand dollars a week, he thought he had everything he could want. While in America, he directed a film about a girl on an ostrich farm, and then one about two men and a pony, and three films starring Soula, none of which had much plot but all of which made money; the unexpected success of these caused the studios to start calling him a genius, because they could no longer call him "that pushy little Rumanian."

His talent, what there was of it, lay in telling simple stories succinctly, with a clearly defined beginning and middle, followed by—his trademark—a shaggy dog ending that remained open to interpretation. Was it, critics wondered each time, testimony to the blank absence of God, or a cry of hope for humanity's will to survive?

He had been lucky in Hollywood, but he missed the Rumania of his childhood, the Marseilles of his youth, the prewar Paris of his adolescence. Politics and common sense eliminating the first two options, he returned to Paris with Soula and their baby, Paula, at the beginning of the fifties. He compensated for the loss of Marseilles by renting a house in the South of France, and began making films that anticipated the New Wave and would go down in movie-history books as "the Groundswell." André Roth, a producer and an old friend, financed his series of *Films Gris* about tramps, vagrants, and refugees. The arbitrary endings were at first criticized for lacking the definition to be found in the films of Samuel Fuller or indeed Jerry Lewis, but soon he became known as "the prime translator of transatlantic anguish." He found himself cornered into international acclaim, and never wondered whether or not he deserved it.

It was Soula's death that brought him the dreadful realization that if he were truly an artist he would be able to throw himself into his work to forget his sorrow. Try as he might, he could find no creative solace in planning where to put the camera or how to rig the body falling out the window, or which side of the bed the girl should be on for the lovers' quarrel. He doubted himself for the first time, and canceled the film he had started.

He filled his days with worry about Paula, which consumed months;

even when she was safely in the hands of Mauricette, he continued to worry about floating croup germs and scalding bath water, and called Klosters every evening to hear from her own lips that she was safe.

He toyed with his own sorrow to see how far it could take him. It interested him that his friends allowed him ample room for misconduct as a widower, and he elbowed his way around in their tolerance for a while until he became aware that he had no particular need to vomit on anyone's carpet or seduce any more teenage girls. The suggestion that he move to Dr. Schweitzer's leper hospital at Lambaréné left him cold ("I should go and lose fingers because my wife drowned? Is this strictly logical?"). Even the smell of rosemary growing by the road outside his house at Eze Village left him cold. He could be neither warmed nor moved.

By the time he met Charlene he had nothing to recommend him but his supposed grief and his concern for his daughter. Once these matters had been taken care of by his hasty marriage, he truly had nothing left. Like many others before him, others in the situation of having few material problems and a deep insufficiency that is perceived as aloofness by outsiders, he turned to the pursuit of ornamentation and rarefied pleasures. Where the soul failed, an assumed noblesse could oblige.

Charlé, still carrying with her the unctuous joviality of a newly arrived houseguest, pleased and proud of her two new names, settled into the Château Rose with only one trepidation: she dreaded that all her efforts at becoming a *Parisienne* would go to waste forty-five minutes outside of Paris. The rent at the Château Rose was not what she would have called high, and she imagined Raoul to be rich enough to afford it. She was obsessed with money, however, and it trickled relentlessly into her conversation. This was a nervous reaction occasioned by the sudden but perfectly reasonable cessation of her alimony.

She was sure Raoul would give her everything she had ever dreamt of and probably more, but she missed the edge that a private income gave her; it took care of the extra scarves and necklaces, the pedicures and waxing sessions. Without her own money, she would no longer be able to absorb the difference between what things cost and what she claimed she had paid for them. Half her cleverness with clothes disappeared with her new status. She told herself Raoul had not married her for her style, but because he was irresistibly attracted to her body and her mind. She did not know he had married her for his daughter.

They moved to the château in May: both nannies, both girls, both newlyweds, both Yorkshire terriers, although Bijou showed signs of wear and tear. Szos sent a cable from Germany, and André Roth sent a basket of champagne and truffles, which came in handy, as it turned out that the place was bare of all essentials, such as frying pans and dishes and mattresses for the nannies. The Vietnamese gentleman who had been so affable to Szos had shipped everything except the furniture; he had even taken the light bulbs.

They walked gingerly through rooms where elegant and extravagant decoration could only be guessed at in the dark. Raoul tried the eggshell-lacquer grand piano, which winced with a wonderful deep tone, and Iris dragged her hand along the strings of a gold harp in the corner of the *grand salon*. They set up a picnic on the dining table, an oval of fruitwood twelve feet long, surrounded by twenty-four Empire chairs with curved backs. While Raoul looked up at the crystal prisms on the chandelier Iris stared at an armless Moor who arched proudly from a pair of golden swirls around his legs.

He was a Venetian concoction, made to hold a torch, fashioned to amuse with his heavy beaded turban; the lecherous grin on his ebony face was meant to convey inebriation. No more than a piece of house jewelry in his time, the Moor had gone through a century and a half of being out of fashion. Armless, he served no purpose. His eyes were ivory set with agate, and his parted lips, open over white teeth, were still pink against the ebony. Iris had never seen a statue smiling before, and she was fascinated and a little worried.

Raoul found candles, and stood on the table to set them in the chandelier. Charlé, who was sunk in one of the chairs, found herself unable to muster a single comment. If this was a château, she was the queen of England.

Looking at Charlé, who was sinking and shrinking with every minute that passed, it struck Raoul that an adequate definition of hell would be to be stuck out here with no one but her for company. He carefully guided the conversation around to the difficulties in running such a large household, to which Charlé agreed. He added that he would need full-time help with his work, as Szos's secretary would be too far away to do impromptu little errands for him anymore, and Charlé agreed once more. He dealt a master blow with the announcement that they needed an expert in fine art to help them bring the Château Rose back to its former splendor, and then produced the name of Jill Adams, at which Paula let out a yelp of delight.

"Can we have Jill again? I miss her so much!" she said.

"Who the hell is this Jill?" asked Charlé, suddenly suspicious.

"She was my secretary ever since Hollywood, and she knows everything.

She knows about art, about decoration, about houses, about films, about Szos, about Paula, about telephones, about missing phone calls and who I hate."

"Well, where's she been all your life?" asked Charlé, who considered that Raoul's life had begun the day he met her.

"She went back to London—she's English—she's been working for Alex Korda, but she'll come back to me," said Raoul. "No problem."

"Are you sure?" asked Charlé.

"I bet you I can get her here by tomorrow." He went to look for the phone and managed to reach London and speak to Jill.

"I don't see why I should come back," she sniffed.

"Because you love me," said Raoul without irony.

Jill had always assumed that Raoul was unaware of her deeper feelings for him. "That's absolutely a lie," she said, a little too emphatically.

"Szos will meet you at the airport tomorrow," he continued. "Just let him know what time."

"Raoul, I can't drop everything just because you call me after one whole year's silence. It isn't fair."

"It's Saintlinger's château," said Raoul. "The Versailles one."

"Oh! The one with the bath in the garden? It's not possible!"

"It is. And it's in terrible condition. You could make it look almost right. You're the only person I know who could."

Jill explained that she would have to stop off before she came, to see her brother, who was a curator at the Victoria and Albert, and pick up whatever she could on Versailles. "By the way," she added, after she had mentally wiped out her London obligations, "are you making any films?"

"I'll have to have some private discussions with you about that," he said, and Jill's heart soared. She knew what private discussions meant, and she regretted that she had let her figure go to seed since she'd been home.

Charlé was not prepared for a rival so soon in her marriage, and greeted Jill with the frosty glance she had practiced on the whores who clung to Saul's associates.

"I'm very glad to meet you," said Jill. "I was most surprised to read that Raoul had gotten married."

"I never knew Raoul had a secretary," responded Charlé.

"What an interesting name you have, is it French?" asked Jill.

"No, Raoul made it up."

"Hmph," said Jill as she set off to look around the Château Rose. A downstairs room had been prepared for her, and Pierre the chauffeur took her bags down. Charlé watched the Englishwoman's rear end retreating toward the staircase and allowed herself a minute of serenity. Jill Adams on first glance had little to recommend her, and Charlé had based her life on hasty judgments. Jill was both colorless (a faded blondness topping pale-blue eyes and transparent skin over an unexcitable circulation), and shapeless (a sedentary adulthood over a horse-borne childhood had put sag in the place of shape). She was only a few years older than Charlé, but something about the size of her upper arms and the condition of her teeth signaled to the world that she was not out to please. Charlé knew about her education. Raoul had spoken at length of Jill's architecture degree and her years of working for I. M. Bergleish, the art historian in Florence who wrote coffee-table books: *The Medici Face* and *Lamb of Gold: Animals in Jewelry through Six Centuries.* Charlé was impressed, because these two volumes had often seemed to her the perfect gifts for intelligent celebrities, and she must have bought them each a dozen times. Under normal circumstances Charlé would have been delighted to ask Jill polite questions about I. M. Bergleish and architecture ("Tell me, Jill, what is the difference between an Ionian and a Corinthian column?"), but she was withholding her admiration until she knew just what the woman was up to.

Paula hurled herself at Jill and clung to her with tears in her eyes, remembering her as part of Soula's life. Iris watched Jill from a distance, impressed by her air of authority and a little wary; no one had bothered to explain by what right this Mademoiselle Adams was suddenly running everything.

Jill inspected the kitchen, which was full of dark dirt; the floor was uneven with congealed bumpy stains, the stove crusted with antique splatters. She began to tremble with excitement at the prospect of having so much to do. Having introduced herself to the two nannies, who had set themselves up in the kitchen, she called Paris to collect her team: a curious amalgam of studio carpenters and forgers, auction-house repairmen and apprentice set decorators. Then she took it upon herself to hire a butler.

The kitchen was decrusted, the fake marble columns repainted, the lichen rubbed off the ceremonial façade, the floors and walls restored to a high sheen. Occasionally Charlé would ask Raoul why all this renovation was necessary on a rented house, and he would answer, "Because it's mine"; Jill would appear out of nowhere muttering about the Victoria and Albert Museum, clutching tracings from the archives of the Musée des Arts

Décoratifs, and Charlé, caught between Raoul's peculiar interpretation of the rental lease and Jill's rabid historicism, could find nothing to say.

Jill, when she was not screaming at the workmen or spelling out words on the telephone, spent her time exuding a quiet sympathy at Raoul. This took the form of listening to him with a pencil and note pad, and writing down most of what he said. Whenever he called for her, her first gesture before seating herself near him—the better to catch his every word—was to take his hand in hers and caress it gently, as if he were an invalid. One day, when Raoul was particularly querulous, he asked her why she had to always look at him as if he were in pain. "To me you've always been a widower," she whispered, betraying both Soula and Charlé in one breath. Raoul allowed himself to smile. He did not care to put himself at a disadvantage by admitting that he, too, thought of himself as a widower, but nothing could have pleased him more than to hear his secretary express his own secret nostalgia.

With Charlé, Jill spoke slowly and a little too loud, as if addressing a backward native in an Indian province. Charlé retaliated by telling Raoul what she wished Jill to know, and thus avoiding direct confrontation. The messages she passed on in this way were all on the order of keeping the workmen out of her bedroom, telling the painters to keep themselves out of sight, and demanding that the carpenters be restrained from banging and hammering before eleven in the morning.

Szos came out as often as he could, feeling proprietary about the Château Rose; as an agent, he could not help thinking that whatever he found was in some way his, and although he had too much class to charge his client a finder's fee, he found it natural that he should be fed, and well, whenever he visited. He was glad Jill had returned: she listened to him when Raoul did not, and was able to steer him toward projects that Szos wanted him to work on.

Over dinner early one summer evening in the oval dining room Szos tried to steer Raoul into a frame of mind conducive to the signing of contracts. Looking around the dining room, and allowing his gaze to linger on the laughing imbecile face of the Moor, he let out a loud groan.

"Indigestion?" asked Raoul.

"I am afraid you are going to waste your talent," said Szos. "These are the best years of your life, and you must not become a vegetable."

"I have no intention of becoming a vegetable," said Raoul.

"Szos," said Jill. "He's only been here three weeks, for God's sake."

"A man must produce. Otherwise his days disappear, and he is gone without a trace."

"You're cheery," said Charlé as she helped herself from the plate that the butler, Eugène, held to her left. "Goody, quenelles. Mauricette's becoming a real *cordon bleu.*"

"Raoul hasn't made a film in over a year," said Szos. "People forget, and although Raoul's work is unforgettable, they can forget even him if he gives them the chance."

"Rot," said Jill.

Szos looked over at the mantelpiece, a construction of red porphyry, and above it at the stained mirror surrounded by gilt waves rising to a crest circled by a trellis. "Sure, you have to clean the décor, but then what?" he said, showing a lack of sensitivity to the magic of curves.

"Szos, don't be a boor," said Jill. Charlé found this remarkably rude of her.

"I have never been intimidated by marble," said Szos, addressing the table. "I once conducted a successful meeting with an Italian Minister of Culture in a palazzo made of so much Carrara marble that it constituted in itself a subprovince of Latium."

"What happened?" asked Raoul.

"Nothing. But I found myself at ease despite the surroundings. When I was a child in Buda, I had an uncle who collected stuffed eagles. They never intimidated me either."

"So what's the problem?" asked Charlé. "Are you intimidated here?" Her inflection betrayed some arrogance.

"Not at all. But you are, and Raoul is paralyzed by it, and Jill is becoming a sort of handmaiden to the glories of the Château Rose. I think it's ridiculous."

There was a silence broken only by the sound of Eugène's shoes as they proceeded through the pantry door, which then creaked shut. Oil for hinges, thought Jill.

"I wanted to discuss an idea with you," said Raoul. "That's why I asked you to come out."

Szos, who had come as a matter of course and without being asked, allowed the little fiction its breadth. "I thought that's why you wanted to see me," he said. "Do you want to talk about it now, or later?"

"Now; why not?" Raoul took a sip from a cut-crystal wineglass, a dark-red *verre de Bohème.* Jill had tried to order plain glasses, but something gaudy and sentimental in Raoul had made him insist on the ruby starbursts. "It's a story about a widower," Raoul began, as Jill put her note pad on the table and Charlé turned her head sharply toward him, as if to stop him.

"A widower, whose dead wife returns. A sort of ghost story, but a love story for ghosts."

"I hate ghost stories," announced Charlé. "They're silly."

"It sounds interesting," said Szos. "Is there any sex in it?"

"That's the silliest thing I've ever heard," said Charlé. "A ghost story!" In the past she had listened as playwrights hired to rewrite Hollywood farces set in the Mediterranean area detailed every banal twist of their plots over drinks in the bar of the George V, and she had repeated their bon mots with enthusiasm and care. She had collected and memorized every detail of the plays, songs and speeches that famous people talked about. But this was different. Raoul was her husband; they lived in a palace. She was important too now, at last; she imagined that being married to Raoul had given her critical judgment in the place of indiscriminate awe; and just to feel the weight of her position, she repeated, "That's the silliest thing!"

Raoul looked at her with an expression of such astonishment that she congratulated herself on having shown what she was made of, and waited for the compliment.

"You think it's silly?" His tone was gracious, even respectful.

Charlé shook her head, pursing her mouth in the manner, she hoped, of an astute critic. "Yes, it is."

"And what allows you to say this?"

"Well, everyone knows ghost stories are like horror movies—I mean, they're just for teenagers, that's all." She glanced briefly at Szos for confirmation, but Szos was staring at the little bread roll on his side plate. She did not look as far as Jill.

"Your long experience of Hollywood has allowed you to form this opinion?"

"Well, it's been years, as you know. . . . Szos, you know I haven't been back in years, but when I was an actress . . ."

"When you were an actress?" inquired Raoul, exceedingly polite.

"Oh," said Charlé, "it wasn't much of a career, but I got around, and everyone knew that those kinds of stories just weren't quality."

She couldn't see Szos, whose eyebrows rose toward the center of his forehead in a form of imploration. Jill's mouth twitched; she had been waiting for this moment.

"Everyone? What everyone? What is this quality you talk about?"

"Quality—" She was beginning to falter, but was still game, determined to make herself heard in a logical and reasoned way. "—like *Gone With the Wind,* that's quality."

"No," said Raoul, very loud, "I want to hear who 'everyone' is first."

"Everyone, you know, producers and directors, everyone—come on, Raoul, you knew them too!"

"Producers!" Raoul was still calm, only louder. "Name one."

"Harry Cohn," said Charlé, naming a man she had once seen across a crowded studio commissary. His was the sort of name the girls at the Magnolia Gardens had whispered; a name that gave film tests and told actresses to lose weight, a name to be reckoned with.

"That imbecile," said Raoul. "He was a friend of yours?"

"No, not at all," she said, quickly adding, "I never liked him."

"Charlene," said Szos, reverting, in his nervous state, to her previous name, "I think it is better not to talk about the past."

"Oh, I don't mind," she said, determined to show her independence.

"Please, I'm interested," purred Raoul. "I want to know how you became an expert on the subject of films." His tone was still gentle, if a little too probing for a question that was so patently unimportant. Charlé felt she was beginning to lose ground; the questioning had gone on too long, and the fixed gaze on her was becoming embarrassing. "Raoul, darling, it's just an opinion."

Raoul put his hands on the table and thrust his chin out toward Szos. "Can you imagine," he asked, "having to listen to this nonsense? Have you ever heard anything so thick, so stupid, so uninformed, so sideways, so secondhand?"

"But—" began Charlé, reaching out toward him across the table.

" *'But'?* You know nothing and I would be grateful if in the future you said nothing."

Charlé shook her head very quickly, back and forth and back again, as if to dissociate herself from everything that had come out of her mouth. "I didn't mean—" she began, and stopped.

Raoul was not even looking at her. He gave Jill an immense smile, and then transferred it to Szos.

"I think it could be wonderful," Szos said. "Is it contemporary?"

Charlé excused herself from the table with a little noise and went through the door to the pantry, for which Jill gave her two black marks: she would have to learn to stay and take it, as if nothing had happened, and she should never use the servants' entrance. Soula never had.

"Was that necessary?" asked Szos, with a little wave of the hand so that Raoul would not take his word as an unmitigated reproach.

"Harry Cohn," said Raoul. "He was the man who wanted to shave Soula's hairline, wasn't he, Jill?"

"He was dreadful," said Jill.

"She just needs to be taught," said Szos. "She's very—"

"Let's talk about something interesting," interrupted Raoul.

"I think the ghost story is wonderful," Jill said to Szos, hoping to sound as if Raoul had discussed it with her at some length.

Charlé was waiting for them in the *grand salon;* she poured the coffee from a tall silver pot into tiny Directoire cups with green edges and handles of gold leaf. Though her eyes were red, there was fresh lipstick on her mouth. Raoul paid her no attention, but Szos changed the number of sugar lumps he wanted, to make her feel part of things: "One—no, darling—two— Wait, no, it's better I only have one."

Jill gave her a gracious smile.

"I like the story," Szos told Raoul, to prove to Charlé that they had talked business throughout her absence, "and I have a little idea about who could work with you on it." As he chattered on, Charlé, having cast abject looks at Raoul's shoes, not yet daring to face the rest of him, rose and quietly walked into the smaller *salon*. There, in the unlit room where swatches of material were pinned to the little bergères and the fire screen had not yet been fixed, she lit a cigarette and peered out at the garden. The fountain was dry, the hedges rugged and unkempt. A single light, from a lamppost that stood at the side of the ornate gate on the far side of the lawn, looked to her almost like a star. She had felt full of self-pity earlier, ready to run away. Now, listening to Raoul's voice steadily drawing out an indistinct story in the next room, punctuated by Szos's little cries of "Brilliant!" which the thickness of his accent made all the more emphatic, she was able to tell herself that Raoul was obviously a genius, and that she was learning, in the most personal and painful way, what it was like to be the wife of a genius. With the clarity of distance—she was some thirty feet away from him, and in another room—she was able to accept the well-known fact that it was not easy to live with a genius, that what was required surpassed mere admiration and devotion and was more in the nature of sacrifice. Having grasped this thought, she quickly put out her cigarette in a little gilt saucer and returned to the *grand salon,* determined to bend herself to Raoul's will, and tickled, in a faintly erotic way, at the prospect.

Her martyrdom was purchased in minor humiliations. Raoul took to saying *"Tais-toi et sois belle,"* a not unkind injunction and a common one among Frenchmen of his generation, whenever she seemed to be about to speak. Szos inveigled him into directing for an American studio a murder mystery set in Paris and starring two actors Charlé was longing to meet: Jean Seberg and Jean-Louis Trintignant. Raoul made it clear that he did not want his wife on the set, nor at dinner when he went out with his actors, nor at the end-of-shooting party, which the producers threw at

La Méditerranée. Charlé considered turning up unannounced, but Jill got wind of her plan from Pierre the chauffeur and managed to restrain her. Jill, having worked on the film, went to the party.

The work on the house stopped during the shooting, which took up most of the summer. In September, while Raoul worked at the cutting room in Paris, the workmen returned and resumed banging and painting. Charlé thought Raoul might be having an affair with a young woman who had been in the film; on Sundays she sometimes picked up the phone to hear him talking to a female voice, and she just as quickly put it down again—she was collecting stigmata. Having separate bedrooms meant that on those nights when Raoul stayed late in Paris, working in the editing room or dining, he said, with old friends, Charlé could never be sure of the time of his return unless she slept in his room; and having tried this once, and awakened to find Raoul standing over her with a glacial expression of polite inquiry on his face, she had resolved never to do it again. He had said just two words: "Get out."

Her own room had a canopy over the bed, blue instead of red as it had been at the Rue Dumont d'Urville. There were panels on the wall picked out in pale blue lines and a fireplace held up by two half-naked bronze doré women. Beside the fireplace was a precious sewing basket on bronze doré feet, an object that Jill had deemed the best thing in the whole place and attempted to move to the *grand salon.* Charlé had resisted: she wanted her bedroom to have some claim to artistic and cultural merit, as if that could entice Raoul into her bed, when all else had failed. It was not a bad marriage; several times a week, after Szos and Jill and a few dinner guests had been dispatched, or after they had returned from dinner in town, Raoul would come to her room, usually when she was almost asleep, and pull off all the sheets with a gesture that Charlé found irritating but for which she was nonetheless grateful, and heave his body over hers and discharge himself into her. She would caress his hair or his shoulders, and try to nuzzle his neck after the brief consummation; as soon as a moment of inattention on her part caused her to let go of his flesh, he would rise and disappear through the tall door into his room.

The girls liked playing in Raoul's room. It was dark green, with a bed shaped like a sleigh and adorned with parts of sphinxes. On the desk there was an inkwell made of three little hinged pyramids, which opened to reveal two inkpots and a queer sort of saltcellar, which Jill informed them was intended to hold sand for drying the ink. They played with his shirts and with his shoes, and looked through his drawers, where they found photographs of Soula. Unlike Charlé, who screamed whenever her things were touched, Raoul enjoyed watching Paula and Iris pull at the knobs on his desk and paw through his books. They gave names to his pipes—the two meerschaums with faces sculpted on their bowls were Isidore and Fritz—and tried fitting their fingers into the niches on the little wooden pipe stands.

Until school started they led a life unrelated to the rest of the world. Charlé, whose only consolation was going to the hairdresser's in Paris, saw no reason to bring the children with her. Jill was busy with Raoul; Raoul was busy with the film; Mauricette was cooking; and only Julie was available to take care of them—impressionable Julie whose fear of rats had become, in the move, a fear of intruders, sudden noises and ghosts.

Soula's trunks were brought out from Paris on Jill's orders; it was Julie who decided to open them. Moved by the natural curiosity of a fan when faced with the prospect of poking through an idol's effects, she showed a perfervid haste in unbuckling the long leather straps that were wound around the Louis Vuitton steamer trunks. As she took out gloves, little crescent-shaped hats wrapped in brown tissue paper, bunches of artificial flowers carefully wedged into plastic boxes, she caressed the objects with the reverence of a pilgrim. It was only when she had gone through each trunk and even tried on some of the less elaborate pieces of clothing—a mink stole the color of lilacs, a tabard made of glittering blue beads—that she brought Paula to the storeroom and showed her the trunks.

"Those are my mother's," said Paula.

"Yes," said Julie.

"Have you opened them?" she asked.

"Non," said Julie, handing Paula a key she had found in the drawer of the largest trunk. It fit none of the locks, but the gesture allowed Paula to feel that she was the first person to look inside the cases. Iris stood at the door, watching Paula as she carefully pulled open the trunks and lifted the tissue paper between each layer of clothing. Paula was too happy to cry: the clothes, the costumes, the flowers and gloves and necklaces were things she had seen in pictures and things she remembered; she had handled them, she told Iris, when she was really young, five or six. Being a full ten months older than Iris, she could use expressions like "really young" and get away with it.

They took to dressing up in the fragments of costume; the dancing-girl boleros from *Insh'Allah,* the huge crinolines from *Midnight on the Plantation,* crinolines that reached up to their shoulders and in which they paraded looking like bright mushrooms. When Jill came back from the studio at night with Raoul and saw them dressed in Soula's things, she congratulated herself on her wisdom: "Let them play," she said to Raoul, who doubted whether it was proper to desecrate Soula's memory in this way. Charlé went to the storeroom alone once, to see if there was anything she wanted; she tried on an evening dress that she vaguely remembered from some film, and although it was only a little too long, she realized there was no way she could allow Raoul to see her in Soula's costume, and put it back with the same feeling of renunciation that had come to color all her dealings with her husband.

Iris loved the house more than Paula did; as long as the doors were left open she could occupy herself roaming from room to room, pretending to be Madame du Barry, looking out the window into the back garden, where she imagined kings and courtiers standing in line outside waiting to pay their *hommages* to her. She had heard enough from Jill about how the Château Rose was a copy of Versailles to be persuaded that they were living at Versailles itself. She told herself that this had to be true, as the very doors themselves were set with long gold bars from the floor to the top, upon which were fixed strange gold boxes and oval gold handles, a little too high for her to reach. Palaces and kings and memories of the comic strip in *France-Soir* that told the story of Angélique, favorite of *le Roy,* combined in her mind to convince her of the importance of her family. She consulted her old history book from the Cours Victor Hugo, for passages dealing with royalty. Past Ambroise Paré tending the wounded, Bernard Palissy burning his furniture, Saint Vincent de Paul and the abandoned babies, there was a picture of Louis XIV at Versailles, holding out his hand to a man who bowed before him.

Louis XIV is the master of France, of the goods and the life of his subjects. He commands alone. He builds a vast palace at Versailles. The palace is surrounded with gardens full of flowers, big trees, statues, vases, fountains with jets of water. At Versailles, the great nobles live near the king: this is the court. From morning to night, the people of the court, who are called courtiers, adore the king like a God. They are proud to be there when the king rises, at the king's meals, at the king's bedtime, at the king's walks. It is they who give the king his clothes, his hat, his cane. They are his servants, his domestics.

Iris not unnaturally concluded that Raoul was the king; and it was further evident that everyone else in the household was in some way his servant. She accepted the necessity of being a courtier, and in her own way contributed to the establishment of obscure rituals that became part of the life of the house. "We must get up before your papa and see him when he wakes up," she told Paula one day. "*Pourquoi?*" asked Paula. "Because it's correct," said Iris; and from then on, the girls were always in Raoul's bedroom by seven-thirty, ready to greet Mauricette as she came in with the tray of black coffee and *biscottes.*

Iris's impression of Raoul as king was further reinforced by certain habits of Jill's. Raoul abhorred shopping, so it was Jill who bought his shirts and ties, even his shoes. She would present these parcels to him on her return from Paris, always in the living room and always within sight of Charlé, who was not allowed to shop for him, on the threadbare excuse that she had never done it before and would not know how.

When Jill had the octagonal fountain fixed and the family gathered on the lawn to watch the first skinny spurt of water rise from the center of the fountain, Iris knew this was just how Louis XIV would have spent an afternoon, and she was proud of them all.

Iris wished for parties as fervently as her mother did, if only to confirm her assumptions about the Château Rose. She wanted hunts in the back garden, balls, a joyous crowd of nobles. She was satisfied with the big windows, vast rooms, beautiful furniture, tapestries, paintings, fountains and gardens (she wondered if the kings had a golden harp as the Château Rose did, and, being unable to find any reference to harps in her history book, concluded that in the matter of harps, the Abime household was superior to that of the kings of France). The only other lack besides courtiers was statues; the armless Moor in the dining room would have to do, standing in for objects that she imagined to be huge blocks of perfect marble fashioned into ladies wearing crinolines not unlike the ones in the trunks in the storeroom. She would stare at the bronze faces on the corners of certain tables, grasp the proud caryatids who held up two of the fireplaces, stroke the fat cherubs who clung to the sides of a pair of blue Chinese vases redone in the manner of the eighteenth century, but none of these objects had the independence or the majesty of a real statue —they were all attached to other things and bound by their function. Only the Moor in the dining room, crowned with his starry turban of painted wood and smiling up at the ceiling, had the semblance of an individual life.

Paula liked the garden, the flowers, the trunks of the trees around which she chased the surviving Yorkshire terrier. She lured Iris into games—Grandmother's footsteps, count the daisies, run to the bottom of the garden and back—games that allowed her to enjoy the wind on her face, the strength of her legs, the speed of her reactions. She had no need to make up stories about the Château Rose: it belonged to her father, and therefore to her, and its hold on her imagination was diminished by the calm certainty of ownership. Her thrills came from her mother's trunks, the private walks she took with Raoul to the village, the photographs of Soula. She had no need to invent anything.

Charlé and Raoul would come and tuck them in at night. In the summer Saint-Germain-en-Laye was infested with mosquitoes that lived on the lake next to the Château Rose, and to guard against them, Jill had put up enormous white nets over the girls' beds. Charlé and Raoul would raise the nets and peck the girls on the cheek, and accede to demands about extra dolls and teddy bears, and then leave, turning out the light.

Sometimes Szos would come in after dinner and sit on Iris's bed; one night Iris, disturbed by his sudden weight, woke and whispered his name, and he raised the net and asked her solemnly, for solemnity had become his mode with her ever since the train ride, if she was happy.

"I'm very happy," she assured him.

"And Paula?"

"She doesn't understand."

"She doesn't?"

"Look over there," she said, pointing at a shelf where dolls were lined up, sitting against the wall. "The dolls. Some of them can move. Sometimes in the morning, very early, you can see them moving. But it's a secret."

"From Paula?" said Szos.

"She doesn't know about it. She wouldn't understand. It's a secret from *them.* The dolls. Shhh . . . they would be very angry if they knew I told you."

"That's reasonable."

"And . . . do you promise you'll never tell anyone, ever ever?"

Szos promised. He was hoping for some revelation about Charlé; he wanted to know if she'd found out about Jeannette Marchais.

"The black man upstairs in the dining room, the statue?"

"Ah, yes." Szos nodded, his lips pursed.

"He's the only person here who knows all the secrets. And he can move too, but I've never seen him."

Paula rolled over in her bed and let out a little groan. Iris turned toward her in alarm, and her hand flew up to cover her mouth.

"It's all right," said Szos. "She didn't hear."

"Are you sure?" asked Iris, with her hand pushing her nose up, her eyes wide with fright. "Please don't tell her, or anyone."

Szos leaned under the net and kissed her. "I promise," he said, and tiptoed out of the room.

8.

At the Court of the Crimson King

In the quiet suburb of Saint-Germain-en-Laye among ugly villas and complacent gardens, beside election posters and a giant sign featuring a black man in a red fez advertising Banania, the Château Rose—born as a joke and long an anachronism—was restored to a glory neither Saintlinger nor Assati had ever given it. The French windows were draped with fringed swags of damask, and the chandeliers were fitted with flickering bulbs ordered from a special house that provided stage lighting.

Seeing the bright lights shining across the lawn and through the newly clipped hedges, the inhabitants of Saint-Germain-en-Laye were intrigued that an "artiste," a man of the *cinéma,* should have chosen to settle in their midst, and even more intrigued that he should be putting on such a show. Solid citizens with a distrust of the capital and its ways, they had feared at first that, like Rubirosa and Françoise Sagan, he would hold orgies and do terrible things with sports cars, but the signs that were fixed along the tasseled iron bars that bordered the property, stern warnings that said PROPRIÉTE PRIVÉE, DEFENSE D'ENTRER, reassured them that here was a man who cared as much about property as they did. Then, too, the people of Saint-Germain-en-Laye, who liked to walk on the wide common next to the Château Rose with muscular German shepherds, living proof to them that they lived in the country, had occasion to see the two little girls, accompanied by a pair of governesses, taking the air like normal children.

The very ordinariness of the children's walks, across the grass and into the village and back again, sucking on lollipops, was a source of great comfort. So was the fact that Monsieur Abime's chauffeur, Pierre, drove very slowly, in an old-fashioned *quarante chevaux;* the Swiss woman haggled at the market like any housewife, and though they liked her less (she was, after all, a foreigner), the kilos of potatoes and solid cuts of meat she bought confirmed to the shopkeepers that she worked for a *patron* with admirably simple tastes. This allowed Monsieur Grandjean, who owned the bar in the main square by the church, to tell his customers, in the strictest confidence, that he knew all about *"les gens du spectacle,"* and that, close up, there was nothing at all unusual or exciting about Monsieur Abime, who came in for a drink now and then; and that this only went to prove that one did not succeed in this world through talent but through cheating.

On the first day of autumn Julie escorted Iris and Paula to the Cours Lamartine, two streets beyond the Château Rose. A summer of playing with costumes and being allowed to stay up until ten had not prepared them for the strict rules of school, and Iris thought the place a comedown from the elegant Cours Victor Hugo. The other pupils had runny noses, and mended sweaters poking out beneath the wrists of their gray pleated smocks. The class sat at gray wooden desks with stains on them, and breathed in chalk dust along with the first principles of sentence construction. They dipped sharp, thin steel nibs into white china inkwells set into a hole at each desk, and scratched out cautious letters between the pale-blue horizontal lines in their exercise books. They cleaned the blackboard for the teacher with checkered rags, and grew indelible ink spots on the second knuckle of their middle fingers.

Paula made friends. She found little girls and boys who enjoyed running around tree trunks, and discovered a talent with rubber footballs; she invited three children back to the Château Rose, and had it not been for Julie's quick thinking—*"il faut en parler à Madame d'abord"*—and stern refusal to allow anyone into the house until both Charlé and Jill had approved the idea, Paula would have infested the Château Rose with local children. "Never," said Charlé when Julie asked her about it later. "Never, ever, are you to bring any child home from school with the girls." It was not a place open to all, she further explained; she saw no reason why local ragamuffins should clutter up the downstairs dining room and the garden. Iris agreed with her. "We aren't *tout le monde,*" she told Paula, "and those others don't have the right to come here."

"But why not?" asked Paula, who had been anxious to show off the garden and introduce her new friends to the surviving Yorkshire terrier; she was sure they had never seen a dog that small.

"Because, that's all," sniffed Iris. Jill had given her the stories of the Comtesse de Ségur for her birthday, and they had replaced the history book in her affections; not only did their tooled red-linen covers and gold lettering give the books the appearance of precious objects, but the woodcuts inside showed Madeleine and Camille, round-faced little aristocrats in long wide dresses, who never mingled with the children of the village, and Iris, who subscribed to the proprieties of the last century, tried to entice Paula into reading the books. "Aren't you happy just being us?" asked Paula. Iris had no answer.

Charlé had sent out change-of-address cards, elegantly disguised as etchings of the Château Rose, postcard size, on deckle-edged hand-milled paper. She had personally addressed every one, sitting at the marquetry desk in the *petit salon;* she had no difficulty in knowing whom to send them to, as her address book contained only names calculated to impress anyone who stole a look through it. Absent from it were electricians, laundries, butchers, schools and doctors, except for Dr. Dax, the heart throb at the American Hospital. In the Rue Dumont d'Urville days the lack of useful numbers had been an impediment to the smooth running of her household, but now she had Jill to take care of all the boring details. The inclusion of the name of Tyler Bromley was her only slip: Maître Mercier had insisted that she have his address *"en cas"* and had made her copy it out in his office: Ezy Vite Juices, Garden Grove Boulevard, Orange County, California. She had skipped Tyler on her first meandering through the B's, but the name caught her eye as she went through them a second time. An urge compounded of the wish to show him how far she had come and a sliver of conscience impelled her to send him a card. To temper the awesome effect of the engraving on the front of the card, she scribbled across it, in the manner of a star giving autographs: "Love to see you—drop by when you're in the neighborhood." The invitation was loose and humorous enough, she hoped, to prevent him from ever taking it seriously; her own gesture in sending it to him would at least ensure that he no longer had to send Iris his postcards of the Watts Tower or crocodiles in the Everglades via Maître Mercier.

Iris was deep in obsessive reveries about courts and kings, and Raoul in his adult way was only slightly less possessed than she was. He began to read the memoirs of Saint-Simon; Jill found she could occupy him for hours with little stories from Marmontel or Chamfort; his surroundings had mellowed his standards to the point where an anecdote about the smell of urine at Versailles was enough to delight him. In the past only a description of a bloody brawl would have engaged his interest to such a degree. Jill took to scratching on doors instead of knocking. Charlé thought she was ruining the paintwork with her nails, unaware that this was strict Louis XIV practice; Jill, as usual, ignored her.

Once the film was done, Raoul retreated to the now splendid Château Rose and decided to conduct all his business out there. To this end a stenographer was imported from Paris and set up in one of the bedrooms in the back, near the girls. Jill had unblocked a secret staircase between her room and Charlé's bathroom; its existence was a source of much excitement, but its unfortunate location meant that it could not be used for the salacious purpose originally intended. The discovery gave Raoul ideas, however; he began asking actresses to spend the night, ostensibly in one of the guest rooms Jill had refurbished. Young scriptwriters came too, and novelists, and sometimes critics. Raoul liked the company of writers: they had strong opinions and got drunk easily, and they provided entertainment. Also, they spoke in French, which disconcerted Jill: she could not follow rapid conversations, and floundered after puns and *contrepètries* like an agitated gundog. Charlé was quickly ignored by all his guests when they saw what little regard her husband had for her: they were his guests, not hers, and only a few foolish young men wasted their time asking her the names of the flowers on the dinner table or the ages of the girls. Jill always cut in with the rapid responses of the trained assistant, and Charlé was left to gaze at her reflection in the mirrored panels. Raoul, used to manipulating actors on a set, easily fell into playing off the inconsistencies of his guests against them; it was easier still to keep Charlé in a state of nervous ingratiation, and Jill alert with efficient selflessness. No matter what he said he wanted, she was always ready to produce it for him: a telephone number, the photograph of a poisoner who had been guillotined in 1910, more valances to frame his windows. When he was surfeited with the adulation accorded him at home, he would take a few days off and go down to Marseilles to hang out with his childhood friends, who inevitably tarnished themselves by suggesting that he put them in a film. Or he would go to Germany, where Szos had introduced him to some fairly interesting women: interesting in that they cared more about the money he gave them than what he said, which was a relief. Once in a while he went to Los Angeles, departing with the entire household massed in tears around the *quarante chevaux,* Paula hugging his legs and Charlé handing him little lists of things she needed from the States, lists that he invariably left in the car at the airport. Although he felt himself growing slack from the imperial status he enjoyed at home, he found the cool reception he received in Hollywood less therapeutic, less bracing than he had hoped. No longer Soula's husband, and with only an unreleased film for currency, he elicited little interest. When he returned, he summoned Szos and blamed him for every indignity he had suffered. "Don Flagel did not return my phone call, and you said he would," he said sternly.

"Maybe he was away. You should have waited for me to come with you."

"You mean I'm not good enough alone? Are you mad? You think I need you?"

"No, no," Szos said, "not at all. It's just that I could have paved the way."

"Does my name mean nothing?" asked Raoul.

"No, wait until the film comes out. Your trip was premature."

"They can come and get me. I'm not going anywhere," announced Raoul.

In the spring the drawing teacher at the Cours Lamartine told the children in her class to draw their fathers. There was nothing unusual in this: the previous week, they had drawn their mothers; and the week before that, themselves. The thirty-two children in their gray smocks smoothed out the thick pieces of grainy yellow paper and set to work. Despite the restrictions of incomplete manual dexterity, they produced recognizable specimens of fatherhood: bearded men in mechanic's uniforms, pipe-puffing train guards, solemn policemen. The businessman fathers were more of a problem, and resulted in sketchy figures in one-button suits with lumpy brown squares at the end of their arms symbolizing briefcases. (Maman, the week before, had been easier: *mamans* were composed of the easy triangle of a skirt, topped by a smaller, inverted triangle for the torso. The teacher believed in escalating difficulties. She was an existentialist.) Papa was giving some trouble as to hair. The pedants made do with coloring in the top of the uneven circles that were the contours of the *papas'* heads, the sunnier children naturally gave their father curls, and the one true artist, a boy of nine named Emmanuel who would one day end up as art director of *Elle* magazine, drew one thin strand that curled upwards and ended in a question mark.

Paula had suffered over Maman; she had labored hard over a princess with the moon behind her but found herself overcome and had been unable to finish. Papa was easy: she started with the pipe, made a nice pair of brown eyes, and found that just the face sufficed. She was used to seeing close-up photographs of her father and felt there was no need to bother with the rest of the body. Sitting next to her, Iris had not yet begun. She wondered if she was required to tell the truth, whether *"Dessinez Papa"* was an order that had to be followed to the letter. She had received two postcards from Tyler: they were signed "Daddy," and Charlé had told her they were from Daddy, but Iris to her own shame had been unable to put a face to this person. She considered drawing a palm tree or a crocodile—these figured on both her cards, and she remembered the ones she had received years before, which also had crocodiles on them, but decided that the teacher would not accept this. She wondered if Paula would mind if she drew Raoul; she was always saying "My daddy is your daddy." Saul she could have drawn, he was easy: checks on the body and two-toned shoes. But then, she would have had to explain Saul to Paula, and she had managed in fourteen months to avoid elaborating on the golf clubs in her closet, on the express order of her mother, who had said one day, "You don't have to tell Paula everything about our life before I married Raoul."

Time was running out. There was a confident rustle of paper at the other desks; hands were shooting up, and the other children were calling, *"Mademoiselle, j'ai fini."* Iris took up her pencil and drew, very badly, a vague stick man to whom she gave straight black hair and a pipe for good measure. "Is that what your *papa* looks like?" asked Paula as Iris held the picture up for the teacher to collect. Iris said, "Sort of," without looking at Paula. "He smoked a pipe too?" continued Paula. Iris shrugged: "All men smoke pipes."

It was decided by Jill that for Paula's birthday Raoul would throw a garden party.

"You'll ask everyone in Paris to come out in the afternoon, and we'll have music on the lawn in front and games for children in the garden in the back," she told him.

"On Sunday," Raoul said, "there's nothing else to do."

"No," said Jill. "On Thursday."

"Everyone will be working," said Raoul. "They won't be able to come."

"Exactly," said Jill. "Why should we make it easy for them?"

A little later Jill showed him a list.

"Don't bore me with details," he said.

"I had an idea," said Jill. "I think we should ask them to come in costume."

Raoul put down the book he was reading—memoirs of Necker, Louis XVI's Minister of Finance—and thought for a minute. *"C'est un peu frivole,"* he said. "I don't want to look like a joke."

"You won't," whispered Jill, "but some people might." And she let out a tremendous braying giggle.

"You're more French than the French," said Raoul.

"Costumes," said Charlé, brushing her hair and watching Iris and Paula in the mirror as they sat on her bed behind her. "I think that's very nice. Was it your idea, Paula?"

"*Non.* Papa and Jill told me. Do we have enough time to have costumes made?"

"I'm sure Jill will take care of everything," answered Charlé. "I have a lot of things to do." She would go to Balmain, now that poor Christian Dior was dead, and have Pierre invent something for her.

Iris lay back on her mother's bed and looked up at the ruched satin canopy, which reminded her of her mother's old bedroom and made her feel safe. She shut her eyes trying to hear the sounds of pigeons; straining, all she could hear was the Saint-Germain train in the distance, the barking of German shepherds on the common, and the burp and splutter of *mobylettes.* "Iris," said Charlé quietly, "get your feet off the bedcover." Iris slid off the satin quilt and went to the chest of drawers, which held all the little picture frames with photographs of the family in them. She looked at the pictures as if it were the first time; after her unsuccessful invention about the pipe, she was looking for particular details. She pulled some of the little chiseled frames forward, to get a better look, but still the images were only of Raoul and Paula and Charlé and herself in various attitudes of familial closeness: hugging one another on a rock during an expedition to the Mont-Saint-Michel, lying on the little steel daybeds on the front terrace, walking down the street in Paris with Szos. There was a wedding picture of Charlé and Raoul alone, and, from the previous Christmas, a picture of Iris and Paula dressed as fairies; they held wands, and their feet were tangled in streamers and ribbons from the presents under the tree. Iris kept looking at the pictures, just in case a tall man with a pipe should have joined Charlé, but none of the pictures dated from before the wedding; Charlé had edited them even more carefully than her address book. "What are you doing there?" asked Charlé. "You know I don't like you playing with my things."

"It's just that I noticed something," said Iris, inventing an insight. "People in pictures always look more pink in photographs than they do in real life." She held up her hand to demonstrate the effect. "Look, I'm not pink at all."

Szos was surprised to receive a printed invitation.

"*Une fête champêtre,*" it said, "*le 15 Mai 1958, au Château Rose.*

Costumes et déguisements." He called Jill. "Am I supposed to get dressed up, or is that just for the extras?"

"It's everyone, Szos. We won't let you in unless you're disguised."

Szos took the threat lightly, but made an appointment with a theatrical costumier. André Roth, who was about to release Raoul's film, called a few journalists and invited them to the party: publicity about Raoul could only help the film. Jeannette Marchais, who had been seeing Raoul on various afternoons in the months since the filming, heard about the party from André Roth and phoned the Château Rose to ask Raoul why she wasn't invited. "It's for my daughter," said Raoul. "You wouldn't enjoy it."

"But everyone's going to be there," whined Jeannette.

"It's my family," he pointed out.

"It's you, too. And why shouldn't I come? I have a right to be there."

"What right is that?" asked Raoul. "Because you sleep with me?"

She recovered quickly: "Well, you have lots of other actresses going. André told me."

"Yes," said Raoul, "actresses are coming. You are right."

"In that case, I can come too."

"You, *ma chère,* are not an actress."

"But I was in the film."

"That doesn't mean you can act," Raoul said, and replaced the receiver. He found it more amusing these days to tell people what he considered to be the truth than to be nice to them. It lifted his spirits; cheered, he went for a stroll in the back garden, down to the little pavilion at the edge of the property. One day, he thought, I'll have Jill make this into a real little house for Paula to play in.

Charlé, who had listened in on the conversation, found her mood lightened by Raoul's words. She had known more or less about Jeannette Marchais for months: Szos had informed her in the name of friendship one day when they lunched together in Paris. If Raoul despised the girl's talent, if he could be so mean to her, then that affair was over, and Charlé could relax. She had not yet grasped that Jeannette Marchais was just a tiny ripple in Raoul's affections, and that there were already three replacements for her.

The week before the fête, Mauricette began making canapés and storing them in the refrigerator, a bold and shiny giant imported from America. On the third day she told Jill, who stood watching her sweat over her pâtés in the kitchen, that she could not continue without proper help, and that Mademoiselle Adams should order the bulk of the food from a *traiteur. Traiteur* yourself, thought Jill, as she dialed La Maison Scott.

"Allô, vous avez des food *pour* a reception *de* one hundred *personnes?"* she challenged them. She was luckier than she had dared hope: Scott not only had chickens ready to be glazed and charlottes ready to be rushed into service, it also had lackey costumes for its hired waiters.

"Parfait!" screamed Jill.

"C'est plus cher avec les perruques," the woman on the other end of the line told her. *"Ils ont mal au crâne après quelques heures."*

"Bien, bien," said Jill, "I'll pay more for the wigs, *c'est parfait."*

Mauricette, relieved, abandoned her canapés and set to work on the cinnamon cookies and raisin cakes, which, being more to her taste, she found easier to make. Charlé complained about the smell of cinnamon and stayed in her bedroom the rest of the week: it reminded her unpleasantly of Eighty-sixth Street.

"My home is inviolate," Raoul told Jill on Thursday morning, while Paula opened her presents at the table in the lower dining room.

"We're having a hundred people here this afternoon, what are you talking about?" asked Jill, diligently picking up stray pieces of ribbon from the floor. She had enough to think about without Raoul getting sensitive on her.

"I don't want journalists all over the house. Who invited them?"

"What are you talking about?"

"France-Presse called this morning and said that eight or twenty photographers were coming out. This is private, who the hell told them to come?"

"Not me," said Jill. "I'll check." She went to the phone in the kitchen.

"Merci, Papa!" shouted Paula, rising from her chair and holding a long dress to her chest. *"C'est une robe de fée."*

"I thought it was time you had one of your own," said Raoul.

Iris was neatly folding the wrapping paper from Paula's presents on the dining table, and casting looks at the two books on art and the big box of paints that had been opened so far. Her own present, a friendship ring that Charlé had helped her pick out at Lido-Bijoux on the Champs-Elysées, was still in its little box, under a blue bow made with American ribbon that somehow stuck to itself if you spat on it. "Open mine," she said, without looking at Paula.

"It's just Eric," screamed Jill from the kitchen. "Your friend Eric Castiglione. There won't be an invasion, it's all right."

Charlé was upstairs in her bedroom with her hairdresser. On the chair by her dressing table was a hatbox with a blue-and-gold-striped headdress in it. "It will hide all your hair," said the hairdresser horrified; he thought he had come an awfully long way for nothing. Charlé sensed his disappointment.

"You could do an Egyptian *maquillage* on me as well, couldn't you?" she asked. "Like Nefertiti, or Cleopatra, *vous savez?*"

"I have no colors," he said. Charlé drummed her fingers on the glass top of the dressing table. "I think there must be some paints downstairs; go look in the dining room. Take these stairs, here—" She pointed to the secret flight through her bathroom. The hairdresser laughed, winked and crept down the stairs, hoping to surprise whoever saw him coming out. When he found himself in an empty bedroom, he fantasized for a moment that this was where Madame Abime kept her lover, although he believed from what she said that she had never been unfaithful to her husband. The bottles of Elizabeth Arden Blue Grass on the chest of drawers, the wrinkled pink nightie on the unmade bed, and the spring curlers covered with pink plastic nets destroyed his fantasy; he paused for a minute, struck by the notion that perhaps it was a woman that Madame Abime loved, and was confused by the various photographs of Raoul wedged between the mirror and its ornate frame. He went through the door to the kitchen, where two hired cooks were at work on the large central table while Mauricette counted the hundreds of little cookies in their pans. One cook was building a Château Rose out of slabs of cake and panels of white frosting tinged with pink. The other was pushing tarragon leaves into place across the bodies of young cooked chickens. Six young men were setting boxes down on the chairs in the vestibule beyond the kitchen; the hairdresser checked them out quickly, and one of them, a swarthy young man with almond eyes and short curly hair, returned his interested look.

The hairdresser knocked on the door of the dining room, which was open.

"Oui?" said Jill, looking up from Paula, around whom she was draping the wide skirt of the new dress. Raoul, seated on a chair with his back to the door, turned in irritation.

"Des couleurs, pour Madame. She needs paints."

Before Jill could answer, Iris seized Paula's new box of watercolors. "Here," she said, "these. Take them. We don't need them right now." Paula raised her hand to stop her present from disappearing so quickly, but the hairdresser was already back in the vestibule, with the paint box in hand.

"And who is *that?*" asked Raoul, huffing to indicate that he had been right to consider the party a rape of his privacy.

"It's Charlé's hairdresser, Raoul." Jill used her humoring tone.

"Those were mine," said Paula in a little voice.

"You'll get them back," said Iris, unable to repress a little smirk. "She needs them; you don't, not right now. You've got a dress to play with." And with the true moral edge of the giftless, she walked away from the table and out through the door into the garden.

It was a warm day; the sun shone down through the dappling leaves of the tall trees, and little patches of yellow light marked the path to the stairs that led around to the front of the house. Iris stood on the gravel, scuffing her school sandals in the dirt beneath, and watched Eugène the butler as he directed sour men in blue overalls carrying cases of champagne to a table between two linden trees. Next to it, two matte speckled-steel washing vats had been draped with sheets and filled with ice. Antoine the gardener stood with his hands on the small of his back, leaning down to watch people from the nursery shove zinnias into the beds of violets under the oak tree. "It's not right," he said. "A violet is a violet, and a zinnia has no place next to it. *C'est bien ça, les gens du cinéma.*"

Jill and Paula, standing outside the dining-room door, waved at Iris. "Jill says that we have to find something to put on the table," shouted Paula. Iris turned and looked at the table: it was covered with a long white cloth, which hung stiffly, creased like paper.

Iris and Paula hurried into the house, past the six young men who had opened their boxes and were taking out white wigs and patting them with the practiced hands of experienced chorus boys. "Lackeys," Iris told Paula, who paused to watch them. "Come on!"

While the hairdresser mixed blue and green in a saucer to try to find the perfect shade of peacock, Charlé was on the phone to Jenny, from the *Tribune.* "What do you mean, you're going to be late?"

"There's a luncheon at the embassy, and I can't get out there till after four. Is that all right?"

"It's a fête champêtre, dear," intoned Charlé, "and that means it starts at two. Well, never mind, and bring anyone really fascinating you run into at the embassy."

"Uh, Charlé, I won't be able to come in costume," added Jenny. "Is that all right?"

"Well, you'll only be here to write about it, after all, so I can bend the rules a little. But everyone will be dressed up. Oh"—this with a little intake of breath—"it's going to be so beautiful."

"Well," said Jenny, "if I bring anyone from the party, they won't be in costume either."

"If they're really fascinating, it won't matter," said Charlé. "Must go now; don't forget your photographer."

Iris and Paula had struggled with the trunk in the storeroom and found what they wanted. Jill was tipping the florists when Eugène, sweating in his yellow-and-black afternoon waistcoat, tapped her on the arm. She turned to see a long swath of cream satin, embroidered with a thousand open-winged birds in flight across a field of roses curling away from curved leaves, undulating out the door. Iris and Paula had placed it over their heads, and as they walked, they separated and closed in on each other, proceeding like a ceremonial Chinese dragon with a touch of the pantomime horse. A gold fringe scurried along the ground, dragging tiny pebbles with it. *"Ça va se salir,"* said Eugène, who had never seen the fabric before but imagined it must be very expensive. Jill remembered it as the bedcover of Catherine the Great in Soula's film *Imperial Wanton,* and was surprised that Soula had managed without her help to coerce the producers into handing it over. She reached for the back that trailed on the ground, and gave each of the girls a kiss. "This is exactly what was needed—you are clever," she said. Eugène reluctantly took the other end and held it up, pulled it taut, and gave it a few shakes. Mauricette came out from the kitchen to watch the dust fly up from the embroidered birds and clucked her tongue against her teeth. Wine stains would never come out of *that.* As Jill and Eugène shook the heavy fabric and let it subside over the table, Paula murmured, "Maybe it is too beautiful." Iris knelt and pulled the fringe straight; touching the wings of the birds and the lozenge-shaped petals of the roses, she opined with childish practicality that it would be awful if someone vomited all over it. "Don't be disgusting," said Paula. "Don't be silly," said Jill. "We haven't asked anyone like that."

Raoul went to have a coffee in the bar in the village. Jill got herself into her costume, a sort of Madame Mère outfit consisting of a black dress with a tapered stiff panel in the front, paniers on the sides, and a black mantilla on her head. Why she had chosen to appear as a dowager queen on a day when she herself had ordered that each guest dress according to his fantasy revealed rather more of her attitude to Raoul's household than she might have wished. While trying on costumes at Pathé, she had convinced herself that black was a good practical color, the paniers and bodice were appropriate to the supposed period of the house, and the mantilla would simplify the problem of her hairdo and allow her to dispense with the services of the queer that Charlé used.

In their bedroom, Iris and Paula were so excited that they could not get dressed; it was Jill, finally, who swept in on a rustle of taffeta and hurried them into their dresses. This afternoon's costumes were too important to leave to Julie. Paula was inserted into her fairy gown first: Iris sat cross-legged on the bed, not daring to move in case she tore the gown in a moment of uncontrollable emotion. Jill fluffed out the skirt as Paula stood still in the middle of the room. Silver and gold threads crossed the bodice; the underskirts of bunched net puffed out the skirt; the sleeves shimmered like the windshield of Raoul's new car when you looked at it through his Polaroid sunglasses. Iris rested her face on her upturned palm and began picking threads out of the white cotton bedcover.

"Come on, we haven't got all day!" Jill rustled over to her and unfolded the costume they had picked out together at Pathé.

"Do I have to wear this?" asked Iris. "I'd much rather be a princess, too."

"This is perfect for you. Come on, Iris, you loved it last week."

Iris cast a disconsolate look at Paula, who was holding her breath in front of the standing mirror and, stiff and resigned, stuck out her arms toward Jill. Jill bounced the silk up from her arms once and then twice, muttering about "a lovely Rigoletto."

"I don't want to be *rigolo,* I want to be pretty," said Iris. She stepped into the ballooning patchwork that Jill had carefully spread on the floor, and allowed Jill to button her into it along her back: she looked down at the bright squares of red and yellow, green and blue and black.

"It's a lovely little jester suit," Jill coaxed. "It's much more interesting than being just a princess."

Iris peered around at Jill, and was a little mollified by the wink she received. She walked to the mirror, turning her feet out the way she had been taught in ballet class long ago. She made a face at herself; decidedly, the costume looked better if you puffed out your cheeks. "Here," said Jill, handing her a stick with little gold bells attached to one end, "you rattle this at people."

Little girls started to arrive, brought from Paris by their parents, who were friends of Raoul's and Jill's. Only one local child came, the son of the owner of Aux Nymphéas, the hotel on the island in the middle of the mosquito-infested lake. He was dressed as some sort of bird. There were little girls in pointed hats—not witches but apothecaries from Molière's plays—and little girls in tutus and little girls in grass skirts, *à la tahitienne,* one of whom, having seen a documentary on Tahiti, essayed lewd hip movements whenever anyone looked at her.

Raoul returned from the village bar and went to change. Charlé was already in her costume, a red dress of pleated chiffon that was Egyptian enough to confirm the intimations of the stiff headdress with the little brass cobra on it poised to strike, but expensive enough, being from Balmain, to reassure her that she was not being vulgar. Raoul granted her a smile from the doorway to his room and opened the box that Jill had left on his bed. As he pulled out the long red gown, he regretted ever having decided to be Cardinal Richelieu. For one thing, he had no religious feelings either way; secondly, red was not a color he had ever been fond of; and last and most important, he knew he would feel like a fool. He sat in an armchair and lit his pipe.

Outside his window he could see a little group of people around the fountain; the water jet was exceptionally lively that day, spraying brightly into the sky, moved this way and that by the breeze. It's a triumph for the plumber, he thought. Bravo, plumber. He watched as little girls joined hands to dance around the fountain while the Yorkshire, a ribbon tied to its collar, danced after them. He thought he recognized his friends among the adults; there was a knight who was normally a novelist, a woman dressed as La Pompadour, and a younger man in tights who must be thinking of himself as a troubadour because he had a guitar. He heard the distant sounds of the little band; an accordion, a fiddle, he thought, or maybe two. He saw Charlé go down the steps in her rippling red pleats and Jill come up from the back, looking like a widowed chicken. He found his diffidence turning to disgust, and then, in a movement he was beginning to recognize, the disgust turned to a peculiar sort of pleasure.

They all look like idiots, he thought, and chuckled; the bonhomie of the sound he found himself making startled him, and he rose from his chair. He was still hesitating about joining the party when he saw Szos puffing up the stairs from the garden; the sight of his agent made him laugh so heartily that he lost all misgivings about it, and he pushed open the window and strode out across the flat stones.

Szos was a little unsure of his costume. The cape was a little warm and the formal cutaway a little tight; but the fangs fit perfectly, and although the nails were ridiculously long and pinched the ends of his fingers where they were fastened on with little metal rings, they made him feel dangerous even if the rest of the outfit did not. He had flapped his arms once or twice as he got out of his car, just to get the feeling of the cape; now that he was within sight of others, he refrained from making any such gestures.

"Szos, you're perfect," said Jill, her skirts scratching against the stone balustrade. He gave her a smile that revealed his long yellow fangs. "Brilliant! Raoul will adore it! Come and meet Vivien Legrand."

Szos pulled away from Jill. "Vivien Legrand, is she here? I didn't know you knew her."

"Everyone's here," said Jill.

Szos busied himself at pulling off his nails. "I can't meet her like this, I do business with her," he muttered. He handed the nails to Jill and unfastened his cape. "I thought it was just going to be family," he hissed. "How can you do this to me?"

Jill gave him an impatient look and left him on the terrace. "I've got things to do," she said. Yves and Annabelle Furet were proceeding toward her up the stairs, followed by a woman covered in gray veils.

"There are six catamites in white wigs down there," said Annabelle Furet to Jill.

"You're a killjoy," said Jill. "Haven't you ever seen a lackey before?"

"I am a dream," said the woman in gray veils.

Szos came across the terrace toward them. The woman in gray veils surveyed his tailcoat, his white shirt, his bow tie. As he leaned forward to say hello, she said, "Yes, thank you very much, I'd like a glass of champagne."

Raoul arrived behind Szos. *"Chéri,"* screamed the woman in the gray veils.

"Suzette," said Raoul.

"But you're not in costume," she said.

Raoul looked down at his tired cord trousers, his tattersall shirt, the sleeve of his dirty suede jacket. "I am disguised as myself," he said. Yves and Annabelle Furet and the two men behind them laughed politely.

André Roth came with an earnest American, who insisted that Raoul had promised him an interview. Little gilt chairs had been set out on the lawn for guests to watch the jugglers; artists, writers, actors, musicians, kept women, a count or two, barkeepers, script girls, socialites and an airplane pilot sat and watched while three young girls played with balls and did daring feats while supporting themselves on one hand. They all clapped when it was over.

Eugène rang a bell in the dining room, and the children, who numbered twenty by now, ran up the stairs. Inside, the huge cake in the shape of the house was enthroned in the center of the table, and the children gathered around Paula. The adults straggled in, eyeing each other's costumes and clutching drinks as emblems of vices that allowed them a dignified distance from such infantile revelry. Paula blew out the candles;

Iris led the applause, having been freed from restraint by her gaudy balloon of a costume. Charlé cut her off and calmly lit the candles again. The children, their faces reaching just over the table, peered at each other: Had something gone wrong? Jill knelt down. "It's because of Monsieur Castiglione," she said, pointing to a tall, gangling man festooned with cameras who stood most inelegantly on a chair. *"Merci,"* he said, nodding at them.

Eric Castiglione had been brave in Indochina, although no one had asked him to be. It would have been easy to avoid the front line and make do with deep-focus pictures of starving orphans taken with an unbiased fifty-millimeter lens, but he would have forever considered himself a coward if he had not donned the wrinkled khaki of a soldier and marched into the undergrowth with battalions of doomed Frenchmen. His photographs of the fall of Dien Bien Phu had been published around the world, won prizes, and the one of the mother and child at the railroad station in Hanoi had made his name. On his return to Paris in 1954 he had found life dull without the proximity of death. His agency sent him to Istanbul, Morocco, Suez, Hungary: he wanted riots, blood in the streets, desolation, despair. All Paris had to offer were fights over parking spaces and altercations in bars. His strength as a war photographer, as far as the papers were concerned, was that he didn't mind which side he was on: he took pictures of the sheer light of lunacy in men's eyes, whether they were patriots or revolutionaries. His contact sheets could serve both sides. One day, returning from an assignment tailing slave traders in the Gulf, he was offered a contract by *Paris Match,* and his girlfriend, a Swedish model, told him she was pregnant and sick of aborting. He signed the contract, married the girl, and now here he was, standing on a chair taking pictures at a ten-year-old's birthday party.

Yet for *Paris Match,* Eric Castiglione was a star. He recorded the sentimental moments in civilian life as they happened to the best-looking, the most famous, notorious or powerful people in France. He shot them all with some measure of inattention, just to show that he had seen weightier moments. He used the highest speed and the tightest shutter, and caught the most poignant look on his subjects' faces just as he said, "I've got it, thank you," and they began to relax. The vicissitudes of the great merely afforded him a living. If he was doing a more careful job than normal that day, or at least using up more rolls of film than he normally apportioned to celebrity reportage, it was because he hoped that Raoul Abime would read his script about war and danger and violence. It was called "Truth Is Everywhere," and it had taken him a good two years to write. He admired Abime: sometimes they drank together at La Rose Rouge.

He guided Raoul to the window as the children waited for their slices of cake, and set the director's profile against the backbends of molding along the wooden shutters. "*Assez,*" said Raoul after a few clicks, "come and have a drink, in the *salon*, away from these monsters." Eric refused: he wanted to set up a really good picture, just Raoul and the family, having tea with the façade behind them. "*Merde,*" said Raoul, but Eric, who knew this to be a pose, promised that it would all be ready and done in ten minutes. Raoul shrugged, caught sight of the great Vivien Legrand going down to the lawn, and followed. He was, he often said, fascinated by her. "So natural, yet so majestic."

Iris watched the Château Rose being cut into small rectangles of white cake, red jam, and white frosting, and slid a look over at the Moor, hoping he wouldn't mind the sacrilege. He had been adorned for the day with a necklace of paper chains; streamers were anchored to his head by a common little piece of Scotch tape, and Iris felt embarrassed for him as she felt embarrassed for herself in her fool's costume. She grabbed her jester's stick and went out to the lawn. Jill was handing a camera to Raoul, who turned it over in his hands. "The new model," he said. "Is there film?" Jill nodded: "Loaded, too." Raoul pulled away from his group and turned toward the house. Carefully he lined the camera up and pushed the button. Jill handed him a cylinder of pink jelly. "You have to count to twenty," she said. Iris shook her stick at them as she passed, and continued walking to the end of the lawn, right up to the gate: she didn't want to look as if she had come outside to have her picture taken. A man outside the gate was paying a taxi driver, and she leaned against the iron bars to watch him. No one ever came to the front, didn't he know that? He was a tall, plump man, obviously a tourist; as he came near the gate, Iris shrank away and pressed her back against the bush. "*Allo!*" shouted the man. "*Parlay-voo?*"

He was bald, and his head rose and rose above his eyebrows. He stuck his hands through the gate and tried to work the huge golden handle inside, but the gate was permanently and severely locked. His assurance terrified Iris. She ran back to the house as fast as she could, keeping along the hedge, and then down the stairs to the garden; she was afraid that if he saw her on the terrace he would harm her, even if there were people between them. The little band was playing "*Malbrough S'en Va-t'en Guerre*" as she skittered down the stairs. Under the trees a few people were eating chicken off little plates, but there was no one there that she could trust. Panting, she ran up the stairs again; her mother, she felt, should be warned.

Szos caught sight of her and waved her over, but she shook her head and started toward the dining room. "Come here, Iris, I want you to meet

Vivien," screamed Jill, and Iris turned, wondering who Vivien was. A woman in white was smiling at her, and making that bird-beak gesture Italians make that means "hello." Looking behind her, Iris saw that the man at the gate had disappeared, so she decided that she no longer had to tell anyone about him; she rattled her stick and marched toward Jill. Raoul, from the terrace, shouted *"Silence!"* and took a Polaroid while Szos, Jill and the woman in white froze and Iris ran to be in the center of the group.

Raoul descended the steps, pulling the film out, and they stopped talking while he unpeeled the photograph from its backing. Then he showed them the picture, which was passed from hand to hand.

"I look like my dentist," said Szos.

"God, I'm fat!" wailed Jill.

Vivien Legrand passed the picture to Iris without saying a word. Iris screamed, "I'm *blurred,*" and handed it back to her, disappointed.

Raoul began to laugh. "Not one of you has looked at the picture," he said. "You only looked at yourselves." Iris felt herself blushing. "Vanity," said Raoul, wagging his finger. Vivien Legrand turned her shiny nose toward him and said, "It is a beautiful picture."

Eric began signaling from the terrace. Raoul excused himself and began to climb back up the stairs when a man emerged from the window of the *petit salon.* "It's the tourist!" Iris said to Szos. "He was at the gate, spying on us."

"Howdy, folks!" said the man. "Anybody seen Charlene? This is the Château Rose, isn't it?" He stepped out onto the terrace. He had a tanned face and his skull was like a well-baked brioche. He was wearing a red-and-white jacket and white trousers, and seemed to have forgotten his socks. In his hands he held a pair of sunglasses.

"Make him go away," ordered Iris, pulling at Szos's coattails; Jill quickened her step and met him at the top of the ceremonial stairs, Madame Mère, flanked by Dracula, confronting a member of the twentieth century. "We're in the middle of a private party," said Jill, who knew the guest list by heart.

"Gee, I thought you were making some kind of film," said the stranger. "I'm just passing through."

"The house is not open to the public," said Jill, sounding like Queen Elizabeth.

He shook his head and passed a hand over the brown skull. Iris saw that he had a small bit of hair behind his ears; she thought he was the ugliest man she had ever seen.

"I'm not the public," he said, and put out his hand. "I'm Tyler Bromley, and Charlene, my wife, asked me to stop by anytime. I didn't expect a fancy-dress party."

Szos cut past Jill and went to the window of the dining room; he could see Charlé behind the glass, talking to the journalist, who looked a little uncomfortable. Szos knocked on the glass, and she pulled the window open. "What is it? Is Eric ready for us?"

Szos felt an insane desire to let out a whoop, but he moderated his voice to suit the grave moment. "Your husband's here. One of your husbands. How many husbands do you have?"

Charlé let out a little scream. "It's a joke! Szos, c'mon!" she said, and turned quickly to the journalist. "He always plays these little jokes on me," she said.

Szos put a hand on her bare, freckled and un-Egyptian shoulder. "You must go out and say hello to him. He asked for you by name."

"By name?"

"Charlene. I haven't heard that name in years."

"Oh, shit!" Charlé pulled her headdress down further on her head and slid through the open window. Tyler was alone, watching the fountain with concentration. Jill had moved back to her group. Only Iris was watching, standing on the steps, hunched in her fool's costume.

"Tyler, how nice of you to come," Charlé said, trying not to look at his bare skull.

He put his sunglasses in his breast pocket and walked toward her. "Charlene," he said, "I would never have known you under that crazy hat. What happened to your hair?"

It was with a great effort of will that she stopped herself from asking what had happened to his. She took his elbow and stared at it so she would not have to look at his face. "What brings you to Paris?" she asked, steering him into the house.

"I was on my way to Sicily; there's a man there who's developed an orange that stays frost-free even on the lowest branches, and Paris was on the way." He paused, sensing he might have bored her. "I wanted to look in on you and my little Iris. Where is she?"

Charlé looked back along the terrace, and realized that she could not avoid anything. "Iris," she called, "Iris." Iris began to run toward them, and Tyler said, "That's her? I thought she was a little boy. Gee, these costumes are confusing." "Iris," she said, "this is your daddy, Tyler." Turning to her former husband, and using a tone more suited to the lightest of badinage, she told him, "It's high time the two of you got to know each other."

Tyler knelt and hugged Iris, who resisted. "She's shy," said Charlé. "Come on, Iris, it's your daddy. Give him a hug." Iris uncrossed her arms and gingerly opened them to the bald stranger.

"Let me see you!" he said, and took her shoulders and pushed her back a little. Iris kept her eyes shut so she would not have to see him.

"Charlé! Charlé!" It was Eric Castiglione calling from the middle of the terrace. "*Viens! C'est prêt!*" Charlé saw that Raoul was already seated with Paula and a tea service had appeared on the little table. The Yorkie was chewing on something at Raoul's feet, and two chairs remained empty. Iris still had her eyes shut, but Tyler, uncomprehending, confused, was looking over at Eric. "I must go, my husband needs me," she said, and began to run along the terrace. Iris, hearing her mother depart, opened her eyes and started after her, but Tyler had her wrist in a firm grip. "Where ya going?" he asked.

"It's the picture," she mumbled, conscious of the new and crippling form duty had suddenly taken.

"Don't you want to talk to your daddy?" he asked, kneeling and ruffling her bangs. "I haven't seen you since you were a tiny little baby." She couldn't move; her eyes were riveted on Charlé sitting with Raoul's arm around her, and Paula leaning against her shoulder. There was still hope, in the form of an empty chair next to Paula.

"I send you cards—have you gotten them?" pursued Tyler. Getting no answer, he stood up. "I'm really knocked out by this place. How about you showing your daddy around?" Iris allowed her hand to be taken while keeping her eyes on the chair. Eric was gesticulating at Charlé and Paula; Jill stood behind him, a glass in her hand.

"Where's your room?" asked Tyler, who had begun by suspecting he had walked into a madhouse and was now sure of it. He tugged a little at her arm; shy was one thing, mute was another. He wished he and Francine had children of their own, and upon this wish came the happy thought that Iris was his, and he tugged harder.

Jill cast a quick, professional glance over toward them, and, wishing to expedite the photo session, which was already seriously eating into the party, she lunged forward and quickly removed the extra chair. With only Paula, Raoul, Charlé and the dog now in his viewfinder, Eric began to shoot.

Iris knew it was all over for her. She allowed Tyler's large hand to pull her into the dining room, where she dutifully pointed out the Hellenic frieze, which she called "Helen's fraise." The speed with which her chair had been eliminated and the way neither Charlé nor Paula had called for her could only confirm that she had no reason to be in the picture. She glanced up at this father who had just been dumped on her; he was looking down at her with a smile that she seemed to recall, showing teeth that were very large and very even.

She showed him the *grand salon* and turned on the switch that activated the lights beneath the floor. "Jeeesus," he said. She plucked a few strings on the harp, and he asked her if she could play; to forestall any admission of inadequacy, she led him rapidly through the *petit salon,* down the stairs, through the dining room and to her bedroom. He whistled at the mosquito-netting canopies over the beds. "Regular little princesses, you both are," he said, sitting on the little armchair that was really only meant for children. She wondered whether to ask him to sit elsewhere, but decided against it. He looked at the toys in the bookcase, the stuffed animals piled in a corner, the two little desks. The accordionist was still playing, and the rhythmic whine of "Les Enfants de la Balle" came through the bedroom window. Tyler looked at his watch: Francine was in the hotel waiting; he had promised to be back at six, but it had taken longer to get out here than he had thought. Iris was looking at him, trying to make him handsome. He beamed at her. "You must be very happy, living in this palace with all these toys," he said, looking at the vase of roses next to him.

Iris burst into tears. She tried to stop, knowing that if she did not he would take her away with him, and then the real end of the world would have come, but she couldn't stop. He took out an immense white handkerchief from his pocket and thrust it at her. "Hey, c'mon, don't cry!" He dabbed at her cheeks; she was heaving with sobs. "What is it, my little, my little . . ." He patted her shoulders.

"I knew it!" Charlé's sharp voice from the door interrupted the beginning of tenderness.

Charlé stamped her foot. "I knew that you'd make her cry! Stop it, Iris, stop it!" She took Tyler's sleeve—the touch of the flesh of his hand on hers would be too much, she thought, too familiar—and pulled him out of the room, leaving Iris alone. In the dining room she challenged him. "What do you want? Why did you have to come and ruin everything? She'll have a trauma about it now, and she hasn't had any up to now, so I don't need you to start confusing her!"

"Charlene," drawled Tyler. "You asked me to drop by. So I did. I don't like the way you're living, with all these oddballs walking around—"

"For Christ's sake, it's a party! Can't you appreciate a bit of fantasy?"

"Sure," he said, "in the right place. Iris seems kind of glum for a little girl of nine."

"You are not getting her back. Now, get out of here, do you hear?" Charlé stood firm. This was a great moment in her life, she thought:

defending her child from a barbarian like Tyler. She pulled off her headdress to give emphasis to what she said, and, incidentally, to increase her resemblance, a dramatic one, to Susan Hayward.

"That's a fine way to welcome a guest," snorted Tyler. He banged the table. "Call me a cab, and I'll go. I'm just going to say good-bye to my little girl." He returned to the bedroom, where Iris lay in a pile of bright silk. "Iris," he said, "Iris." She sat up and pulled the mosquito netting around her.

"I don't expect you to understand," he said. "But always remember, I'm on your side. I'm your daddy and I love you." He put down one of his cards—a business card, unfortunately, because he didn't have his private address printed on anything (Francine said it was vulgar)—on the bed next to Iris. "Anytime you need me, just call collect. Collect, okay?" He bent down and kissed her wet forehead, and left the room.

Iris looked at the card and dropped it as if it were burning. She stayed in the room until all the guests had left and night had fallen and she could hear Raoul and Charlé laughing with Jill and Szos in the lower dining room. Paula came in. "What happened?" she asked.

"I was indisposed," said Iris. It was Charlé's favorite excuse for staying in bed, and the only alibi Iris could think of.

"You're too young to be indisposed," said Paula. "Who was that man? Charlé wouldn't tell me."

Iris blessed her mother for the first time in her life. "A relation," she said, "an uncle."

"Jill said he was your father."

"She doesn't know anything," said Iris. "Let's talk about something else."

But she knew that on the terrace that afternoon she had been marked with the indelible taint of the ordinary; and that no matter what happened, she would never be a princess in a shimmering gown.

Later, after a dinner of soup and leftover boeuf en gêlée, she overcame her fear of the arms that stick out of walls and the snakes that lie on the edge of carpets, and climbed up to the dining room. The streamers still hung from the chandelier, but otherwise the room had been put back to order. She tiptoed over to the Moor and kissed his shiny black cheek. "Make me one of you," she whispered. "Please."

Part II
SOCIAL LIFE

9.

The Land of Little Houses

Every spring Antoine the gardener burned rubbish in the back of the garden, behind the little pavilion that had been restored and now served as a playhouse for Paula and Iris. The eight sides of the outside wall had been re-covered with a green trellis, and inside, a low banquette ran along under the windows. It was here that the girls spent their afternoons when school was over, and most of their Sundays. Charlé, too, wished she could have a retreat to go to, but she was condemned to stay in the Château Rose and submit to whatever Raoul had on his mind. These days, with the unexpected success of two films to shore up his status as a director, there was a constant stream of newspaper reporters, women described as old friends and men from Marseilles who drank a great deal of red wine. Jill steered the guests and visitors around with the condescending air of a grand chamberlain, and offered casual hints as to how they should behave—little things, such as "Raoul hates being interrupted," or "Charlé only likes to hear about flowers and gardens, she's got a green thumb." Charlé had no such thing as a green thumb, and was vexed that everyone insisted on talking to her as if she were a gardener. Jill's tactics in the matter of cowing guests had attained such a state of refinement that Raoul often found them discomfited before he even opened his mouth. The atmosphere in the main house was edgy, particularly when there were overnight visitors. No one felt at home: if the walls and moldings and mirrors and drapes didn't get to them, the harp did, or the echoes of their words on the marble floors.

Charlé had planned her escape many times: flying to New York, driving to Deauville, or simply hiding out in Szos's extra bedroom in Paris. The escape, she knew, would be easy; the problem was what to do once she had made the move, and about this she had no idea whatsoever. She needed a man to give her impetus; if anyone had held her hand and told her she deserved better than this, she would gladly have abandoned Iris and run off with him; but her life was to all appearances the height of self-indulgent luxury, and Raoul's little barbs seemed to visitors to be no more than evidence of his charming individualistic character. Worst of all, although her face and figure were still holding up fairly well, whatever sparkle Charlene had possessed as she twinkled and giggled on the arm of Saul Hyott had been dimmed in Charlé by the superior blaze of Raoul. She was discovering that fame demands only one thing from those closest to it, and that is insignificance.

At Jill's suggestion she went to an English health farm that spring; Jill had said it would relax her, and Charlé took advantage of the opportunity to get herself back into shape. Maybe it was the little pouches at the sides of her mouth that were keeping her saviors away, or the manner in which her stomach bulged out just a little below her waistline.

Iris and Paula now spoke mostly in French; it was Raoul's language, and the language of his visitors. English had become the language of subterfuge: they used it to lie to Jill about whether they had finished their homework, and to lie to Charlé about whether they had taken their baths. Charlé occasionally suggested that an effort in the direction of learning to read and write in English would prepare them for something she called "an international future," but Iris and Paula felt that their brains were already overtaxed by the Cours Lamartine, and loudly resisted the notion that they needed another skill. For them, the real world ended at the gates of the Château Rose. School was a punishment endurable only because they were in the same class, thanks to Paula's refusing to push herself and Iris working as hard as she could to keep up. Paris was only a place where they went shopping.

In the pavilion they told each other entrancing stories, playing with pieces of costume and jewelry, and inventing plays in which they were both the heroine. The real was unintelligible to them, a dreary invention of strangers who didn't understand; the fantastic was the bedrock of their experience. Iris, without telling anyone about it, still talked to the Moor.

One day, when Jill was in the downstairs dining room reading the papers, they heard her calling them. "Paula! Iris!" she shouted, smoothing down the pages of the *Herald Tribune* as she opened it on the table. On the chair next to her was a pile of twenty copies that she had sent Pierre to get at the station in Saint-Germain-en-Laye. "You must both look at the paper! Your father's gotten a wonderful review." Paula came in and leaned her elbows on the table. "What does it say?" she asked. Jill said, "It's right there, black on white—can't you read?" Iris and Paula looked at each other and sighed. The headline said, "Abime Film Breaks New Ground." Iris pretended to read; Paula, more conscious of her own wishes and less inclined to maintain a false front, nudged Jill. "You know we can't. Go on, Jill, please!" Jill looked at them both with theatrical reproach, took her glasses from the case on the table, set them on her nose, and, with a mutter of "Frog savages!" intoned: " '*Les Archanges du Mégot,* which opened yesterday at the Pathé Elysée, is the finest work yet to come from Raoul Abime.' " Paula beamed with pride and settled comfortably on the table to listen. Iris rearranged herself in her chair. Jill continued: " 'In this simple story about tramps, a story so bleak and dark that the violently erotic scenes come as necessary relief, Abime has at last proved himself a master. Colas and Pignolle, the two tramps, swig from broken bottles beneath the bridges of the Seine and exchange pleasantries about death while floodwaters threaten to engulf their sordid shanty homes. When Madeleine, a rich *femme du monde,* is saved from suicide by Colas, Abime makes the erotic sparks fly. The ensuing drama has tragic proportions, and the ending is elegant, earth-shattering and unexpected. Nicole Amiette and Richard Beulot are outstanding as the fleshly Madeleine and the dour Colas, while Gérard Blery's performance puts him forever among the ranks of the great.' There!" Jill put down the paper, and turned to Paula, her head inclined as if she were addressing a puppy. "Whose father is a little genius?" she asked. Paula smiled back.

Iris withdrew. She had taken to withdrawing on occasions such as these. Ever since it had been made clear to her that fathers could not be chosen but were immutably imposed by an arbitrary fate, her attitude toward Raoul had been one of awe, of nervous admiration. The proprietary love that Paula acted on with such wholehearted spontaneity was something that she could not share. Iris was unsure of her reactions, ill at ease, constrained. She felt herself unqualified to give the right response on every occasion, and her voice came out as a croak, which sounded like a sneer, when she meant it to express the greatest approval. She deciphered clues in her environment and adapted her behavior to what she thought was expected not of a daughter but of a bystander. Unlike Paula, who would roll around in the dirt, climb trees, or dance on the downstairs dining-room table at the least sign of interest from Raoul, Iris needed prodding. If asked to perform, she would; if everyone else was doing it, then Iris would fling herself into the part of a gay, extrovert, creative child. But most of the time she watched.

Since Charlé was away and it was the first day of their Easter holiday, Raoul decided to take the girls to lunch at the new drugstore on the Champs-Elysées. They changed into American dresses and waited for him in the kitchen. Paula had a handbag, a castoff from Charlé in pale-blue leather with a zipper across the top. She was almost thirteen, and three inches taller than Iris. Iris resented this, and resented the handbag as a sure token of Paula's maturity. Not to be defeated, she stole a manila envelope from Jill's office and put a pair of gloves in it, along with a notebook and a pencil. "Raoul says we're going to the Louvre first, and I might need to write something down," she told Paula, who did not like having the symbol of her seniority eclipsed by an envelope. "Come on, Raoul's waiting," said Jill. In Charlé's absence she replaced her, mothering the girls with inflexible jollity, sitting at the head of the dinner table in makeup and jewelry, and sleeping with Raoul.

Raoul stood outside the garage, impatiently tapping his foot as the elderly Pierre attempted to start the Citroën. *"Ça va pas, ça va pas"* issued from the driver's seat, but Raoul didn't want to hear any complaints. He was anxious to get to Paris: first the Louvre, then lunch, and after lunch, he would hand the girls over to Szos, who would take them to a movie. His afternoon, free of interviews, meetings and discussions, shimmered before him in the remembered shape of a nubile young Lebanese woman he had met, and mastered, the week before. She would be waiting for him at four o'clock in her apartment on the Rue Jacob. Raoul took a deep breath of the bracing spring air, marred just a little by the burning pile of trash, and stretched out his arms. He blessed health farms and the vanity of women.

"Nous voici," said Paula, creeping up behind him and followed by Iris. Pierre steered the car out of the garage, and they hopped into the backseat

well before Raoul took the wheel because they did not want to miss the thrilling moment when the hydraulic pumps raised the car's rear end.

The twenty-one kilometers that separated the idyllic if suburban life of the Château Rose from the center of Paris were usually covered by Raoul's chauffeur in half an hour. Pierre took every care, stopped at red lights, and seemed to have a nose for traffic jams and a destiny to be caught in them once he had sniffed them out. When Raoul drove, the trees and power lines sped past the windows, red lights existed only for other cars, and the Citroën emitted an unmistakable smell of burning rubber. Iris and Paula loved it, their hands clawing deep into the springy woolen upholstery of the seats, their knees bouncing against the sides of the car. Every time Raoul revved the engine they let out a yell; but Iris took care never to yell louder than Paula, no matter how fast Raoul went.

Raoul parked the car on the Rue de Rivoli. The visit to the Louvre seemed absurd and unnecessary to him. He was hungry, and anxious to be done with lunch. He locked the door and crossed the street without waiting for the girls. Five buses, a motorcycle and three small cars hurled themselves at him; he darted elegantly among them but when he got to the Tuileries side his heart was beating hard. He should phone Szos's secretary, he thought, and get rid of the children before lunch. Hands linked, they remained at the opposite curb. Raoul was about to wave them across to him when he felt a foreboding. It's just idiocy, he told himself. They're old enough to cross the street. He raised his arm. At that instant, Raoul in mid-wave, Iris and Paula about to step off the curb and cross over to him in the sparse traffic between a pair of red lights, a pigeon in mid-swoop across the sunny street, at that moment a little gray van like the one they had just missed on the Boulevard Ney, parked thirty feet from the girls, exploded with an impossibly loud noise; shards of bent corrugated tôle fell through the air, a deep gray cloud billowed out from the remains of the van, three people fell in their tracks underneath the arches, cars braked and skidded, a workman in the process of crossing was felled by something sharp and fast made of steel and rubber and lead and fifteen shop windows shattered at once.

Then came the smell of smoke, a smell like that in the garden when Antoine burned his garbage, allied to a worse odor: that of burning flesh, and with it the cries of pain and angry shouts.

Raoul was already running across the street, in what seemed to him slow motion, impossibly slow and defeated somehow by the smoke and the sounds. Finally he reached the space between two cars where the girls had been standing, and they weren't there. He scanned that part of the pavement where their feet should have been, focused on it as if they could be found between the smooth gray rectangles, as the smoke rose and blew toward him through the arches. Then he burst into a cry of such depth that it was a howl.

"Papa!" he heard.

Iris and Paula were on the ground between a car and the sturdy base of an arch, entwined like monkeys. Raoul stumbled to them and bent down. "Okay? okay? okay? okay? okay?" was all he could say. Iris had a bruise beginning on the side of her face, but Paula was untouched. Quickly he helped them up, and ran toward his car, his hands now trembling so violently he could barely open the door. He pushed them in the front seat, and was trying to fit the key into the ignition just as the sirens of police vans coming up the street split his head in half.

"Was that a *plastic?*" asked Paula through chattering teeth.

"Oui."

"The Algerians?" asked Iris.

Raoul ignored her question. "What happened to you? You could have died, my God, you could have both died."

"I don't know," said Iris, "we were just standing there, and then there was the boom!—and we got pushed away."

"You could have died," said Paula to her father.

Suddenly a policeman stood in front of the car, both hands on its hood. *"Pas le droit de quitter le lieu d'un crime,"* he said.

Raoul gave up trying to start the car and threw his head back in resignation. The policeman came to the window. Raoul's eyes were closed, so it was Iris who had to lean over him and wind down the window.

"Identité, s'il vous plaît," said the flic.

Raoul opened his eyes, and said in French, "We have almost just died, all of us, and you want my papers?"

The policeman saluted. Ten or so of his colleagues were running past him now, toward the exploded van. "Five dead" could be heard from far away. "Five dead."

Raoul took out his wallet and handed it to the policeman without bothering to remove his *carte d'identité* and only present that. He felt incapable of the most minor actions. The policeman flipped through the solid wad of news clippings—reviews, had he cared to read them, of *Les Archanges du Mégot*—and honorably bypassed the several fifty-thousand-franc notes; then he found Raoul's ID and saluted again. *"Mes respects, Monsieur Abime,"* he said, and turned away from the window quickly, without returning the wallet. His friend Alphonse, the main photographer for *France-Soir,* had to be somewhere around. He peered at the wreck up the street and screamed, "Alphonse, leave that shit alone, come here, it's a good one!" Alphonse took a few more pictures of the burning pile, a close-up of the dead workman's back in the middle of the street, and, satisfied, trotted over to the car. The flic jerked his thumb at the window. *"C'est Abime, le réalisateur, vas y, c'est une pige de plus."* Alphonse raised his antique Leica, Raoul raised his hand but not fast enough, Paula raised her head in plenty of time, and Iris kept on crying into her palms. The policeman, proud of his quick thinking, saluted once more and said to Raoul, *"Vous pouvez rentrer chez vous maintenant, m'sieur,"* with the tone of one giving much needed advice, and handed Raoul back his wallet.

It was several hours later when the Citroën purred into the garden of the Château Rose; Raoul had gone first to the American Hospital, where he had made sure Iris and Paula were each given tranquilizing shots. And just for good measure he hired an intern to drive them home while he sat in the back with the two sleeping girls. He was trembling from his brogues to his collarbone, and he had even neglected to call Jill—or the Lebanese, what was her name? Jill, who had been waiting for them since the sun went down, came to the door and was relieved at first to see that it was the Citroën, and then aghast to see a man in a white smock at the wheel. She dashed into the garden and was at the car door before Raoul could open it. Paula's head lolled on his shoulder, Iris's was tucked between the edge of the seat and the window. Raoul unfolded himself from the car and took a deep breath of garden air, and retched violently as he caught the lingering scent of burning rubber. Jill turned to the intern. "What the hell's going on?" she asked as Raoul vomited straight onto the gravel.

Jill called Charlé in England while Raoul had a bath and Julie and Mauricette sat vigil at the girls' bedside.

Charlé was appalled. "How could he take them anywhere where that could happen?" she asked Jill in a whine.

"It was the Rue de Rivoli, Charlé," said Jill.

"My God, no!" said Charlé. "Which part of it?"

Jill racked her brains to remember which part of the street, then remembered that she hadn't been told. "Charlé, I don't know which part," she said. "Does it matter?"

Charlé had ordered some hats at Paulette and couldn't help wondering if that had been blown away too. "Oh my God," she continued. "Are they really all right? Is this going to be a trauma?"

"They're out for the count now, and I think they'll survive," said Jill. "After all, I was in London all through the Blitz and it didn't affect me one bit."

"These are delicate children," said Charlé. "Delicate children. My God, is Paris safe? Was it Algerians?"

"Probably. Raoul's having a bath right now. He was pretty shaken up, and the intern wasn't there, so he doesn't know."

"Intern!" The connection was already bad, but Charlé's screech didn't help. Jill held the receiver away from her ear.

Charlé's sobs came over as hisses and spittings, with a sniffle here and there. But her voice was clear: "I want the children in London at once. I'll meet them at the airport; you just let me know when you can get them over here. Right now. I won't have my babies blown up—" The line went dead.

Jill sat on the side of Raoul's bed. She smoothed her hair and patted her skirt and became very British. "Charlé thinks the girls should go to London right now, that Paris isn't safe, and I must say I agree with her. You should go to London tomorrow."

"Why?" asked Raoul.

"It's just not safe here."

"So. A bomb went off in the street."

Jill put her hand on Raoul's knee. "Thirty men were wounded this afternoon at the Bourse. They were bombing all over Paris. Really, Raoul, think of the children."

"Then, you go. I'm fine." Raoul gave a harrumph and sucked on his pipe.

Charlé, in tears, met them at the gate in London. The head of the customs hall had refused to allow her through to greet her children at the airfield, and she felt slighted; this kind of abusive behavior always came her way when she was without Raoul. Paula jumped into her arms, no mean feat for a thirteen-year-old, while Iris stared. Jill nodded approvingly at the square-faced driver, who relieved her of her baggage, and amid questions about revolution, war and safety, they made their way to a waiting Daimler.

Iris's first impression was disappointment with the landscape. Small, dark brick houses glued together, row upon row of grim and modest brick, adorned by an endlessly repeated zigzag of pale painted fretwork that followed the angles of the roofs. The pilot had talked about the low ceiling, and she decided that the houses, too, were low ceiling, like the sky, low ceiling and horrible. The colors of the street were green and brown, a dark bright green like the paint on certain bicycles, and a brown that lacked conviction, a sort of leftover brown. Above these rolled the folds of the moist English ceiling, sagging into darker gray curves of rain nearby, and of incipient rain in the distance. Dank; to her, "*sinistre*."

Charlé told Jill about the health farm, and about the friends who just happened to have an empty mews house at a split second's notice, but only for a week or two.

"Well, I don't think we'll be staying much longer; after all, this mess is going to blow over soon, and we shouldn't start behaving like displaced persons, should we?" said Jill.

"Well, I'm terrified. On the radio this morning there was all kinds of talk about parachutists falling out of the sky and I don't think Raoul is safe. He should be with us."

The car pulled into Belgrave Square, swung smoothly around half of its cream perimeter and turned into a smaller street where only the lower halves of the houses were painted white and the ubiquitous brown brick covered the other stories. Iris began to feel chilled; to her relief, the car turned again and carefully nosed down into a tiny cobbled street. It came to a stop by a tiny house, smaller than even the other dwarfs' dwellings in the street, and painted bright blue. "What is this?" asked Iris.

"It's sweet," exclaimed Paula.

"It's a mews!" cried Jill to Charlé's irritation; she had wanted to explain what a mews was. "It's the Lewises' house," she explained, very loud, to drown out Jill's explanation about mewses and horses.

The girls climbed out of the car, and looked at the little window boxes on the windows, and the little doors that opened, for some reason, on the top floors, with winches and pulleys hanging over them. The houses on the street were painted every shade of yellow, blue, pink; there was even one that was purple. The driver took the bags out of the back and waited patiently while Charlé searched through the various pockets of her fairly new Hermès alligator bag. Finally she drew out a horseshoe from which dangled a long chain with five keys; she tried every one in turn.

"Let me help you," said Jill as Charlé struggled at the turquoise door.

"I was here this morning, I did it then, it must work . . . there!" Triumphantly she swept the door open into a miniature living room, where two tiny chintz sofas faced each other across a small leather-topped table on which rested some ten copies of *Country Life.* Jill led the way in. She felt at home.

"Is this a house for children?" asked Iris at the door. "Because if it is, it's very nice of you to think of us, but we'd rather—"

"—stay with you!" said Paula.

"We'll all be here," said Charlé. "There's room for us all, there's even a maid's room for Jill." She caught herself: "It's a miracle to have an extra bedroom in a mews house," she said to Jill.

"I know. It's always been my dream to live in one of these, but nowadays they're much too expensive for real people."

"The Lewises are real people," said Charlé. "They own a great house in the country, a stately seat, and this is just their *pied à terre.* They let me have it the moment I told them about my problem—aren't they wonderful?"

"Lewis? Lewis?" asked Jill from a window that she had wrenched open.

"Arbuthnot-Lewis," Charlé enunciated, "Arbuthnot-Lewis."

"Oh, the Earl of Umberline." Jill gave a little laugh and settled on the sofa.

Over the mantelpiece hung a portrait of a man in uniform: in the grate was an electric fire with coals made of fat chips of orange glass. Charlé went to a tiny mother-of-pearl chest and opened it to reveal bottles and a silver tray. As she made a drink, Iris and Paula, taking the tiny steps two by two, went to the top floor. There they discovered a yellow room with twin beds covered in dark-green velvet; a linen cupboard stocked with five little towels and a cake of lavender soap; a bright orange bathroom with prints of stags and foxes framed in gold on its walls; and a large bedroom with a ceiling that was interrupted by jagged angles, all neatly delineated by frayed pink braid, pink rose wallpaper that had peeled a little just below the window, a dressing table with a set of silver brushes and a mirror, and a large bed with a headboard carved like a choir screen. Jill came up, glanced briefly at the rose room, pointed to the smaller room from the door and said, "This is my idea of sheer bliss." Then she went down again.

That evening a new friend of Charlé's, a homosexual screenwriter whom she had met at the health farm and who happened to be a "great fan" of Raoul's, came to take them out to dinner. He chose a Mexican-Cuban restaurant near Harrods where Jill said she used to go with her student friends. Charlé talked about clothes for fifty minutes, while Iris and Paula, both California babies, tasted the first guacamole and corn chips of their lives.

Jimmy Kieron was more inclined to talk about the manifestations of doom than about the vagaries of Paris fashion, and heroically managed to steer Charlé toward the subject of the fate of France. She tut-tutted the whole thing.

"But it is a full-scale revolt against De Gaulle," said Jimmy Kieron. "Surely that's pretty alarming."

"Enough to get us out of the country as fast as possible, but I don't think it's worrisome," said Jill.

Jimmy Kieron continued: "I saw in the paper today that Raoul"—although he had not met Raoul, he used the first name on the strength of his familiarity with Charlé—"was caught in a bomb attack yesterday. Awful business. Surely that's what persuaded him to—"

Charlé cut him off. "What paper?" she asked.

"Actually, the *Sunday Express,* with a picture. Didn't you see it?"

Charlé looked agitated. "No, I didn't. What kind of picture? Was it big?"

"Yes, it was Raoul and his daughter."

At the word "daughter," Iris and Paula stopped eating and looked up. A benign look crossed their faces.

"Who?" asked Iris.

"Raoul Abime," said Jimmy Kieron, who obviously felt that full names should be given when speaking to children.

"Not me?" asked Paula.

Jimmy Kieron looked at her. "Well, maybe it was you. Whichever one is his daughter, that's what the paper said."

"But we were *both* in the car," said Iris, as she put down her knife and fork.

"It was terrible," explained Jill with the confidence of one who had been the first to hear the news. "They were all on the Rue de Rivoli and . . . "

As Jill recounted the story to Jimmy Kieron, Charlé was preoccupied with thoughts of her own. Her ten days at the health farm had contracted some of the pouches she was beginning to exhibit beneath her eyes and below the exterior edges of her lips; she had met some seven or eight interesting people, of whom Jimmy Kieron ranked possibly fifth, behind the landed Lewises, a fat Greek gentleman who owned a yacht (she assumed that a fleet of tankers kept the yacht afloat on a sea of Greek millions), and two young Englishmen who were reducing on a bet. Her intention in going to the health farm had been more positively carnal than aesthetic, and in that respect she had come away empty-handed. She had unfinished business to complete in England: she was determined to find herself a lover. Paris was out of the question; she would have to stay in London longer. As her imagination shriveled at the challenge of conjuring up the lucky fellow, the restaurant reasserted itself and Charlé caught the end of Jill's story.

"And then the police cars came, all along the Rue de Rivoli, and they had *paniers à salade* too, and people were screaming everywhere," said Iris.

"It was awful, awful, awful!" said Paula.

"And then we got into the car, but Raoul couldn't open the door, he was shaking so hard, and we were in pieces, all of us," continued Iris.

"Go on, go on, it's wonderful!" said Jimmy Kieron.

"I don't think they should, really," said Jill.

"No, no, no," said Jimmy Kieron, waving his small, plump hand in the air over his rum and Coca-Cola. "Such life! Such detail! These girls are born actresses!"

Paula and Iris hurtled into the next scene, flattered to be described as actresses, with Iris harboring only the wisp of a doubt whether "actress" was quite the correct word to describe two such brave victims.

"Blood, blood, everywhere!" said Iris.

"And then I can't remember," interrupted Paula, selfishly, to Iris's mind, since she was not advancing the story. "I just fainted."

"I didn't know you'd fainted," said Jill, who nudged Charlé.

"I did, I did, it all went dark, terribly black!"

"Fascinating," said Jimmy Kieron. "And Raoul was shaking?"

"Yes, shaking," confirmed Iris. "His hands were like little leaves in the breeze, when the *aquilon* is blowing."

"The *aquilon?*" asked Jimmy Kieron.

"North wind," said Iris, lowering her eyes and taking a modest sip from her virgin tropical punch. Then, using logic on the worrying question of press coverage, she raised her hand as she did in class. "Wait. Since Paula fainted, I must be the one in the picture!"

Jimmy Kieron nodded, as if he had been waiting for the correct answer. Charlé dangled her bracelet in the direction of a package of Du Maurier cigarettes. "You were probably both in the picture," she said, to cut the subject short. "Now, who wants some dessert?"

While the girls ordered coconut-chocolate sundaes, Charlé fixed Jimmy Kieron with her long green eyes and murmured quietly, "If you've still got the picture lying around at home—I mean the paper—I'd like to have a look, you know, to see what they said?"

Jimmy Kieron said he'd look for it.

That night when the girls were fast asleep in the buttercup-yellow bedroom of Jill's dreams, Charlé managed to get through to Paris and Raoul.

"I'm glad you called; it's impossible to get a line out."

"Have you been at home all evening?"

"Yes. Szos is staying here. It's safer. De Gaulle has been on the television, in uniform, giving us the *Français Françaises* routine."

"God, what a bore," said Charlé.

"Look, I'm not afraid of anything, you know that. But Debré has been on the radio, and they're talking about paratroopers coming down at Orly or Le Bourget, a seizure of power. It could be bad or it could be bullshit."

"Well, don't you know?" screeched Charlé.

"No one knows. I'm glad you're there. I'm going to do what has to be done, and I'll keep in touch."

"What has to be done? You don't even know what's happening!"

"There's talk of blocking the roads from the airports, in case of a march into Paris. Just remember, Charlé, I'll be fine."

Szos asked to be put on the line.

"Are they going to kill De Gaulle?" asked Charlé.

"Crap. It's all about Algeria. There is no—" Szos stopped himself because Raoul was hitting his arm; he looked up; Raoul was shaking his head like a clown in a pantomime, making his hands into planes and dive-bombing the small marble-topped table that held three cups of tea and two glasses of brandy. Szos continued in a new vein: "But it's bad, Charlé. There is danger. It's lucky that you and Jill and the girls are there. They have closed the airdromes. There is a curfew, and God only knows what can happen in the next few days. Stay in London."

In London, Charlé closed her eyes and emitted a sigh of relief. In Saint-Germain-en-Laye, Raoul closed his eyes and did the same thing. "Well, I guess I'd better go now," said Szos. "We are having a convocation of the servants. Raoul is arming them with his hunting rifles. Call us tomorrow." Szos hung up hastily, as the laughter coming from Raoul and the genial if overweight Lebanese girl on the couch grew louder. In London, Charlé replaced the receiver pensively; her own interests were nothing compared with the brave historical sweep of the moment they were living. Stranded in England by war and revolution, she thought as she poured herself a brandy, What a life you're having.

Jill found it all rather a romp, she said. She was proud of the fearlessness she had acquired in the war, and whenever it was tested she was happy to be able to feel it, almost touch it, as everyone around her crumpled. She believed Americans were made of an inferior colonial substance, evanescent and fragile, an aeruginous metal which, unlike her own tempered steel, had no weight and attracted germs.

Charlé thought she would go stark staring mad if she had to spend the whole time with Jill. Luckily, Jimmy Kieron called and invited her to a cocktail party to be given by a dear friend of his, one Dara Devenish. "Mad as a hatter, of course" was the way he described her, "but the bats in her belfry are inherited and in her lucid moments she's divine. And, of course, the rest of her inheritance more than makes up for her occasional vagaries." Charlé looked forward to meeting this woman who had a private church, even if it was overrun with vermin.

Dara Devenish lived in a house that seemed to be scattered among three plots of land, its various reception rooms connected by glassed-in walkways. It was near the river, in Chelsea, a spot that was already blessed with the renown bestowed on it by that group of amusing acquaintances of the Queen's sister who went by the name of the Chelsea set. Dara Devenish had been one of them, and still was; there was a rumor that she had been a guest at the wedding itself, which Jimmy Kieron passed on to Charlé so that his new friend would feel at home. Charlé betrayed the limitations of her world by asking what wedding he was talking about. When he told her, she said, "Oh, of course, Margaret!" as if they had been girlhood friends, although she had to admit that no, they had never met.

At Dara's house Charlé found what she had come to England to find: a lover. At Charlé's particular stage in life it did not matter what kind, which was lucky because Dara's friends and guests did not include anyone who could have been called famous according to Charlé's increasingly strict canons. But just as one relaxes certain sartorial rules when one is abroad, Charlé allowed her standards to slip because it was convenient and no one was to know in any case. Gripping a shallow glass of champagne into which orange juice had been poured by a kindly-looking butler, she wandered between the second sons of earls and the cousins of dukes, fascinated by the neighing chatter and amazed at how closely the scene resembled *The Reluctant Debutante.* She imagined herself in the Kay Kendall role, and consequently flared her nostrils and raised one eyebrow whenever anyone addressed himself to her, which was not as often as she might have wished. Dara had greeted her with a "Splendid!" and bussed Jimmy Kieron busily and told him, "That rat Miles is here tonight so you'd better go hold his willy at once"—instructions which he followed, abandoning Charlé. She wondered if her Givenchy suit didn't look a little too sharp and thought that might be why the women were giving her a wide berth. Or maybe it was the futuristic shrapnel on her shoulder that put them off. They all seemed to be wearing bouffant sleeveless dresses in bright silks, discolored under the arms and not quite zipped up properly in the back. She got a whiff or two of odors that she was used to smelling only on servants and wondered about British standards of hygiene, and then told herself that she was just being silly because, after all, Jill always smelled wonderfully of lavender and Blue Grass. She liked Dara, despite her brusqueness, because she had noticed a large safety pin like a baby's diaper pin holding together her hyacinth print silk dress at the waist and it reminded her of Gertie Tamlyn, who never sewed up a tear, back in the old days. She wondered what Dara's inheritance was, and took a close look at the paintings to see if they were Reynolds or Turner, the two

English painters whom she knew to be worth a fortune. They weren't; they were rather pallid street scenes of Dutch towns, so she figured the money was probably discreet. She was gazing at a collection of spotted china spaniels on the mantelpiece and memorizing the host's names on the impressive lineup of thick white cards that leaned on the spaniel's forelegs when behind her she heard a loud "I say, I say, I say!" She turned around.

A youngish man stood looking at her. Next to him a sullen girl in a wrinkled pink dress was saying, "Charles, that's so awful and common and boring I can't imagine why you always do it." But the man was ignoring her; he had eyes only for Charlé.

"I'm Charles Frantwell," he said, extending a hand that was fleshy but adequate.

"And I'm Charlé," she said with a giggle designed to make him feel at home. "Charlé Abime." She waited for the question about whether she was married to Raoul Abime, but it did not come. Instead he said, "Oh, I say, we're twins, or something, what fun! And you're an American. Are you here for the season? It's a bit early."

This was the longest series of words Charles Frantwell would ever launch at Charlé. He led her toward the bar, where she explained about the terrible events in France and her flight to London. She then explained about Raoul and Jill and the daughters, and Frantwell was smitten. They sneaked out of the party, leaving Jimmy Kieron to feel enormously guilty when he realized that he had lost his charge, and went to dinner at Wilton's. She noticed the way he treated the waitresses, an utter disdain redeemed only by the sort of familiarity a small boy might attempt with his nanny. He was so English, she thought. It was difficult eating dinner with permanently flared nostrils, but she managed. She fancied she might even be in love; here was a solid person, not a crazed Eastern European with an uncertain future in an uncertain country. She was dining with the finest flower of—what was it?—the Rock of Gibraltar.

Frantwell could just as well have been called James or Willie or David. There was nothing about him to distinguish him from other Englishmen of his age (thirty-five), his class (landed upper), his education (scant learning at Harrow and two years in the Guards), his occupation (something in the City), or his income (from work, small; from family investments, large). Large, too, were his ears, his hips, his behind, and his tailor's bills, which ran into the thousands for disguising the latter two features beneath impeccable navy pinstripes. His jaw hung open in the perpetual expectation of mirth; his rosy and almost transparent nostrils fell back onto his cheeks like those of a newborn baby; his watery blue eyes faced the world with a mixture of benign superiority and knowingness. It was the knowingness that principally attracted Charlé, for there was little to appreciate in him besides his bloodline, and at their first meeting she had not yet heard all about it, though inexorably she would. It was his trump card, that lineage, which on a clear day in the dens of certain genealogists could be seen to stretch right back to the man who fed the horses on Noah's ark.

Frantwell was taken for granted in London—as were the rest of his ilk who were not distinguished by the possession of athletic prowess, libidinous mothers or gigantic schlongs, or by the ability to achieve water racing speeds in excess of one hundred and fifty miles an hour. Indeed, the post-debutantes had long been repelled by the greasy strands of his gray-brown hair, slicked back over a now balding pate with an unguent that smelled curiously like a curdled lemon tartlet. His habit of saying "I say," as many times as the market could take, was borrowed from a popular television comedian, and struck his peers, as we have seen, as endlessly banal. To Charlé it was a magic phrase, the very epitome of Englishness.

He took her home, to a flat so dingy that at first she thought it had to be part of a boarding house, until she noticed the Turner above the mantelpiece.

He offered her a brandy; she glittered at him in the tidy little room and they talked for several minutes about the trees of Ovington Square, which were visible behind the glass of his windows. She wondered if she was doing the right thing when she asked him to sit by her, but the sight of a row of silver cups and the confirmation that they had been won at polo endorsed her whim. "Shall we?" she said.

He threw himself on her in his narrow lumpy bed, which dipped in the middle of its bunting mattress and swayed dangerously, the mattress knocking into the polished mahogany head- and foot-boards; these bore little inlaid Sheraton medallions of pale blond wood, which she had leisure to admire when he took her from the rear. She ignored the detail that his elbows landed, as if guided by radar, smack on her breasts. She ignored the antennae of sticky hair that rose to plaster themselves over the pillow, the enthusiastic hips that ground away at her coccyx or at the mattress, the knees that crushed her tender bloated calves. Gratefully she shut her eyes and thought of England.

The girls were less besotted with the hub of the Empire. They waited sullenly to go home, convinced that what had happened in the Rue de

Rivoli was worse than anything that could be happening now. The day after their arrival, France had been immobilized by a general strike, but the day after that—the day of Dara's party—everything was on its way back to normal. By the end of the week Jill had returned to Paris and Raoul had phoned Charlé to tell her it was safe to come back, but she insisted on staying a little longer, saying it was so good for the girls. Paula hated Charlé for delaying her reunion with her father, whom she missed acutely. Iris, feeling protective of her mother, was convinced that Raoul was up to no good behind Charlé's back, and that her mother was a fool to prolong an inane visit for so long. But Charlé told the girls that they were making wonderful and necessary progress in reading and writing English, and that one more week would ensure that they would no longer need Jill to translate the *Herald Tribune* for them.

Their reading took the form of deciphering the small billboards on which the news vendors displayed their headlines. The girls competed in shouting them out: " 'Mother of Four Dies in Blaze'!" Paula would scream as soon as she had worked her way through the letters, to which Iris would respond, in slightly slower English, " 'Man, Eighteen, Rapes Girl, Four.' "

"Listen!" Paula would nudge Iris: "That one says 'Battered Baby's Mother Convicted.' What's 'convicted'?" As their walk took them past another vendor Iris would then scream, " 'Tortured Girl, Seven, Raped by Gang.' " The meaning of these sentences did not penetrate at once, such was their pride in the accomplishment of reading English, but a while later, over lunch or tea, they would exchange scared glances and whispers about the strange habits of the English. Iris told Charlé over lunch at Marcel's on Sloane Street that she thought the English hated children. "They hit them and murder them and beat them and shred them all the time." Charlé wasn't sure what the shredding was all about. The connection between *carottes rapées* and rape eluded her.

The girls felt threat everywhere; their responses to it varied according to their characters. On the mornings when Jill marched them to Harrods, leaving Charlé to lounge in bed and make phone calls, they passed certain disturbing spots, areas of grass and weed, protected by small low walls, where a bomb had fallen some twenty years ago. The traces of staircases and the hardy wallpaper that still adhered to the walls of adjacent buildings—relics of houses long ago exploded by buzz bombs—were fascinating at first, surreal, pleasing to eyes that had been trained to enjoy surprises. But for Paula, the daily appreciation of these empty spaces soon deepened into a brooding on the meaning of the event that had caused them. Iris enjoyed finding new evidence of the defective taste of the late inhabitants —"Purple walls and yellow paper! Really!" but Paula wondered if their relatives ever came along to put flowers in the little patches of wasteland and shed tears right there on the sidewalk. Inevitably, by the time they got to Harrods, the only thing that could cheer her up was a quick bit of sleight of hand in the costume-jewelry department. Paula never took anything big; cotton daisy brooches with yellow felt centers and sometimes a silk geranium were the extent of her spoils, but Iris, although she dimly apprehended the need for such release, was horrified at the idea of being caught and thrown into prison. Jill never noticed; she bought a lot of brown pigskin gloves and inner soles and sewing kits. Charlé never went shopping with them, for she said she had to go to the doctor's every afternoon, which was worrying; Jill thought that it was hypochondria; Iris, with her backstairs mind, that it was tuberculosis; and Paula, with prescience, that it had to be a man.

Their greatest joy was television, an artifact that was denied them at the Château Rose because Raoul did not want a set in the house. Enthralled, they watched the dancing toucans of the Guinness commercials, the baritone delivery man from Esso Blue, the seraglio splendor of Turkish delight—chocolate bars "full of Eastern promise," and, as they found out for themselves, full too of a sticky pink jelly that tasted like cheap soap. They sang along with "Rael-Brook Toplin, the shirt you don't iron." They loved Desmond Morris, who gave tea parties for chimpanzees, and they had a passion for Fury the sensitive stallion, an import from America. Still, they were glad when their exile was over and Charlé took them back to the airport. Iris wasn't sure about the tall, silly-looking man who came with them and gave Charlé a little box when he saw them off at the gate. Paula waited until they had landed to tell Iris, while Charlé fussed with passports, that he was almost certainly her lover.

"My mother doesn't have lovers!" Iris told her, furious.

"My father does," said Paula, smirking.

Iris didn't know what to say.

In the next four years, Charlé contrived visits to the hypothetical doctor in London at least once a month. Occasionally Raoul asked Jill whether she thought there was anything really wrong with Charlé, to which Jill would let out a prodigious and triumphant harrumph. Charlé almost confided in Szos one day at lunch, for the thrill of having so limp a clandestine lover as Frantwell had abated rapidly and she was soon maintaining the relationship only for the form, and what was form without witnesses? Szos headed her off when he sensed a confession coming; he had been stuck in the middle once before and was not going to allow it to happen again. Instead, he treated her to a long and somewhat confusing dissertation about European marital customs, the moral of which was that in an adult marriage each partner does as much of whatever he wants on the side and takes care only to not interfere with the running of the household and the education of the children.

So she resigned herself to continuing her secret little visits, during which she met no one save Frantwell's charlady, saw very little theater, as Frantwell couldn't abide culture, and had to spend two days shopping for every night of polite intercourse. For the second time in her life, she wound up with an extraordinary number of twin sets.

10.

Villa Stallatico

Villa Stallatico rose from the rocky shore of the Baie de Villefranche on high concrete posts that met as arches and almost looked like stalactites; it was erroneously assumed by the families who rented the house for the summer that its name derived from this curious resemblance. The villa was a landlocked pleasure craft, a citadel on the sea for those who preferred to swim from their own jetty rather than from the precarious wooden ladders of yachts. The jetty, a wrinkled and scored concrete runway, imposed the villa's rights some forty feet into the Mediterranean. The portion of water that it dominated was hairy with seaweed, alive with squid, and shot through with silver fish that moved with the flashing speed of arbitrary thoughts.

It had been built by a German baron in the early years of the century, and furnished by him with doors stolen from the municipal buildings of the historic lower Rhine. The ubiquitous dark wood was adorned with grotesques, masks, and adamant but unspecific leaves. The floors throughout were the local dark-red tile, polished to a dangerous shine. The villa clung to the face of the rock with grim caution. For all its sprawl, the house was only one room deep, applied to the granite like a vast abstract frieze with cubbyholes. The baron at his death had left the house to his stepnephew, a Dutch composer of minimal talent, who had added to the master bedroom a dais that was set with delft tiles depicting sailboats moving toward the horizon, in monotonous repetition of the idea of freedom. The bed reposed on this dais, and it was here that every summer Raoul and Charlé made up their differences and revived their marriage.

They had been married nine years. In that time Raoul had had three or four successes, one negligible failure and several passionate affairs. He had lost a bit more hair and been given a retrospective—unfortunately, on television on Saturday nights, so that nobody who had a country house could watch it.

Despite their differences, Raoul and Charlé agreed that it was important to lead a normal life for the girls. Jill had found the villa years before, when she was a young assistant of I. M. Bergleish, and had always thought it the ideal place for a family holiday. When Raoul told her he needed just such a place, she had arranged the rental through a friend on the coast.

Every year on June thirtieth, Charlé and the girls flew down from Paris accompanied by Jill to begin a two-month holiday. Raoul always came a little later, making the most of his weeks alone with whomever he chose, at the château or in a hotel. He liked the idea of family holidays more than he liked the reality: for him a crushing problem that extended to all things, including his art.

Iris and Paula called it Villa Troglodyte. They pointed out its defects to visitors with an aristocratic glee that seemed like the self-deprecation of the very fortunate. They were no longer the tiny costumed brats of the Château Rose; the onset of their teens had afforded them a more acute vision of the world. They went in to Paris from Saint-Germain-en-Laye three times a week, to dance classes and films; and now knew more about Algeria than anyone else in their class. Although Paula was older than Iris, she remained in the same grade as hers. "She just won't study," the teachers told Charlé, reproof in their voices. Paula didn't care.

For the first few years at the villa, when they were thirteen and fourteen, walks into Saint-Jean for ice creams sufficed to keep them amused. Jill had her own room, a sort of cabin in the garden just past the balcony of Raoul and Charlé's room. She had an office in one of the maid's rooms down a steep curling staircase beyond the kitchen, where she made whatever phone calls the French Post Office allowed through its frayed circuitry. She complained that she had to make her way through the length of the entire house—half a cliff face, at least—to get to her office from her room. Charlé resented that Jill had two rooms to call her own, while she didn't even have one.

Iris and Paula did not complain about their room: it had the distinct advantage of being situated in a little house of its own, to the right of the front door. Two heraldic lions grasping shields snarled on either side of the heavy oak door, and ants swarmed around the three steps leading up to it; but inside, it was cool and dark and big, with its own dressing room and bathroom. The window over Paula's bed gave directly onto a little patio that was the first thing a visitor saw of the house. Iris, fearful by nature, had from the first chosen the bed jammed into a corner on the other side of the room, and every year thereafter she reclaimed it as her own. She liked the feeling of being surrounded by masonry. Paula liked the feeling of being nearer to the center of things.

Paula at seventeen was a romantic. The previous winter she had engraved on her wrist in blue ink the motto: *Vis Jeune, Meurs Jeune, Et Sois Un Beau Cadavre* (Live young, die young, and be a beautiful corpse). The influence of her contemporaries was evident in this act: easy despair, theatricality, and the sluttishness of self-tattooing. Paula smoked, in secret, too much, and worried about getting lines on her face, which was beginning to resemble Soula's. Her dark hair was down past her shoulders with long bangs that she washed every morning, even when she didn't wash the rest of her hair. Her legs were long, her ankles fine, her hips a little wide. Her silhouette had class, and she knew it. She spent long hours in front of secluded mirrors, jutting her hip out in a contrapposto worthy of a Praxiteles, sucking in her cheeks and glowering at her green eyes from beneath her fringe. Class, she would think, I am class. The elegance of her proportions sometimes moved her to tears, and never more than in the summers when the innocent reflection of her long legs topped by the triangle of an orange bikini bottom, glimpsed in a slice of picture window or part of the hall mirror, allowed her to be struck by the harmony of her own slender lines. She felt wasted in a life composed of school and the Château Rose. The mirrors showed her that her body was an asset, an incalculable prize, an amazing bonus, and she regretted each day that passed without its perfection being recorded. She consulted *Elle* and *Vogue* with peevish discontent, offended that it was not she, Paula Abime, wearing the striped ribbed sweaters across her skinny rib cage, and flat silver shoes at the end of her long, narrow feet. She felt she was going to spoil unless something happened soon, and brooded about this as she lay on her bed. "An unexploited orchard of loveliness," she tried; then, in an unconscious tribute to Donne, with a quiver in her voice, "a virgin continent."

Charlé did not believe in publicity for people younger and more photogenic than herself. Her rationalization was, as she told the girls, "There's plenty of time for that later, you don't want your life eaten up by it now." She had refused one director's offer to test Paula for the child's part in his version of *The Innocents;* she had refused the entreaties of another to test Paula for the part of Zazie; she had refused the pleas of Le Printemps, the department store, to have Paula model their Emmanuelle Khanh clothes in their *Idée Junior* show. There were offers for Paula and none for Iris for two reasons: the obvious one, that the name Abime was better known than Bromley; and the subtle one, that Paula was decidedly more attractive. Even Charlé found herself in the curious position of being a stepmother who favored her stepchild over her own daughter. It wasn't anything one could pin down, just a general impression Paula emitted, even to those who had neither met nor seen her, that she was, in some mysterious way, a natural.

The nicest thing that could be said of Iris at sixteen was that she was not a natural. She lacked the ease and spontaneous grace of Paula. She lacked the assurance most daughters have that their mother is on their side; she was wary, confused and easily intimidated. She was awed by names. Iris was smaller than Paula, rounder, squatter. Her face was that of the Florida Bronsteins, which puzzled her. She lacked her mother's red hair and her sharp little features. Her eyebrows, were it not for judicious and constant plucking, would have met at the bridge of her nose. Whereas Paula bloomed in the sun, Iris withered, came out in spots, squinted and perspired.

"La jetée est privé-é-é-é-é-é!" Charlé, in a turquoise voile jacket that billowed in the breeze, leaned over her balcony and waved a fist at the fisherman who had installed himself on the concrete jetty. Iris and Paula, who were having breakfast on the terrace outside the dining room, looked up at Charlé. Iris rose and peered over the railing. "Ugh, he's got squids all over the jetty again," she said. Paula dipped the tip of a croissant into an open jar of sour cherry jam, and sucked the jam from the croissant. "Someone should go down and show him who's the boss," she said, with the tiniest trace of a French accent.

Charlé's heels—conical appurtenances beneath slender wooden soles attached to the feet by green silk ties—clattered down the steps. Taking a cigarette from the ill-hidden packet under Paula's sun hat and wagging a finger at the girl for smoking, Charlé walked over to the balcony and, shading her eyes with one hand, scanned the horizon. In case the girls wondered what she was doing, she turned toward them and, leaning her elbows on the railing, said with a conspiratorial smile: "Don Flagel's yacht is coming in around noon, and we're all going on the boat for lunch." Seeing no change of expression on Paula's features, she asked, "Isn't that interesting? Aren't you excited?"

Iris, who had been manifesting every symptom of excitement just beyond the range of Charlé's gaze, shouted, "I am! Very!" to attract her mother's attention.

Charlé gave her a short smile and frowned at Paula. "Well?" she inquired.

"Do I have to go?" asked Paula.

"Look," said Charlé, "we're all going. Even Raoul's going. Don is an old friend of his and a dear friend of mine. Paula, you've seen him every year. Come on!"

Paula uttered an inaudible "Oh," and rose from the table. As she disappeared into the dining room Charlé turned toward Iris and addressed her as if she were Paula's nanny. "I don't know what I'm going to do with her. Don't you see she gets more difficult every day?"

"It's a stage she's going through," said Iris sagely, and got up to follow Paula.

Paula had gone to the garden room, a hexagon of glass and stucco with mats of ragged coconut fiber on the floor and three broken-down canvas-covered sofas. She was shuffling a pack of cards, elbows resting on her skinny brown knees.

Iris subsided into one of the sofas and watched Paula wordlessly. Finally, with the slow and painfully precise enunciation of the infinitely bored, Paula spoke. "I was planning to go over to Saint-Jean and sit at the café and see who was around, just let things happen," she said. "I don't want to be stuck on a boat with a bunch of Raoul's old fart friends."

"But, Paula, something wonderful could happen on the boat—"

"Your mother will flirt with Don Flagel and my father will flirt with Don Flagel's whore and there will be something like a mousse for lunch and then you'll get seasick. It's not a wonderful prospect."

Iris changed tactics, feeling she had been caught climbing. Sticking her rounded legs out in front of her, and surreptitiously pinching the little flow of fat that seeped beneath the hem of her shorts, she allowed herself to contract Paula's point of view.

"We're young and beautiful and we need men!" she exclaimed, in an eerie, unconvinced falsetto.

Paula stopped dealing herself a set of solitaire. "Right," she mumbled.

"And," continued Iris, "we need them now, before we shrivel up and get old."

Paula put down the cards and crossed her arms on her chest. "Sometimes," she said, "just before my period, I have this terrible urge—to be—" She sighed with longing. "—kissed."

"Ooooh!" said Iris. "Me too."

"It's so strong. It takes me over. I feel it everywhere."

Iris nodded vigorously.

"Sometimes if there's someone around, I let him."

"Who?"

"You know, Michel from school, or that André. But that's not it. You know?"

Iris shook her head sadly. "It never is." She was still far from receiving the numinous seal of a first kiss, but had been keeping up a certain pretense about it for the past six months.

Paula sighed again, and went to the record player. Iris followed her; they deliberated silently over Charles Aznavour or Dionne Warwick, and Aznavour won. Paula pushed the record onto the spindle, flicked the switch, and hurried back to the sofa so as to be prone when the first notes came out of the loudspeakers. Iris did the same. *"Tu veux / Parce que tu sens gronder en toi / ces choses qui n'ont pas de nom / et qu'on appelle l'amour / tu veux,"* sang the deep voice with its throaty catch that could equally represent barely repressed lust or a bad cold.

Iris gazed out to sea, her eyes filled with tears.

Paula gazed down at her perfect legs and grasped her right forearm with her left hand. The metal of the little snake ring on her middle finger was hot against her flesh. She could feel her damp hair clinging to the back of her neck. She breathed in slowly, to prepare herself for the onslaught of the next verse.

"Tu veux sentir en toi / la tendre déchirure / qui affolle les sens / et fait de toi une femme / tu veux."

Iris contemplated the tender tearing that would make her a woman, and shuddered. Paula remained with her eyes half closed, imagining herself being rent asunder by the tender ministrations of the man conjured up by the song: world-weary, older, knowing, deep-voiced, a touch bronchial and infinitely concerned with pleasing her.

They waited for the song to end, and then quietly left the room: Paula, to go lie on the terrace and offer her body to the sun while she daydreamed further about the unknown lover; Iris, more practical, to hide in their bathroom behind a locked set of doors and stimulate herself with an erotic book called *Les Chansons de Bilitis* by Pierre Louÿs. Apart from the release these moments afforded her, she treasured this particular volume over the other works of erotica discovered in the study bookcase because of its one line about virgins: "Those who wait the longest want it the most." It made her feel important.

Meanwhile, over the two speakers in the garden room, the five speakers in the living room and the two horn-shaped speakers on the dining terrace, Charles Aznavour was singing in a booming whisper about having been young yesterday, when he caressed the wind without thought of the morn.

Two hours later a big fat yacht pulled into the bay of Villefranche. Charlé, from her dressing table, where she was applying a glowing copper lipstick, followed the stately passage of the boat to its mooring in the center of the bay. Her eyes were not up to telling her that small figures in white and aqua blue disported themselves on deck; ten minutes later she could just make out the launch coming toward the jetty, propelled along the steel-blue water by twin plumes of spray.

Iris and Paula waited on the jetty. Paula was dressed in white trousers and a black T-shirt printed with the points of the compass in white ink; Iris, still in her bathing suit, held flippers in her hand, and a bag of clothes was at her feet. She had so actively sympathized with Paula's initial disgust at the idea of luncheon on the yacht that she had decided to swim out. Raoul was descending the hundred stone steps down to the sea; his short-sleeved safari jacket, the color of *crème fraîche*, flapped open as he walked. In his right hand he held an unlit pipe by the stem. Wraparound sunglasses obscured that part of his face that was still attractive; his chin, like the rest of his face, was suntanned, but sagging, and swayed with his gait.

The launch had reached the jetty before Charlé was ready. Raoul and Paula screamed at her to hurry; Iris, undecided whether to show her independence by risking the swim or give in and go by launch, held on to the thick metal rails of the ladder at the end of the jetty, dangling one leg in the lukewarm sea. The sailors, one of whom was anxious to tie the launch to the rails, stared at her with curiosity. "Ahem," he said, holding the rope, "ahem." Raoul thought about lighting his pipe and decided against it. He heard the sailor, and looked down at Iris, who was staring at the water as if it held a message for her.

"You're going to swim?" he asked without much interest.

"Yes," replied Iris eagerly, glad to have been noticed.

"Very good. You'd better start now. We'll get there before you," he added unnecessarily.

"I'll enjoy the exercise," answered Iris. Pausing to pull on her flippers, she pushed her bag over to Paula, and with a little wave, like a paratrooper bailing out over enemy territory, she jumped into the water.

"Brave girl," Raoul said to Paula.

"She's just showing off," she answered.

"I suppose you have your reasons for not doing the same," said Raoul.

Paula's eyes filled with tears. "Oh, Papa!" she said. Raoul looked blank for a second as Paula reproached him with her sobs. "How could you ever forget?" she asked.

He put his arm around her, and shortly after having assumed the consoling posture, he remembered Soula's death. He gave his daughter a hug.

Charlé, clattering down the steps in thong sandals with little clusters of blue beads on the insteps, was struck by the tenderness of the scene before her. Paula with her head on Raoul's shoulder, Raoul holding her in one arm and his pipe in the other. "My family," she screamed from the shower stall at the base of the cliff, and staggered toward them on her high heels. The two sailors saluted her; they had been instructed by Don Flagel, a punctilious gallant, to salute ladies every time. Charlé acknowledged their gesture with a little wave of her hand, and allowed Raoul to help her into the launch. Paula followed, carrying Iris's clothes. Charlé sat down on the pillows at the back, and as the launch snorted off into the water she ran a hand through her hair. Reaching out to Raoul and Paula, who still held hands, she confided: "I'm so happy that we're all together." Paula smiled at Raoul, who smiled at Charlé.

Don Flagel was waiting for them at the port side of his boat. The letters spelling out *Shulamith* could be made out along the side of the boat. The flag of Liberia floated over the aft deck. Flagel was heavyset, bald, short, with a bad-tempered face. He always came to Paris for four weeks in the spring and took a suite at the George V. Charlé gave a cocktail party for him every year, and every year he patted Paula and Iris on the cheek and told Charlé that they were "developing," a word that caused deep shame in the girls, who took it to be an assessment of their "obus," as schoolyard gossip deemed them. Paula looked on Don Flagel as a sort of hurdle to be reckoned with, a person whose approval she would need to be allowed into the next stage of her life. For that she hated him, and tried to avoid him.

"Don't fall," said Don Flagel as the launch was tied to the teak ladder and Charlé attempted to change boats. He held out a short, hairless arm and waved it in the air, as if to conduct his guests safely on board. Charlé managed to get the heel of one of her sandals caught in the little square holes of the ladder; Raoul waited for her to regain her balance before attempting to follow her up the steps. Paula squinted into the sun and wondered if her hair, blown by the breeze, looked as alluring as she hoped. She tugged at her T-shirt and stepped onto the ladder.

Flagel preceded Raoul and Charlé toward the stern, which had been turned by the addition of a semicircle of wide banquettes into what was then known as a conversation pit. In this pit of navy canvas and bamboo sat three people: a tall blonde dressed for a formal lunch in a white silk shirt, a small brunette clad only in a pink bikini, and a short dark man who leaped to his feet when he saw Raoul. Charlé nodded to the women, whom she assumed to be whores, and watched Raoul being hugged by the dark man. "Arto!" exclaimed Raoul. "Charlé, you remember Arto!"

Charlé looked blank.

"Don't you remember me?" asked Arto.

"I'm sorry, I don't think we ever . . ."

"We met at the circus—" began Arto, who was interrupted by Don Flagel, who asked, "When you still had your snake act?"

Arto shot him a look of strained loyalty. "I have never, ever worked in a circus," he said politely. "Only the best clubs."

"Charlé, Arto was at our wedding," explained Raoul.

Charlé extended her hand to the Peruvian.

"Arto is my secretary," said Flagel. "Anything you need he can get you. He's a genius." This impelled Charlé to shake Arto's hand with a warmth that the dim memory of his presence at her wedding had failed to elicit.

Paula felt herself nudged by Charlé, and stepped forward. She gave Flagel her hand, and smiled. "Paula," said Charlé.

"Of course," said Flagel. Then: "Beautiful, beautiful."

The two women rose from their cushions and, nodding silently at Paula as they passed, went forward to the saloon. "Mimi and Irka," said Flagel, a note of apology in his voice. He clapped his hands. "Melchior!"

A tall Balinese in white Indian trousers and a waiter's jacket glided out of the saloon. He inclined his head. Raoul waited for him to raise his hands to his forehead, and was rewarded. After the bow, which Flagel accepted as his due, Melchior asked Charlé what she wanted to drink. Puzzled by his thick guttural accent, she could not answer at first. Raoul ordered a beer, Paula asked for a Pimm's, and Charlé decided upon orange juice.

They all sat down on the banquette. Paula twisted around to observe Iris's progress across the glassy blue water and saw the yellow rubber cap bobbing among the short waves, at what seemed like a considerable distance away.

"Why is that Indian German?" asked Charlé.

"He's Dutch," said Flagel. "Very reliable. His name's Van der Akker."

"How come?" Charlé was fascinated.

"Enough talk about the servants," said Flagel. Turning to Raoul, he put a hand on the director's knee, set his drink down on a table and asked in a shout that fancied itself conspiratorial: "So! When are you going to direct a film for me?"

Raoul laughed down at his shoes and lit his pipe. "Don, you know I've always wanted to make something with you. Just a case of the right thing."

"At the right time," added Arto, eager to clue himself in on major creative moments.

To Raoul, interference was something one demanded of one's own employees at strategic moments; one did not accept it from the employees of others. With enormous restraint he said, "That's right, Arto, at the right time."

Flagel put his free hand on Charlé's knee. "And where is your little girl?" he asked. Charlé's face registered bafflement—wasn't her little girl right there with them? She looked toward Paula, who was still leaning over the railing, then back at Flagel as she realized he meant Iris.

"She's . . . " she began, and cast about wildly in her mind for a possible answer to the question. Raoul saved her. "She decided to swim out," he said.

"She's a brave girl," added Charlé, assimilating the news with the social dexterity of a true professional.

Flagel looked at his watch. His feet showed his impatience: the white moccasins drummed against the deck, as if Flagel were running. Raoul inquired if Iris's athletic efforts were going to delay something. "Just lunch," said Flagel. "Jean-Jacques was making a seafood soufflé."

"How wonderful!" exclaimed Charlé.

"The chef likes guests to be on time," explained Flagel. "It's one of his quirks. Raoul, we must talk. Paula, why don't you see the girls. They will show you where to sunbathe."

Paula rose obediently and went into the saloon while Raoul was dragged to the base of the flagpole for a business discussion and Charlé found herself with nothing better to do than watch her daughter's progress through the water.

Irka and Mimi were tinkering with the cassettes lined up next to the stereo player and barely acknowledged Paula's arrival. She joined them, selected Frank Sinatra and inserted the tape into the machine. "He'll kill you if he finds out," said Irka in a thick German accent. "He doesn't like women to touch the machinery."

Paula giggled. Mimi smiled at her; then the two women took her by the arm and led her to the upper deck. At the top of a perfectly polished mahogany gangway was a little corral full of cushions, their ownership marked by different bottles of suntan oil. Irka peeled off her bikini top while Mimi unbuttoned her shirt, and both lay flat on their backs, half naked, uttering little sighs.

"Is good," said Mimi.

Paula realized this was no time to act shy, and pulled off her T-shirt. She fell to her knees while doing so, just in case a crew member happened to be standing at the prow with his eyes on the sun deck. Giving a sigh as contented and melodious, she hoped, as those of her two new friends, she lay down. Once prone she was grateful, because the boat's movement, though slight, had been making her feel a little peculiar.

In the water, Iris was losing strength. The ship still seemed to be miles away; she found that when she sighted it and tried to swim faster, she simply exhausted herself. The answer was pacing, but long regular strokes and even breathing didn't seem to advance her at all. It would have been better, of course, if she had been doing the crawl, but all she had ever mastered was the breaststroke, and its laborious movements, unsuited to waves, bored and frustrated her. There were things on the surface of the water that kept bumping into her arms, her shoulders, her face: plastic bottles of mineral water, the occasional waterborne turd, plastic netting, sodden empty cement bags. It's not even Sunday, she thought, and the sea is full of *merde.* At first she had occupied herself with counting strokes; when that failed to entertain her, she began a monologue about her own prowess that included the word "spunky" in its main theme. Spunky little thing, she said to herself, courageous and devoted and strong and spunky, fearless, brave, went behind enemy lines, parachuted into occupied France, a medal for spunk— After half an hour the monologue was stilled by increasing panic. The boat loomed nearer, but a Riva and its water skier had cut across her line of sight, and she experienced a few minutes of staccato heartbeats, followed by the image of Raoul delivering a funeral oration lauding her spunk, as the wake of the motorboat forced her to dog-paddle until the sea regained its relative calm; when it did, she realized with horror that the dog-paddling had exhausted her, and that it was possible she would never reach the boat. She turned on her back and floated for a few minutes to calm down. Almost immediately the image of the giant propellers of the boat installed itself in her head, and she whirled around in the water to see where she was going. The boat was only about a hundred yards away; she saw the back of Charlé's head and, at the bridge, a captain wearing a cap—and then she saw another Riva coming at her from the right. Sure of instant death, she threw up her hand, yelled *"Attention!"* subsided too low in the water and swallowed a jugful of salty water with the nasty aftertaste, once she had spat and retched it out, of fresh gasoline.

The Riva, bucking elegantly like a horse in a canter, drew a curve around her and pulled to a stop. Its driver, a tall, bronzed young man with longish hair and a yachting cap, leaned over the edge. *"Ça va?"* he inquired.

Iris ignored him. She was most particular about not speaking to strangers. She had never allowed a man to pick her up, did not approve of the process, and even at a time like this she felt that personal danger was no excuse for letting her morals slip. She heard another *"Ça va?"* and slipped under water in an attempt to forestall any further overtures on the part of the young man. She opened her eyes, and thought that she could see, in the glaucous blur, the silhouettes of the twin screws. She rose to the surface as fast as she could, and yelled *"Au secours"* the moment she felt air. The young man in the yachting cap dropped to the floor of his boat and held his hands over the edge. She reached for them and was drawn up, bumping against the wooden hull and scratching herself on the chrome bolts. In the Riva, she lay gasping like a beached fish, and conscious, despite her winded state, of the shape of her upper thighs. She pulled off the absurd yellow cap and her hair, half wet, fell down in a tangled lump. *"Vous alliez où, exactement?"* asked the young man. She looked up at him: he was about twenty—the ideal age; his features were regular, his eyebrows did not meet in the middle, he was tall and thin. Awed by such perfection, and afraid of being caught looking at it with anything more than a passing, casual interest, she sat up and pointed to the boat with great seriousness. *"Là,"* she said.

Assuming an air as serious as her own, he pulled the throttle and steered the Riva toward the port side of the *Shulamith.* Iris perched behind him, looking at his broad shoulders, glancing at his tiny ass, which rested on the back of the driver's seat. A pack of Gitanes stuck out of the pocket of his white trousers; his feet were bare, but a pair of American sneakers lay next to her, behind the leather-covered seat. She hoped briefly that he might be an American, perhaps a college student vacationing in the South of France, but decided that was too much to hope for, and resigned herself to the conclusion that there was doubtless a class barrier between them. Sixteen years of Charlé and nine years of Jill had taught her almost everything there was to know about class barriers.

Just before they drew up to the ladder, he turned and looked at her with eyes that were pale green, paler and greener for his deep tan. With a flash of white teeth and a crinkling of the eyes—she noticed a little stubble on his chin and around his cheeks, and added a few years to his age, and felt weak thinking of the manliness that had forced that stubble through the skin—he asked if she really wanted to go on board the *Shulamith.* Iris said nothing. To throw herself into a wild adventure with this stranger in his flashy Riva was everything she had ever dreamt of; soon her hair would be dry enough to stream behind her in the wind, and if she stood with her bottom muscles clenched she would feel almost streamlined. Anything could happen. She was incapable of an innocent thought about picnics or sallies around the bay; she saw the pastimes of youth as mere alibis for fornication, and, in her mind, the consequences of abandoning the *Shulamith* ran the gamut from the ignominy of failing in one's social duty to turn up at lunch, to the inconvenience of becoming a kidnapping victim, with milestones of disgrace in between: the shame of defloration, the horror of rape, the debasement of perversion, the loss of her reputation and self-esteem. She could conceive of no redeeming pleasure.

There was also the slight chance that having pulled away from the *Shulamith* and gone off hitting the waves with this stranger, she would not be missed. What if there was somebody wonderful on board? An actor, a director, somebody really interesting? She wavered. The young man stopped crinkling his eyes, gave an impatient little snort, and tied up to the yacht.

Now Iris had no idea what to do. Getting out of the boat and saying thank you with a smile was a maneuver she immediately rejected. She felt a tip was perhaps in order. "I would invite you on board," she said in English, just in case he was the college student of her dreams, "but it's not mine, and as you know, er, one has to ask the captain's permission. But maybe you could, um, wait and I'll . . ."

The young man was smiling at her with the watchful yet placid expression of the Great Sphinx. She blushed. From the railing above them came a sort of roar. It was Flagel, flanked by Charlé and Raoul.

"Come on board!" he ordered.

"I'm coming, I'm coming!" screamed Iris, scurrying onto the ladder.

"Both of you!"

The young man touched his hat, not in deference but to adjust its angle, and followed her up the steps.

Iris decided that she had made a catch, after all. Charlé held out trembling bejeweled hands to her (her summer jewelry, turquoises and corals) but Iris deferred her mother's hug until after the introductions. "Raoul, Don, Mom, this is the gentleman who saved me," she said. She loved using "gentleman" to describe men; it also was less weighted with the sexual overtones contained in the word "man." Smiling at him as he boarded, she said, "I'm terribly sorry, in all the confusion I didn't get your name."

"Alain Velle," he said, and stuck out his hand at Don Flagel, in what seemed the full knowledge that Flagel was not only the owner of the *Shulamith* but also an extremely important man.

Raoul surveyed Iris. "You had problems crossing the channel?" he asked.

"Yes, no, I mean . . ."

Flagel patted Monsieur Velle on the back. "You must stay for lunch," he said, slightly offhand despite the booming voice. "If Jean-Jacques allows it. Melchior!"

Melchior was sent to ask the cook if Iris's rescuer could partake of the seafood soufflé, and Flagel, whose latest project (a story about a Greek shepherd during World War II) Raoul had just dismissed, decided to make the best of an afternoon that seemed wasted before it had even begun. By the time Melchior returned to announce that the cook said one more guest was acceptable, Flagel had found out that Monsieur Velle was a student at the Sorbonne completing a law degree only to please his father, for he had ambitions to become a songwriter and performer. These personal details interested Flagel little; it was Velle's profile that fascinated him, and the peculiar green of his eyes. Just like Errol, he thought, and sought a second opinion from Raoul. "I never knew him," said Raoul, adding unnecessarily, "I'm of a different generation." "But you've seen him on film, surely," said Flagel, a touch impatient; all he was asking for was a yes that would pay tribute to his perspicacity. "No, I never liked the romantic genre," said Raoul.

Scuffling was averted by the arrival of Mimi and Irka, with Paula in their wake. Alain Velle rose to be introduced; his presence elicited guarded interest from the women, who knew the extent of Flagel's jealousy and had no desire to be put ashore so early on in the cruise. But Paula, who was blissfully free of constraint, greeted him with frank interest. He seemed to like what he saw. Iris had been watching him carefully ever since he set foot on board (she felt it was safe to look him over now that they were no longer alone, now that she was protected by the presence of her mother and therefore free to give her version of flirtation, which meant staring from under her fringe and passing an ashtray before it was asked for); she saw the green eyes widen at the sight of Mimi and Irka, and practically pop out when Paula came forward. Iris watched Paula sit down beside the young man as if it were the most natural thing in the world, pull a Gitane from the packet he held on the wooden arm of his director's chair, and lean forward for a light despite Charlé's tentative and unheeded admonition not to smoke. Iris even saw the look Paula gave him as he pulled his match away from the tip of her cigarette, a look of such insolent calm that Iris was shocked. To interrupt the atmosphere that was beginning to build up, she leaned forward in an attempt to reach his packet of cigarettes and knocked it to the floor. He bent down to retrieve it, and replaced it on the arm of his chair. Iris was left leaning forward in her chair in mid-movement. She was about to try again when a look from Charlé stopped her: "What are you doing, honey?" asked her mother.

Iris decided to be bold. After all, Paula was bold and nobody minded. "I wanted a cigarette," she said.

"Oh, no, not you too! My baby doesn't smoke!" said Charlé.

Iris felt herself reddening; she subsided back into her chair and kicked her feet against the smooth deck. "Go change," said Charlé. "I think your things are around here somewhere. Paula knows." Paula, without removing her gaze from Monsieur Velle's face, pointed to the little canvas bag on the cushions. As Iris rose, Flagel muttered, "Be quick, lunch is soon."

"Where do I go?" she asked. Mimi pointed to a door down the side of the covered deck.

When Iris had changed and returned to the stern, she found no trace of the party save Raoul's pipe nestling in a clean ashtray. At once her heart beat faster: she had managed to be late for lunch. She scurried up a ladder to an upper deck with Raoul's pipe in her hand. There was no one there. She went back down the ladder, through the saloon—where a plaque that said "God, your sea is so big and my boat is so small" briefly caught her attention—opened two brassbound doors, crossed a marble hall where an incongruous bouquet of orchids topped a short square pillar, and opened another door; she was in the dining room at last. All eyes turned to her.

"I brought Raoul his pipe," she said helpfully as she almost ran to the empty seat, between Mimi and Irka, at the opposite end of the table from Flagel.

"We do not smoke in the dining room," said Flagel.

"I couldn't find you," she continued. "I thought you'd be eating upstairs." A white-coated steward handed her the silver spoon that matched a silver basket holding a soufflé dish in which lay a prolapsed wedge of crabbed and musseled egg white looming in a pond of cold béchamel. She helped herself and ate quickly to catch up. Everyone else was on the veal Orloff.

"The soufflé would have broken in the wind," said Mimi, which took some effort to understand. Flagel continued talking to Raoul, while Paula and Monsieur Velle had reached the point of bantering.

"Oh, *peut-être* I prefer The Animals, *alors.* The ass of the rising sun," he was saying in a falsetto.

"Absolutely!" said Paula. "Me too."

"My *musique* is *très différent.* You must listen to it."

"I'd love to," said Paula, fingering her bread crumbs. So far she had eaten one asparagus spear and two slices of tomato from her salad plate. She did not believe in eating in public, and had been confirmed in this view by a recent reading of *Gone With the Wind.*

Alain Velle was trying desperately to remember the names of some of Raoul Abime's movies. He had recognized him at once, and felt it incumbent on him to question the director about his work, but he did not want to look like a fool. As for Don Flagel, he knew that he was *le plus grand impresario du cinéma américain,* and that sufficed. He held his breath as he listened to the words of these two titans.

"How is Szos?" asked Flagel. "I haven't seen him in a long time."

"Very well," said Raoul. "I had lunch with him last week."

"What do you do?" said Iris to Mimi.

"We are models," she said, indicating Irka as well.

"Oh!" Iris could not have been happier had she met all four Beatles. "Models! How wonderful." Paula shot a look at the two women and smiled at them. She felt a bond between them and her due to her future destiny as a model. Iris wanted to know everything.

"Are you photographic models?" she asked.

Mimi said, "No."

Slight disappointment for Iris. Paula returned her attention to Alain Velle. Flagel asked Raoul if Szos was "still hondling." Raoul said, "*Quoi?*" Alain Velle asked him if he had enjoyed making *Les Amants.* Raoul said, "I am not Louis Malle," and softened it with a paternal laugh.

Iris persisted. "Showroom models?"

"No," said Irka.

Iris tried to think what other kinds of models there were. She tried one more time. "You work in couture houses?"

Mimi and Irka looked at her and didn't bother to answer.

"I just saw Richard and Elizabeth," said Don Flagel.

"Oh, Dick and Liz, how wonderful," said Charlé. "How are they?"

"Fighting like cats," he said. Melchior came in, bowed, and announced that there was a call for Monsieur Flagel on the ship-to-shore. Flagel frowned. "Melchior, I am not to be disturbed when I am dining with guests," he said.

"It is Mr. Wyler," said Melchior.

"Excuse me," said Flagel as he got up from the table and puckered his napkin onto the table. "Business."

After he had gone, Charlé gave a little laugh that stilled all conversation around the table. "Well! It's work, work, work, all the time, isn't it?" she said to the assembled company.

"He wants me to direct something about a shepherd," Raoul whispered to her. "He's getting senile."

"Monsieur Abime," said Alain Velle, "do you enjoy working with Jeanne Moreau?"

Raoul considered. "I have never worked with Jeanne Moreau," he answered after a pause, "as far as I know."

"Alain is a musician. He doesn't know much about films," Paula explained in his defense.

"Really, I don't like the *cinéma* at all," said Monsieur Velle, "to tell the truth."

Raoul's eyes lit up. "Not at all?" he asked.

Monsieur Velle shook his head and inclined his chin forward. "I hate it."

"Good," said Raoul. "That's a relief."

Flagel returned. "He's in Antibes, so I asked him over for drinks. Tally is with him. They just returned from Africa."

"Oh, how wonderful," said Charlé. "I haven't seen them in so long!"

Coffee was served in the saloon. Don Flagel inserted *Strangers in the Night* into the cassette player, removed it and checked it for dust; then he inserted it anew and clicked on the machine.

Paula gave Iris a wink; she meant it to be no more than a friendly and conspiratorial comment on the lunch, but Iris, hoping that it carried a secret message, came over to her and whispered in her ear, "What is it? What's up?"

Paula tried to shake her away gently. "Nothing, go back and sit down."

"What is it?" asked Iris again.

"Tell you later," said Paula.

Charlé sat on the white sofa between Mimi and Irka. She noticed that they both wore the same Cartier watch, the new model with the octagonal dial.

"That's the new model," she said to Mimi. "Isn't it?"

"Yes, the octagonal dial."

"I really like it," said Charlé.

"I like your sandals," said Irka.

Charlé surveyed the clusters of beads on her insteps. "They're fun, aren't they? I got them down here."

"Oh, we never shop on the Côte!" said Mimi.

"Except Cartier," interjected Flagel, who was sitting nearby in an overstuffed armchair. "You can work up a lot of saliva for Cartier."

Irka shrugged her shoulders. Mimi said, "We don't get that much at Cartier."

"You get enough," said Flagel.

"Listen, Don, I'm tired," said Raoul, who hated being on anyone else's property as much as he hated talk about shopping. "I think I should take my family back to the house."

"Oh, no!" Charlé cried, the prospect of a happy reunion with Tally and Willy Wyler receding from her. "Not yet!"

Arto, who had not said much of anything during lunch, was occupied at the bar making brandy Alexanders. "Don't go," he said to Raoul. "You can rest in one of the staterooms."

"Of course! Mimi, show him the Eric Ambler suite," ordered Flagel. Mimi rose and took Raoul's arm. "It's very calm down there, you won't hear a thing," she said.

Charlé watched them leave with narrowed eyes. She turned to Arto and asked when the Alexanders would be ready. He carried one over to her and sat by her side. "You haven't changed at all," he said.

"Thank you," said Charlé.

On the deck, Paula and Alain Velle stood by the rail.

"You have a very exciting life," he said.

"What's exciting?" asked Paula. He moved a fraction nearer. "These people," he explained, "this *milieu du cinéma,* it's so new to me."

She looked at his eyes. Under the shade of the upper deck, they were darker, but she was not inclined to notice differences in tone. She was looking into his eyes because he had shown every sign of being smitten by her, and had exhibited certain symptoms of discomfort which she wanted to add to. A light sweat beaded his upper lip, and his unshaved beard had made some progress since Iris first noticed it some hours before. "Why don't you shave?" Paula asked, and held her hand toward his face.

He took the hand and squeezed it, then rubbed her palm against his cheek. "You don't like it?" he asked. "Ouch!" she shouted, and took her hand away.

Iris appeared behind them. "I'm bored," she said, very loud, to announce her presence.

"If you're bored, go back to the house," suggested Paula with a heinous lack of sympathy. "You could swim."

"I can't do that!" said Iris. She joined Alain Velle at the rail. "That's our house," she said, pointing to the Villa Stallatico, which reared from the water like an octopus. Velle seemed unimpressed. He put an arm around Paula, who accepted it with absent grace, imperceptibly bending toward him.

Iris returned to the saloon, where her mother and Arto were standing at the bar while he made a new batch of brandy Alexanders, and went through to the library. Flagel's shipboard library was a legend in Hollywood circles: it had every volume ever offered by the Great Books Club, the Collectors Book Club, and three or four other purveyors of mail-order culture. These were arranged in special bookcases built into the walls of the cabin and secured by brass strips padlocked at the sides. Anyone desirous of improving his mind had to first choose the volume he was attracted to, then ring for Melchior, who would liberate the chosen book, secure its cellmates, and write the title in a gold-edged red-leather ledger. This effectively discouraged reading on board the *Shulamith,* which was Flagel's intention: he liked to have undivided attention from his guests.

Iris ran her fingers along the titles. *A Connecticut Yankee in King Arthur's Court* briefly arrested her hand, but she decided against it, being unsure what Connecticut meant, but surmising it to be the tale of a flag-waving Indian. Finally she decided on *Our Lady of the Flowers*, which was ensconced in a different case near the porthole, along with *The Story of O* and Frank Harris's *My Life and Loves.* Melchior signed it out for her, raising one velvety eyebrow, but Iris felt no guilt at choosing something from the pornography bookshelf because she knew Jean Genet to be Literature. She and Paula had studied *The Maids* at school, and *The Balcony.* She was proud of resisting the more enticing titles, such as *Lolita,* and felt that her choice showed a combination of daring and restraint that marked her as a highly sophisticated individual. She settled into a small sofa by the porthole and opened the book, and took a cigarette from the silver goblet on the table next to her but neglected to light it.

She was dismayed to find she couldn't figure out what sex anyone in the book belonged to, but soldiered on doggedly through at least twenty pages. Her reading was interrupted by the sound of a motorboat sputtering away from the *Shulamith.* She looked out the porthole and saw Paula standing up behind Alain Velle, headed toward the open sea. She ran into the saloon, the book still in her hand.

Charlé and Arto were on the sofa, sipping fresh brandy Alexanders. Don Flagel, changed into white pants and a short-sleeved white shirt, had an arm around Irka, who was trying to put on a high-heeled gold sandal.

"Paula's gone off with that man!" said Iris.

"Where did that book come from?" asked Flagel.

"The library."

"Well, you shouldn't take books out of the library," he said, ever the perfect host. He clapped his hands and Melchior appeared. "The book," said Flagel. Melchior removed it from Iris's hand.

"But, Mum, Paula's gone off with that man!"

Charlé looked at her blearily, uncomprehending. "How nice," she said.

"But is she safe?" asked Iris.

Arto joined in. "Of course she's safe, he's studying law."

"Where's Raoul?" asked Iris, agitated by a righteous anger.

"Don't bother him now, he's napping," snapped Charlé.

Iris turned to her mother. "Don't you care what happens to Paula? She could get violated!"

"Ah," said Flagel. "What an interesting word. 'Violated.' What do you suppose it means, Irka?"

Irka just giggled and nudged Flagel in the region of his ribs.

"She means raped," explained Arto to Flagel. Charlé twisted toward Arto, squinted at him through an Alexander haze and said, "Don't be ridiculous. She's too young."

Iris ran out of the room and went down the stairs to the staterooms. There she found herself in a long narrow corridor with shining mahogany walls on which views of London in the early nineteenth century alternated with artistically arranged black-and-white photographs of various movie stars. The impetus to warn Raoul of Paula's fate was somewhat dulled by the large number of closed doors that lined the corridor. She knocked at the first one, sprang back, retreated down the corridor, where she waited behind a bend until she could be sure that no one had answered. She knocked on one more door, this time holding her breath with her heart pounding away, and was immensely relieved that once again no one answered. She had visions of Raoul fast asleep and angry at being roused. Having failed in her mission to alert Raoul, she decided that rather than go back to the snakepit of a saloon, she would retire into a stateroom herself and while away the rest of the afternoon with a nap. She could have returned to the villa, but that would mean swimming again, or, worse still, commandeering the launch and disturbing the sailors who were no doubt lolling around the galley reading *Playboy* and exchanging lewd jokes. Steeling herself for the ordeal of opening a door without being bidden to do so, she marched down to the end of the passageway and grabbed a well-polished brass handle, which she turned and pushed in one swift determined movement.

She was inside the cabin before she realized that it was occupied. In the dim light provided by the round portholes over which gray linen tweed had been drawn as blinds, she could see a figure in the bed. Iris ran back toward the door and closed it as fast as she could without banging it.

She stood panting, leaning against the door. Was it Raoul? If so, why did he look so huge? Was that Mimi lying across Raoul's belly? Unsure of what she had seen, but sure that it was of momentous and somewhat sinister significance, she tiptoed back down the passage and opened the first door she had knocked on. It was a tiny cabin all paneled in rich wood, with a profusion of musical scores framed in brass on the walls. She locked the door carefully, lay down on the bunk, and tried to figure out whom she had seen in the other cabin while idly and mechanically fingering her crotch.

The Riva was slapping into the waves with a force that slightly alarmed Paula; as they rounded the point, the waves grew larger, and twice the Riva thumped into deep trenches and was almost swallowed into the choppy water. Each time Paula gripped Alain Velle's shoulder muscles in panic, and each time he took his hand off the wheel and squeezed her hand. As they passed the giant statue of the Virgin and headed for the harbor at Saint-Jean, Paula found herself standing very close to him and she decided to play it cool. She retired to the flat back of the boat and stretched out on the wet boards, feeling it inappropriate to start rooting around for a towel. He glanced around to see what she was doing, and seeing the long golden body laid out with feet towards him, he took the hint—he was not a slow man—and cut the engine. Under her, Paula felt the onset of a deep swell and almost rolled over the edge of the boat. Alain caught her and placed himself beside her.

"Ça va?" he inquired.

Paula nodded at him. She felt only a slight seasickness, and that was masked by a rather interested feeling she perceived at the pit of her stomach. Funny, she thought, I'm not expecting my period. Alain Velle's face approached her shoulder, which she found an odd target until the pressure of his even white teeth on her hot salty flesh convinced her otherwise. She turned her face toward him, wondering, and finding it salacious to wonder, what kind of a kisser he was, and after the shock of his undeniable halitosis she found that he was a rather good one. She threw her arms back over her head and allowed her mouth to be invaded by his, grateful for the pressure of his torso against her rib cage, and conscious only of the rhythm of the sea, the rhythm of his tongue, and what a pretty picture they must make. As his hands rose to her T-shirt and began stroking the compass points, ignoring for the most part North and South and concentrating on East and West, Paula even forgot about the picture. When she pulled her T-shirt off, it was with only the slightest prompting from him, and she was almost as amenable to removing her white jeans. Glancing up only to see if there were any other pleasure craft in the vicinity, Alain Velle began the job of seduction in earnest. Paula pushed his hand away five, six times, and then allowed it to occupy the top of her thighs.

Alain Velle, who had somehow expected more resistance, found himself torn between the urge to press his entirely tanned body onto the white areas of Paula's bikini lines—what else was a Riva for?—and the natural reticence any man of honor would feel at wresting pleasure from the daughter of such important people on the first day of their acquaintance. He put a square, well-manicured, tanned, golden-haired hand on her lower stomach, the fingers splayed out toward her navel and her hips, and administered a long kiss. Then he looked into her bright green eyes and asked, just to make sure, *"Tu veux?"*

Paula, gratified beyond her wildest daydreams, nodded vigorously. Here it was at last, someone who understood exactly the import the moment had for her, who knew just what she wanted and how, who might understand the importance of *la tendre déchirure.*

Alain Velle stole Paula's virginity between three-forty-five and three-forty-nine that afternoon. They were covered with a large beach towel on which was printed a subway map of London, where Alain said he liked to get his cashmeres. In truth, he wore only Shetlands, and the Riva was borrowed from his Milanese friend Ignazio Pinazzi, who was in the hospital with a broken collarbone, but did she need to be told everything?

He did what he had to do; she failed to do anything to stop him. Afterwards they lay in the back of the Riva, Paula on her stomach in a reaction of prudery, a belated attempt to claim her breasts and pubis as her own, and they smoked cigarettes and watched the dark-blue water hitting the hull as the chrome bolts by their heads became crusted with salt. After a few drags on her cigarette, Paula began to feel faint.

"What is in this?" she asked.

"You noticed something? I'm glad. It never works with me."

"But what is it?" Paula was a little indignant. Why was this idiot trying to drug her *after* he'd done It? What was the point?

"It's nothing much. They're dipped in red wine and then dried in the sun. You are lucky to feel something."

She shut her eyes and tried to feel more dizzy. It was a dizziness that somehow precluded nausea, obliterated seasickness with its own superior disorientation. She found herself eager to discuss the doctored cigarette at great length, as a means of avoiding talking about the somewhat painful and profoundly unexciting process Alain Velle had just put her through. She did not want to be rude, although she would not have minded showing signs of ingratitude, but for that she would have had to be quite certain what was worthy of gratitude and what missed the mark, and although his kissing certainly rated pretty high, despite the bad breath, she had nothing to compare the rest to, and fell back on describing those physical symptoms with which she felt most at ease.

"It makes my eyes prickle," she said.

"Yes, it's supposed to."

She took another drag. "And my arms feel heavy."

Velle nodded with as much energy as he could muster.

"Didn't it do anything to you?" she asked plaintively.

Velle temporarily misunderstood. "For me, it was wonderful," he assured her.

"How did you learn how to do it?" she asked.

"Quoi?" He smiled, flattered.

"Dip cigarettes in red wine."

"Oh, everyone does it," he said, dismissive.

Paula, whose threshold of boredom was notoriously low, thought for a second or two about doing It again, decided against it, and pulled on her T-shirt. Velle's eyes were closed; his arms were thrown back over his head, exhibiting thickets of black hair in the hollows of his armpits. He had pulled on his shorts again, but the red-and-black striped-webbing belt lay unfastened on the deck, its twin snakes unjoined. A tiny stain nestled near his crotch on his right thigh.

"I'd like to go home," Paula said.

He didn't say a word, but stretched himself as if awaking from a long and refreshing sleep and pulled himself up to a sitting position, put on his cap again, and sat behind the wheel.

"Où?" he asked.

Paula pointed out to sea. Alain Velle saluted and started the motor. Paula lay back, thinking that she had just become a Woman, and wondered if she was going to tell Iris all about it or just drop a couple of disturbing hints.

On the boat, Iris was shaking hands with William Wyler and his wife and six other people whose names she failed to hear properly. Charlé was in her element, chattering to her old friends, her drunkenness quite dispelled. Raoul exchanged glances with Mimi, which Don Flagel intercepted, understood, and was grateful for, because he liked the feeling that Raoul owed him one.

In the late afternoon, when the sea had turned to lead and the floating garbage took on the look of semiprecious stones, the launch from the *Shulamith* returned Raoul and Charlé and Iris to the Villa Stallatico, where they found Alain Velle and Paula playing gin rummy in the garden room. Charlé invited him to stay for dinner, and he accepted. Raoul said something about a script conference in Antibes with Gérard Defly, and left in his Mercedes. After a dull dinner during which Charlé read French *Vogue,* Paula and Monsieur Velle were silent, and Iris found all her attempts at conversation rebuffed by the other members of the party, the young gentleman departed in his Riva and Paula kissed him good-bye on the jetty.

Later, in bed, Iris turned over toward her stepsister and asked, "How could you have?" It was the best way she had of phrasing it, for it implied her disgust and her feelings of betrayal without, she thought, sounding too jealous. Paula took a long drag on her cigarette—she was lying flat on her back, her thin voile nightie rumpled across her chest—and, without looking at Iris, said in a voice that was deeper than usual and for once bereft of its slight French accent, "It's an affair of the flesh. Just that." Iris wondered if she had lost her chance; then she realized that Alain Velle was thus a rapist, after all, which made her a lucky girl for having escaped his evil designs. The suspicion that he was hers by right worried her a little; to go to sleep she had to remind herself that she was not the type to give herself to the first passerby.

11.
Coming Out

The Monte Carlo galas at the Sporting d'Eté were Charlé's passion. Every summer she looked forward to the five or six August nights that would be spent beneath the stars down by the beach in the casino's outdoor ballroom. Raoul hated these functions, and the only serious disagreements that he allowed himself with her during their summer truces were about the galas. Eventually he would give in, and after enduring two hours of idle conversation with the other occupants of their table, a quick fox trot on the dance floor lit from beneath, and half an hour of a floor show that owed its very existence to the proposition that there could be a context in which tall horse-faced English girls with silicone breasts and weak chins constituted alluring sex objects, he would retire to the casino and gamble away as much as he could before his good luck caught up with him and inexorably made him come out richer than he had been going in. Charlé would stay at the table, usually drunk, laughing and winking at whoever her companions were. For these evenings she liked to gather sundry households from up and down the coast, preferably bored industrial millionaires who by dint of hard work had amassed the fortunes to buy themselves huge houses by the water, but who had failed to make the right connections on the way up and therefore found themselves stranded on a littoral of closed doors. Many were English couples, whom she had met during her London visits.

The English were grumbling then, but they were still rich, the pound still being a sturdy green brick worth its weight in white asparagus. Charlé made sure to promise them a fine time beneath the palms by the calm blue sea should they actually rent the houses they were considering long-distance. They were so grateful for everything she arranged for them—lunch parties, trips to the perfume factories at Grasse, introductions to film stars passing through, dinners at the Chèvre d'Or or the Colombe d'Or up in the hills, all faithfully reported in *Nice Matin*—that they inevitably bought the gala tickets and insisted on inviting Charlé and Raoul as the merest token of reciprocity. "You see," Charlé would explain to Raoul, "we don't even have to pay for our fun!" To which he would reply, "They can buy you but not me!"

It was decided that Iris and Paula would attend their first adult gala that summer. "Paula being just seventeen, it's absolutely correct for her to go," said Jill, "but Iris is still a little young."

Charlé applied some Charles of the Ritz Sun Creme on her nose, and replied, "That may be the fact, but in France everything's looser, and, anyway, does it make any difference?"

"In England it would. After all, the moment a young girl puts on a long dress, she is offering herself in marriage." Jill got up, her cardboard binders under her arm. "I have to go downstairs and type up some letters for Raoul. You decide what's best."

"It's already decided," said Charlé.

On her way down to her office, Jill passed Iris, who was sitting on the steps by the telephone table and intently consulting a matchbook. She looked up guiltily, but Jill paid no attention to her and simply muttered in passing, "Don't sit on stone, you'll get piles."

"Piles?" shouted Iris.

"Hemorrhoids," Jill explained, and continued on.

When Jill was safely out of earshot, Iris picked up the phone and dialed. The South of France telephone system always made her nervous: the rolling beeps preceding the connection always sounded like a sort of police siren, with their sententious overtones. She waited. At last the number rang. At that moment she heard Paula's soft footsteps on the stairs above her and hastily returned the receiver to its cradle.

"Hi, what're you doing?" asked Paula, her eyes still puffy and minuscule with sleep.

"Oh, nothing."

"Calling your lover? C'mon, *allons manger.*"

On the terrace Iris folded her arms and pinched the flesh above her elbows.

"It will be great tonight, won't it?" said Paula.

"So-so. What are you expecting?"

"Well, what are you?"

"Nothing much." Iris fingered the cap off Paula's brioche. "Paula . . ."

"Yes?"

"Are you going to take Alain with you?"

"Of course not!" Paula burst out laughing, but not too loud. She was proud of the cynical attitudes she managed to muster in herself but didn't want Charlé to get wind of them.

Iris's eyes were wide with astonishment, and then she looked down at the table. "N.O.C.D.?"

"Quite."

Iris nodded wisely. Terrible problem, this N.O.C.D. It had started the previous fall, when Charlé was urged by Jill to hand over the girls to a "young people's dinner party" at the British embassy. At that dinner Paula had discovered that English boys her age were even duller than the French variety, and Iris had learned from the mouths of three overweight pre-debutantes the ultimate dismissive phrase Not Our Class Dearie. She had adopted it at first with the total confidence of one who is sure of her status, and Paula had borrowed it and made it her own, as she tended to do with anything she borrowed, be it a scarf, a pair of shoes, a pencil or a bottle of Invisible Liquid Makeup.

"But who will you dance with?" asked Iris.

"You're always worrying!"

"Don't you think we should have Mum get us those heated rollers so we can do things to our hair?"

"I don't know about you, *chérie*, but I'm going into Nice with her to get my hair done. Didn't she book you an appointment as well?"

Iris shook her head, trying to look unconcerned, but when Paula had left the table and started down the stairs to sunbathe, she allowed her eyes to fill with tears. It seemed at that moment utterly typical of Charlé to exclude her from those activities that guarantee a woman's allure. Once she was sure that Paula was safely down on the jetty, and had heard the angry clicks coming from Jill's typewriter in the office, she ran to the phone and took the matchbook cover out of her jeans. She dialed again, and this time the number actually rang.

"Thérèse-Isabelle."

"Bonjour." Iris inquired if they had kept the dress for her; the woman at Thérèse-Isabelle informed her they would not keep it past noon, and reminded her the price was five hundred francs.

Iris now had the problem of extracting five hundred francs—a sum so vast that she could barely contemplate it—from some member of the household. But the dress was worth it. It was, to Iris, the supreme incarnation of elegance. Keeping its form and color sharply in mind, she climbed up to Charlé's bedroom and hovered by the half-open door, where she could hear little slaps coming from the bathroom beyond. She walked in quietly. Charlé was applying a thick white cream to her legs and rubbing it slowly in upward motions toward the tops of her thighs, slapping as she went. Iris saw her white plastic bag lying open on the floor by the dressing table but decided against theft, as she knew that before she could separate the precious five bills of one hundred francs, or even if, by a miracle, she quickly found a bill of the right denomination bearing the likeness of Molière, Charlé would catch and challenge her. She entered the bathroom and sat on the lid of the toilet seat.

"You excited about tonight, cherub?" asked Charlé without looking up.

"Mmhnn." Iris decided to play it cool.

"Have you thought what you're going to wear yet?"

Iris, ever the type to blanch at opportunity, recoiled. She blushed. She contemplated the almost certain gift of five hundred francs that Charlé was about to bestow on her, and mumbled a thanks.

"Why, don't thank me, honey, I just think you should wear that nice blue dress."

"Which one?"

"The one with the sort of big flowers on it. That you got at that boutique near us. Cannelle, was it called?"

"Mum! It's made of furniture fabric!"

"It's very nice."

"It's a sundress! You can't wear a sundress to a gala!"

Charlé stood up and patted her hair in place. She grabbed Iris's hands and massaged them briefly. "Here, it'll do your hands good," she said. "They can get dry in the sun, you know." Iris pulled away and stormed over to the wide mirror over the sink where she repressed the urge to hurl the giant bottle of Pierre Cardin Amadis against the porcelain. Grabbing the small box of mascara that lay open on the counter, its center a small dark arroyo glistening with Charlé's spittle, she began to desultorily apply the blackened mucus to her lashes. Charlé let out an irritated sigh and left the room.

"What's Paula going to wear?" Iris shouted, deeply unconcerned. The question brought Charlé back to the door. She suggested that Paula might wear her version of the blue dress, the pink one.

Iris threw the mascara into the sink and whirled around. "You just have no respect for us, that's all!" she shouted. "We're being launched, introduced, brought out tonight, and you want us to look like deck chairs! You're a bitch! And what's more, why aren't you taking *me* to the hairdresser too?"

After Iris had run out of the room and across the hall to her own quarters, Charlé sat on the bed to put on her sandals. They were excellent Jourdan ones, brand new, a perfect shade of brandy. She reasoned that the child was just like her father, ungrateful and probably paranoid. She wondered what to do about her. She felt a surge of anger that Iris should so misunderstand her—of course she had booked a hairdresser's appointment for her as well, did Iris take her for a wicked witch of the West or something? She considered how different Paula was: cheery, uncomplicated, unspoiled. The fact that Paula had never exhibited any of these attributes did not disturb Charlé, for to assess Paula as the positive child in her life was comforting. Nor did she extend her hereditary analysis of Iris to Paula; had she considered for a second what traits the combined characters of Soula Tithe and Raoul Abime would deposit in the soul of their child, she would have had ample reason to tear her hair out.

She sat at the dressing table and drummed her fingers on the glass. Maybe she should let them get dressed up a little. But then, she wouldn't want her friend the photographer from *Nice Matin* (who made the galas into milestones in her social career and in the lives of her English friends) to see the size and shape of her children. She wished she had never thought of asking the kids to go. But there was no way of stopping them now. She threw a longing glance at a pair of imaginary *broderie anglaise* smocks with pink ribbons and flat Mary Janes, and took her purse out of her bag. Three thousand francs. Holding back a basic thousand for herself, and then another thousand for good measure, she counted out three hundred francs for each girl. That should do it. Stunned by her own generosity, and afraid of its losing its impact unless she acted on it at once, she went to the window and called to Paula on the jetty far below. Paula sat up and turned and squinted and held a hand over her eyes, and shook her head. Faintly Charlé heard a sharp "What?" float up to her. She leaned further out the window and waved the wad of hundred-franc notes. Paula rose to her feet and began running toward the stairs, and Charlé pulled away from the window, wonderfully warmed by the idea that she could wave money at Soula and Raoul's daughter and get an immediate response.

As Paula climbed the steps she was thinking about Alain Velle. The limited effect of his exertions on her body had not sufficed to make her imagine she was in love with him. Since that first day she had seen him almost every day, gone driving in his car, a small red convertible, and sneaked several more sessions of grunting in between the requisite meals and elegant strolls together. By now she was bored. Paula had been blessed since birth with a divine indifference to convention, as her father saw it. She was aware of the world only as something that either stood in her way or made her feel good. Monsieur Velle, who talked much of synthesizers and obscure doings at the *fac de droit,* was, she decided, no more than a conduit to other, more interesting young men. The encumbrance of her virginity had been nicely disposed of, and looking at the matter realistically, she supposed it greedy of her to expect anything more from their physical contact than she did from the dentist. Her impacted womanhood —she imagined something like a baby tooth falling out and being replaced with a nice white shining new fang—was a problem that had been dealt with, and now she could proceed with having a good time. Paula had the distinct feeling that life would be kind to her.

In Jill's office, Iris was sitting by the window sharpening pencils. "You really should sharpen them more often," she told Jill helpfully as she screwed a pencil into the steel blade of a tiny sharpener made of transparent yellow plastic. Jill smiled absently and took another puff from the cigarette burning in the Ricard ashtray on her right. "If you do them all, I'll let you file," she said. Iris sighed. "If you don't want to, I can get along perfectly well without you, you know," added Jill.

"Can you pay me?" asked Iris boldly, glancing at the travel alarm clock that said ten-thirty. An hour to go, and then she would lose the dress.

"Pay you?" asked Jill. "I thought you did this because you liked helping."

"It's just that I need money, desperately."

Jill stopped typing at once and looked up, her face a caricature of alarm. "What have you been up to now?" she asked. "Is it drugs? Drink? Men?"

Iris giggled, delighted at the absurdity of the question. She loved Jill when she teased her like that.

"Okay, what is it? Have you gone through your allowance already?"

"No! I still have fifty francs, but I need another four hundred."

"Four hundred! That's thirty pounds. What have you been doing—gambling?"

"I need a dress for tonight. And Mum won't give me a penny, and I have no money at all in the world—"

"Don't give me that nonsense," said Jill as she resumed typing.

Iris stood up. "It's true! And you know she prefers Paula. You know it—come on, admit it! And she doesn't want me to look pretty or anything."

Jill was fond enough of Iris, but not to the extent of doing what she now did, which was to take a silk wallet out of her purse—the one screen-printed with a reproduction of Gainsborough's *Blue Boy,* in which she kept the large bills—and remove from it four hundred-franc notes, and hand them one by one to Iris across the desk. It was Jill's dislike of Charlé that prompted the gesture, allied to the spinsterish sentiment that it was high time Paula stopped getting everything her own way. And, to be absolutely clear about it, Jill told herself that Iris needed all the help she could get, because she was beginning to look a little Jewish around the edges (a Jew, she thought, would describe the look as intense, dumpy, nervous), and since that wouldn't do in Jill's book, she didn't see how it could get by in anyone else's. She patted Iris's hand and said, "Run along now and get yourself a pretty dress." Iris stood up and went to hug her benefactress, but Jill made a great fuss about pushing her away and laughing. "What can I do for *you?*" asked Iris with that rising, childish inflection at the end of her question that innocently presupposed there were ways in which she could repay Jill. "Just remember you don't look good in prints," said Jill, patting her on her rounded bottom. "Run along now, I've got work to do." When Iris had left the room in a flurry of "Oh, Jill, I love you's," Jill took out the ledger bound in dimpled black paper and wrote in the petty-cash column, next to "Disbursements": "Entertainment—400 francs."

Iris still needed fifty francs, to say nothing of the fifteen or so she would need for the taxi to Beaulieu and back. She wafted into the cool kitchen and leaned against the cerulean tiles, watching Toinette pound basil in a mortar. Toinette turned around, glared, and asked what *"ma petite"* wanted. *"Rien du tout,"* said Iris, and then explained that she was going into Villefranche with Mademoiselle Jill, and Madame Abime wanted them to pick up some spices and things, and could she, Iris, have some of the housekeeping money? A hundred francs would do. Toinette threw the pestle down on the table, then reached into the pocket of her apron and extracted a wad of notes, thicker even than the ones secreted about the persons of Jill and Charlé. Raoul had grown to like lavish food; he had therefore authorized Jill to give Toinette four thousand francs a month, with no questions asked. Charlé, who knew in her gut that even if they ate lobster twenty times a day there was no way that Toinette could spend that amount, had elected Toinette unofficial banker; she borrowed freely from her, on the twin conditions that neither Jill nor Raoul should know, and that Toinette would be paid back more or less in full.

The cook handed Iris the cash, and said, *"Vous me donnerez le reçu, hein?"* Iris said, *"Oui, oui,"* very fast, and ran out of the kitchen.

By the front door, she ran straight into Paula, who handed her three hundred francs. "What's this?" asked Iris, guilty and flushed.

"It's from Charlé. To get something to wear tonight."

"Why didn't she give it to me herself?" asked Iris, sensing a plot.

"She called for you and so did I, but you didn't answer. Want to go shopping now?"

"I can't," said Iris, eyeing Paula's little Cartier watch with the sapphire in its winder; she had had one just the same but had lost it. The time was now VIII to XII. "I've got to run," she said.

When Raoul came back from a lengthy conference in Antibes that evening, he found the Peddleby-Marshes and Ian Gloskow seated on his terrace clucking about the price of diesel fuel, watching their yacht roll in the bay, and drinking kir. Frank and Gladys Peddleby-Marsh owned the *Glycoma,* the longest and thinnest boat in the waters of the Mediterranean. Their permanent guest was Ian Gloskow, who was rumored to be the lover of one or both of them, but no one knew for sure. Raoul had evolved ways of coping with Charlé's friends; he dozed, he drank, he snarled. But with the Peddleby-Marshes he was on his best behavior, for he believed the rumor about their ménage and hoped that by being pleasant to them he would one day be taken into their confidence. He thought them worse than fools, of course, and sociologically reprehensible, but the whiff of their original sex life kept his usual disdainful hauteur in check; with them he still carried himself with hauteur, of course, but it was an amenable, friendly hauteur. Ian Gloskow rose to kiss him as he arrived, while Frank and Gladys remarked in tandem that he was not yet dressed. Frank was crackling in a starched-front shirt with diamond-and-ebony studs, while Gladys looked like an ambulatory seed catalogue in a chiffon creation by the foremost London couturière. The Peddleby-Marsh diamonds, wrested from the very graves and funeral pyres of colonial India minutes before Gandhi had put his foot down, glistened at her neck. Charlé winked like a harbor at night: a couple of thousand rhinestones sought their mates across her gown's inky surface of navy blue sequins. Raoul winced slightly as he noticed the way her arms sprang from the armholes of the tight dress like marzipan, freckled, soft, with no definition other than that imposed by the shoulder straps. He asked about the girls.

"They're dressing. They've been fussing all day. I gave them some money and they were very excited."

"I hope they haven't made themselves look cheap," Raoul said. "Where's Jill? Isn't she coming tonight?"

"Yes, she is. But she had a date. She's gone to Monte Carlo to pick him up."

Raoul laughed, letting the Peddleby-Marshes and Ian Gloskow in on the incongruity of Jill's having a date. Charlé suggested that he change.

"Yes, old boy!" said Frank. "Slip on one of your dellybars, what?" said Ian. Raoul looked piqued. "I only wear djellabas at home," he murmured. "Who's Jill bringing, anyway?"

"Jimmy Kieron."

Raoul looked satisfied. "That *pédé*." He rubbed his hands together and peered down at the sea, which yielded no new information. Then he went to change.

At nine o'clock they rose, a little drunk, their boredom with each other momentarily assuaged by the anticipation of the evening. Raoul patted his jacket, where behind the gold buttons nestled ten thousand francs, casino fodder. They proceeded up the stairs.

Iris and Paula met the party at the front door. In the dark, very little could be discerned of their apparel, as they wore enveloping Portuguese shawls. They all clambered into the car, a long Lincoln hired for these occasions by Charlé. Iris stared at her fingernails most of the way, trying to gauge whether they were like little shells—an attribute she desired also for her ears—or whether they looked like stubby pieces of animal horn despite the five coats of nacreous glaze she had spent an hour applying. It was hard to tell in the dark car, and she was grateful every time a streetlight illuminated the corner where she sat. Paula was gazing first at Gladys, then at Frank, then at Ian. She thought Gladys was not bad-looking for an old woman, and that Frank had a certain allure about him. The shirt studs belonged on a gangster, of course, but the face had a blanched, well-boiled look, aseptic, kind, a little sinister. She wondered if she was ready for sinister men yet—she could swear Don Flagel had looked at her with rather more attention than usual, had looked straight at her breasts. Then her thoughts turned back to Ian Gloskow. He was decidedly different: there were those startled dark-blue eyes that reached almost to the edge of his hairy eyebrows, that soft upper lip that twitched just before he spoke, that air of surprise which made him look vulnerable, accessible. She speculated briefly on the probable size of his cock, and then couldn't look at him. God, life was complicated. "*Paulette*," said Raoul from the front seat, "*regarde-moi*." She looked at her father, and he made the dreadful sound of teeth clicking against his tongue. "You're wearing too much makeup," he said in French, as if to keep this observation secret, as if no one else in the whole car had ever heard a word of French. Paula let out a secret little "*Merde!*" which only Iris caught.

The Peddleby-Marshes discussed the length of the journey for the length of the journey; Ian Gloskow and Raoul discussed whether or not Alain Delon was a handsome man, a subject which did not ordinarily arrest Raoul's attention but which intrigued him for the way it seemed to worry Ian Gloskow. When the car drew up to the casino, a uniformed doorman opened the door for Raoul, and the party stepped out onto the warm sidewalk. Raoul took Charlé's arm as three local photographers raised their cameras to their eyes and bounced their flashes off the overhanging balcony. Frank and Gladys glanced pleasantly at the gentlemen of the press, indicating that although they usually refused such offers, tonight as a favor they would grant their images in celluloid as an act of goodwill. A sleepy youngster from the *Journal de Menton* snapped—on the contact sheet it would be no more than a blur—and Ian Gloskow, a girl on each arm, marched through to the door.

"Well, let's see you," said Charlé to Iris as she tried to pull the shawl from her daughter's shoulders. Iris held it fast against her; in the hall of the casino, jostled in the wakes of immaculate couples, the men handsome in their evening jackets, the women slim pillars of silk the colors of precious stones, their hair perfect lacquered spheres in shades of lemon drop, caramel and amber, Iris felt like a misshapen aberration of nature. Her brave and modern choice of dress no longer seemed anything but inappropriate; she did not want to be caught in the same glance as these polished beauties.

Paula meanwhile was undergoing a trauma of her own, which had less to do with appearance than with jealousy. She was watching Raoul greet and be greeted by various women, some of whom he introduced to Charlé and their guests, some of whom he acknowledged with only an inclination of his head; they were not all beautiful, not all terribly young, but each seemed to know him well and be eager to touch him. They appeared to have husbands or escorts, waiting for them impatiently at the door to the ballroom, and they pointed these men out to Raoul with tiny gestures accompanied by little shrugs. It annoyed Paula that he should allow the evidence of his present and former intimacies to intrude on his evening with her.

Paula had long since made her peace with the idea of Charlé. Her stepmother was a sort of spendthrift secretary and housekeeper, a guardian, a pain in the neck: she was not a rival for Raoul's affections—that Paula was sure about—and it delighted her every time she read in the paper about a woman Raoul was seen with, or when she answered the phone at the villa and a soft voice timidly asked for him and then left some ridiculous message about veal chops or the car being fixed. These were testaments to her father's good taste in not being faithful to Charlé. But to have to gaze upon the women and see that they were actually pretty ordinary, and had freckles or downy upper lips, was disillusioning.

Ian Gloskow was gazing at her in rank admiration. He thought it awfully clever of her to have made herself look like one of those Arab boys you can buy in Marrakesh; her eyes were rimmed with kohl (which he liked to use himself upon occasion, but only below the latitude of Casablanca), her lashes seemed purple in the neon light, and her lips were dark red. As he was admiring her, Raoul left the woman he was talking to and grabbed his daughter's arm. "You are going to remove that jam from your mouth at once," he said. A blonde passing by goosed him, and he turned to acknowledge the touch with a slight smile. "Now go, and take Iris. She looks more miserable than I've ever seen her." He led Charlé into the ballroom.

At the door to the powder room a small fussy woman in black relieved the girls of their capes, and tapped the saucer on the counter. Paula straightened her dress, a white shift that barely covered her bottom, and retied the black velvet ribbon at her neck. She could see her legs only down to her knees in the mirror, and stepped back to get the full effect. To the American lady who was dabbing powder on a sunburned nose in the far corner of the room, Paula looked like a daguerreotype revised by a one-hand magazine; to Paula, Paula looked like a sort of angel or a nymph or the lead dancer in a Rhythmic Ballet. The shift had been purchased that afternoon around the corner from the hairdresser's, and looked it. Skimpy and a little shiny, the only form it could complement was one that as yet remained in two dimensions.

Iris contemplated her own image and thought at first that there was a fault in the glass, or that the mirror had been taken from a fun house. A covert look over at Paula, who looked, alas, flat and perfect in the glass, confirmed her worst fears. She had made the wrong choice.

"Do you think it's nice?" she asked in a timid voice. Paula glanced briefly at her—she was removing her lipstick carefully with a Kleenex borrowed from the American woman with sunburn—and nodded. "Pretty."

Iris didn't believe her. The dress was a knitted tube of different-colored metallic threads with a plastic yoke at the neck that looked like some sort of drafting instrument. Into the yoke were screwed four rhinestone-topped bolts. She turned for the side view to see if her neck jutted out of the plastic the way the young Marchioness of Fedder's neck did in a large color picture in British *Vogue,* the picture that had first alerted her to the existence of the dress. Her neck did not jut; it seemed to emerge from the square of plastic like that of a penitent in the stocks. To compound the caricature, the dress was a size too small, and hugged her body like a stocking. It followed the rounded line of her bottom and retreated at once below it to her thighs, delineating the incipient steatopygia that was Iris's nemesis.

"We'd better make our entrance," said Paula casually, brushing her hair with Iris's brush. "Come on." Iris remained rooted to the spot. Her nose was shining again and she had no powder. The face was wrong, the dress was wrong, she should have stayed at home. Paula tugged on her arm. "Come *on,* you look fine!" and pulled her out the door.

They crossed the hall gingerly, not quite sure how to find the ballroom. Iris reflected that if Raoul had any human kindness at all, he would have waited for them, but she did not share her feelings with Paula. She wanted to appear self-sufficient and eager for fun. Paula, for all her misgivings, was enjoying ambling across the foyer, allowing herself to be looked at. Her new white gladiator sandals threatened to come undone at the knee and cascade down her legs, her skirt was short enough to embarrass even herself, but all she was aware of was the pleasant metallic cool of her chain-mail shoulder bag and the looks she was getting. Iris was walking like a royalist to the guillotine, repeating to herself Charlé's daily admonition to stand up straight and forgetting to use her favorite word "spunk" at a time when she needed it the most. They came to the door of the ballroom, and, beyond, they saw a sky dotted with stars, a dance floor, tables stretching out like the avenues from the Etoile.

"We've got to cross the dance floor!" cried Iris.

Paula did not even hear her. With one step she crossed into the illuminated arena, heading for the far side without knowing where the table was, but keeping to a straight line nonetheless. Iris started off after her, but was busy scanning the tables; she tripped on the raised edge of the large glass tiles that made up the floor and dropped her bag; she bent over to retrieve it, sweating and blushing and being eminently aware of what an idiot she must look, how everyone must be laughing at her. She sneaked a look from her kneeling position, just to make sure; but the people at the nearest table were looking at each other, and the waiters were busy carrying trays, so she was able to rise again with some degree of self-possession. Once up, she realized that Paula had disappeared, and stopped in her tracks. A quivering scintillation near the far edge of the dance floor signaled her mother's presence, and she hastened toward it, and as she did so she caught sight of a young woman and an older man pointing at her, the young woman laughing and the older man shaking his head in a knowing way. She felt the urge to break into a run so as to escape the sadism of these strangers, but thought better of it when she realized what her bottom would do while being so rapidly transported in its thin metallic sheathing. By the time she reached the far side of the floor she was so relieved that she attempted to take the four wide steps that led down to the level of the tables in one go, and failed. She careened into a waiter, who held her by the elbows until she had regained her balance. "*Quelle table?*" he asked discreetly.

"Raoul Abime," said Iris.

"*Vous n'aviez qu'à me le dire, mademoiselle,*" said the headwaiter as he pushed her toward a spot from which Charlé, standing, was waving at her. Before Iris could sit down Charlé had fallen on her like a hatbox out of a closet. "Guess who's here!" she shrieked. Iris's heart beat faster. Who could it be? The man of her dreams? Marlon Brando? Alain Delon? Hervé Vilar, who sang "*J'ai envie de vivre avec toi*" on the radio? Charles Aznavour? "Who?" she asked in an urgent shout.

Charlé shot a look at Raoul and regained her composure. "Sit down," she hissed, seating herself and adjusting the bra straps that were beginning to stir from the armholes of her dress. Iris took her seat on a chair wedged between Frank Peddleby-Marsh and her mother. She put her little crochet evening bag on her lap and the hairbrush fell out. A waiter poured champagne into her glass.

"Who is it?" she asked her mother.

"It's just terrible, it's so embarrassing!" was all the information Charlé found fit to vouchsafe.

"But, Mum," pleaded Iris, "you were so worked up about it just a minute ago! What is it?"

"Shh!" Charlé ended the conversation abruptly and dug into the bowl of caviar that a waiter proffered on her left. Iris waited for her mother to help herself, and then for the caviar to come to her. Iris's hand was out for the spoon, but to her surprise she found that the waiter served her and that she was not allowed to touch the deep bowl, its black lining gleaming like a geode. She attempted to take the spoon anyway, following her mother's example, and found her hand being abruptly nudged back to the table as the waiter emitted a sharp "Tsk! tsk!" She decided the evening was not going to go well.

After two spoonfuls of caviar had been put on each plate—Raoul, like Charlé, allowed to help himself, the rest of the party served like schoolchildren—there was a general reaching for toast and munching of *tartines* to the accompaniment of grateful yet mechanical oohing and aahing. "Just the thing for breakfast," said Ian Gloskow to Paula, who rather hated the stuff. Not so Iris, who knew its price and its rarity, and was overly noisy in her expressions of contentment.

Then came the meat, some sort of animal cloaked in sauce, its identity obscured by pepper and champagne. Iris attempted to flirt with Ian Gloskow, who, being on the other side of the table from her, and fully three seats away, was incapable of discerning any intention in her loud remarks to him about the balmy weather and number of stars in the sky other than that of keeping him from his dinner and ruining his evening.

Just as Charlé began to cut her meat with a gusto she normally reserved for attacking the dead skin that formed on the soles of her feet, Raoul said he had seen someone on the other side of the enclosure and vanished. He did not bother to elaborate on the identity or indeed the sex of the person. Charlé allowed him to go with a little trill of a laugh. His departure relieved her enormously: there was one encounter she knew was bound to take place that evening, and Raoul's absence decreased his chances of witnessing it.

Dessert came and went in the form of *barquettes* of strawberries manned by mint leaves and Charlé began to relax, within the confines of an anxiety that held her like a canvas dress one size too small. She was laughing with Frank over Iris's head about the way the shutterbugs were gathering at the door by the stage, ready to snap Silvano the teenage heart throb, who would be the main attraction of the floor show. There were many other things she could have been laughing about, for Frank and Gladys had provided the table with endless examples of the mindlessness of their Maltese sailors, the high prices at the Rhul in Nice, and the perils of sailing too close to the shores of Sardinia, but she had been unable to concentrate on what anyone was saying long enough to understand the reason for the various punch lines. She had heard "And then he fried the lentils!" and simulated a laugh with a little wrinkling of her nose, and she had heard "the bugger was only ten feet deep!" and been too distracted to join in the guffaw that Ian Gloskow, ever the thoughtful guest, had provided as a finale to that particular story. Paula was watching the room for a glimpse of her father, feeling betrayed and elaborating on schemes of revenge that involved utilizing her new trick of opening her legs and letting a man push his thing into her, in baroque and shocking public exhibitions. In those rare moments when she was not contemplating the creation of a *scandale,* she was wondering wistfully if this was all there was to social life. She was rarely wistful, but as she had recently become aware of subtle intimations from mirrors and men's eyes that her youth was not to go by unappreciated, she wanted to know that there would be some fun in it for her. So far, as we have seen, sex had proved to be below her expectations, and now, being launched by her father and stepmother was providing her with all the excitement of dining at an open-air convention for the geriatric.

Iris had no such misgivings: she thought it was all wonderful, if slightly intimidating. She had recovered from the waiter's rebuff and comforted herself with the thought that, obviously, only important people could be allowed to help themselves to caviar, and when she became an important person, she, too, would be allowed to grasp the silver spoon. And if the women all looked a million times better and sleeker than she could right now, it was only a matter of time; after all, these were women, real *femmes du monde,* and decades of care had gone into buffing their sheen, and their taste had been formed by couturiers, not simply by magazines. She had decided that the dress that so embarrassed her was in fact defensible, a true creation of a prêt-à-porter, an emblem of 1966, and that she was in a way a patroness, albeit a very young one, of an emerging art form, that of fashion for the masses. Not that the masses could afford a five-hundred-franc creation, of course, but it was a step in the direction of democracy, it was a political act. As her reasoning escalated into fervid self-justification she began to sit up straighter; her unruly and abundant flesh began to matter less as she concluded that she had shown a form of aesthetic bravery in endorsing what *Elle* might call a "difficult" look, and anyone watching Iris would have been surprised to notice in the last few minutes of dinner that the young girl who had been so self-conscious and uncomfortable at the start of the evening was beginning to assume the demeanor of a rather smug dowager.

Someone in fact was watching; and just as the lights dimmed in preparation for the onslaught of music and color that was to lull the couples who had paid three hundred francs a head into a feeling that their money's worth was leaping at them across the concealed footlights, he made his move. Charlé saw him as he laboriously lowered himself into the seat next to Paula. She screamed, "Saul!"

Iris's head whirled from the stage, where a profusion of pastied nipples were launching an attack on her sensibilities, to the man who had just sat down. She had not heard the name for almost ten years. She recognized the face at once, although the gray skin had developed new valances and ruchings, having aged in the manner of a slipcover on a sofa. She gave him a huge smile, which she instantly changed to a look of polite if cheerful inquiry, in case Charlé minded her being happy to see him.

Charlé's reaction confirmed Iris's need for caution. Turning to Paula, Charlé said slowly and deliberately, "I can't see Jill anywhere. Can you? She would have come up to us if she had seen us. Where do you think she is?"

Gladys joined in the inquiry, unaware of how much she was helping Charlé. "Yes, where is the woman? I'd have liked to talk to her."

Charlé continued. "Darling, why don't you go find her? I'm sure she's somewhere here. Go on, find her for us, and have a chat with her. Don't worry, Silvano won't be on until much much later. The guest star always comes on at the end." She made the gesture of pulling Paula's chair away from the table, and Paula rose without noticing that it was the wrinkled-looking man who had caused such agitation in her stepmother.

"Well," said Saul, indulgent. He assumed that Charlé had to dispatch the young woman for reasons he ignored. He nodded at Frank and Gladys, who nodded back guardedly; they had not been introduced, nor was the face familiar from the publications they subscribed to. Ian Gloskow gave Saul his standard flabbergasted "Hello," which Saul interpreted to mean that his presence had managed to screw up the evening for these nice strangers.

"Hey, Charlene, I'm sorry if—" he began.

"Nonsense," said Charlé in the voice of Dara Devenish, which she borrowed on occasions like this. "I couldn't be more delighted to see you. Frank, Gladys, Ian, this is Saul Hyott, an old friend of mine." She made the introductions with an adamantine smile. Iris's jaw dropped at the description of the man who, she was almost certain, had been her mother's lover—there was no other word for it; after all, her memory was excellent and hadn't they shared a bedroom back in Paris? Her mother's eyes turned toward her with messages, orders to do something, behave in a certain way, but what?

"You remember Iris," said Charlé in a tone that could have sweetened the coffee for a whole regiment. Iris chose to look demure; that was a good look—eyes lowered, lips a trifle apart, nostrils flared just enough to give definition to her nose.

"My my my," said Saul, "when I saw you the last time you were just a tiny, tiny little girl."

"Not that tiny," corrected Charlé. "She must have been at least seven."

"Age of reason, here in France," said Ian Gloskow.

"I remember *you,* " said Iris, emboldened by Gloskow's reminder of her French roots.

"Do you?" asked Saul, scratching his ear and beaming at her. "What do you remember?"

"You played golf a lot," she said. Her mother was looking at her with her half-opened mouth stretched across a smile, her eyebrows raised, a look of ebullient expectancy animating her features. Iris went for it: "And you were always traveling, and you brought me presents every time you came home."

"How wonderful!" exclaimed Gladys at the same moment that Charlé was screaming, "That's lovely! You've got a fabulous memory!"

"Oh," said Ian Gloskow, holding fast to the thread of the exchange, and wishing to turn it into a general conversation that would provide occasion for comment from all present. "Where did you live?"

"In Paris," said Saul, who then ruined the cosmopolitan effect by adding, "France."

"Yes, well," said Charlé, shrill and bright and very American, "what brings you back here now, huh?"

"Remember the Hi-Fliers?"

Charlé nodded.

"The what?" Frank opened his mouth for the first time since Saul's arrival. "Of course, the horse? Won at Saratoga in, let me see, '52, '53?"

Saul, who had brightened at the mention of racehorses, hastened to correct him. "No, that was High Flivver. The Hi-Fliers were my dancing troupe. Great girls, great gams. I disbanded them when I moved to Paris, but a few years later—"

"I say, since you're on your life story, wouldn't you like a brandy, old man?" asked Ian Gloskow. Saul looked pleased at the offer. Ian snapped his fingers for a waiter. Gladys leaned forward, her diamonds quivering. "You're in the entertainment field, then, Mr. Hyott?" She pronounced it "High-art."

"Well, yes, I am. After Paris, where— Oh, thank you"—he picked up the brandy—"something of a distressing personal nature occurred—" He took a double sip, and they all watched the rise of the dewlaps over the descent of the brandy, except Charlé, who was opening her bag to take out her compact and powder her nose, and then Saul continued, "—which made me stop and take stock. I returned to the States and took my old life in hand again."

"How fascinating!" said Gladys.

Frank reflected on the strange pomposity of Americans when discussing their private lives; he liked to generalize upon the merest insights, and congratulated himself on his knowledge of both human nature and the United States. "Go on," he said.

"Well, and I don't mind admitting this, I was pretty shook up by what had happened—"

"What happened? Had your wife died?" asked Gladys solicitously, having calculated his age by a quick count of the folds and assuming that widowerhood was the only opportunity for tragedy open to a man his age.

"What?" asked Saul, then answered himself. "No, not at all. Well, in a manner of speaking, maybe."

Charlé was still powdering her nose.

"So I went back, and picked up the pieces. Called up all my girls, and bless the little cuties, they were all waiting for me. So I got—"

"That's great!" exclaimed Charlé, snapping her compact shut with a loud click. Saul gazed at her with sadness in his baggy eyes. "You think so, sweetheart?"

Charlé waved her compact at him, in a gesture of backstage solidarity. Saul's eyes went to the compact, a small box of platinum adorned with flattened chrysanthemums in red and yellow gold. It had a topaz clasp in the shape of a C. "Hey, you've still got it!" he said. Charlé looked at the compact. "Why, yes," she said.

"I think that's remarkable, a man who remembers a woman's *things,*" said Gladys, who rather liked Saul for it.

"Well, you see, I couldn't forget how much that co—"

Charlé cut him off. "Saul always had an eye for the finer things in life," she told the others. Saul sat back in his chair, and extracting a cigar from his breast pocket, he nipped the end off it with his right incisors. Frank, who had rather been hoping to be offered one—he was a generous man, but was too mean to buy his own cigars—extracted a Mexican gold peso from his pocket and handed it to Saul. "Use this, you'll find it does a neater job," he said, activating the mechanism by which the peso revealed itself to have been flayed like an Aztec sacrifice and slipped over a thin circle of silver with a guillotine mechanism across its central hole. Saul waved it away. "Don't use the gimmicks, they ruin the flavor," he said.

Leaning back toward the table and emitting a pall of smoke toward Iris, he went on, "My life turned out to be just great." Ian Gloskow repressed a yawn. Couldn't he get to the point? Was there a point? "The Hi-Fliers really took off this time around—we made a picture, maybe you saw it, *Belles of the Field?*" His audience looked blank. "Nuns, they were nuns who saved a flyer, get the joke? Anyway, it was a smash hit in the States; now they're topliners at Vegas, and here we are!"

"My husband's a director, he may have seen it," said Charlé.

"Here *who* are?" asked Ian Gloskow, still hoping for a point.

"Me and my wife. And the Fliers. That's who we're watching."

All heads turned to watch the stage, as if to confirm that the Fliers were worth watching, and then back to Saul.

"Your wife," said Charlé in dull, noncommittal tones. She had not turned to watch the stage.

"Sheila. You remember Sheila?"

Charlé almost choked. "McCoy?" she asked.

"Wetherly. You might have known her in L.A."

Charlé shook her head. "She's a great gal, and I can't wait to introduce you." In a lower tone he added, "Wetherly, Wetherly, you know? The airplane factory."

"She owns it?" asked Charlé dully.

"Her folks. Real old money."

"Oh, Wetherly!" said Frank. "Of course. Wetherly Aviation. Know it like the back of my hand."

"You see?" said Saul in tones of triumphant vindication.

"That's just wonderful, Saul," said Charlé. "Gee, I wonder where Raoul has got to."

"Shall I go look?" asked Iris, grateful for the opportunity to get away from something she did not understand but heartily disliked.

Charlé took her daughter's hand. "Yes, go see if you can find Paula," she said. "And then come back to watch Silvano with us."

"Silvano. I handle him. He's very hot right now," said Saul as he waved his cigar.

"You do?" Iris was impressed.

Not so the Peddleby-Marshes. "Who he?" asked Gladys.

"Star of the evening, dear, who we're waiting for," whispered Ian, who hated it when Gladys showed her age and used advertising lingo.

"Wow," said Iris. Dara Devenish once more possessed Charlé. "I have never in my life heard you use such common language," she said. "Can't you find a more articulate expression?" Iris stood up.

"Hey, I'll come with you," said Saul, and rose with Iris, taking her arm. Casting a cheery "*Bonsoir,* folks" at the table, he led Iris away.

Charlé let out a theatrical sigh of relief and threw her hands palms down on the table, as if crushing a pair of moths. Gladys opened her mouth to ask who this extraordinary person was, but Charlé forestalled her. "That awful man!" she said to her three friends. "I thought we'd never be rid of him."

"He seemed very fond of you," said Frank.

"And of Iris. What a kind face he has," added Gladys.

Charlé shook her head and took a cigarette from her gold-and-topaz case. Hitting it against the tablecloth (like a navvy, thought Ian, who knew a thing or two about navvies), she did her best to shatter their illusions. "He's just awful. A second-rate leech. Yech!" She emitted a faint raspberry and allowed Frank to lean across the table and light her cigarette.

"Still, he seemed awfully fond of *you,* " said Ian coyly. "As if he carried a torch for you."

"Oh God! Can you imagine anything worse! Spare me!" shouted Charlé, wheezing with sincere giggles. "The very idea!"

Across the room, Iris, with her hand in the firm and dry grip of Saul's large palm, was searching for her stepsister while Saul was looking for the secret door into the casino. He had located it that afternoon during the rehearsal, but now in the dark he was lost, and the milling regiment of waiters served to confuse him further. Iris saw Paula sitting with Jill and Jimmy Kieron and two other men, and motioned Saul toward their table, but he held back.

"Don't you want to meet my stepsister?" she asked.

"Who are the others?"

"Raoul's secretary, and some writers."

"Crap. Let's go gamble," muttered Saul. Iris knew this was not what Charlé had had in mind at all when she sent her away from the table, and tried to carry out her mother's wishes. "We can't leave now, I have to listen to Silvano with Mum afterwards."

"C'mon, come keep me company," he said.

"Where is your wife?" asked Iris, ever conscious of the laws of propriety and her duty to uphold them.

Saul had just spied the door. Iris found herself propelled mercilessly toward a part of the wall paneling depicting three storks, one of which seemed to be about to lay an egg. "Where are we going?" she demanded, indignant.

"Relax. It's me, Uncle Saul," he said, pushing one of the storks. The finale of the Hi-Fliers was bringing down a shower of paper rose petals onto the stage. "We'll miss Silvano," said Iris.

"No, we won't, there's the dog act first, and the magician, the effing ventriloquist, and a bunch of slant-eyed dames who juggle plates. C'mon."

He was holding the panel open; beyond it she could see a long white room with green baize-covered tables in it. "That's the casino!" she said.

"What else is new? Of course it's the casino. C'mon, I'm holding the door open for you, glamour girl."

Iris hesitated again. "Saul, I can't. I'm not twenty-one yet."

He pushed her in just as a headwaiter came over and started fussing, saying *"Interdit! Interdit!"* Saul showed the man his casino identification and slipped through.

The panel shut behind them. Iris stood riveted to the spot, aware of her transgression. She was weighing which was worse: hurting Saul's feelings and making him think she was a prim ninny or breaking casino rules.

Saul was being saluted by all the croupiers. "They all seem to know you," Iris pointed out as she caught up with him.

" 'Course they do. Most of 'em used to work for me. Hey, lemme look at you!" he said. In the clean, crisp air conditioning of the casino he felt alive again. He turned and took her by the shoulders. Iris held her breath. She supposed in that instant that she had been a beautiful child, and that time had not improved her. Saul said nothing, and the expression on his face did not change. His benevolent camaraderie remained. She had hoped for some dim flicker of—astonishment? admiration? But she didn't dare ask.

"You look like an attractive kook," he said.

She didn't know what to make of this. He could have said "beauty," or "glamour girl," as he had years earlier.

" 'Kook'?"

"Yeah." He saw her face had fallen, and it reminded him of Charlene one day in L.A. when her look had betrayed the same endearing despair. "Hey, that's a *good* thing to be," he said in the voice he used for the youngest of his dancers. "It's interesting."

Iris just nodded. "Wanna drink?" he asked, heading for the bar. "I can't drink," she said. "Mum doesn't like me to."

Saul didn't answer. At the bar he asked for a whiskey on the rocks and a champagne cocktail. "Oh, champagne," said Iris. "I drink *that* all the time."

"Prosit," said Saul, and drained his glass.

Iris sipped at her champagne. A small sugar cube was noisily disintegrating in the bottom of the glass. "I remember now," she said slowly. "You used to go to that place with lamps like, uh, pawnbroker balls." She hated having to say a provocative word like "balls," even to an avuncular figure like Saul, and therefore repeated "pawnbroker." Saul looked gratified. "Yeah, that was Enghien. But you never came there, how did you know that, you bright little tyke, huh?"

Iris smiled. "It was on all the posters. I used to pass them on the way to school and think of you under those funny little lamps."

Saul looked at her with something resembling fatherly love in his eyes.

"Your mother hasn't changed. She's as pretty as ever," he offered. Iris agreed eagerly: "Isn't she?"

One of the croupiers who had been watching them with beady eyes came over to offer a handshake to Saul and glance meaningfully, in the best croupier tradition, at the young girl with him. Saul shook his head. "I'm sure she's twenty-one, Francis, because she is my daughter. Francis, Mademoiselle Iris Hyott." Iris put out her hand prettily, enjoying the subterfuge. When Francis had retreated, his mind perhaps not entirely at rest, but a nice hundred-franc bill nestling in his palm where Saul had deposited it, Saul leaned on the bar and cocked his head at Iris. "Your sister, she okay?" he asked.

"She's great. Why didn't you want . . . I'd love it if you wanted to meet her."

Saul pushed an invisible Paula away in the air. "Naw," he said. "You're the only teenager I want to know."

Iris beamed and felt confident enough to hoist herself on a barstool, metallic stocking dress or not. Saul pointed to her costume. "That what they're wearing in Paris these days?" he asked. She shook her head. "I got it down here. At a nice shop. It's my first piece of real fashion, do you know what I mean?"

Saul didn't. "It's a bit short, but you've got cute young knees. And that thing around your neck looks like a ride at Coney Island, but why not, huh?" He beamed. Iris felt happier than she had been in years.

"I miss you," she said.

Saul's eyebrows rose, taking his eyelids with them. "Ya do?" he asked.

Iris then had to overstate. "We all do."

Saul shook his head. "Your mother doesn't miss me. She walked out on me. Eight years ago."

Iris felt she had just learned the secret of the ages. It was even more important, more fascinating than knowing who had been sleeping in the cabin on Don Flagel's yacht. And it had more bearing on her very own life, her Paris life, her pre-Raoul life. She grabbed the statement and worried it a little, like a dog with a slipper.

"*She* walked out on you? Is that what happened?"

She giggled a little. Here was Saul back in her life, telling her secrets about her mother. It was precious, a moment to hold on to. She wanted more. "Why?" she asked. It was a daring thing to do, but what could stop her? She was already breaking the law just by being there. "Why?" she asked again.

"Basically," said Saul, looking deep into her eyes, an experience that provided more pleasure for him than it did for Iris, who found herself fascinated by the loose lower lids that swung beneath his eyes like hammocks. "Basically, your mother's always been a whore."

Stunned, Iris could not reply. It was a trap. Of course it was a trap, to make her break the law first and then to lure her into sins beyond redemption and then to be nice to her, to soften her up so she would be absolutely trusting when the blow came. A disgusting trap. She threw her glass down on the bar, where it shattered and the slivers went into the olives and the nuts and the little fish-shaped crackers. Then she wished for a more violent gesture, but her only missile left was her bag, and she didn't want to throw that. She thought of spitting, and did not. (Bodily secretions should be kept within the body, it had something to do with one of the dirty books, an Indian one maybe, that she had been reading in the toilet.) She wanted to slap Saul or claw at his face, but she was afraid of the texture of that skin against her hand, under her pearly nails. She said nothing and hoped to look forbidding.

"Hey, don't react like that, sweetpea," he said. "You're a big girl now, and you should know the truth."

"That is not the truth," she enunciated, the Maid of Orléans confronting the British.

"Well, not strictly the truth, I mean she didn't turn tricks or anything. But her values are dollars and cents. She hasn't got an ounce of loyalty in her body."

"Go to hell!" shouted Iris; she turned on her stool and edged off it and marched toward a clearly marked door.

Once outside, she found the ladies' room, where she sat on a stool in front of a mirror and sobbed until even her Swimprufe mascara ran down her face to mingle with the rose-colored blush-on, the squamous white Mary Quant Cheek Lighter, the several layers of Invisible Veil, and the cheery-pink lip gloss into a dark and runny mess that hung at the edge of her chin and marked her forearm like India ink when she wiped it away.

An old woman with white hair was being delivered at the door by a young man who was the image of Dorian Gray. "Take *care,* darling," he said as she came into the powder room. "I'm fine, pigeon," she shouted back, using her silver mesh handbag like a paddle to propel herself along, teetering on unseen high heels beneath a silvery white sheath that matched her hair and refrained from following the lines of her body. She caught sight of Iris as she was proceeding toward the stalls. "Are you all right, dearie?" she asked in the same quivering falsetto she had used on her Dorian. Iris nodded and sniffed. "Here, dear, here's my handbag, you keep hold of it while I go attend to nature's call," said the old woman. "You'll find everything you need in there."

Iris opened the clasp of the bag and found a comb, a brush, some powder, a little cake of rouge, some mascara—bright blue—in a tiny little tube with its own equally tiny brush, a small spray bottle of Ecusson perfume, and two tiny beans wrapped in white net and cotton. She set the objects on the counter in front of her, washed her face, cursed Saul again, and began to paint herself. After ten minutes the old woman reappeared, her dress hitched up in back. "Can you help me, dear, I seem to be caught in my girdle," she said. Iris sprang up and went to pull the woman's dress down in the back, and as she patted it into place she felt under the thin fabric a strange series of bumps and girders. "Just the corset, dear, don't be scared. Now!" The old woman allowed Iris to help her down onto one of the little stools, and she watched with interest while Iris rouged her cheeks. "Funny, I never did it that way," she said. "I always put it up high, like this." Taking the powder puff she showed Iris what she meant. Iris began to sob again.

"All right, 'fess up. Man trouble?" she asked.

Iris smiled at the absurdity of the idea. "No. I've just been insulted. Or rather, my . . . I've just been gravely insulted." She was too loyal, too shocked to repeat what Saul had said, even to a total stranger.

"Left you for another girl?"

"No, it's not a man. Well, it is, but not what you think."

The old woman laughed. "Oh, honey, keep away from *them!*" she said. "They're *nothing* but trouble, with a capital *T!*"

Iris looked puzzled. "Who are?" she asked.

"The fairies. Keep away from the fairies."

Iris began to sniffle.

"Here, have a Kleenex." The woman dug into her purse again, and found, not a Kleenex, but an embroidered handkerchief of chiffon with rhinestones on it. "Blow between the stones or you'll scrape your nose off," she advised. Iris wondered if the old woman had ever been a whore. She wanted to know about whores. Maybe, she thought, whores were good things. She tried to imagine a way she could bring it up. She could ask, "Have you ever known a whore?" No, that was ridiculous. The old woman winked at her, and taking one of the little white beans, broke it under her own nose. She threw her head back and then thrust the bean under Iris's face. "Quick, before it goes away, smell it, smell it!" Iris leaned forward to take a sniff. She supposed it was perfume.

The smell hit her like a truck. School lavatories, a doctor's office, trains going up her nostrils. She grabbed her nose and choked, but before she could gag she felt a tremendous void in her head, a neat clean vacuum, and then a jolt. She rose with it and sat down again abruptly. When she had recovered her breath, she asked angrily, "What was that?" and jumped up and grabbed her little bag and stood near the door. It had to be part of a plot, the whole thing was a plot: Saul, this crazy old woman poisoning her . . .

"Ammonia. Spirits of. Clears your head. When I was your age, I wouldn't have dreamed of going out without them. In case I felt faint. Very good when you've had too much to drink and you want to keep your wits about you."

Iris leaned against the door. "I must go now," she said. "Do you want me for anything else?"

The old woman turned to her, her down puff in hand, a colony of white powder on the bridge of her nose. "Nothing, dear. Just have a good life. Oh, and if you see my boyfriend out there, would you tell him I'm coming?" Iris inclined her head. Maybe she could get a job as a companion to this nice old lady. The son was so beautiful. She opened the door and looked into the hall. "I can't see him," she said.

"Oh, well, if you do . . ." The old woman's voice trailed off as the door shut on its hydraulic hinges.

Iris began to cross the foyer. From behind a pillar came Dorian Gray. She was about to say, "Your mother's in there," when he took her by the arm. "I say," he asked in one of those English-for-Export voices that she had learned to detest. "Have you seen my girlfriend? She went into the ladies' loo about twenty minutes ago and . . ."

12.
La Belle Paula

"Who is that man?" asked Jill, who had seen Iris cross the room on the arm of a baggy middle-aged stranger. Paula felt a minuscule twinge of anger. "I don't know," she answered, feeling that she had every right to know. "Maybe he's helping her find the loo," offered Jill. Jimmy Kieron sniggered into his drink. He didn't find Jill funny very often, but she had spent the early part of the evening regaling him with the tale of Iris's four hundred francs, which he had found hilarious, and he had laughed even harder, though to himself, when Paula had come over to their table looking rather cheap and wrinkled and he saw that Jill's plan had worked. Now that Jill was in her cups, she was barely able to string three words together, but Jimmy Kieron was so grateful to her for the earlier entertainment that he continued to bray whenever she opened her mouth. He found Paula lacking in charm; she talked to him with what he took for a certain amount of condescension. On Paula's part this was nothing more than a sign of a sublime lack of interest in the person and actions of Jimmy Kieron, whom she had long ago figured to be a writer and nothing more. Writers slunk into rooms looking at their fingernails, and headed straight for the bar even if they weren't drunks; they liked to make remarks about the bomb affecting the genes of people and birds; they told long stories about people she had never heard of, whom they referred to by nicknames; they were touchy about everything but personal hygiene, a point on which they enjoyed failing. Worst of all, the only attention they paid to her was of the most unwelcome sort: they didn't look; they asked questions about how she felt and whether she was happy, and inevitably, regularly, excruciatingly, they asked if she remembered her mother. Writers had no feelings for anyone but themselves. They had bitter laughs and insatiable curiosity about the shortcomings and misadventures of everyone else who had ever lived. Raoul liked to remark behind their backs that the accepted notion that writers are intelligent was a gross exaggeration, and Paula agreed wholeheartedly. If they were so clever, she thought, looking at Jimmy Kieron and particularizing her generic disdain, why couldn't they get their crooked brown teeth fixed and get the spot of egg off their stupid bow ties?

Paula was a little drunk. She calculated, as a measure of discipline, how much champagne she had put away since the beginning of the evening, and was inordinately pleased to come up with a figure of seven glasses of her own, four of Iris's, and half a split drunk directly from the bottle at Jill and Jimmy's table. She was flushed, coated with the spangled aspic of a light sweat mixed with some handfuls of Bain de Soleil she had used to accentuate her exquisite tan, and happy. Jill had told her that Raoul had gone to ground (Jill was fond of hunting expressions, though the only horses she had seen in the last twenty years were employed at the track) in the arbor of orange trees behind the casino with a fine Florentine filly, an expression whose fricative alliteration had almost caused her to mislay her upper lip once and for all inside her nostrils. Paula hoped her father had a princess in the bushes, at least. For the time being she forgave him, and felt an accomplice in what she saw as his noble lechery.

The dog act came and went onstage, as did the Japanese jugglers, the ventriloquist and two singing sisters who had seen better days. Jimmy Kieron was whispering to his two cronies throughout these acts; he didn't like to watch dogs being tortured, it was one of his sentimentalities. His friends were locals, more or less: a cousin of his, who lived on the Cap not far from the Abimes' monstrous house, and his lover, who owned a restaurant. Jill was drunk, and gurgled gently to herself while watching the blurred stage. She was rather proud of her defiance in going to the gala separately tonight instead of playing bleeding gooseberry to the Abime ménage, nanny to the awkward girls, telephonist to Raoul, and spokeswoman for England to their friends.

Paula was even more bored than she had been at Charlé's table, but the idea of returning there did not tempt her. She waited patiently through the acts, wondering whether she would have a better view of Silvano at this table or her father's. Idly and without clapping, she watched as a handsome young man walked onto the stage. He was tall and young and his hair was daringly long for the place and the audience. He had a German name. He was a magician, but a magician without a cape, a top hat, or a moustache. Instead he wore a beige three-piece suit. Paula had a moment of sympathy for his probable discomfort locked into that vest, and a moment of interest when he announced that he was going to read the minds of members of the audience. She longed to have her mind read, and perked up. The magician demanded volunteers and gave his personal guarantee that they would not have to go up onstage. Paula lost interest. Not so Gladys Peddleby-Marsh, who began agitating a napkin from Charlé's table. The magician noticed her, but elected to divulge the secret thoughts of a round gentleman nearer the center of the arena. He concentrated with his hands on his eyes as the man stood up and remained still, watched intently by the women at his table.

"You are worried about your son," the magician said. The round gentleman shook his head emphatically. "Yes, yes," insisted the magician. "You wonder where he is and what he is doing." The round man burst out laughing, and so did the people around him. The magician looked bemused for an instant, then asked, "Was I correct? Would you tell the spectators if I was right?" The man was handed a microphone. "My son"—he said it in French—"is Silvano. And I'm wondering when he's going to come on!"

The audience laughed. Paula clapped, and waited for the next message from the telepathic wonder. It was to a woman in green who stood up at the very end of the room, and who, according to the magician, wished she had bet on number three. A moment of puzzlement was followed by vigorous nodding. "The third husband," she shouted with a firm conviction that needed no microphone. The audience clapped. The mind reader was gifted enough to divine a certain dissatisfaction in their applause, and with an imperious signal, sent the orchestra into an eerie Cha-cha-cha. "Now," he said in English, "I will take the most beautiful woman here away where no one can see her."

Paula looked at the other tables to see whom he would choose. That blonde? The one, like her, in white? A spotlight scanned the audience. It stopped on Paula. Jill, who had been having a quiet snooze, shielded her eyes rapidly. "What the fuck's going on?" she snorted. Paula stood up and dutifully made her way between the tables to the stage, where a waiter showed her the steps. The magician was beckoning, holding his hand out to her. She climbed up to him, unaware of any movement save his imperative direction toward the center of the stage. For motives best known to themselves the audience clapped, and although she was surprised, it was the kind of surprise with which one receives a present on one's birthday. *"Merci,"* she whispered. He winked at her. "This beautiful mademoiselle will now vanish." He pronounced it "vaneeshe."

At Charlé's table, Frank and Gladys were in paroxysms of delight. "Look at her, isn't she beautiful!" exclaimed Gladys. Charlé thanked her. Ian Gloskow wished she had touched up her makeup just a bit before going onstage, but kept the thought to himself. Frank looked appreciatively at the long legs and wished he were sitting just a touch nearer. That short skirt . . .

A box was wheeled onstage. "Oh Christ," said Jimmy Kieron. "If we haven't seen this a million times . . ." Jill gave him a smirk.

The box was six feet high, rectangular. Its armature was some sort of metal painted white, and it was made of clear glass, a fact which the magician demonstrated by stepping inside it for all to gaze upon him in his three-piece glory. He stepped out again. Paula, who had weathered thirty seconds of standing onstage alone with nothing better to do than watch him enter and leave the box, was feeling a little nervous. One of her sandals was coming undone again, and she could hardly bend down to do it up, as everyone would be able to see her fanny. To her relief, the magician stood facing her again, and taking her hand, he led her into the box to the strains of "Walk On By." He whispered in her ear as he helped her in, "You are the most beautiful, I have been watching you all evening." She felt herself blush. "Scared?" he said. She nodded. He turned to the audience. "This young woman is scared. So she should be. She is going where no one has ever been." Paula's face registered alarm, and he quickly hid it by standing directly in front of her. "There's nothing to be scared about," he whispered, and added, "What are you doing later?" She opened her mouth to speak, but he closed the glass door and she was locked into the booth. She saw him retreat to the apron of the stage, which had earlier been the dance floor, and heard him indistinctly through the glass. His voice sounded vaguely ominous. He turned toward her and waved his hands in the air. Tiny concealed bulbs lit up inside the box and suddenly she was blinded. She could still distinguish the audience, and she heard the loud clapping that greeted what must have been her disappearance.

Quickly she looked down at her arms, which were there; the hem of her dress, which was already coming undone; her feet. The lights made the box stifling, and the lack of air made her feel dizzy. She was beginning to hear a faint yet insistent buzzing in her ears when she discerned through the glare that the magician was approaching; he pulled the door open, allowing the heat to escape and be fanned by the warm damp air of the night. She started to walk out, but he shut the door a fraction. "Ladies and gentlemen," he said, "*vous voyez,* there is no one in there!" The audience applauded again, warmly this time. Paula began to dislike what was happening; she tried to signal her misgivings to her jailer, but he looked right through her, and whether that was a function of the illusion or simply professionalism on his part she couldn't tell. He shut the door tight once more. He saw me a second ago, he saw me, she reassured herself, and grabbed her elbows and felt the ring with the snake head on her finger; she stared down at her feet, which were looking a little washed out by the bright light. She felt the ringing in her ears again and wished she had stayed with Jill.

Charlé was watching with a look of tender concern on her face. At her own table, Jill was rocking herself back and forth, watching through lowered lids. Raoul slid in at the back of the room, and stood with his arm around a tall woman in an emerald-green sheath. "Do you like magicians?" she asked him. "I like it when they saw women in half," he answered.

Down by the bar the maître d'hôtel was searching for Eric Castiglione, whom the manager had specifically requested for the end of the magician act. "The girl's cute and she'll make a nice picture" had been the explanation. The maître d'hôtel did not enjoy being sent on missions rounding up drunk members of the press; he could not repress the urge to linger as he passed each table, an inquisitive smile on his face, a "*Tout va bien?*" hovering about his mouth. Therefore it took him a good twenty minutes to find Eric Castiglione, what with various guests calling out to him—"*Henri!*"—and assuring him that everything was *très bien.* Castiglione was standing against a pillar, talking with Raoul Abime, who was puffing on his pipe and occasionally knocking ash into an ashtray on a table whose occupants did not seem to mind. Eric Castiglione was experienced enough to know that he was about to be called upon by the summer management to pay for his free room, free dinners and free drinks. "*Oui?*" he said, cocking an eyebrow in a manner that only a man who had spent half his life with his left eye closed could master. "The stage," indicated Henri, "a photo." "*Je n'en doute pas,*" said Eric in tones of subtle irony—being rude to the employees of the company that provided him with his summer vacation was his only way of proving that he was his own man. "Your instruments?" asked Henri, who preferred not to use strictly technical terms when dealing with the tools of a profession for which he had not been trained. Castiglione reached into the pocket of his formal evening trousers and handed Henri a small red cloakroom ticket. He did not like walking around with a camera; that was something he could leave to the younger men, like Claude Azoulay; Eric Castiglione had dignity.

"Who're you going to do?" asked Raoul, squinting at the illuminated box onstage.

"The girl in there. She's pretty, *jeune fille,* Greek type. Want to come with me?"

Raoul said, "Why not," and then asked, *"Type grec?"*

Eric made the gesture of cutting off any protuberances from his chest and patted his own ass. "Flat," he said with a wink.

Eric Castiglione and Raoul arrived in the wings just as the magician ordered the lights back on in the house, and off in the box. Raoul saw Paula in profile inside the coffin, her head in her hands. You idiot, he thought, you're onstage, stand up straight and smile. He could not repress an angry gesture. Eric Castiglione, who was winding film into his Leica (he wasn't going to drag an assistant to the coast for three weeks; after all, he went to war alone), caught Raoul's pummeling on the elbow. "What is it?" he asked.

"My daughter, and she's behaving herself like a provincial."

"C'est Paula?" breathed Eric Castiglione, delighted. Father-daughter picture—Raoul Abime welcomes the child of Soula Tithe to the limelight —and she's his daughter—reunion on the coast (how was Eric to know that they were staying together? He rarely budged from Monte Carlo)— the cygnet grown up. "How old is she?" he asked.

Paula was being helped out of the box by the magician; the crowd was applauding vigorously. Her face glistened with sweat, but she stretched her neck regally as she took the magician's hand. What was happening was not entirely to her taste, but she was glad enough to have avoided dying in the box and decided to make the best of it now. She saluted the crowd with the smile of a survivor.

Eric propelled Raoul forward onto the stage. He turned back toward Eric, mouthing *"Merde,"* but the magician reached for him and dragged him to the center of the stage. The magician was still unaware of their identity and relationship, but long training in inhospitable beer cellars and the clubs of Geneva had taught him never to allow anything on his stage to look unplanned. Proudly he held out his hand to indicate Raoul, then Paula. "*Mesdames, messieurs,*" he intoned, "*ce soir j'ai la surprise de vos vies.*" He caught the eye of the bandleader, who was mouthing "*Anglais*" at him, and translated at once, which also gave him time to think. "Ladies and gentlemen, tonight the surprise of your life. I have brought onstage a man who is for this young woman—"

Right on cue, Paula said "Papa!"

The magician's finest hour came and went in the space of that second. As Paula and Raoul embraced, albeit a trifle gingerly, he thought that the gods had truly blessed him. To elevate the crowning moment of his career yet further, Eric Castiglione, the ace photographer from *Paris Match*, was there, at his feet, his camera a magic mirror. The magician gave a huge smile at the lens and put his arms around the man and his daughter as the curtain came down amid thunderous applause. Eric Castiglione waved him away; the framing he had, with the shirred drapes in the background, was almost an Oscar shot, and the magician didn't belong; he would not move, however, and the curtain came up again on the scene in time for the entire audience to witness Eric Castiglione gesturing rudely at the magician, who was finally forced to obey; he stepped to the left and disconsolately left the stage.

Charlé, who found herself standing on her chair screaming with delight, clambered down again when the photography session started and said to her friends and neighbors that she didn't know what had come over her; then she planted a fervent kiss on Gladys's cheek and on Frank's, and ordered another bottle of champagne. "Quite a surprise, eh?" asked Ian Gloskow, a master of the redundant, while Charlé repowdered her nose.

Onstage Paula watched her father for direction, as autonomy was obviously no longer possible. And yet, for all her deference, Raoul noticed with alarm that when Eric started snapping, Paula's eyes went automatically to the camera and her lips jutted out in an approximation of Soula's famous sulk. He tightened his hug a little to make her stop. She might have winced, but neither he nor the camera saw it. "Come on, let's do this in private at least," he whispered, and led her offstage when the curtains joined for a second time. "I hate publicity," he muttered to her as they reached the safety of the wings, but Eric Castiglione had followed them and was once more at their feet. "*Assez, Eric, merde,*" he said in a gruff but kindly voice. Eric shook his head and reloaded. "*La première page,* the cover!" he said.

Already the set for Silvano was being dragged onstage, with a great clunking of thick wooden amplifiers and a scuffling of sneakered stagehands' feet. "Let's go somewhere quiet," pleaded Raoul, but he was unheard. Eric held up his flash, then gave it to a stagehand to hold. Paula's eyes opened brightly for the twenty clicks that followed, and Raoul deposited his hands in a variety of unerogenous sites about her body.

A rising tide of props enveloped them; Silvano's show was, as the French say, *bien fourni,* and he performed onstage with umbrellas, hand puppets that he sang to, palm trees he stood under, a paper moon. Raoul took Paula's hand. "Enough now, we go back to the table. Eric, *ciao.*" Paula resisted him; she wanted to wait for Silvano, perhaps even brush against the famous silver jeans just an instant, and she was rewarded. The singer stood behind them, polite as a boarding-school boy, his thick black hair rising to a lacquered dome and falling away behind his ears in sheaves. Paula smiled at him, a truer smile than the one she had given the camera, a grateful smile, a young smile. He reciprocated. Raoul, impatient, tapped his foot and then decided to expedite matters. "*Silvano, bonne chance.* I'm Raoul Abime, and I'd like you to come to my table after your show. This is my daughter Paula."

"*'Soir,*" said Silvano. He was busy concentrating, but recognized Raoul from the fan magazines and didn't want to be rude to anyone who could help him. Not yet, at least. Also, he wanted to get onstage and they were blocking his way. He gave Paula a kiss on the cheek as he passed by, and Raoul was at last able to steer her back into the audience, where they joined Iris, who was staggering back from the ladies' room. Paula could not resist asking, "Did you see?" but Iris said sadly, with tears in her eyes, "No, I only just came back. What?" and Paula felt so well disposed toward poor unhappy Iris that she did not elaborate. With the Olympian charity of the fortunate, she said, "Nothing." They sat down next to each other while Charlé greeted Raoul with little claps, which provoked a series of angry ssh's from the people around them. Silvano had begun to sing.

Now, Silvano was not Aznavour by several long shots—he was twenty years younger and eight inches taller, with a voice whose principal charm was that it seemed to belong either to a castrato or to a boy whose balls were in the process of descending as he sang. But old women loved him no less than young girls did, for to young girls he was an androgynous peer and to old women he was the kept boy of their dreams. He sang of living together for the space of an afternoon, of taking the fast road to the other side of love, of losing a companion in the sandpile and finding an angel in the café fifteen years later. He gave nostalgia to youth, and handed youth over to the rueful nostalgia of the older generation, trussed and larded on a platter. Women wept.

Silvano arrived at the Abimes' table, after an ovation lasting several minutes and a triumphant progress through the auditorium. The curtains parted onstage to reveal the orchestra miraculously transported there, and the stage lit up from beneath and once more became a dance floor. Paula wriggled her shoulders out of her dress and leaned forward, once the necessary and inaudible introductions had been made. "You were wonderful," she said in French. *"Merci,"* he said, and kissed her hand.

Once they were home, the girls stayed on their balcony watching the sea turn pink for dawn, talking about Silvano and assessing their chances of meeting him again. "Of course," said Iris sleepily, crumbling the calamine lotion that was drying into its chalky nightly mask on her face, "you're the one he's *really* interested in." Paula tut-tutted the idea; she was removing the pink nail polish from her toes, where it had lingered all evening without once attracting the hostile attention of Charlé; she could not hope to have such luck last into the next day. "Nonsense, he liked you. Maybe we'll both see him again."

"But you're the one he talked to."

Paula was brimming over with love that night. "He saw *you*, too," she said. "All you had to do was talk to him."

The summer ended with sharp equinox winds whipping the flotsam onto the jetty, and Toinette screaming about migraines, and the cat that came with the house run over by Vivien Legrand, who had come to see Raoul about a film they were to do together. It was Vivien Legrand, furthermore, who informed them that *stallatico* meant a type of manure found in stables; an uncommon word, she said, but not a pleasant one. Charlé and the girls journeyed north by plane while Jill and Raoul took the train down to Rome, where Vivien Legrand and Alfonso Ercole were waiting for them.

At the Paris airport, Iris headed directly to the newsstand to buy the latest copies of *Elle* and *Marie Claire,* which were somehow unavailable in the South; and there she saw on the cover of *Paris Match* the photograph of Paula and Raoul that no one had remembered to mention to her. At first she was stunned to find her stepsister's image in a stack on a kiosk; then she was excited, breathless, amazed, even grateful, jealous only as an afterthought. Then she read the headline. *"La petite Soula Tithe avec son père Raoul Abime—tendre réunion."* Then she was indignant at the false information, righteous with superior knowledge. She took a magazine and slapped it on the counter. The newswoman looked up at her through half-moon glasses. *"Ça sera deux francs, ma petite,"* she said. Iris threw down two francs, then took three more copies of *Paris Match* and slapped them down on top of it. To the pile she added the *Elle,* the *Marie Claire,* a *Marie France,* a *Vingt-Ans* and a *Salut les Copains,* in case there was a picture of Silvano inside. *"Ohé, du calme, du calme,"* cautioned the woman.

Paula came up to Iris, and looked at the stack. "Did you get *Salut les Copains?*" she asked.

"You won't believe this, you won't bloody believe this!" blurted Iris. "You won't believe it!"

Paula looked at her in wonder. "You've forgotten your money?" she asked. Iris threw a ten-franc bill at the vendor and riffled through the covers until she found *Match,* and pulled it out. "Look!" she said. "Look!" Paula's face registered amazement, joy, an enchanted calm. "That's me and Raoul," she said, and, taking the magazine, held it up to Charlé, who was tottering along on new stiletto heels (purchased in Nice in the event that she should have to look up-to-date before she had a chance to go shopping), followed by two porters wheeling before them the annual booty of tar-stained couture bathing suits, torn batiste shirts and wrinkled Puccis, all encased in a burial mound of brightly padlocked beige Gucci luggage. "Oh," said Charlé, putting her hands to her mouth and clouting her chest with her brown alligator Hermès bag. "It's Raoul!"

"But look!" screamed Iris. "They've got your name wrong."

"*My* name?" asked Charlé.

"Mine, she means," said Paula, who was reading and rereading the cover lines with a puzzled expression. "They call me Soula Tithe."

"Oh, no!" cried Charlé. "How awful!"

"Come," said Iris with dignity, "Pierre must be waiting," and she led the way, leaving Paula and Charlé to pore over the cover in the middle of the arrival hall of Orly Airport like a pair of tourists examining a street map.

But in the car she sneaked at look at one of the other copies, which she kept beneath the *Marie Claire* that promised to unveil the future of its readers via the rediscovered method of the Arab horoscope.

Paula examined her own image critically, silently, she hoped with a professional eye. The mouth was almost right, but not quite. There was work to do there. And maybe Raoul had been right about the dress, after all—it seemed a little heavy in the picture. She was able to be critical and calm because, try as she might, she could not find anything in her image to offend her.

13.
Rough Personalities

The great Vivien Legrand was no longer young, but this did not stop her from behaving at times as if puberty lay in her future rather than in the far distant past. She had been married for seventeen years to Attico dell'Arco, a painter of Greek origins whose fame was to be, if anything, posthumous. They went their separate ways, Attico remaining in Positano, Vivien staying in hotels all over the world while she starred in films for which she had been hired to provide a gritty quality of reality. She was beautiful in the manner of a windswept monument, of a lush field two hours before harvest, of a storm at sea. She had, in her time, been called heraldic, hieratic, crude, barbaric, earthy (very often), a force of nature, and a gift from God. In her private life she managed to combine the qualities of hetaera and harridan, and it was her private life that influenced the lives of both Charlé and Paula, and to a certain extent that of Iris. Had it not been for her sudden all-consuming lust for Raoul Abime, Charlé's two-year exile in London, with all its consequences, might never have come about. Anyone with adult wits about them would have noticed after a week or two that Raoul was far from being a prize, and politely allowed time and careers to effect the necessary separation, which could later be deemed in sad tones "inevitable." Vivien Legrand, who had spent a lifetime nurturing and expanding an unbridled sensuality that brought her to the limits of polymorphous perversity, found Raoul such a fascinating and tricky object upon which to exercise her passions that she could not let go.

It had started in the lobby of the Grand Hotel in Rome. Raoul and Jill, edgy and restless from an endless trip on the *rapido* through the thigh of Italy, had retired to their suite upon arrival. Alfonso Ercole, Vivien Legrand's agent, had called to inform them that the meeting would take place in the suite at seven o'clock. Jill told him that sounded adequate. Needled by Jill's lack of enthusiasm, Alfonso told Vivien that, for a change, she could spend as long putting on her clothes as she needed to. "It doesn't matter if we are late, we have to show them who you are," he told her. Consequently, Vivien puttered around her villa on the Appia for several hours, made a few phone calls and generously killed time as the sun was setting. When it was dark, she finally sat down at her dressing table and began slapping her cheeks to bring some color to them. She had her maid pull out one of the black silk housedresses that Fabiani had made for her after a pattern copied from her own mother's favorite garment, and carefully buttoned it so that some portions of her blood-red silk slip remained visible. Taking an ivory-handled hairbrush, she tangled her hair with her head bent over, then snapped her head back so that an aureole of dark waves rose from her forehead like the snakes on the head of the Medusa. Grabbing a worn raffia basket, embroidered with now frayed woolen flowers and the word *Capri,* she signaled to her chauffeur that she was ready.

As she descended the stairs, Alfonso cried *"Brava!"*

"Do I look good?" she asked, one hand on her chest.

"Not only do you look wonderful," said Alfonso, "but it is also nine o'clock. Abime will be green. You are a genius."

Vivien gave a little snort of satisfaction and tossed her head. She might be the daughter of a concierge from Nice, but she was a star, and entitled to make people wait.

Jill told Raoul at eight-thirty that it was ridiculous to wait any longer. "You begin shooting in three days, anyway. You'll have plenty of time to see her, you know her already, so what's this silly meeting about?" she demanded. Raoul said nothing. He was sitting on the sofa near enough to a copy of *Time* magazine to have been reading it, but reading did not interest him. His large feet, shod in suede shoes with inadequately fine laces, rested on the coffee table. He was holding his pipe in his hand and staring into space. Knowing his moods, Jill busied herself with the lists of things she had to do while in Rome: the antique dealers to visit, the doctors to bribe, the assistants to round up, the reliable contessa to be tracked down. At nine she looked up from the heavily gilded desk and offered the thought that they might as well order up from room service, since the bloody woman obviously was not going to arrive.

"*Pas du tout,*" said Raoul. "Let's go out to dinner." He shook himself and rose. "We could go to George's, or that ridiculous place where they have pictures of failures all over the walls."

Jill was beset by sudden timidity. "What if she comes and finds we're gone?" she asked.

"*Tant pis.* I'll show her who's the boss. *Merde.*" This last was by way of encouragement.

Jill shook her head. "My hair's a mess. I should do something to it before we go out."

"You still won't win any beauty prizes, so just get your bag and *viens vite.* I don't want to be here when she comes." He hurried her out the door so fast that he left the key inside. Jill was well trained enough to exclaim that it was her fault when its absence was discovered in the lift. Raoul just nodded.

The concierge at the desk winked mechanically at Signor Abime. He remembered an incident a few years ago with the *poverina* Signora Abime, the first one, and a masseur, and he felt this entitled him to wink. Raoul took it as a mark of friendliness and, as was usual in these cases, offered a blank and surprised stare in return. Jill made a sign to the doorman, who bolted outside in search of a taxi; Raoul followed him to the door and stood jingling the multinational change in his pocket and looking at the neon sign across the street that said MAGYAR CUKRASZDA until he realized with distaste that it was the shopfront of a Hungarian pastry shop that Charlé always insisted on visiting on her rare trips to Rome. This unpleasant reminder of his domestic affiliations plunged him deeper into the gloom which his most recent holiday at the Villa Stallatico had left him in place of a suntan. Eight years ago, he thought, he had tried to elude the traps of romantic larceny by choosing a woman who appealed to him only in a limited area, and whose main function was to serve as mother to Paula. The small portion of his sexual taste that inclined to short redheads with thin bodies had remained constant, but Charlé had physically outgrown the mold that pleased him, and her other attributes, whose very unattractiveness he had originally counted as virtues in that they allowed him to feel at all times superior to her and thus immune to any sticky webs of affection she might seek to cast around him, were now at such a distance from what he considered tolerable that it took the greatest effort for him to refrain from hitting her every time she opened her mouth.

In long discussions with Szos he had sought to define the problem. "Marriage is an institution for morons and idealists. I am neither yet—right, Szos?" Szos nodded. "And except in the case of Soula, who was remarkable, I consider marriage as holy as dry cleaning and good cooking. A household convenience."

"What else?" added Szos, not as a question but as confirmation of the piercing veracity of Raoul's statement.

"Now, if you were to get married, you would understand perhaps a little better what I mean."

"Please," begged Szos, "leave me out of this."

"One does not exalt the duties of hygiene. One does not talk about the joys of ventilation, or accounting, or whatever else it is that *bon bourgeois* are supposed to do. One does not; I do not; the bourgeois do. They talk of little else. I've heard those women talking—with relish!—about quiches and *thé à l'anglaise,* about *régimes.* For them, it counts. For us, for us who make something, who care about deeper things, who wrestle with ideas, who have to prove . . ." He was clutching his napkin as he spoke, making it his unfathomable enemy, a world of undisclosed ideas, unscaled peaks, and unrealized creations. It was a slightly stained, much laundered piece of cotton damask, but Szos watched it, riveted to the symbol of every challenge to which he had failed to rise, every uncrossed, unburned bridge. "Yes," he muttered, "indeed."

"We have other things to do than occupy ourselves with smoothness, with surface. That's for maids, for carpenters. I must have danger!" He slapped the table. "Danger! insecurity, hunger, danger!"

"A minute," said Szos, fearing the worst. "You have to do the Vivien Legrand film first; it's signed and there is no changing plans now. Then there's the script that Mo Silverman is writing for you. Then once you've done that, you can take a few months off and have danger. But not right now, please, Raoul, think of—"

"What?" challenged Raoul. "My daughter? That's why I married that imbecile. No, Szos, it's time to think of me. I'm fifty. Fifty-one. That is old."

"Charlé is a good friend," interjected Szos, in a tone that shrank the statement down to the size of an irrelevant aside. Raoul, who always paid more attention to the tone of voice than what was actually being said—

an old habit left over from the days of post–synced sound—used the time to take a bite of bread and continued, "The danger I am talking about is an emotional danger."

"Where do you propose to find it?" asked Szos.

"Nowhere. That is why I am angry. I am fifty, it is all over; *baiser les nanas* doesn't interest me anymore, the only pleasure left is work."

Szos breathed a sigh of relief. This discontent was just another little luxury of Raoul's. He had never thought of his client as an idealist. It was odd what age did to a man.

"For myself," said Szos, summing himself up, "I long ago learned that nothing really very interesting was going to happen to me, so I decided to spend time with people who interested me, and make money out of them. My needs are simple. Some good conversation, occasional sex, decent food. That suffices."

"Conversation!" Raoul spat the word out like a profanity. "If I contented myself with conversation, I would not have the soul to make films. What if films were nothing but conversation, *hein,* Szos? Who would pay to watch two men talking about what's wrong with their lives? No one! The public wants to see tests, challenges, drama—drama is what society needs to expurgate its sin of failing to live. How can I give them drama, tied to the obligations of my daughter's education and the running of a ridiculous *faux château,* the mindless demands of my *arriviste* wife, a regiment of false values? How can I know anymore what it is to suffer, to need, to wish, to hope? How can I tell a story that will move people, when nothing moves me anymore?"

"Mo Silverman is a good writer, I think you can trust him" was all that Szos had to offer in the way of consolation.

Snatches of these conversations lingered in Raoul's brain as he stared at the Hungarian shopfront. He was embarrassed to have revealed himself to Szos as naïve, like an adolescent; but wasn't this unexpected surge of longing a sign that he was in fact as young as ever? A reassurance that all was not over? He might have been hard on Charlé: *dur avec elle, la pauvre,* what can she understand, after all? The neon sign flashed off. It was ten-thirty and Charlé was *après tout une conne.*

Jill stood waiting by the door of a tiny Fiat 600 taxicab, an insufficient vehicle if ever she had seen one. "Can't you get us anything better?" she demanded of the porter, who shook his head. "Raoul!" she cried, "Raoul!" He stirred from his spot and shambled toward the miniature taxi. As he was about to get in, a car drew up and Alfonso Ercole got out and ran past them in the direction of the lobby, followed by the statuesque and unbuttoned Vivien Legrand. Jill hissed, "It's them."

Raoul took her arm. "They can wait; I'm going to have dinner," he said.

"You can't," said Jill. "You simply can't. Go in there and say hello, at least."

Raoul looked at her with the hurt eyes of a betrayed senator. *"Et tu, quoque,"* he said, and turned on his heels and entered the hotel once again. Jill pushed five hundred lire at the driver and followed Raoul.

Alfonso Ercole was tapping on the concierge's desk with a rolled-up copy of *Novella 2000.* The concierge was looking mournful. Vivien Legrand was surveying the hall with the uncharmed attitude of a grand duchess bidden into a hovel. Raoul crept up behind them, noiseless on his crepe soles. Vivien Legrand whirled around, her flesh following the movement at a discreet interval. "You!" she said, and grabbing Alfonso's magazine, she hit Raoul on the cheek with it. Then she laughed. Her head went back, the Medusa curls tumbled, the middle button on her housedress flew open, the gold chains that encircled her neck rose and fell, while those that darted between the folds of silk and lace and flesh at her décolletage seemed to throb with the sound.

"You are several hours late, and Miss Adams and I were just going out to find some food."

"This is inexcusable," said Alfonso.

"Damn well is," added Jill. "Two hours late!"

"Caro!" screamed Vivien Legrand, dropping the magazine. "I have been waiting so long for this moment, and now you abandon me! You have no heart!" She wrapped her arms around Raoul and gave a loud sob into his jacket. Jill noticed that they were exactly the same height.

Raoul felt the humid silk and heaving body against him as an interesting form of offense, like being called an Algerian or being accused of theft. Vivien Legrand's operatic advance had nothing to do with him, but by being so gratuitous and generously futile, it amused him. He smiled.

"Why don't you ask them to come to dinner with us?" whispered Jill.

Raoul ignored her. "Now that you are here, what plans do you have?" he inquired of his star.

Vivien Legrand was looking at him carefully. He really looked much better at night. "Let us go upstairs and discuss everything," she commanded, excluding the other two.

"I'm hungry," said Jill, a trifle louder than she should have.

"Why don't you and Alphonse go eat dinner," said Raoul, his eyes fixed on Miss Legrand. "You have so many details to make lists of."

"That's right," said Vivien Legrand, "Raoul and I will take care of the essential things. Go, Alfonso. I'll see you later."

"Vivien, you look wonderful," said Raoul. His tone was rich, his voice sincere. Vivien was even more vulnerable to nuances of tone than Raoul, and felt her feelings toward him shift a little. She refrained from tossing her head and waited silently for the next compliment.

"You've gained a little weight, but it suits you," he said.

"Let us go up to the suite," she said.

"The key is inside. Go up to the second floor and get the maid to let you in. I'll be with you in a minute."

She looked surprised, an expression that so ill-suited her heroic features that Raoul was pleased. If he could still disconcert, there was hope. Shivering slightly, Vivien Legrand nodded. This had the elements of an interesting plot; it would have been beneath her as a *comédienne* and as a woman to ask where he was going or what he was going to do first, and how long it would take him. She turned on her high heels and went toward the elevators. A bellboy who had been observing the scene and knew enough French to have followed the conversation helpfully gave her the room number just as she stepped into the elevator. *"Trecento cinquanta sette,"* he said with a wink. Her hand came away from her rib cage, where it had been compressing her loudly beating heart, and slapped the bellboy on the cheek as the doors to the elevator closed. He was to treasure that day forever.

Alone in the hall, Raoul looked around. He considered having a drink at the bar; just sitting in a chair in the colonnade, eating a quick veal paillard in the hotel, going for a quiet walk. The veal paillard proved to be the most appealing idea, and he went out into the street to hail a cab. He would go down to the Grappolo d'Oro, where he and Soula had eaten so many times, and have a nice bowl of spaghetti with squid sauce and think about things. Miss Legrand could wait.

Which she did. She waited standing in front of the fireplace, where a pile of logs belied the fact that the flue had been closed up years before. She looked at herself in the mirror, lay on the sofa, picked up a newspaper, looked in Jill's briefcase, grew bored, restless, angry and, finally, panicked. She decided to go back to the Appia; she phoned downstairs to discover that her driver had left with Signor Ercole and the *signora inglese,* swore at the concierge and hung up. She decided that leaving was cowardly, an admission of defeat, almost as bad as staying. She resented the hungry flush of expectation that Raoul had cast her into; her position was untenable. Grabbing her straw bag, she marched to the door and slammed it shut behind her, an act that she regretted at once, as she was not sure that she wanted to leave and she did not care to ask the maid to let her in one more time. She felt hungry, more for sex than for food. Majestic and unstoppable, she sailed down the corridor, took the magnificent stairway and descended into the hall. There she went to the reception desk and demanded the best suite. *"L'appartamento imperiale, quello per i cardinali o i re,"* she ordered, tapping her unpolished fingernails on the polished mahogany of the counter. She was led to the second-best suite, which she found to her liking; it was three times the size of Raoul's. She tipped Dario, the young manager, with a pat on the shoulder, rang for room service, and when the waiter arrived holding the tall white menu card, she took it out of his hand, threw it on the floor and led him to the bed in the cream-and-gold bedroom.

He wasn't the best-looking young waiter in the world—a little scrawny, with a speech impediment and a rash on the small of his back. These details didn't bother Vivien Legrand in the least; all she wanted was a little snack, to take the edge off her appetite and give her strength for the next round.

At the Grappolo d'Oro, Raoul picked at some winkles in garlic sauce and thought about revolutions, dead friends, the paucity of life. He did not think about emotional danger anymore. Some unconscious part of him had apprehended the outcome of his relations with Vivien Legrand, and therefore cut off any coherent signals about them. He was in his usual state of mordant sentimentality, which in a man who so loudly professed disgust for all manifestations of romanticism took the form of cynical despair. Paula had inherited it, but in her it was tempered by a faith in the future. Raoul's future, as far as he could see, was in his past, ruined (*Abimé,* he thought in French, *abimé par Abime*) by deaths and made unclear by layers of disillusionment. He ate a peach, but it was late in the year for peaches and he found nò pleasure in it. The only thing that pleased him was thinking of the awkward lies Jill and that silly operetta agent must be telling each other. Even the prospect of a furious Vivien Legrand was only mildly amusing. He considered the discord that would rule the shooting, thought briefly about the script—a nonsensical affair about a fishwife who inherits a whorehouse in Rome and becomes a marchesa—and ordered a Sambuca.

Jill and Alfonso Ercole arrived back at the hotel long before Raoul. Alfonso was surprised to learn that his client had taken a suite there, but not at all surprised that she would not take his call from the lobby. He let her chauffeur drive him home.

Raoul was handed his key at the desk and wondered how it had gotten there; he deduced that Vivien Legrand must have left in a huff, and decided that she was not as strong as he had hoped.

Hardly had he slipped himself between the fine batiste sheets of his bed than the telephone rang. Smiling, he waited for Jill to answer it; he heard her grumbling from across the living room that it was his line and not hers, and couldn't he pick it up? He reached out an arm and did so. A voluminous *"Caro!"* assaulted his ears.

"Ah, Vivien," he said. "How enchanting to hear your voice."

"Where are you? I am waiting," she said. Her tone was slightly bored.

"I'm in bed," he announced, sitting up.

"So am I," she said and hung up. He was a trifle puzzled, but cheered. At least she was fighting. Charlé would have been in tears hours ago. He turned off the light.

A knock resounded at the living-room door. He shouted for Jill, but got no response. A voice on the other side of the door shouted *"Permesso!"* —more a warning than a question; a key rummaged in the door, and a waiter arrived at the door to his room. Raoul glared at him.

The waiter was carrying with some difficulty a jeroboam of champagne in a huge bucket. Raoul shook his head. *"Sì, sì,"* said the waiter, a young man. The *"sì"* came out of his mouth in a cloud of spittle. He heaved the bucket onto the marble-topped chest of drawers by the windows. Raoul tried to explain that the management had already sent their champagne to him hours ago, there had to be a mistake, the champagne was in the *salone,* the boy could go see for himself. Shaking his head, the waiter opened the monstrous bottle and poured a glass—one of two that were on the tray—and brought it over to Raoul. In the warm glow of the bedside lamp, Raoul saw something glitter at the waiter's neck. Chains. He thought as he reluctantly took the glass that it was shocking for the hotel to allow its employees to dress like Folies Bergère dancers. Then he remembered the chains from Vivien's neck, beckoned the boy back and reached for the necklace. The waiter produced a piece of paper from his pocket. On it was written "140." Nothing else. Raoul took three hundred lire from the bedside table (he was always a poor tipper) and waved them at the boy. They were refused, and the waiter left the room. Raoul took a sip of champagne, swung his legs over the side of the bed and began to laugh.

There was some doubt about the sincerity of the gesture; indeed, the bottle was too big, the provenance of the waiter's chains was murky; Raoul reached for the phone to ask the concierge to verify Vivien Legrand's presence on the premises, but thought better of it. Rising, he went to his traveling bag and extracted from it a toothbrush. He carried this to Jill's room, where he knocked on the door. There was no sound. Annoyed, he pushed the door open. Jill was sitting up in bed, reading *Variety* and frowning. She looked up, hopeful, and put the paper down, instinctively making room for Raoul on the bed. "Did you have a good evening?" she asked, in her own version of sweetness.

Raoul waved the toothbrush and stayed on his feet by her side. "There's a terrible problem," he explained.

"Oh dear!" Jill's hands flew up to her face. If her professional mode consisted in remaining unflappable, at private moments that she hoped would also be personal she took on the attributes of shrinking frailty. Raoul continued, "It's Vivien Legrand. You have to help me patch something up, or the film will be a disaster."

"Anything, what is it?"

"She left this in my room. You have to take it to her." He held up the toothbrush.

"But she lives out on the Appia!"

He shook his head. "She's in room one-forty. I can't explain it all now—just bring this down to her." Jill got out of bed and pulled on her dressing gown, telling herself in no uncertain terms that she was a ninny to have expected anything else. She grabbed a little brutally for the toothbrush, and received a kiss on her head from Raoul. "Then what do I do?" she asked a little crossly. "Watch her brush her teeth?" Raoul said nothing and padded back to his room.

Vivien Legrand was waiting for the knock on her door, and had positioned herself in the salon of her suite. She was not expecting Jill, whose personal aesthetics were jolted by the sight of an enormous and quite naked woman with curls of hair cascading down her shoulders. Jill mustered a "Good evening" out of her own good breeding, while Vivien could not repress a violent exclamation of "*Connasse.*" The two women stared each other down. Vivien Legrand did not bother to cover herself, and alleviated the "*connasse*" with a somewhat predatory smile. Jill stuck the toothbrush out in front of her as she might brandish a crucifix at a vampire. "This is yours, Raoul says," she announced, and turned on her slippered heels and proceeded up the hall to the elevators. In her suite Vivien Legrand sat down to consider the toothbrush.

It was a definite deadlock. Alarmingly discomfited, she went to the mirror over the mantelpiece and imagined herself as Anna Magnani; she flared her nostrils and made a fist, which she shook at the mirror. Being French rather than Italian, a detail that had often been overlooked by those who employed her, she shouted "*Imbécile!*" at herself. In moments of stress such as this, she reverted to her own nationality for the simple reason that, as a Frenchwoman, she was unique and unbeatable. As an Italian, she was just one of a slew of imposing fortyish sluts. She sat on the damask-covered armchair and began to think.

Back in Raoul's suite, Jill hissed to him that if he ever made her confront a naked giantess again, she would leave him. "Tell me," asked Raoul, managing to convey indifference, "was she wearing chains around her neck?"

"Nothing at all but a lot of hair!" screamed Jill. "Hairy bush and hairy armpits, revolting woman!"

Raoul was delighted that his hunch about the chains had been correct. Jill was still standing in the doorway of his room, and he wondered if he should comfort her in the usual way. But next to the prospect of measuring himself against his titanic adversary, Jill seemed dull and familiar; and anyway, he reasoned, as he bade her a definitive good-night, the night was not yet over. He picked up the phone and called room 220.

There was no answer. He hung up, then tried again a minute later, sipping his champagne. Still no answer. He heard a knock on the door of the *salone.* Quickly he heaved first the jeroboam and then the bucket into his closet, put the tray under the bed, and shoved the glasses behind the curtains. Then he slowly crossed the room and went to open the door. Vivien stood there, fully dressed. "Are you going somewhere?" he asked.

"Ask me in for a drink," she said, and swept past him through the dark living room into the bedroom, where the light was pink and welcoming. Raoul followed, hanging back slightly. Vivien Legrand scanned the room. Raoul passed in front of her, went into the bathroom, filled a tumbler with water, and carried it back to her.

"You were thirsty?" he inquired, handing her the glass.

She looked at the glass, with its opaque pale-pink streaks from Raoul's mouthwash, and took it without missing a beat; she abruptly crossed in front of him and entered the bathroom. Raoul followed. At the sink she turned toward him, and taking the toothbrush from her bra, where it was stuck like a dinner-table rose, she opened the tube of dentifrice that lay on the ledge and carefully squeezed half an inch of the stuff onto the brush. As Raoul watched, she carefully and vigorously brushed her teeth, rinsed her mouth with the glass of water he had given her, and then broke the glass in the sink. Then she took Raoul's razor—a gold-plated Gillette safety model—ran the hot water, picked up the tube of shaving cream and handed it to him. "I don't like rough cheeks," she said. Raoul obediently went to the sink and shaved his chin. He glanced at her as he did so, glad to be amused. When he finished he turned to her, but she was already in the bedroom.

"*Assez,*" she said from the bed. "Let's be serious now for a few minutes."

The hygienic prelude was eminently in the spirit of contradiction that had ruled the evening, for it was followed by acts of such utter and rank carnality that at times Raoul imagined he was sinking into an abyss of feminine effluvia, exhalations and emissions beyond his wettest dreams, parcels of flesh taking body and then, seemingly, taking root beneath his hands, his groin, his mouth, his entire body contained, absorbed and then rejected in spasms and enfolded again, consumed, sucked in, torn at, pounded on. It was exhausting; once or twice he attempted to tell her his age, to suggest a certain restraint to the hungry animal in his bed, but was silenced by little slaps on his mouth. After much heaving and groaning, and seismic cantering from Vivien Legrand, Raoul came. This made a nice change for him, and as he fell face first into a satiated and gloomless sleep, he had a second to reflect that he felt oddly content.

Vivien Legrand could not go to sleep immediately. She turned on the lamp, which she had been careful to switch off before Raoul came to bed, and went to wash herself in the bidet. This was a habit she clung to because it allowed her leisure to be alone and think after moments of intimacy, which is how she thought of sex. Straddling the cold china and splashing herself with Aqua Velva soap, she decided that it would be impractical for her to continue visiting Raoul at the hotel; she was sure that the lobby was already full of *paparazzi.* Nor did she want him to have to commute out to the Appia; directing a film was hard enough without an extra hour in the car every evening, and she didn't want an exhausted director in bed or on the set. It was simplest if she kept him at the house. There would be no problem with Attico, and the secretary woman would be useful for teaching her English. Delighted with her arrangement, she dried herself carefully and returned to bed.

Before Raoul awoke she had called the driver and the maid and arranged for the transfer of Monsieur Abime out to the Appia. She dressed and ordered breakfast for herself and Jill in the *salone;* when it arrived, she tipped the waiter (who knew all about his second-floor colleague's wild night, and hovered suggestively by the door until she hit him on the bottom with a cushion to speed his exit) and went to Jill's door. "*Cara!*" she cried. "Breakfast! *Il caffè!*" Jill peered at her through the half-shut door. Vivien planted a kiss on her cheek. "Come," she said, leading Jill into the living room and sitting her down at the rolling table. "We have so much to talk about. What sign are you?"

Before the day was out, a bemused Raoul and a delighted Jill were installed in a rambling house at the end of an alley of cypresses, just beyond the tomb of Cecilia Metella on the Via Appia Antica. Raoul had not expected, much less actually desired, this turn of events, but the house seemed a comfortable place to be, despite some atrocious paintings in ochre and black which Jill knew to be Attico dell'Arco works and upon which she politely refrained from commenting. Vivien Legrand was full of benevolence that day; she wept when Raoul attempted to explain that he had a daughter to think of, tore her hair out when Jill said the telephone didn't seem to be working too well, and kept quiet when Charlé's name came up. She told Jill that she had *"il biondo Tiziano"* hair, which no one had ever told Jill before for the good reason that she didn't. She told Raoul that she had known at once he was a Taurus, because he had real balls. She ordered roses put in Jill's room and had a pipe rack fetched from Rome for Raoul's traveling collection of pipes. Raoul was in a daze, which he interpreted as resignation; he could as well have called it happiness, but that was not the kind of thing he liked to admit, even to himself. While Vivien was having her pre-dinner bath he sat with Jill in the living room, in front of an unseasonably roaring fire, drinking brandy and soda. "I . . ." he began uncertainly.

"It's all right," said Jill, a touch impatient.

"You see, it's—"

"For the best," said Jill, willing "it" to last.

He looked into the fire. "What can I say?" he asked. "It's *force majeure.* She is definitely *force majeure.*"

Information about the shocking liaison spread from paper to paper according to the principle of communication between vessels, but the news did not reach Paris at once. The delay allowed Charlé and the girls to settle back into the Château Rose, secure in the belief that life was to go on as before. This hope began to crumble as Paula's picture on the cover of *Paris Match* incited a score of publications to track her down and invite her to be photographed for their pages. The first three sets of pictures were taken by Eric Castiglione, who did not want to let go of his discovery. Paula assumed that this meant he was in love with her, and allowed him to take her out to dinner. Unfortunately, Iris accompanied them and talked incessantly throughout the meal, amusing Eric but ruining the seductive atmosphere that Paula had hoped for.

Charlé took Iris shopping, and they returned to the Château Rose each afternoon laden with corduroy culottes, skirts, ribbed sweaters, suede suits fashioned like blue jeans. These extensive purchases dimmed in Iris's eyes next to Paula's little souvenirs of her days posing for *Elle,* the plastic brooches and chenille scarves that she would leave casually on the bed, and which Iris would pick up and finger longingly as artifacts of a distant place too hermetic and fabulous to be accurately described.

Charlé invited Eric Castiglione out to the house for drinks: a peculiar invitation requiring one and a half hours of driving at peak rush hour for a single glass of vodka. She wanted to tell him not to let this magazine thing go too far for Paula, as the girl had a school year ahead of her, exams to pass, a future to think about. Paula and Iris listened as Charlé spoke, both gazing at Eric with longing eyes. Iris wondered what the chances were of his needing an assistant; Paula, how long it would take for him to try to seduce her.

It was perhaps Charlé's ill-conceived invitation that prompted Eric to call Raoul in Rome and offer his services for a *Grand Reportage* on Vivien Legrand.

Raoul was delighted to have Eric act as the executioner of his marriage. The Italian gossip rags had printed wild surmise; their habitual conjecture was considered questionable even by the laundresses, novice nuns and schoolgirls for whom it was written, and Raoul wanted the irrefutable stamp of *Paris Match* on his new liaison. Eric followed them around Rome, catching shots of Raoul steering the towering Vivien into restaurants, into cars, along the ilex-bordered walk of her house on the Appia. These were better than the *paparazzi*'s shots, where her face was often obscured by one of her baskets held up to shield her from the flash, Raoul's back was turned to the camera, and the close-ups of them showed open-mouthed surprise—an unincriminating emotion. Eric's were full of the gross animal feeling that bound Vivien to Raoul.

To Eric's chagrin, *Paris Match* did not publish all his photos, and he ended up selling the rejects to the popular evening papers in both France and Italy. So it was that, two weeks after the return to the Château Rose, Charlé found herself in the space of a day confronted with nine different reports of Raoul's infidelity. She tried to reach him in Rome, but the Grand Hotel said he had checked out long ago. She sent a telegram to Alfonso Ercole, asking him to intercede on her behalf: Ercole wired back that he could do nothing when it came to affairs of the heart. Raging, and surprised at the speed of her actions, she booked three seats to London for herself and the girls. Iris was excited to be running away; Paula protested that Charlé was not her mother and that she could very well stay in the Château Rose alone and continue her career as a model until the first day of school, when, she swore, she would of course resume her studies. Charlé insisted that Paula come with her; she thought of the girl as a useful hostage, and argued that Paula was too young to live alone in what she called "the country."

In the excitement of packing and stealing tranquilizers from Charlé's bathroom to give Paula, who was having hysterics in her pavilion in the garden and threatening to fly to Rome to join her father, Iris forgot to make the ritual tour through the Château Rose that preceded her other, calmer departures. She did not go up to the dining room to bid good-bye to the Moor, and only remembered him in the middle of the night. It was too late and she was too tired to get up and walk through the house to perform this rite, and she felt that the Moor would not mind. She was sure they would be back within a few weeks when the whole thing had blown over.

Szos went down to Rome, where the expansive Vivien invited him to stay at her house. He declined, knowing how difficult it was to persuade young men to accompany him all the way out to the Appia for the night. They asked for ludicrously inflated carfare back to Rome. He visited the set, however, and came to dine every night. Raoul was benign, having at last met his match. Jill, not yet having discovered Vivien's weaknesses, was on her best behavior.

Raoul took Szos walking toward the swimming pool in the warm September night. "Well? Will it last?" asked Szos, to remind Raoul that he had seen them come and go.

"I don't think so," said Raoul. "That's why I'm enjoying it."

Clever woman, thought Szos.

14.
London Life

Unlike their flight from the insurrection of 1961, this trip was badly planned. There was no one to meet them at the airport, no kind Mr. Barnes with his Daimler, and no Arbuthnot-Lewis mews house to stay in. Charlé checked into the Westbury, a hotel the girls had never heard of. Iris set about making their rooms look interesting by draping her scarves over the pleated chiffon lampshades and throwing Charlé's on the high backs of wing chairs. Paula remained prostrate on the linden-green coverlet of her bed in an attitude of absolute dejection. Charlé started phoning her friends—Dara Devenish first, then Frantwell, who could still serve some purpose, Jimmy Kieron, the Lewises at their country seat. As she filled her little Hermès date book with lunches and dinners for the months ahead, the vengeful misery that had taken possession of her yielded to a new ambition, that of conquering London.

The girls were enrolled at the Lycée. Despite Paula's poor record, the fact that they were transferring from a superior institution in the homeland assisted them in gaining immediate entry into the class of Première, where they would study for their *bachot* just as if they had never left Saint-Germain-en-Laye. With an efficient dispatch born of panic, Charlé found a rental agent and, through him, an apartment in less than a week, and sent for Mauricette, whose loyalty was her newest and single remaining article of faith. Julie was abandoned to the devices and whims of Matilde, the Saint-Germain-en-Laye cook. When Iris protested, Charlé snapped back bitterly from the couch, where she had her feet up before an evening at the theater with Dara Devenish, that Julie was nothing but a star-struck little cow who deserved everything she had coming to her. "She was my first nanny," sobbed Iris, heaving dramatically.

"She was not," snapped her mother. "Your first nanny was a fat Negro woman called Hannah. "When I was still with your lovely father, Tyler . . ." Oh no, thought Iris, she's going to start that again.

Paula, after sinking into a catatonic despondency that had led to the loss of a few pounds and meant that she was now flatter than ever, rallied for two reasons. First, Raoul called her the second night they were in London, a person-to-person call, which flattered her because she did not realize its purpose was to ensure that he did not have to trade words with Charlé; he had assured her that whatever happened he would always be her father, a fact she had not doubted for one second but of which it was nonetheless pleasant to be reminded; he had added that Vivien's house in Rome had a room that was being prepared especially for her. In view of the delicacy of the situation, Paula did not inquire whether there was room for Iris there as well; she was old enough to know that the protagonists in a steamy affair of the senses had no mind left to think about extra beds for people who weren't even relations. She kept quiet to Iris and Charlé about the substance of the phone calls.

The second reason had to do with her career. She had realized dimly that London had become interesting in the past year; certainly the clothes there were nicer, cheaper and more amusing than those in Paris, and there were the Beatles, although, strictly speaking and as everyone knew, they came from Liverpool. But she had not known until they arrived that London had the potential to become the center of the world. On their first day there the girls had gone to Abingdon Road, drawn by the unquestionable magnet of a tiny shop called Biba's. They knew about Biba's because among the pre-debutantes in Paris and even in Saint-Germain-en-Laye its reputation was established as *le seul endroit.* Paula had looked so exquisitely tall and flat in the little striped dresses, so mysterious in the crochet cloche hats, that the manageress, a girl whose aspirations to flatness were dashed by a pair of unsightly protuberances on her chest, had automatically called up a reporter and photographer friend from the *Sun.* The photographer's nimble patter convinced Paula, who needed some instruction as to vocabulary, that she was truly a dolly bird, quite fab, and really switched on. Crowned with these epithets, Paula managed to persuade Iris to stay in the shop until the last dress had been photographed; she was particularly attached to the stark black-and-white broad stripes of three yards of curtain fabric that passed as an evening gown.

They moved into the apartment, which was decently situated on the south side of Eaton Square. The front hall smelled of tapioca pudding, even if it was 1966. For decoration the landlord had provided a red carpet, a marble bust of an obscure senator with short spit curls licking at his impassive face, a mirror trimmed in thin gold leaf, and a table with turned-out legs that made it look like a drunk on all fours. On this table lay some forlorn bills addressed to such dreary-sounding people as "Miss E. Hatchett" and "Reginald Lofting, Esq." Paula picked them up and threw them down again, disappointed. Her experience at Biba's had left her with the certainty that London was full of interesting people who were longing to meet her; her neighbors' names canceled two out before she even began. The pictures in the *Sun* weren't out yet, and she found herself stilling all thought, more or less as she did in front of the camera, so as to speed them safely through to publication. Iris, standing in the hall while Charlé told a shirt-sleeved porter where to put the bags and to please hold the lift, was seized by a precise and ineradicable view of her future, which she knew to be the size, shape and color of that grim, staid hall.

The flat was under the roof, low-ceilinged, but extensive. Net curtains blotted the already scant light from the windows, and everything inside looked faded. The gray-green sofas in the drawing room, the pale blue-gray bedcovers in the second bedroom, which was to be the girls', the exhausted primrose of the main bedroom's fabrics, all conspired to make the place looked used, bled of life. Everything that was not dyed a halfhearted shade was sharply polished wood, dark almost to blackness, fashioned into such novel items as telephone tables, butler's tables, sideboards and trolleys.

"Ça manque de mystère," declared Paula.

"I think she must think it's aristocratic, or something," announced Iris, in an act of betrayal toward her mother, whose taste she tended to follow in all matters. She felt unreasonably proud of this rebellion.

In the bedroom, Paula found an old copy of the *Weekend Telegraph Magazine* and began reading with laborious pleasure, spelling out the occasional word aloud. "What is it?" asked Iris. Paula sat up on the bed and said, "Listen to this: 'London is where the action is, the gayest, most un . . . un . . . un-in-ee-bee'—*merde*—'the most, and in a wholly new, very modern sense, the most coolly elegant city in the world.' " She let out a relieved sigh, closed the magazine, and smiled at Iris. "I think it's wonderful that we're here. We'll probably meet the Beatles, and I can't wait to make the scene."

"Make the scene? Go onstage? You're going to act, suddenly?"

"Make the scene. Be groovy. It's what that man from the *Sun* said. You have to make the scene."

Iris sat down next to Paula and looked at her gravely. "I don't think you should start going out with every photographer that you meet. Famous reporters from *Paris Match* are one thing, I mean, that's interesting, but some man from a newspaper *populaire* is different. You must remember who you—"

"Iris," Paula interrupted. "You're in London now, don't you think you should start speaking English?"

The pictures came out in the *Sun* at the end of their first week at Eaton Square. Charlé had been puzzled by Paula's insistence that the porter bring them this ratty little paper with its headlines about Harold. When Iris brought her the double-page spread of Paula, entitled "Paris Dolly Digs Groovy Boutique Scene," she understood it was imperative that she take Paula's career in hand at once. Offering her stepdaughter the first official gin and tonic of her life, she sat her down for what she deemed an important chat, but was in fact a rambling diatribe in which she extolled her own love for Raoul and bemoaned the speed with which times were changing. Paula was bewildered, but allowed her to draw arcane parallels between the practiced perfection of French couture and the wild youthful spirit of English miniskirts, which she then applied as symbols of the old life they were leaving behind and the brave new country they had come to. Paula, who had less of an attachment to clothes than either Charlé or Iris, found some difficulty in following her line of reasoning, but sensed that Charlé had some surprise planned. She was right.

The day before they were to begin school, when Iris had already bought all the *cahiers* for both of them at a small shop that supplied French notebooks to the Lycée, Charlé took the girls to lunch at the Connaught with Dara Devenish. Paula thought Dara was probably a terrible lesbian, because she stared at women the whole time and always tried to kiss her near the mouth. In fact Dara was merely shortsighted and ill coordinated, but Paula would not countenance these weaknesses as explanations.

Dara was waiting for them when they arrived, wearing the sort of coat a highwayman might choose if he planned to go to the moon; it was made of a silvery plastic that crackled when she moved her arms. She had refused to surrender it to the cloakroom because underneath she still had on an old flowered pinafore she wore to weed the flower beds in; she'd been doing a spot of autumn tidying in the garden, and figured that if she kept her new coat on she wouldn't have to change underneath. Her hair, which was reddish, had been pinned up on top of her head with what she knew to be haste but which Charlé took for the unmistakable style of the truly confident; it tumbled and writhed across a regiment of little skewers, down to her shoulders. Dara saw Charlé come in in her square-cut short white coat which showed a great deal more than her knees, followed by the two girls, one of whom at least seemed to have become quite grown up. "What courage!" she said to her hostess as she sat down, to which Charlé replied, "Courrèges." "I know," said Dara, "that's what I meant. Not for me, all that boxy stuff. Now, what shall we drink? My, Paula, you look fabulous or should I say 'fab'?"

Paula squirmed, and was reproved by a look from Charlé, who immediately brought up the object of the lunch.

"You saw the *Sun*, of course," she began. Dara frowned. "You mean that beastly new rag that taxi drivers read? Never touch it." Charlé quickly took the folded pages from her bag and gave them to Dara, who nodded appreciatively once she had put on her glasses. "Very pretty," she told Paula, who thanked her with lowered lids, not wanting to risk one of Dara's long lingering looks. Iris finished the melba toast.

"Well, you see," said Charlé. "I think it's an awful pity to waste Paula on a paper like that. I was wondering about your goddaughter. She could help."

"You mean Sally, at *Vogue.* It's no problem, dear. In fact, had I seen what Paula looks like these days I'd have suggested it myself."

"What does Sally do?" asked Iris.

"Personalities. Of course you're the one with the personality, but when *Vogue* say 'personality' they mean long legs and a name, so you're out. They'll be mad for Paula."

Iris was flattered to be told she had a personality when all she had ever been credited with were bad moods. Paula knew exactly what a personality meant, and was glad to be deemed devoid of it: bushy eyebrows, fat thighs, and an uneven and resentful temperament. She ordered a plain grilled sole, in case there were photographers in her future.

After lunch Dara swept off to make a phone call from the ladies' room while Charlé squeezed Paula's hand. "See what I do for you?" she whispered. Iris ate her bread-and-butter pudding and pretended she was deaf.

Five minutes later Dara sailed back to the table. "She's there, and I'm going to take Paula over right now. C'mon, stringbean, we're off. Thanks for the grub, Charlie. I'll be on the blower later with all the gory details."

Dara Devenish and her coat swept through the fifth-floor corridor of *Vogue* like an invading army, Paula trailing behind in the role of the spoils. Sally the goddaughter was found sitting at a desk piled high with paper, cards, gloves and shoes. She was a tall plump girl with reading glasses shoved on top of her back-combed honey-blond hair. Her columnar legs were encased in high black patent boots, much higher than any Paula had seen in Paris, and her body was the battlefield for opposing camps of black and white stripes. "Well!" she screeched as Dara and Paula stood at the door. "Come in! I'm on the phone to Paris, bloody collections, but I'll be off in a tic. Grab a pew." Various other females who were folding garments around her stared curiously at Paula; they had seen Dara many times before, and although the presence of Lord Devenish's ex-wife was always the seal of social approval, they didn't much care for social approval and she truly looked a fright. An older woman shushed Sally from a distant desk, and then rose to examine Paula more carefully. Paula's leather jacket had a gamin air that she rather enjoyed; taking a checked barrow boy's cap from a pile of hats near the door, she shoved it on Paula's head without any ceremony. "Hello Dara dear," she murmured. "Where did you find this sweet, sweet face?"

"She's my discovery," said Dara. "How's Alfred?"

"Sick with fright. He's standing for the seat that just fell vacant when old Borrington toppled off the branch in Twickenham last month, and his agent says if he doesn't get in this time he'll have to resign from the rolls."

Paula didn't understand a word, and decided that if she was called upon to comment on this impenetrable string of circumstances, she would have to pretend to be French. Dara would just have to understand. Sally hung up the phone, screaming, "Silly frogs, I could murder them all." Paula quickly abandoned the option of being French, but luckily Dara and the woman carried on as if Paula were deaf and mute.

"So! This is her! Dara told me who you were," said Sally, rising to shake Paula's hand, "and I'm Sally Meadows. I do the personalities; I say, I must tell you we're all crazy about your mother here. Look!" As she spoke she pulled several sheets of paper off the pinboard that covered one wall, and revealed a studio picture of Soula Tithe, thinly veiled and heavily lashed, in her early role of Onoria in the epic *Huns of Italy*. Paula gasped: she was shocked and elated to find the familiar picture of her mother, a jeweled hand resting on her shoulder, in these foreign surroundings. She went up to the picture to touch it, but Sally warned her off. "Fingermarks, you know, simply impossible to get off." Paula let her fingers hover near the surface of the shiny print just to annoy Sally, and to state her symbolic ownership of the picture. "There's quite a vogue of her coming back, you know," continued Sally. "Although Dietrich is far more popular, really, because they showed *Shanghai Express* last spring on the BBC, and the following week there wasn't a boutique around that didn't have black feathers and little beaded skullcaps. But Soula Tithe, well, it's a more subtle sort of allure, because—"

"Oh Sally, shut up!" said Dara, who had quite exhausted the subject of Alfred's political career.

"Tell me, Paula," whinnied Sally, raising her voice, undaunted. "Would you like to do some pictures?" Paula said nothing. She thought how much easier it was to deal with men, really; they simply told you what they wanted to do and steered you into it. She cast around the room hoping to see a man lurking somewhere, and, failing to find one, looked back at Sally and nodded her head.

"Good! We're just about to do all the Christmas issue, fucking late, but we can't help it."

"Sally, your language is impossible," sniffed Dara, who had been going through the correspondence on her goddaughter's desk, adding, "What dreadful things you get invited to! Openings of clubs and pubs and launchings of cars! No wonder you're such a wreck whenever I see you."

Sally motioned to Paula to sit down, and took a sheet of paper and asked her to write down her vital statistics. "I don't know them in inches," said Paula. "Will meters do?"

Sally looked at her body. "You're nice and flat-chested, and you've got great legs. Just write down your dress size, which must be eight, and your shoe size, that's all that matters. Have you ever done this before?"

"Oh, I've modeled quite a lot," said Paula. "*Elle*, mostly."

"What issues?" asked Sally beadily. "I've never seen you before, and I've got total recall about photographs, really I do."

"Oh," said Paula casually, "the cover of *Match* last month, and *Elle* comes out about three weeks from now. And then—"

"Sally," said Dara. "I didn't bring Paula Abime, the stepdaughter of my closest friend, here so that you could grill her like some detective."

"I just wanted to make sure no one else had bagged her," said Sally.

Charlé was delighted when Paula told her what the prospects were at

Vogue; Paula's future success seemed assured, and Charlé was glad to feel in some way responsible for it.

On the way home after their first day at school, the girls decided that the Lycée was too large, too noisy and poorly staffed; that the place where Paula's new friends had steered them for lunch, an establishment called the Joyride, was disgusting; that the English class went much too fast for their liking; and that the sooner they got out of there the better. They had, however, learned a slew of new words: fab, gear, smashing, super, spastic (for inadequate), swinging, to snog (to kiss), mod—a trifle *démodé*, being a year old at least, but still viable—posh for chic, a word they had heard Jill use but had always taken to be a mispronunciation of the French for "pocket," and trendy.

Vogue had called. Paula was needed at Hanover Square the next day at ten-thirty. She let out a whoop of joy and threw her books down on the floor. Iris looked at her with solicitude. "I hope it's going to be all right," she said.

"Why shouldn't it?" asked Paula.

"Nothing," said Iris, "nothing at all."

Paula went to *Vogue* in a leather jacket and a pair of turquoise velvet jeans that exaggerated the length of her legs by failing to cover her ankles. On her feet she wore her brown moccasins, and she borrowed a tweedy shirt of Iris's to put over her T-shirt. She had drawn all the right lines around, over, under and beyond her eyes, filled in her lids with white cream and the lid crease with some grease labeled "hazel." She had used the Helena Rubinstein scimitar mascara, she had whitened her mouth. Sally Meadows pronounced herself pleased with Paula's efforts, and even more important, Ted Billingsgate winked at her.

Ted Billingsgate was the leader of the group of East End photographers responsible for the revolution in fashion, sexual mores, photoengraving and body alignment that was giving England its new name. If Bailey had created Shrimpton, Billingsgate had created Whitebait, a model originally named Winifred Burke, who had won her *nom de pose* when Billingsgate confided to Bailey, Duffy and Donovan that with her you could eat the whole thing, head, tail, and all. Whitebait's face was to be seen in posters all over London, mooning over a single Pretty Polly stocking; the rest of her attributes were well represented in *Vogue* and *Queen,* and her wardrobe was the subject of *London Life*'s inaugural investigation into the closets of the famous.

Ted and Whitebait had drifted apart a little in recent weeks, and he was searching for a new face. Looking at this Abime chick over from Paris with her silly blue trousers and her uptight shirt, he wondered if she might not be the one. He'd have to see the face without all that makeup, after sex, of course, before he knew for sure. All the bints looked alike with the black liner and the white mouth. You couldn't tell a real beauty till you'd fucked her, he liked to say. But not until the session was over: it wasn't professional to fuck a new girl before you even worked with her; if it went well, then it could be a partnership and they could both tell the world to fuck off, and if it didn't they could tell each other to fuck off. But trying to pull her in front of the *Vogue* skirts the first time they met was strictly amateur, and whatever he was, Ted Billingsgate wasn't an amateur. An article in the *Sunday Times Colour Magazine* on him had described him as "edgy, sceptical, dry, resilient; animated by pure high-octane nervous energy, switched on, a twenty-five-year-old amalgam of youth, vitality, tough professionalism, full of excitement and life yet with a beady native shrewdness and an awareness of fashion that makes him one of the prime movers of the new Britain."

He also liked to pick his nose when he was driving his dark-blue Morgan, especially when it was parked at traffic lights. Then he'd flip the little slugs out the window onto the next car, his pleasure being particularly acute if it was a Rolls with some snobby old marchioness wrinkling up her face at him in the backseat. He was proud of his origins as a fish gutter's son; and whenever some star-struck stranger who'd read the dossier on him came on with a lot of poses, he'd let her know where he stood. "Wiv me, there's only three things that count: havin' a laugh an' a pint wiv me mates, havin' a shag with a nice bit of crumpet, and watchin' the box."

It was inevitable that Paula should conceive a design to sleep with him as soon as possible; the ambition grew within her as she felt him watching her try on the various dresses at *Vogue,* defined itself when they all piled into his Morgan to go to the park, and grew unbearable while he photographed her, for he was in the habit of coaxing his models along with intimate endearments, which (although devalued for him by automatic and casual usage) fell on Paula like so many declarations of love. "That's it, sweetheart, beautiful, my lovely, gorgeous, what a bird!" he shouted as she ran between the trees wearing bunny trench coats, tweed knickerbocker suits, quilted miniskirts, muff-bearing jackets, vested shifts and lamé culottes. "Cor! Do that again!" he roared when she cocked a leg over a bench. "That's what I call defying the laws of decency. Beautiful, you really do it to me, more, more, more, MORE! I can't take it, stop! Stop, I'm coming!" he yelled, causing Paula to stop and await further instructions. Sally, who was standing next to Billingsgate, her neck festooned with belts, just shook her head and shouted, "Carry on!"

"That's right!" screamed Ted. "Carry on turning me on! I love you, you're the best thing I've ever seen. That's it, you're a natural, sweetheart, that's it, what a turn-on. I can't bear it, gimme, gimme, gimme! More!"

Iris was not consoled that night when Paula told her about the day, confessing her attraction to the dashing man who had molded her, she swore she could *feel* it, molded her through his camera lens.

"What do you mean?" asked Iris, who was longing to tell her about the hot surges occasioned by Stogie, a cigar-smoking ruffian from the Lycée who had been occupying her daydreams for all of two days.

"Well, it's as if he controlled me, he made me do whatever he thought of just by looking through the camera at me. It's as if . . . he were creating me, controlling me, no, more than that, as if I were in bed with him even though we were in the middle of Hyde Park with that stupid fat girl watching and all sorts of other people there."

"In bed with you?" Iris was bemused. "Like he was doing it with you? Flesh to flesh? Like his *bête* was inside you, and everything?"

Paula withdrew from the clinical description, which she found a little embarrassing. "No, more . . . spiritually. It was so beautiful, oh Iris!"

"Huh," grunted Iris. "Are you going to see him again?"

"Tonight," said Paula. "That's the best bit, so I kept it for last. He's picking me up at nine and he's taking me to dinner."

"And?"

"And, well, maybe. I mean, of course. Iris, I'm in love!"

"You coming to school tomorrow?" inquired Iris.

"If I'm not working," said Paula. "I'll know later tonight."

Later that night, at three in the morning, Iris was woken by Paula cascading into the room with little flapping noises. She sat up in bed. "Well?" she asked, a squadron leader confronting a returning pilot.

"Yes, yes, yes, yes yes," breathed Paula as she threw herself back on her own bed. "A billion and a half times yes."

Iris clambered out of bed and sat by Paula's side. "Did you take precautions?" she asked dourly.

"Precautions?" replied Paula. "Why, nobody saw us."

Iris kept her worries to herself. If Paula had to have a baby and then put it up for adoption, that was her business. "Tell me more," she ordered.

"Well, he took me to this place that was Italian and downstairs and very noisy—"

"Was it the Terrazza? That's where they all go." Iris had been reading her magazines.

"I can't remember—the what? Anyway, it was full of people he knew, his best friends—"

"Famous people?" Iris hoped not, and was, on her own terms, reassured.

"Famous? Well, I don't know. Other photographers and men who are art directors, advertising men, and a man who owns a nightclub."

"The Ad Lib?"

"I think so. Because we would have gone there if we hadn't gone to his pad."

Pad, thought Iris, the wonder of it! His pad!

"Was it fab?" she insisted on asking.

"The pad? Pretty groovy. But oh, he was so wonderful, I can't tell you. He touched me all over first, and then he gave me something to smoke."

"Drugs! He gave you drugs to drug you and make you lose yourself and lose all control of your senses! You must be insane letting him do that to you!"

"And then, don't be silly, I knew what I was doing, I'm not new at this like some people—I'm sorry, I didn't mean that. Well, he made me do something a little disgusting but he really liked it, so it was all right. I suppose."

"What? What?" asked Iris, impatient. "With his thing?"

"You mustn't ever tell I told you this," said Paula sitting up and lowering her voice still further, "but he made me put it in my mouth."

"EErgh!" Iris stood up with her hand over her mouth. "In your mouth? Prostitutes do that, he was treating you like a prostitute!"

Paula shook her head, wise and rich with secrets. "It's quite common, he said. I suppose they just don't do it a lot in France yet."

"And then?" urged Iris, the thrill of disgust abating, leaving her eager for more nausea.

"Then . . ." Paula sank back on to the bed, her voice dreamy. "Then he put it, oh Iris . . . I can't describe it to you. You'll just have to wait and see. He even wanted me to spend the night, not like that stupid Eric Castiglione, who wouldn't come near me . . ." Aha, Iris thought, Eric Castiglione wouldn't touch her, there must be something good about him after all. "It was fab. It was great. I'm so in love."

"Did it hurt?" asked Iris.

"Hurt? Well, it's never very comfortable. But that's what women have to put up with, and it doesn't matter, and anyway, he says that after a while your cunt gets wet if you do it enough."

"He talked to you about your cunt? He said that word?"

"Shh," said Paula. "You're ruining it like this. Anyway, I want to go to sleep now."

Iris lay awake until dawn, stretching the information she had received into long strands of conjecture, weaving it into a pattern of terrifying rituals and anticipating how she would behave when faced with such challenges. When she could no longer unravel her tangled apprehensions, she finally fell asleep, beatifically happy because the one sure fact in the whole skein was that *Vogue* had only chosen Paula because they had seen at first glance that she was no more than a loose and whorish individual. No true personality, she told herself, would stand for that kind of rough treatment.

15.

To Each Her Own

Paula thought of London as her lucky break; to Charlé it was a *coup de jeune;* to Iris it was merely hell, for whereas Paula was basically unassuming enough to consider that she needed luck in order to succeed as a person hired to wear clothes in front of cameras, and Charlé was gullible enough to believe that the proximity of a great many young girls in short skirts was enough to magically transform her into one of their number, Iris lacked the docility of spirit enjoyed by both her mother and her stepsister, and was only irritated and depressed by the glamour of London. Not that it failed to touch her; she was as helpless in the face of a magazine stand as Paula was passive on the cover of those magazines, as disarmed by the publicity that served as credo in the sixties as any other consumer. But instead of infusing her with the conviction that she was living in the best place at the best time, the picture books, the posters, the records, the cosmetic wrappers, the magazine articles and the television documentaries only served to inflame Iris with the itchy notion that she was missing out. On free love, on thin thighs, on The Pill, on nightclubs and pop stars and a certain kind of fame. As Paula's career took off (into orbit, as the debased scientific phraseology of the day would have it), Iris reflected bitterly that it seemed that Paula was getting all the prizes for just being there. And since she was there too, in the same place at the same time, her bed not five feet away from that of the wonder girl, she found it unnerving and almost uncanny that all of the bounty flowing Paula's way managed so effectively to avoid her own person. Being as yet incapable of forming a philosophy that could protect her from the pain of being undiscovered, uninvited, unphotographed, unwanted, undesired, and unsought, she took the only option open to her, that of being bitter. In her bitterness she attained a despairing set to her face, which attracted some of the young men at the Lycée, those who had considered suicide and liked girls who looked as if they had, too. It would have taken a more than average astuteness to divine that her misery was caused not by the subcutaneous stirrings of philosophical questions, but by the slings and arrows of outrageous superficiality.

It was not a good time for the soul. All that was irrelevant was busily being sanctified by ex–public school boys and working-class girls on the make with a reckless glee that owed a great part of its energy to the hope the perpetrators had that they were committing sacrilege. If the old idols had been class and respectability, the new ones were form and an instantaneity that denied both past and future. It was not a time, it was a moment; there was no progression, no alignment of days leading into years and aging all they contained. There was, instead, a series of snapshots, frozen two hundred and fiftieths of a second, printed on shiny paper, adorned with captions, bound into magazines, and disseminated as *The Word,* that moment's version of *The Word*, which was, of course, *The Latest Word.*

There were discotheque parties for people born under the same sign, for people with the same surname, for people with the same cars. There were fashion shows and fashion shootings, and somehow these two activities, which in normal times serve to move the merchandise from the manufacturers' racks into stores and on to the backs of customers, became the *summum bonum* of the moment.

They had arrived in September; by May of the following year Paula was the living symbol of Swinging London. Her canonization had been effected by repeated images that spread her aura around the city. Her commitments to *Vogue* and Ted Billingsgate had forced her to abandon the Lycée before any of the professors had a chance to find out her name, but they learned it soon enough through the newspapers. There were shots of Paula modeling dresses, arriving at restaurant openings and fur sales, crossing the threshold of movie houses for premieres. Sometimes one could discern the heavy outline of Ted Billingsgate next to her; less often, but more poignantly, the skinny one of Jed Ocker, the pop star, who was recording a song dedicated to her entitled "Paula, La, La, La." There were pictures of her in the gossip columns of the *Express* and the *Mail,* in the *Evening Standard*'s small news pages, which they liked to perk up with a pretty girl between the stories about fired bus drivers and housewives who'd found fortunes in their attics. Paula appeared on chat shows, nodding mutely but vigorously when she was asked what she liked about London, and puffing on her menthol cigarettes. She was the star at charity fashion shows, where she danced down the runway to the joyful contrapunto of the Beatles; she gave beauty advice and grooming hints on the Friday-night all-teen pop hour, which was called *On Your Mark, Get Set, Go,* and was hosted by one Mark Roger, who served as the Apollo to her Venus.

It was impossible to buy a copy of the *Financial Times* at a newsstand without seeing Paula Abime staring down from the covers of different magazines, with the edges of twelve different collars encroaching on her skin, and the bristles of false eyelashes rimming twelve different versions, due to printing errors, of the color of her eyes. She was the canon of ideal beauty against which all women were measured. To men she was an artifact, the correct thing to be seen with. To women she was a yardstick by which to measure their shortcomings. Neither of these roles demanded of her anything other than that she stay thin, keep her hair clean and her powder dry.

Paula's main relationship at Eaton Square was with the large square mirror in the bathroom, before which she performed feats of engineering with miniature centipedes of false eyelashes; here she improvised new tricks with liquid eye-liner, a dot at the edge of each canthus, a fringe of diagonal hatchings beneath each eye, extensions in the style of Ra and that of Nefertiti. She knew that other models thought it best to keep the face clean when they weren't working, but she felt she owed it to the public to look her best. Carefully she would rub on the powder rouge: high for an Oriental effect, low for the precious Garbo effect, none at all for a crisply cadaverous effect. Her hair, which during the day was subjected to every whim and fancy of fashion—being crammed into stockings and stifled under wigs of red or green or blue Dynel (a chemical substance that attained the state of fine if slightly sticky strands and which passed that year for hair), secured with stationer's rubber bands, backcombed around daisy chains, and ironed—required what she thought of as first aid when she was at home. So it was with the solicitude of a nurse that she carefully brushed it every evening, checking the ends for forked splits and hampering their progress with the application of her burning cigarette end, a trick Vidal Sassoon had taught her. Twice a week she poured olive oil on her head and spent two hours turbanned in front of the television set. Her body too was oiled before her bath, so that dead skin could slip off. Her nails she merely buffed, after an application of Mavala strengthener, which ensured that she would be more likely to break a tooth than succeed in dislodging a sliver of hangnail. She would check her weight, a steady seven stone seven on the British scale (which Charlé had hastened to buy at Harrods), and pummeled herself with net bags of seaweed and a hemp glove to discourage any cellulite that might have designs on her buttocks. All this took a considerable amount of time, so that from the moment she returned home after a hard day on the no-seam paper until the doorbell rang to announce the arrival of Ted, Jed or Mark, she did not see anyone but herself.

Charlé made little jokes to her new circle of friends about Paula's timetable. "I'm not even sure she *eats* at home," she would say, provoking gales of laughter because the question, of course, was whether she *slept* there, and on this subject Charlé was loyally mute. In some deep basement of her mind languished the thought that since Paula was having such a success, maybe she should hold out until someone really marvelous came along; next to this relic loomed the even rustier notion that photographers were not very important people, but over this one was thrown the gaudy fact, now six years old, that Princess Margaret was married to one, which bestowed on the misgiving a jeweled surface that made it somehow decorative, while doing nothing to diminish its size.

Charlé was in a quandary: much as she loved the youth and energy of London, she had become aware ever since Raoul's escape that there truly was something a little unreliable about creative people, and she was using her time to track down a good, solid millionaire. Raoul's monthly checks were adequate, but not inspiring.

Paula's triumph served Charlé in two ways: it gave her the opportunity to feel generous for allowing it to happen; and it gave her a convenient social handle in a town where Raoul's name was unpronounceable without affecting the sort of French accent that most Londoners resented, and, when pronounced properly, met with a stony lack of recognition. But Paula Abime ("Abbim" was the favored way of saying it) was a name that spoke bound volumes of *Vogue,* and she used it freely, confident that it was fittingly modest to present herself as Paula's stepmother. Religiously she bought every magazine that bore the girl's likeness, and congratulated herself on the discipline that forced her to whisk each issue off the coffee table the minute it was out of date, and store it with the others in one of the spare closets. She sensed that back numbers brought bad luck.

Raoul might be turning into a back number himself, she suspected, and the part of her that longed for topical relevance was relieved that he was still in Rome. There was no divorce in sight; it seemed that Vivien Legrand was still married to someone else, at least according to Szos, who came to London regularly to check on the new young actors who were proceeding straight from drama school to the pages of the *Sunday Times Colour Magazine* and thence to starring roles as mute, tormented souls. "Also, there is no divorce in Italy," explained Szos, although Charlé was well aware of the fact, having followed the long trail of bitter frustration that had attended the efforts of Sophia Loren and Carlo Ponti to wed. "How are Carlo and Sophia?" had been Charlé's automatic rejoinder, to which Szos had shrugged his shoulders and looked blank. "You know I don't speak to him anymore, Charlene!" he had said in such definitive tones that Charlé allowed the disaffection Szos implied to spread itself over the Italian peninsula and embrace everyone on it from Antonioni to the Pope. "Yes, Italy is finished," she concluded, with relief. Vivien Legrand, Raoul, Roberta cut-velvet handbags, Fellini, buggy rides, Capri, the goddamn Tower of Pisa—you could keep them all as far as she was concerned. They were old news.

And she was new, which was almost the same as being young. Vidal Sassoon had transformed her hair from an uncertain swirl that heralded middle age to a pair of sharp curtains that obscured one eye at a time and rose precipitately in the back, allowing her to turn up the collar of her mink trench coat and look as casual as any Cockney out of art school. No longer was it red, but a strong and shadeless black, which created an unexpected physical likeness between herself and Paula.

Her preference for Paula over Iris was half survival instinct, half nostalgia for what she knew to be the only important relationship in her life. No matter what Raoul had done, or failed to do, the idea of him was still potent enough to claim her loyalty. The memory of his position in Paris ten years earlier still served to make her think better of herself because he had chosen her.

Even Dara, who made a noisy fuss over being immune to the celebrity of people who had to work for a living, never failed to quietly brief her friends on Charlé's status. Charles Frantwell asked Dara one evening when they sat alone in Lord Vizreader's Wiltshire drawing room whether "I'm expected to take care of her since she's arrived bag and baggage."

He liked expressions like that, and repeated "bag and baggage," prompting Dara to assure him that Charlé had nothing of the sort in mind. He disappeared from that particular house party with such haste that it crossed Dara's mind that his only reason for attending had been to ascertain his degree of responsibility toward Charlé. Indeed, shortly thereafter he married a kind, round-eyed girl from Suffolk, who hadn't been in London long enough to hear that he wasn't desirable. Dara was immune to guilt, but a certain amount of good manners pushed her to introduce her American friend to financial wizards, chairmen of well-known companies, merchant bankers with six homes in five countries and the like, millionaire lords with mad wives who never set brogue out of Scotland, divorced dukes, property magnates. "It's funny, I always thought you liked the arty types," she told Charlé one day, to which Charlé replied, "But they *look* arty, and they're so much more attentive!" By which she meant that they wore their hair a little longer than Charles Frantwell did, bought their shirts at Turnbull and Asser, and drove fast, low cars.

They would have been content to take her to Covent Garden and to drinks in the second-floor drawing rooms of narrow, ornate houses in Belgravia, the way one exhibits a curiosity. She was looking for love, but was wise enough never to talk of herself (a course that would have made the British anxious) but to dwell instead on her travels, the places she had been and the people she had met. Her escorts had a hearty appetite for gossip; they thought of themselves as leading dull lives, and this battered hummingbird (as the Viscount Celroy had once described her, in a moment of great weakness) seemed to have known everyone who was anyone on the Continent. She jabbered for her supper at Mirabelle, but to her great dismay, the content of her stories never quite sufficed to get her invited away for the weekend, and this became the fixed and nagging sore point in her life.

As much as Charlé told herself that she was ripe for unconditional admission into the ranks of the ruling class by the sole virtue of her record, she could not help being dazzled by Paula's life, and comparing her own to it. One evening in the toilet during a dinner party she smoked a joint with a friend of Dara's son. It didn't have any physical effect on her, but the mere idea of dabbling in drugs made her feel infinitely superior to the hapless oil tycoon who was lunching her that week. She wondered if she was missing out, but justified her choice by the logical reasoning of the shopper: it was better to stick with the tried and true, the quality, rather than attempt to keep up with the endless list of new faces, new names, most of which appeared as phone messages for Paula on the pad by the telephone in the living room at Eaton Square. They might be *in* today, but who knew where they were headed?

Little did she know that the member of Parliament whose slow and sometimes stuttering speech suggested to her the holy gravitas of the statesman was a notorious homosexual whose interest in women began and ended with his mother, and whose entire parliamentary career had consisted in attempting to pass bills forbidding the shooting of migratory geese. She had no inkling that the duke who played footsie with her at Dara's dinner table was really Dara's lover. She failed to notice the signals emitted by Lord Vizreader (whom she found fascinating) to the effect that his sympathies lay with the dead leaders of the Third Reich.

All she knew was that they sought her out. Their curiosity about the mores of Continental notables was enchanting; never had she found such good listeners. She could hold their interest with lists of celebrities who were known to take hard drugs, beat their wives, crash their cars in the Bois de Boulogne, buy Dom Pérignon for their servants. When drunk, a not uncommon state, she would extend the list of malefactors to include Raoul, and impart the secret sorrows that had made her marriage, as she confessed, "a living hell." Offers to relieve her of the physical burden of celibacy she received with a steely "No." She was going to hold out until she was asked away for the weekend. Occasionally, over a second brandy at Annabel's, just when her paunchy swain was weighing the advantages of losing half an hour's sleep in her company, she would add, "—not in London." The hint was too subtle, however. The oil tycoon, the divorced duke and the merchant banker, all of whom had regular mistresses, often themselves married to other men, oftener still married to their best friend, took it to mean that for obscure reasons the woman could only succumb to the temptations of the flesh when in Paris; and though she was known to be good value socially, until Ben-Abi happened upon her, she did not strike any of the men who took her out as someone to get one's schedule in a mess over.

Ben-Abi was Egyptian and French. He was in stocks the way his ancestors had been in sand, up to his neck and occasionally beyond it. Being Egyptian and French—he always added that "and," rather than allowing his nationality to be hyphenated—he found it banal to content himself with his best friends' wives, and as his best friends were those very Englishmen with whom Charlé was playing, xenophobes to a man, they would have found it rather repulsive of their own wives to jump in the sack with someone whose money they respected but who was, after all, only a brown man. Being very rich, he feared the greed of strangers more than he noticed their prejudices, and he believed in marriage. Dara, who had met him when one of her penurious moments had forced her into selling the lesser of her two landscapes by Devis, had found out that he was recently divorced and had sensed at once that he was looking for a new wife. He had asked her questions about the Duchess of Argyll, questions so leading that the implication he was in the market for matrimony could not have been lost on a deaf mute. He had inquired whether Dara had ever run across Rita Hayworth, the late Kay Kendall or Diana Dors. His taste seemed eclectic, but the outrageous price he paid for her picture of the nasty little fields and the gummy stream convinced her that here was an essentially desirable bachelor. She didn't mind the French and Egyptian provenance, and his slight French accent made her place him next to Charlé at her very next dinner party.

Although he would have preferred to ally himself to some member of the aristocracy, he was charmed by Charlé, who herself would have preferred a blue blood, but was attracted by his French accent and his deep tan. "We are both outsiders," he whispered to her over coffee in Dara's drawing room, where the space left by the lesser Devis had been filled by an Augustus John oil sketch of Dara's mother. Charlé sighed. "The English don't understand," she hazarded, taking him for a Frenchman. He told her about his art collection; she riposted with tales of the Château Rose, which aroused his interest at once: he thought she meant the one in the Loire Valley. They were instantly attracted to each other.

In May of 1967, two national opinion polls, two glossy magazines and three popular papers all named Paula Girl of the Year. Iris was eating her breakfast in the kitchen when she caught sight of the headlines. "Paula's Our Bird!" said the *Mirror.* "Chick of the Year!" said the *Express.* "Daily Mail's Top Dolly!" said the *Daily Mail.* Shit! thought Iris, and as she did the shock turned to excitement and then awe; she thought of waking Charlé to show her, and then, remembering that Paula was actually sleeping at home that morning, she grabbed the papers off the kitchen counter and ran into the bedroom.

Paula had a pillow over her head. Iris sat down and shook her.

"You're the Girl of the Year!" whispered Iris, and then she realized how silly that sounded. "I mean, the papers are calling you the Girl of the Year, Paula!"

Paula opened her eyes. "I had a terrible scene with Ted last night, oh God!"

"It doesn't matter," said Iris, convinced that her news could heal anything. "You've been named Girl of the Year."

"What are you talking about?" asked Paula, stirring in her nightgown. Iris held the papers in front of her, like a newsboy allowing passersby to read the headlines. The *Daily Mail* said "Meet Paula, the Face of '67." The *Express* said "Movie Star's Daughter Is Girl of the Year." The *Daily Mirror* said "Cor! What a Dolly!" over a picture of Paula in a miniskirt sniffing a bouquet of daisies. Paula sat up. "Oh, that!"

" 'Oh, that'? Is that all? Paula, it's incredible!"

"What do you mean, 'incredible'?" asked Paula, a trifle miffed.

"Well, coming like that, Girl of the Year! Nothing ever happens to *me.*"

"But the agency said that it was going to happen. It's just work, Iris, and I'm so miserable." Paula retreated to the comfort of her pillow. "If you knew what a number Ted laid on me, you'd get me a cup of tea."

Iris put the papers down carefully on the chest of drawers. "I'll get some more copies on my way to school," she said, and then proceeded to hover. Getting a cup of tea would be in some way to indulge Paula's stubborn ingratitude in the face of amazing honor. She opened the *Daily Mail* and read aloud: " 'Two independent polls have independently named Paula Abime, the eighteen-year-old daughter of the late movie star Soula Tithe, Girl of the Year. Paula, eighteen, has the biggest smile and the longest legs in the business, according to her manager, Peter Reynie. Our fashion editor, Anne Chiclet, knew it before anyone else, and Paula was photographed this week in the season's latest gear.' Paula, there's three pictures of you here, you look wonderful!" Paula was listening and pretending not to. It was easier for Iris to express wonder and joy at the findings of the opinion polls than to compliment Paula on her appearance in the photographs, but she had made a brave effort. "Got a fag?" Paula asked as Iris continued reading: " '—a bunny-hair dress, four pounds seventeen and six at Bus Stop, worn with a bunny muff and Moyra Bowler shoes, seven pounds'—God, that's expensive, seven-pound shoes—and here it says 'The sexy Paula,' and they've got you in a black crochet dress, twelve pounds, at Maxine Leighton—Jesus, twelve pounds!—worn with openwork black lace tights (to order at Liberty's) and sexy strappy sandals, eight—"

"I don't want to hear the prices," said Paula, converted. "Just tell me what else it says."

Iris turned to the *Express.* " 'She's been linked with William Piggot

Brown, with composer John Barry, with Jed Ocker, but she says her heart belongs to Ted Billingsgate,' " she read.

Paula gave a sigh. She had found the fag she wanted in her handbag, which gaped by the side of her bed. A pair of dirty tights protruded from its bright yellow maw. She wondered if Ted would read it, and what he would think when he did. Surely that would make him take it all back. I am not a foul little scrubber, she said to herself. "Go on," she told Iris.

Iris took a breath: " 'In a few short months Paula Abime, eighteen, has become the face of '67. She's taller than most models, and still lives at home.' "

"What does that mean?" sneered Paula. "I mean, what's it got to do wiv anything?" Iris hated it when Paula spoke secondhand Cockney.

" 'Two independent research organizations asked seven thousand people who they thought the face of '67 was, and they all named Paula as the girl most girls would most like to be.' " A brief smile pursed Paula's mouth. " ' "She can look like a duchess or a charlady," said Ted Billingsgate, the Svengali of the fashion set with the Don Juan touch.' "

"Wait a minute," said Paula. "What was that?"

"The Svengali of the—"

"No, before that. A duchess or a what?"

Iris started to repeat the paragraph, but Paula, coerced out of bed by the hint of a slight, was at her side. She ran her finger under the words to make sure she was reading them right, and her lips moved as she found the word "charlady." It crossed Iris's mind that Paula was really very stupid.

"Charlady! How fucking dare he!"

"I think he means, earthy, sort of, you know, real?" Iris was being gentle.

"*Une bonne!*" snorted Paula as she retreated to bed. "What about some tea, since you've woken me at this ungodly hour?"

Iris turned to her, exasperated. "I'm not your maid," she announced. "One would think you might be grateful; after all, I come in with this wonderful news, and all you can do is complain about Ted."

Paula gave a loud sigh, the sigh of the wise. "You don't understand anything," she began, and drew another breath, as if what she was about to explain was so complicated that she was not sure she could get it right without a scrupulous and grueling effort of concentration. "I've known about it for weeks. I posed for the *Mail* on Monday. And they didn't pay me, because they said it was publicity and you're supposed to be grateful they print your name."

"But they always print your name!"

"Not on fashion pictures. And it only means I'll get more work. I don't see why it's so important to you. Really. And Ted told me I was a scrubber last night because he thinks me and Mark Roger are havin' a scene, and if I can't work with Ted anymore, I'm finished! And who named me that, anyway? Bunch of effing nobodies. It's not as if people I respected thought I was great." With that she snuffled down into her pillow. Iris stood by the door, perplexed, somehow wounded. She went back to her breakfast, and decided to leave the papers just to show Paula that she didn't give a damn about her.

When the door had shut behind Iris, Paula stealthily rose, grabbed the papers off the dresser and returned to bed. Lighting another cigarette, she read the headlines. Her face didn't mean much to her anymore; she could only see it as looking less good than it should—too fat, dumb. But it was different with her name; she always felt a tiny shiver come over her when she caught her name in print, like that first chill when she took her clothes off in a cold dressing room; and here, seeing it in bold type, large, on the front page, the shiver was almost a tremor. Carefully she grasped the paper and opened it; it was the *Mail.* She ran her eyes along the print, fast, seeking to grasp at once everything that was being said and thought about her, but it was the dim story about bunny-hair dresses. She took up the *Express,* found the page, and after an instant of still and satisfied communion with her name, read the story several times before she understood it. Iris had not bothered to read the end.

"Like Shrimpton before, and Twiggy, and Sue Murray, Paula has the look that spells today, and men can't seem to get enough of her. She's at Dolly's every night, and Terry Horsenden-Farr is naming his new discotheque after the groovy American beauty. What does the girl who has everyone want?" A moment of good sense stopped her: she had misread "everything" as "everyone," was offended by the suggestion of sluttish behavior, and read on: " 'I just want everything to be beautiful,' says Paula, 'for everyone.' The raven-haired beauty, 5'11", thinks her arch rivals Jean Shrimpton, Celia Coddington, Sue Murray and Twiggy are all 'fantastic.' Does she feel jealous of Ted Billingsgate's carryings-on with other models?' " Paula held her breath for the answer. " 'Not at all,' she says, 'what we have together is really beautiful and nothing can come between us.' " She read this with profound relief, forgetting that she had said it herself. The last sentence of the article, hanging like a loose thread above the ad for do-it-yourself home extensions, was more ominous: "How long can a gilded butterfly last in this age of industrial disputes? Carry on grooving, Paula, and maybe next year a British bird will catch everyone's fancy."

She shut the paper quickly, and carefully replaced it with the others on the dresser, telling herself that she had not read them. She tried to go back to sleep. Well, it is really beautiful what we've got between us, she thought, and no one can ruin that. And then she remembered the scene last night in Dolly's, when Ted had thrown a glass of vodka at Mark Roger and then hit her, and told her he was going home with that Tamara chick. He'll read the papers today and he'll see that I really love him, she told herself.

On her way to school Iris bought the *Daily Mail,* the *Daily Express* and the *Daily Mirror,* two copies of each. She spent that day receiving congratulations on her sister's triumph. In three terms she had managed to eliminate the degrading distance implied by the prefix "step," and none of her classmates was sufficiently interested to probe the intricacies of her blood relationships. Anyone who failed to mention Paula to her that day was eventually confronted with subtle non sequiturs that began, "Paula was in such a state this morning, she was so excited about what's happening to her," leaving them no recourse but to inquire what the excitement was all about. To which Iris, rolling her eyes and looking away, would produce a copy of one of the papers and hand it over, saying, "Didn't you see? It doesn't mean anything but work, of course, but the way she's carrying on you'd think it was the end of the world."

Despite all evidence to the contrary, it had been decided by Charlé and Paula that Iris was intelligent; instinctively they heeded nature's law of compensation, which doomed Iris to be considered bright because she lacked the length of limb to be considered beautiful. She was unwilling to study, uninterested in anything save trivia: her curiosity hungered only for snacks, and the banquet that the Lycée offered seemed to her rigorous and untempting. She feasted instead on the stuff of magazines and horoscopes, while giving her family every indication that her mind was exclusively occupied with Kant. At school her social currency consisted of her privileged insights into fashionable life, garnered from clues in the form of Paula's torn tights, Paula's invitations to parties and openings, Paula's phone messages and the gossip columns of her favorite newspapers. She had gathered about her the audience most likely to be enraptured, girls who shared the same aspirations as she did. Girls who had Sassoon cuts, initiates of fashion with strapped shoes, white stockings, shoulder bags, sometimes even, as a daring touch, a lover.

At times Charlé attempted to arrange a date for Iris with one of her acquaintances' children. She was most taken with the idea of Lord Vizreader's son Valentine, who was at Westminster School, but Iris bristled haughtily at the suggestion. For all that she liked names, she limited her interest to those who were said to be in some way responsible for the present ebullient condition of the gray and gloomy capital. Inherited names, the legacy of ancestors who had built abbeys, repelled invaders, sunk the Armada, or merely been close personal friends of the more open-handed monarchs, failed entirely to capture her attention. She was not being difficult; though she longed to meet the designers and photographers and hairdressers and artists who were profiled at length in the *Sunday Times Colour Magazine,* and sometimes had disturbing dreams about finding herself next to one of the Beatles, she wished modestly that when the time came for her to be asked out to dinner by a man, he should have earned, at least once, the typographical tribute of having his name set in print in any of the publications that she so actively perused.

When Eric Castiglione came to London on a shopping expedition, he called and left repeated messages for Paula. But by then—it was a full week after she had been named Girl of the Year—Paula's time was so little her own that there was no way she could give her first benefactor even five minutes of it.

At the third phone call, Iris timidly came on the line. "Do you remember me?" she asked.

"Ah, oui!" said Eric, unguarded.

"I'd love to see you, we could go dancing at some of the clubs." Eric, who had failed to bring his Swede on account of Paula, allowed himself only one more question before submitting: "Do you know where the Kings Road is?"

"I go there every Saturday," said Iris. "I'll take you, and we can lunch at Alvaro's, it's great."

"Okay," said Eric. "And tell Paula I just saw her father in Rome and he sends lots of love."

"To me, too?" asked Iris.

"Bien sûr, bien sûr," said Eric a little vaguely.

Iris could not decide what to wear. Paula's affair with Ted Billingsgate had resumed, and her portion of the shared bedroom was nothing more than a wasteland of heaped crocheted minidresses and beaded skullcaps, none of which Mauricette would touch for fear of getting a disease. In the closet, where Iris vainly sought the perfect outfit in which to go shopping with a member of the fourth estate, Paula's fox coat—her first major purchase—hung forlornly, its horizontal bands of fur torn from their leather moorings about the elbows. Beside it, tiny Lurex sweater dresses were straining against the sharp shoulders of dry cleaners' hangers. Next to them, Iris's collection of crepon Jean Cacharel blouses (she was faithful to Paris, and a girl at school could get them wholesale) looked dreadfully innocent. At last she selected her own leather blouson from last fall, though the day was warm, and a yellow suede skirt stiff with snap fastenings.

Eric came to pick her up, hoping for a glimpse of Paula. "She's out being interviewed by Smith Clark," Charlé told him; she was hanging around hoping to hear something about Raoul, for she had seen a new story in *Paris Match* about the Roman lovebirds, and knew the pictures were Eric's. But Eric, sitting on the couch and exclaiming about the pastoral effect of the treetops outside the windows, was not going to tell her anything. In desperation Charlé asked, "Well, where are you kids eating?"

"I booked Alvaro's," said Iris with a certain pride; it had been one of her ambitions to eat there. Charlé nodded with approval and proceeded to her bedroom, gaily waving good-bye to Eric.

"Qu'est-ce que c'est Alvaro?" asked Eric as they stood in the balmy street waiting for a cab to chug into view.

"C'est formidable," said Iris. "It's where all the people who write about London go to see what's happening."

"You don't know anywhere more authentic?" asked Eric, adding, "Is the food good?"

The first person they saw as they came through the crowded doorway of the tiny Italian restaurant was Paula. With her was a large and bland-looking man who, despite his Prince of Wales checked suit and long hair, bore the unmistakable mark of being an American, in that he was staring about him in utter and rapt fascination. Everyone else at the tables was acting like Paula, either mooning at the centerpieces, contemplating the fringes on their thin antique-market scarves, or frowning at the quilted domes of bread on their side plates. *"Tiens!"* exclaimed Eric. "Ah ha!" Iris said, as if she had planned the whole thing as a wonderful surprise for Eric.

Paula straightened herself as if for a yawn, and caught sight of them as she was throwing her head back. She waved, and Eric was upon her. Iris hung back, riveted by Smith Clark, whom she had seen on television at least three times that week. He had written a book about dinner parties in Atlanta, Houston, Dallas, San Francisco and New York. It was all true and it was a best seller.

"What are you doing here?" asked Paula. Iris started to explain: "Eric came to shop." Paula pursed her mouth; her resemblance to her mother was most acute when she did this, and Smith Clark took out a little notebook to note this down. "I *meant,*" continued Paula, in a tone that was almost surly, "what made you come *here?*"

"Your sister insisted," said Eric.

"Your sister!" cried Smith Clark, and then he held out his hand most formally. "I'm Smith Clark, I'm interviewing your sister. For the *Observer,* do you know it?"

"What, the Sunday paper?" asked Iris.

"Of course she knows it, she's an intellectual," said Paula with grace. She'd explain later that Iris was not really related at all.

"Eric Castiglione, *Paris Match.*" Eric's voice was twice as deep as Smith Clark's, and the hand he held out was twice as large and considerably hairier than the writer's.

"I've heard of it, of course," said Smith Clark, and then with a note of dismay: "Are you joining us? We're working—at least I'm having fun but poor Paula is working hard."

"We've got a table," said Iris; quickly she turned away to hide the flush that was beginning to cover her face. She felt that she had overreached by even going to Alvaro's, and the rejection she felt was only justice being done. A round man with a moustache caught her wavering uncertainly in the middle of the room. "*Signorina, posso aiutare?*" he asked.

"I booked a table," she whispered, hoping Paula and Smith Clark hadn't heard. In a perfect world, Eric would have booked it. The man with the moustache opened his arms wide to embrace the room, the girls in Biba trouser suits, the hollow-cheeked blond men, the crowd that seemed to her unfocused eye to be made up of only the most exciting people in London, a fact she could not confirm, not daring to look at anyone too closely until she had secured a table for herself.

"Is full, is completely full," said the man with the moustache. He was wearing a dish towel draped around his waist.

"I'd like to speak to Alvaro," she said.

"I am Alvaro," said the man with the moustache as he crossed his arms.

"Look," she whispered to him. "Do you see that man there?" She pointed at Paula's table, where Eric had taken root and was glaring at Smith Clark.

"Smith Clark," said Alvaro, "journalist. Very good writer."

"No, no, the other one. He's Eric Castiglione and he's from *Paris Match* and he's in London doing a story about it."

Alvaro shrugged. "So is everyone else here," he said.

"But he's the best photographer in Europe. He just did Vivien Legrand in Rome, and he's here to take pictures."

"Vivien Legrand! She is spectacular," conceded Alvaro. Slowly he raised his arm to summon one of his waiters. By the window, three people were rising from their table; a girl in a Hungarian embroidered blouse and tight red velvet jeans, and two men, both in jeans jackets, both wearing little necklaces of beads. An Afghan hound emerged from under the tablecloth, whimpering with the effort. "Your table," said Alvaro. Iris turned and faced the room with a magnificent smile.

All through lunch, Iris kept staring at Paula's table. She figured that everything was wrong, that she should be the one exchanging tidbits about the Hellenic conscience with Smith Clark, and Paula should be allowing Eric to look into her eyes. As it was, Eric was pumping her about the best places for *les Shetlands,* and she was having to explain that Shetlands were not where it was at anymore as far as London was concerned. He asked about pubs; she told him about clubs, Dolly's, Sibylla's, the forthcoming Paula's. "You mean she is opening a nightclub?" he asked, looking across the room at Paula for confirmation.

"No, not her, but it's being named for her."

"Who's doing this?" He sounded outraged.

"What's wrong with it? Terry Horsenden-Farr. He's great." She said this without ever having met him, but she liked the Renaissance eyelids Mr. Farr exhibited in his pictures in the columns.

"Is he her lover?" asked Eric. He said "*son mec.*"

Iris laughed. "Oh, no! That's Ted."

"Billingsgate? I know him. It's not possible."

"Eric, I don't know where you've been. Everyone knows it."

"Does Raoul?"

Iris fell silent, conscious of betrayal. Eric asked if Paula took drugs. Seeking to impress, Iris answered as accurately as she could. She liked being questioned. It made her feel responsible, trusted. "Of course, doesn't everybody? I mean just pot, really, and hash, that's all people take in London." She stressed London: she had heard from a girl at the Lycée that French photographers were into opium, and opiated hash, and strange things like that. She didn't want Eric to think that London was anywhere near as decadent.

When Eric had heard his fill of alarming news, he set about repaying

Iris. He told her how Raoul divided his time between the Château Rose and Rome; Iris said "I know." He told her that Vivien Legrand was *"une grande bonne femme,"* and that she and Paula shouldn't blame Raoul for being attracted to her. "We don't," said Iris.

"How's school?" he said.

"It's my life," said Iris. She did not wish to appear as mindless and insubstantial as every other girl in the room. "You're still intelligent," said Eric, the way one would say, "There's still life in the old dog." Iris looked down modestly at her zabaglione. "I'm doing my *bachot* next month," she said.

"It's very good that you study," he said. "Excellent, everyone else is wasting their time. What will you do after?" Iris considered, breaking little pieces of breadstick, and looked up to see Eric's head swivel helplessly toward Paula. She turned and saw Smith Clark writing something in his little notebook.

Paula was not enjoying the interview. She wished she were sitting with Eric. They could talk about Paris, and she would find out how Raoul was. She missed her father, although she knew that if she were living in Paris or Rome, none of the wonderful things that were happening would ever have occurred.

"Do you like London?" she asked Smith Clark. It was the first question she had put to him.

"I'm astounded. Why, it's even hot here!"

"I know," she said, smiling proudly. "Ted says the climate changed when the mentality changed. He says we've created a totally new environment, and that the old codgers haven't got a chance."

"Do you agree?" asked the writer, his Mark Cross pen poised over the fake morocco of his little book.

Paula squirmed in her chair and threw both her legs straight out, like unwanted croquet mallets. Her purple-and-white-striped vest dress was so short that he got a glimpse of delectable blue underpants, his favorite garment. He smiled benignly, to encourage her.

"I don't know—I mean, it's me that a lot of it is happening to. I'm in the middle, I don't know anymore." She gave him a huge smile, the same one that had just been contracted to sell Virgin Wool to the United States. Then Iris was standing behind them. They both looked up.

"Where can Eric get groovy men's clothes?" asked Iris plaintively.

Paula looked blank.

"I need to get some things too," said Smith Clark.

"Great! We can all go shopping together!" said Paula. Iris was amazed at her boldness. She would never suggest going shopping to a man. The implications were somewhat embarrassing, if not entirely sordid.

They went out into the sunny street and joined the ambling parade of shoppers. They stopped at every window, Smith Clark being most attracted to those that displayed peacock ties and wide-lapeled suits; while he was absorbed in contemplating them, Eric took Paula aside to suggest dancing, dining, to hint at possible quiet moments alone in Hyde Park Hotel, where he was staying because it was so *"anglais"*; Paula would have none of this; she began every refusal with "Ted . . ." and Eric was reduced to telling her that she was even more beautiful than she had been last fall.

Iris walked neatly beside Smith Clark and joined him at the windows. She had never thought about men's clothes before. Once she leaned toward him, careful not to intrude, and said, "I saw you on television." He smiled. "Did you read my book?" he asked. "Not yet," she said. "You'd like it," he said, which was what he said to sell more books. She vowed to buy it at once.

Eric wanted shoes. *"Des* Church's," he kept repeating.

"Never 'eard of 'em," said Paula in her Ted voice, but Smith Clark had, and the two men joined forces to find a shoe store, where Iris took Paula aside and repeated everything she had heard about Raoul. Then Smith Clark insisted they go to John Michael, and Eric expressed the hope that they might have something to fit him. *"Des épaules de footballeur,"* he said, pointing to his shoulders, which seemed large to him, living in a country of puny men, but which looked perfectly average to Smith Clark.

At John Michael they had to press through a throng of men taking belts off racks and trying on barrow-boy caps; Smith Clark led the way to the basement, where the three-piece suits were kept. Iris looked at herself in the mirror. Her legs were short, their shape uninspiring; under the studded miniskirt the two pairs of underpants that she always wore, so as to be sure to commit no unconscious indecency, bulged inelegantly. She sucked in her cheeks and retied the chiffon scarf that held her hair back in a low ponytail. Her looks might improve when she hit thirty; that was what one of the girls at school had said, but that was late to begin modeling, that was when the skin began to give up. One of the louvered dressing-room doors opened a crack, and she saw a slice of male body, the horizontal line of bright red briefs. Quickly she turned away, hoping it wasn't anybody she knew.

Charlé had returned bright-eyed and babbling from a weekend in the country, her vocabulary suddenly full of follies and grottoes, venison and port. She was hinting that her summer might be spent in Capri, with

Ben-Abi, after "the June parties" that were suddenly her prerogative, when they had been no more than her dream three days earlier. Matters were precipitated by a phone call from Raoul; uncharacteristically, he asked to speak to Charlé, who covered the receiver as she took the phone and announced to Iris that it never rained without pouring. Then setting her face into the bitter mask of the abandoned wife, she snapped, "Yes?" Iris left the room; she did not like witnessing Charlé's performances. When she heard the bell that signaled the end of the call, she returned to the living room, pretending to search for a book. She was bending over the magazines on the little lacquer coffee table when Charlé, snorting smoke from her Du Maurier, let out an angry sort of "Huh!"

"What is it, Mum?" asked Iris obediently.

"That beast!" screamed Charlé. "He wants Paula in Rome."

Iris repressed a smile. "That's awful, Mum, really awful. It'll mean the end of her career. Ted will never wait for her."

"It's not that bad," said Charlé, settling into the sofa with a glass of whiskey. "It's only for a few weeks. But that Vivien had her filthy clutches into him, it's obvious."

"But you don't mind, do you? I mean, you've got a boyfriend now, and everything."

"Have you been gossiping about me?" hissed Charlé.

"I'd never ever do a thing like that," said Iris, "but isn't Ben-Abi taking you to Capri, and all?"

Charlé was disappointed. She longed to be gossiped about, even by her own daughter. "I suppose you're right," she said. "He is, after all, her real father, and I'm getting back on my own two feet again. Believe me, honey, it wasn't easy." She liked the feeling that she was able to confide in her daughter; it was like having a friend who wouldn't compete. "And we still have each other, don't we?"

"I'll miss the villa," said Iris. "Do you suppose Raoul will keep it?"

Charlé shrugged. "That's up to Jill," she said, and they both giggled at the image of Jill grimly running Raoul's life no matter what.

Charlé refused to see Paula off at the airport, but Iris went along for the ride, hoping there would be photographers at the gate. There were, but she had bidden her stepsister good-bye at the passport counter, so all she got out of the trip was a bar of Toblerone that she purchased at the magazine stand. As she rode back alone in the shivering black cab she wondered why Ted Billingsgate hadn't come with Paula.

A week later she sat for the *baccalauréat* exams. With her throughout the week of silent concentrated hours was a copy of Smith Clark's book

Dinners Divine. It was her favorite book, for he concluded in his afterword that the most important thing in the world was status.

A few weeks later an immense brass tray supported by little black legs appeared in the living room, and on it was a gigantic bouquet of exotic flowers. "What are all those things?" asked Iris.

"From Abi. Isn't it wonderful? It's a Moroccan table."

"I thought he was Egyptian," sniffed Iris.

"He is, but, darling, after Capri we flew down to Marrakesh for a couple of days—he goes there all the time—and it was wonderful!"

Iris saw it at once. Charlé was about to go live in a tent with this greasy little man. She let out a loud sigh.

"Iris," began Charlé, "it's time I had my own life."

"Me too."

Charlé ignored this and continued, "Abi and I are deeply in love." Iris nodded vaguely. "And we are getting married."

"Are you and Raoul divorced?" Iris inquired coldly.

"No, but we will be."

"And where are we going to live? Alexandria? Thebes?"

Charlé was finding Iris unhelpful, and it surprised her that her daughter could be so insular, so lacking in poetry. "Look, Iris, you'll be eighteen soon. There's no reason why you should have to live with me anymore. Especially since you seem to give yourself the right to approve or disapprove of the man I'm in love with."

Iris murmured, "Sorry."

"Paula can take care of herself, thank God. You're a different problem."

"I really like him," said Iris, hoping to reconquer her mother with one sentence. "Really," she added for emphasis.

Charlé, whose own passion for Abi was based on greed for his money and nostalgia for French accents, did not feel that there was anything *louche* in marrying an Egyptian. Iris was one of the few people, along with Lord Vizreader and Dara's maid, who were openly reserved about Abi, and though it was easy enough, though socially damaging, to avoid Lord Vizreader, and difficult but manageable to avoid Dara's maid, her own daughter was another matter. "I think," she said, "that you should go to college."

"Yeah," said Iris. "Because I'm such a brain."

"No," said Charlé, in one of the colder pronouncements of her life. "Because it's time you and I saw less of each other."

Iris felt as if one of her mother's high heels had pierced through her rib cage. Her perceptions were not acute enough for her to realize that the dialogue her mother was using was lovers' talk, the choice of words inappropriate.

"What will I do?" she wailed, like any lover.

"Study and make friends your own age. You've been around grown-ups all your life and it hasn't been good for you, no sirree."

"Paula's not a grown-up!"

"Paula's been a grown-up since the day she was born."

"I'll be separated from Paula—my God, what are you doing to me, you're breaking up the family to fuck an Arab!"

Charlé stood up to go and slap Iris but thought better of it. "You've just done it, my dear," she said. "That's it. You'd better apply to whatever college will take you, and judging by your English, I'd say you should try for a French university, if they'll take you."

"Why shouldn't I get into Oxford? I can study French there," screamed Iris. "If Valentine Vizreader can get in, so can I." Charlé tapped her foot. "He is the son of a peer of the realm, it's different for him. You're an American."

"I am not," shouted Iris, and then she took a deep breath. "Only sort of," she added lamely.

Charlé began to see a way out of her problem. When Iris had stalked disconsolately out of the room, she poured herself a drink and called Ben-Abi at the Dorchester. Having assured herself that he truly loved her, she called Tyler in Orange County to ask for his assistance with Iris's education.

So it was that Iris Bromley's European childhood came to an end. Three months later she was enrolled at Frances Lyle College, a liberal university near New York dedicated to educating young women of large fortune and unstable temperament.

Part III
REAL LIFE

16.

Hair

One morning in the dining hall of Frances Lyle College, Iris read in her copy of the New York *Daily News* that Raoul Abime had sold his Paris residence, which the paper called the Rose Castle. She felt immediate outrage; the name was all wrong, and furthermore Raoul had never owned it and therefore could not possibly be selling it.

She resumed eating her toast, cinnamon and raisin bread charred to a satisfying black and bent under a load of apple butter; but barely had she taken a bite when her outrage deepened, dispelling her appetite. She was hurt that she should have had to find out about so deeply personal a matter from the gray pages of a tabloid. She felt betrayed: Raoul's reasons for ceasing to rent the Château Rose were doubtless important to him, but irrelevant to her. It was his presumption in acting on them without consulting anyone that angered her. For the Château Rose was a part of her past, and although she expected little from her former stepfather, she had never imagined that he would dispose of her childhood in so cavalier a manner.

She read the item again, just to make sure. It was in Suzy Knickerbocker's column, between a paragraph about Marisa Berenson and the

Baron Arnaud de Rosnay and something about the Spanish ambassador.

She scooped up the paper, and with it a French Lit. text entitled *French Romantic Writers: Sorrow, Spleen and Sex.* She would phone Paula at once. At the door of the dining hall she was stopped by the urge to go down to the mailroom and see if there was something in her box; the number of important letters Iris had received in the three years she had been at Frances Lyle could be counted on one finger, but she believed in synchronicity and last-minute rescues. She clattered down the stairs in her new clogs and peered through the glass on her box. A piece of paper curled against its side. Quickly she opened the little door, and pulled out a handcrafted mimeographed sheet announcing that Laura Hohenzollern had canaries for sale.

The campus was quiet around eleven in the morning, which was Iris's preferred time, and she had so arranged her classes that her presence was never required before the afternoon. Slowly she trudged up the bosky hillocks upon which Frances Lyle had seen fit to establish her institution —"Dedicated to drawing out the living spark of the spirit from the pure hearts of young women," it said on the brochure and the college's letterhead—and arrived at the door to her dormitory, an ancient building by American standards, erected at the time of the First World War. Its Tudor gables and leaded windows would have had a certain charm had it not been for generations of institutional neglect and the weekly use of disinfectant. It was named after one of the college's principal benefactors, and its lack of glamour resided principally in its unromantic name of Kleinwort.

She had not always been stationed in Kleinwort; her first year she had been in Avery, a nice plain name that led to jokes about aviaries from the few young men she managed to encounter during her forays into New York City. The second year she had been in a dorm called Tobaschelli, named after a minor opera singer who had been taught at Frances Lyle and whose grateful family had donated an edifice of white stone in the manner of the Pitti Palace, but with fewer windows. That entire year she had received no letters at all; she figured it was laziness on the part of her correspondents, faced with such an unwieldy name; she dared not face the fact of their indifference, and if she ever met anyone in the mailroom that year as she opened her empty box, she would improvise sparkling discourses on the unreliability of the mail from Europe. The other girls hated her for being so European when she was as American as they were; anyone who could speak French like that and insisted on speaking it at times when it was neither appropriate nor likely to be understood should at least have a French name. They found Iris pretentious, loud and resentful.

She had every right to be resentful: her mother, stepfather, second stepfather, stepsister and even Jill Adams seemed to have contracted as a body to forget her, and it was only with the most enormous effort on her part that some semblance of contact continued. They'll see me again and I will have become just like the people around me, she thought. I will have lost every trace of civilization. She pictured herself with a small cotton square over her hair and tied at the nape of her neck, a navy smock, a joint in one hand, talking about the SDS and Timothy Leary and flying saucers. That'll show them, she thought, but she knew that nothing she could do was likely to produce any great shock in Charlé or Paula. And, despite the clogs from a Scandinavian shop specializing in clumsy footwear, she had not changed that much.

She had put on a few pounds with the pill: her stomach bulged, as did her thighs; her jowls were heavier than they should have been and the flesh around her ankles was clogged with water. She was still a virgin, but determined to be prepared. Opportunity had presented itself several times in the last three years, but inevitably it came with a moustache, a VW van, and an invitation to get stoned, and Iris found all three of these factors rebarbative; nor did they constitute an equal trade for the prize of her virginity. She prided herself on being too sophisticated to be dazzled by fast cars and a nodding acquaintance with headwaiters, but she would not countenance the idea of a man who had anything less than a reputation. She was too humble to demand fame, but someone like a magazine writer or perhaps an art director would be, in her own terms, powerful enough to interest her. There were few magazine writers and art directors hanging around the campus of Frances Lyle, and as they were not a breed upon whom the aspirations of other Frances Lyle girls were fastened, she did not meet them when she spent weekends in town with her new friends.

Her hair was long, like that of the five hundred other girls on campus. Frances Lyle was known for its students' hair; they wore it down to their hips or beyond, flew it like banners, swung it like swallowtail pennants; hair—chestnut and dull brown, blond streaked with taupe, impenetrable black, sun-crinkled red—was the ensign of the college; no girls at Smith and Vassar dared foster such unbridled growth. Frances Lyle girls talked often and furiously about hair; its feeding and upkeep and length and life-span. They held drying sessions in front of the fireplaces in each dorm, for they believed that electricity was bad for hair. They put mayonnaise on it, mashed avocadoes, lemon juice, vinegar, raw eggs, oil of almonds, honey. They affected a peculiar ponytail in which the ends of the hair were placed over the top of the head, in the manner of sumo wrestlers, and fastened with imitation tortoiseshell clasps. They did not wear buns, which they found professorial and too restricting, uptight. Occasionally they wore braids hanging down over their chests, in the style favored by the betrayed but passionate Indian braves in Westerns. They did not wear makeup, which they considered artificial and old-fashioned, and only in this did Iris differ from the rest, for she could not resist eye-liner; at moments of great stress, when she wondered what her purpose was on earth and what her future held, she would barricade herself in her room and carefully groom her face, imitating in every detail the careful ritual that she had watched Paula perform. Then she would look in the mirror at the image she had created, which, with a bit of sucking in at the cheeks and the correct tilt of her head, almost resembled that of Paula in the magazines, and she would feel reassured.

The dissatisfactions of her generation were growing into an ideology, soon to be called the Women's Movement, but at that time they were still confined to savage acts against pretty girls, such as tearing up their clothes and throwing away their false lashes when they weren't looking. Pretty girls were called sellouts, traitors, victims of consumerism; rap sessions were held in the dorms after the hair-drying sessions, in which the more politically oriented and less sexually driven girls—usually potential great beauties of above-average height, the objects of homosexual fantasies—pointed out that the greatest enemy was Man: Man made the products and invented the advertising to corrupt and enslave women; Man wanted nothing more than to keep women in the servile and second-rate state of breeders and baby minders; Man was a Heel.

Still Iris kept taking the nauseous little white pills in their twenty-four-pill cards of silver paper and plastic (with rounded edges to suggest feminine pliability); still she longed to be fucked and dreamt of phalluses, sometimes in the form of growing castles, sometimes in the form of cucumbers, and most often disguised as wriggling pink and yellow worms. She didn't tell anyone about this. As far as her classmates were concerned, she was a sophisticate who had been intimate with the Yardbirds and the Kinks if not the Beatles back in London. She was embarrassed about her physical longings, particularly as she had talked herself into the awkward position of seeming to know more than she actually did about matters of the flesh. This misconception was fostered by the walls of her room, which exhibited provocative quotes from French Romantic poets amid a profusion of pictures torn from magazines and newspapers. These were fixed to the walls with Scotch tape and cunning little wedges of putty in such a way that the surface of the wall was completely hidden by the shingles of torn paper. The other girls thought the pictures represented the men in her life, but they were Paula's men. Her friends peered with an admiration devoid of envy at the haggard young faces under spiky long hair. " 'Michael Preston, lead guitar of the Thamesmen,' " they read out, " 'Frank Studer, bright new star.' " "Oh wow! 'Jared Gartner, Fellini's discovery'—Iris, why don't you bring any of them back here?"

Iris would shrug and say, "They're not much fun anyway."

She settled herself on her bed, which was covered like every other bed in the dorm with an Indian bedspread from Azuma, in teal and curry, and smiled at the pictures on her walls, at Paula and Vivien and Raoul and Jill. There was a tiny picture of Charlé, who had been renamed Charlie by Ben-Abi, in a little frame hidden behind a postcard, upon which was printed an injunction to "Go Placidly Amid the Noise and Haste."

The phone rang. It was Charlé-Charlie. "How's my little baby?" she began, a startling overture for her. "Ben-Abi had to go to Beirut, so I came here. How are you?"

"Mother," said Iris in a warning voice, "I'm busy. I'll ring you back after my class."

"Very well," said Charlie, a little put out by Iris's brusque disregard for the news of her arrival. "I'm at the Pierre."

Iris hung up with a sigh. Charlie had been to New York four times in three years, and yet each time she expected Iris to act as if her visit was important. Iris had told her roommate, one Honey Rittensporn, that she felt nothing for her mother, and Honey's grave acceptance of this revelation had made Iris realize they shared a common problem.

She had known when she left London that family would be inevitable in New York the way yellow fever was inevitable in the tropics. She had dutifully visited her grandmother in the East Eighties and said polite words to her grandfather Eddie, looked at the family album, noticed that her mother was wearing a large bow in her hair on Easter Sunday in 1933, drunk a dark wine called Bull's Blood, and contrived to disappear without leaving her private number at Frances Lyle. The meeting with her father had contained fewer risks of prolonged contact, as he commuted between Florida and California and rarely came to New York, which he called "the Apple," with the excuse, he told her, guffawing, that he preferred oranges. Nonetheless, when she first arrived, she had been obliged to meet him at the Waldorf-Astoria, where she sat in the enormous lobby staring at every bald head she saw with fearful expectancy, remembering the intruder at the Château Rose. She hoped his skull would stick out in the crowd; it was the one sure thing she remembered about him.

When a man with a Beatle fringe came over to her and asked, "Iris?" she was startled to recognize a semblance of her own features beneath the thick, shining thatch. He had foiled her again.

Over dinner in a Japanese restaurant, where she watched horrified as pieces of meat shriveled in their own fat on the searing steel plate in the center of the table, he told her she had a grove or two to call her own. He seemed proud of this: she took it to mean that he had named some orange after her. He told her he was sure she had the boys up at Frances Lyle standing in line to get a date with her; she told him primly that it was an all-girl school. He said he was glad to know that, as he was paying for her education, which she found an ungracious thing for him to mention. He commented on her slight accent with proprietary pride, as if he were responsible for her time in London. She listened while he told her stories about frost and weather, while she fiddled with chopsticks and tried not to look at him.

She had been ready to make an effort to know him, but the incongruity of finding him disguised as a Beatle shocked her and offended her good taste. It was better to be an orphan than to be related to such a foolish disguise. The wig released her from the duty to be more than slightly polite. He invited her out West to meet his new wife and the twins. She asked what had happened to his old wife. "Francine, bless her heart, passed away," he said. "She got bubonic plague from a squirrel." Iris thought Francine sounded pretty interesting and wondered why all the interesting people were, one way or another, out of reach. She wasn't sure about the expression "passed away." Raoul had never said that about Soula; it sounded maudlin. As they parted he reminded her about the groves and invited her to stay anytime her busy social schedule—that was what he called it, "a busy social schedule," as if anybody had such a thing anymore—allowed her some time for her family. She promised she'd come, and never went. He phoned sometimes, to ask what she was doing over the holidays. She spent the holidays in London with Charlie and Ben-Abi, she told him, but thanks anyway.

Family aside, Iris had to tell Paula about the Château Rose. She knew she was in Los Angeles: she had read her name in the EUROPE TO U.S. list in *Variety* just two days ago. The acting teacher had a subscription to *Variety,* ostensibly to prepare his students for the jargon and rigors of professional life, but in fact to check out opportunities for himself and stay abreast of any developments that might prove beneficial to an ambitious young director of the Brechtian school of musical comedy. Iris, who sometimes helped with costumes and makeup on workshop productions, always looked for it in his office. She tried to remember which hotel Paula had been at last time, and decided to try them all. "I would like five numbers in Los Angeles, California," she told the operator. She gave the Beverly Hills Hotel, the Beverly Wilshire, Don Flagel's house, the Chateau Marmont and Paula's agency, which was called Talent and Beauty, Inc. Panic had triggered in her an ingenuity that was later to become an asset, although the operator found it just a lot of extra work. She checked her watch; a quarter to twelve, therefore a quarter to nine in L.A. She wondered how correct it would be to wake Paula, and reassured herself by reminding herself of the news. This was a grave matter, she decided, no time for niceties.

"Beverly Hills Ho-tel," said a distant voice. Iris had not set foot in Los Angeles since the day she had left tucked under Charlene's arm, but she fancied she recognized an undertone of melons and sunshine in the voice, some supermarket memory perhaps, and felt homesick.

"Paula Abime," she said with authority.

"Person to person," added the long-distance operator, ever mindful of form and wishing to hurry through her list.

"One mo-ment, please." Iris allowed herself a smile: right the first time. *BzzzzBzzzz.* "I'm sorry," said the hotel operator, "she's not in. Would you like to leave a message?"

"No message," said Iris. She called Charlie and announced she would come into town for the weekend. "I'd love that," said Charlie, "just love it."

Iris packed two Pucci minidresses and some pink elephant-leg pants into a Gucci hold-all that Paula had given her after her first trip to Rome. She added two of her curly wigs, and packed all her makeup. She would cut French Lit. and the special class on Toussaint L'Ouverture, Caribbean hero, which was really part of Black Studies but was taught in French.

At Grand Central Station she checked the bookstall to see if there was anything she wanted, and bought *Women's Wear Daily.* Sometimes a stray Frances Lyle debutante was caught in its *Eye* pages, and more often she found Smith Clark there. Although she had not spoken to him since London, she saw his picture so often that he felt like one of her closest friends. The adoration she lavished on her walls of pictures had contaminated her emotions to the extent that whenever she saw a published picture of someone she had met, she felt it as a sign from them, a response, a communication.

She bought a Hershey bar for moral support, and went to the coffee shop inside Grand Central. Perhaps she should phone him; he was sure to be interested in news about Raoul. She looked through the sea-blue pages of her little leather address book. His address was secondhand, gleaned from Paula, and it was in any case not his but the address of Esquire Magazine, 488 Madison Avenue. His phone number was a dud. No one had warned her about answering services, and in her first eager weeks in America she had repeatedly called him, as well as some other names and numbers that Charlie had given her, only to find that everyone in New York had at his command rosters of servants answering the phone and offering to take messages without being able to confirm or deny that their employers were at home. Discouraged by the guarded tone of these replies, Iris left no messages, and eventually gave up calling. She was sure she would run into Smith Clark if only she went to the right restaurant and sat in the vicinity of the right tables.

She took her bag with her to Bendel's, where she tried to decide between a pair of papier-mâché earrings and a large Maltese cross by Kenneth Jay Lane, which was set with stones the color of breath mints. Then she walked up Fifth Avenue to the Pierre. It was early spring, neither warm nor cold.

Charlie opened the door to Iris looking more ornate than usual, and lightly pecked her cheek, where she left a smear of sugared bronze. Then she stood back. "Don't you ever get anything dry-cleaned?" she asked, staring at the coffee stains on Iris's Courrèges coat.

"Oh, Mother," said Iris, who had exhumed the coat from the back of her closet especially to please Charlie, "can't I do anything right?" She put her bag down and attempted a hug, which was declined by Charlie with a gesture that implicated the heavy embroidery on the front of her caftan in the necessity to keep a safe distance. "Come see what Allegro's done," said Charlie with a rising trill, leading the way into the apartment, which was Ben-Abi's New York pièd-a-terre, or, as he and Charlie applauded themselves for calling it, pièd-en-l'air. "Who's Allegro?" asked Iris. "Wonderful new decorator. Met him in Marrakesh. One of the boys, if you know what I mean, but really such a sweetheart, and so much imagination!"

Iris gasped. Upon four smallish rooms Allegro Spitz had lavished every illusion he had about the past of Europe and of Asia. A chandelier made of eighteen scimitars threatened the front hall, with a wink to Damocles; the living room contained four Buddhas of varying sizes and degrees of holiness, a battalion of wedding boxes from Japan, lampshades pleated and ruffled like ball gowns, several Louis Quinze armchairs of doubtful origin, a savonnerie carpet from Portugal in tones of pink and lime green, and some twelve wooden saints from churches the length and breadth of Italy. Incensories hung on chains from the ceiling, like evening bags; they threw a Moorish light that allowed the grouping of fat little sofas to aspire to some kinship with the ottomans they would have been had Mr. Spitz's vision had any consistency.

On the walls were prints of London in the 1820's, which gave a stern note of monotony that acted like a tranquilizer on the agitated room; alas, they were interspersed with torchères protruding from the walls at intervals unrelated to those of the incensories; and the bulbs of these were capped with neat little shades. Iris, whose taste was not yet formed, still knew a mess when she saw one; she longed to throw Indian bedspreads over everything. "Whew," she said.

"It's original, isn't it?" asked Charlie. Her daughter's opinion was only mildly interesting to her, but as in the matter of her husband's nationality, she felt she could easily be at a disadvantage if she allowed anything but rapture to be expressed regarding her choice. Iris said nothing, and sat down on one of the little settees. Charlie, rustling in her emerald robes, sat facing her across a tiny glass table upon which was displayed a collection of Art Nouveau silver boxes. "Those are pretty," said Iris, pointing at them. Charlie remembered that she liked little shining things. "I especially like this one," said Iris, picking up one in the shape of a woman turning into a butterfly.

"Please don't, darling—each has a specific position." Charlie batted her hand at Iris, who gave a loud sigh. "I'm serious, darling. Allegro showed me how to place them all for the best effect, but I can't remember what he said, so put it back where you got it from." She watched as Iris replaced the box, and pushed it with her forefinger to make sure it lay where it belonged.

"Did you read about the Château Rose?" Iris asked.

"No. Did it burn down?" asked Charlie with a mean little laugh.

"Raoul got rid of it," said Iris. Even now she felt herself choke on the news, but Charlie seemed untouched. "Isn't it awful?" she prompted.

Charlie looked over at her. "Really, Iris, you exaggerate so much! What's awful? I suppose the fishwife didn't like it."

"But doesn't it matter to you?"

"No," said Charlie, lighting a cigarette. "Why should it? It was just a place, and all that is a long time ago now."

Abruptly Iris leaned forward and pounced on a chocolate-covered cherry in the little black lacquer bowl, where it was displayed among truffles and almonds. As she brought it to her mouth, Charlie shouted, "Calories!" and Iris reversed the motion without pause and replaced it with its confrères.

"It was home," began Iris, "for eight years, and it was the most beautiful place I've ever lived in. It was . . ."

Charlie blew smoke out of her nostrils and stared at the curtains, uncertain about the length of the fringe on the swags. "*House and Garden* are coming to look at it next week," she retaliated. "They've heard this is the bravest room in New York."

Iris gave up.

"It's time to call Mother," said Charlie. "She says she hasn't heard from you in months. You should be more considerate, at least of her feelings. She is *my* mother, you know."

"I've been busy," snorted Iris. "Study, study, study. And there's a lot more going on these days. Civil disobedience. Draft resisting. Sit-ins. Demonstrations."

Charlie now gave a critical little harrumph. "Well, don't go burning *your* bra," she said. "Not with your figure."

Iris glanced down at her breasts; she was doing the best she could, which mainly entailed not sitting up straight. "Mum," she pleaded, "that's not the important thing. It's the issues. The important thing is Vietnam." She pronounced the name with the correct emphasis of one who knows all the facts and has given lifeblood to the cause.

"You're there to get an education," said Charlie. "Just don't forget that."

Iris held her breath until it was clear that Charlie's intention to call Coquette had been no more than an idle threat. Assuming an expression of uncritical excitement, she worked her voice into a chirp. "Well, what's up tonight?"

"This wonderful hairdresser from London is coming to do my hair, and then we're going out with Sheila McCoy and her new boyfriend, he's something in television, he runs one of the networks, I think. I just don't keep up with New York things enough anymore. What are your plans?"

Iris was confused. "Oh, Mum, I came in just to see you!" she said. If Charlie didn't mean to take her along tonight, who was the other half of the "we" she was talking about? The idea of seeing Sheila McCoy thrilled her. It had been at least fifteen years since she had laid eyes on her, but she held on to the memory of her two meetings with the singer with the tenacity of a real fan. "I'll come with you," she said.

"No beau?" inquired Charlie.

"Let's not go into it," said Iris.

"Peines de coeur? Tu veux dire à Maman?" asked Charlie in her most intimate French, which since her latest marriage had acquired, at least to Iris's purist ear, an unctuous North African inflection that made her wince.

Iris shook her head.

"You know, I saw Valentine Vizreader at Christmas. It's a pity you didn't come to Saint Moritz with us this year. He asked about you."

Iris, who had lunched once with Valentine Vizreader the previous summer and had been saddened but not surprised to hear from his cherry-red lips that he had had a revelation to the effect that his proclivities lay in the direction of boys several years his junior, batted her eyelids twice at her mother and rose to go to the bathroom. "They're all fairies in London," she called from the hall. "It's the school system."

Left alone in the living room, Charlie bit into the cherry that Iris had valiantly resisted and wondered if her daughter was going to turn into a lesbian. It would be acceptable if she was still living in France, she thought, but not if Ben-Abi decided to move back to New York. What do you tell your girlfriends when your daughter is a lesbian? she wondered.

In the toilet Iris wished she had a lover. As recently as January she had gone on a blind date arranged by Honey Rittensporn. As they sat drinking beer in a dark-red bar she had found herself repelled by the distinct difference in class between herself and the young carpenter from New Haven, but she was aware of the holiness of good honest work with the hands and attempted to honor it with a descent into the basement of the auditorium, where there were spare mattresses used for just such philosophical gropings. She had found that she preferred to keep her underpants on, and, returning alone and unblemished to the dorm, had extracted from a blushing Honey Rittensporn the information that the young man was in fact her drug connection. Iris had then gone three weeks without speaking to Honey, sensing disparagement in the girl's choice of a lover for her. Honey broke the silence by explaining: "I'd always heard you say that you liked a bit of uncomplicated fucking." Iris was truly in a corner.

She watched the hairdresser from the door of Charlie's bedroom. He was blond, with skinny hips, tight jeans, a floppy sweater gliding over his bare chest. With his hands on his hips he was staring at Charlie's reflection in the mirror. He turned as she came in, and she saw that his face was a little like Valentine Vizreader's. Even better, she recognized it from the pages of *London Life* and felt an immediate pang of homesickness that she interpreted, wrongly, as attraction.

"Iris, Nick," muttered Charlie.

"Hi, sweetheart, ain't I seen you somewhere before?"

Iris quickly checked her reflection in the mirror to see who it was that she looked like. Finding no traces of either Lynn Redgrave or Charlotte Rampling, she nonetheless gave him a smile and sat on the edge of the bed, which was awash with printed roses quilted into bubbles.

"Well?" asked Charlie.

"Shall we touch up the color? My partner Ted's a genius colorist, and he's opening a shop here next week."

Iris rose and quietly left the room.

"It's not going gray, is it?" asked Charlie.

"No, but it could be brighter," reassured Nick. He snipped at some stray ends. "We could shape it a little, make it sharp, y'know?"

His scissors sought perfection through the dull black strands. "Organic, like," he said, "is a great new color. It's developed in by Ted himself, all alone. Genius, he is."

"I'll be back in England next week," she sighed. Then: "I'm worried about Iris."

"Yeah?" he asked, paying little attention.

She was determined to confide in him, since he was to be her escort for the night. It would make them closer.

"She on drugs then?" It was for him a casual question. Charlie screamed. "Did I hurt you?" he asked.

"Iris wouldn't know a drug if it bit her," exclaimed Charlie.

"Wants to run off with some hippie?"

"She hates hippies. I think she hates hippies. I don't see her much, and I'm not sure what her life really *is,*" said the concerned mother. "She can't handle money," she said after a pause, with a glance at Nick, which he took to mean that there was a great deal of money to be handled. "Well, it's a good thing *you* can," he said, in the spirit of flattery; Charlie was not sure how to take this.

In the guest room, Iris lit a joint and lay back on the yellow moiré cushions of the bed. She wanted tonight to be the night. Maybe Sheila McCoy's boyfriend would have a friend; with this hope, she dozed off after carefully stubbing out her joint. She was awakened by a soft knock on the door, and sat up on the bed. "It's almost time to go," said Nick's voice. "Get ready." She thought it might be correct to ask him what she should wear: hairdressers loved giving advice. "Wait!" she shouted, rising from the bed. "I want you to help me." She opened the door.

"Yeah?" he asked.

"What can I do to myself to look fabulous tonight?" she asked with naïve trust.

He narrowed his eyes. "Lose twenty pounds and get a suntan," he answered.

Iris might not have come if Charlie, having shouted through the door several times that it was time to go, hadn't had the inspiration to say, "We're meeting Sheila at Elaine's—we can't just leave her sitting there." The mention of Elaine's was enough to make Iris forget that in the eyes of the hairdresser she was pallid and overweight. Elaine's was where Paula reportedly dined when she was in town, where Jeanne Moreau dined, where Gay Talese and Tom Wolfe and perhaps even Smith Clark hung out; it was where people were noticed, even if they didn't need to be. Warren Beatty went there with Julie Christie; art directors went there; Iris told herself that the hand of destiny was writing the menu tonight, and she was suddenly fearless.

The taxi took them far uptown, and let them off on a drafty sidewalk where odd pieces of paper blew off from stacks of trash. In the restaurant there was a jukebox next to the door, and the room was dark. Had it not been for the sign on the window that said ELAINE'S, Iris would have thought they had come to an ordinary bar, of the kind she made it her business to avoid. Charlie darted forward, having spotted Sheila sitting with a stocky young man near the rear, by the toilets. Nick stopped to say hello to a pair of models sitting at one of the tables; Iris looked at the walls, where book jackets were displayed under posters for art shows in a manner that proclaimed Elaine's to be a home for bohemians, artists and intellectuals.

Despite this omen, the conversation at the table cleaved fast to the only common ground there was between a singing star, a wealthy expatriate, a television executive, a hairdresser and a college girl. They talked about restaurants and airplane food, with occasional digressions into gossip about the people who walked in and were greeted by a fat woman, the owner, who managed to be both surly and effusive.

"Do you still go to Petruschka in Paris? God, it was wonderful. Remember those drunken evenings there with what's-his-name?" asked Sheila.

"It's called Rasputin," corrected Charlie, "and yes, we still go."

"Men come and go, huh, but restaurants go on forever," suggested Iris, trying to catch the light tone that her mother was so good at. For this she received the reward of Charlie's back, which left her free to make eyes at Sheila McCoy's young man.

"Didn't I read about you in the *Village Voice?*" she asked, confident that she was correct: she had cut the piece out, for it had listed "seventy men for the seventies," and she was grateful for any tips that came her way. "Me?" said the young man, whose full name was Bennison Hack III, although Sheila addressed him as Plumface. "I really don't remember," he countered deftly, forcing her to declare herself either a fan, a groupie, or what he called a "media sucker." She proved to be all three by knowing what his position was on Vietnam, where he had worked before BTV (the New York *Herald Tribune*), and what page his picture was on in the *Voice.* He could not help being enchanted by such dogged devotion from a new acquaintance, and as a reward he asked her what she wanted to do when she graduated.

"I'd like to be like you," she said without a trace of shame.

"Why is that?" he asked, making himself as much the elder statesman as his boyish mien allowed.

"Well, you've managed to combine political idealism with being a success," said Iris, mouthing the ambition of her politicized classmates.

"It's not easy," admitted Bennison Hack with a frown.

"Nothing worthwhile ever is," rejoined Iris, quoting her professor.

"I like you, you're wise," said Bennison with feeling. "If there's ever anything I can do for you, just give me a call."

"May I really?" asked Iris, stirred out of caution by hope.

"Sure," he answered. "It's part of my professional responsibility to root out the bright ones." To this he added a little laugh. Iris pushed her address book at him, and he inserted his name under that of Drue Heinz, a grande dame whose address Iris had filched from Charlie's book, although they had not yet been introduced.

"Oh, Drue," said Bennison, whose eye for detail never rested. "How is she?"

Iris changed the subject.

It was a successful evening even before Nick leaned over and mouthed "Let's split." In ordinary times she would have ignored the order, but the exchange with Bennison Hack had buttressed her confidence to such a degree that she no longer feared the contagion of Nick's mediocre status. Charlie was battened into her usual rut of frosty chit-chat with Sheila, who had decided to ignore Nick, and Bennison Hack had been occupying himself with saying hello to the people at other tables between making short phone calls at the pay phone. A woman in a piano shawl and a tight bun had walked through handing out buttons advertising a rock band's new album, and Iris had received one like a sacramental wafer. There seemed to be nothing left to do at Elaine's except leave.

"Oh, Nick, we're going to Arthur," screamed Charlie as the young man rose. "How can we go dancing without you?"

Nick whispered in her ear: "I thought I'd cheer Iris up a bit, make everyone's life easier"; Charlie turned a surprised smile on him. It would definitely be cozier with just Sheila and Bennison; much as she wanted a young man to dance with, she felt a certain reluctance on Sheila's part to open up to Nick, and she realized that Sheila just didn't know how different things were in London, where hairdressers were a vital and exciting part of the scene. "Well, if you think you can cheer her up," she whispered back, "go ahead and have a go." And to that she added a lascivious little giggle meant to encourage Nick to do whatever he wanted with Iris; it made her feel democratic.

"Where are you takin' me?" she asked outside, eliding her consonants to make him feel at home. He extracted a joint from his pocket and hailed a cab with the joint held aloft. "You don't want to get busted," she screamed, and tried to lower his arm. He winked at her. A cab drew up, and they got in, Iris conscious of the prophetic intimacy of sitting on the same backseat. "Where to?" asked the driver, forcing a decision. Iris looked at Nick; he had put his hand on her knee, which had set up in her an unexpected trembling. "Do you want to go dancing?" he queried politely, perceptibly increasing his pressure on her knee. Iris opened her mouth but no sound came out. He watched her mouth and realized that its shape had potential. "Let's go back to my hotel, and get"—he leaned toward her—"stoned." She nodded. "The Berkeley," he ordered, and sat back in the seat, rolling the little twist of paper between his fingers. Iris was conscious of not breathing, and chided herself for being so weak as to be affected by the mere placement of a hand upon her knee. She slid a look over at his knee, wishing that she dared raise her eyes just a little to encompass that portion of his anatomy that was described in the pornographic books she bought in garage sales as "the place where his legs met." She did not allow further consideration of this spot to do more than graze her mind, fearing that it would provoke an agitation that she could not disguise. She focused on her breathing and attempted to rationalize her actions as rapidly as possible, for the cab was speeding. "It's time I got rid of it, high time, this is the perfect moment," she told herself. Nick said nothing. She glanced at him and reconsidered: "But a hairdresser? Hairdressers are homosexual. What am I doing?"

There were few preliminaries in the hotel room: they puffed their way through a second joint; he invited her to join him on the small beige tweed couch and she did. The television was on; it had been on when they came in, Iris still blushing from the look the receptionist had given her, which she thought was full of reproach but was no more than the effect of severe astigmatism. William Holden in Africa with a team of braying elephants attended Nick's slow and disingenuous efforts to grasp her breasts and Iris's efforts to convince herself that this was indeed what she wanted him to do.

"I can go play poker with my mate Ted," he suggested, "if you don't want to do it. I mean, it doesn't matter to me."

"Ted Billingsgate?" asked Iris, distracted out of lust by the familiar name. She sat up.

"No, Ted Cohen. He's a genius colorist."

"Oh." Iris let herself fall back onto the cushions, and turned her head toward the screen. She was still deliberating. It would probably hurt. She felt herself oddly immobilized, and also she wanted to throw up. "I feel sick," she said.

"Must've been something you ate," said Nick without much charity. She didn't want to be left alone in a strange hotel room, and she had no intention of returning to Charlie's apartment. "Don't leave me," she whispered. His presence would be enough to let her think she was doing something. "Stay."

"Fair enough," he said, much to her regret. It was one of those catchy phrases that reminded her of everything she hated about England, principally its lack of enthusiasm for her. It offended her sufficiently to impel her out of the sofa to a standing position: she would leave. Nick took her movement as a cue and slipped his hand inside her dress. She left it there. He pulled her toward a door near the TV set. "Where are you going?" she asked, alarmed. "To the bedroom," he answered, adding with pride, "It's a suite."

He went to turn on the light on the bedside table, but she cried out "No!" The light from the living room was bad enough. She found herself rooted to the foot of the bed. Nick was bending over, pulling down his trousers. She saw his meager bottom outlined with light.

I can't, she thought, I can't.

He turned toward her. There it was, bobbing slightly, pointing straight at her. He took her by the shoulders and laid her down on the bed. Her legs were stiffly held together. He pushed up her short skirt and pulled at the waistband of her tights. With cold hands she helped him, careful to avoid contact with the object that now rested between them like a cool puppy. She unbuttoned the top of her dress and pulled her arms out, grateful that she had remembered to shave her armpits. He looked at her breasts, which slipped away from each other and rested, upturned but slanted, on her upper arms. "Oh wow," he said, reaching for a sharp pink nipple.

"I'm a virgin," she said with extreme difficulty.

"Oh wow," he repeated. There was a few minutes' silent truce. He lit a cigarette, and rose and went to the bathroom. She heard urine splashing on enamel, and thought how close to nature he was, how simple, how uncouth. When he came back, he put his hand on her hair, betraying a certain expertise as he ruffled it and gauged its texture, and then he said, "I'm very gentle." He lay on top of her, and, to her enormous surprise managed to slip himself into her without exerting himself too much; to her even greater surprise, she felt no pain. "You really a virgin?" he asked, as he moved gingerly inside her. She bit her lip, wondering whether this interesting stroking within her merited a scream or a muffled cry, and nodded. She felt a few more soft rubs, and counted them; after seven he was motionless. She stroked his back, which was thin, all ribs and soft skin, and decided that the feeling of a man on top of her wasn't at all bad. Then he pulled himself out of her, and the pleasant contact was replaced by the sudden embarrassment of ooze between her legs. She sat up and grabbed the bedspread, and throwing it around her, she stood up; after a moment's hasty readjustment—she had managed to cover her shoulders while leaving her pubis and bottom bare—she retreated to the bathroom.

She closed the door carefully, and then turned on the light. She saw in the mirror that her face had never looked so puffy, so formless; her eyes were half closed, as if stricken with allergy. Oh well, she thought, at last, and splashed her face. Then she looked at herself again and laughed. A drop of white glue fell from between her legs and landed on the tiled floor with a splat.

She spent the night there, crawling toward Nick to try touching his back, retreating to try to sleep, dreaming of crumbling teeth and tired tulips. In the morning she called Charlie and said she'd have lunch with her midweek; she felt that any other announcement would provide the prelude to some form of recrimination.

"May I ask where you are?"

"I'm back at school," she lied.

Nick's partner Ted came in and announced she had just the kind of hair he wanted to try his new color on; Iris willingly took to Nick's bathroom, where she sat all day with a towel around her shoulders. By early evening Ted had finished, and Iris's black hair was now a glittering shade of copper, like that of certain usherettes and cashiers. "Camp, isn't it?" grinned Nick. Iris thought it was fabulous, and said so. She felt a little uncomfortable with Nick now that the deed had been done, and wanted to return to Frances Lyle and think about the meaning of it all before she did it again, but he started plucking her eyebrows and snipping at her hair, and somehow it was eleven at night. She hoped he would take her to Elaine's, but he said it wasn't his scene, and ordered from room service. They ate in bed, with the TV staring at them from the doorway, and Iris decided that sin was boring. Then he lay on top of her again. This time she counted to fourteen before he stopped, and she kissed him afterward. Later, in the night, she tried to interest him in her body, but he mumbled, "You'll break it off if you go on like that," so she gave up.

The next day he looked at her new red hair and announced that he had to give it some shape. He was opening up a salon in New York next month, and he wanted to get his statement right. She hoped he would make her his model, and returned willingly again to the bathroom. After four hours in front of the sink, he had cut twenty-two inches from her hair. "See, I told you," he said as she stared at herself. "You look like a new chick." She agreed: like a newly hatched little pullet.

"I must go back to school," said Iris. She took a bath, changing the water twice, and regretted that she had left all her other clothes at Charlie's.

The first thing Iris did at the dorm was change into clothes that she thought might go with the shaggy copper head that was now hers. She was delighted to find when she stepped on the scale that she had lost four pounds, and attributed the miracle to sex, rather than the irregular meals she had been having for the last thirty hours.

That evening, when she came into the dining hall, where ninety percent of the Frances Lyle students were gathered to stage a sit-in, she sensed that people were looking at her in a new way. A group of girls carrying placards on which were pasted Revlon ads and pages from fashion magazines stared at her. She went up to them, braving it out, and asked what the placards were about. "I thought this was going to be a sit-in about the war—what's this other stuff?"

"This degrades women!" shouted Shawna Manners, pointing to a photograph where a model's ear was being raped by a fat sable brush tipped with pink rouge.

"Of course," said Iris hurriedly.

"And we're burning later," said another girl. "Fashion magazines. All of them. Jean Shrimpton in effigy. Your Paula. All the traitors."

"Traitors," said Iris. She was trying to conjure up the feeling of Nick's cock inside her, but what had been scant sensation was now almost imperceptible. At least her nipples were sore.

"Iris!" Honey Rittensporn screamed at her from the tea urns across the hall. She ran over to Iris, carrying a sheaf of leaflets. "My God," she said. "You look absolutely, utterly, too, too divinely incredible! What happened?"

Iris was tempted to tell her, but then her secret would be out. "Nothing," she said, "just the usual—Elaine's and a few fucks, you know."

"But your hair!" screamed Honey, louder than she should have in that company. "Your hair is a masterpiece! You must give me the name of your hairdresser!"

17.

Horror Vacui

Iris couldn't sleep that night. She lay in bed and watched the dawn, which came upon the campus in the guise of fog. Nature around Frances Lyle was conducive not to reverie but to the seeking of shelter. Hybrid bushes, trees brought from distant places, and planted with great ceremony and later adorned with little plaques to explain who had given them, alternated with thick unruly woods and angry looming boulders. The grass, even in the absence of dogs, was sparse and looked chewed up; the bumps and ridges of the Glenarm fault, which ran directly beneath the main line of buildings, hunkered and cringed in an image of geological hysteria. As landscapes go, the place lacked tranquillity.

When it was almost light, Iris got out of bed and put a record on. It was one that Paula had given her in London, and its title, "From the Underworld," was something that Iris thought might have some bearing on her peculiar state of mind. She sat on the bed and smoked a cigarette, looking at her feet, listening for a message.

> "Out of the land of shadows and darkness
> You are returning towards the morning light."

These lines afforded some comfort; not so the next.

> "Don't turn around now, I hear you whisper
> In my ear
> If you should turn now, all that you want now
> Will vanish like a passing dream."

As the music trailed off she began to weep, without finding any release in her tears. She rose to shut off the record player, a college model in which the turntable swiveled out like a Murphy bed.

She began to skim through her room, looking for reassurance. The phrase "identity crisis" came to her mind. Her classmates had all had theirs. Her professors, most of them Frenchmen transported to America, said she was suffering from culture shock; they had been saying it for years. "Don't worry, one acclimatizes," her literature professor had said. The Freudian analyst she had visited three times at the end of her first year, on the advice of her adviser, had claimed she harbored a deep-seated rejection of man. In mid-room, Iris stopped and thought about that. No, she did not want to see Nick again. But neither did she reject man. She began to pace again. She opened her closet. The time spent in boutiques and department stores, shoring up and caulking her image as a girl-of-the-world had provided her with every invention fashion could spew up in those years. The wigs were on the top shelf; hanging from the rail were leather miniskirts, chenille sweaters, caftans from Israel. She rummaged through her drawers, looking for a clue. She found granny glasses, bangles from Bombay, buttons from her buttoned boots. She went to her desk and looked at her collection of pads of writing paper arbitrarily adorned with the features of Marilyn Monroe and Mata Hari, the multicolored note jotters she never used, the felt pens in the shape of rockets or feathers. She riffled through various boxes on her dresser; such appellations as Desk Set or Jewelry Tidy regularly drove her mad with acquisitive lust, and she had several of each, believing that her changing moods would require seasonal changes of color and shape in these items. This morning they yielded no pleasure.

She went to the pictures on the walls, staring at Raoul for a long time. "I miss you," she said. *"Tu me manques."*

She looked at herself in the bathroom mirror and shook her head at the unfamiliar face. She looked not trendy, not chic, not elegant, not even like a boy. She looked simply shorn, like a collaborator in 1944. She would not allow herself the dull feminine reaction of mourning for lost locks, she was better than that. She returned to the bed and attempted to excite herself, but her body was like a friend who had been consorting with enemies: it didn't want to know any more.

She couldn't sleep; she decided to read, but a glimpse of the forbidding titles on her bookshelves sent her looking for a copy of *Cosmopolitan* under her bed. "How to Keep Your Man," it said on the cover. She sought another reason to read it. "How to Lose Fifteen Pounds Fast!" held her interest. She read about grapefruit and hard-boiled eggs—old news—and then turned to the horoscope. "Lucky girl!" it said. "Star opportunities shine down on you this month, and a bright witty Gemini keeps you positively tingling through the full moon. This is your month!" She read on, momentarily arrested: Iris consumed Metrecal, Mayor Lindsay, and Bonnie and Clyde berets indiscriminately; the *Cosmopolitan* horoscope was as believable as the rest. "An intrepid Sagittarius takes you hiking, skiing, or snorkeling mid-month." She let the magazine drop to the floor: didn't they know she hated sports?

Fifteen cigarettes later, the sun was high over the Tudor bell tower and Iris was reading a book called *Elegance,* which had alphabetical headings for such things as Shoes, Trousers, Velvet, Undergarments, Wool, Yearly Review, and Zibeline. Part of her mind was occupied with visions of herself on a jagged mountain road, being held by a man who covered her eyes and touched her body. She soothed the excitation with bland prose about the care of real silk stockings. Noises began in the dorm: the clattering of clogs on wooden floors, the banging of doors, the hurried typing of last-minute additions to term papers. In the bathroom she heard Honey turn on the shower, and the splash of water on tiles reminded her of Nick's hotel room. Determined not to be distracted by an emotion that she found puzzling and inappropriate, she read on: "Small circular pads should be sewn into the armpits of all fine garments by your maid. The damage done to silk by modern-day deodorants is one of the things a chic woman must guard against."

"Iris?" called Honey. "Will you listen for my phone? Jerry's calling and I don't want to miss it. Iris?" Honey opened the door; Iris lay back on her bed, *Elegance* in her hand, eyes closed, snoring slightly.

When Honey had gone to breakfast and the dorm was quiet again, save for the frantic typing that Iris deduced to be Katie Milford working on her Hegel three doors down, Iris finished the book and went into the bathroom. She opened the medicine cabinet; she was hoping Honey had left her Valium behind, but as usual she had taken them with her to her first class. The only drugs to be found were Midol and No-Doz. A joke of Saul's about the moron tiptoeing past the medicine cabinet flashed through her mind, and she tiptoed back to bed.

At noon the bell tower chimed, waking her. Sunshine filled the room. Spring was upon her, with its horrible imperative to be happy. She sat up in her crumpled nightgown and tried to remember if she had a class.

She went to her diary; on the advice of Honey, her biorhythm scores were heavily marked on the upper corners of every page.

To her surprise, she saw that they had risen through the previous week, to culminate on Friday; marked in ink was the evidence that she had been on an intellectual, physical and emotional high. She had been waiting for the three sets of numbers to coincide ever since Honey had taught her how to calculate rhythms. "Triple highs are the best things that can happen to you," Honey had assured her.

I got laid by a hairdresser, thought Iris. If that was the best that a triple high could bring her, there seemed little point in going on. The pictures on the wall smiled at her blindly from the pinnacles of better lives. Iris looked at the pictures of Michael Preston and Frank Studer facing Paula's wall. The only way she could justify to herself the aberrant act of pinning them up was to have them facing Paula so that the correspondence would be logical to her own eyes, if obscure to those of her visitors. She looked over at Paula, reigning over the wall by her desk, painted in camouflage to look like an antelope, decked in tulle, self-sufficient in her perfection.

She turned to Raoul's wall: black-and-white pictures of him at airports, or hunched behind microphones at press conferences, surrounded a color portrait of him chewing on his pipe, with the word "Perennial" inlaid under his chin; it was torn from *Life.* Iris had composed a frieze of tender scenes between Vivien and Raoul, posed for Italian and French magazines that she had tracked down at Rizzoli's international bookstore in the city. She had still not visited the house on the Appia, but felt she knew it well, particularly the living room with its fumed oak beams and tiled fireplace. That was where Vivien liked to sit on an ottoman in front of the fire, looking tenderly at one of her Labradors. There was a sofa, Iris knew, behind the ottoman, although it wasn't visible in every picture, and in the latest layouts it seemed to have been re-covered, going from blurred orange to blurred blue. There were poplars on the grounds, and somewhere a swimming pool. Szos had told her there was a little temple, which he described as an early Roman latrine in ruins, but she imagined a temple of Vesta, the site of dark mysteries performed by the superior and doubtless magical Vivien, the sorceress, the enchantress.

Iris looked to the pictures for confirmation of her own existence. She had collected these fragments of other people's lives with an ardor unsuspected by her schoolmates. She thought of Paula and Raoul and Vivien as parts of herself, their lives as her own. The duty she imposed on herself to become the curator of the disparate scraps of evidence they left in their trail seemed to her, in normal times, to be the only logical means of countering the effects that time and forgetfulness had wrought on her property, her past, her family. The silent worship she sent up to the clippings was not something she usually perceived as misplaced or sacrilegious. The components of her true life were scattered; the clippings were her only defense against feeling abandoned.

She felt just now like—she struggled for comparisons—Napoleon on Elba, Napoleon on St. Helena, Churchill in the wilderness, a feral child. Abandoned.

She was wide awake but exhausted, bleary and uncoordinated. She sat down at her desk: study was supposed to ease pain, everyone said that. As she had elected to study French, and had managed in three years to go over the same subjects she had been taught from the age of four, she could only remember two occasions on which she had been conscious of truly studying. They had both involved staying up all night in the dorm kitchen and eating some twenty or thirty pieces of toasted whole-wheat bread spread with little squares of butter filched from the dining hall; her memory of those nights was not of what she had been reading, but of the difficulty of spreading the hard butter on the soft bread, and of the cool butter and the warm crumbs as they went down her throat.

She turned to her bookshelf for solace and illumination. Set texts on *La Vie sous la Deuxième République* and mimeographed lectures on light images in George Sand's correspondence were jammed alongside books chosen solely for their apparent complexity. Although she still couldn't write a sentence in English that said what she meant, she reveled in the notion of the intellectual superiority that her second language had bestowed upon her. Hermetic titles and impenetrable names delighted her for their apparent weightiness, and she had assembled the most opaque gems the college bookstore had to offer. Her shelves exhibited Hildesheimer flanked by Honegger, Dobzhansky with Husserl, and two copies of Wittgenstein: a title such as *Tractatus Logico-philosophicus* fulfilled her every requirement. She had never tried to read the last, and was consequently undaunted by the difficulty of the ideas within.

When buying the books, she generally felt she wanted to know what was in them, but the desire in itself was insufficient. A kind of blankness descended on her whenever she reached for even an assigned textbook, and despite her willingness to be violated by great ideas and irrevocably changed from within, she was unable to summon up the necessary receptivity. Still, the shelves impressed her visitors from outside the college as much as the clippings impressed the Frances Lyle girls, and for Iris that was enough. Being unable to grasp anything more than the surface of things, she had made her home in the shallows, and long ago settled for appearance over reality. She was content to seem glamorous to the intellectual and intellectual to the glamorous. The twin misapprehensions combined, on good days, to make her feel that she was living a full, rich life.

Maybe, she thought, everything really is okay, I'm just *inquiète.* She felt . . . the French for it translated as "terraced by a deaf anguish," which didn't sound right in English, but that was the feeling. A triple high is probably very heady, like really good grass, she told herself. She would call Paula.

The operator at the Beverly Hills Hotel had an even cheerier voice today. "I'll put you right through," she said. The phone rang in the room.

"Yeah." A man's voice.

"Is Paula there?" Iris looked at her watch: twelve-thirty. It wasn't too early.

"Who is this?" He sounded asleep, and angry.

"It's her sister."

A muffled sound. "She hasn't got a sister," said the man. Then he hung up.

Iris let the receiver dangle at the end of her arm. Her heart was beating too fast. She tried to calm herself with the idea that she had been connected to the wrong room; but the man had said "Paula," she was almost sure she had heard him. Maybe someone was playing a joke on her. Maybe Paula had picked up some stranger who didn't know about her real life, her real attachments. She pondered whether to try again.

What was the use? She looked at her Paula wall. Paula, who truly did not care, Paula, for whom she was nobody.

She took her mat knife from the bureau drawer, adjusted its blade and, without thinking about it, sliced across the back of her hand. She was squeamish about the curve of her thumbs, the inside of her knees, the veins at her wrist. The back of her hand was less fragile and thus less intimidating.

The skin separated easily; she didn't look.

The blood came out in regular spurts, like water from a pump. It was dark, and warm. She watched it flow out to cover her hand, then held her hand up so it would run down her arm. I can do anything, she thought. She felt brave. Then the blood slowed a little, the pumping seemed to abate. She shook her arm to get it going again, and remembered that warm water encouraged blood to flow.

She rose gingerly, fearing that she would be too faint to walk, and was disappointed to find herself able to negotiate the few feet to the bathroom. Perhaps a little deeper, she thought, and held the point of the blade to her hand.

A new eddy rose through the gash, and as she looked at it she felt a sudden nausea at the sight. That was her hand? She wanted to run away from it.

She decided she should call for help, then felt like an idiot; she contemplated the deep rivulets on her arm that moments ago had provided such a pleasant feeling of power, and found them theatrical, ridiculous. Quickly she rinsed them off, and then ran into the corridor and shouted "Help!" in a small, unconvinced voice, squeezing her arm to make the blood flow a little more. After the third "Help!" Katie Milford, with a face like thunder and her glasses askew, came out and glared at her. Iris held out her arm and Katie ran toward her.

"It's an accident," she said. Katie didn't believe her, but helped her back to bed.

It was lucky for Iris that she developed mononucleosis a few days later. Otherwise she would have had to finish the semester like all the other girls who aspired to be ordinary people and called it being real; she would have had to study and simulate a semblance of enthusiasm for the spring.

This way she found herself in the infirmary, surrounded by flowers, visited by Charlie, who was about to leave for Capri when Iris called her to tell her the news. "I'll stay and take care of you," she announced. "What do you need?"

"Nothing," said Iris. "Just tell Paula I'm sick. She's in Los Angeles, at the Beverly Hills Hotel. I'm really sick."

Charlie came up in a limousine and brought her what she humbly called "light reading matter," not knowing that Iris seldom read anything else. There were journals on decoration and a great many movie magazines, which Iris found odd, for they seemed well thumbed, secondhand almost. "Paula will come and see you next week," Charlie told her. "And maybe Ben will come to New York, and if he does, we'll both come up and see you, wouldn't that be nice?"

A week later Paula arrived at the infirmary; she wore a black ciré jumpsuit and carried an immense bunch of flowers. Iris had no way of knowing that the flowers had been in Paula's hotel room when she checked into the Plaza, a gift from a cosmetic company that was wooing her for a coast-to-coast promotion of its new lip gel; the sight of the flowers convinced her that Paula cared.

"You look fabulous," said Iris, in as weak a voice as she could achieve.

"You look awful," said Paula cheerfully.

Iris motioned to her to come nearer. "Look," she said, pointing to her hand, where a puckered line crossed the back of the wrist, red on white.

"You didn't!" said Paula.

"I did."

"But why?" Paula wrinkled her nose, solicitous but disapproving.

"Love," said Iris.

Paula nodded knowingly. "Who're you telling," she said. "Aren't men awful?"

"I have to get out of here," said Iris.

"Yeah, it looks pretty drab," said Paula. Iris was propped up in bed, her short copper hair sticking out like something on top of a Raggedy Ann.

"Your hair," said Paula. "I don't know if it's you. I had a doll like that once, I think. Who did it?"

"A friend," said Iris. "He's opening a shop in New York."

Paula looked out the window. "What a lot of girls," she said; the infirmary faced the dining hall, and the girls were streaming in for lunch.

"I'm not made for college," said Iris. "They're all babies. I belong in the real world."

"Hah!" said Paula with feeling. "The real world is pretty dreadful too, let me assure you."

"Who was that man you were with in L.A.?" asked Iris very quickly.

"Who?"

"When I called you. About two weeks ago. At the Beverly Wilshire, and he answered the phone."

Paula was looking at her with a sudden mistrust, a narrowing of the nostrils that Iris recognized from the old days as meaning "Keep out of my business."

"I probably got the wrong number," she said hastily.

"I was at the Beverly Hills Hotel, not at the Wilshire," said Paula. Iris remembered that she had called the Beverly Hills, and said nothing.

Paula could have told Iris about going to bed with the male model who had been in the ads with her, but she didn't see why she should. He wasn't a very interesting catch, and, anyway, she didn't want it getting around that she was sleeping with male models.

"I must go now," said Paula, after looking at her watch. "They're waiting for me in town."

Iris didn't ask who they were; she didn't care to show any more interest in Paula's affairs.

"I'll be in Paris this summer," said Paula. "Why don't you come out and stay with me?"

"But where are you staying? Didn't Raoul give up the Château Rose?"

"Why should I stay at the Château Rose?" asked Paula. "I've got my own apartment now."

18.

The Eyes and Ears of the World

Iris lost no time: she had learned during her vigil of hysteria and longing that she could not survive without changing something in her life, and being unprepared to relinquish the teachings of her youth, she sought to advance into the world that was represented by the pictures on her walls. She called Bennison Hack at BTV and was granted an interview, during which she dropped as many names as she could think of and admitted, willfully, that she could not type. Bennison Hack did not pause to inquire whether she could read and write English: it was not the sort of question one asked a Frances Lyle girl. She told him she wanted a summer job, but that she would consider something longer as well. He told her that all the summer jobs at BTV were taken by girls from other colleges. She suggested that she could interview people on the air; TV journalism seemed to her, as it did to most people, to consist of walking around with a microphone in one hand followed by a camera. Bennison Hack, a little defensively, told her that it took a good ten years to get in front of the news. Iris was emboldened by despair, by the memory of the chapel bells tolling as she lay on her bed with the truth of her insufficiency choking her, and was determined not to be discouraged. "I'd be very good," she said. "At anything to do with fame."

"Fame?" he asked. "What qualifies you for that?"

"I've spent my whole life among famous people," she answered, anxious to make this statement sound grave and meaningful. Seeing that he was showing interest, she continued: "They're the only kind of people I feel comfortable with. I feel unnatural with the others."

Bennison Hack knew what she was talking about: his mother had begun calling him from Illinois to ask him if he had *changed* when his success with BTV had put his face on the cover of *Time* magazine. "Name a few," he said.

"My stepfather Raoul Abime, and Vivien Legrand . . ." She saw there was little reaction to either of these, the merest flicker perhaps for Vivien, but nothing to hang a career on. She began inflating: "And Don Flagel, of course, and Albert Camus, and Jean Paul Sartre, and Truman Capote and Elizabeth Taylor, and Maria Callas and David Frost and, of course, my stepsister, Paula Abime."

"The model? I think maybe you could do something for a magazine. Go see my friend Julian Sorrel at *Gentleman.* That's about all I can think of. You may get lucky there."

A week later—a week in which Iris, staying with her mother at the Pierre, discovered that a certain Mike seemed to be leaving an inordinate number of messages for her mother, and that her mother always crumpled up the little slips on which the hotel wrote the messages and put them carefully in her handbag—Iris went to see Julian Sorrel. Being mainly paneled in mahogany with a nautical theme, the offices of *Gentleman* reminded her of Saul's dressing room and her bedroom at the Rue Dumont d'Urville. There were as many tall blondes with streaked hair, high-bridged noses and thin legs in flat moccasins occupying the desks at *Gentleman* as there had been at BTV. She sat across the mahogany desk from Julian Sorrel and watched him for clues. Sorrel was older than Bennison Hack III, and his days as a wonder boy had been wasted on the unresponsive public of the early fifties, the days when wonder horses and wonder dogs and wonder drugs attracted more attention than the efforts of ambitious young journalists. Iris saw a confident-looking man, burlier than Bennison Hack, red in the face and therefore, to her, beefy, in a rumpled summer suit of heavy linen. He had dark hair, a decent amount of it, and the way it stuck out over and behind his ears gave him what she took to be a look of Byronic distraction. She thought he was larger than life rather than overweight, interestingly casual about his clothes rather than slovenly, sexually attractive rather than simply in a position to help her.

Julian Sorrel's twenty years of manipulating the curiosity of his readers, first as a gossip columnist and arson reporter, later as a newspaper editor, and on and on until he was at last the *éminence virile* of *Gentleman* magazine, had earned him two cynical certainties to which he clung as talismans against getting suckered into his own game. The first was the conviction that most human actions, with the exception of defecating and paying bills, sprang from the urge to be known. He imagined the entire human race to be driven by a passion to see its three and a half billion names in print, for in twenty years he had not met a single being who did not want to be written about. He saw the efforts of performers to outdo themselves as lust for good reviews, the randiness of young people of both sexes as no more than a desire to be gossiped about, and campaign speeches, balls, dinner parties, weekends in the country, procreation, even lunacy and suicide, as no more than grist for his mill and therefore merely examples of the endless, fearful, screaming, immemorial desire of mankind to be talked about, if only, as a last resort, posthumously. (If anyone disputed him on this point, he would say, "It is a well-known fact that people who attempt suicide are only trying to draw attention to themselves. Why shouldn't the same be true of those who succeed?") He had sometimes, on train journeys or plane trips, at odd moments when he was not occupied with gathering news or being beamed at, considered writing a history of this urge called "From Tom-toms to Press Releases."

"So," he said to Iris. "You want your name in the papers?"

"Not my name," she said. "I'm not like that."

Julian Sorrel smiled to himself. He appraised her with what he called his "working-girl eye," which called upon a less stringent set of standards than those he imposed on actresses, models and society women who could afford to have themselves improved. Her litany of names had not struck him as particularly exceptional, being a hodgepodge of the late fifties and the most obvious cultural beacons of the year they were at present consuming, 1970. He fixed a point just beyond her head, a trick of his to disconcert beginners, and asked her why she wanted to be a journalist.

"I never said I wanted to be a journalist—just that I wanted to write for you," she answered.

"Yes, about this stepsister of yours. Are you prepared to tell everything about her?"

"What do you mean by 'everything'?"

"My dear," he said—it gave him a kindly avuncular air, this "my dear," and he only used it on people he was planning never to see again, as he did not want to find himself, *ever,* in a position where he had to match actions to his words—"My dear, unless you are prepared to tell everything you know about the subject of a profile, you might as well become a publicist. Publicists are paid by people to get their names in the papers. I'm sure your model stepsister has one."

"She doesn't," said Iris.

"That's just what a good, loyal, well-paid publicist would say. Now, as all you're offering me is the fact that you are obscurely related to this very pretty but, let's face it, pretty irrelevant girl, I'm afraid there's nothing I can do for you."

Iris felt salvation, which had been hovering in the room, to have suddenly departed. "Oh God," she moaned. "Isn't there anything I can do?"

"Research," said Julian Sorrel flatly, which was the same suggestion as Bennison Hack had put forward. "Or, you could come up with a story idea. Like, for instance, do pretty girls have more fun? Now, that's an idea."

"What about it?" asked Iris, hope renewed.

"It's been done a million times before." He sat back on his leather swivel chair, and tilted it so as to effect the greatest possible distance between himself and Iris without actually getting up. The plump young girl across the desk from him had a look of savage hunger in her round brown eyes, one he had not seen since earlier that morning while shuffling through a sheet of contacts of Biafran refugees.

"Journalism is not a way to make a living. The pay is low; only the top one percent earn anything worth investing," he said.

"I have a private income," she said, almost certain she was speaking the truth.

"That's not good. Journalism requires hunger. Unless you want to make your mark, you should forget it. It's tough."

"I don't mind," said Iris.

"The day will come," said Julian Sorrel, "when you have to choose between protecting the interests of your friends and getting a story. Are you sure you know which choice you'd make?"

Iris remained silent. She was anxious to use the capital she had, the stock of acquaintances that her mother had so lovingly built up. She was not sure if she should waste it all at the very beginning of her adult life. She was silenced not by ethics but by social bookkeeping.

"Why don't you try fashion? It's easy for girls, and I could send you to someone I know."

"I'll try anything," answered Iris.

A week later Iris went to see one Joe Johansen at the offices of a publication called *Style,* a weekly magazine devoted to secondhand aperçus on contemporary life gleaned from other publications. *Style,* a sort of fan magazine for those whose greatest joy in life was shopping, prided itself on photographs of the young and celebrated and every other page housed a gossip column where the names of designers appeared in bold type. Even the college girls who had not secured posts in the research department of BTV, the reception desks of *Gentleman,* or jobs as rovers at Condé Nast, thought *Style* was a little too fluffy. It was Iris's luck that *Style*'s second-string party critic had been taken ill with food poisoning the day before she went to see Johansen.

She recited her list of names to him.

"So," said Johansen, a young man with a round, exhausted face, wearing a seersucker suit and a bow tie in the hues of a tomato sandwich on white bread, "you know everybody and you're rich. How come we haven't met before?"

"I was in Europe," said Iris grandly.

"Julian," he continued, "who, by the way, started me off in journalism, so I won't hear a word against him—does he still cough into his handkerchief and then look at it, by the way—anyway, Julian said you have an article on Paula Abime. Where is it?"

Iris looked at a poster on the wall advertising a fashion show at Bloomingdale's, and tried to imagine where the article might be if she had written it. The phone rang, and Johansen answered it. By the time he hung up, he had forgotten his question, and looked instead at her short copper hair. "Nice cut," he said with the discriminating accent of an expert.

"Nick Smith, he's just opened a shop here, I could write about him," she said.

"Fine," said Johansen, "three hundred words."

"Is that all?" asked Iris. She felt on safe territory: there was something about the shameless consumerism of the magazine and the wholehearted way Johansen had pinned all his invitations to his wall that reminded her of London in the sixties.

"What else do you want?" Exasperation returned to his voice the Nebraska twang he had spent seven years eliminating.

"A job."

"She could replace Bunny," came a voice from a desk behind Johansen.

"Who asked you anything?" he said, turning to the girl who had spoken. "Bunny's practically our main contributor."

"Ah, shit," said the girl. "All he does is review B parties. She could fill in."

"Do you think you could do it?" Johansen asked her. "It's not easy."

"What would I have to do?"

"Come back here at eight tonight with a notepad and a pencil. I'll take you to a press party for the Fly-by-Nites and then we'll go on to a Warhol thing."

Johansen fixed her with a solemn stare. "Just how much do you know about parties?" he inquired.

Iris had already risen to go home and get ready for the night's assignment. "What should I know? I've been to thousands." She thought she'd add a little embroidery. "When I was a debutante in London, there were at least three a night."

"Debutantes can't spell," said Johansen.

"Johansen," said the girl behind him again, "you can't spell."

"Exactly," he said. "Oh, well; look your best. See you later."

Iris returned to the Pierre and told Charlie she had a job. "What is it, dear?" asked her mother.

"Reviewing parties," said Iris with pride. Charlie felt an instant pang: surely she was better qualified than Iris for such a job. "I'm going to a charity thing at the Met," she said with unconcealed satisfaction. "All the top people in New York will be there. Maybe you can write about it."

Iris wore her Emily Bates dress from London. It looked from a distance like a melting ice-cream cone, and on closer inspection it revealed to Johansen such a profusion of conflicting patterns that it was safer to stare at Iris's face than attempt to trace the squiggles to their illogical conclusions. Some parts of the dress, identifiable only as *bits* for their refusal to assume the status of sleeves or bodice or skirt, were the same shade as her hair, which was why she had chosen this particular garment in which to make her entry into New York night life.

"Heavens," he said.

"Aren't you changing?" asked Iris with a glance at his wrinkled stripes.

"I don't have to change," he said. "They take me as I am." He gave his bow tie a little tug to loosen it. Iris feared for a second that Johansen might turn out to be a real person, a breed she had encountered rarely enough but one that always intimidated her with subtle hints about her moral inadequacies. Her fear was dispelled when he elaborated: "If I want to go somewhere in my wrinkled suit, do you know what happens? The next day everyone is going everywhere in wrinkled suits. That's power."

"Power?" asked Iris.

"I lead, they follow. Do you know how many people read *Style?* Eighty thousand in New York alone, and we're sold in the drugstore of the Beverly Hills Hotel. That's astounding. It's enormous. I'm a trend-setter. Now . . ." He led her into the elevator lobby without pausing for breath. "We all know how tacky trends are when everybody follows them. Trends are shit. They're beyond the pale. Take your dress, for instance."

The elevator door shut on them, and Iris felt herself blushing. It was a year old, but she was sure there wasn't another in New York like it. "That dress is an Emily Bates from London. It's fun. It's expensive. It's beautifully made."

"Why, thank you," said Iris, as if she had been laboring over its random seams herself. "I didn't know you knew about Emily Bates."

"My dear, I am *Style!* How could I not know an Emily Bates when I see one? Who do you think you're talking to? Some amateur?" As he drew out the syllables of the word "amateur" Iris realized that Johansen was homosexual: until then, she had been able to think of him as nothing more than a chubby young man with a definite attitude.

"So this month you're unique," he continued as he hailed a cab on Lexington Avenue. "There's not one other dress like that in this city. Next year there'll be a hundred, and in five years there will be Emily Bates *sunglasses*, Emily Bates *candy bars*, Emily Bates tacky, tacky *lingerie* made of cling-glo Moygashel triple-blend *nylon*, and then I sincerely hope for you that you will no longer be wearing Emily Bates anything!"

"You think she's going to be so successful?" asked Iris.

He gave her a furious look. "Success," he said, "is beside the point."

"Of course," said Iris.

"Be a trend-setter," said Johansen, "like me. When I launched Manny Mongoose, no one would touch him. They all said, 'Who would wear plastic shoes? Plastic shoes are for *poor* children in *Third World* countries! And I just smiled and wore my plastic shoes and changed them every day—you know, blue ones one day and yellow the next and pink, green, and then bam! After I'd run pictures of Liza Minnelli and Diane Von Furstenberg wearing plastic shoes, every socialite in town wanted them, and a year later every secretary in every office is wearing Manny Mongoose plastic sandals! That's power!"

The cab drew up at a restaurant in the East Thirties, and Iris waited while Johansen paid; through the windows of the restaurant she could see a crowd of people in a yellow haze.

"It's the New York Free Soup Kitchen for the Blind," said Johansen, steering her out of the cab with his elbows. "It's a cute place, but it's been used for just too many press parties this year and it's getting a little tired. Oh, there's Bob! Hi, Bob!"

A small, thin man was standing on the sidewalk, clutching a camera; he looked up and smiled at Johansen, revealing an enormous mouthful of bright teeth. Johansen nudged Iris: "Bob, this is Iris. She's going to be working for us, but take her picture anyway, because of the dress, and anyway she doesn't work for us yet. We have a strict rule"—he was addressing Iris now—"that we never, ever, under any circumstances photograph staff. Now walk towards Bob and smile— Oh, wait a minute." He held her back and pulled a handkerchief from his back pocket. "You have lipstick on your teeth. Here, open your mouth." Iris bared her teeth and Johansen rubbed the linen quickly across her incisors. "Now, go!"

Iris walked toward Bob, who let off three flashes at her and then put down his camera. "Okay, come on, let's go inside," screamed Johansen. Bob gathered up his camera bag that lay at his feet. "Not you!" screamed Johansen, "or is everybody here already?"

"Susan Superstar and Maria Braun came in together, and Jared Gartner was supposed to be here, but I haven't seen him and I've been here since seven-thirty," said Bob.

"Stay out there!" shouted Johansen as he pushed Iris through a glass door made opaque by a thick film of finger marks, and then stood at the entrance to the room with a look of defiance on his face. A few people turned and a woman came toward them, trying to hide the fact that she was hurrying by throwing little "hellos" to her left and right. "Johansen!" she shouted. "Baby!"

"This is amazing! Emily, isn't this incredible!" Iris was looking at the woman's dress, stunned. Apart from a few divergences in the number of squiggles and patches of random lace, it was the same as the one she was wearing. "Emily Bates, this is Iris, who is, as you can see, a fan of yours. I didn't know you were in town!"

"I just got in," said the woman, who had purple hair. She looked Iris up and down, and smiled at her. "You've got it on backwards," she hissed. "Go change in the loo." As Iris retreated to the toilet Emily shouted after her, "It's always nice to meet a fan!"

The dress looked as improbable reversed as it had originally. Iris took out a joint, lit it, took a deep puff, and instantly regretted it; it was her first joint since the mononucleosis, and it went directly to her heart, where it set up palpitations. "I won't drink, I don't have to get stoned, it's all going to be fine!" she said to the mirror. She stubbed out the joint, put it back in her bag, and took out the notebook. "Look professional," she muttered, pushing the door.

"Good, you're back," said Johansen. "Now, this is Pauline; she owns a model agency, and she's the one who imposed, positively decreed, girls with big noses last year."

"Long noses," corrected Pauline. "Big noses aren't good, but long noses are."

"Hello," said Iris, conscious of the fleeting pink shadow of her own nose looming in the center of her field of vision. Pauline didn't return the greeting; she was peering through the mass of huddled bottoms and shiny tops. "Isn't that Rafael Hernando there?" she asked Johansen, who stood on tiptoe and half shut his eyes.

"Yes, it is. Remember how nice he looked in *Vogue* when they photographed him in his house in Morocco? It's a shame he's wearing that safari suit. It's so unsexy." Having delivered his pronouncement, Johansen relaxed his arches and returned to his normal height.

"What do I do?" asked Iris, holding up the pad so her new boss could see it. He slapped her hand down. "Put that away, it's too tacky to be seen reporting. Keep everything in your head, and go to the toilet to write things down." She began to replace it in her bag but he grabbed her wrist. "Wait, there's one thing you need it for, and that's for the names. Always try to get the names right. Just don't wave it in people's faces—next thing you know, they'll be asking you to read their quotes back at them."

Someone handed her a glass of white wine; as she raised it to her mouth she felt her arm being pulled away and half the wine went down the front of her dress. "There's Maria Braun, she's the lead singer of the Fly-by-Nites. Write down everything she's wearing. Quick!" Iris listed khaki shorts, black stockings, silver shoes, a red Boy Scout shirt and gold hair, and then looked at the face; buck teeth protruded from a bright-red mouth, little blue eyes like a rat's swiveled under plucked brows. The eyes rested on Johansen, and Maria Braun opened her mouth and emitted a cry like a banshee in childbirth. Then she was delivering bright-red kisses all over his pallid sweating face. "You super cutie!" he said. "You're the cat's pajamas!"

"He always talks like that," Pauline said to Iris. "He's trying to bring back the fifties. I don't think it'll work."

"Oh, I'm sure it will," said Iris, fired with newborn loyalty.

"That's Redd Blue, the guitarist," hissed Johansen. Iris glanced up and quickly wrote on her pad: "Hand-painted beard on face, black shirt open to the waist, salami in jeans." She stopped writing to examine the bulge at his crotch at greater leisure, but Johansen hit her again: "It's only Saran Wrap, sweetie, keep writing. I didn't think that could fool anyone anymore, where have you been?"

"In the infirmary, I've had mono—"

"Well, how did you get it? Don't answer that, I don't want to know. Look, there's Fred Paine, he's into very dirty things and he's got six rhinestone brooches on his lapel—now, that's news!"

A red-haired girl came up to them; she cast a practiced eye over Iris's hair, and muttered, "Vegetable dye?" as she leaned forward to kiss Johansen. "Yes, it is," said Iris. "Iris, this is Mona Mount, the singing model. Remember these names. Mona, where's the hound?"

Mona whistled; people's legs were seen buckling, a young man leaped backwards, a girl gathered up her skirt, and a large Labrador squirmed through the crowd to arrive panting and delighted at his mistress's feet. "This is Chuckles. He goes everywhere with Mona." Iris wrote down "Chuckles/w/Mona."

"Enough. Let's go to the end of the room and then come back. I'll teach you how to work a party," said Johansen. Iris followed him through a mass of wet satin shirts, tight suede jeans, clinging antique dresses, bristling thrift-shop embroideries. She felt the thick satin of her dress being ripped by Navajo artifacts, pointed pins and spiky cut glass, but was resigned to the hazards of her new profession. A man's long hair got tangled in the beads at her shoulders; she pulled, he cursed, neither apologized. "Shit, it's the English!" said Johansen, and she didn't know what he meant until she reached where he was, which was soggy with beery breath. "Drummers," he explained, "let's get out of here," and pulled her into a clearing. "Ah!" he said, "watch out! Here she comes! No escape! It's Bridget!"

A small dark woman approached them, wearing dark glasses with windshield wipers on them. "Johansen," she shouted, separating every syllable, "you genius!" She wore a long black dress and a black jacket over it.

"Never trust anyone who calls you a genius," said Johansen to Iris as he extended his arms with a deft show of reluctance at the tiny figure. "Iris, this is Bridget Oligovsky." Iris held out her hand; the woman was older, and could be expected to shake hands, at least. But all she did was glare up at Iris. "You new on *Style?* I know every member of the staff and it's sure you're not on a date with Johansen."

"She's new, she's new," he assured her.

"Hey, this is a real magazine society evening," said Bridget.

"Huh?" prompted Johansen.

"Well, everyone here has been photographed for a magazine. That's magazine society. Except me, I'm the only one. Johansen just won't put me in *Style.* He's a pig. Still, I keep trying." She gave a loud sigh, wagged her finger at a passing young girl, and pinned Johansen against the wall. Iris wrote Oligovsky on her notepad, and then, catching a look of desperation on Johansen's face, addressed his tormentor, "Mrs. Oligovsky, do those windshield wipers work?"

She looked up at Iris. "Of course they do. My boyfriend gave them to me. Look." She turned a knob by her ear and the wipers began their circuit across the lenses. Iris thought she could see Mrs. Oligovsky's eyes slowly crossing in time with them; she smiled over at Johansen.

"Who was that?" asked Iris when the woman had moved on.

"She's a scourge. She was married to a famous poet once, and she owns a gallery, but she's the pits. All she wants is publicity. Never ever write about her, ever."

"But everyone is saying hello to her," remarked Iris. "They all seem to know her."

"Nobody writes about her. She just isn't interesting. She's trying so hard the whole time, it's painful. Now come over here and oh my God! Look!"

Johansen had pushed open a door and through it Iris saw tables set for dinner. "I can't believe this," said Johansen. "This is bigger than I thought. I'd better put you on the list." He went off to make Iris official, and returned with a small girl carrying a clipboard. "This is Sally, and she's the most important woman in New York." Iris wrote down "Sally." "No, no," said Johansen. "Never write about a PR. Sally's the best PR in New York and she handles everyone who is *anyone*, but we never write about her, do we, dearie?"

Sally gave him a sick little smile and held out her hand to Iris, who was glad to see that at least one person recognized the normal rules of etiquette.

"I've put you between Rafael Hernando and Ritzy Cracker," said Sally.

"Take notes," instructed Johansen as an older woman with a tiny bun and large ear lobes grabbed him by the neck and pulled him away.

Iris recognized everyone at the table, and each face gave her the same kind of smile, not entirely welcoming but acknowledging her presence at the table as a fairly interesting vicissitude. A thin-faced man with long hair she recognized as Dixie Dodger, a sometime drummer for the Rolling Stones; Berio Lucchese, the interior decorator who had made waterbeds fashionable, was unmistakable with his slicked-back hair and onyx cigarette holder into which was screwed a Nat Sherman mauve Cigarettello; there was a dark young man whom she had seen in perfume ads and in Andy Warhol's *Interview* magazine. She knew he was a baron, and what remained of her Frances Lyle social conscience told her to dislike him, so she granted him a socialistic sneer. A noisy Italian girl, dressed as a Pierrot with a rhinestone monocle, hugged someone whose face was familiar, some kind of fashion photographer, said to be a Pygmalion to the undiscovered beauties of New York and Paris. She blew him a kiss; you never knew. A man with ringlets introduced himself as a conceptual architect, and Rafael Hernando nudged her and whispered, "He once built a balsa-wood model of a toilet and he's never gotten over it."

She put her notepad on the table. It would explain her presence, and the table would keep it steady. The people around her registered the notebook and granted her great smiles. "Take down every word I say, and if you get anything wrong I'll pull out all your hair," said the creature on her right, as he breathed stale tobacco and licorice into her face. "I'm Ritzy Cracker," he said. "But next week I'm going back to my original name, so make the best of it." Iris's pen was poised in the air. "Write it *down,* I said," urged Ritzy Cracker.

A waitress, a sullen girl with braids tied on top of her head, slammed down plates of warm lamb and peas in front of them. "Aaah!" screamed Ritzy Cracker, "institution food! Just like Riker's Island! I love it."

"Have you ever been in prison?" asked Iris.

"Honey, I was born in prison. Write it down, write it down!"

"What's your connection to tonight?" Iris was enjoying herself: the semblance of thoroughness made her feel important.

Ritzy Cracker slapped her hand. "Naughty child, you haven't done your homework! I'm an original Fly-by-Nite!"

He turned to the waitress, who was negotiating the difficult passage between two tables: "Oh, miss, how much is this plate of slop? Because I don't think I can afford to eat here, I haven't got a penny to balance on my nose!"

"It's a party," shouted Mrs. Oligovsky. "It's free."

"Caviar!" shrilled Ritzy Cracker. "I want caviar!" Opposite Iris, the noisy Italian girl raised her eyes to the patron saint of bouncers. Mona Mount, on the other side of the nameless baron, brought her fist down on a bread roll as if to smite all noisy faggots from the face of this earth. Much further down the table, Johansen extended an upraised thumb in Iris's direction.

Coffee was served out of large tin urns; dessert was individual portions of fruitcake wrapped in cellophane envelopes. Johansen took Iris's cake away from her and announced, "Now we go downtown. Come on. Bob's outside waiting. Well, did you write down everything? Did you notice how

Esmeralda, she was right in front of you, had a *diamond* in her front tooth? They're all doing it in Europe, I'm surprised you haven't got one. Hurry up!"

In the cab he asked her if she had spoken to Rafael Hernando. Iris looked blank, and flipped through her notepad. "You turkey, you were sitting right next to him! I wanted you to find out all about his new collection! What were you doing there, snoozing?"

"I was listening to that funny man Ritzy Cracker. God, he's witty," said Iris, attempting to make a pronouncement of her own.

"My dear," said Johansen, solemn once more. "You have just made the biggest gaffe of your career. Ritzy Cracker is finished. He was fun"—he made a moue— "ten years ago, *maybe,* and that's stretching it. He had his day with Warhol, but now he's finished. I mean, he cleans houses for a living! Oh, you're useless!" He crossed his arms over his chest and turned away from Iris, staring out the window.

She tried to save herself. "That kitchen reminded me of the Coupole," she said. Johansen remained immovable in his sulk. Iris felt tears coming to her eyes, but Bob gave her a wink and, holding up his camera to his face, let off a flash. "Ow!" said Iris.

"You fuckup," muttered Johansen. "How many times have I told you never to do that in a taxicab? What if a buggy was passing by right now and you startled the horse, huh, did you think about that?" While she and Bob went up to the loft in a freight elevator, which was being hoisted by an elderly janitor in red overalls, Johansen remained downstairs, busily talking with Rafael Hernando to make up for Iris's lapse.

"Do you know Eric Castiglione, the great *Paris Match* photographer?" she asked Bob.

"I always go to Paris for the collections," he answered, leaving it at that. He walked ahead of her into the huge room before them; she tried hovering, and realized that she did not want Bob to think she was waiting for Johansen, so she followed in the wake of Bob's flash, which was going off with irregular frenzy.

The room was so big that the groups of people standing in it seemed more like beleaguered wagon trains in a desert than guests at the same party. There was spilled white wine in silver patches on the floor, and in the corner a camel dozed, with a black girl on its back dressed as a houri. Little white plastic cups rolled here and there to music coming from speakers half as high as the walls, and on those walls were three screens, one with TV ads from the fifties and the others with more conventional light shows. Some people were standing in front of the ads, watching them and bursting into loud laughter every time the image of a happy family was projected. Iris went nearer; there was a tap on her shoulder. "What did I tell you, it's the fifties!" said Johansen. "Write it down!"

At four o'clock in the morning Iris, still in her stained dress to keep hold of the feeling of the evening, was hard at work on her fifth draft of the party critique Johansen had instructed her to hand in by ten. Her Olivetti, a present from Szos, was resting on a folded blanket on top of Charlie's intaglio dining table, but still the noise echoed off the hard edges of the scimitars overhead. Iris looked up now and then, alerted to the loud staccato of the Olivetti keys by some change in the rhythm of the air conditioner's humming. She need not have worried: Charlie was fast asleep seven blocks away, curled in the arms of Mike Mullen, investment banker, aging bounder and billionaire.

Iris listed what everyone had been wearing, conscious of her duty to be an effective witness to the passing scene. Figuring this to be insufficient, she added a short paragraph about the party. She wrote it in French first, and then translated it.

La soirée du soup kitchen pour les aveugles ne manquait pas de brio, mais hélas les excentricités d'une certaine Madame Oligovsky . . . It read: "The evening at the Soup Kitchen for the Blind did not lack brio, but alas the eccentricities of a certain Mrs. Oligovsky contributed to an unquiet atmosphere. If it was not for the brilliant spirit of Mr. Ritzy Cracker, guests would have been submitted to listening to a monologue that had nothing of original . . ."

At ten o'clock Iris had finished. She had worked all night, and unlike similar nights at Frances Lyle, she had not once felt the need for toast. Charlie came in and let out a cry when she saw Iris huddled over the dining table. "You'll ruin it with that typewriter, you're insane!" she said to forestall her daughter's questions. Iris frowned a little, but in her state she barely registered her mother's ball gown, her mink wrap, her good jewelry. "I won't ruin it," she said. "I put this blanket underneath."

"You are not to mess up this place!" continued Charlie. "This is my apartment!"

"I just wrote my first article," said Iris, "for publication."

"You've been typing all night in your best dress? It'll be ruined. Honestly, Iris, you have no respect for property, your own or anyone else's."

Iris went on typing.

"Is someone paying you for this?" asked Charlie.

"Yes, they are actually," said Iris in her debutante accent, as she tore the last piece of paper out of her typewriter. What could her mother know about the passion and heartache that went into making a name for oneself? Charlie hustled into her room to change into a robe. Iris followed her, and watched her undo the side fastenings of her flower-sprinkled organdy. Charlie caught her looking at her. "I forgot my key," she said. "I had to stay at Mike's. Don't worry, he's got a huge apartment. A triplex."

"I didn't say anything," said Iris.

"You were thinking," said Charlie.

Iris, summarily bathed and now wearing an antique market dress that she hoped would impress Johansen as much as the Emily Bates rags had, arrived at the office of *Style* a little before noon.

"He's not here yet," said the girl who sat behind him. "And I'm Angela."

Iris waited by his desk, reading back copies of *Style,* most of which she had read before during her years at Frances Lyle. The only ones she didn't know by heart were the summer issues that she had missed while on holiday in England.

"Twelve pages!" said Johansen when she handed her work to him.

"It's all in there," said Iris, pleased with the speed and accuracy of her work.

He picked a felt-tip pen from an ivory canister and began scribbling on his message pad. "I suppose I'd better read it," he mumbled.

Iris controlled her urge to say Yes please, at once, and fixed the rings on her fingers with abstracted concentration.

He frowned as he read it, and Iris heard the felt-tip pen's muffled scratching across the pages. She glanced over to see her careful translation disappear under the fine blue stripes of his disapproval.

"You don't like it?" she asked under her breath, so that if by chance he wasn't listening she could pretend she hadn't said a word.

"This reads funny," he said. "But all the details are there."

Angela, behind him, winked at her.

He set the pages back down on the desk, and then shook them together and handed them over to Angela. "This can go to the printer's once you've proofed it," he said.

"Do you want to know how to spell my name?" asked Iris.

"It's okay," said Angela. "You put it at the top of every page."

"Are you sure you want this job?" asked Johansen, folding his hands over his little paunch. Iris sat down facing him. She felt that the previous evening had given them something of a relationship, and she leaned forward, as if talking to an old friend. "That's the question everyone asks me," she said. "I don't understand. Why wouldn't I want to write for your magazine? What's so awful about it that I don't know yet?"

Johansen could sometimes be wise. "Iris, it's not that the life is bad. The pay isn't so good, but you're rich, so that doesn't matter." (Iris was pleased that this fiction about her was beginning to take hold. "Rich" was a nice adjective.) "I'm just wondering, do you think you could take the pace? Parties every night, pictures to be captioned, fashion shows, there's a lot to do. You have to be at the balls and on the ball at all times." Iris was nodding her head with impatience: none of this daunted her, nor would it have daunted anyone else. "But, this is the thing: you're going to be writing about people. Famous people. And you aren't going to be writing about yourself. I don't want to ever see one word about your own moods, opinions or whatever. Manny Mongoose may be out, but he's more important than you are. If you're here just to make a name for yourself, forget it. We have a public to serve."

"I wouldn't dream of pushing myself forward," promised Iris.

"Good. Just remember: everyone you meet is more important than you are."

"Absolutely," said Iris, fervent, fiery in her devotion to this new humility.

"One more thing, and then I'll give you your invitations for the week. *I* am *Style;* you just work for it. No getting a big head."

Iris put her hands to her hair to signify that she would keep the size of her head in check.

He pushed over a folder of cards and papers. "And when Bunny gets back, you're out, unless you're really useful to me."

Iris nodded and opened the file. "Won't you be coming with me anymore?" she asked.

"No," said Johansen. "I've shown you the ropes. I only go to the A parties."

19.

The Vocabulary of Fashion

Iris was so happy at having become a member of the staff of *Style* that she did not question her mother about the absurdity of claiming to have lost her key when she lived in a hotel. Ben-Abi did not return to New York and Charlie did not return to London; Iris overheard no phone calls, saw no telegrams, intercepted no letters to prove that Charlie's marriage was falling apart. It was simply dissipating itself, the threads failing to join, connections not made, questions not answered, questions not asked. Had Charlie wished it away she could not have made it disappear faster. Mike Mullen, known as the Chairman, took to picking her up at the Pierre before taking her to the festive gatherings of boards on which he sat, official dinners of committees that he chaired; sitting loomed large in Mike Mullen's life; his name and his reputation were such that official bodies and headwaiters were always pushing seats at him, and universities regularly clamored for him to endow Mike Mullen chairs of Commerce and Finance. Charlie was tired of Ben-Abi's wild nomadic ways—Capri one day, Marrakesh the next, side trips to Johannesburg and Asmara, endless new vistas. She was ready for a sedentary life, and she tossed her curls at Mike Mullen. He had never had much of a liking for foreigners, but she was an All-American foreigner, and he liked short women.

Charlie suggested that Iris should find her own place to live, since she was now earning a living. Iris pointed out that she was earning only a hundred and twenty-five dollars a week, nothing you could live on. Charlie said, "Your father can support you, ask him. I've taken care of you all my life, now it's his turn." She did not count the Frances Lyle fees as support.

Iris called Tyler at the Ezy-Vite offices and explained that she had gone into journalism. "Does that mean you've dropped out of school?" he asked.

"No, I'm working for the summer. I'm a real journalist," she said.

"That's great," he said, adding, "I'll let you write about me anytime." It was his little joke, but Iris took it as an order.

"I'd love to," she said, "that would be great."

"Is there anything I can do to help you? You want some brochures about the new plant, some info on oranges?"

"I need an apartment first," said Iris, cleaving to the point.

"Call my lawyer," he said. "Don Minerva at Ticon, Chicago, and Luzt. There's a little something coming to you when you turn twenty-one."

"I'll be twenty-one in a few months," she reminded him.

"What's the paper called?"

She sensed that if he heard the word *Style* he would know at once that he and his oranges were of no interest to her. "*Gentleman,*" she said.

"Isn't that full of pin-ups?" he asked.

"No, it's all about relevant issues of today," she said. "Like the war, and civil disobedience, and—"

"Don't go getting involved with any long-haired Commies," he warned her. "They're everywhere. Watch your step."

Don Minerva explained to Iris that she could expect an income of two thousand dollars a month from the day she turned twenty-one. "It's all from your groves, so it isn't really a trust fund," he said.

"Can I have some of it now?" she asked.

"Only the day after your birthday. I could, though I don't usually do this, advance you something."

"Yes, please," said Iris.

"There will be a small brokerage charge, of course. Nothing much, say fifteen percent."

"Fine, fine," said Iris, anxious to get the money.

She found a sublet in a small building off Lexington Avenue, just a few blocks from the offices of *Style.* The floors were bare, there were green plants withering on the windowsill, and the owner, who was going away to Canada for a year, attempted to sublet her cat to Iris along with the apartment, but Iris was firm. "Animals tend to die around me," she said, "especially cats. It's just my karma." The owner was a little worried about Iris's karma, but as she wanted five hundred dollars for one room plus kitchen plus bath, and Iris was the first person who seemed willing to pay it, she took her cat to Canada and wished the plants good luck.

Iris put Indian bedspreads on the couch, the dining table, and over the curtain rail. She inserted a piece of card with her name on it into the mailbox and tipped the doorman five dollars so that he would string together the white plastic letters spelling her name in the gray box on the wall where all the tenants were listed. She got a telephone and was listed with 411. Don Minerva gave her a checkbook from Banker's Trust and that too had her name on it, but the address was that of Ticon, Chicago, and Luzt. She felt rich.

Within the month she had attended seventy-nine parties, at the rate of two and a half per night, written about twenty-four of them, captioned one thousand and two sheets of Bob's contacts, and met a young art director from *Gentleman* who, she ascertained, was a friend of Eric Castiglione's. In the swift confusion of her new life, Iris did not want to mislay her true feelings; the only means she had for distinguishing them from fleeting interest or social excitement was their relation to the past. Thus, when Philip Ross, former cartoonist and current art director of *Gentleman,* said, "Eric Castiglione? He's one of my best friends," she knew that it was safe to take the young man to her bed.

By the end of August she was on the masthead of *Style,* at the end of a list of "social critics" that included the wives of certain bankers, the daughter of a marchioness, the sister of a singing star, and every boy Johansen had ever been to bed with and cared to remember. Her prose had not improved; Johansen had found the best way to deal with it was to cut out all the verbs and string the names together. This created an effect of claustrophobia and unease (further enhanced by the jamming together of capitalized words, TRASH, TREND, GEAR, and also GROOVY), which reproduced for the reader the sensation of being at the very loud parties that they were reading about. Iris felt that she was working very hard, harder than anyone else on the masthead. None of the other names ever showed their faces at the office.

Bunny, the man she was replacing, was spotted at an Andy Warhol party acting as one of the hosts. This clue was interpreted to mean that he had defected, and Johansen found out that while Bunny had been convalescing at Montauk, a fifth column of Warhol apostles had stolen upon him and recruited him for *Interview.* "The job's yours," Johansen told Iris. She weighed the opportunity, and decided that it would be churlish to insist on pursuing an education. She told no one but Paula of her design; she wrote to her, enclosing three copies of *Style,* and claiming in seven pages of purple felt-tip scribbles to have found complete happiness in the real world, where she intended to stay.

She felt that the dark night of her insufficiency had passed, and that at last she could lay claim to being a whole person. The weekly printing of her name above her column, the raised letters of her name on her business cards from *Style* (above the paper's motto, "It's the only thing that counts"), her name in the framed panel in the hall of her building —all assured her that she existed.

Johansen was teaching her the tricks of his profession. She came into the office one day bearing a shopping bag from a department store. "Are you mad?" he asked. She looked at her bag; under folds of grayish tissue paper was sequestered a brand-new skirt. She patted it. "Did you pay full price for whatever's in there?" he continued. Iris said "Of course." Didn't rich people pay full price? She wondered if his influence over her was supposed to extend to personal matters of budget.

"Get it wholesale, you idiot!" he hissed. "What do you think *Style* is all about?"

"But I only cover parties," she said, acting ethical, "not fashion."

Johansen shook his head. "Parties are *Style,* fashion is *Style,* it's all the same thing. Can't you take care of yourself?"

She interpreted this to mean that she was free to exploit her position to its fullest. She took to phoning companies that made dear little Victorian dresses, designers of clinging garments in man-made fabrics, boutiques that stocked imports from East and West, and, having introduced herself, proceeded to rhapsodize on the wonderful taste they had, sliding gently into a hint that she would write about them for *Style.* As she set up the time and date of these putative interviews, she would add a casual, shimmering little aside about the antebellum gown, the exceptional four-way dress, the circumcision cape, and within days—sometimes within hours—these items would materialize on her desk at *Style.* If the hopeful donors were green enough to go along with the flattery, there would be a little note stapled to the package; if they were so hard-boiled that they understood the terms of the exchange, they dispensed with the note. Each time she solicited a gift this way, Iris felt a little pang; she calmed herself with the reminder that most of what she wanted was not yet available to the public, and what she was doing was merely trend spotting. "Calm down," Angela told her. "Everyone does it here." The addition of the "here" implied to Iris that mores at the *New York Times, Vogue* and *Women's Wear Daily* were more old-fashioned in this regard. The enigmatic questions Julian Sorrel had thrown at her about ethical choices had no bearing on this particular problem: Iris told herself that personal interest was an abstract consideration that had nothing to do with her. Fashion was a different world.

The algebra of favors became familiar to her. During the summer she learned, partly from Johansen and partly from candid observation, that every time she was asked to lunch it was to write about her host, when she was asked to dinner it was to write about the host and the food, and if she was invited to a private party it was to write about the host, the food and all the other guests. Press parties required only that she write about who or what was being launched. Her social life had been born fully staffed under these conditions, and she wisely saw no reason to complain. She learned to turn her minor power so that it caught the light and showed to best advantage: she had done her article on Nick and his salon, which was called Snip! (the exclamation mark was his tribute to British musicals of the sixties). She called Snip! "the biggest thing to hit women on the head since cavemen promenaded themselves with clubs," a line that Johansen promptly amended to "the wittiest, ritziest salon since men came out of caves," which did not quite coincide with what she meant, but she had learned not to quibble when Johansen got busy with the blue pencil. To show Nick that he was not singled out for her attention, she rapidly wrote about five other hairdressers in Manhattan. They all insisted they be allowed to do her hair for free, and she took her Hairtoday to Snip!, and her Snip!-sheared head to Kenneth, causing her look to change weekly, as she called forth ever-greater efforts all around.

The art director, Philip Ross, had endured a period of great fame in his early twenties and was living out what he thought of as his twilight thirties in the offices of *Gentleman.* He sometimes suspected that Iris was with him only because of his job; she insisted on coming up to see him at the office almost every day, and, when she was at *Gentleman,* kept darting into the corridor outside Julian Sorrel's office. As for sex, she seemed to get the same amount of pleasure from being touched, pumped or pounded by him as she did from picking her toenails. Iris assured him that what she felt for him was the purest love, the sort that springs unbidden into the hearts of young shepherdesses in obscure rural dales.

He doubted this, as he had doubted everything she said since the day she told him she had been brought up in a pink marble palace. Philip Ross was not a very patient young man, and without pausing to investigate further, he decided that she was suffering from infantile delusions. Had it not been for his lust for parties and noisy activity, and Iris's plentiful invitations to such affairs, he would not have spent more than one night with her.

Iris found Philip a little paranoid, but irresistible. Her visits to *Gentleman* were prompted by a desire to be seen by Julian Sorrel, now that she was no longer a miserable college girl looking for a job. She had the good sense to know that *Gentleman* was an infinitely more respectable publication than the superfluous rag she worked for, and when she watched Philip laying out the somber portraits of Mao and John Kenneth Galbraith, Ho Chi Minh, Nixon and Eugene McCarthy (this last captioned: "Why isn't this man crying?"), she felt she could see the touch of Julian Sorrel's incisive mind in Philip's every pencil stroke. She breathed in what she took to be a purer and more responsible air than the fashionable breeze on Lexington Avenue. When Philip worked on weekends, she would, unbidden, bring him unwanted sandwiches, and pause to admire his pretty arms as they protruded from his timeless football sweater, and then creep into Julian Sorrel's office, where she would stare at the editor's chair with the awed self-surrender, the devout unction that her chosen icons summoned up in her. She did not want to be Julian Sorrel; she had no designs on the chair as the symbol of the editorship on the venerable magazine; she hoped only that its occupant would deign once more to notice her, and perhaps have the grace to comment on her progress. Her respect for what she considered his superior values prevented her from approaching him openly. That would have been a form of trespassing, while creeping around his empty office on a Sunday afternoon and glancing at the top letters on his desk was an acceptable form of worship.

When Sorrel's name came up—and it came up often—she was assailed by the urge to say that she knew him. She was stopped by a holy dread of being told that he had found her fingerprints in his office, and hated her. She held firmly to the belief that if she excelled herself, he would deign to swoop down from his heights of relevance and carry her back up into his world of cultural integrity, his meaningful Olympus.

She did not gift him, but on his envoy, Philip, she lavished shirts from Turnbull and Asser's New York shop, which he never wore, and tickets to old films at the Museum of Modern Art, for which he always arrived late. She attempted to circumscribe Philip's movements with enticing invitations, and to change his appearance. Johansen referred to Philip Ross as her *lover*, making the word sound as slimy and grotesque as he obviously imagined their sex life must be. There was something thrilling in being considered both highly professional and decadent by the same man. "Try getting his look together a little better," Johansen elaborated when they all found themselves at a party that combined the attributes of both Johansen-worthy A and Iris-duty B.

Johansen taught her a system he called the vocabulary of fashion; more than a lexicon for his publication, it was an early semiotic device by which a pair of pants could be seen as both more and less than a pair of pants: a signifier of masculinity or a rejection of femininity, which could be used to enhance or confuse the message of what went over them: a shirt with a sharp collar was in the same mode, a dress was antithetical and therefore contrapuntal to the pants, and so on. Only the staff of *Style* and a handful of fawning designers knew what Johansen meant when he talked about ties as homunculi, or jackets as bourgeois archetypes, but Iris loved it.

They sat together at fashion shows, and Johansen would say, "Watch the details. The general effect is only there to confuse you."

She honed her eye in the showrooms of Seventh Avenue, refined it further in the vast emporia of Oriental imports downtown, and constructed out of her taste a system of belief. She felt fully justified in notifying Frances Lyle that she would not be returning, and cabling her father to that effect, for she was able to add, "I'm learning so much more this way." She could recite at will the difference between batiste and voile, the various methods of dyeing by tying, the infinitesimal differences between Hungarian cross-stitch and Rumanian side stitch, which was essential for distinguishing the real tundra blouses from the fakes streaming out of Bucharest. By Christmas she knew her stuff, which was prudent of her, as Johansen hired a house for Christmas in Litchfield, Connecticut, and filled it with young designers for a weekend of Socratic questions on the order of "When is a dress not a dress?" Iris received excellent marks for her knowledge of the multiple meanings of clothes, but not for her practice of adding imported cheddar to the canned Swedish meatballs.

Her science extended eventually to people; by Easter she could not only tell the difference between a debutante and a plain girl, but also the varieties of debutante: reluctant, rebellious, drugged, subversive, cosmetically corrected, libidinous, lesbian. The difference, too, in black models, between those originating in Ethiopia, those from Jamaica, those whose parents were from Jamaica but who had grown up in Queens, those with real Ibo blood and those who only claimed it. She knew most phony titles, could predict the future of a singer's or an actress's career by the colors they wore (yellow bombed; purple had to be careful not to burn out too fast; black, unless leather, was a loser).

Her twin gifts for watching people and making snap judgments were being fully used.

"You're fat," Johansen told her one day. "Do something about it." She was stunned: for her protector, her mentor, to turn on her with disparaging remarks about her body was the last thing she had ever expected. She burst into tears and hid in the toilet, which at *Style* was on the outside landing, reached by a single key shared by all the female members of the staff. She was unable, therefore, to hear him banging on the outer door two hours later, begging her to come out. When she finally emerged, she found a note on her desk.

> *Clothes hang better on a thin person, everyone knows that.*
> *And Halston says he doesn't do samples in a size twelve.*
> *Dr. Kronkheit 976-1212.*

She saw the wisdom in Johansen's warning at once, and made an appointment.

Dr. Kronkheit gave her pastel pills in colors that inspired Iris to suggest a line of "dexy-dream" sweaters to a Seventh Avenue manufacturer. The pills made her vibrate like a leaf in a gale; the first weeks she thought she would die of jangling before she lost a pound, but then her body began to shrink horizontally as it appeared to grow vertically. Her heart, which had done its racing only when she called Europe, heard bad news, or approached Julian Sorrel's office door, now knocked against her chest with the insistence of a taxi meter. Her tussles in bed with Philip became even less interesting to her than they had been before; her fascination with such things as the conjoining of two different patterns rose dramatically, enabling her to tout aesthetic misalliance with passion. The finding of a stock of 1930 enamel belt buckles in a dingy shop on Thirty-seventh Street made her ears ring and her legs tingle, signs that she associated with a form of sexual pleasure. She was obsessed, increasingly, with aligning the pencils on her desk according to color, picking up lint from carpets, and making lists of what she had to do six or seven times over. This frenetic concentration struck Johansen as evidence of a healthy professional development. He didn't pay much attention to Iris's chronic quivering: he liked it when people trembled in his presence.

She had been at *Style* almost a year when Philip Ross invited her to a party at Julian Sorrel's. She had been waiting for this moment for so long that at first she didn't register, and then let out such an almighty squeal that Philip at once regretted having phoned her. They had not seen each other much, to put it in the bland terms by which such relationships are described. He found her increasingly overbearing and mannered; in her new boniness she was attractive, but he preferred the company of less verbose, and better shaped, young ballet dancers. Iris thought Julian Sorrel was overworking him, and attributed the distracted distance he exhibited to artistic preoccupation. She was now, thanks to the pills, wonderfully thin; thanks to the magazine, wonderfully elegant. What more could a man want?

Dressing for Julian Sorrel was a test. She stood naked in front of her closet, where presents from manufacturers hung next to designer samples: her attainment of a size four had been greeted with wild jubilation by all the fashion people who wanted their names in *Style.* Standing in front of the closet, what she felt was not the mere idle dissatisfaction of a young woman greedy for clothes; she was, she knew, the still point of the turning mode. As her lightly sweating palms adhered to the flaccid suede of endless variations on the earthy feeling of the Southwest—a feeling she was keen to promote, having been unreasonably smitten by a photograph of a desert in which two stout Indians squatted, sheathed in suede—combinations of possibility ran through her head. At length she decided to get herself up as a sort of tragic maroon and mauve Garbo of Chinese extraction: she felt she had been seen enough in her New Mexico beads and wattles, and now that she had cheekbones, she might as well use them. The Chinese element, an avant-garde touch for 1971, came from a pair of brown sandals with wooden soles, which she had obtained in the usual manner.

The Good Earth, she thought, as she fastened the rudimentary rope straps around her ankles. She cast a brief look at the ceiling in the manner of one trying to discern a swarm of locusts from afar. Two chiffon scarves were wound around her head, a tunic covered her to mid-knee, and wrinkled purple trousers protruded from beneath. The wrinkles were a deliberate part of the ensemble; the Good Earth Chinese look might have been associated with laundries in the minds of certain racists, but not in the ideal Gobi Desert for which she was dressing.

Philip arrived with his assistant. Iris's heavily rouged eyebrows in the Ch'i style rose at the sight of the girl, and in her kitchen she muttered, "Why'd you bring her?" as she handed him a lukewarm orange juice.

"It's a staff party," he explained, looking down at his Manny Mongoose plastic shoes. Iris looked down too, and allowed herself a little smirk. She liked his blind spots about trends; they proved that he was heterosexual. "Manny Mongoose," she allowed herself to say, in her capacity as pitiless critic of the passing scene. "I didn't know he still made those things."

20.

Room at the Top

Julian Sorrel's apartment was not decorated, and this struck Iris as a sign that he must be poorer than she had imagined. There were shelves buckling under thousands of books, shelves listing dangerously with yet more books, a few green plants, open windows and white walls; the furniture that was not being sat upon was covered with drinks, and none of it was remarkable.

"Hello," said their host. He stood, flushed and healthy, sweating a little, welcoming his guests in the central hall.

Iris bristled at his greeting. He should have said, "I'm so glad to see you here." That was what the host of every single party had said to her since she had begun at *Style.* They then took her around to introduce their guests and spell their names for her. They made sure she had a drink. They made a little fuss over her. "Hello" was no longer good enough. Philip was shaking Julian Sorrel's hand; the assistant waited to do the same. Iris decided she wouldn't say anything, and swept grandly past them.

In the living room she perceived a great number of important bodies, among them that of Smith Clark, talking to Antonioni. Antonioni recognized her. *"Buon giorno,"* said the sad Italian. Iris kissed him. They had been at the same table just a few weeks before, and they had talked about Paula and Vivien Legrand. Iris asked Antonioni if he had thought of casting Paula in his next film. "No," he said. She looked at Smith Clark, waiting for him to recognize her. He was looking at her with some puzzlement.

"I know you!" he said.

"London," she said.

"Last month?" he asked.

"No, four years ago."

"What a memory you have!" He beamed at her. He had not changed; to Iris's eye, it seemed that he was even wearing the same shirt, an idea she dismissed at once.

"Will you remind me of your name?"

"Iris Bromley." She wished he had not made her say it; under her breath she murmured, "Paula Abime, remember when you interviewed us?"

The chins wobbled a second or two; the eyes clouded over in an effort to remember. "Oh!" he said at last. "You're the model! I remembered you as taller."

Julian Sorrel appeared and Iris smiled up at him. He put an arm on her shoulder, and she engagingly put her arm around his waist, discerning there, to her disgust, an undeniable bolster of excess flesh.

"I've been following your progress," he said in her ear. "It's quite remarkable."

She felt a flush from her ear lobes straight down to her crotch, an area so rarely visited by anything of that nature that unconsciously she scratched herself. "Smith, do you know Iris Bromley, scourge of *Style?*" asked Julian Sorrel, propelling her toward Smith Clark, who ran a hand through his hair. "Oh, *Style,*" he said, as if that explained his lapse of memory. "I thought you said London."

"I did," snapped Iris, and feeling that she owed Julian Sorrel an explanation, since Smith Clark was so patently unworthy of one: "Years ago," she said, stressing *years* to imply, at the periphery of her words, that perhaps Smith Clark was just a little passé, "Smith Clark"—the full name, to show respect and also a little distance—"interviewed my stepsister in London. He was the first journalist I'd ever met and I was wildly impressed." To this she added a snicker, which Julian Sorrel took to mean that journalists of Clark's ilk didn't impress her anymore.

"I thought you liked journalists," said Sorrel, holding her arm a little tighter.

"Some of them," she said.

Iris left her admirers and went in pursuit of Philip, whom she found huddled in a room with a small, lithe girl in turquoise tights; in Iris's vocabulary of fashion, the hue and pattern of the tights spelled out that her goose was cooked as far as Philip was concerned, and she left them to whatever they wanted to do. She knew she should be taking notes; she had spotted Tiny Tim, so she had a story, but she wasn't sure how to proceed. She did not want Julian Sorrel to see her with the notebook, much as she wanted him to read her piece about his party when it came out. She sensed that if she started taking notes there, in front of all the other writers, she would advertise that she was not part of the hallowed group. Clutching her bag, she watched as a man who had written about the Chicago riots from the point of view of the police talked to a tall girl who had written about the Vietnam war from the point of view of the whores in Saigon; she spied a young man who had been a student at Kent State on the day of the shootings, and was busy parlaying this incredible good luck into a series of articles on "The Student as Victim of Society."

An exiled Czech film director whom she recognized from the well-illustrated interviews he had given held forth to a group of young women about the dangers of living in the Plaza Hotel. He was short and blond, but because of what she knew about him, namely, that he had many girlfriends and smoked an occasional pipe, she fancied there was some resemblance to Raoul. The director waved a hand in her direction and continued talking. Rather than obey his invitation, she stared at a point just to the right of his head. Into that indefinite region composed of a bit of wall, the trailing ends of a hanging fern and the top of a high-backed chair, came the unmistakable face of Eric Castiglione. Iris sprang forward, knowing she was saved.

"Who are these broads?" he asked in French, after they had embraced and he had commented that she looked older, but beautiful.

"The men are the most important people in New York. They're the opinion makers. The women are just secretaries," answered Iris, with a disdainful glance at the cleverly made-up but distinctly colorless young women who punctuated the masthead names of the party. "Camp followers," she added. Eric allowed her to take his arm just as Julian Sorrel returned. "Good, you know the ace," said Sorrel. "He's my new find."

"I think I was the first to tell you about him," said Iris. "In fact, I'm sure I was."

"I'm sending him to Cambodia," announced Julian Sorrel, raising his voice.

"He photographed my sister's birthday party," retorted Iris, almost shrill.

"He's a war photographer," said Julian Sorrel. "He does wars." Then, for no apparent reason, he asked her, "Is the hired help giving you trouble?"

"Who?"

"Phil Ross. He's a punk. Leave him alone."

"Well, send me somewhere," she offered, her chin jutting out.

"Can you type yet?"

"My secretary does it for me," she said, and to further reinforce her credentials as a powerhouse in American journalism, she tugged at Eric's arm, announcing, "Let's go to Elaine's."

"I can't," said Eric. "*J'peux pas,* Ilka is waiting for me."

"Who's she?"

"My wife."

"Oh, well," said Iris, undefeated. "Have you seen Paula recently?"

"She is a star," said Eric. Sorrel tapped Iris on the shoulder, as if to knight her. "That's right, you were going to do a piece on her for us," he said.

"I'll do it now," said Iris.

"Let me think about it," said Julian Sorrel.

Iris was still waiting for him to think about it when the last guests left Julian Sorrel's apartment; Philip had left an hour before, claiming urgent business back at the office, which Iris rightly took to be the slim chance in turquoise tights waiting for him on the corner, a hunch she verified with a quick glance out the window. She would not have transgressed the law of cocktail-party hospitality had she not felt Julian Sorrel's hand on her buttocks and heard his voice say, "Stick around," in a curiously uninflected manner.

Out of the office, Sorrel was no longer the Godhead. She decided that now was the time to further her career in a manner honored by tradition and literature, and the decision had bestowed on her the sort of calm that is known to those who have decided Not to Think for a given period of time; even the effects of her last diet pill were muted, and her palms only slightly moist.

"Well! What a jamboree," huffed Sorrel, throwing himself on his white sofa. "Did you enjoy it?" He took a swig from one of the glasses on the table.

Iris, using *Style* jargon, answered, "I feel at home with trend-setters, but opinion makers are a different breed." The remark fell way below his hopes. He felt he had better ask her her age.

"Twenty-two."

"Not really."

"Yes, really," she said.

"Somehow you seem older," he said.

She took her college ID card, still valid but quite useless in her new life, and shoved it at Julian Sorrel.

"I see," he said, looking at the picture of the square-jawed, slightly fierce freshman that had been laminated for posterity. He handed it back without another word; as she went to replace it in her bag, she remembered it was time for another pill. Holding up the little transparent plastic box with its pastel gremlins rattling inside, she asked if she could have a glass of water.

"Those uppers, downers, or something even more sinister?" he asked.

"Diet pills," she said proudly.

"You shouldn't take that stuff," he said. "That's what makes you old before your time. Puts lines on your face. My first wife went that route. I had to put her away finally."

"Put her away?" asked Iris, a little shocked at his cruelty but gratified to be privy to his family secrets.

"She became a pillhead. An upper-middle-class junkie. It's an American Tragedy." With that he took another swig, this time from a different glass. "Jesus, vermouth!" he said, wiping his lips. "Who the hell was drinking vermouth?"

"I think I was," said Iris. "It's one of the things allowed on Dr. Kronkheit's diet."

"There may be a story in this," muttered Sorrel; he was unsure whether to allow the evening to drift gently into carnality, or let it rest as an exchange of story ideas. There was something a little driven about the girl that made him want to put a pillow over her face, and it was only the shape of her lower lip that tempted him to shove the same pillow behind her hips and have his way with her. It was obvious she was ready to do anything to get into his good graces; and being a Southerner, and romantic, he was happier when a woman seemed a little less interested. He shifted slightly on his couch. Food would not be a bad idea. "Hungry?" he asked.

Iris still had the pill in her hand. She wondered whether just for once she could do without the evening pill—"To prevent the midnight munchies" was how the doctor had explained the need for a 10:00 P.M. amphetamine—and show that she was as lusty and oral as the next girl. A small voice inside her whispered "Discipline," and she popped the pill in her mouth, determined to honor both her diet and her commitment to professional advancement. "Sure, I'm hungry," she said.

"We could call out for pizza," said Julian Sorrel, pulling himself up from the couch and proceeding toward the kitchen. While he was gone she examined the room, which at first had struck her by its blandness; now that the guests were gone, and despite the glasses and ashtrays agglomerated on every surface, she saw that it was a place of decided interest. On the walls were lithographs by Pop artists, some of them signed "To the Big J." A small group of pictures, black-and-white photographs, revealed that Julian Sorrel had in his time shaken hands with Harry Truman, Harry Belafonte, Humphrey Bogart, Eleanor Roosevelt, Cardinal Spellman, Robert Moses, Fiorello La Guardia, Meyer Lansky, Marilyn Monroe and three astronauts. She knew who the people were because each picture bore on its frame a little brass plate with the date and names engraved in Times Bold. She felt a coincidence of outlook with Julian Sorrel, and this relaxed her to the extent that she returned to the sofa and was able to sit down without feeling like a trespasser.

"Fine! Pizza's coming up, and I've got some beer in the icebox."

Beer, thought Iris, that's all I need. But rather than tell him that she never drank beer because it was the major No-no on Dr. Kronkheit's list, along with bananas, fried onions and Brie, she gave a brave little smile. As we have said, she was ready to do anything that night. Boldly she placed her Good Earth feet on the coffee table, in an attitude of loose expectancy. Julian Sorrel began picking up the debris, carrying ten glasses at a time with his fingers shoved down into them.

"Can I help?" she asked. He didn't answer; she let him make two trips before deciding that his silence was probably affirmative. She followed him to the kitchen, where among dirty coffee cups and piles of newspapers she found a tray. Gay and domestic, she darted back to the living room and loaded the tray with glasses.

"You're organized, I like that," he said as she carried the tray into the kitchen. She wondered if she was auditioning for the part of the maid, and asked languidly whether his cleaning woman couldn't do all this.

"Sure, but I hate to leave a mess for her," he said.

Intimidated by servants, she thought, lower-class background, societal guilt, liberal. At that moment, these were endearing qualities.

"What the hell do you see in Ross?" he asked later, as he snuffled down a limp wedge of pizza heavy with extra cheese and pepperoni.

"Why, don't you like him?" She was picking the mozzarella off her slice, and trying to be subtle about leaving the crust. She thought Philip would be flattered to know that his boss and his girlfriend were discussing him. For the purposes of this insight, she forgot that she no longer counted as his girlfriend.

"Well, who is he? What's he ever done to earn your admiration?" He asked the question in the full knowledge that Iris admired him; and seeing her stop chewing to consider the matter, he launched into his theory of love, which owed as much to Pierre Corneille as it did to the ethics of the New York meritocracy.

"You've got to understand something," he began as Iris fixed her shining Dexedrine eyes on him. "When you came to my office the first time"—(he remembers! she thought, exalted)—"you were just another college kid. Now you've got a name in this town, a little name, but still a name. You can go up or down with that. If you want to keep hanging around with the fashion faggots and screwing the occasional hairdresser"—(here she blushed deeply, astounded that he should know so much about her, and wondering, gratefully, who had taken the trouble to gossip about her)—"and running after mediocre art directors, that's your choice. But just think what you've got available to you!" She cocked her head, to encourage him to press details upon her. "Some of the best minds in New York were here tonight. Did you talk to any of them? You've got to be direct in this world, unless you want to settle down with some guy nobody's ever heard of, and make babies and clean the house."

"God, no!" said Iris.

"Well, that's the option most girls take. But the way I've always seen it, you have to look up to someone to be able to love them. You've got to be convinced they've got something you don't have, and it's by going after that—magic, charisma, accomplishments—that you're living up to your potential. Everything else is just settling for what's easy, for what's available. You want to know why I became a journalist?"

Iris nodded.

"I wanted to ball Betty Grable. My older brother was in the army, and he kept writing Mom all these letters about Betty Grable, and I was only fourteen, but I figured that while he was away in Europe fighting, I could seize my chance to get to Betty Grable before him. We competed a lot, you see."

"I see," said Iris.

"So I became a cub reporter on the Eatonville *Gazette,* that's where we lived, Eatonville, South Carolina. And I covered every fire that happened after three-thirty, that's when school got out, and every nasty little murder in the rough part of town."

"Ugh," said Iris.

"Experience, experience! By the time I was twenty-one, I was editing the goddamn paper"—here he let out a contented sigh and seized another slice of pizza from the floppy box that rested on the coffee table, and he shoved it into his mouth before continuing, a little muffled: "There wasn't an aspect of life in Eatonville that I didn't write about. By the time I was twenty-three, I was finished with that hometown stuff. I'd interviewed everyone important who ever came down there, *Time* magazine called me up to New York, then I went to *Life,* that's where I did all the Alger Hiss stuff, then *Gentleman* called me up and that was that. By the time I hit the quarter-century, I'd interviewed everyone who was ever anyone in the whole United States."

"Did you ever get to ball Betty Grable?" asked Iris, emboldened into folding her elbow above her head in a Grable pose, to suggest she was as desirable as any pin-up.

"No," he said with a practiced sigh. "She was entertaining troops overseas, and by the time she came home she was a back number."

"Well," said Iris, "I suppose that's the way it goes."

"Now about love. My first wife was the most beautiful debutante of her day. I followed everything she did from a distance, for four years; she took over from Betty Grable for me. I even kept cuttings about her, can you imagine that?"

"Yes," said Iris.

"And by the time I met her I knew exactly how to handle her; you don't flatter a girl who's got everything, you put her down. That's how to get them. We were married a month after we met. I did a profile on her old man and that got me her parents' blessing."

"I suppose they were very rich," said Iris.

"Hey"—this in a reproving tone, his hand held forward as if to halt a flow of critical traffic—"it wasn't the money. Money isn't the important thing. It's glamour. That's what I wanted. We were very happy, for about six years. Beautiful apartment, beautiful little kids, beautiful dog, the works. She was in *Vogue* almost every month."

"What went wrong—I mean, apart from the pills?" asked Iris, in an effort to be direct.

"Who told you about the pills?" he asked, suspicious.

"You did, earlier. When I took my pill."

"Oh yeah." To support the excuse that his inattention was due to drink, he finished his glass of beer before continuing. "You better get off those things, you know. I had to put her away in the end."

Iris suppressed an "I know." She felt she was not only listening well but also handling him, a feminine art to which she was unaccustomed. It felt good, and was easy; no more than a question of keeping her mouth shut.

"So then there was Magda. Beautiful model, exotic. That didn't last long. Same problem."

"Oh?" said Iris.

"Yes, premature ejaculation."

"Oh," said Iris, now shocked. He saw her redden and enjoyed it.

"Don't be embarrassed. My shrink has taught me to express things that formerly I would have, well, dissimulated."

"Yes, yes," said Iris, cheering herself with the reminder that he hadn't said "impotence."

"Now the actress. That was more like it. You know, it took me almost twenty years to discover that what I really admire is talent. I'm passing this along to you because I like you. Talent, that's the thing. Unless someone's got talent, a hotline to the gods, you know, what are they? Just bodies. Ambulatory flesh. Extras."

"Extras, yes, you're right!" cried Iris, full of revelation. She wanted to hug him, a desire reinforced by his admission that he liked her.

"Talent, that's the thing."

"You've got talent," she hazarded.

"I do?" He cocked an eyebrow at her and folded an arm behind his head. A quiet belch slowly worked its way up his chest and emerged as a small, immobile cloud of pepperoni.

"Yes, you do such amazing things at *Gentleman,* that's talent," she said, feeling herself on slightly shaky ground. She summoned up to memory a few examples: "That cover with the ape and Joe Louis? And the list of five hundred forgotten names in transatlantic literature? And the series on medicine-cabinet contents? I mean, that's really brilliant."

"You think so?" he asked, gazing up at the ceiling.

"Brilliant," she said with such feeling that he looked modestly down at his shoes.

" 'Every writer owes God only one thing, and that is to be a witness to his time.' Know who said that? Goethe."

Iris nodded, feeling as a Frances Lyle girl that she should be familiar with the quote.

He sat up suddenly. "I'm going to tell you something I'd like you to keep quiet, just for the moment. Okay?"

She nodded so eagerly that he was touched, and instead of continuing, he reached out a large hand and fondled her neck for an instant before speaking.

"Gossip," he said at last. "Gossip is the coming thing. Never mind articles. Never mind trying to define or witness your time. Gossip is what history's made of, the interesting part of history anyway, and as contemporary historians it's up to us to produce it."

"It?" She knew the hand on her shoulder was an invitation, or perhaps an order; either way she was prepared to acquiesce and obey, and awaited a further signal.

"Gossip. I'm going to be leaving . . . Hey," he said with a large smile, "let's continue this in bed, shall we?"

"Sure," said Iris, trying to be as casual as he was. "Why not?"

His bed was six square feet of buckled sheets, torn newspaper and depressed pillows, with scatterings of sunflower seeds and Oreo crumbs. From its condition Iris deduced, correctly, that the actress, whoever she was, no longer figured in Julian Sorrel's life, and that here was a man alone. As she separated the components of her costume and unveiled her angular body, thoughts of housekeeping and cohabitation sparked off possibilities in her mind that she had not contemplated before. It was only when she lay under the tall and heavy body and discovered that premature ejaculation meant an even briefer version of her exertions with Nick the hairdresser that an iota of doubt crept into her mind. She cheered herself, once he had rolled off her and proceeded to the icebox in search of something refreshing, with the thought that at least he had not required her to do anything sticky and perverse; he had in fact not required her to do much at all, and she propped herself on a pair of exhausted pillows and concluded that they had several things in common: talent, an appreciation of fame and a lack of interest in sex that she saw as a sign of aristocratic detachment.

He returned, splendidly naked and unashamed of his girth, bearing two pieces of chocolate cake on a Lusterware plate and a glass of milk. "Well," he said, lowering himself onto the bed, "that was nice!"

Iris didn't answer, sure that as a man of refinement he would not wish to engage in a discussion; too late she remembered the shrink.

"That *was* nice, wasn't it?" he repeated in a new tone.

"Oh, yes!" she said. "I feel much better with you now." She hoped that sounded honest and soul-baring enough.

"You didn't come," he said solemnly, as if he had divined a dark secret, as if it took great perspicacity to notice that a woman who lies immobile during seventy-five seconds and then lets out a relieved sigh through rounded lips was not thrashing in the throes of animal passion.

"I never do," she said gaily, and reached for the second piece of cake: she needed at least one more sin to show for tonight.

"Funny, that's a common problem," he said. Then he put his arm around her, a long arm with golden hairs on it and soft muscles as cozy as his pillows. Iris leaned back on him.

"Now, as I was saying: Gossip is the thing," he continued.

"I'm sure you're right," she said.

"I'll give you a quiz. Lemme see. Okay. Who is Warren Beatty with this week?"

"Julie Christie?" she said.

"Good enough. Um, what's Frank Sinatra's middle name?"

"I don't know."

"Albert."

"I don't see the point of this," said Iris.

"Okay, this'll get you," he said. "What's the name of Christina Onassis's husband?"

"Joseph Bolker. Los Angeles real estate man."

"Too easy."

"Hey, it's like Trivia. You know Trivia?"

"Sure, what was the name of the fourth Stooge, and all that. This is going to be bigger. What do people want to read about? Stars. Who is a star? Anybody famous, anybody who's been on TV. It's the biggest subject in the world."

"What about important things?" asked Iris.

"That's a very young question," he said, tenderly enough. "I'll tell you the big things. The seven big-time sins. Money, drugs, adultery, embezzlement, homosexuality, divorce, tax evasion."

"What about Sloth, Envy—"

"Back numbers. Everyone's lazy and everyone's envious, they swear the whole time, the old stuff is the fabric of everyone's lives. It's the new sins that people are fascinated by, you know why?"

"No."

"Only the rich and famous or the brave can afford them. Mr. Average just can't hack it. One divorce and he's paying alimony for the rest of his life. Only Mickey Rooney, the millionaires of this world can afford a string of wives. Some little guy embezzles, he gets caught. Only the great can get away with it."

"But what does it mean?" asked Iris.

"Imagine a magazine that's all about what people get away with. Hanky-panky on Olympus, if you like. Not the *National Enquirer,* that's small potatoes. Think big!"

"You're going to start a magazine!" said Iris, sitting up.

"It's a secret. Launching it next year."

"If you're telling me, that means that you trust me," she said. "So you'll let me work with you? Please?"

He patted her skinny rump.

"Oh God," she said, putting aside what now seemed to her to be old-fashioned longings for meaning, "how wonderful! Oh, Julian!"

"Hey," he said, his Southern accent suddenly pronounced, "it's them against us!"

21.

Them Against Us

At first it was easy for Iris. The magazine, *Lookout* by name and gaudy by nature, was launched at a party that took up every room of the Tavern on the Green. The first issue in January of 1972 contained an article by her, which had taken several weeks to research and a month to write; its final stages had been supervised by both of *Lookout*'s rewrite men, which had saved her job. It was called "Kronkheit—Diet Doctor to the Stars and Godsend to Pillheads," and it landed the doctor in jail for a term that he has still not served out. Various people, including Johansen, who thought she was mad to leave *Style,* explained that she would make a lot of people sore if she went ahead with her piece, to say nothing of the danger she was putting herself in. "If you put him in jail, you'll get fat again," Johansen had pleaded.

"I don't care," Iris had answered, full of a reforming zeal that owed its life to Julian's frequent injunctions to tell the truth; this truth was nearer to the prejudices of Middle America than to any objective reality, for Sorrel said, "The point is to tell Peoria what they always thought." It was in the service of this commercially viable ideal that Iris had found the courage to approach her doctor, and, simpering, ask him for an interview.

Notions of Liberty, Justice, and Success had attended her stealthy examination of his records and the subsequent phone calls to patients who had moved to Connecticut, coincidentally all to the same quiet institution near New Milford, from which they told her about the slide, slow for some and astoundingly rapid for others, into what she later called, in print, "drug-dependent delusions." The two letters that she received from the mothers of heroin addicts, although irrelevant to the problems of amphetamine users, made her feel that she had performed a service to humanity not that far removed from the exertions of Mother Teresa of Calcutta.

Unlike the rest of Dr. Kronkheit's clients, who were forced to seek another of the dwindling breed of speed pushers in New York, she had amassed enough pastel pills to last her several years; her glint diminished only on those days when she made the mistake of taking too weak a pill in the morning. She saw nothing odd about having denounced the very weaknesses she lived on, just as she saw nothing wrong in printing a list of the names of the rich matrons and bug-eyed actresses who had been diminished by Doctor K.'s ministrations. Her view of her role in life was influenced by Sorrel's endless references to journalists being "if not above, then next to, the law."

The fourth estate was a state of grace.

Her good luck in sleeping with the editor before he had launched his publication meant that no matter how many long-haired lady photographers or sharp-hipped women writers ran after Julian, she was the first lady of his new harem, and, as such, had certain rights, including those of interrupting meetings, discussing things with him in private late at night, and being able to give her ideas to him without asking for an appointment.

The affair was kept quiet, out of a shared sense of protocol; and the random nights that they spent together gave them a pleasant sense of complicity. He liked it that Iris took him and the magazine seriously; he was having problems with his friends, the great minds of New York who had filled his apartment that spring evening: they said he was running after irrelevancy, or worse, that he had sold out, turned his back on Meaning, that he might as well print his rag on small rectangles of green paper, since all it was about was money. He gave up trying to explain to his friends that he was creating the next trend with his bare hands and his sleeves rolled up; he didn't want to appear defensive. Instead, he printed their names in the first of his yearly In and Out lists, which were more virulent than the version *Women's Wear Daily* had been doing, for he appended explanations as to each victim's fall from grace. They lived down these attacks without much difficulty, as no one in the intellectual hub of New York would admit to reading *Lookout,* but their stock among the inhabitants of Middle America and the purchasers of checkout-counter magazines declined rapidly, and for years they had trouble getting on talk shows.

One of Iris's bright suggestions, in bed late one night, was that Eric Castiglione should to go Persia to photograph a ball that the Shah was holding. (In his haste to leave *Gentleman,* Julian had neglected to carry out all the necessary formalities for Eric's trip to Cambodia, and the photographer, a little disillusioned but determined to strike out into the New World, was still hanging around New York.) Julian thought this made brilliant sense, and offered her a slice of imported Swiss cheese as a reward. Now that she felt at ease with him, she was able to refuse it.

He set her to work on a series of stories that were ideally suited to her background and temperament, making use as they did of the contents of her address book, and proceeding chronologically backwards from her newest acquaintances to her oldest friends. The first was called "Can Bennison Hack It?" an in-depth examination of the career of the man that *Lookout* described shatteringly on its cover as "Former Wunderkind, the Fat Boy of TV." Bennison Hack had questioned Julian's reasons for sinking so low, and this was retaliation. Iris interviewed her first benefactor, asking innocuous questions in a quiet voice and asking him to repeat each answer twice, as she laboriously wrote them down in longhand in a spiral book; a Sony was calmly recording from inside her handbag, which enabled her to make a great show of putting down the notepad every time the phone rang and crossing to the window in his office, so as to allow the Sony to tape his off-the-record conversations. She had learned to be cunning, and excelled at all forms of dissimulation.

But as she finished her first draft Julian Sorrel came by her desk and read a page, giving her odd looks as he read. She was brave enough to ask him if it was all right. "Do you always write in French?"

"Sort of," she admitted.

"And you haven't been found out yet?"

"I was writing gossip for two years, Julian!" she said.

"Never call me Julian in the office," he hissed, returning her page to the pile. "And learn to write plain English. Read Hemingway."

She read Hemingway for three straight months, and learned. To write. Short sentences. In English.

Then she interviewed Sheila McCoy, whom Bennison had left on some trivial excuse a few months earlier. The singer, who had bombed at the Winter Garden and was going through an early change of life, was full of unexpected gems, so much so that when, a few weeks later, Julian suggested that Iris do a profile (which *Lookout* called a "Silhouette") on Sheila McCoy, Iris tried to dissuade him. "She told me Bennison Hack wet his bed, for God's sake, that's wonderful stuff! I can't turn on her after that!" Iris told Sorrel.

"Oh, so she's a great friend of yours, huh?" he asked.

"A friend? No, but she's a—what's the word—she's a source."

"Fine, so go find another source. She's a subject now. I want everything, her beginnings, her movie career, the fact that she was an alcoholic in the fifties, her affair with Saul Hyott, the works. I hear she's a lesbian as well. Get to it!"

"Saul Hyott? How do you know about Saul Hyott?" asked Iris. His was the last name she expected to hear mentioned. She was torn between the violent desire to explain that he had been like a father to her and the need to know more.

"My dear, there isn't anything I don't know about the Mob," he said. "Now get to it!"

"But what is it about Saul Hyott? What's he do?" she asked, with a remarkably cautious choice of tense.

"Oh, Iris, read *Variety,* will you? He's just taken over Transatlantic International Pictures."

"Oh," she said. "Okay, I'll do Sheila." She left the office, and, instead of phoning Sheila McCoy, began daydreaming about the terrible situations she could find herself in. Saul's identity as a gangster was news to her, but not entirely startling; it explained the casinos, and made Charlie look heroic for leaving him. She imagined that one day Julian Sorrel would order her to interview Saul, and out of loyalty she would have to refuse; her job would be on the line, and Julian's old warning about personal interest suddenly struck her.

So that's what he meant, she thought, personal interest versus the freedom of the press. It gave her a feeling of power. Having treated herself to several scenes in which Saul begged her not to reveal his secrets while she stood firm, her hand on a Bible, tears running down her cheeks, she at last started assembling a file on Sheila McCoy. And then she ran into the problem, headed item number three, of the singer's relationship with Saul. Rather than bring up what she considered a knotty personal problem, which, if presented wrongly, could make her look both amateurish and incompetent in Sorrel's eyes, she decided to bring it to her mother.

She tracked Charlie down in Virginia, where she and Mike Mullen were staying with some of his vassals. She was divorced now from Ben-Abi, but Mike Mullen had not yet asked to marry her. Charlie felt she was losing her touch, and, in her insecurity, was happy to hear from Iris.

"Darling, how sweet of you to call," she said in a mellow voice.

"Mum, can you have lunch next week?" asked Iris. "It's important."

"You're getting married!" said Charlie.

"Not at all. It's work," said Iris, using the word as a shield against Charlie's middle-class expectations.

"Oh no you don't," said Charlie. "I saw what you wrote about Benny Hack, and it's a crying shame that they let you get away with it." Charlie had always defended her friends, and as she grew older she extended the perimeters of her benevolent protection to include recent acquaintances.

"Mum, it's about Saul," said Iris.

"Saul? Why on earth are you bringing him up all of a sudden?"

Iris wondered whether to explain about the article on Sheila, and found it better to dissemble: "He's become head of a studio, did you hear?"

"A studio?" The irony was a little hard for her to take.

"Yes, in Hollywood. Isn't that funny? Should I tell Sheila?"

"Sheila McCoy? Why would you tell her?"

Iris saw the occasion to sneak it in: "Well, she had an affair with him, didn't she?"

From Virginia came a silence, and then a little cough, followed by Charlie's anger. "Is that what you cook up in that filthy magazine of yours?" she hissed. "The maids here read it, and let me tell you that Muppy and Ham confiscate it when they find it backstairs. If you go spreading any nasty rumors like that, I'll have your hide!"

"Mum, it's not a rumor. I mean, you know it's true, come on." This was Iris's less successful version of what Julian Sorrel called the ingenue technique. When he used it, the line went: "Why would you lie to me when you know I know? Don't you remember, you told me yourself last time I saw you." Still, it worked, mainly thanks to the blood tie, which allows for untold mistakes in presentation.

"How long have you known?" breathed Charlie.

"Ages."

"Oh really? Sheila admitted it to me just last year. She really felt awful about it, you know, carrying on with him when we were all in Paris."

"Yes, that part was rough," said Iris, scribbling rapidly in perfect shorthand.

"All the time I thought it was just that he had to go to the country, can you believe it?"

"You thought it was the casinos," said Iris.

"That's right! Oh, darling, it's so nice to be able to talk freely with you. I feel we never have. Maybe it's because you're finally growing up . . ."

Iris deftly steered Charlie away from the irrelevancies of sentiment.

"That's why you left him for Raoul, right?" she suggested.

"Well, I didn't know, but that Christmas, that week just before Christmas, he was with her, and I thought he was in the country! Isn't it odd how things work out? And I felt, can you believe it, I felt guilty about leaving him for Raoul."

"That's rough," said Iris.

"I could have killed Sheila when she told me, because of all the bad feelings I had, back then. And then I thought, Why bother? She's given me so much pleasure for so many years, what's a little thing like that? I mean, why should I be angry? I value her friendship too much. It's as if Paula did something like that to you, you know?"

"Oh, Paula," said Iris with disdain. She had been spared too many thoughts about Paula since she had begun her time with Julian Sorrel.

She quickly phoned Sheila McCoy, bearing plentiful good wishes from Charlie, and inquiring whether the flowers she had sent as thanks for Sheila's help with the Hack piece had arrived.

"Of course, they did, sweetheart! And they were gorgeous. I would have thanked you for them, but I've been so goddamn busy!"

"Oh?" said Iris, sensing a handle for her story.

"Yes, I'm going to cut an album again. *Favorites from Now and Then,* don't you love the title? I've got a great, great young producer, he's arranged all sorts of good people, and I'm working with him now."

"I know!" said Iris, and as if the thought had just struck her: "Let's do a piece on you!"

"Oh, there's no need to," purred Sheila McCoy.

"No, no, I insist! It will be wonderful, all about your comeback." This was foolhardy; the singer roared at her, "Comeback? I never went away! What do you mean, 'comeback'?"

"Well, your new album, you know." Iris was still easily rattled. "You know, a new album, that's news! Oh, please, let me do a story on it! I'd be so grateful, really!"

"Well, if it helps *you,*" said Sheila McCoy. "After all, you're just starting out."

When the piece appeared, all the details of Sheila McCoy's life were laid out in alliterative indignation. "Strenuously resisting Sapphic leanings stemming from convent days in a depressed mill town, the sleek songbird flew to the top—and plunged to the bottom. She mingled with the Mob.

She battled the bottle. She learned to love life. At the expense of five broken marriages, a string of disappointed girlfriends, and a family she never sees." Sheila threatened to sue, but her lawyer, in cahoots with *Lookout*'s lawyer, explained that there was no way to prove that she didn't have lesbian tendencies because everybody had them, and the piece had in effect pointed out that she had never given in to them, which proved that she was not homosexual. Sheila McCoy, muttering, "The little bitch," between cries of "My audience, what will they think?" vowed to destroy Iris any way she could.

Julian Sorrel was delighted with Iris's work. "You're incredible," he told her. "I don't know anybody else who can put aside personal feelings like you do, and just forge ahead and tell it like it is. That's a precious gift, you know."

Iris felt herself glow, and waited for him to pronounce the word "talent"; since he did not, she modestly told herself that she had to do even better before he would anoint her. She was holding on to the idea that if she did something really spectacular, Julian Sorrel would fall in love with her and give her a column with her picture on top of it. She found little to delight her in their moments of intimacy, and was dimly aware that his stock as a prize New Yorker had diminished since the birth of *Lookout;* she needed only to use her eyes to know that he was overweight and balding; still, as the only world she believed in was the one he ruled over, she was certain she could not do better than to become Mrs. Julian Sorrel. Without, of course, giving up her work.

The next assignment was handed out by the object of her love and admiration with the express purpose of testing her. They were having lunch at the Veau d'Or one day when Iris spotted Szos, seated at a table between two young women. She was surprised to see him in New York, and in that sort of company, and waved wildly at him until a waiter asked her to kindly stop agitating herself in that way and offered to convey a note to her target. Szos waved back, to the annoyance of the waiter who had hoped he would scribble an answer; and as Iris was finishing her salad he came over. Iris hugged him across the table, and introduced him to Julian Sorrel, who shook Szos's hand as if it were a found object: he was not wild about foreigners.

"Sit down, sit down and tell me everything!" said Iris, and Szos, without glancing at Sorrel to see if he approved, lowered himself into the third chair at their table.

"Raoul is coming to America to lecture at some things called summer schools, Vivien is in Rome with Paula, the French have discovered that

Paula can't act, but the Italians will never know, and I'm moving to New York," he said in one breath.

"That's awful about Paula," said Iris, emphatically concerned.

"Nonsense, it's the truth, and you've always known it," said Szos.

At the word "truth" Julian Sorrel automatically reached for the little brown notebook he carried everywhere with him. Iris saw out of the corner of her eye that he was writing "Paula Abime: Washout" in his neat little hand, and she wished she had not seen it. Quickly she tried to change the subject.

"Why is Raoul lecturing? Isn't he making a film?"

This made Szos uncomfortable. He remarked that she seemed to be very thin, and was she getting enough rest, as she obviously wasn't getting enough food to keep a canary happy.

"Of course she isn't getting enough rest," said Julian Sorrel, addressing Szos for the first time. "This is New York. Nobody sleeps in New York."

"I hope that isn't true," said Szos, "since I'm moving here."

"Oh yes, you said that, when are you coming? Have you got an apartment yet?" said Iris.

Szos held up his hands. "All in good time. I have to organize my clients first. If they cannot get put in jail here, I will have to maybe change professions."

"Put in jail?" Julian said to Iris.

"I think he means arrested, isn't that what you meant, Szos, if they can't get arrested?"

"My very words, exactly."

"But why move here?" asked Iris.

"You want me to go back to Budapest? Paris is slow. There is nothing to do now that Gaumont has taken over everything, and all the directors want to do is masturbate with eight-millimeter cameras, and all the actresses are short peasant redheads with acne. The glamour is gone."

"Sounds awful," said Julian Sorrel.

Szos nodded sagely. "It has changed so much, Iris, you would not believe it. It's a different world."

"Oh God, don't say that!" said Iris, before pulling herself together enough to make a connection. "Szos," she said, loud enough to attract the attention of the messenger waiter once more, "you've come over because Saul's a movie mogul now, isn't that it?"

Szos gave the smile of a man who has been cornered into the truth. "What can I say?" he said.

"You've said it," said Julian.

Back at the office he took out his notebook and called Iris into his room. For once, she went with trepidation.

"I've got three names here," he said, scanning the little pages, "and I want you to pick the one you'll start with. One, Paula Abime."

"I'd have to go to Europe to find out if it's true what he said about her acting," she said quickly. She had never been sent farther than Washington, and a long trip was a mark of Julian's esteem.

"Two, Raoul Abime on a lecture tour. Co-eds scream for the Svengali of Cinema, that sort of thing."

"He was my stepfather," said Iris.

"I know," he said with a little groan. "Three, Saul Hyott." He looked at her. "Unless you're going to tell me he was your stepfather as well?"

"As a matter of fact," Iris began, "he—" Seeing Julian Sorrel's implacable eye on her, she considered briefly whether to shock him with it now or keep the information for her eventual file on Saul, and said, "He isn't interesting. Not yet; let's do something with his studio later. I'll do Raoul on tour. That should be nice."

"Nice? What's that silly little word doing in here?"

"Interesting," she said as she left the room.

"Remember, no puff pieces!" he screamed at her through his open door.

Later a little note appeared on her desk, in his immaculate writing. "Who is Vivien?" it said.

If he had asked Paula that question, she would have answered, "The most wonderful woman in the world." In the two years that had given Iris her vocation to report on the doings of her betters, Paula had remained the same, untouched by time or experience. Fashion photographers counted this a blessing. "Still a kid," they told her, or more often, as she worked in Paris, *"T'as pas changée."* Inevitably the urge to act had come upon her, and Szos had engineered the necessary vehicles for her elongated form.

"She is so sensitive," he told skeptical directors. "She feels everything, and she shows it on her face." He did not add that the disorder passed fast. This sensitivity had long been admired by photographers. Billingsgate still remarked, when asked about her in interviews for books on the golden days of the sixties, that "all you had to do was say 'You're a flower,' and she'd start bloomin' bloomin'." Szos tried to spin this empathy of hers into a career. "You are a natural," he said, "and when you turn those green eyes on the camera, old men will cry out." The best he could come up with, however, was a low-budget all-French effort in which she pressed on the camera a wide-eyed, intense, but ultimately vacuous stare. The reviews for this film, *Rien,* in which she played the quintessential turn-of-the-decade part known as *la fille* (the girl)—a creature endowed with long legs, long hair, wearing a short skirt, and carrying in every shot a pair of jingling car keys permanently affixed to her fist—a showy part with few lines and half a love scene, where in the best tradition of French farce *la fille* (the girl) was quite naked and *l'homme* (the man) kept on his trousers with the knife-sharp creases, the reviews mentioned her as a beauty, which pleased her, and a cipher, which pleased Szos as he took it to mean symbolic, mysterious, when in fact the reviewers meant it as the mathematical symbol for zero.

The next film offered Paula the chance to play "a girl of today," a slight improvement on "the girl," in that it gave her the opportunity to act out scenes of daily life that the less acute critics could interpret as fleshing out the part. She was seen taking a bath, boiling a little pan of water, watering a pair of geraniums on a balcony, talking to a cat, buying a stick of bread, and running down a flight of steep steps to catch the Métro, which could be heard rumbling in direct sound. The film, *Les Noix* in French (*Gang Warfare* in English, due to one of those misunderstandings with the distributor's subcontracted subtitling firm), was praised for its social realism: there was a particularly grisly scene where the male lead was seen skinning the very same cat that Paula had earlier talked to. The only praise Paula received was for the length of her legs, this time encased in jeans for every scene save for the one, of course, where she took the bath. Szos told her not to worry: "Katie Hepburn started out just like you," he assured her, without one iota of truth. "It will just take a little longer."

Paula waited one year before again committing her image to film; during that year she went from being "a girl of today" to being a bird in a gilded cage, for lack of anything better to do. When she first took over her father's old apartment in Paris, she imagined it was to get away from Ted Billingsgate. Raoul had said, "This is yours," and she had taken his word for it. He spent most of his time in Rome directing strange films starring Vivien or Anglophile Neapolitans with names like Hugh Killarney. Raoul told her he regretted having nothing that would be good for her, and she accepted this with equanimity, knowing that she had to make her own way. She tinkered with a baron, toyed with a singer, lost her head for three days over a soft pretty young man about to play Christ in a musical, and allowed a marquis with a thin mouth to court her. When he gave her a marquetry commode from his family castle, she knew he was serious. The marquis, who was from a fine Catholic family, was only trying to annoy his mother, a Paris-hating lesbian who lived in the Auvergne and raised pigs; she was opposed to performers as a race and to Paula in particular; she did not like mixed blood. The French gutter press, which had not ceased delighting in Paula's activities since her birth on the cover of *Paris Match,* called her a *croqueuse d'hommes,* or man-muncher. The marquis's mother thought this was proof of her unsuitability. The marquis, whose name was Hugo de Vigny, took Paula to numerous balls, *générales,* opening nights and art gallery *vernissages.* He liked being seen with her. He offered to pay for certain necessities—the Rue de Berri apartment was in a sad state of disrepair—and Paula, who was choosy about what modeling she did now that she was an actress, could not help but accept. Her fallow period did not allow her to indulge in repair of the boiler, nor in new curtains nor a new car. He installed carpet on the walls as well as the floor of Raoul's old bedroom, and took her on frequent trips to exotic places where the sun has no sooner set than it is replaced by blue lights meant to repel insects. Paula soon found herself indebted to him; she did not suppose he would want repayment, but she knew what was said about people with thin mouths.

One night, lying on the silk sheets he had given her, he told her that her beauty and her *douceur* (sweetness) deserved the best. "But it's as if you were keeping me," she whispered. *"Ce n'est pas bien."*

"Tiens donc," he had answered, "don't be so solemn. Americans are solemn, that's why I hate them. Life is to be lived, not analyzed."

Thus reassured, Paula returned to the enjoyment of everything he had to give her. Whenever her emotions were touched, which was often, she abandoned thought. She could assimilate information, but was incapable of filing it. She was misled by certain convictions, born of misunderstood statements and half-imagined promises, which had begun as the mechanical encouragements of photographers, hairdressers, fashion editors, designers and the midnight reassurances of the men she slept with. "You're beautiful," they told her, "you're beautiful." When she was not in a situation where those around her depended on her beauty for their livelihood, she would ask, forlorn, fervent—"Am I beautiful?" No one commented, as they had for Iris, on the fact that she could speak French, and she believed all she had was her beauty.

She was understandably depressed when, in May of 1973, she turned twenty-four. The ghastly quarter-century was almost upon her, and she was not yet a star, nor even an actress, nor—the sentimental thought touched her—married and a mother. Hugo de Vigny gave her a pendant, which he had ordered to his specifications from Chaumet, his family's jewelers. The words *Carpe Diem* were fashioned out of gold, and the dot of the *i* of *Diem* was a two-carat diamond. Paula expected a diadem or a tiara when she saw the box, but was nonetheless deeply touched when she saw the necklace. "It means enjoy the day," he said. By the next morning she had forgotten what the words meant, and later felt a little funny wearing the name of a fish around her neck; she did not forget his injunction to be happy, however, and proceeded to act lighthearted and pleasure-loving. This was not alien to her nature, and she availed herself of the task with such ease that Szos began to wonder if she wouldn't make a nice light comedienne. He had long cherished an idea of Paula as a quiet homebody, shy and retiring, and her loud giggles and sharp driving in heavy traffic as a performance. He had suggested her for the part of a woman of the world in a film that was old-fashioned enough to confer on that character the luxury of a name, Violetta. "Miss Abime's performance as Violetta belongs on the runway of a fashion house," the *International Herald Tribune* said; this was the only review in English, as once again the film failed to be bought for America and even the normally stalwart and indiscriminate Cork Film Festival board turned it down.

At this sad juncture in her life a rash of nervous origin settled upon Paula's upper chest and Hugo decided to go skiing in Chile. She dined one night with her father, who was on his way to the Balkans, he said, for a cure. "You should see Vivien," he told her.

"I'll see her with you when you come back," she said. He didn't tell her that he thought it was over with Vivien.

Then Paula herself ran into Vivien, at the hairdresser's. "You need a holiday, *ma petite,*" Vivien said, feeling maternal now that Raoul was safely dispatched and she had no need to prove anything to him. "Why don't you come down and stay with me? Your room's still there in my house, you can stay as long as you want, spend the summer."

Szos took her to lunch and told her not to be depressed. "This happens at the beginning of every career, you're just too beautiful, the dumb critics don't understand. And everyone gets rashes." Paula went back to the Rue de Berri and called Vivien in Rome, who asked her to bring down six *baguettes* and some *savon de Marseille.*

Vivien was a gift from the gods. She didn't stop telling Paula what to do with her life, and provided her with an endless store of adages, bromides, slogans, mottoes and philosophical guidelines. "A woman isn't a woman until she has suffered." "A man isn't a man until he has found the right woman." "The only person you must never lie to is yourself." "Producers think we actresses are horsemeat. It's up to us to treat them like the butchers they are, and only send our maids to see them." "A woman under thirty is a girl; a woman over thirty is a woman, and a woman over forty is on her own." "A true woman will always follow her heart, for that is what makes her a woman." The endless repetition of these words gave Paula a sense of womanhood that soothed her anguish at growing older. She didn't have many people to practice on at the villa. The few young men who strayed past Vivien's gates were quickly routed by the gardener with a rake, or by Vivien with a sharp line of inquiry that led either straight out the back gate or up the massive wooden stairs, *"alla Tudor,"* to her bedroom. "Don't do anything, let them come to you," Vivien told Paula whenever the younger woman expressed a desire to go into Rome to see who was around and hang out. "At my age a woman must give in to her appetites," she explained. "One does not diet after fifty. When you are young, you must mortify the flesh to keep it pure. No sex without reason!" Paula showed her impatience: "I'm sure there are all sorts of old friends I could see at Babington's," she said.

"Sono mascalzoni, lasciali," said Vivien, which meant, "You don't leave here without me."

Szos, by a natural chain of events, had replaced Alfonso Ercole as Vivien's agent. He never referred to the string of bad deals and broken contracts Vivien had beguiled Raoul into; he was discreet, and wished never to offend. Vivien Legrand made good money in Italy: people were afraid of incurring her wrath, and no check made out to her ever bounced. Szos had given up on Raoul; the Balkan project, a low-budget documentary about potters, was the best French television could come up with, and Szos had managed to persuade him into doing it by invoking racial roots.

When Szos came to Rome, Paula saw that the Italian Szos was a freer person, a happier man. He usually brought with him some form of companion, who would sit looking at him with dutiful eyes and then, when Szos's back was turned, throw Paula a wink. Vivien intercepted one of these signals, and later called Paula into her room. "A woman never takes away a *froscio*'s little friend," she warned. "Never."

"But why?" asked Paula, relieved that someone had made eyes at her.

"They have diseases," said Vivien.

On his third visit to the house, Szos brought, along with a new friend, the news that he had found a wonderful part for Paula. *"Ah sì?"* Vivien asked, giving Szos a warning look. He added quickly, "It's not anything you would play, lots of nude scenes."

"Paula is like a daughter to me, the daughter I never had," said Vivien, "I only want the best for her. What nude scenes?"

"Not too many," he said. "Necessary, tasteful. It's that book by Cyril Croton, *These Lustful Stones.*"

Vivien was at a loss; she made the face of one who is trying to remember a long-forgotten book, but as she never read, it was mere mime.

"A tragic story," added Szos helpfully.

"That's good, she needs to do tragedy. A woman is a woman only when she has suffered."

"Oh, tragedy!" Paula was lying on the blue sofa, patting one of the Labradors, a daily task she had taken over from Vivien. She knew what tragedy was: Hugo skiing in Chile. "Do I get to die?" she asked.

"You suffer," said Szos, rolling his *r*'s, "you love, you are tormented, you go to a convent, you try to purify yourself, you come out, you kill your lover, you die," he promised.

Paula saw a panoply of profound experiences arrayed within her grasp. "How wonderful! How do I do it?"

"From the heart, my child, from the heart!" cried Vivien. *"Il cuore!"* She clutched her heart.

"How do I get the part?" asked Paula, nodding vigorously at Vivien to show she understood.

"The producer is coming here next week. He's an old friend. We will have it all organized for you. And the star, do you know who he is?"

Both women shook their heads, Vivien waiting to hear the name of a former lover, Paula that of a future one.

"Did you see *Scorpion?*" asked Szos, leaning on the couch and making little claws with his hands. He looked more like Peter Lorre than ever.

His friend said, "It was wonderful."

"Scorpion," repeated Szos.

Paula cried out. "Oh no! He's incredible, and what's more, I think I met him once!"

"What, who?" asked Vivien crossly.

"Kid Crane!" said Paula. He's that wonderful, wonderful, beautiful actor, that English actor, you know, his last one was *Scorpion* . . ."

"Lo so," muttered Vivien.

"The film about the—oh, Szos—what was it about?"

"A mercenary who terrorizes an orphanage," said Szos.

"You mean *La piccola storia delle ragazze che sentivano venire il lupo una sera di novembre?"* asked Vivien, her memory jogged by the plot. "Of course I saw it. The man is a genius!" Beaming approval, she settled back on her couch. Having named the ominous title, she felt chilly. Like all great actresses, she was afflicted with an emotional homeostasis that impelled her to live whatever she conjured up in her mind, and turning to Szos, she asked him to throw another log on the fire. The friend, a sweet-faced German, rose and accomplished her bidding.

"We will plan everything," said Szos. "Campaign. We will persuade him."

"Who do we have to persuade?" asked Vivien, joining the game.

"The director, and the producer. The director is some young man called Frank Laredo. The producer is an old friend of mine."

Who?" asked Paula.

"Saul Hyott," said Szos.

22.
The Important Things in Life

Iris went to interview Raoul at the Algonquin Hotel when he arrived from Yalta. Raoul greeted her at the door to his suite with puffy eyes and a tender hug. He had not been prepared to see her look so pretty.

His clothes smelled of his old pipe tobacco; the sunglasses lying on the drop-front desk were the same shape as the ones she remembered, and he was still wearing suede shoes. Iris felt that she was confronting him for the first time as an equal, and wanted to impart this to him; but no sooner had she taken off her coat and sat on the little sofa than the phone rang, and he was lost to the stranger on the line. She looked around the room; it seemed incongruous that he should be staying in a place associated with drunken wits in the twenties and down-at-the-heel publishers when she had noted his progress through the needle-spire three-star hotels of Fifth Avenue; she suspected there was some tragic flaw in him that had lately come to light and forced him down into this ignominy.

It was Julian Sorrel who had started her thinking about tragic flaws; he said everyone had them, and all you had to do to predict a man's future was to isolate his basic personal Achilles' heel from all the other personality defects, which were no more than red herrings and could usually be recognized by the fact that those were faults he talked about, while flaw number one remained a touchy subject and thus a secret. She had no guilt about looking at her stepfather with a journalist's pitiless eye; had she known how much empathy and how much hope most writers carry with them into an interview, she would have been shocked at their lack of moral fiber. These days, she enjoyed thinking of herself as stern, cold, adamantine with integrity. It was all part of the job, and in this particular case, the man had gone and disposed of the Château Rose without asking her opinion.

She noticed that his shoes could have used a going-over with a soft gum rubber, that his shirt was missing a button on one cuff, that his thinning hair had discharged a little snowfall of dandruff on his black jacket. As he talked on, in French and English, with his mysterious caller, she rose and signified that she had to go to the bathroom; he pointed to the bedroom door, and as she passed the bed she saw, sticking out from under a virgin copy of the *New York Times,* the unmistakable cover of *Penthouse.* In the bathroom, she, a true disciple of Julian Sorrel, went through the little leather kit resting on the side of the sink, and inventoried a full supply of Dexedrine, Valium five's and Valium ten's, lithium, something called Limbitrol, Gelusil pills, Maalox liquid and five whole boxes of Optalidon, which was the one patent pill she had not encountered before. The Aqua Velva she opened and sniffed, just to re-create the old days, and regretted it at once; as the pale blue smell of mornings in the garden at the Château Rose set off a rattling chain of memories, she felt her objectivity slipping. She replaced the bottle, examined the Gillette double-blade razor, riffled through the side pockets to discover nothing more revealing than a tweezer and a German instrument that she dimly remembered as being useful for ingrown toenails, and completed her tour of inspection by taking seven Dexedrine pills from their little tube, just in case. These she slipped into the pocket of her army trousers; then she flushed the toilet, ran the water, and returned to Raoul.

He had just hung up. *"Alors, ma petite, ça fait longtemps,"* he said, placing affectionate hands on her shoulders. *"Dieu t'es maigre!"*

"I don't speak French so well anymore," she said with a touch of dryness which Raoul found unappealing; he thought she could make an effort.

"So, you're a journalist and you're going to interview me, *hein?*" he said, lighting his pipe.

"Yes," she said. "But I want to come on the lecture tour with you. It will be more interesting that way."

"Twenty-two days? *Tu es folle?*" He rolled his eyes at her. "I hear they are the Stations of the Cross, every day a new torment; isn't it better we talk here?"

"No, I've got to come with you. *Après tout*"—she hazarded the French to avoid alienating him by the inference of what she was about to say—"I don't see Jill and we can't let you go alone."

"C'est mignon," he said. "That's sweet." Iris had used the "we" without thinking, as an automatic journalist's reflex against expressing a personal concern; this little *nous* had sounded to his ears as if the whole household of loving, attentive women still existed, and beyond it the Château Rose, and outside that the two gardens, intimate and sprawling in the back, formal and contained in the front, with the lone Yorkie yapping on the steps, and Szos at the dinner table, busy, grim, and resolved to drag Raoul out of the whole precious edifice of costume and daydream and toward reality, so that Raoul forgot for a moment where he was, as the warmth of remembered safety engulfed him; and the noise of Samsonite suitcases banging against the stair rails outside, in the tenth-floor corridor of the Algonquin Hotel, could have been Jill lugging some new discovery in a crate across the main landing. Then a voice outside said, "Oh, honey, look at the cartoons! They're originals!" and the spell was broken. Raoul pulled himself together, looked at Iris for a clue as to what he had been saying, saw her mouth "Jill" and gave a little "Aha! *Bien.* She is in America now, but in California. She works for a movie studio."

"I thought she'd never leave you," said Iris.

"Oh, we were never really together," said Raoul, inadvertently dropping another secret into Iris's past. She digested this with a flickering memory of Paula having once told her something of the sort, and said, "I just can't imagine you without Jill. It's much harder than imagining you without Mum."

"Well, Jill was more part of my life, *je suppose,*" he said.

"It's just odd," said Iris, at a loss for suitable words.

"We all need signposts," said Raoul.

"So who does the work for you?" she asked.

"Work? There isn't any work. My signposts are gone, too. Szos talks only about moving to New York. I wasted five years in Rome, it's my fault, we all make mistakes. I've just made a documentary on pottery in the Balkans. What you learn, Iris, is that every year you are more fallible. Every year there are more mistakes you can make."

"Oh yes?" She was interested now. The curtain rising on the fatal flaw? But his next words caught her unawares: he was still sly, wise to the ways of journalists. "How have you been?" he asked.

She had been waiting for a statement, not a question, and had to give the answer some thought. "Oh, I work so hard I don't know how I've been."

"But your father, he gives you money, *non?*"

"Yes, Tyler gave me groves; I get the money from them. I get two thousand dollars a month," she said, remembering that Paula had complained that Raoul gave her nothing, that she had to scrounge money off Jill and Vivien Legrand and even work for what she spent.

"So you don't have to work, why do you work so hard? Life is beautiful, you're young, you're crazy to work like that."

"I work because I love it, not because I want to," she said. "And anyway, I think the real danger for a woman is to do nothing and just allow the man in her life to give her an identity." Fearing that this might smack of repellent polemic to a man who considered that the only job fit for a woman was to play another woman on the screen, she added, "Don't you agree? I mean, don't you work because you love it?"

"It's a different problem. One, I am an artist, not a worker. Two, I haven't worked in a long time."

"Why not?" she asked brightly.

"Why not? You are asking me? Ask the studios! Ask the French public! Ask Gaumont! Ask the Comité des Lectrices of *Elle* who voted me *"un phallocrate rétrograde!"*"

He stuck a brass tamper into the bowl of his pipe and crossed his legs. "I am a victim of the public," he said. "No one will finance me to do what I want, and what they want me to do I won't do. Don Flagel came to me again; this time it was seven airmen or soldiers or corporals stuck in Yugoslavia during the war, escaping in a hay truck. International cast. Millions of dollars. Twelve weeks in Brno, or Sfügg, or Tem, they have such places. I said, '*Vas te faire foutre!* I make personal films'!"

"But that's the wave of the future—I mean, all the Americans are making personal films, right?"

"The Americans. Not the Europeans. There is no more dialogue between the Americans and France, *c'est fini.* Why do you think I am lecturing, traveling like a salesman, from college to college, across an America that I have never seen? You can take notes, Iris, I don't mind."

It never occurred to Iris that she could demand a private talk instead. Why should she? Far safer to put their relations on a public level, with the spiral-bound notebooks between them. She turned on the little Sony at the same time, just to protect herself.

Raoul, for the interview, slipped into a detached objectivity that allowed him to blame history, rather than himself, for his lack of success.

"The golden age is over, and the parameters, the limits of the hexagon are now closing in on those who think France has any message for the world. We have been shown to be traitors, collaborators, and the world is against us."

"But you're Rumanian," she said quietly, to steer him toward autobiography. She scrunched comfortably down in the chair.

"Not important anymore. My identity is French. I am a poor man, Iris, a poor man."

"You lost all your money?"

"It went, it went."

"But what are you going to do now?" she asked with some impatience.

There was a tone of self-pity to the rest of his ramblings, and his extrapolations on the fickleness of women seemed to reflect somehow on Iris, via Charlie, and he had little to say about Paula. She came away, after three hours, with the distinct realization that there was very little of what he had said that she could use; only his promise that she could come with him on the trip "if she didn't mind being bored" held any hope for the piece.

The trip did not reveal any further insights into her former stepfather; he was tetchy at airports, drank brandy on planes, retired to his motel room on arrival at each stop, met her for dinner in the lobby of these places, spoke sharply to her photographer, who was none other than Bob from *Style,* who had been promoted to *Lookout* because he was fast on his feet and knew how to bribe doormen. Over their plates of steaming roast ribs or London-cut New York steaks, Raoul enjoyed quizzing Bob about the kind of lenses he used, in between complaining about the food and eyeing the waitresses, but to Iris's chagrin he never revealed anything about his own technique to Bob, nor even made an actual pass at one of the co-eds. They traveled, all three, in a sort of vacuum of bad food and orange bedrooms that uniformly boasted matching sets of double beds, usually covered in textured, fitted turquoise spreads, and wall panels depicting the old West in a tentative inky hand, blown up to nightmare size and laminated black on white. The heads of the departments that had summoned Raoul (departments called Cinema Arts in some places, Video Studios in others, Audio-Visual Cultural History and, regrettably, in a women's junior college next to a pair of magnificent waterfalls, Movie Magic) listed his accomplishments, fawned, toadied, simpered, scraped, and expressed gratitude while handing him the $3,500 check for each appearance. Raoul accepted their praise and their money with cool tolerance. To his audiences of eager young men and flirtatious but slightly confused young women, who thought they were seeing Roger Vadim more often than not, he talked about the need for dreams, for freedom of expression, and for beauty in a world that as his trip progressed he increasingly described as ugly, callow, stupid, and bland.

"He talks a lot, but he doesn't say anything," Iris heard a student complain at Wayne State, the day before they reached Lazarin: had she not been so loyal, or rather, so torn between two loyalties, to Raoul and to Julian Sorrel, she would have turned to the student and said, "Don't I know it!" She contented herself with saying very loud, so as to be overheard, "Some people just don't know how to read subtext."

The situation was saved, and Iris's reputation rescued from the dangerous reefs of puffery, six days into the tour. Raoul had spoken at five colleges in the Midwest, and was on his way to the auditorium at Lazarin, with Iris and the head of the Cinema Studies department trotting behind him down a pale-green corridor, when suddenly he clutched his stomach, doubled over, leaned into the wall for support, dropped his pipe, let out an indignant *"Ça alors!"* and fell to the ground. The head of Cinema Studies was particularly worried: "Just about the same thing happened to King Vidor here last week," he said. "We'd hate it to get around. Maybe it's the dining-hall food . . ." Iris knelt over Raoul, weeping. Ohio was so very far from anywhere either of them called home.

Raoul was put in a hospital, where a pair of doctors diagnosed a mild heart attack. "Are you sure it wasn't a stroke?" asked Iris, who had recently written about "the stroke personality" in *Lookout,* and thought that Raoul fitted it exactly.

"No," said the first doctor, "it's a heart attack."

"You're sure it's not anything he ate?" asked the head of the Cinema Studies department.

"We're sure, all right," said the doctor.

"Will he live?" asked Iris, an elegy forming in her mind.

"Sure he'll live," said the doctor.

Bob took pictures of Raoul in the hospital while he lay asleep, his mouth agape, a solitary bouquet of scarlet carnations from the Lazarin dining-hall staff rising apologetically from his bedside table. Iris waited for him to awake, and, clutching his hand, asked him tenderly what he wanted now. "I feel responsible," she said. "I've got to get you back to New York. Szos said he'd fly in if you needed him."

"I don't want to see Szos. It's his fault, he should keep away from me," he said. He told her he wanted to be left in the hospital there, he was comfortable, the nurses weren't too bad-looking, everything was fine. "Go back to New York, *vraiment,*" he urged. Iris pondered whether to hang around Ohio, acting like Raoul's daughter; the prospect would have been more tempting a few years ago, but she had work to do. Just before leaving, she called Paula in Rome to tell her the news. "Oh my God," was Paula's reaction, to which Iris hastened to assure her that Raoul was recovering without any problems. "I'd come, I really would," said Paula's faint little voice from Rome, "but there's a director I have to meet this week about a film, and I'm afraid that if I'm not here, I'll mess up my chances. And it's a part I really want, too."

"What is it?" asked Iris, a trifle appalled at Paula's single-mindedness, which was almost equal to her own.

"About a girl who's so passionately in love that she kills her lover. And she's called Paulina. It's for me! Pray for me, will you?"

Iris gave her the number of the hospital, sent Raoul's love, and took a plane to New York with Bob.

She was in the process of writing the story—"Legendary Storyteller Raoul Abime Collapses on the Road"—when Julian informed her that Paula had just arrived in New York. "It's not possible!" said Iris. "She decided to stay in Rome!" She was protecting her second paragraph, which stated without a trace of irony that Raoul's daughter, "starlet" Paula Abime, was heartbrokenly staying on in Rome to pursue her career, because her father wanted it that way. Iris was then using a great many adverbs like the casually infelicitous "heartbrokenly," and she wanted to hold on to this one. "How do you know?" she asked Julian.

"A friend of mine just flew in from Rome, and she was on the plane. He says she's really pretty."

"Oh, not so much anymore," said Iris with authority. "Where's she staying?"

"My friend dropped her at the Plaza. Why doesn't she have dinner with us tonight?"

"I didn't know we were having dinner tonight," said Iris. "And anyway, I'm working."

She called Paula.

"Oh darling, I'm so glad you called," said Paula. "I was trying to reach you. I'm going to Ohio tomorrow."

"But why did you come? He's going to be okay, that's what the doctors said."

"Iris, I just couldn't leave him there!" said Paula. "Just think of it, all alone in the middle of nowhere, with no friends, and no relatives, and no one who loves him— It's too awful!"

Iris said she'd be right over; she wanted to see the workings of compassion at firsthand. "More material!" she shouted at Sorrel as she ran out of the office with a new tape in her Sony and a new ballpoint in her hand.

Paula's demeanor perfectly expressed the meaning of the word "distraught"; she had two cigarettes burning in different ashtrays, with one in her mouth; and half her hair was caught inside the neckline of her sweater. Iris pulled it out and smoothed it down, true to her years at *Style,* and ordered a bottle of vodka from room service while Paula sat on the bed, intermittently crying and cursing herself.

"Don't you see? How could I be such a selfish bitch, just running after my own career? It disgusts me, it really does."

"Don't blame yourself," said Iris, noting with a certain satisfaction that Paula had brown indentations curving from her tear ducts down to her cheeks, and that her boots were worn down at the heels.

"But it's all right for you, you were with him! I had to hear about it over the phone, it's much worse. Oh, Iris, how is he?"

Iris spent ten minutes reassuring her and then tried to flesh out the limits of Paula's compassion. "Would you really give everything up like that just to go see him?"

Paula nodded.

"But Paula, there's a plane every two hours for Ohio. You could have gone straight on from the airport."

"I didn't want him to see me like this. You know he's always hated women who look unhappy. I'm going to have my hair done in the morning, and get a good night's rest first, so I'll really cheer him up. You know, after I told you I was staying, I went for a walk in the garden and suddenly what I do seemed so unimportant—"

"Your career!" said Iris.

"My career. Three rotten films. They only want me for my face and my body. That's not a career. Oh, Iris, don't you want to give it all up, too, and just have babies?"

"No!" Iris didn't know how to begin expressing her disgust. "I don't know how you can think like that, Paula. What about London and all the things that have happened to you since?"

"You wouldn't understand," said Paula. "I'm twenty-five, almost. It's over."

"You're just depressed," said Iris. "You'll get over it."

Julian took them both out to dinner at Elaine's, where Paula's presence ensured that for once he was not snubbed by his old friends. Clay Felker came over and shook hands with him, nodded at Iris, and sat to chat with

Paula. Nick Smith, now an established New York hairdresser with his own line of organic hair-care items, attempted to come over but was routed in good time by a providential waiter who spilled a plateful of calamari over him, sending him to the toilet instead. Richard Avedon deposited a kiss on Paula's forehead, and a woman with a tiny bun the size of a cherry tomato and rouged ear lobes attempted to inveigle Iris over to her table, with raucous cries of "The divine one!" which Iris sagely ignored. Sorrel found Paula charming, unaffected (Iris later privately ascribed this opinion to her dirty hair) and beautiful. As they dropped her off at the Plaza, while Iris and Paula were hugging each other in a renewal of sisterly affection, he took out his notebook to write: "Paula Abime: victim of the image." Excited into new conceptions of life by this insight, he dragged Iris back to his place, where he spent half the night quizzing her about Paula.

The story came out two weeks later: "Daughter drops everything for the father she loves," said the line on the cover; inside, Iris's story espoused a morality that was Manichean in its conception of success as a dark hellhole, of failure as a necessary ordeal on the path to redemption. "Abandoning the easy glitter of laid-back Roman holidays, princes and Ferraris, young actress Paula Abime fled to Lazarin, Ohio, where her father, the great movie director of the fifties, Raoul Abime, lay dying in a public hospital. 'Only love counts,' said the tear-stained starlet, who has tasted the bitter fruit of fame and has learned, through unspeakable torments, the importance of family feelings. Raoul Abime was participating in a voluntary educational program . . ."

The Southern states reordered that issue: the local ministers, having learned the touching tale from their wives and daughters who read *Lookout* regularly, had enjoined their congregations to read the article and draw from it a lesson. Julian Sorrel gave Iris a raise, and asked if she had heard anything from Raoul or Paula. "They're in Los Angeles now," she said. "I don't know if they've seen it."

Paula was desultorily shopping for nail polish remover and magazines in the basement drugstore at the Beverly Hills Hotel when a picture caught her eye. It was Raoul's face, eyes closed, a greenish cast hovering over his complexion and bleeding onto the rest of the composition, which consisted of a sheet, a bunch of bright red carnations and an inset photograph of herself looking downcast. Being of a mind that rebelled at paying for pictures of herself, she shoved the magazine into her canvas holdall and proceeded back upstairs, where she made herself comfortable in one of the fat easy chairs in the lobby and read Iris's version of her conversion. It did not strike her that there was anything presumptuous in Iris's description of her as a "broken jet-set bud," nor did she find the account of Raoul's collapse sensational. "Clutching his chest but stoically repressing any sounds of pain, the great director fell to the hard floor, seriously ill"; the words brought tears to her eyes. She felt she should thank Iris for telling the story so that thousands of strangers would be as moved as she was, and began sobbing.

Having finished reading about her selfless devotion in *Lookout,* she glanced at her watch, a gift from Hugo. It was not yet time to go back to the hospital; Raoul did not have strict visiting hours, but Paula had found, after the first pleasure of the reunion (which was sweetened by his awareness of what she had sacrificed to be near him), that spending her time at Raoul's bedside was a dull affair. The doctors in Ohio had told her what he must do to keep well, and had suggested that he stay in bed for a while; but once Paula had wandered around Lazarin for half a day, finding nothing more to her liking than a Save-Mart that stocked oil lamps, mouse traps, bird feeders and inflatable rafts, she had decided, in selfless fashion, that it would be better for Raoul to be in the hospital in Los Angeles, where he had friends and she could go shopping. They had traveled like Florence Nightingale and half the Crimean army, with a stretcher and a drip bottle attending Raoul, and a young doctor attending Paula. Don Flagel, contrite and generous, had offered Paula his guest room, but Raoul, with the capriciousness of an invalid, had forbidden her to accept it. She stayed at the Beverly Hills Hotel, which was delighted to have her back, but because this was a private visit, she could not afford the usual suite, and was instead in a tiny room threatened by a banyan tree at the window, so she spent most of her time in the lobby.

She leafed through the magazine, started reading Iris's story again, and was caught by the last paragraph. "While her father recovers, Paula Abime has set a new goal for herself: 'All I want to do is get married and have babies,' she confided to a close friend. 'Those are the only important things in life.' " She let out a sigh, and felt very wise for having expressed such sentiments, particularly as the last line said: "This point of view may not be what the feminists want to hear, but then Paula Abime at heart is just an old-fashioned girl." Paula had not spent enough time in New York to be familiar with the current status of old-fashioned girls; the description sounded near enough to Vivien's "real woman" to reassure her that she was on the right track.

As Paula sat there, her hands lying idly on her lap, daydreaming about how she was to attain the goals that seemed to have suddenly become hers, a man in a pale-pink suit watched her from the concierge's desk. "Who's that one?" he asked the man behind the desk, who leaned over and said, "I'm new here, I don't know. I don't recall seeing her on TV, so I don't think she's anybody."

Satisfied with his answer, the man in the pink suit strode boldly over to Paula. "Hi!" he said.

She looked up. She was so used to people in Europe coming up to her and saluting her with a familiarity grounded on a lengthy acquaintance with her image on paper that she smiled back, automatically gracious. Then a doubt wound itself around her; the man, with his curious topping of smooth brown hair, his wide tanned face, his brown eyes, looked oddly familiar; she groped for a name, sure that she must have met him, indeed even talked to him, so familiar were the features. She thought she might have met him with Hugo, perhaps in the Caribbean. "Hello," she said, trying to sound warm, wondering whether to append the "darling!" she granted to people whose names she remembered. "Wanna come to the Polo Lounge and have a drink?" asked the man. Sure that this meant they had been introduced, Paula smiled and rose, leaving the magazine to roll into the corner of the armchair between the cushion and the arm. Once she was standing, she realized that she was taller than he, and as she looked down and saw the pleading in the brown eyes, she caught sight of an arrangement of nose, eyes and mouth that, viewed from that angle, suggested someone that she knew very well, and at that particular moment regarded with love. "Are you Iris's father?" she asked, with a delighted look on her face like a parent that has just solved its child's riddle.

"Who's Iris?" asked the man, hurt at being taken for a father.

"I thought you were Iris's father," said Paula. "Iris, Charlie's daughter."

"I don't know any Iris," he said.

"I'm awfully sorry," continued Paula in her soft voice, lacquered with French inflections and drawn out with Italian languor. "I thought you were someone I knew."

"I thought you were working the joint," said the man in pink.

"Working?"

"Are you a working girl?" he said.

"No, I'm not," she said, full of her new goal. "I'm a wife and mother."

Once she had shaken off the man, she went up to her room. She sat on her bed, which, despite the modest dimensions of the room, was a standard Hollywood king-size, and made a list of the men she could marry, with Hugo at the top of the list. When she had finished, she looked at the twelve names, crossed out five, then two more, then three, leaving Hugo de Vigny and Ted Billingsgate, for whom she still carried, if not a torch, at least a pocket flashlight. She tried to visualize laughing babies, first little French ones in lace christening gowns, then English ones eating oatmeal out of bowls printed with bunnies and mice in raincoats. Preferring the ethereal lace versions, she crossed out Ted and asked the operator to connect her to Hugo's number in Paris. It seemed entirely logical to her that now that her mind was made up, Hugo would fall in with her wishes.

Before she could be connected to Paris, Szos reached her; he was calling from New York. Without pausing to inquire after Raoul's health, he said, "There you are! Stay there. The producer of *These Lustful Stones* will be calling you the moment I tell him where you are. He's excited to meet you. He's turned down everyone else for the part, and I think it's yours."

"But, Szos," said Paula. "I don't want to do that anymore."

"Nerves," said Szos, "just nerves."

23.
The Sights of Rome

Toward the beginning of October, it was announced that Paula Abime was to star in *These Lustful Stones,* to be shot in Rome, directed by the wonderboy Frank Laredo, financed by Transatlantic International Pictures, and co-starring the famous Anglo-American actor Kid Crane. Both Julian Sorrel and Iris were struck with the same thought at the same time, while reading identical issues of the *New York Post,* and they collided in the open space between her desk and his office.

"Italy!" said Iris.

"Italy!" said Julian Sorrel.

"Can I really?" asked Iris.

"It seems worth it," said Julian Sorrel. "Come on in and discuss it."

The points against going were that Iris did not speak Italian, knew no one in Rome other than Paula, and had backed the wrong prophecy when she had written that Paula was ready to give up her career. The points in favor were the extraordinary confluence of stories she could write: a profile of Vivien Legrand, a profile of Kid Crane and a story on Paula. "If you're going to get mushy about Paula, I can't let you go," he warned. "But be sure to give her my best regards. I'd love to come myself, but I'll be much too busy here."

"On what?" asked Iris, protecting her turf.

"Nothing you'd be good for," he said with nonchalance.

She sensed some change of heart had taken place in him, and that it entailed some demotion for her. She asked again, insistent this time, transgressing the unspoken agreement of their collaboration, which was that she would never question him, but only support the thrust of his enthusiasms.

"What stories?"

He ran his hand down a list that his secretary had typed up. It was headed VITAL ISSUES and the words themselves offended Iris.

Behind him on the wall were displayed the ninety-seven covers of *Lookout* to date: singers grabbing their mates, punch-drunk boxers, a solemn deposed empress, pretty girls and handsome movie stars in equal amounts, here and there a famous child. The logo was a uniform blue, a color said by marketing organizations to appeal to manual workers, civil servants, members of the armed forces and housewives. The color reproduction, garish at first, had straightened itself out, and by scanning the covers the eye could detect a turn toward pinks and red and away from yellow and acid green. Only the recent cover of Raoul, the third from the last, stood out as unpleasant with its chartreuse hue, a little like a *memento mori* by Hans Baldung Grien among the healthy smiles.

Looking at the wall, which had provided her with reason for pride and had been the image of encouragement to her from the first issue, she felt alienated for the first time. Once more she said, "What stories?" Her voice sounded shrill, though she did not raise it. "Iris, you're getting very good at the showbiz stuff, and the American stories are just politics. Nothing that you'd be any good at." The word "politics" reverberated in her with the resonance that she had always sensed in certain abstract nouns: Meaning, Government, Protest, and Caucus had the same solemn and impenetrable aura, and a large part of her euphoria at *Lookout* consisted in her conviction that she had left these words, with all their attendant obligations and unfulfillable challenges, well behind her, immured at Frances Lyle, locked into the heads of the New York intellectuals that Julian Sorrel no longer bothered talking to. Her faith in Julian Sorrel and all his works relied on the supposition that he too had turned against those looming concepts, and his seeming endorsement of frivolity, his appetite for the carnage of gossip, were to Iris proof that here was a grown man (respected, competent, a star in his field) who shared her view of the world. And now he was babbling those words again, dragging rocks of relevance into the magazine, and she felt her own contribution etiolate, fray at the edges, soon to be revealed as no more than the single leaf on top of the cherry on top of the icing on top of a frivolous cake that was too sweet to tempt any but the weakest and most self-indulgent, with its superfluity compounded by being several days too old.

"What stories?" she asked again.

"Oh look!" he cried out, annoyed. "First of all, it's none of your business, and second, you're just not the person to do them. There's a women's conference in the Southwest, that's not for you! There's an investigation on the contents of the blacklist, Jane Fonda and all that, I've put a really bright girl onto that, who used to write for the *Berkeley Barb*, she really knows what she's doing. Then there's one on the prisoners of war and their families, the readjustment—you know, half these guys have divorced their wives since they've been home." Iris was relieved to hear him point this out: if he still found divorce a newsworthy subject, all was not lost. "And there's a piece on the political cinema in Hollywood, and the girl who's trying to unite the hookers. None of that is for you, right?" Iris shook her head. "Okay, so what are you complaining about? You're going to Europe, you'll do a wonderful job. So that's it."

With his hand he made a gesture she had seen a hundred times before, though never before to her: it meant Leave me alone, the meeting's over. As she left the room she heard him calling, "Get me the White House," to his secretary, and it was with a feeling of doom that she regained her desk. Her apprehension doubled when she recognized a tall and handsome girl, with an indomitable smile and real cowboy saddlebags slung across her shoulder, who was waiting outside his office: she recognized the tall correspondent from wire pictures as "the last woman in Saigon" who had covered the last two years of the Vietnam war. Julian was getting serious.

And then she had not heard a word from Raoul about her piece, not a word from Paula since their evening in New York, nothing but a little postcard from Szos announcing that his new address would be 770 Park Avenue, beginning October first. Only Charlie had communicated with her: a letter, on stationery headed Pelican Bay, Maine. "I'm glad the old bastard got what he deserved," Charlie had written with characteristic generosity, "but why you had to betray me is beyond me, and Mike thinks you're a little offhand in this regard, too. Still, I suppose that's what it takes to get to the top these days. Call Mother, please, for me. Love, Charlie."

It did not worry her that her mother was calling her a traitor: she knew that the only reason Charlie had read the piece was to see if she had been mentioned, and Iris had decided, with the punctiliousness of a good reporter, not to bring any blood relatives into the article. Still she longed for reassurance that some member of the clan appreciated her efforts, and she called Szos's new office every day until she left for Rome. At first there was no answer, then a secretary materialized on the wire to announce that Mr. Shows was not in town yet; she was as yet unaware of the correct pronunciation. The day Iris was leaving she dialed the number one more time, and knew, the moment the girl said "Ferdinand Tsotz," that he had arrived. To her relief she was put straight through.

"Oh, Iris," said Szos. "Did you get my message?"

"What message?"

"I called weeks ago to say that I liked your piece on Raoul."

"Really?" asked Iris, investing his compliment with the power of absolution.

"Yes. It was careful, and there was nothing harmful in it," he said.

"I'm off to Rome, right now," she said, and thought she detected a sigh.

"Fellini?" he asked wistfully.

"Paula, and the movie, and Vivien, isn't it great?"

"I'll see you there. Good-bye, and good luck," he said. It was unsatisfactory, but she made do with it.

She felt brave boarding the plane, if only because this was her first assignment abroad. Over her shoulder swung a Louis Vuitton document case; in her traveling bag were twenty-five virgin tapes, in case she couldn't get the right quality in Rome, and two of the office tape recorders were in her suitcase. She squinted at the stewardesses, who all looked like Claudia Cardinale, though not quite as hefty, and checked that her $3,000 in traveler's checks were safely in the zippered part of her handbag. Then she took two Valium, dispensed with the evening dexedrine, and fell asleep.

The plane landed in a pink-and-blue dawn at Fiumicino airport: Iris held her breath as she watched the sky rise up and crossed her fingers. She couldn't have named what it was she wished for, only that she wanted it desperately. On the way in from the airport she watched for signs of Italy in a singularly banal landscape. She had been away from Europe so long that the merest stone house would have been a potent symbol of the vital stock of the past. In the absence of anything that could provide her with an instant illumination, she fell to speculating about the availability of those irresistible sweaters, striped and gnarled in endless colors, that were called Missoni and cost hundreds of dollars in New York. From this she extrapolated a witty Vivien Legrand, clad in random zigzag streaks, chuckling throatily and wondering out loud why she hadn't had the pleasure of meeting Iris before. To which she would pull herself up, fling back her hair with a graceful gesture, and say something wise about Paula and Raoul. Since writing the article she felt she had their number: Paula was a sweet bumpkin who could be pushed around, and Raoul was a self-dramatizing jerk. Although neither of these estimates was strictly accurate, they had taken on the appearance of truth in the past weeks, and had been confirmed by Paula's and Raoul's silence.

"Eccoci quà," said the driver as he drove through a gate in a wall of massy stones, which appeared to be penetrated by a pyramid. Iris turned to see more of this peculiar coupling, but it was gone, and now a delicate temple, with fluted pillars that seemed from a distance to be marked by the bites of giant teeth, stood on a rise to the left. "Bocca della Verità," recited the driver wearily as he sped past the colonnade where the hungry medallion was already out of sight. "Teatro di Marcello," he murmured just as he passed the curved arches at the edge of the road, and Iris turned again, convinced he had misnamed the Colosseum. *"Monumento,"* he intoned as he swerved past the Victor Emmanuel Monument, which Iris, with remarkable conformity to general opinion, decided looked like a wedding cake. "Mussolini," said the driver pointing to the Palazzo Venezia on the left, which Iris watched recede, wondering why they would have such a large monument to a Fascist. The cab sputtered down a dark street. He drove her to the Piazza del Popolo so he could have the pleasure of naming it, swung around the obelisk, darted back up the Via del Babuino, said "Piazza di Spagna" as he drove past a small stone boat imprisoned in an oval indentation in the center of the road; Iris looked up, saw a tower of steps, and recognized them from a hundred postcards.

The Hassler was expecting her; a gloved bellboy took her up to her room, showed her that the closet doors opened, as did the windows, demonstrated the door on the small refrigerator, and wished her a pleasant stay. Quickly she unpacked, hung up her clothes, lined the virgin tapes along the back of the mirrored dressing table; then she allowed herself a first impression of Rome by opening the windows and stepping onto her balcony. She saw domes in the distance, a mauve haze farther still, and walls every shade of brown and red; nearer, the Obelisk seemed close enough to touch, and across the street she watched two uniformed chauffeurs smoking cigarettes as they each leaned against their car, one on a Jaguar, one on a Rolls-Royce. The cobblestones, plump and laid out in a pleasing pattern, gave the illusion of being closer than they were; she felt she could touch them. It was warm, and she leaned on the balustrade, hoping to watch some scenes of Roman life; but it was eight o'clock in the morning, and on the Piazza Trinità dei Monti no one stirred but the chauffeurs.

The public relations woman met her in the bar late that afternoon. She was a sturdy American with close-cropped hair and a tailored suit that struck Iris as remarkably unassuming, even dowdy; glancing down at the woman's shoes, which she discerned to be copies of an expensive type of moccasin that she herself would never wear, she began to worry about the range and quality of Italian goods *in situ.* The woman, who was named Grace Gregory, had with her a pile of imperfectly Xeroxed handouts, which she insisted on calling "exclusives." She had ordered them both Camparis. After inquiries as to the flight and the room, and assurances that she would do everything in her power to help, she began to outline Iris's visit: "Tomorrow you can come on the set and talk to Frank Laredo. Then I'll introduce you to Paula Abime, and you can maybe talk to her the next day."

"I know her already," said Iris. "We were brought up together."

Grace Gregory did not take this in at once; she soldiered on: "She's very shy and doesn't like talking to the press."

"Wait a minute," said Iris. "I know her. We were brought up together."

"You were?" said the PR, favoring Iris with a stare through pale lashes. "Why, isn't that amazing!"

"She was my stepsister," said Iris. "My mother was married to her father."

"Oh, that must have been before Vivien Legrand," said the PR with the air of one who has solved a mystery.

"Yes, it was," confirmed Iris.

"Well, I have strict instructions from the producer that Paula is not to give any interviews unchaperoned. He wants to make sure she doesn't give away the plot."

"But it's a well-known book," said Iris.

"Be that as it may," said Grace Gregory with finality, "I have to be there."

Iris ignored the threat, and passed on to Laredo. "Do you chaperone the director too, or do I get to speak to him alone?" she asked.

"Frank likes to talk to the press heart to heart. But you'll have trouble getting an exclusive, you know. I've got five people here all waiting in line to see him. He's a very, very interesting man."

Iris nodded, resigned to a fight; it could come later.

"And of course you're dying to talk to Kid Crane," said Grace. "I bet."

"Well, actually, no," said Iris, to show she could be difficult, too.

Grace Gregory stroked the lap of her skirt, a tentative beige gabardine that Iris decided would, in the language of fashion, be absolutely silent. Grace then leaned toward her, in the manner of a neighbor on a long bus ride. "Let's be friends," she announced. "It's much easier that way."

"Sure," said Iris, offhand, and waited a few seconds before asking where Paula was staying.

"She's out on the Appia, at a house where she stays," said Grace, the proud keeper of privileged information.

"You mean Vivien Legrand's house," said Iris, continuing quickly so as not to react to the look of embattled dismay on the PR's face. "I'd have thought it would be simpler for her to stay in town."

"The Via Appia," said Grace through pursed lips, "is near the studios. That is why Roman movie stars have their houses there."

"Well," asked Iris impatiently, "who else is in the movie? Who else is there I can talk to?"

"Isn't that enough?" asked the PR, her hand on her stack of paper. "How much are you going to do?"

"As many stories as I can," said Iris.

"The producer was most anxious for you to have all the help I could give," said Grace, separating the words as if she were reading them from a typewritten memo.

"Who's he?" asked Iris.

"Saul Hyott, I thought you knew that. And he's staying at the hotel, just like Kid Crane and Frank Laredo."

Iris jumped out of her chair, intending to run to the porter's desk and leave a note for Saul, and then thought better of it; she smiled down at Grace Gregory, a little sheepish to have shown such haste, and leaned over for a potato chip. "Going somewhere?" asked the PR. "No, I'm just twitchy. I slept all day, I need some air." Grace Gregory offered to show her Rome, and Iris, feeling obligated to fulfill the duties of a tourist, accepted.

As they left the hotel, Grace Gregory explained that Transatlantic International Pictures were glad to have publicity in *Lookout,* a statement Iris found imprecise enough to wish to challenge it with a dismissive little "Why?"

"Because, apparently—I've never seen it, you understand, it doesn't come to Rome; magazines are really a problem here unless you buy them secondhand, at full price, from the stands on the Via Veneto, where they get them from the hotels like the Excelsior where all the tourists stay—well, apparently, it's very popular."

"It's the number one fastest-growing popular magazine," said Iris with firmness.

"Yes, that's what I mean. It reaches more people than the quality ones do."

"Saul Hyott's a very good friend of mine," Iris said. "I must leave a note for him before I go." Leaving the PR on the outside steps, Iris returned to the porter, who gave her three sheets of paper. Assuming, for the sake of the note, a greater friendship than had ever existed between them, and forgetting, for the sake of her assignment, their meeting in Monte Carlo some years before, she wrote in her best truckling style: "Saul, isn't it great? I can't believe we've been brought together like this. Absolutely dying to see you. Love, Iris."

Grace Gregory waited outside, folded into a tiny black Fiat. She drove Iris down the Via Gregoriana, the car vibrating miserably over the uneven street. "It's an antique," shouted Grace over the grinding of gears and the rattling of what sounded like empty tunafish cans in the back. "They don't make them like this anymore. I would get a Mini if I could, that's what I really want, but I can't afford one. Now, do you want to see the Trevi Fountain?" Before Iris could answer, she turned into a street, and came to a sudden stop. The wide basin was roped off; a vendor sold chestnuts from a little cart, and children played at the edge of the water. Rising up onto the high wall of the palazzo behind it, the effervescent architecture of stone, carved to resemble rocks, looked to Iris like a film set. "Tell me something about it," she asked.

"Well, in '55 Vivien Legrand shot that wonderful scene here, where her lover throws her in the water. You should have seen it: it took all night. She had to fall in the fountain five, ten, fifteen times; she was screaming at Visconti in the end, she was so angry, and she was throwing things. We had to rope off both entrances to the piazza, but the crowd kept breaking through: they heard she'd be naked, so there was no way to stop them. They were like animals!" Grace Gregory evidently found pleasure in the story; her forehead sweated lightly and her pale lashes flapped over her eyes as she continued, "I had the job of my life trying to get the people out of there. And Luchino was furious." She added, in a sigh, "It was different in the old days." "I know," said Iris. She wondered how long the woman had lived in Rome: she stressed the syllables of certain words with an increase in volume that Iris found both irritating and inaesthetic, and supposed this was the way one went native in Italy. Grace Gregory reminded her of Jill, a more hopeless Jill with no houses to play with, no art history to throw around, and instead of a single Raoul, a changing cast of tyrants.

The tour of Rome, which took in the same sights that the taxi driver had pointed out that morning, was punctuated with anecdotes about Visconti, Fellini, Robert Aldrich, Dino De Laurentiis (Grace Gregory took great care to give both *i*'s their due), Sophia Loren and Anna Magnani. The Bocca della Verità was the excuse for a long story about Audrey Hepburn and Gregory Peck shooting the scene in *Roman Holiday* where he pretends his hand has been grabbed by something inside the medallion. Grace Gregory became so carried away with the story she insisted that Iris get out of the car and examine the very place where she had stood while the scene was filmed: she, Grace Gregory, not Audrey Hepburn. Iris found the wholehearted association that the PR was making between her life story and Iris's place in the world more than a little annoying; and the annoyance was compounded when, pausing for a *cappuccino* in the Piazza del Popolo, at a *caffè* that had a good view of the movie stars' restaurant, Il Bolognese, Grace Gregory said, "If you're lucky, maybe somebody will take you there."

"I'm sure I'll be eating there," said Iris, defending her birthright: where else was she supposed to eat, anyway?

"Is there anywhere else you'd like to see?" asked Grace Gregory as she sped around the Colosseum, leaving Iris perplexed as to the identity of the slice of amphitheater she remembered from the morning. Iris mentioned the Pantheon. "You'll have to go there by yourself, it's in a pedestrian area," said Grace, pushing the accelerator to heave the little car up the slope to the hotel. "There!" she said, as the car swerved to a halt in front of the Hassler. "I'll pick you up tomorrow morning at ten. I'm sure you'll just want to rest and take it easy tonight."

Iris waited until she had disappeared down the hill again, and then crossed the little piazza to the top of the Spanish Steps. Down below she could see shopfronts winking up at her, their lights on. A lust for new sweaters overtook her and she ran down the stairs, ignoring Keats's house to the left, oblivious to the view. She crossed the Piazza di Spagna fearlessly, her eyes on the window of a shop on a central corner, which displayed exactly what she wanted. Once inside, she pointed at everything, and dragged armfuls of clothes into the little dressing room.

When she climbed back up the steps, slowly this time, baffled by the strange distance between the worn stone treads and their uneven surface, she was carrying seven shopping bags, which contained all the components necessary for a new look. The rush of buying had calmed her somewhat, but she could not rid herself of a certain unease, which was caused partly by Julian's shift in attitude and partly by the contact with Grace Gregory, which had disturbed her for reasons she couldn't name. She paused for an instant on the steps of the hotel to look behind her at the Roman lights coming from Roman kitchens and living rooms in Roman houses in the deepening Roman twilight, to pay homage to the distance she had come, and to attempt to salute her new surroundings. It was warm; she was not used to being warm in late October.

As she crossed the lobby to the elevator she saw a television set in the bar with people clustered around it. She wondered about the reputed elegance of the Hassler Hotel.

In her room she opened her packages and contemplated the bold stripes, the dislocated chevrons, the tympanic checks that would set her apart from the herd when she returned to New York. Then the doubt came back, the feeling that for all its outward signs of luxury, the trip might prove to be one of those times when the people she wanted to see wouldn't call back, the smiles she got would be aimed at someone else, and the essential superfluity of her existence would be demonstrated to her in some awful way. To meet the doubt head-on, she called Vivien Legrand's number and asked for Paula.

"Who is calling?" a voice asked in slow and careful English.

"Iris."

"Iris?"

"Iris Bromley."

"Are you a friend of hers? Is it personal?"

Goaded into belligerence, Iris screamed, "Yes!"

"I am sorry she is in the bath," said the voice, and the phone was hung up.

Iris dialed again. "Look!" she said, "I want to leave a message for Paula Abime, will you please take it?"

"Non capisco inglese," said the voice.

"This is her sister, Iris, speaking," she continued, "and I am at the Hassler Hotel. She can call me when she gets out of the bath. Okay?"

"Are you a friend?" asked the voice again.

Iris banged down the receiver, uttering a resonant "Fuck!" She grabbed her wrist: her pulse was throbbing. She tried to remember if she had taken too many pills that day. She put on a new sweater and an old pair of trousers, determined to go out and have dinner alone, to prove she didn't need any of them. In the lobby the television was still on. "Tell me," she said to the concierge, "what are they watching?" There was a tone of disapproval in her voice. "Sports?"

"No, signorina, the news," he said. "Mr. Laredo asked for it."

The news, she thought, the fucking news is following me everywhere! I don't want the news! Rome isn't supposed to be like New York. Outside, the piazza was silent, and she cursed again, wishing she had noticed earlier that there were no restaurants around. Under her arm she had a copy of *Cosmopolitan* that she had bought at the airport and not yet read, armament against anyone who presumed to look at her too long. Defeated, she turned back into the hotel, just as a tall man with dark hair moved away from the group by the television set. He started walking toward her, his hands in the pockets of his jacket, a look of such dejection on his face that at first she only recognized the emotion, not the features. His eyes looked at her briefly before returning to fix on the floor, and in that instant she recognized the pale-blue stare of Kid Crane, and altered her path imperceptibly, so as not to appear to be walking straight at the movie star. Them against us, she told herself: from now on they could run after her.

Kid Crane pushed through the revolving door and was out into the night, where he lit a cigarette and buttoned his jacket. The news on television angered and depressed him. Having become too famous too fast, and particularly since his face had been on the cover of *Time,* he felt that his equals were the great of this world, heads of governments, presidents, party chairmen, ministers of defense. The war between Egypt and Israel affected him personally, too, because he had once made a film with Topol, which had left with him warm personal feelings for all sabras, all Israelis, all Jews. His reality was that of people who are never in their own country, who relate to the world as an impossibly international place whose news is condensed into handy weeklies; in Rome, he stayed in touch with the decisions of his peers in the handsome pages of the *International Herald Tribune,* where the daily information was alarmingly pure, unclogged by parochial trivia. Being an actor, he had a dramatic turn of mind that allowed him to apprehend the shape of tragedy looming at the end of every situation. More than any other man in Rome that night, more than President Leone, who was sitting up at an emergency meeting of his cabinet, more than the Israeli, Soviet and Egyptian ambassadors, more than the worried strategists at the American embassy, more than the solemn newsmen and twitching fifth-column moles gathered around the telexes at the Foreign Press Club, Kid Crane was worried about the Yom Kippur war.

He would go for a walk; he needed the air. He started off toward the Villa Medici, and was stopped by the thought that he might miss something if he went too far; then told himself that he would find a television in any bar he wandered into down below, beyond the Piazza di Spagna. As he started down the stairs he longed for a serene stretch of land. Towns reminded him too much of his childhood in Manchester, the dark close houses and the clean little gardens all so prim and correct. Theater had helped him break from those streets a little, and films even more: because films had taken him to America, where he had learned about land, its glorious expanse that reduced all rules to nothing, the scope and privacy of sand and grass and trees and rocks, the supreme privacy of places where nobody lived, where you could own a few thousand acres without having been born into them and where there were no little picket fences, no deep areaways for dustbins and neat garbage.

Kid Crane—born Christopher Cranham, renamed by Universal in 1962—was a sensual man, powerfully endowed with what acting coaches call sense memory. He could project a variety of emotions, which helped in his vocation, and also lose himself in certain basic pleasures, which interfered with the serenity of his private life. As he skipped down the stairs he conjured up the sound of grasshoppers, the rough edges of wheat against his hand, the grip of cowboy boots and the asperities of irregular earth under his feet, avoided imaginary cow dung, kicked stones that were not there, looked at an absent moon and heard a distant imaginary pickup truck. Like all good English sensualists, he had built an adobe house in Taos, and it was toward that that he began running. The visions faded halfway down, to be replaced by Malibu, where he also had a house; he took the last set of steps with the surf pounding on his left and little wooden houses on his right, the imaginary moon now behind Malibu clouds, his bare feet hitting dry, hard, cold sand, sharp with a million crushed shells, and then splashing through the slick of a cold wave, the sand soft and giving, cold mud, ice cream, running through pins and yogurt, his feet tingling with remembered twilight marathons toward Paradise Cove. He was jolted by the last step, the one that did not lead to another but seemed to rise again as the stairs turned flat. He hunched his shoulders and proceeded down a dark street. Here there was no possibility of projecting Malibu or New Mexico; the stone walls with their cantilevered streetlamps were implacably urban. He thought of Jack the Ripper, a part he had played to much acclaim. He leered at two young girls, who skittered toward him down the narrow street; they recognized him and began to giggle, and he gave a sheepish smile. Suddenly he held up his hand and hit the wall. "They'll cut off the oil!" he shouted, his trained voice reverberating on the tufa walls. Possessed with the need to do something, at the very least to communicate the insight that had shot through him like a thunderbolt, he looked for a bar, a place with a phone.

Men thought of Kid Crane as naïve, when they weren't busy wondering aloud if he wasn't a faggot: his first starring role as Rupert Brooke had been a little too sensitive. Those who worked with him found him self-absorbed; women found him driven, often toward them; and the press had dubbed him a wild man, because he had emerged in a generation of English actors who drank too much, quoted Shakespeare in bars and nightclubs, and had been married four times. Kid Crane thought of himself as the sum of everything going on in the world, a reflection of the moment, a mirror. The great Swiss director Tannenbaum had once told him: "You are the mirror for our inconsistencies, you absorb the essence of the truth and breathe it at the audience." And Kid Crane believed him, every word.

He turned toward the Corso—he was beginning to know Rome, when he bothered to pay attention to his surroundings—and there, to his relief, he saw a sign that spelled out BAR in thick blue capital letters, and walked in. He scanned the walls: posters of Switzerland, Coca-Cola medallions, a cheerful girl stroking her cheek with an artichoke and saying, in a gold-rimmed bubble, "Ah—Cynar." No television. He took a coin out of his pocket and banged it on the counter; two men playing cards looked up, and a young boy shaking a pinball machine looked around and uttered an impatient "Shhh!" From behind a curtain of multicolored plastic ribbons came a small man with the face of a disappointed prune, thinning hair and a towel wrapped around his trousers, on which he was wiping his hand. Raising his hand to his mouth to remove the cigarette that dangled there, and squinting so as not to get a parting shot of smoke in his eyes, he said *"Sì?"*

"Eurh," said Kid Crane. *"Non c'è una televisione?"* His Italian was rotten, but his deep voice gave it a semblance of authenticity.

"No," said the man, sticking the cigarette back in his mouth.

"Allora, un caffè," said Kid Crane. He rather liked the way the *allora* had reverberated through his rib cage; it was not a word he had tried before, as it implied an ease and familiarity with the language that he would have been too shy to aspire to among the crew of the film. He respected crews, and knew they would see through him at once. *"Allora,"* he repeated, purely for his pleasure.

"Allora?" said the owner, thrusting up his chin. *"Va bene?"*

"Ah," said Kid Crane, *"sì."* He wondered how far his Italian would take him if he attempted to discuss the war. Then the actor took over from the man, and kicked the doubts aside. *"Questa guerra,"* he said. *"Terribile."*

"La fin'" said the owner.

"Sì, sì," said Kid Crane with emphasis. *"La fin' del mondo,"* stopping himself just in time from adding *"cane,"* as in the film.

The owner clapped his yellowed hands together: *"L'apocalisse!"* he cried. This was lost on his customer, who nonetheless added another *"Terribile!"* to the fund of conjecture.

"Chiuderanno il petrolio," came the cobblestone voice of one of the cardplayers.

"Il petrolio, sì," said Kid Crane, turning toward him and toasting him with his *espresso.*

"Petrolio, finito!" exclaimed the owner, with an unexpected look of glee on his face.

"Gli ebrei, tutti morti!" cackled the second cardplayer. Kid Crane was puzzled. *"Ebrei?"* he asked the owner, who hunched his back, then pushed down his nose, crossed his eyes, took a thousand-lire note from his pocket and rubbed it in his hand: *"Juss!"* he said. *"Ebrei! Israeliti tutti morti!"* He made a good, if old-fashioned, Shylock.

"Peccato! Erano bravi!" shouted the first cardplayer.

Kid Crane left a smaller tip than he would have before the playful impersonation, which he took to be the sign of a deep-rooted anti-Semitism, and added to his worries about the world as he retraced his path up the Spanish Steps. He dreaded returning to the hotel; in the few weeks since he had been in Rome, he had conceived an irrational dislike of Frank Laredo, which was useful on the set, where his role required an impassive hauteur, but torture in the close enforced friendliness of the hotel. He wasn't wild about the gangster, either, and he regretted having left his wife in London. Laredo was a little young, a little intense, not really on his level; Paula was even more of a kid. There was no one he felt at ease with in Rome, no one who was really part of his world. He had agreed to do the film for the money, but his agent had warned him that he was going to be with a bunch of greenhorns, and now he was beginning to feel it.

"Signor Crane," trilled the concierge, who was well drilled in the protocol of stroking. *"Come va?"* Kid Crane nodded at him, extended a hand for his key, and was handed a message with it. "Latest news bad," it read, "Laredo." He went to the bar, where Frank Laredo, uncombed, unshaved, unbathed, his eyes drooping from fatigue, waved him over. "They've been stopped at the Nile," he screamed.

"Oh my God!" said Kid, resonant with feeling. "It's not possible."

A woman in a print dress, sitting at another table, leaned forward to her husband. "Honey, we should go back tomorrow, while we still can."

"Nothing's gonna happen," said the husband. "Stop worrying."

Kid Crane longed to be able to do something; he glanced over at Laredo, who at thirty-four was a catalogue of the ravages drugs can wreak on a man's face, and opted for quoting Lear's final speech, a part he had never played but whose bleak aridity he fancied he would one day be up to.

Iris had dined on a piece of sole, a salad and a fruit salad. She was just leaving the dining room, with her eyes downcast so as not to catch the smirks of the waiters who had shown their contempt for women who dine alone, when she saw Saul arriving at the door. All thought of measure left her, and she darted forward in a rush of excitement, crying "Saul!" Taken aback by such evident affection, he opened his arms wide to receive her in a hug.

"Let's see you! The girl reporter!" he said. She pulled away from him and saw that the dewlaps had grown, the hair had thinned, the tan was darker than ever. "How's your studio?" she giggled. He slapped her on the back without answering; a tall woman with elaborately curved black hair in which reposed a rhinestone daisy waited behind him to be introduced, but he led Iris toward the bar. "Come, I want you to meet the gang," he said, indicating the two men crouched at a table next to the portable TV. The daisy woman followed three steps behind. "Frank," said Saul with the commanding tones of a proprietor, "I'd like you to meet my little stepdaughter, Iris, who's a big journalist from *Lookout.*" Frank stared up at her through his eyebrows, and raised his hand, mumbling an indistinct greeting.

Kid Crane had stood up, in deference more to the idea of the studio head rather than to the person of Saul Hyott. He shook Iris's hand and favored her with a second glance, and said, "Pleased to meet you," with an inflection of such pure sincerity that Iris, already mollified by the stare, felt her knees weaken. Pulling herself together, she threw him a contemptuous "Hi!" and turned toward Saul, the very picture of respect.

"Well," said Saul, having ordered a bottle of champagne, "I'm sure glad to catch you before I go."

Iris thought he was addressing her, and leaned over to assure him that she was as grateful as he was to have the chance of this encounter, but he was patting Laredo's knee and Laredo was nodding, his head thrust back. Kid Crane pulled up the cuff of his shirt to look at his watch, and glanced nervously at the television set. "No more news until midnight, buddy," said Laredo, "and that's by special dispensation from the Pope."

"Why do you have to watch it down here, don't all the rooms have TV?" asked Iris.

"The reception," said Kid Crane. "The reception's better on this one than the ones upstairs."

Saul and Laredo were muttering to each other about footage and overage, terms that Iris recognized from Raoul's similar mutterings with producers. Saul patted her on the shoulder. "Iris, I'd love to catch up with you, but Frank and I have to have a talk, it's important. Do you mind?"

"How long are you staying?" she asked quickly.

"I'm leaving tomorrow. Tell you what, let's have breakfast on the roof tomorrow morning at eight. You'll love the roof. Great view. Then you can tell me everything."

Iris rose, miserable to find herself dismissed by someone for whom she had pretended respect, and accorded a curt "Good-night" to the assembled company. Kid Crane rose, being a gentleman, and found that both Saul and Laredo were bidding him good-night. Resigned to missing the last broadcast, he left the bar.

Iris was facing him as she stood at the concierge's desk, her key in hand. The depression she felt gave her an attractive slouch, pulled down the corners of her mouth that was too often set in an ingratiating smile, and the jet lag had conferred on her skin an enticing pallor. The brown and red random threads of her sweater looked like the fine pelt of some furtive and dangerous animal. Kid Crane thought of New Mexico, of having her under a purple sage. He walked straight toward her, and as the concierge held out his key he leaned over to her and said, "Some family hour, eh?"

"He's not my family," she said. "He was an accident of my mother's. I'm not responsible." As she said it she realized that if Saul had asked her to sit in on the meeting, she would be defending him to the last.

"Did you just get in?" he asked.

My God, she thought, here's one person in Rome who's talking to me. She looked up and touched her forehead. "This morning. I slept all day."

"I'm going for a walk," he improvised. "D'you want to come?"

She looked past him at the door, as if the question would be decided on the merits of what lay just outside the hotel. "There's nothing there," she said. "I looked, earlier, but there's just the steps."

He followed her gaze, and seemed to accept this view of things, and took his key from the concierge, as if giving up on the idea. Iris decided it was silly to turn down the first nice offer that had come her way. "But let's go see if they haven't got a temple lurking somewhere in the vicinity," she said. "I'd love to see something else besides the hotel." She figured now was not the time to go into her conducted tour of the afternoon.

"C'mon," he said rapidly, as if to a team of boys, or huskies. He had once played an explorer in the Far North, and certain words, such as "Mush!" "Whoa" and "C'mon," had clung to him ever since like burrs.

Outside, Iris took a few steps and waited. Kid Crane drew up alongside her. "Well, which way?" she said.

He pointed to a taxicab that was parked across the street. "That's what I call a real walk!" she said, taking him for a cozy urban sissy like herself. He preceded her to the car; the driver was listening to the radio. *"Come va?"* inquired Kid Crane through the window. The driver shook his head. *"Male."*

"Jesus!" said Kid Crane. "I wish there were some way to get the dope on what's going on! You're a journalist," he said, "where do the foreign correspondents go? You must know that."

Iris leaped at the opportunity to be of use. She searched through her bag for a little card that Mack, the former war correspondent of the *New York Times,* now at *Lookout,* had given her: RADIO STAMPA, it said, *55 Via della Mercede.* "This is it," she said, holding it up. "It's the telex place, and it's also the press club."

He looked at his watch again. She could get the news for him; he'd have her later. "God, it's getting late," he said. He wasn't going to any press club to get mobbed.

"Oh, I don't mind," she said, suddenly pliant. "I'd love to go."

"Would you?" he asked, keen as a little boy.

"Sure, no problem," she assured him.

"Great." He consulted his watch again. "I'll see you back here later. I'll see what I can get on TV. Come up to my room when you get back."

"Won't you be asleep?" she called from inside the cab, feeling tricked.

"Even if I am, I'll wake up," he answered.

The cab let her off in a small street where all the shopfronts were dark, and the only traffic was an occasional scooter. She pushed the high painted door of number fifty-five, and followed the signs that said RADIO STAMPA up the stairs. Three flights up, a glass door barred the way, with a hubbub of voices and the click-whirr-pinging of machines coming from behind it. She went in.

"Sì, signorina?" said a man in a white coat, an ink-stained lab assistant.

"Look, I don't speak Italian, and I'm from *Lookout* in New York, and I'd like to know the news," she said, loud enough to be heard over the machines and to cover the absurdity of her demand.

The white coat called over another white coat, who went to fetch a burly Frenchman in a gray suit from a table where he was scribbling in longhand. *"Oui?"* said the Frenchman.

She repeated her request.

"It's all over. They've stopped the war. Go down and look in the bar."

Thanking him, and repressing the guilt that she felt for interrupting a newsman at his task, she went down a flight and found the bar. A group of men were sitting next to a radio, and another group at the bar counter. Conscious of being the only woman, but now possessed of the information from upstairs, which at least put her on a par with the men, she walked over to the nearest group and introduced herself; then, with a sigh, she said, "It's all over, isn't it?"

An Englishman insisted she sit down, and handed her a sheet of paper bearing the Reuters dispatch. "Before you read this, do you want a drink?" he said with great kindness. She shook her head. "I've got to go back to the hotel. I just had to know."

"We all did. Old Gerry there, man in fatigues looking pissed off, he was leaving in the morning for Cairo. Now his trip's blown."

"How awful," she said, solicitous. She knew how hard it was to get a trip organized.

"But *Lookout* isn't interested in this, is it?" said the Englishman. "I tried to sell them a story a few months ago, and they said nothing political."

"It's changing," she said, as one who knew.

"Is that why you're here?" he asked.

She was about to tell him the truth, but the aura of tense concern in the smoky bar was so attractive that she did not want to dissociate herself from it by misplaced candor. "Yes," she lied, and then sought to diffuse the untruth by giving a wry little chuckle and adding, "I suppose until just now, I mean."

"Look, you can have the dispatch, we've all used it," he said, adding generosity to his virtues. She thanked him, refused a drink again and left, promising to return. Downstairs she waited inside the big door, afraid to go out, unsure how to find a cab alone at that hour. Finally she opened the door and looked out; the street was still empty. She stepped out, gingerly, clasping the sheet of paper in her hand. She told herself that a true journalist was afraid of nothing, and began to walk in the direction of a square, where some twenty taxis idly waited at a stand.

In the hotel elevator she pressed her floor, five, and then the eighth, Kid Crane's. The doors opened at the fifth floor, and she waited for them to close again: they opened at the eighth and she was immobilized by doubt. Should she wake him? What if he was not asleep? She stepped out just as the door slid closed again, and looked for 807. She listened. No sound of radio, no television, no running water. She leaned closer to detect sleep, snores perhaps. Still nothing. Her fear of closed doors was based on a deep and ancient conviction that if a door was shut, it was intended specifically to shut her out.

She folded the paper, took out a pen and scribbled, "I hope this tells you all you want to know," and slipped it under the door. Then she ran down the corridor and rang for the elevator; she saw the red light of the emergency staircase next to it and ran down the three flights to her room. She did not want to be caught intruding.

"I'll tell you about films," said Saul over a pair of fried kidneys that passed for an English breakfast in the Hassler rooftop restaurant. "Movies are like gambling. It's all craps; a throw of the dice, a spin of the wheel, a turn of the cards."

"Yes," said Iris, "but that doesn't tell me how come you're the head of a studio now." She really wanted to know, in view of her future exposé, so she made her tone as simpering as she could, her expression vague.

"Some of my friends bought Transatlantic International, and I was the best person they could think of to run it."

"Saul," she said, a congratulatory purr.

"Hey, I've been in show business since years before you was born, glamour girl," he said. "I bet Charlene never told you about the Hi-Fliers, did she? No, she wouldn't, she was always jealous of them. There's nothing I don't know about bookkeeping against the odds, if you know what I mean."

"Double entry?" she suggested.

He put out a hand. "Hey, that's not funny. No, it's how to make a profit when you're dealing with air. What's a movie? Air!"

"Raoul wouldn't agree," said Iris, incautious.

"Raoul?" said Saul. "Who the fuck is Raoul? Oh, Raoul! What does he know? He's finished. The future's in American movies."

"Why are you doing this film, then?" she asked. "An Italian subject, here in Italy, why not do it in Los Angeles?"

"Reality. Reality's the big thing," he said. "Laredo's a killer with reality. He's American. The script's American. The star's American, and the girl's American."

"But the story's set in Milan," Iris put in.

"And the studio is here. We got Italian extras, Italian lighting. The whole thing'll look so Italian you can smell it." He put his fingers to his mouth in imitation of a popular TV advertisement for spaghetti sauce, and kissed his nails. "Unhumm!" he said, his eyes rolling toward the ceiling. "Da reala ting!"

"Who's financing it?" she asked, shuddering at his lack of elegance and sounding sharper than she wished to. He opened up his napkin and brought it up to his mouth, as if to distance himself from what he was saying: "Transatlantic International, of course. Who else could afford such a big picture?"

"But Paula's sort of an unknown," said Iris. "Isn't she?"

"Soula Tithe's daughter? She's going to be hot. She's gorgeous, and even if I'm not crazy about her father, she'll go far."

"I'll tell her you said so," Iris assured him.

24.

The Magic of Hotel Suites

Grace Gregory met her on the set. Today she was wearing wide-bottomed jeans made of a material thicker and darker than denim, the seams outlined in white stitching that gave her body a peculiar resemblance to a battleship. Thick-soled sandals adhered to her feet with lanyards, and she wore Argyle socks. In her arms she held a metal clipboard. "You're late," she said.

"The car was late picking me up," said Iris.

"I've told everyone you're here," said Grace Gregory.

"Thank you," said Iris.

"It's my job," said Grace Gregory.

The set represented three connecting rooms: a great hall in the baronial manner of Piedmont, with coffered ceilings, fireplaces surrounded by thick blocks of stone, an intaglio floor cleverly made of linoleum. Next to it was a bedroom, dark green, immense, with a four-poster bed against one wall; Grace Gregory led Iris through a small door to another bedroom, which was hung with white lace draperies, and decorated with a prie-dieu, two crucifixes, and a single bed. "This is where she gives herself to him," whispered the PR. "It's her bedroom."

Iris commented on how well built the set was, which elicited from the PR the name of the designer, together with a garbled list of his credits and praises for his talent. Two giant projectors poured spring sunshine through the window; Iris was about to remark on the subtlety of the lighting, but wishing to be spared any more superfluous names and biographies, she inquired instead how soon she could see Paula. Grace Gregory told her that Paula was being made up now, and would see her after lunch.

To disperse her growing feeling of frustration, Iris lit a cigarette. "Not on the set," said Grace Gregory. Iris looked around for somewhere other than the masterpiece of the floor to put out the cigarette, and found a film-can lid already full of butts. She turned to say something to the obnoxious woman, and spotted an electrician shaking out a match. "What about him?" she asked.

"Oh, it's different for the crew," she said. "They're working, they can do what they like. Frank Laredo's a health nut, he doesn't like visitors or anyone not involved on the film to smoke. He says it's a way of keeping the pollution down." With that, she offered Iris a piece of candy shaped like a coffee bean.

Iris wondered at the lack of activity; the PR explained that a scene was being lit on another set. "Why don't we go to where they *are* working?" asked Iris.

"Okay," said the PR, "if you want, but you must be very quiet."

They stood behind the camera, the sound men, the grips, the focus puller, the script girl, the makeup man and the hairdressers; the group of people, massed together like a human pyramid, rose to a point in the person of the young man holding the mike just above Laredo's head. Iris stood on her toes, crouched to see between legs, gave up and settled cross-legged on the floor. She would concentrate on the sounds.

"My father is a strict man," came Paula's voice, unconvinced and reedy. "He counts his money and watches me like a hawk."

"Your father is my friend. It is your brother I do not trust," said the baritone that she knew to be Kid Crane's.

"Cut, and fuck it to hell!" said Frank Laredo's voice.

"I think we should get out of here," Grace Gregory whispered. "He's having another fit." Iris stood up again. One of the crew winked at her: she felt that gave her license to stay.

Paula turned to face them, wearing a long blue dress with white lace on the sleeves and around her throat, her hair in a long braid; she looked at Iris, unseeing. The bright lights, thought Iris, that's why she can't see me. Frank Laredo was talking to her, eye to eye; they were the same height. Suddenly Paula put her hands up to her eyes, and turned from the director and marched straight toward Iris, who involuntarily beamed at her and started forward. "Paula," she said softly.

"I can't talk now, can't you see I'm—" muttered Paula, pulling her dress to her with a sharp tug and drawing away. The hairdresser went to her and put an arm on her shoulder, and she leaned her head on him as she continued toward the back of the stage.

"It's like this every day," said Grace Gregory. "She lets him throw her. She just hasn't got the experience."

Iris told herself that Paula had not recognized her.

She felt two hands on her shoulders, the confident grip of a massage. "Thank you for the note," she heard. The hands left her shoulders, and Kid Crane came around to face her. He was unrecognizable; his hair was plastered down with some sort of grease, a beard was laid along his chin, yards of white silk circled his neck to end in a graceful knot; the high collar of a riding coat framed his head, and in gloved hands he carried a silver-topped cane.

Grace took over: "Iris, this is Kid Crane; Kid, this is Iris Bromley, from *Lookout.*"

Iris began to say "We've met," but Kid Crane forestalled her. "How do you do, Miss Bromley, it's a great pleasure to meet you. I've heard you're the best newshound in New York, or indeed Rome." Taking her hand in his, he raised it to his lips and applied a delicate kiss worthy of a marchese, barely touching the skin. She returned the compliment with a curtsy. Grace Gregory watched them with a look of solid disgust on her face.

"He's always playing around like that," said Grace outside, on the way to Laredo's office. "I think he's a bit weak in the head, but the Italians love it." Iris said nothing. It was a long time since anyone had invited her to play a game. "I'd like to see Paula first," she said. "Can we go to her dressing room?"

"I think it's a bad idea right now," said the PR. "Let's wait until after lunch."

The two women faced each other off over lunch in the huge dimly lit commissary of Cinecittà. Over *osso bucco* and thick red wine, Grace Gregory explained that the Italian cinema was in a sad state of decline. "You should have seen it fifteen years ago," she said. "*Hercules Unchained* and Visconti and Rossellini, no, Rossellini was already finished, Fellini, Vittorio De Sica, those were the days." Iris said as little as possible; she had no ideas about Italian cinema, and did not want any either.

"Of course you're dying to interview Kid Crane," said the PR, licking the marrow from her slice of bone.

"Not necessarily," Iris said.

"You're not? He's a big star," said the PR.

"Look, I'd like to see Paula now. I've finished eating."

"She'll be in her dressing room," said Grace Gregory, resigned. "I'll show you the way."

"No thank you," said Iris, standing up.

Paula had gone home for the day, and Laredo, hurling expletives at the crew and kicking the occasional chair, was rehearsing Kid Crane in a scene with Ermengildo Scola, who played Paula's father.

Grace asked her if she wanted to stay and watch, but Iris declined, and asked for a car back to town. To her relief, she was allowed to go alone.

She gave the driver the address of Vivien Legrand's house on the Appia; he made a few faces, and then turned to her: *"È la casa della Legràn, no?"* She nodded. *"Va bene,"* he shouted, accelerating past a railroad crossing. Soon he drew up to a pair of iron gates. *"È qui,"* he said; he got out of the car and pulled on a bellrope that protruded from one of the stone pillars. A gardener in blue limped up to the gate; Iris, who had left the car, saw an avenue of cypresses leading in a curve toward a clump of bushes, behind which she divined the house to be. "Miss Abime. *Je suis sa soeur,*" she shouted, using French in the absence of Italian. But the gardener only shook his head; she repeated her demand. He crossed his arms in front of him.

"No," said the driver, an experienced translator.

Iris stamped her foot and threw herself back into the car.

She decided to return to Radio Stampa, that warm and welcoming hub of information where she felt in touch with the pulse of current events. In the telex room, the Frenchman from the night before was still seated at the same desk, still scribbling in longhand. He gave her the latest Reuters dispatch, which he had just finished turning into impeccable French, and she read it at a nearby café. The war was truly over, but the Arab states seemed to be organizing themselves to make demands on what Reuters quoted them as calling "the Imperialist West." She felt the churnings of history and conceded that Julian might have a point, after all. Then she went shopping again.

Back at the hotel, she found a note from Grace Gregory: "Kid Crane will have dinner with you tonight, you lucky girl. Meet him in the bar at eight." She felt it was only fitting, and went up to the eighth floor to push the new telex under his door.

"Thank you," he said in the bar at eight-fifteen, when she joined him, after having changed her outfit three times, as if her living still depended on it. "I think it's bad news," she said in a concerned voice, grave and a little deeper than usual. He stared into his glass and shook his head slowly. "Not good," he said.

"How was the rest of the day?" she asked, determined to squeeze some copy out of the evening.

"A waste. That stupid little cunt Paula threw her shit fit—and she went home to sleep off the bollocking Laredo gave her."

He took her to dinner at Il Bolognese; "I'm not sure you'll like it," he apologized. "It's sort of commercial, and crass, but it's the only place I've been in Rome." As they came through the door a table of Americans set up the unmistakable nudging and winking of those who have recognized a star; Iris stood up straighter, and was glad she had chosen the new silk shirt.

When Kid Crane had ordered, he said, "It's too boring always talking about me. How was your day?"

"It was pretty awful," said Iris. "Let's not go into it."

The English part of Kid Crane admired reserve, and he probed just enough to hear about Paula's relationship with Iris, and her irritating disappearing acts. "You won't ever tell her what I said about her, will you?" he asked. "Not that I meant it, but still it would be so awful for her." He put himself in the part of the young actress who hears the star has been complaining about her, and shuddered.

"Well," said Iris, "I'd rather hear about you."

"Oh me!" said Kid Crane. "Is this an interview?"

"Why not?" asked Iris, pleased that he assumed there was room for doubt, and hoping that her answer left a margin into which could be inserted small notations of a personal nature, asides, further inquiries about her state of mind—who knew, even a touch here and there.

But Kid Crane was resigned to the inevitable. "Well, I was born in Manchester, RADA, Bristol Old Vic, Royal Court, you know, the usual early-sixties nonsense. Then after the David Lean picture, in '57, I went to Hollywood." Iris turned on her Sony; she felt the first click under her fingers, but the next sensation, that of the tape engaging, the slow regular hum, did not happen. "Wait a minute," she said, and took the machine out of her bag. Kid Crane started when he saw it. "You were recording me?" he asked.

"I always do," she said. "In case of lawsuits."

"I hope you never have a lawsuit against me," he said.

"Usually it's the other way around," she assured him as she opened the plastic lid and pushed on the stanchions. "It's broken," she said.

"Never mind," he said. "I'm much happier without it."

"But it slows you down if I take notes," she explained.

"Don't take notes. You can do it properly another day. It's all right." He took her hand and gave it a light squeeze; the hand was moist, small, trembling slightly. He found he could not let go of it. "Are you all right?" he asked, to cover the surprise he felt. "Fine," she said, feeling herself tremble a little more than usual.

He released her hand and began talking about his wife. "You've heard of her, of course," he said. "Arabella Grant."

"Oh, sure, the painter, isn't she?"

"Very talented. She has a studio in our house in Malibu, and she goes there every day to work, and nothing can disturb her, or nothing could until Alexandra. Alexandra disturbs everyone."

Iris was silent. He began talking about Malibu, and Arabella's paintings, the air and light of a place she could not remember. She watched his hand as he plucked the air between his fingers, stroked sentences away from his mouth, his fingers fanned out to define gradations of feeling, groping at the concept buried in an anecdote.

She wondered what those hands would feel like all over her.

"How long," she asked, "how long have you been married?"

"Four years," he said.

She had to resume the interview. "How old is Arabella?"

"Arabella is twenty-eight, and Alexandra is not yet a year old."

"How sweet," said Iris with an utter lack of feeling.

"It took me a long time to find her; three marriages and twenty years," he said with pride. The list of Arabella's exploits took them through their plates of boiled meats; Iris found that she could eat even less than usual. She kept glancing up at Kid Crane, and every time the pale-blue eyes looked at her she felt a physical presence on her body. She told herself that was why the man was a star, and reminded herself that she only liked blond men. Then, lest she get too big for her crushed boots, she told herself that movie stars did not go for journalists.

"You're not eating," he said, having come to the end of his paean to Arabella. "That must be why you're so thin." His hand reached out and touched the space at the opening of her shirt, where beneath the collarbone that jutted out like Audrey Hepburn's, her ribs made ridges under the white skin; his fingers touched her there, and then withdrew.

Her teeth began to chatter, silently at first, part of an exquisite wave of vibrations that radiated out from her sternum.

"I'm sorry," he said. "I didn't mean to do that."

She put her napkin up to her mouth, and lowered her eyes; he had to be aware of her state, or he wouldn't have said anything, she thought. She gave a loud sigh and addressed the fate of the world to tide them over the shock. "What do you think is going to happen with the Middle East?" she asked.

"The end of the world, they were saying in Rome last night."

"Oh?" she asked, jealous to hear that he had gone out without her and seen people in the know.

"It's just my feeling. Thank you for the dispatches, by the way. I really appreciate them."

"You think the Arabs will cut off the oil?" she asked.

"That's it! Hey, you're bright!"

Iris felt blessed. He rolled some nodules of bread between his fingers. "They'll cut that off, and the lights will go off all over Europe. No more heating, no more electricity, no more cars, no more industry—the Dark Ages!"

His gloom was so catching at close quarters that she felt herself about to cry. "What will we do?" she asked.

"Live in huts, hunt in packs, return to our primitive state, hunter-gatherers, nude men in the bush, feasting on giant rats . . ." He saw it all: the decline of the West accentuated a hundredfold, cities crumbling, decay creeping in from abandoned railroad sidings, a heavy fog like the one in *Soylent Green,* which he had much admired—particularly Edward G. Robinson's performance—weeds running wild through cracked concrete, water gushing through tarmac from rusted, rotten mains. "Anarchy, destruction, and plague," he said.

This time it was her turn to put out her hand; the pale-blue eyes had in them a visionary fear; he was no longer a movie star, nor even an actor, but a frightened child medium in a trance. She took his fingers in her hand and said, "Not that bad, come on!" in jocular New York tones. He focused on her and pushed his black hair off his forehead, where a lock had fallen forward.

"I'm sorry," he said. "I get carried away sometimes."

Over coffee they changed subjects again, back to her; but the trembling had not abated, and when his shoes accidentally brushed the instep of her boot, she froze her foot there, to await the next contact. "So this must be like being back in the bosom of your family," he said, "what with Mr. Hyott and Miss Abime and such."

"I suppose so," said Iris, "though it's not as if my family ever had much of a bosom." There was something she longed to explain to him, about time and distance and the faculty certain people had of forgetting who they were, but she found it hard to find a formulation for it that did not sound like sour jealousy, the bitterness of the unsuccessful. "We've all gone different ways," she said at last. He found her a good-looking girl, with her brave square jaw and her dark eyes, and the sort of bony frailty that he liked in women, the kind Arabella had had before Alexandra.

"I like being away from my family," he said, suddenly cheering up. "It's painful trying to be the same person all the time. It's limiting." She tried to decide whether she would write about Kid Crane's disaffection for married life. Did it mean he hated his wife? Would that make a story? Would Julian care? Did she care? That was something she didn't want to think about.

"And an actor, least of all," he was saying. "An actor, I think, is all the parts he plays and all the ones he wants to play, plus all the things he's ever wanted to be. That's hell on a relationship."

She gave him a knowing sign to encourage him.

"You have that problem? Do you live with an actor?"

"No, my boyfriend's an editor. He's brilliant."

He asked for the bill, and she kept her *Lookout* credit card in her purse. She would let him pay, like a date. This detail excited her.

Outside the restaurant he took her arm, to steer her across the small street that separated them from a church. Her arm was very thin, and through the fabric of her coat he could feel a small, fine tendon descending from her shoulder to her elbow that reminded him of the legs of certain puppies, miniature breeds, Pekingese, Chihuahuas.

They walked up the Via del Babuino without talking; she longed to take his hand but was afraid of seeming coy, and he was stopping to look in the windows of antique shops with a dutiful curiosity. Now and then a rush, as of cold air, ran through her at the idea that she was walking down a Roman street with Kid Crane. When the open space of the Piazza di Spagna was in sight, she stopped at a bar, to prolong their separation from the world that waited at the top of the steps in the Hassler. They drank their brandies at the zinc-rimmed counter, standing elbow to elbow, each conscious of a warm and deliberate pressure, a flow of something magnetic that anesthetized the rest of their bodies. Nothing had been transgressed yet; this was what was called flirtation, irresistible but harmless.

"I haven't talked to anyone for quite a while," he said; he felt her stiffen a little, wondered if he had said too much, and diffused his words into a general statement of his condition in Rome: "I always try to stay lonely, you know, when I'm working, it's the best thing for concentration, but after a while, especially *here,* I was beginning to feel cut off from any sort of real contact."

"You mean it would have been as nice talking to anyone else, or do you mean you like talking to me?" she challenged, overtaken by an unfamiliar boldness. She was silent a moment. "I suppose it's you," he said, and detached his arm from hers, to negate the words.

As they climbed the steps, slowly, stopping at each broad landing to forestall any unattractive breathlessness, they talked about books. "Boy, did I bring books!" he said. "Every nineteenth-century novel about passionate love I could find. Problem is, they're"—now his voice became British, an imitation of Noel Coward—"terribly, terribly dreary."

"I like books that just overwhelm you, and leave you feeling torn and wounded," she said. The blue eyes stopped on hers, inquisitive, amused, the eyebrows raised above them in interest. "Really?" he said. She felt herself blush. "No, really," he said, looking down at the steps that shone a little in the moonlight, "I'd love to have a book do all that to me." Or anything, he added, silently. She was unable to think of any titles at the moment to support her tastes, and climbed on silently.

They stood next to each other at the concierge's desk. "Eight-oh-seven," he said, as she said, "Five-two-three." The concierge unhooked their keys from the wall of cubicles, and handed them each a message. Iris kept hers closed. Kid Crane had taken both keys, and kept them in his hand. "Would you like a drink?" he asked. As he handed her a key the sleeve of his coat hovered over her wrist and then withdrew. She gripped her key; she waited.

He opened his message. "Aha!" he said, glancing from the note to her face. "I've got to make a phone call. Why don't you come up afterwards, we can continue our talk, in my room."

She followed him to the elevator. "Sure," she said. "Is it big? Mine's tiny." She blushed again: what the hell was she saying?

"Huge," he said casually, "the biggest in Rome." Then he stared at his key, examining its heavy graven tag. "What a silly mistake," he said, "we've got each other's keys." He handed her his, and gracefully grabbed his own. She got off on the fifth floor. "Ten minutes," he said.

In her room Iris sat down on the edge of the bed, legs together, hands on her knees, keeping herself very tight and still. Either, she told herself, he is seducing me because he is a seducer, that's all the roles he's played, and that's how he proceeds—I shouldn't take it personally, it's not necessarily directed at me, it's just his way of being, he's lonely and bored, it's not anything I should take personally, I could be any girl—or else he wants good press.

She caught herself in the mirror; as ever, her face disappointed her, too needy those brown eyes, and the mouth too wide, too shapeless and overdefined at the same time. Look at you, she thought, wake up. Onto the mirror shimmered a more graceful set of features, the delicate eyebrows and strong short nose of Paula, the small mouth that even to Iris had always had something of the flower about it, the look of calm grace that she had always wanted. She took a deep breath, but it only agitated her further; the inside muscles of her thighs were throbbing, and deep in her pelvis an aching fist opened and closed. She crossed her legs and opened her message. *"Signor Sorrel da New York,"* she read. She heard herself describing him to Kid Crane as her boyfriend, and heard herself saying, "My boyfriend called," and didn't like the word anymore. Nothing in her had ever throbbed for Julian. Or for anyone. Making an effort to control her gestures, she rose from the bed and took off her boots. As she was brushing her teeth the phone sounded its glottal buzz. Against her will, she answered with a voluptuous "Hello."

"I'm waiting for you," said Kid Crane. "My call's over."

She was out of her room and up the emergency stairs before she had time to think. Outside his door she stood in her stocking feet with her hand on her chest, trying to slow her breathing, waiting to calm down. He opened the door before she knocked.

From his windows there could be seen an infinity of domes, of rooftops, of rousing bronze statues and, in the distance, the dull white of the Victor Emmanuel Monument. The curtains were pulled back; a Mozart piano concerto coming from a portable tape deck filled the room with music; a bowl of fruit on the coffee table looked like a still life. Everywhere were candles: in tall holders in front of the mirror above the fireplace, on either side of the sofa in double-branched candelabras, in portable candlesticks on every little table. "It's beautiful," she said. She looked for the bedroom door, and saw it was half open, and dark beyond.

"I never have any electric lights in here," he said, and added, lest she think it was done specially for her as part of a seduction scene, "It's all for character. Things feel different by candlelight."

"Raoul used to do that," she said. "When I was a child, we always had candles."

"I don't want to hear about Raoul," he said. "What would you like to drink?"

"Anything," she said. He went to his refrigerator, which she was pleased to observe was the same make and size as the one in her room, and she looked at the books on the table. *Madame Bovary, Anna Karenina, Nana:* all women's stories, she thought.

"It's a different world here," he said, handing her a glass. He was looking down on her in the flickering gloom; he had taken off his tie, and two of his shirt buttons were undone. She longed to reach up and touch him, but she convinced herself that it would be the wrong thing to do. She felt at home there, more at home than she had felt anywhere for years; the long room was familiar, with its thick silk drapes rustling slightly by the open window, as were the lines of the indistinct furniture, the little ovals of light growing out of each table, the waves of darkness that seemed to come and go like clouds around them. "I feel good here," she said.

"So do I." They sat there, saying nothing, feeling trust in the shifting shadows. Iris relaxed in the obscurity, which gave her the sensation of being inconspicuous, almost invisible. Soon she felt she should make conversation. "How was your phone call?" she asked.

"Telephones," he said. "I hate them."

He's had a fight with her, she thought with joy. Angry for allowing herself this lapse, she stood up. "You have to get up early, I really mustn't keep you," she said with formality.

"That's very considerate," he said. "I'll see you out."

They parted at the door without a kiss or even another tentative skimming touch. "See you at the studio," he called down the hall to her.

When she went to bed, Iris found she was imagining his body on hers, next to hers, alongside hers. She knew it wasn't love.

25.

Keeper of All Secrets

What had to happen happened the next day at four o'clock in the afternoon. Iris had gone to the studio and waited patiently on a chair, guarded by Grace Gregory; Laredo had spoken a few kind words to her, and Paula had thrown herself in her arms, sobbing that Iris had not even tried to get in touch with her. Iris was so far beyond thinking of Paula anymore that she responded just coolly enough to elicit an invitation to come and stay at the house on the Appia, starting the following weekend. She barely listened; she had her eyes on Kid Crane, who could be seen crossing and recrossing the back of the set, dressed in a cape but without makeup, muttering to himself. "He's being sent home early today," explained Grace, who followed Iris's anxious gaze. "It's all on Paula this afternoon, to catch up on lost time."

Iris contrived to return to the hotel as early as he did. She left a note for him, which she had spent the ride home roughing out, in varying degrees of irresistibility. She'd tried "I'm free this afternoon, too, let's have tea." Then there was "Why don't you call me if you're free this afternoon?" followed by "Doing nothing this afternoon, hear you're not either, let's talk some more," which led to "Loved meeting you last night, let's see each other again, am in my room," which became "I'm free, are you?" which she dismissed in favor of "Call me, I'm in this afternoon." This was what she wrote on the Hassler's crested paper before returning upstairs. She should have called Vivien Legrand, she should have stayed to talk to Frank Laredo, she should have been watching Paula to determine what sort of actress she was, but all she could think of was sex. She took a bath, shaved her legs, shaved her armpits, powdered herself all over, ran a stream of Jicky down her back straight from the wide neck of the perfume bottle, rubbed it in beneath her breasts, and spent fifteen minutes outlining her eyes. Then she dressed herself again and lay back on her bed and waited. When the phone buzzed, she let it ring, imagining what she would say. What she said was "Oh, you got my note! How nice!" He offered to take her for yet another walk; "I'll pick you up in your room, or are you busy?"

"No, I'll just get ready," she said.

True to the fiction of a walk, he was wearing an overcoat when she opened the door; she felt a strange license from him to do whatever she wished, and crossed her legs and leaned on the door and said, "You won't need that here, let me take it off." She reached up for the shoulders of the coat as he turned around, but he kept turning and was facing her, very close. She clasped her arms around him and stretched her neck so that her mouth could reach his. They kissed against the door, and she found she was pushing herself into his body. He closed the door behind him, and locked it. She pulled him toward the bed; the little fist in her belly was awake again, opening and closing, stirring for life. She pulled his tie off. His mouth was half open; she kissed it again, and their mouths continued the messages from the night before. "I've been thinking of you all day," he said. She didn't answer. The night and half a day apart had provided the right gestation period for lust, and what had been set off the previous evening by accidental and then deliberate proximity had grown into a shared compulsion.

She took off her shirt, then her silk camisole. She went to the window and pulled the curtains shut, not entirely, just enough; she felt him watching the movement of her breasts as she moved, and liked that he was looking at them. She pulled off her skirt standing in front of him, and put out a hand to touch his chest, and lowered her head to be kissed again. His skin felt oddly intangible to her; his body was the same temperature as hers, and instead of the expected shock of unfamiliar epidermis, she met the reverberation of a warmth exactly like her own. With, for once, no fluttering uncertainty or fear of censure, she pulled down the zipper of his trousers and knelt to feel inside his briefs; hardly had she clutched at his cock, and found it smooth and stout, than he was standing and pulling off the rest of his clothes, his mouth on the top of her head. He pulled her onto the bed; she saw dark forearms, thick with hair, well shaped, the arc of a raised knee, a corner of smooth shoulder; she felt the strong flat chest to which she pressed her breasts, the long torso, the strength in his thighs pushing her legs apart, but her legs were already apart, opened in a sudden and ecstatic movement, to receive the simple, delicious, straight, long, bold, relentless and serious cock that was slowly rising into her.

The path it made widened, parted slowly to accommodate it. She felt him in her as flesh, muscle, blood, heat. No embellishment was necessary for either of them to show that they were receiving pleasure: no crying out, no pressing, pinching, pummeling or heaving. All was intent, deliberate, animated by the rhythm of pumping blood, lit by the electricity of nerves. She felt the shape of his body beneath her hand, but not his skin: their textures had melted together, blended by a common sweat. She was oblivious for once to the social distractions of such moments, the hair that needs to be removed from the mouth, the elbow that must be resituated for comfort. The little words of encouragement or dissuasion that attend such first encounters were left unsaid: both heard only the orders of their common body. For the first time, Iris was not Iris, nor even the pastiche of someone else, but wholly a body, and no more. Freed of all baggage and all assumptions, she swam and soared through him as he swam and dug through her. Kid Crane was, unusually for him, himself. The reality he best understood, that of his body in action, was confirmed by hers. They flailed and inched and trembled, and when they came, they howled.

Their selves returned to them gradually, scraps and tatters falling back on to them from the walls and corners of the room to which they had been dispersed.

"I feel great," said the American part of Kid Crane.

"Oh God, yes," said Iris, being Paula.

"You really love it," said the roué in Kid Crane with a disturbing glance of his blue eyes.

"You're just wonderful," said Iris, the fan.

They scattered the constraint with another embrace that began with touchings and fingerings and ended, much like the first, ecstatic. This time it was Iris who broke the spell. "I feel very happy," she said, trying to stay neutral; the implication of her words alerted him to the protocol of random fucking, and, consulting his watch, he told her it was eight o'clock and she should run a bath.

The problems came to her in the bath, after the first surge of heat. Was this an affair, or what? She glanced at herself in the mirror. Perhaps Paula was the one who should be having an affair with him. She wondered if it was her place to act as if she were having an affair, and concluded that she had a responsibility to protect his position, and discretion would be the best course. As the bath water ran out, she wrapped a towel around her, and saw that she had a red mark from his teeth on her shoulder. She opened the door and looked in the bedroom. He was gone. A note on the bed, printed in capitals like a ransom note, said "Call me."

Kid Crane had listened to the splashing in the bath while he smoked a cigarette, feeling good. His hands had sought the still-damp patches on the bed, and followed their outlines, trying to divine what moments had left them there. The tension that had been bothering him for a few days was gone, replaced by a satisfied calm. He was happy she had wanted him as much as he had wanted her; it had obviated the need for any more silly exchanges, and put the whole thing on a nice, straightforward level. He liked people who were direct, as he so rarely could be. And he congratulated himself on having seen this thing in her from the first glance, this reckless animal that had gone for him, he remembered happily, like a ferret. He ran his hand over his chest, then down to his stomach, to check how his weight was doing with all this pasta; satisfied, he scratched his pubic hair, and laid his hand in a paternal clasp on his cock. As he did so, the face of Arabella came to him, and he quickly lit another cigarette. There was nothing to be guilty about; God only knew what she was doing in London with all her old art-school friends, and what happened on trips didn't count, she knew that. An actor, anyway, had to be free to experience whatever he needed to feed his imagination, fill his sense memory with a store of delight. After all, he was an artist. For Arabella it was different, a painter was a visual animal, but then wasn't a painter an artist too? Sure, but landscapes were the things that turned her on, light and shadow, not sex. No painter needed sex for inspiration. Unwilling but dutiful, his mind wandered to Picasso. Yes, but Picasso was a man. Women painters weren't the same. Having calmed himself with coffee-table-book rationalization, he found he was sitting up on the bed, and feeling dizzy. An actor needs to live out everything he feels, he told himself. I wanted the girl, I've had her, it was lovely, a nice way to spend an afternoon. Then he caught sight of the cassettes lined up on the dressing table, and it came back to him that she was a journalist. The fear that she would write about him made him jump to his feet; he looked at himself in the mirror of the closet, no longer cocky, but unsure.

He saw it all. She would write about this and he would be disgraced, shown up. He had started out fine, but then he had slipped into being personal. His greatest fault, he knew, was being personal, too open to the auras and expectations of others. He had a sudden insight that Arabella was coming to Rome; she might have landed already. Their conversation the previous night had been unsatisfying, and she usually came running when he was vague with her. She could smell another woman a thousand miles away. He saw her arriving downstairs, talking to the concierge, finding his key was gone, getting a bellboy to take her up to the room; opening the door, looking around, wondering where he was. He pulled his trousers off the floor, wishing he could take a bath here, but she was still in the bathroom, and he did not want her—this her, Iris—to know what was going through his head, she knew too much already. As he pulled on his shirt the thought struck him that perhaps she was even a spy, able to get those telex printouts with such ease, pretending not to speak the language but fearless about going out into the night to find a press club she claimed she'd never been to.

He told himself he was ridiculous, this was going too far. Still, the little spy movie, a low-budget affair with hand-held cameras and extras taken from the street, unfolded in his mind: he was some sort of ambassador, and she was a spy, and he thought he could pull the wool over her eyes about, say, America's involvement in Italy, whatever that might be, and his chauffeur would be his sort of aide-de-camp as well, and she would fall in love with him and confess her role, unless in the new way of women she put her work before her heart and steeled herself to turn him in. But to whom? As he thrashed out this problem he saw himself riding around in a big official limousine, not minding the starving crowds jeering at him because his real mission was to save them all from some unnamed disaster, and that was what the girl didn't know. Unexpectedly, as he finished tying his shoelaces, the girl turned into Hedda Hopper, and at the same time the imaginary Arabella drummed her fingers on the marquetry top of the table by the window in the living room of his suite. He took a pen from the desk, and on the little pad by the phone he wrote, "Must run: urgent." Then, still the ambassador, he tore it off the pad, realizing that his spidery but still-correct copperplate writing was unique in Rome, and could identify him unfailingly; this time he printed his message. Then, quietly, he opened the door, and shut it without noise. It was better if she called him: if Arabella was upstairs, he wouldn't be able to call.

He was relieved to find she wasn't there, and to confirm that she was still in London he put in a call to her. Then he took a long bath, although, once the danger of his wife's presence had disappeared, he found the smell of lavender and cunt that hovered about him extremely pleasant. Arabella, it turned out, had gone to the country for a few days, to Wales, the maid said. He asked to speak to Alexandra, who burbled at him, and he hung up, reassured. He buzzed Iris's room, but there was no answer. Foolish girl, he thought, we could have had dinner. He didn't want to get dressed again, but ordered dinner in his room; just as he was finishing his cheese a piece of paper was slipped under the door. He saw before he picked it up that it was a telex printout, and a fondness for Iris mingled with the return of the scenario about the ambassador and the spy. When he read it, he saw that it was not about the conferences following the end of the Yom Kippur war, but about beef prices in Austria. He laughed at the joke, and then wondered what she meant by it: did she think of him as meat? He took to bed the last resonant smells of her body and the determination to ask her what she thought beef prices in Austria had to do with him.

Iris was not on the set the next day; Kid Crane found himself doing strange things, wandering down corridors toward Grace Gregory's office, turning back before he reached her door, stopping in at the commissary at lunchtime, although he normally never left his dressing room. He wanted to see Iris, to touch her in subtle places while others looked on, to ask her what she meant by the last Telex; and he dreaded seeing her as well, dreaded having her come upon him at a moment when he was unprepared, concentrating on his part, listening to Laredo, or standing on his mark while the lighting cameraman measured the distance to the tip of his nose. In the wanting to see her there was no guilt, nothing but a simple and direct urge to take a look at what he had wrought and offer himself for confirmation; in the wanting to see her before she saw him there was an element of self-protection. In the middle of a scene with Sebastiana Grampelli, who played his wife and was confronting him with evidence of his liaison with Paulina, he imagined Iris typing out a story about him; he quickly put the dread to rest with the reminder that she had enjoyed it, if anything, more than he had, and that this would keep her quiet.

Iris was out at Vivien Legrand's house: Paula had called at midnight, after Iris's short visit to the Press Club, and had invited her to spend the day.

The road to the house from Rome was different from the one she had taken from the studio: it was the real Appia Antica, with tombs along its sides like sentry boxes, and the worn uneven paving that the Romans had set down. The day was gray, and a sad wind blew through the little trees that clustered at intervals along the road; after admiring the tombs, Iris began to find them somewhat depressing, unfitting markers for a residential street.

The gardener pulled the gates open with a smile this time, and the taxi took the curved drive right up to a graveled terrace. As she paid, Paula came out, wearing a long caftan, her hair hanging down, a cup of coffee in her hand. She looked pale and soft around the mouth, unhealthy. "I just got up," she explained, drawing Iris inside. A small, fat woman with an apron brought a tray of fruit and cheese to them in the living room. Iris recognized the turquoise couches and was glad they had stayed long enough for her to see them. "Is Vivien here?" she asked.

"She'll be down later. She's being massaged," said Paula, picking a fresh litchi from the bowl. She began to peel it, and then put it down. "Oh Iris, it's so awful, I don't know what I'm going to do!" she said.

"What is it? Laredo? Is it the film?"

Paula shook her head. "It's better. It's worse. I'm so glad you're here."

"Is Raoul all right?" asked Iris quickly.

"He's fine, he's still in Los Angeles, and Szos has arranged some kind of retrospective for him, in Indiana, I think. Iris, are you my friend?"

"What do you mean, am I your friend? I'm your sister!" said Iris, flattered to see Paula so vulnerable, delighted at the question, and unable to give a mere yes. "I'm the closest person to you in the world," she added. "I mean, we don't see each other much, but I think of you as another me, you know that," she said, taking Paula's hand. She was prepared to back her statement of allegiance with still more testimony, but Paula stopped her: "I'm pregnant. I don't think I'll be able to finish the film."

"Who?" asked Iris.

"Hugo. Oh, Iris, isn't it wonderful?"

"Don't you use anything?" asked Iris irritably. She had never been pregnant.

Paula shook her head. "What you said about me wanting babies—well, it's true, the film sort of happened when I'd already made up my mind. So when Hugo came to be with me in Los Angeles—well, it happened."

"Is he going to marry you?" asked Iris.

"Of course he's going to marry me," said Paula a little sharply. "It's not like I just fell into bed with him for the first time, you know."

I won't tell her about Kid Crane, thought Iris, she wouldn't understand. "What's the problem, then? It's everything you wanted."

"I'm vomiting every morning, and look at me, I look like hell, and I've got nude scenes coming up in a couple of weeks, and well, look!" She pulled up the caftan to her chest, to reveal, bulging neatly over a pair of black silk bikini panties, a perfectly spherical stomach. "And look," she said, tracing a line from her navel downwards, "it's even growing hair! I can't be seen like this!"

"Well, at least your tits will look good," said Iris, a little tactless.

"No! The nipples are getting big and horrible, really ugly. It's just not possible, that's all."

"Have you told Laredo?" asked Iris.

"How can I?" said Paula, beginning to cry now in earnest. "He'll take me for a complete idiot. Or he'll take me to get an abortion."

"Well, you could have an abortion, and then get pregnant again later," advised Iris with practical cool. "I don't think it hurts anymore. Don't people go to London for that all the time?"

"No, here they go to Switzerland. And I'm not having an abortion."

A pair of Labradors trotted through the door and came to lick Paula's hands. "Look at them," she said, "aren't they sweet?"

"Paula," said Iris, "does Vivien think you should have an abortion?"

"Vivien thinks it's more important to be a woman than to be an actress," said Paula. "But it's easy for her."

"She's a star," said Iris.

"And she's never been able to have children. Iris, I'm going to have this baby."

"Well," said Iris, "since it screws up the film a little, you should tell Saul."

"He's left," said Paula. "Anyway, he's a shit."

Iris looked Paula in the eye. "What do you mean, a shit?"

"He's tried to stop Papa from working in Los Angeles. His studio won't use Papa, and the other studios won't either. He's a shit, and I haven't said one word to him since the day I got the part."

"But it's your big chance!" said Iris impatiently. "Don't you understand, Paula, this is your first big part in a real American film, you could become a star! And now you want to throw it all away, for nothing! Wake up! You're incredibly lucky, you've always had everything you wanted. Now you've got a chance that any actress would kill for, and you're getting sentimental."

"But Iris, you said it yourself, that's not what's important."

Iris had run out of Julian's philosophy—he had never given her any tips about the dilemma of Career vs. Motherhood, and she had never given the problem much thought on her own. "The actors," she continued a little lamely, "the crew, you've got a professional responsibility toward them, haven't you thought of that?"

"Iris, you haven't got a heart!" screamed Paula with fine drama.

"That's not true!" said Iris. "I do too!"

"You've never been in love!" Paula shouted back.

"Yes I have!" screamed Iris. "I am! Right now!"

"Well, then," said Paula, triumphant at having won her point, and neglecting to pump Iris on the details, "you should understand! There are times when you have to choose between what's important and what's not. That's what a crisis is. That's what Vivien says, and—" Rising from the couch and clutching her stomach, which, without the gesture, would have remained invisible beneath the billowing orange silk, she made her way toward the fireplace, where she gripped the high stone mantel and leaned from it like a trailing vine. "—now is a crisis and I *am* doing the right thing."

Iris opened and closed her hands, brought them together, went to her bag for a cigarette, and lit it. "I don't know what I can do," she said. "I mean, I'd like to help, but I don't see how I can."

"You think work's the most important thing in the world, don't you?" hissed Paula. "That's what Szos says, you're possessed by work. You're afraid to live, that's why you're so crazy about work. It's not the same thing with me."

Iris enjoyed being described as possessed, and took it as a compliment, which softened her slightly. "You must see Hugo, I think that's the thing," she said.

Paula sobbed onto her own shoulder. "I haven't told him, either," Iris heard her say.

"You're a lunatic," cried Iris, coming up to her. "The baby is the most important thing, and you haven't told him?"

"Last summer I told him I didn't want to get married. And he didn't mention it again in Los Angeles, so I figured I'd wait until I saw him. So when I didn't get my period I tried to get him to come down to Rome so I could tell him, because I couldn't tell him over the phone, it wouldn't be romantic enough, and he still hasn't come."

Iris felt as if Paula had thrown all the pieces of a puzzle onto the floor and was asking her to straighten out the pattern. Horror at Paula's lack of professional integrity, nay, professional gratitude, was replaced by a feeling of impotence. She had never met Hugo. She could think of ways to save the film, to save Paula's career, but saving a relationship was a problem she had never dealt with. As she tried to remember some of the truisms about love that she had run across, and cast her mind back to Frances Lyle, where the subject was discussed more than in the offices of either *Style* (where everyone you fucked was called a "trick") or *Lookout* (where the marriages of the articles' subjects were made to be broken, and sexual contact between colleagues amounted only to an occasional rubbing together of groins between assignments), Iris realized she was unprepared for the role of confidante that Paula had so blindly assigned her.

"Alors, mes chéries, ça va?" Vivien Legrand swept into the room, wearing an afternoon housedress of printed silk, high-heeled shoes, and carrying a basket. *"Enchantée,"* she said to Iris, who went to shake her hand.

They ate lunch in a dining room filled with eucalyptus blossoms, whose slightly medicinal smell gave the coddled eggs on their plates a curious aftertaste. Vivien was being charming; she asked Iris about her work, her impressions of Rome, her impression of Laredo, what she thought of Kid Crane: "I think he is a major star," she told Iris. "He has a magnetism I cannot believe."

"Oh yes," said Iris. "He's really wonderful. I like him a lot."

"And his wife, you should see her!" said Vivien. "A beauty! Never an ounce of makeup, natural, a real woman!" Real women seemed to be a little too highly regarded these days, and Iris hated them all.

Vivien gave Iris some flowers from the garden when she left and sent her back to Rome with the chauffeur; Paula waved her off, sending her bereft looks and making dialing motions. "You must interview me whenever you want," said Vivien.

The concierge pushed a message across the counter to her: "Mr. Crane called from the studio," it said. She wanted to call him back at once, but, influenced by Vivien, decided she would be a woman, and wait. She lay down on her bed and fell asleep and dreamed of a man in an overcoat bending over her, straddling her, making her come with no more than a warm breath. The phone woke her; it was Kid, back in his room. "Come down," she said at once.

"Come up here," he said. "It's more comfortable."

She took her bottle of perfume, threw it in her bag, and ran up the emergency stairs. Paula's problem receded from her as she ran, and by the time she stood outside his door she was just flesh longing to be touched, simple flesh. They came together curiously, to see if the feeling was the same, and then made love, merging with deliberate and painful gentleness. "I called you," he said when they had been together four hours, five. "I know," she said, "but I knew you'd be back." Assailed by a fear of sounding too assured, she added, "After all, you live here, too."

"Where were you?" he asked.

"With Paula. On the Appia."

"Oh," he said indolently, his hand on her leg. "How is she?" Iris sat up. "Fine," she said, a little doubtful. She knew she owed it to him as her lover to tell him everything; but doubt whether he was her lover or just a movie star amusing himself in the usual way, rather the way Raoul used to with all those beehived women, stopped her, and she forgot Paula in her concern. She had ample evidence that she wanted him physically, and that he wanted her as well. But the situation was unclear, and it worried her. She wanted to be able to ask him, but apprehended that a simple question such as "What am I to you?" might slice the evening like a knife. Still, she could not resist a hint.

"Vivien Legrand was talking about your wife," she said. "I hear she's beautiful."

"I told you that," said Kid Crane. "She is."

To ease the discomfort, Iris went to the bathroom and splashed her face. When she returned, he was sitting up on the bed. "What do you want from life?" he asked.

"Oh, me?" she said. "Nothing."

"Do you want babies, a husband, a house in the country, what?"

"None of that! I hate babies. I don't like the country. And I don't want to get married." She thought that would please him, and it did. Good, he thought, that's one problem dealt with. He pressed on: "But what do you want?"

"Just to work," she said.

"Work?" He hoped she wasn't going to say "act," as they often did.

"Write my articles, you know, travel, like this, but more."

"You'd never write about us, I trust," he said.

"Oh, of course not," she hastened to assure him. "Never! This is private, it's our secret, isn't it?"

"Yes," he said, "it's our secret." He gave her a kiss out of relief. But she had to add to it: "No one must ever know, I think, don't you?"

"You're right, that's the way it should be, a secret," he replied.

"Good," she said. "That's the best way."

"We must tread lightly," he said. "Very lightly."

She thought she understood; she wanted to understand, to have something else between them besides the sex, which she knew to be, in its force, impersonal: to have a credo in common, a shared belief in something, was better than to be no more than silent crashing molecules, and if that credo was no more than the solemn agreement to keep what was between them a secret, then it at least defined them as a secret, with all the rules and definitions that go with secrets: it gave them an existence, an identity, and it was definitely better than nothing.

In the next days she became almost as proud of the secret as of the ease and joy that was between her and Kid Crane when they were alone. She went on the set, where she would sit with Paula and hold her hands, reassuring her that everything was going to be fine, that she was keeping Paula's secret. "I'm good at secrets," she told her one day, thrilled at the irony. She interviewed Laredo and transcribed the tape, intending to send Julian a story on "Wild West's Wonder Boy Tackles Unholy Passion in Eternal City," but she never wrote it, for by the time Kid Crane had returned to the hotel and put in his evening call to Arabella, it was time for her to go up to his suite and forget about everything but him.

For Kid Crane the arrangement worked beautifully; he no longer worried too much about the fate of the world, being more concerned with keeping Arabella amused on the phone so that she would not conceive of coming to Rome; he no longer had to eat out, he could stay in his candlelit room, which he had made his entire universe, and enjoy the very delights of love that he had to simulate on the set with Paula.

They crept into each other's rooms, guided by desire and restrained by a deliberate and exquisitely painful caution that added to their pleasure; sensing the drama of their lust, they crept up and down the backstairs, dreading yet hoping for ambush on the landings, seeing sex in the pattern of the corridor carpets, excited to the point that for each of them the cold metal doorknob of the other's door was a physical harbinger of the excesses to come. Whatever he wanted her to do she did, led by him as if on a leash into his own melting mirror. She longed for him to rise above her, pitiless, selfish, inexorable and yet pathetic; he did. He longed for her to curl around him, above him, under him, to grip him, to suck the essence out of him and into her and to conquer and exterminate him from within and grant to him that he became her; she did.

Where Iris, in the dark, was abandoned and fearless, Paula, beneath the arc lights, was tight, awkward and removed, even in so simple a thing as a three-quarter-profile kiss. From time to time he would express to Iris his amazement that two women brought up together—he called her a woman, which she loved—could be so different, which accentuated the deep internal pride Iris felt with him, and raised the fact of her sleeping with him to a universal triumph, not only over her physical misgivings of the past, but also over Paula, over the image and memory and obsession of Paula as a superior being, now revealed by the mouth of her lover to be no more than a spotlit sham.

The tension on the set was remarkable; Paula brooded over her secret but still told no one; Hugo was coming any day, and she would not let it out until she was sure that he would marry her. The wardrobe girl and the costume designer had noticed something, and the makeup man saw telltale patches on her forehead, and added some more Erase each day under her eyes, but, good Catholics all, and people of a sunny morality, they said nothing. Laredo suddenly found her sweet, where before she had only been maudlin, and he spoke to her with greater kindness, exercising his wrath instead on Kid Crane, who approached his love scenes with such confidence that he was blowing them all. Grace Gregory took Iris around by the arm, muttering that something fishy was going on, and Iris placated her with an interview on "The Life and Times of a Roman PR." She had no intention of even transcribing the tape, but she knew how powerful a drug it was for people to talk about themselves, and she allowed the woman two and a half hours of monologue into the second of her machines. Embarrassed at having revealed her weakness for her own life story, Grace asked if Iris had enough of everyone. "After all," she said, "you've been here two weeks, haven't you gotten all the stories you need?"

"I still have to do Vivien Legrand."

"But you've gotten everyone in the movie, haven't you? How was your interview with Kid Crane, by the way? I never asked."

Kid Crane was standing next to them watching Paula totter through a ballroom scene; he looked over at Iris and made a motion with his thumbs down, which she first read as a comment on Paula's dancing, and then understood to be a cue. "Terrible," she answered. "I'll have to do it again."

"Oh dear, I don't know if he'll want to be interviewed all over," moaned Grace Gregory. "He keeps pretty much to himself these days, and hates going out."

Iris looked past her and saw Kid Crane repress a smile. "See if you can persuade him," she urged the PR. "If you can't do it, nobody can."

"I'll talk to him alone, later," promised Grace. "I'll leave a message at your hotel. I've tried calling you in the evenings, but you're never in your room."

"I have friends in Rome," said Iris, loud, so that Kid Crane would know she was not betraying him. "I go out a lot." For this she received an inclination of his head; he then turned away quickly, scanning the set.

Grace Gregory approached Kid Crane in his dressing room, and began with: "I know you despise all journalists."

"I don't despise anyone!" he said. "Wait a minute."

"Yes, you do! That poor, poor girl, all alone here, and she represents a very important magazine."

"I'll speak to her, I promise," he said.

"I know you need your isolation there in the penthouse, and all those candles and things, but just one dinner isn't asking too much, is it?"

"Wait a minute," he said sharply. "Who told you about the candles?"

"Everyone knows about the candles," said Grace Gregory. "It's been in the paper."

"What do you mean? That's private! Who told the press?"

"The room-service waiter at the hotel told me, and I put it out. It's a nice touch: Kid Crane, twentieth-century actor, gets into his nineteenth-century breeches by candlelight."

Bloody hell, thought Kid Crane from Manchester, the room waiter.

The formalities of a second interview were set for the following Sunday. The government had just passed an edict barring all use of gasoline on Sundays, and although the production manager was trying to import foreign license plates to put on the company's cars so that they could circulate with the dispensation accorded to tourists, these had not yet arrived. Iris, dressed in a semblance of casual clothes, cashmere trousers and a checked jacket, met Kid Crane in the lobby and shook his hand with great deliberation. He too was dressed for an afternoon in the country, a tweed jacket and galoshes. They left the hotel making loud small talk, of the variety of "How have you been?" and "Are you enjoying Rome?" The staff watched them, amused at the comedy they were playing: no one employed in the hotel had remained unaware of the nocturnal whereabouts of the Signorina Bromley.

They walked down toward the Piazza Venezia, and turned left toward the Forum. "It's nice, this walk," he said.

"Just being alone with you in the fresh air is enough," she said. They passed groups of people, Romans divested of their cars, trudging across the streets, dragging children and grandmothers behind them.

"I suppose they're all trying to get to restaurants," said Iris. "Usually they go by car."

He held up his finger to his ear. "Listen," he said, "it's incredible, the quiet. I'll bet it hasn't been this quiet for two thousand years."

Gradually even the sound of shoes and canes was behind them; they walked along the edge of the Forum. "Let's go in," he said. "I've never been there."

They turned back and found the entrance. Iris went up to pay, but Kid Crane took out his wallet. Apart from the first dinner, it was the only thing he had ever bought her, and she took the little piece of paper that he handed her and held it with tenderness. "It's chillier here," he said, turning up the collar of his jacket. She took a cashmere scarf out of her bag; it was wrapped around the Sony to protect it, but she undid it and handed it to him. "This'll keep you warm," she said. To her delight, he put it around his neck.

She let him walk a little ahead of her on the Via Sacra, and watched the movement of his long legs as he climbed the hill. She thought of the feeling of those legs, of the perfect volume of the ass above them, of his weight, his smell, his skin on hers. I love him, she thought, I want to be his. She ran a little to catch up with him. "It's rum, isn't it?" he said, pointing to the ruined buildings on the left. "They've still got their great bronze doors but inside it's all pigeon shit."

"You haven't been inside," she said. "How do you know?"

"They had cows grazing here in the eighteenth century," he said. "I've seen drawings. They didn't realize what history they had under their pasture. Used the stones to build houses with, ignorant peasants!"

His knowledge and compassion astonished her; she had heard him talk about Shakespeare, just a little, and had seen his books, but his opinions on the topography of Rome had so far remained hidden.

"Have you ever played Julius Caesar?" she asked.

"Never," he said. "But Brutus, twice." He stopped in front of the Arch of Titus, and looked up. "See the eight-branched candlestick? That's when they looted the Temple at Jerusalem," he said. "And furthermore, no Jew must walk beneath the arch. It would transgress something or other."

"Where did you learn all this?" she asked.

"Hah!" he said. "And you thought I was just another pretty face. You don't get to be forty, my girl, without learning a thing or two. Let's go to the top."

He had never told her his age before, and she took this revelation as a gift, the second that day. They climbed the Palatine; for a while there was nothing to see but vegetation, modern weeds, the modern feet of a modern family in front of them. Then the path flattened, and a little sign hung on a rope across two stones said VIETATO L'INGRESSO.

"Let's go in there," he said.

"Is it allowed?" she asked.

"What are you, a tourist?" he asked, throwing a leg over the rope. She followed, thinking that she would follow him everywhere.

"Temples! Gods! Pan! The worship of Priapus!" he shouted, pointing out a harmless tree, some steps and a puddle of water. The puddle had possibilities: it was formed by the overflow from a little fountain, where water poured into a trough through the grimacing mouth of a round medallion face. He plunged his head into the stone basin and pulled it out, intoning, "I've just been purified, there's not a sin in the world can stick to me anymore, go on, shove your whole body in there, you temptress, be baptized by the gods of rut and anointed into eternal orgasm." His voice had become British, theatrical, resonant.

A poet, she thought, he's a poet. She put her fingers in; the water was cold. He pulled her away from the fountain and groped at the waistband of her trousers. "Here, under the tree," he said.

"Someone will see us," she whispered.

"No one comes here, it's a sacred grove dedicated to Pan, and only adulterers are allowed. Come on." He pulled her under a short mulberry tree. "That's a sacred tree," he said, "it likes people to fuck under it, it makes berries out of spilt come, it makes flowers out of spilt seeds, it needs lovers under it. Can't you see it's begging us?" He rolled over onto her. Lovers, she thought, he said "lovers." They labored to please the tree. She reached for his face, just before he came. "Say my name," she said; his eyes registered surprise. "You've never said my name," she whispered. "Never."

He said something, a word which ended with an *a*. "What?" she hissed, pinching his shoulder through the jacket. "What?"

"Aaaaah!" he said. "Aw!"

She felt the rough rocks under her, and the dried winter grass, and the sharp spikes of burrs and dry flowers. She put her hand over her face. "Come on," he said, standing up, manic with energy as he did up his pants. "Pan's happy now, and the tree's delighted, it's time to go visiting." He dragged her back toward the official path and led her up to a plateau, where a tall Oriental pine wafted its green branches over flattened stone walls.

He felt wonderful. It was hard to be in Rome and not feel the demands of gods seeping into one's marrow. He was open to it all, a willing sacrifice. He had given the grove a tribute, now he could ask for something back.

"You didn't say my name," complained Iris.

"Look," he said, ignoring her. "Those must be foundations of basements, aren't they odd?" He was pointing at regular square holes in the ground.

"You didn't say my name," she repeated. He took her by the shoulders and fixed her in the eye. "Iris Iris Iris Iris Iris Iris Iris Bromley, journalist, okay?"

"Is that all I am?" she asked.

"No," he said. "It's not." He walked on. She ran after him. "Look," he said, delighted, pointing to a signpost. "That's the house of the Empress Livia."

"Livia," repeated Iris. "The wife of Augustus."

"I've got an uncle Augustus. Let's go and see if she's in and have tea with her. My uncle Augustus was always most fond of her, and I should see how the old girl's doing." Iris followed him. Livia's house was the only preserved building on the hill; it had walls, a few leaded windows, a pot here and there, to indicate the scale and shape of everyday objects. There was a wide atrium, barred by an iron gate. He pushed it open. "Good afternoon, Livia," he said, making Iris giggle.

He bent down, completely serious, and addressed a space by the window in the center of the biggest room. "I've come to bring you a young woman I'm very fond of. Iris, this is my aunt Livia. Livia, Miss Iris Bromley, who thinks I don't remember her name." He motioned Iris to sit down, and she crossed her legs and settled her cashmered bottom on the dusty mosaics of the floor. "Two sugars, Livia, as ever," he said, sitting down himself. "And I believe my friend will have the same." He handed Iris an imaginary cup, and took a sip of tea from his own. "Now, Auntie, I've got a problem to discuss with you, but first of all, of course, how's the old Empire doing? Okay? Augustus, eh? Well, he was always a problem like that. And the grandchildren? Claudius still masturbating all over the courtyard, naughty boy! Caligula's being nice to Drusilla, that's good to hear. And little Britannicus, still a pansy? Oh well, that's what an English education does for a boy." Even his accent had become more British, Oxford and BBC proper. He was reveling in his game.

Sitting on the floor a little behind the strange, possessed man who was, just as he claimed, so many men, Iris felt an adoration rising in her, a feeling as pagan as the entire Palatine Hill. As he improvised his babble to Livia, a respect for his imagination, his ease with words, even what she figured to be a striking command of ancient history, his confident juggling of reality and nonsense, took hold of her, and she felt humbled by his talent. Earlier, on the hill, his conversation with the gods had reduced her to feeling mortal, an intruder from a prosaic world; an old feeling of discomfort and an old awareness of some incurable lack had begun creeping into her, and now it settled in comfortably, made welcome by the sense of trespass that she felt in Livia's house. She knew something splendid was happening, and she also knew that its splendor excluded her. She longed to touch him, to take his hand, but could not move toward him. The force of his attention was directed so strongly to something else in that Roman room that she felt a chill.

"The problem, Livia, is this. I'm in love. What can I do? You know my dear lady wife almost as well as I do, and she's a wonderful woman, if a little artsy. Even Tiberius likes her, and I know Caligula's dying to mate her with one of his pet gryphons. But you and I know that one woman is not enough, and, Livia, perhaps you haven't enjoyed her company as much lately as you used to? Only a thought, don't let me influence you in the least. I know what these arranged marriages are, don't think I fail to understand your problems. But mine is that I've fallen in love . . ."

The second time she heard it, Iris drew in a sharp breath. Her immediate reaction was to wonder whom he had fallen in love with. She knew with pitiless and morbid modesty that it was not she. Paula, she thought, or perhaps some Roman whore he saw at lunchtime?

"You're wise, Livia," he continued. "You've been through this a few times yourself, I daresay. No, I don't agree about poison. In your day, perhaps, but nowadays forensic science . . ."

Iris suddenly remembered the Moor. It was the same thing talking to the Moor at the Château Rose, except that with the Moor she prayed for a response. She rose to her feet and went out the door, to lean against a wall in the dim afternoon light of November and look blindly at the sign, in three languages, that told the story of Livia's house. Kid Crane didn't have to grovel to the gods; he told them what was on his mind, and felt so at ease with the unseen and the immortal that he could banter with them. And there was something heavy, something disquieting in Livia's house. Iris was used to feeling humbled by Kid Crane when they were not alone, humbled by the way others looked at him and waited for him to talk. But in the bare old empty earthen room, they had been alone, and yet something else had humbled her, reduced her.

Her adoration. The intensity of his game and the pleasure he took in it had forced her to stand back and adore him from the outside, and in the moment of adoration there had been no communion. By the very act of adoring him she had cut herself off from the object of her beseeching heat, she had been unable to understand his words, and his confession was proof to her that she did not count.

She touched the rough stone wall and told herself she had no right to expect more. At least, she told herself, he had shown her what sex could be. Upon this cynical thought she felt a jealousy so desperate and murderous that she wanted to pull the stones from the wall and hurl them into Livia's house. Instead she took the little paved walk up the hill away from the house, and stood on the plateau of the Palatine ruins looking over at the tree.

Inside the house, Kid Crane stopped talking, and Livia dissolved. He felt an asshole for having declared himself, and doubly silly for having resorted to a conceit that he suddenly remembered as the central ploy of a nauseating film, starring Leslie Caron and a bunch of puppets, called *Lili.* He stood up and carefully brushed his trousers with all the mundane concern of a man who values his suits from Huntsman. Then he went to find Iris. He was a little ashamed, and a little shy.

"I know I don't mean shit to you," mumbled Iris as they descended the hill, surrounded now by crowds of children, nuns, mothers. "What are you talking about?" he asked, irritated more at himself than at her. "Never mind," she said.

Iris did not want to go up to his room when they returned from their walk. He only asked her once, before turning his head away in the elevator as the door slid closed. As Iris sat down on her bed, still trying to assimilate the unpleasant feelings that were assailing her, the phone rang. It was Grace Gregory. "How was the interview?" she asked.

"Terrible," said Iris. "He didn't say a word, and all he wanted to do was walk around Rome."

"Is this some kind of a game he's playing?" asked the PR, concerned.

"Maybe," said Iris.

"Well, here's some important news. Paula's been kicked off the film."

Iris choked. "Why didn't she tell me?" she wailed.

"Well, I'm telling you," said Grace Gregory, full of herself. "It turns out she's pregnant—"

"Oh no." The secret was out.

"Oh yes, so much for your stepsister! She's being replaced by that little redhead Elsa Verity."

"I must speak to Paula," said Iris.

"Need a quote fast, right?" said Grace Gregory.

Paula was crying so hard that Iris could make no sense of what she said over the phone; Vivien Legrand took over: "You must go with her. She is going to Gstaad tomorrow, she will marry her marquis, who waits for her there, she will be a real woman at last."

Iris was more than happy to be of service. She picked up Paula in a taxi the next morning, took her to the airport, and made her smoke a cigarette and drink a brandy before they boarded. "It's bad for the baby," announced Paula.

"Fuck the baby," answered Iris.

A silver-gray Mercedes met them at Geneva airport. "Why didn't Hugo come to Rome?" asked Iris, as the car slid along the road rising through the mountains, where a light rain was falling.

"He was going to come but heard the weather report and wanted to get some skiing done."

"Does he know I'm coming?" asked Iris.

"I don't know," said Paula, which meant he didn't. She wiped her eyes with a Kleenex.

Two hours later the car drew into the tiny main street of Gstaad. Paula woke up and nudged Iris. "Look, isn't it sweet? You should see it in the winter, with snow. That's where we get the bread, and there's the Olden Hotel, and that's where Elizabeth Taylor gets her hats." The car went up an incline, curved around a hairpin bend, passed a Disneyland pile that Paula explained was the Palace Hotel, continued up the road a little, and drew to a stop in front of a high wall. "We walk from here," said Paula, holding her heart. "God, I'm so excited!" She pushed the iron door in the wall and ran across a small courtyard that could hardly qualify as a walk, knocked on a door, which was opened by a large woman who reminded Iris of Mauricette, delivered a perfunctory hello, and disappeared up a wooden staircase. Iris looked at the driver for instructions on what to do; he pointed at the door and said, "Go in."

In a large room with dark pine walls Paula was wrapped around a smallish man with the bushy eyebrows of a Spaniard. Iris knocked on the side of the door and waited to be told to enter; the clutching couple paid no attention to her, so she walked in. "Ahem," she said.

"Bonjour," said the man, and to Paula, detaching her arms from around his neck, *"Tu veux, chérie?"* He advanced toward Iris, rigid and stately to compensate for his lack of size. "Hugo de Vigny."

"Iris Bromley."

"You are the secretary to Paula?" he asked as a proper host. Iris didn't even bother to answer. She went to Paula and hugged her; "Will you be all right?" she asked. Paula nodded. "Good, now I'm going to go back to Rome. I don't think you need me here."

"There are no more planes today," said Hugo, coming toward them. Iris saw that he was a little barrel-chested in his Argyle V-neck, his legs a little short in their corduroy après-ski trousers. "Please stay at least for the night."

Iris watched the two of them over dinner; Paula would glance nervously at him, then follow that with a quick slithering movement of her arm over to his shoulders, which she grasped and kneaded as she pulled her chin down, her clean dark curls tumbling around her neck, her gold earrings dancing as she inclined her head, while her gold bracelets tinkled and clanked, and she would look at him through half-closed eyes with longing tempered by assurance and gurgle endearments. Iris watched, mesmerized by the confidence that informed every proprietary gesture, from the way she patted his napkin down on his knees to the way her knuckles brushed his sallow cheek, where a six o'clock shadow was spiking through. Everything she did, even the way she criticized the radishes in their crystal bowl ("Hugo, these are really disgusting! How can you allow her to serve you this? They're old!") and helped herself freely from his plate ("*Chéri*, I'm ravenous, I'll finish your potatoes") reflected her absolute certainty that she was the only woman in his life and he was lucky to have her. Iris tried separating each gesture from the string of graceful movements so she could use them herself when she needed to. Once she saw a tight little smile on Hugo's face, intercepted by the maid's arm as she served him his mousse, and she thought Paula might be overestimating her chances.

While Hugo took a phone call from Los Angeles ("He's got property there," Paula said with admiration in her voice, "I've seen it, a supermarket plaza and a whole lot of buildings"), Iris pulled her over to the couch and asked in her ear if she had told him.

"Not yet, darling, but he'll love it," said Paula. "I told you, I wasn't going to say a word over the phone."

"Paula, how long since you've seen him?" she asked.

"S-o-o-o long! Two months at least."

"Why did he want you to come here? Why didn't he come to Rome?"

"I told you. Why?"

"I just think it's odd being here, out of season, not a soul around, it's as if he wanted to hide you!" said Iris.

"Nobody would want to do that!" said Paula. "Are you crazy? You have the weirdest view of the world." Then, loud, to Hugo—"Darling, is anyone else coming up here?"

"*Non,*" he shouted from the telephone. "*Pourquoi?*"

"You see," said Paula. "He wanted to be alone with me."

"Well, I'm leaving tomorrow," said Iris.

She left them talking on the sofa, and went to a room that the maid had shown her earlier. Everything in it was blue and white, from the lampshades to the carpet. She slipped between sprigged sheets, pulled the checked duvet over her, and listened slyly for the screams of a fight. None came, and she fell asleep thinking of Kid Crane. She saw him walking alone on the Palatine Hill, throwing golden offerings; just before she fell asleep she saw him with a turban on his head, or a halo, something golden.

When she came down to breakfast Hugo was already up. "Paula sleeps," he said, pouring her some coffee. Then, "*Je m'excuse de ma gaffe, hier,* I didn't know Paula had a sister."

"It's okay," said Iris, weary of the eternal issue.

"I would like you to know we are getting married," he said. "I'm very glad she did not do those nude scenes, my family would not have let me marry her."

"I don't understand," she said.

He shook his head. "*Actrices* are *très mal vues* by my father; my uncle is archbishop of Paris; we are an old Catholic family. *Vous savez, la vieille France.*"

Iris sighed at her toast and nodded. "*Ah, oui,*" she said. She did not like being called *vous* by her future stepbrother-in-law.

She left a note for Paula. "Congratulations, bravo," it said.

When she arrived at Geneva she called Gstaad: there was an hour and a half to kill before the plane left. She fingered the ticket she had bought with the money Vivien Legrand had pressed on her, and asked for Paula.

"Darling! I'm so glad you called."

"I just wanted to congratulate you. Hugo told me at breakfast. You did it!"

"There's just one thing," said Paula. "I haven't told him yet."

"You're mad! He must have noticed."

"He did, but he didn't say anything. I'll tell him later—listen, he wants babies too."

"Paula, you've got to tell him." Iris was stern now, righteousness exacerbated by the vision of Paula's happiness, even if the object of her desires was squat and pompous.

"Will you come to the wedding and write about it?" asked Paula.

Iris felt brushed away like a piece of lint.

26.

To Love and to Trust

There were three messages waiting for her at the Hassler, and one was from Julian. She called him at once, holding the others from Kid Crane in her hand, feeling them for support.

"You're crazy," he began. "You've disappeared on me. Three weeks!"

"Personal business," she retorted.

"Oh yes? like what? Love or family?"

"Family," she said.

"You bet it is. Your Paula gets kicked off the movie, and runs away to Switzerland, and you don't even call me about it? She's worth another story right now. Get to it."

"I can't, Julian."

"Are you getting soft over there? What is it, the pasta?"

"It's just that Paula and I are very close again, and I can't write about her. Not now. But listen, she'll be getting married soon, and we can have the exclusive."

"To whom?" he asked, peremptory.

"Hugo de Vigny. Family of the archbishop of Paris. Old French Catholics, couldn't be grander. Eric Castiglione can take the pictures. I'm sure there'll be a ball."

"What have you being doing meanwhile? Spending our money? Losing your objectivity, what else?"

"I've interviewed . . ." She thought. She could do Vivien Legrand quickly and send it off; she certainly couldn't use the Grace Gregory placebo, and Laredo, though transcribed, was incoherent. The pause grew longer.

"Iris, have you done Kid Crane?" He was impatient now, shouting.

"Yes," she said quickly.

"Well, telex it at once. We've got a hole in the next issue; if we get it in two days, no later, we can use it. Some pictures of him just came in, with that wife, Annabella or Arabella, a real beauty. Have you got the whole story?"

"What whole story?" she asked.

"The other wives, the background, the drinking, the fucking around, all that."

"He doesn't drink much," she said.

"Listen, I don't want a puff piece either. None of this Mr. Wonderful sensitive actor in touch with the spinning wheels of creation. Give me the dirt." It sounded horribly like an order.

"What if there is no dirt?" she countered. "What if there's not an ounce of dirt, what about that?"

"Don't be snippy! There's always dirt. Is his wife down there? Ask her. How much does she spend shopping?"

"No, his wife isn't here," she shouted.

"Okay, then, it's simple. Who's he fucking? Iris, for God's sake, you know how to write a story!"

"What about Vivien Legrand?" she offered weakly. She had sunk to the bed, and lay curled around the receiver like a large question mark.

"Late-fifties nostalgia, forget it. Just get me Crane. Did you find any story on Saul Hyott the shyster?"

"No, he's gone."

"So what the hell's keeping you so long? Have you forgotten you have a job to do?"

"No," she said, quietly at first, then repeated it louder, "No."

"You're one of the best," he said—he knew when to crack the whip, and when to wave the carrot—"so pull yourself together. Remember, it's them against us."

She started to ask the operator for Kid Crane's room and changed her mind. Instead she called the room waiter, and gave him a note. It said,

"Call me I'm back how are you." She asked the boy to push it under the door of room 807.

It was past midnight when she heard a knock on her door; she had dozed off, exhausted and full of Paula's problems. When she shut her eyes she kept seeing herself in a frilly little bridesmaid dress, like something she had worn as a child, standing behind Paula who was dressed as a bride. It was a persistent and nasty picture; she would have preferred grinning chimeras to the image of herself as a perpetual lady-in-waiting. The knock made her sit up. "Who is it?" she asked. She heard Kid Crane's voice, and went to the door. "I was away," she said as she opened it. He put his arms around her. His face was cold from the outdoors. "I missed you," he said. "I had to go out to dinner."

"Oh yes?" she asked, preceding him back to the bed, where she sat down, turned on the weak bedside light, and lit a cigarette. There was such ease between them, she thought, it had to be all right.

"Business," he said. "I had to see Elsa Verity, she just came in to replace Paula."

The rage she had felt outside Livia's house came back and she threw the cigarette across the room. "What are you doing?" he asked.

"I'm sorry," she said, getting down on her knees by the dressing table to look for the cigarette. "It was a reflex. I'm very nervous. I was with Paula, it's all a mess. I'm overtired."

He went and held her, and steered her onto the bed.

"Cigarette," she said. "It'll burn the place down."

"Never mind," he said, pushing her sweater up, "not important."

This time he was trembling more than she was. She reacted from a store of violence: bit him and drew blood, scratched his back, pulled at his cock. "Calm down," he said. He didn't like being marked.

"I'll have to leave soon," she told him, sitting on the edge of the tub while he took his bath. It was a small tub, uncomfortably wedged between sharply angled tile walls. She tried to appear unconcerned, as if it were the same to her whether she stayed or left or watched him bathe. She concentrated on doing nothing at all. She watched his features move with unsaid things as he turned the soap in his hands: his wide cheekbones, his eyes, the blue pale tonight, fragile, reacting to some inner dialogue. "You can say it out loud," she prompted. "It's very good when you do." He gave her a smile and returned his attention to the soap, a gelid translucent pain hovering over him. "I'm sorry I hurt you," she said. He pulled his shoulders in a little, as if his sense of touch were so acute that it reacted to the very word "hurt." She remembered how his face above her sometimes took on the blank serenity of a statue, immobilized in the act of feeling pleasure.

"Was it a nice trip?" he asked, his voice reverberating against the tiles and amplified by the deep oblong of water that lapped around his knees, his chest, the upper part of his arms, encircling them with the pale green of Badedas, and allowed his hands out, only his hands with the soap in them, going from hand to hand as if it were a game he was playing, not a bath he was taking.

"Okay," she said, remembering that Hugo de Catholic Family had taken her for Paula's secretary, and loath to start explaining that the whole trip was about marriage, not about dismissal. It would sound too banal to him, too banal to allow it into the confines of their secret.

"I went shopping yesterday, I bought myself a Missoni cardigan," he said. She had seen it on him when he came in, had noticed at once that he was carrying on him an artifact of fashion in gray and bronze and purple and yellow, and she had wanted to know how he had come upon it. "I like their stuff a lot," she hazarded. "I have some of it too."

He rose, the water falling away from him with loud slapping noises; she reached for the towel and handed it to him, but he had already leaned over and taken the terrycloth robe off the back of the door. He put it over his shoulders and stepped out of the bath.

"Who helped you pick it out?" she asked. Slowly he took the robe off his shoulders and put his arms through the sleeves; then, making the face of an enraged but perfectly controlled samurai at himself in the mirror, he tied the belt with a martial thrust and left the bathroom.

He was lying on the bed. She came and sat by his side, pushing the robe open across his legs; the rough texture grated on the skin of her knuckles, but under her palms his legs were moist. She wanted to take off her clothes and just lie on top of him, dive into him, dive into his body. She wanted to disappear into him.

"I love you," she said.

Kid Crane saw Arabella's face. Impassive, listening, watching. He recoiled without anything in his body moving, without an eyelid descending, without the tensing of a single muscle. His mouth remained closed, his hands stayed by his side, his feet did not twitch, but he seemed to be moving away from Iris, changing shape, diminishing. The bed around him was suddenly wider, longer, and the distance between them became immeasurable. Her hands were still beneath the robe, but though she was still holding his legs, she could no longer feel them, only a dull, dense, and fairly hard agglomeration of matter that she had never touched before.

"Look," he said. "I can't say that to you."

"I know," she answered quickly. "I wasn't expecting you to." She stood up, and found herself turning around and around. "Really," she said, "I understand, you've got a wife you love. It must be hard. I'm not asking for anything, I'm not. I'm happy we have what we have." She got down on her hands and knees and peered under the bed.

"What are you looking for?" he asked.

Dignity, she thought. "Let's go out to dinner," she said. "I haven't eaten. I'm looking for my shoes."

"It's past two in the morning, there's nowhere to eat." He sat up. "You have the same problem, don't you?" he said. "You've got a boyfriend. People have affairs all the time."

Oh, good, it's an affair, she thought, now I know. "It's not the same. Anyway, you know what he wants? He wants me to interview you."

Kid Crane let out a laugh that would not have disgraced Falstaff; he lay back on the bed to give it its full due, and then rolled over and leaned down to where she sat now, on the floor.

"I'll lose my job if I don't," she said, her lower lip jutting out.

"Fine," he said. "No problem. Anything to keep your job for you. That's the important thing, isn't it?"

She nodded, determined to convince him, and by association, herself.

"Tell Gracie we'll do it tomorrow. Have the old bag book us a table." He began fishing for his trousers on the floor.

"Not unless you stay the night," she said.

"Hey, I'm the one doing you a favor," he said. "Remember that." He stood up to pull the trousers on, and pushed his arms into his shirt. "If all you wanted was an interview," he continued in drawing-room-comedy accents, "you could have spared me an awful lot of trouble." The sudden bitchery brought her to her feet again; he sounded just like her mother. She wanted to hit him. She wanted to tell him that she didn't want the interview, that the last thing she wanted to do with him was sit across a Sony from him and gather his life and loves into the tape.

"I'm good," she said. "I'm really good. You'll see. I'm not doing it because he asked me, but because I want to. I want to write about you. I think you're fantastic, really fantastic, and no one's ever done a really good piece on you. You'll see."

She let him leave, and when he was gone she went to look for the cigarette. There was a long burn in the dark-green silk drapes down at the bottom, where it had wedged standing up next to the wastebasket.

The next night they faced each other over a thick white tablecloth in the Fontanella Borghese. The owner came to offer them white truffles (it was the season) and grated them onto their dishes of pasta. The smell of old socks that came from the truffles was not at first ingratiating, but there was so much else in the taste—woods, perfume, a smear of cognac, more old socks, mushrooms, breeze, a calm brown taste—that Iris was enchanted with them. Kid Crane turned the machine on himself, with the look on his face of a man going to the gallows. He told her, without stopping for breath, an official version of his life. He mentioned the streets of Manchester for local color, praised the Old Vic in Bristol, praised the Royal Court, praised David Lean, praised Robert Bolt, Richard Attenborough, Peter Ustinov, Yvonne Mitchell, Peter O'Toole, a good friend about whom he told two mildly entertaining stories, praised Arnold Wesker and Harold Pinter and said a few deservedly harsh words about John Osborne's decline into xenophobic paranoia.

The next course came—*vitello* for her, a T-bone steak for him—and he passed on to his Hollywood period; he praised Lana Turner ("I didn't know you made a film with her," said Iris, to which he answered, "If you haven't read the script, don't pass comments"), extolled Natalie Wood, delicately skirted around the question of Hollywood directors, went on to praise King Vidor ("A genius: I wish I could have worked with him"), expressed untold admiration for John Huston ("Now there's a man!"), mentioned in passing his divorce from an English Anne and his marriage to a French Véronique, praised Gregory Peck, whose wife was also called Véronique, extemporized for a few minutes on the art of Robert Altman, whom he had unfortunately not met yet, divorced Véronique ("Different cultures, different worlds don't mix," with a significant look at Iris), discoursed on the war film as an art form, yes or no? (he thought yes in peacetime, when the subject could be handled in the abstract, no in times of war, when polemic and propaganda made the expression naïve). He discussed his various houses, mentioned his two attempts at playing Shakespeare in the Mark Taper Forum ("Romeo yes, Hamlet no. Long Beach is better for Hamlet"), examined the problem of the expatriate movie star, compared himself, but modestly, for he admired their talent, to David Niven, Leslie Howard, Charles Boyer, remembered Jean-Pierre Aumont and had to agree that French was better for farce, was reminded of what a fascist Adolphe Menjou had been, told one anecdote about Mae West, met and married one Sylvia who seemed to disappear quickly, for with dessert he concluded his life story with a triumphant flourish in which Arabella Grant, former English debutante, landed beauty from Scottish stock but with profound emotional ties to Wales, a dog called Silver, recently deceased but still alive in his heart, Alexandra, a gurgling blond baby, a three-level house in Malibu, an antique Packard, a housekeeper from El Salvador and a host of dependable friends, mostly writers ("Have you heard of Bob Towne? Well, you will") or artists ("Ed Ruscha, now there's an eye for you!"), all were woven into a multicolored, sun-drenched, self-sufficient garland that rose and curved around him, crowning his achievements with the roseate glow of pure happiness.

"*Voilà!*" he said. "Got enough?"

She pushed down the knob on the tape and put the machine back in her bag. "Yes, thank you," she said dully. If she had ever imagined there could be the smallest, most insignificant cranny in his life into which she could fit, she now knew what a miracle it was that he had found time to dally with her at all. Dally, she thought, trifle, play, idle, fool around. Abuse. She got up from the table and went to pay the bill. "Why did you do that?" he asked when she returned. "I always pay when I take an interview out to dinner," she said, folding the bill and putting it carefully in the envelope where she kept her receipts. "I have to transcribe it tonight," she said. "And write it."

They started to walk back to the hotel in silence. A cab passed by, and she whistled for it the way she did in New York. As she got in she asked, "Can I give you a lift?" but he waved his arm in front of his face, and made a few gymnastics movements. She sped off in the car.

As he walked along the street, Kid Crane wondered what had happened. He was glad he had phoned Arabella and asked her to come down: he felt he was losing his grip on things. He had, at one point in the last ten days, been able to envision a world where he could spend his nights with Iris and his days on the set and have his marriage on the end of a telephone. It had seemed a neat and adequate solution, elegant even, practical as long as *These Lustful Stones* continued, which it would now for a long time, with all the scenes to be reshot on Elsa Verity. He loved being married, he liked having a child at last, he liked Arabella. He disliked Alexandra only when she woke screaming at dawn, and that had been spared him long enough that he had almost forgotten about it; he liked everything about Arabella except the weight she couldn't take off since Alexandra was born, but that would go, and the smell of turpentine and the clinging odor of linseed oil, but if she wasn't painting she smelled just fine.

But he liked sleeping with Iris better.

No, he didn't. It was the excitement of the illicit, he was old enough to know that; the shock of the new nude, the unfamiliar was always more interesting, especially to an actor. But Iris was not unfamiliar; she was perfect. No, no one was perfect. The journalist was horrendous, vile, prying, snooping, sneaking, testing, dropping little snatches of information only to glean more. No, that was Louella, that was Hedda, not Iris. But she cared about her job! She thought that writing about other people was important! She thought writing about him was important! Him, Kid Crane, né Christopher Cranham, the least important, most diffuse, unspecific, modest, humble little mummer in the world.

He walked on. I should keep the driver at night, too, it's more convenient, he thought.

Arabella would arrive and she would go first to look at the ceiling in Saint Peter's, she'd call it paying a visit, then she'd hunt down every chiaroscuro mural she could remember, then she'd drag him along to temples she had found on the far side of Rome. But he wouldn't take her to the Palatine Hill. That was his, and Iris's.

When he got back to his room he called Iris.

"Listen," he said, "I love you."

She put down the phone without answering. The Olivetti in front of her had already spewed out five pages of his ego; by the width of the tape left, plus the three other sides, she had another twenty or so pages left to do. "For a simple boy from the provinces, London was like a dream," she typed out. "And the renaissance hadn't even started yet, Ken Tynan was still in short pants, but I could smell it coming, the sap and rise of English talent."

"Crap," she said, and stopped typing.

She pulled the page out of the typewriter, screwed it up, and muttered, "Them against us, them against us," several times. She put a fresh piece of paper in, turned the Sony on again, and began typing.

"There's only one thing I've ever believed in," his voice rang out, deep despite the tinny machine, "and that's honesty. I told my teacher at RADA that he was a fool, and I almost got kicked out, but I was glad I'd done it. It's the same with relationships: I tell Arabella everything, and she tells me everything, it's better that way."

Crap, she thought, and despised him for lying to his wife; then it struck her that perhaps he was not lying, and had told Arabella all about her, and the two of them had laughed about it over the telephone, the gullible, toadying little journalist panting into his suite every night, truckling and fucking, desperate for his sperm, his presence, feeling elevated by his attention, dragged up out of the mire of oblivion by his superior touch . . .

She stopped the tape, then ran it forward, decided it wasn't going fast enough, stopped it, opened the lid, pushed it out, turned it around, put it back, snapped the lid shut, turned it on again: the Hollywood period.

"At first those old columnists were delighted to have some fresh young blood around, and they linked me to every starlet there was. Poor Sandra Dee! The number of times she was dating me when we'd never even met!"

He's boring, she thought. She pushed the fast-forward button.

"It's a system, that's all. I figure, you don't fight against the system when it's on your side, know what I mean, sweetheart?"—this in suggestive Northern tones. "Elizabeth Taylor was getting suspended every week, I just kept quiet and had a ball on the side."

She ran it back: "—a ball on the side."

She turned it off. She lit a cigarette and thought of Julian. Them against us suddenly didn't mean anything; it had as little to do with what she felt as a ball on the side.

She was suddenly very tired, and reached into her bag for the little box of pills. She took a blue one, they were good enough to go all night on, and put it at the side of her mouth. As she took out the tape and opened the second one, she swallowed it. The piece has to be in New York in a day, she told herself. He's boring and he's married. Get to it.

"I've learned a lot recently, so much that it surprised me, because I thought when I was twenty-five that I knew everything there was to know. I've learned to respect people, women particularly, they seem to be coming into their own these days, and you have to listen to them. Women have new rights, new identities, they don't have to belong to a man anymore."

She felt herself being pulled back toward him; and thought with pity of Paula, in her mountain cabin with her little bear.

"I don't think there's a man alive today who can force a woman to do something against her will."

She stopped the tape. Was Julian forcing her? She was tired of hearing about women: she pressed the fast forward again.

"And I've got to admit that I've never been so happy with anybody as with Arabella. I never thought she'd have me, you know, a boy from the provinces like me, just an actor."

I look up to you, she thought. I'd have you. The tape went on.

"Saul Hyott, now there's what you call a genius and a gentleman. He's unfailingly polite, and his vast experience has allowed him to bring new conceptions to running a studio. He's turned Transatlantic International around in the space of a few months."

I don't want to hear this self-serving, self-promoting crap, she thought.

I don't want to be his pipeline to approval. I don't want to tell the world about him. I don't want to tell Julian, I don't want to tell Paula, I don't want to tell anyone.

Quickly, before she could falter, she gathered up the tape from the desk and pulled the other one out of the machine. With febrile fingers she plucked at the bare celluloid between the plastic guards, and pulled it out, and out, until the wheels hummed as the tape swirled forth. Then she opened her window and threw both cassettes as far as she could. Giddy with relief, she shut the window and sat on the bed.

Now, she thought, I'll sleep. But the blue pill was holding her up, racing words and pictures through her mind like those little tin cars with wheels you push against the floor a few times, fast, to make them go. She wished she had a joint, but Rory at *Lookout* had warned her three times about Italian drug laws and she had left her grass at home. She wondered if what's-his-name upstairs would have any, but dismissed the thought as she cheered herself for having forgotten his name. No old-fashioned matinée idol took drugs, and that's all he was. A vestigial Clark Gable. A leftover. She thought of the Press Club, and its grimy secondhand aura came back to her. Drink, that's all those pressmen understood.

Why had she ever thought of herself as an outsider? she wondered. Who had said, "You stand there, a little apart and to the side, and watch and keep quiet, and don't get in the way. Don't intrude. This isn't your place, it's ours"?

She went to pee, a long stream that kept her glued to the toilet seat when she wanted to be doing something else, but she didn't know what. She dried herself, and washed her hands carefully, and watched her hands on the soap, and passed it from her left to her right hand and back again, over and over, until she remembered that it was Kid Crane's movement in the bath yesterday, or some other day. She held her hands under the fizzing bubbles of the tap, and found herself admiring the device that made the water froth like cappuccino foam. I'll put one of those in when I get home, she thought. I must find out where they got it.

She came back into the bedroom, and was dissatisfied with the bed. She could not change its position, but she turned the coverlet inside out, and then she changed the armchair from the window to a spot near the bed where it looked cozy, even if it blocked the entrance to the room.

She watched the dawn come up, sitting in the armchair with her feet on the bed. She drank a Cointreau, a Benedictine, and two Sambucas from the bar; the Sambucas reminded her of the Marie Brizard anisette she and Paula used to drink, lying on the sofas on the lowest terrace, all through the boring summer nights at Villa Stallatico.

When it was light out, Iris peered from her window to see if she could discern the discarded cassettes lying anywhere on the street. When she could not find them, she decided that what she'd done was in effect a good thing, and she put in a call to Julian Sorrel. The sleepy hotel operator informed her that it was two in the morning in New York, and this strengthened her resolve. She was bound to annoy him one way or another, so there was no sense in waiting until he was awake.

"Julian," she told him, a note of reproach in her voice, which she hoped would mask her feeling that she had it coming to her, "I can't work for you anymore. I've made up my mind, and it's final."

She waited for the answer.

"Julian, are you awake?" She could hear her echo, and tried to ignore it.

"Now I am," he said among clicks and buzzes.

"That's it, I'm leaving."

"So you finally had to choose," he answered.

27. Retreat

Perhaps it was panic, the fear of being unable to make sense of what was happening, or the presentiment that if she tried to alter things to suit herself, the retribution would be terrible. Iris, having told Julian that she was leaving, packed her new clothes; filled out her expense sheet; counted the *Lookout* traveler's checks. She wanted to leave Rome as fast as possible. It had defeated her, and she did not want to allow it to do any further harm. She did not leave a note for Kid Crane. She started one, but when it ran into ten pages—pages asking what she was to him, pages that mentioned Malibu and pages where the ink ran under her confused tears—she tore it up. The feeling was not frustration. It was a terrible split inside her between what she knew she could do, which was to praise and describe and write up and imply, and what she must do, which was to go up to his room and lie on his bed and reach for him and be silent and passive. Like, her thought continued, like Paula would be. Her adult confidence had been built on rejecting and denigrating Paula's ways. She could not betray herself now, even if it would solve everything. What, she asked herself, would it solve? She had never done anything reckless in her life; recklessness now would be to say "Help me." He might say "Who are you?" He might say "I can't." She had to leave.

She called Paula in Gstaad and was told that she had returned to Paris. She called Paris and Paula said, "Come stay with me. I need you." She did not pause to think that this would be a good thing to say to Kid Crane. She booked a flight to Paris.

On the plane she allowed herself the sacrilege of imagining Kid Crane next to her, both of them heading for Malibu. She tried to remember California, but only the melons in the supermarket and the pink paint in the house on Coldwater Canyon came back to her. The plane gave a lurch, and she stopped thinking about Kid Crane, in case she had infringed on something and had caused the momentary failure in its progress through the sky.

It had been warm in Rome. The dark mid-November cold of Paris brought back memories of her knees freezing above insufficient gray knee socks on school walks. It was a wet cold, with the sky a ponderous gray too severe to allow the entertaining possibility of snow. The only patches of bright color on the way in from the airport were the red posters for *Scorpion,* with the face of Kid Crane painted in lurid tones of sunburn, his hair raven-black, with electric-blue highlights that made a cobalt halo around his head. At first she smiled at them, sending him secret signals from the cab seat. Then she tired of it, but every time another red poster loomed into view, she wanted to understand why there were so many of them on the way to Paula's apartment. When she got out on the Rue de Berri, there was one across the street, with him glaring down at her. She could not resist a parting glance as she rang the concierge's bell.

"It's all over," said Paula as she opened the door.

Iris put down her bags. "Not again," she said. She slipped the shopping bags full of new Roman sweaters off her shoulders.

They sat in the living room, with its strange pieces of inflatable furniture. Paula clasped her hands together. "It all happened the day after you left."

The day after I left, thought Iris, not a good day.

Paula got up; she was wearing another of her caftans, with an old crew-neck cashmere sweater over it. She glided a little unsurely toward the kitchen. "I'll make us something," she said. Iris looked around the room; there were a few grand old pieces of furniture, and she recognized the harp from the Château Rose. "Did Raoul take the furniture with him when he moved out?" she shouted to Paula.

"It's all in storage. There's hundreds of boxes in storage," Paula shouted back. Iris looked through the books on the coffee table; there were anthologies of erotic writing, copies of *Vogue,* magazines for skiers and boat owners. The apartment looked like a showroom at Bloomingdale's, but dustier. "Tea or instant?" Paula shouted, and Iris said "Tea," thinking of England. Paula returned with a little lacquered tray on which were a heavy clay teapot and two little rice-pattern cups. She poured the tea with great care. It tasted sour and sad. There was no sugar.

Then, wrapping herself in an old checked blanket that Iris recognized from somewhere, Paula lay on the bearskin rug and leaned her elbow on the animal's stuffed head, and, between lighting cigarettes with little Italian wax matches that kept breaking and rubbing her sleeve against her eyes, explained what had happened.

"He doesn't want a child out of wedlock, and it would have been out of wedlock because everyone would have known I was pregnant before we got married."

"That's bullshit," said Iris.

"Not to him, and not to his family. He even said terrible things like how was I sure it was his child, and things you can't imagine."

Be specific, thought Iris. It was not easy following Paula's story. There were asides about how he had ruined her, and diatribes against the heartlessness of French men, and disparaging comments on his performance in bed, and tantalizing hints as to his peculiar tastes—"If you knew some of the things he wanted me to do, like with other girls, you wouldn't believe it!"—mingled with endless paraphrases wherein Hugo de Vigny expressed a deep and true love for her, but was constrained by his ancestors to behave in a way befitting his station and his class, and with these came her replies, as far as she could remember them in all the emotion and ghastliness of the moment, expressions of love as true and deep as his, but free of any of his constraints, as her ancestors were Rumanians (she said the word with pride) and obscure Americans and she herself was a free spirit, an artist, *à la limite,* even a bohemian, though, as Iris could confirm, by no means a hippie.

Iris listened, nodding her head when Paula took the part of Paula, shaking it vehemently and making clucking noises with her teeth when Paula was being Hugo de Vigny, heartless wretch, scion of a bunch of pigheaded, tight-lipped fascists. When Paula began to falter, and the same phrases returned a second and a third time, Iris let her own mind wander, and it ran straight down to Rome, where it circled the idea of Kid Crane and pulled at all the possible things he could be doing now, of which wondering what had happened to Iris was the main contender, although fucking with Elsa Verity and sitting in the bath playing with a bar of soap tied in honorable second place.

At last Paula's droning stopped, and she lay back on the bearskin in a position worthy of Soula Tithe, with her arms behind her head and her profile capping the animal's furry skull like a hat.

"Will you keep the baby?"

"It's only two months," said Paula, suddenly capable of precise medical calculations, and therefore open to coldhearted possibilities for self-preservation. Noticing this reversal, Iris suddenly felt winded. The haste with which she had left Rome had conferred on her an energy that she had mistaken for firm resolve. Now that the flight from the enchantment of Kid Crane's hotel suite had lost its impetus and the journey was becalmed in the still waters of Paula's pain, Iris felt purpose draining from her, to be replaced by anxiety.

"We've both blown it," she said.

"What have you blown?" asked Paula. "You're a real career girl, you're fine."

Iris cleared her throat to get Paula's full attention, and signify the importance of what she was about to reveal.

"I've just lost my job, and I've lost the man I love."

"You mean you got fired, just like me? You too?"

Iris started to say No, I quit, and as a matter of fact I quit the man as well, but Paula was sitting up now with a look of rapturous enlightenment on her face. "And your guy dropped you too," she was saying. "That fat editor in New York? It's just as well, he was awful, and slimy, I don't know how you could have gone out with him!"

Iris wavered. She could tell Paula everything; Paula had told her everything, but something in her wanted to go on protecting Kid Crane's secret. And Paula was so trusting, so vulnerable, so distraught; the news might confuse her as much as the reality had confused Iris.

"He *is* slimy, isn't he?" she said. Then she nodded, accepting that Julian had rejected her, taking on the full weight of his opprobrium, making it count, making it exist, allowing it to move her, to upset her, almost to the degree that Paula was upset by Hugo, to make things even, though not to the point of utter despair, which would have been hers only if she had felt anything for him beyond awe and ambition. So strong was the assumed emotion that she found herself crying, and then crying for Kid Crane, and Paula joined her in this diversion and they reached for each other and hugged like sisters.

Paula marveled that Iris's misery was as intense as her own. "There,

there, it's all right," she said, stroking Iris's hair. "You know, it's really odd, but the same thing has happened to both of us at the same time, like we're twins or something." She smoothed her hair and wrapped the blanket around both of them, and made a little room for Iris on the bearskin rug. "Just like we were twins," she said, "or born under the same sign." Iris valued Paula's feelings of kinship, and felt the other girl's state to be too fragile for her to start dotting *i*'s and crossing *t*'s and pointing out that she had not been fired, she had made a moral choice.

"What will we do?" she asked, feeling herself on safe ground in assuming, since she had willingly erased them, that the differences between them were now gone, forgotten. The bearskin rug had become a raft in the middle of the dirty floor.

"I could stay with Raoul," said Paula. "He's taken a house in Los Angeles."

"With what money?" asked Iris.

"He's doing some film," said Paula, defensive. "I've heard it's a nice house."

"I could stay with *my* father," said Iris, wincing.

"Then I could act in America, and maybe work with Raoul," said Paula.

Iris kept her mouth shut. She could not work with Tyler. At what, counting orange crates?

"Did you really lose your job?" whispered Paula. Iris nodded. "I'm so glad," said Paula. "We're really in the same boat."

So as not to answer, Iris sat back, cross-legged, in the middle of the bearskin and made the motion of rowing with her arms. "One, two," she said. "One, two, come on Paula, pull yourself together, the shore's in sight, *un peu d'effort!*" She stuck her tongue out with imaginary effort. Paula sat up and faced Iris, stuck out her arms and pumped them back and forth, but without moving her shoulders. Even just playing make-believe, she's not very convincing, thought Iris. Paula tugged at something with her right hand. "I've caught a crab, I've caught a crab!" she shouted. She began to laugh, and Iris did too. They collapsed across the rug, their heads on the parquet pond, laughing and holding their stomachs, laughing till the rug wrinkled up on their legs and they rolled over each other across the floor.

"Stop, my stomach!" screamed Paula.

"The baby?" panted Iris.

"I don't think it's that easy," said Paula between gasps. "If only it were." Then they laughed even more, holding their bellies and screaming between loud intakes of air, and yelling and panting and screeching with delight.

"Do you want more tea?" asked Paula when the frenzy had passed.

"No," said Iris. "It was really disgusting."

"Wasn't it," said Paula. "Iris, I adore you."

Iris felt her eyes fill with tears again, but this time she felt it would be wrong to share them. She looked away, and went to her bag for a cigarette.

"This tea *is* shit," said Paula, getting up off the floor. "It's that tea all the French drink because they think it's refined. *Le thé anglais.* They figure anything the English put in their mouths has to be shit, so they drink this shitty tea." She carried the tray into the kitchen, and Iris followed her, puffing on a Muratti, holding the box in her hand. "Take that out of my sight," said Paula. "Those particular cigarettes remind me of Rome, and I never want to set foot in that dump again as long as I live. It almost destroyed me."

"It wasn't too healthy for Raoul either," said Iris, leaning against the wall, which, like the cabinet, was painted a dark forest green; under the single neon tube on the ceiling, the narrow room looked like the corridor of a train.

"Didn't do you much good either, dear," said Paula in a British accent. She took a *biscotte* from a cardboard box, smelled it, and replaced it. Iris opened the refrigerator door and looked inside. A tinfoil plate held two *oeufs en gelée,* one of which was growing a fine specimen of mold. "You should throw this out," she said, closing the door. Paula shrugged. "Two adult women starving to death in a kitchen," she said.

"If this were New York," said Iris, "we could call a takeout."

"In Paris we're the takeout. Oh God, who can we get to take us out?"

They retreated to the bedroom, where Paula sat on the very bed where Charlie's blow job had changed all their lives sixteen years before, and went through her address book. "We could call Eric Castiglione," she said. "It would be just like old times."

"Forget it," said Iris. "He's moved to New York."

"That's right," said Paula, "I forgot. Shows where my head's been."

"Who else is there?" asked Iris.

"Szos is gone, too. He'd have been perfect. Nothing less than La Tour d'Argent, and loads of free advice."

"Darlink, never touch a man! Zey arr for me!" Iris's imitation was a little timid, but Paula laughed and said, "You're dreadful."

Having read through her book, she put it down. "You know, there's really no one left here. They're all in America."

Before they left for New York, Iris and Paula took the train out to Saint-Germain-en-Laye. Iris had insisted on seeing the Château Rose one more time and Paula was easy to convince. They had slept in the same bed, made up in the same bathroom mirror, and eaten the same omelets for three days without a fight, and had taken to referring to themselves as the brokenhearted bosom-buddy blossoms. Iris had indulged Paula by listening to the descriptions of Hugo's houses that would have been hers, descriptions that lacked the telling details Iris would have given them; Paula compensated for this vagueness with lists of such attributes as "tons of atmosphere" and "hundreds and thousands of flowers in the gardens." Paula had not had to indulge Iris once. Iris had seen to that: she felt, and knew, that her only hope of redemption, of being accepted back into the world she had come from, was to make herself as agreeable as possible, round off the cynical edges, and replace any movements of rebellion with a kind and compassionate attitude. She had brought up the Château Rose as a place that needed a visit, anthropomorphizing the fake château until its loneliness struck Paula as something to be remedied at once. On the train they talked about the Cours Lamartine, and Jill and Julie, and Szos as a vampire. Iris remembered the Moor, this time with fear. She had let him down.

They were uncertain whether to walk from the station, and unsure of the way: they had never come by train before, and the station was in an unfamiliar part of the village. A taxi drove by slowly, a suburban taxi with a slow pace and a puttering engine, and they flagged it down. "Le Château Rose," said Iris with authority.

"Le musée?" asked the driver.

"Non, le Château Rose," repeated Paula.

"C'est ça, le musée."

The girls looked at each other and got in the car. On the way they passed the old *place du marché,* with its church and its cafés, and Iris thought she saw, up in a side street, the old *papeterie* where she had dawdled among the schoolbooks. "The trees are so ugly," murmured Paula, with her concern for nature. They had been pruned that year, and held out their dark branches like amputated fingers, the white wood bare at the knuckles. The cab puttered past rows of new houses with pale-green iron gates in designs of semicircles and unkeyed squares, with new sun porches and verandas and, doubtless, new plantings under the chilly black earth of their flower beds.

"It looks like New Jersey," said Iris.

"No, it's a little more chic," said Paula, who had never seen New Jersey. Then the cab made a turn in a familiar place, between two walls, and they felt the Château Rose approaching.

We're home, thought Paula.

"You know," said Iris, "we don't belong anywhere."

The cab skirted the empty common. "I'm glad that hasn't changed," said Paula as the cab took on the road that was the direct approach to the main gate. *"Mais non,"* said Iris. "We go in by the side gate." The driver shook his head.

The main gates were open. "You're lucky, it's open," he said, "it isn't open every day." They paid and got out, and he handed them a card. *"Vous m'appellez, pour le retour,"* he said.

"Let's have him wait," said Paula.

"Don't be silly," said Iris. "We want to take a look around."

There was a little sentinel box at the left of the gate, and in it a uniformed attendant was slumbering over a tin cup of coffee. *"Deux,"* he said, looking at them. *"Dix francs."*

Iris paid. They walked along the gravel of the front garden. The fountain was off. The hedges that hid the iron fence on either side of them were well clipped. The windows on the façade were dulled. One of the doors was open, the last French window on the right, where the dining room was. A woman, wearing a coat with a red sweater wrapped over her shoulders and woolen gloves, stood just inside, by a little table. A placard behind her on the terra-cotta wall, said: LE MUSÉE DE LA VALLÉE DE L'OISE.

"C'est quoi, ici?" asked Iris in a high voice. The woman pointed at the sign. "Yes, but what does that mean?" asked Iris.

"Eh bé," said the woman in French. "What does it mean, asking what does it mean?"

They walked through the rooms where nothing of what they knew remained except the marble floors. The drapes were gone, replaced by *"exemples de tapisserie de la vallée de l'Oise,"* thick modern panels of rugs depicting the flora and fauna of the marshy flats around Saint-Germain-en-Laye. The living-room furniture was gathered in the center of the room, surrounded by a red rope. *"Exemples de meubles du 19ème siècle,"* read a little card sticking up from a holder on the floor. "I always thought that stuff was eighteenth-century," said Iris. Paula said nothing. She was looking at the winter garden, where nothing now bloomed, nor even grew save for a few Hollywood chewing-gum wrappers. Iris, not normally a neat housekeeper, crossed another red silk rope to pick them up. They returned to the little drawing room, tiptoeing across the floor. At the door Paula turned around and looked back. "Do you realize they shoved that furniture right over the marble sun?" she said.

"What do they know?" asked Iris.

The mirror was still above the chimneypiece in the *petit salon,* but the chairs that Jill had had re-covered were gone. Paula had not placed much stock in visiting the place for its own sake; she was doing it for Iris, and the different disposition of the furniture, the absence of certain pieces, the strange and ugly new curtains, did not affect her as much as Iris, who was looking around her, her fist in her mouth, searching for something and close to tears. For Paula it was the temperature that bothered her; the government, it was obvious, had not seen fit to heat the little museum, and the cold coming from the floors reverberated off the tall glass windows and made her feel she was in a tomb. Despite the cold, the air inside the rooms had a strange old smell, schoolchildren's breath on an enforced visit, the accumulated fug of listless exclamations. She felt she would catch a cold if she stayed there too long. "It's too small to be a museum," she said. "It looks second-rate this way."

Iris didn't answer. She had gone through the door to the dining room again, the heels of her boots echoing on the floors now with a determined and aggressive sound. Pulling the fur collar of her cardigan around her face, Paula followed.

Iris was standing in the center of the room where the dining table had been. The little woman behind the table by the door was looking at her with suspicion, ready to leave her post and attack her, it seemed, if she committed any sin against state property. Iris looked up at the chandelier, and saw that the branches had been fitted with electric bulbs. Slowly she turned her eyes to the right of the fireplace. Instead of the Moor, there was an easel on which were displayed leaflets describing the history and geography of the Île de France.

"C'est tout?" asked Paula, addressing the woman. She wanted to go downstairs.

"C'est tout."

Paula pointed to the floor. *"Et en bas?"*

"Des caves," said the woman.

Iris turned and glared at her. "It's not true," she said in French. "There aren't just caves down there, there are bedrooms and dining rooms and bathrooms. I want to go down, and so does my friend."

"Pas possible," said the woman. *"C'est interdit."*

"Come on," said Iris, heading for the service door to the stairs. "Fuck her."

It was locked. *"C'est pas permis!"* screamed the woman, darting forward from her table.

"Je m'excuse," said Paula. *"Nous vivions ici dans le temps."* Iris heard her, and realized that Paula's French was better than hers. She was still pulling at the door handle when the woman's hands came down on hers. *"Merde!"* she said. *"Laissez moi!"* I sound like an American tourist, she thought.

"Pardon, madame," Paula began, all unction and gravity, and in perfect French: "We both used to live here. Could we go down and take a look?"

The woman let forth a stream of outrage. *"Non, mais,* who do you think you are, miss? This is government property now, and it is expressly forbidden to let anyone in. *Voyons, vous n'êtes pas chez vous ici!"*

She spoke so fast that Iris had trouble following. Paula was easier to understand.

"Mais si, this was our home!" said Paula. She turned to Iris. "Forget it," she said.

They looked at the back garden through the drawing-room window again, and saw that it had sprung benches, and that the gardener's house had grown an awning, on which was written CAFÉ, but it was shuttered. Iris let out a little "Oh!"

"What did you expect?" asked Paula, putting her hand on Iris's shoulder. "There's never any sense in going back."

Iris looked at her. "How did you know that?" she asked.

"That's what Vivien always says."

They walked to the station; it was a long walk, and they lost their way several times, and their discouragement and exhaustion grew as the flat vistas of wide suburban streets offered only the prospect of more sidewalks and more hedges, more driveways and more endless expanses of front lawns. Their feet grew cold, and Iris, who had forgotten her gloves, put her frozen hands in her pockets. They blew little clouds of breath ahead of them, and looked down to watch the pattern of the flagstones, which, being on a smaller scale than the ample villas, had the superior attraction of succeeding each other at a faster rate.

They stopped at a café on the *place du marché.* Paula ordered a *croque-monsieur;* the memory of the bubbling cheese sandwiches with petals of ham curling inside made Iris salivate, despite the pink pill she had taken on the train. The waiter brought a square of white bread, scarred with the brown grid of a grill. Paula picked it up and bit into it, and pulled it away from her mouth with a cry of disgust. Strings of white cheese and a long dry flake of ham hung out of the sandwich. "It's cold!" she groaned.

"Garçon!" shouted Iris.

The waiter came over and apologized: the *croque-monsieur* was of the best make, it came from the manufacturer who sold all the *croques-monsieur* to all the airports and train stations in the country, and this was the Bar de la Gare. "But it's cold," said Iris. The waiter apologized again: perhaps it had not been in the Super Grill long enough to thaw out.

They left for New York the next day. Szos invited Paula to stay in his guest room, so she declined the offer of Iris's couch. Iris hugged Paula tight when she was dropped off in front of her building: she was afraid of losing everything that they had just begun to share. Paula told her New York was just a tiny, brief interruption. They could resume their brokenhearted bosom-buddy blossoms act in Los Angeles.

Iris was stunned to find her apartment unchanged, when she had changed so much in the month she had been away. The service took an hour to read out all her messages; she noticed that they had tailed off in recent days. Charlie had called seven times.

Iris made herself a cup of coffee and turned on the TV; she was startled to find that less had happened on *As the World Turns* than in her own life. She decided she should write to her father. The $2,000 a month was now important, and in her panic she sensed that for that very reason it might disappear. She had hoped to avoid action, confrontation, by leaving *Lookout:* the notion that new problems might flower from that decision did not strike her, but she found herself beset with a sudden worry about her livelihood.

She wanted to call Julian Sorrel, but could not. In her week with Paula she had improvised diatribes against the editor as an opportunistic New York wolf, who had abused her body and her address book in equal measure. "He just wanted to use me," she had told Paula again and again, and Paula, sighing, would answer, "Hugo just used me too, to bring some glamour into his boring little life." Iris had come to see Julian Sorrel through Paula's eyes; furthermore, she did not trust herself, once she had him on the line, to refrain from telling him about Paula and the fiasco with the marquis.

She wished for Kid Crane, and was stunned to think of the alacrity with which she had turned against him. On the blank afternoon of her return, while everyone else in New York was busy doing what had to be done to get ahead and make a name and carve out territory in the harsh vertical world, Iris settled on her couch to try to think. In pursuit of her own pleasure, she had betrayed all the laws that Julian had taught her, and she had betrayed the person she had made of herself, the person Julian had made her. She listed those traits he had commended in her—vitality, ruthlessness, drive, brightness, sharpness, her legendary spunk—and they gleamed so brightly in the New York afternoon that her fall in Rome seemed in contrast to be a moment of soggy weakness. A fever in the body sent expressly to test her, to distract her from the important thing in life, the pursuit of personal success.

Success? She took a tranquilizer to slide her through the early dusk, and when she awoke three hours later at nine, the phone was ringing.

It was a jubilant Charlie. "I'm calling from Los Angeles," she announced, brisk and sunny.

"I can't believe you're there," said Iris. "That's just where I want to go."

"Well, dear," said Charlie, "we looked and looked for a place to spend the winters. The country houses on the East Coast are nice, but the weather is so punishing, and Connecticut is full of dead Indians, and Virginia is fine for Mike but I don't ride, so what would I do? Florida is full of old Jews, except for Palm Beach, and Mike's ex-wife is queen there, so it wouldn't be healthy to be that close. The South is *hors de question*, and nothing happens there except shopping centers and there isn't an ounce of social life except in Houston, and ever since Mike refused to bail out some dumb cattle baron he's been *persona non grata* there, so scratch that! Then there's San Francisco, that's where his family's from, but the boredom! You can't believe it! All they do is talk about rotten second-rate French food in their silly little French restaurants, I had to laugh. And the country around there is a little wild, the trees are much too big, and there's barbed wire all over the place."

"Yes," said Iris wearily.

"Then we went down to L.A., I wanted to go and take a look, I hadn't been there since that time Raoul didn't win the Oscar, and do you know, it's simply divune!"

"Divune?"

"That's how they say it here, di*vune*. And it is!"

Iris was not happy that her mother had beaten her to California.

"The ease of the way of life! The easy opulence! The houses are pretty, just like the Château Rose, but the plumbing works, everything works, and there are hordes of nice Mexicans just dying to become maids and chauffeurs instead of that surly Black Power stuff they give you back East. Of course I'm not sure about their cooking, but they're very willing. Well, you don't see that in Boston, my word, not anymore. And we found this divune house, Ronald Colman built it and Doris Day or Judy Holliday or one of those blondes lived in it, and it's got a fountain in front!"

"Good," said Iris, sleepily reaching for the clock. She wondered why Paula and Szos hadn't called her for dinner, or whether the service had picked it up.

"It's absolute heaven! And twelve bathrooms and about three powder rooms so that when I have a big party nobody'll have to stand in line. And Carrara marble all the way from Italy. I'm going to redo it bit by bit, or maybe all at the the same time, it depends how Allegro's time goes, you know?"

"But, Mum, what about Mike's banks and his chairman things? Doesn't he have to be in New York?"

"Darling, as Mike says, when you're A number one, they come to you. And the Philharmonic has asked me to be on its board, it's like coming home again. Now here's our address—2715 Bird of Paradise Lane, corner of Jacaranda Drive, which is just up the road from Muscipula Drive." She then gave Iris two phone numbers, paused for breath, and inquired after her health.

"I've quit my job, I've decided it's time for me to live a bit."

"That's wonderful, darling," said Charlie in her real-estate gush. "You can become the person you were always meant to be."

"Who's that?" asked Iris, intrigued.

"It's a wonderful book I've been reading. It's called *How to Become the Person You Were Always Meant to Be.* It's taught me so much!"

"Can I come out and stay with you and Mike?" asked Iris.

"Oh," said Charlie. "We're going to have a full house over Christmas. I don't know if we'll have room."

"Well, make room," said Iris. "I'm your daughter."

Iris stayed in New York long enough to find out that New York no longer needed her. She could not phone any of her friends on *Lookout*: the only thing she had to hold on to was the certainty that she had made an irreversible moral choice to abandon the precincts of gossip. Going back on it before she had even started her new life would leave her with nothing. She did not go to the few parties she was invited to because she did not want to run into Johansen or Julian. She and Paula ate lunch at the Russian Tea Room, and made plans. "I have one more month," said Paula, "then I can make up my mind." She patted her stomach.

"Don't do that, people are looking at you," said Iris. "They might infer something."

"What does 'infer' mean?" asked Paula.

Iris sighed, but gently. "They'll make connections."

"I don't care what anyone says about me," said Paula.

Paula left for Los Angeles with Szos on the fifteenth of December. Szos was determined that she have a rapid and hygienic abortion in the best hospital in Beverly Hills; to this end he lectured Paula on her foolishness. When she quoted Vivien's theories of real womanhood at him, he waved the name away impatiently. "Vot does she know?" he said as they buckled their safety belts for takeoff. "She just wanted to make sure you would never become a star."

"Your soul has withered," Paula told him.

"Does your father know? He will die!" said Szos. "We put you in hospital before you see him."

"He won't mind," said Paula. Raoul, she knew, would like it that she was brave enough to flout convention.

Iris went to one party, on a street where she had once gone to purchase plastic tubing for a happening at Frances Lyle. She went up in an elevator propelled by ropes into a huge room like the first loft she had seen, except that instead of a light show there were plants growing in high baskets from the People's Republic of China. One or two people asked her how her trip had been, and she gave sad, mysterious smiles. A few others asked why she had left *Lookout;* had she been fired or had she quit? She told them she had quit because she had become aware of irreconcilable differences between her view of the world and Julian Sorrel's. This sounded as if she had been fired, and the listeners nodded their heads sympathetically.

She walked through the cold streets astounded that she could put one foot in front of the other. She thought of Kid Crane constantly, and his name ran through her head: his real name, which he had told her as part of their secret. She preferred the dignity of Christopher to Kid. She wished she had never accepted the need to have a secret; the spice had turned to poison, she saw now. Removed from the breathless pounding, from the greedy ghosts of Rome, she saw the affair as a deep and ill-fated meeting of souls, an aborted idyll. He would be bound to return to Malibu; she would be in California. The West Coast held hope.

She visited Eric Castiglione and his wife in their small apartment on Thirty-third Street. Eric admitted, over the third bottle of good wine, that New York had disappointed him. "I haven't photographed anything but parties in two years," he said. "I wasn't made for this." They ate pâté from a tin and watched Natalie Wood on television in *Miracle on Thirty-fourth*

Street. Both Eric and Ilka remarked that it was possibly a good omen to be just one street away from a miracle.

"C'est quand même formidable, l'Amérique," said Eric. *"La télévision."*

A French journalist who was staying with the Castigliones for a month to try to write a novel about America made it clear to Iris that he would appreciate her company on the Staten Island ferry. The ferry was very cold and took an age to cross to the island. Once there, he said, "I've seen it," and they went back to New York. She took him to bed with her, trying to extract from his body the same pleasure she had been initiated to in Rome, but to no avail. She resented his cock, withdrew from his fingers, turned away from his mouth, and found herself shrinking from his touch as she sought to dazzle him with her new science. The resources she had discovered in herself with Kid Crane went untapped, and her bold, lewd and unafraid advances upon the most secret recesses of the Frenchman's body, although they delighted him, left her disgusted.

On the twenty-third of December she boarded a plane for Los Angeles, having sublet her apartment. She took with her her new Roman clothes and the last three boxes of pastel pills.

As the plane circled over an enormous expanse of pale beige earth stamped with tiny gray boxes the pilot announced, "We are landing in Los Angeles, which used to be the center of the world and I leave it to you to find out why it isn't anymore." Iris put out her cigarette and wondered what ignominies the pilot had suffered at the hands of what starlet, and gazed down. There was sunshine. She hoped she was home.

28.

The Only Place to Be

A hot sunset waited outside the airport building. The sky was pink, orange, yellow, cobalt, turquoise, purple, violet, bright red. Tall palm trees were silhouetted black against this effulgence. They really were the way they looked on Tyler's postcards. "Wow," said Iris. She got into a cab; the driver pointed at the sky. "It's because of an earthquake in Yucatán, they say. There's all kinds of stones in the sky, that makes the color."

She gave him the address: Bird of Paradise, Jacaranda, Muscipula.

"Bel Air," he said; Bel Air, she thought, beautiful air.

She felt ecstatic, as bright as the sky, as calm as the hot still afternoon. She wanted to see reality under different skies, in different air, and already they both exceeded what she had imagined. To find herself there, not as a tourist, not as a stranger, not as a reporter. She saw, outside the window, an oil well pumping away on a little ridge next to the road, and mountains in the distance. Her town, the town where she had been born, the town where, someone had once said and Julian Sorrel had often repeated, there was no there there. But her family was there: Paula, Charlie, Raoul, even Jill and Saul, and Szos. The cab pulled onto a series of indecipherable freeways. The radio was on, playing familiar old favorites. The Beach Boys sang "Surfin' USA." She let her head bob from left to right.

Then they were on a long green road; she saw by looking at the signs on the cross streets that it was Sunset Boulevard. Arriving at sunset, on Sunset. She sensed that this calm vacuum of a town was full of answers. Why else would they all have gathered here?

The cab turned through an ornate gate with guardposts on either side, and a sign in gold that proclaimed BEL AIR. As it rose through narrow roads bristling with dark-green hedges and leafy perennials, Iris prepared herself for Charlie, just a little: she combed her hair and powdered her face. The cab drew into a graveled drive flanked by two swollen fluted columns. A uniformed woman with black hair and a brown face came through the front door, which was taller than the house. "Miss Iris?" she said. There was a reindeer on the roof, trailing a silver banner that said "Merry Xmas."

The house was remarkable for the casual dispersion of its rooms, which straggled through the large garden in the back like extra tents in a bivouac. There were rooms on either side of the pool, which was set with dark-blue tiles. There were rooms that followed each other under cover of an arbor of monkey-puzzle trees down to the Paestum columns, rooms that dawdled along past the tennis court, rooms that gathered humbly behind the kitchen and were intended for the staff. Charlie came out of the house as Iris stood in the garden, where night had caused a hundred sprinklers to spring into action.

"My darling!" she shouted. Iris turned. Charlie was wearing a lime-green dress; her hair was red again, she was slimmer, and, as Iris took the brick path up to the wide terrace, where Charlie waited for her, she saw that her mother's chin had changed. "You look wonderful!" she exclaimed.

"I had to go to a cocktail for the CARE committee, that's why I wasn't here to meet you," said Charlie. Iris felt her mother's thin wrist, her bony back. "You look different," she said.

"Just the tiniest tuck, and it was absolutely painless," said Charlie. "Come inside, it gets chilly around now."

Mike Mullen shook Iris's hand. "Charlie tells me you've left that awful magazine," he said. "I think that's a very wise move."

Iris had the good sense not to explain the moral thrust behind her decision. Mike Mullen was not a man who allowed petty questions of ethics to slow him down. She smiled and thanked him, and accepted a drink, which he presented as "one of my unbeatable bullshots."

After dinner, which was served in a mirrored room full of metal flamingos raising their beaks to the ceiling, Iris followed her mother to one of the powder rooms. "I think he's wonderful," she said.

"He still hasn't married me, that's all," said Charlie, examining her teeth in the mirror. "Three and a half years! And I got divorced from Ben-Abi!"

"Why won't he marry you?" asked Iris.

"Who knows? He says it's sexier living together. I think he read it somewhere. Still, I don't really mind."

On Christmas Eve forty people came for eggnog and Swedish specialties prepared by the caterer of the moment, one Mr. Blomgren. On Christmas Day Iris called Paula, and got Raoul. She didn't want to mention the baby in case Raoul didn't know, but her tact was superfluous.

"She's vomiting right now, she'll call you back," he said. *"Ça va?"*

"I'm fine. Raoul, is she . . ."

"Paula is keeping the baby. It was too late to do anything else."

"Oh my God," said Iris.

"Non, c'est très bien. Life must go on. It's funny, no? When do we see you?"

That afternoon Mike, Charlie and Iris were invited to a sit-down Christmas dinner for one hundred people at the house of a man who made airplanes. There was a footman behind every other chair, stuck there like a decoration. Each guest received a tiny airplane: tiepins for the men, brooches for the women. "I'm so glad to meet you," the hostess told Iris, "I just love all the mean things you write about people."

"I don't do that anymore," she said.

During the day Iris kept to her room, a magnificent suite of travertine marble and late Mughal hangings. There were immense pillows on everything, and little tables made of yucca-caudex slices. When Mike Mullen told her she could take her pick of the cars in the garage, any she wanted except the Bugatti, she refused, without explaining that she could not drive. The other houseguests materialized on the twenty-sixth, having spent their Christmases in Boca Raton or Palm Beach. The living room reverberated with the cackles of men who owned Kansas City or the aerospace industry. Charlie chattered with their wives, all of them dressed in loose shirts and matching trousers in strange jewel colors, jade, amethyst, beryl, with necklaces and bracelets to match their outfits. Iris could not tell anyone's age. Some women who talked about their grandchildren had perfect little noses and tight young faces and bouncing blond pageboys; some had faces that went with grandchildren, but had creaseless eyelids and firm chins. The men were wide and brash, like Mike Mullen, though without his foursquare pomposity.

Charlie announced she would give a dinner on the thirtieth to welcome Iris. "I can't invite Raoul and Paula," she told her daughter. "Mike wouldn't like it."

"Just Paula, then?" suggested Iris.

"Raoul wouldn't like it," said Charlie.

On the day of her dinner Iris put on her silk pajamas from Rome and watched the sunset. Guests were expected at seven. Charlie said you couldn't bend the rules, people in California ate early. The Yucatán colors blazed, and Iris stood on her little terrace to breathe in the sunset. None of the plants around the house had any odor, not even the one that sprouted beneath the bedroom windows, labeled "Mediterranean lavender" by a diligent gardener. Instead, there was always a vague scent of gasoline. Iris had ordered a basket of lilies for Paula on Charlie's account at The Garden of Eden. She lit a cigarette and was thankful for the taste of tobacco.

She couldn't stay in the house much longer. Her original delight at being in Los Angeles had not found anything more to thrive on; there were still the sunsets, but the sprawling house, its baying guests and the reindeer on the roof all were proving as inodorous as the greenery. She looked at her watch, a present from Charlie. In a few minutes she'd have to go into the living room. She wished acutely for Paula. The inevitability of Paula's baby suggested to Iris that Los Angeles was a place full of consequences: the end of lives, long rivers of pain and plenty, getting or not getting what you want, the end of things, a place where events came to die. Consequences of sperm and hubris and also, maybe, of hope. Szos would be at dinner: he'd know how to get Kid Crane's phone number. It would be cheating to get it through *Lookout*.

She was not seated next to Szos, but was next to her host, Mike, who alternated between talking to the man two seats away from him about the goddamn Arabs and massaging his chest. There were many courses: shrimp, crab, fish, salads, imported cheeses announced as such by little flags on them that said "Imported," and two mountains of fruit in enormous silver bowls carried in by the uniformed Mexican and her twin sister. Charlie, at the other end of the table, rose to propose a toast to her daughter. Iris bowed her head as Charlie raised her glass. She heard a peculiar sound from her left.

"Rgh!" said Mike Mullen. His face was red. She thought it polite to ignore his indigestion and faced her mother. "Rgh," said Mike Mullen again, and then he lurched up from the table, sending a cut-glass carafe flying, and reeled back toward a silver-gilt console. His arm went smashing onto the glass top of the console, sending it off its supports. Some of the men guests had risen and watched in dumb alarm. A woman screamed, "It's a coronary, Harry did the same thing when he had his!"

"A doctor!" screeched Charlie. The guests looked at each other: they owned oil wells, they owned mountains, they owned planes, but none of them had a local doctor. Harry's wife was on her feet, and at Mike Mullen's side, supporting him. "Get him to lie down. Oh God, I wish Harry was here, he'd know what to do."

"Where's Harry?" asked Iris.

"He died last year," said the young Lockheed executive on her right.

Mike Mullen was laid out on one of the peach sofas in the living room while several millionaires fought to be the first to phone the paramedics. "Get my doctor, my doctor!" screamed Charlie, as she stood over Mike with her fist in her mouth. Iris ran from her to Szos, to the phone. "The same thing happened to me once," said Szos. "But it was an overdose of pep pills."

Iris went into the kitchen to get some water. A radio on the marble pastry counter was playing "California Dreamin'." "The water is in the crystal jug on the bar," said the butler. Iris ran back into the living room, her high heels skidding on the marble pond of the floor. "Calm down," said Szos. "There's nothing to do." She went to hold her mother, who pushed her away with an involuntary jerk of her back. The guests stood in uneasy knots between the living room and the dining room. Those who were not houseguests wondered whether they could leave; those who wanted favors from Mike Mullen pondered how best to have their devotion noticed. The houseguests, with the proprietary ease of regulars, took pieces of fruit from the table, but ate them standing up, on alert.

"Rgh!" went Mike Mullen. Someone had loosened his shirt, but his face was purple. His white hair, which usually hugged his head under a careful slick of Vitalis, stood up against the cushions.

"Give him chocolate," suggested someone.

"Don't be stupid," said Iris.

Charlie knelt on the floor, clasping his hands in hers. "Don't die, Mikey," she whispered. "Don't die."

Iris knelt by her, holding a cut-crystal glass of water. Charlie shook her head. "Where are the fucking paramedics?" asked someone. The uniformed Mexicans, eight of them, stood in the embrasure of the kitchen door. Szos offered anyone who wanted one a port. Someone opened a copy of *Architectural Digest* and tried fanning Mike Mullen's face with it. The doorbell rang. The Mexicans sprinted for it as a man.

Mike Mullen's body rose on the sofa. "Rgh!" he went one more time. Sweat was pouring down his collar. He tried another "Rgh." His body arched up above the pillows. His eyes opened wide, to see the Carrara marble ceiling one more time. Then his body fell back onto the sofa, and was still.

"No, no, no," Charlie was keening, reaching for his hands. "No, no, no."

The paramedics, two strapping young men with long hair and big white teeth, covered the distance from the front door in two seconds. They looked down at the man on the sofa. One of them picked up his wrist, and replaced it on his chest. Then he closed Mike Mullen's eyes. "He's gone," he said.

Charlie was not allowed at the funeral: Mike Mullen's ex-wife flew in from Palm Beach with a retinue of Mullens and two teenage boys, the rightful heirs to the Mullen millions. Iris sat on a peach sofa—not Mullen's deathbed but its mate—in front of the fireplace, where a trio of lignite logs glowed over a gas flame. She held her mother's hand. Charlie held a box of Kleenex in her other hand. Her hair was pulled back in a covered rubber band, and behind her ears, Iris could see two little white marks where her neck had been trimmed. Charlie found comfort in the flames. "Raoul said I was a flame the night he met me," she told Iris. Iris squeezed her hand, and suggested that Charlie eat something. The houseguests had dispersed: they all wanted to go to the funeral, and felt it might be tricky to stay in the house with Charlie if she wasn't going. It was simpler for them to check into the Bel Air Hotel and go from there in a procession of black limousines.

"Would you like to see Raoul?" Iris asked, offering to call him.

"Tyler," said Charlie. "I want to see Tyler."

"I don't have his home number," said Iris.

"He lives in Placentia," said Charlie. "Look him up."

"Tyler and Elizabeth are away," said the person who answered the phone. "Is there any message?" Iris looked over at her mother, curled like a shrimp on the couch. "Tell him his daughter called," she said, and gave the number.

Paula came over, driving a chartreuse-green Mustang and wearing a Greek dress that was cleverly pleated across the stomach. She hugged

Charlie. To Iris she said, "You can come and stay with us, but maybe your mother needs you." Iris nodded. "I'll see you and Raoul later." She watched Paula drive off in the old car.

Paula picked up Raoul at the Cock 'n Bull, on Sunset, where he was having a meeting with a seedy little producer. As they drove down to his little house in West Hollywood, Paula said, "You ate meat."

"Paula, I was hungry, and it was lunchtime."

"I don't think you should eat meat," she said.

The discovery of Quinn's Nutrition Center on Melrose Avenue had converted Paula to vegetables and vitamin pills in a scant two weeks. Never one for reading much besides horoscopes or magazines, she had found the leaflets at Quinn's about Total Health and Holistic Pregnancy easy to read and utterly absorbing.

"How was Charlé?" he asked as Paula parked the car.

"Destroyed. You should go see her."

Raoul didn't answer. He got out of the car and crossed the three feet of grass to his splintered wooden porch. Paula went to the kitchen, where she took some powdered bone meal and calcium, and some choline pills to keep the lipids running smoothly through her blood. Then she soaked the new ficus plant in the sink. Then she went to rest in her bedroom, where a poster of *Bride of Attila* was taped above her bed. She had found it in a shop that sold movie memorabilia on her second day in Los Angeles. For fifteen dollars she had been able to buy the huge picture of her own mother, glowering under a fringe of gold coins, a red veil stretched across her face, blue lines extending her eyes upwards.

At four, Sam Chester arrived, as he did every day. He was a former journalist who claimed to have known Raoul in Paris, though neither Paula nor Raoul could remember him. He and Raoul were working together on a script about a gang of underpaid reporters who get together to rob a bank. A silly story, but one for which a producer who put up $25,000—up front—and Raoul needed the money. He enjoyed working with Chester: here, at least, was a man who took pride in having known him. They faced each other, sitting in bamboo-sided armchairs, drinking coffee out of mugs that came with the house and had "The Poseidon Adventure" inscribed on them. Toward evening Paula came out of her room, dressed now in a T-shirt that divulged her shape. She went to take the ficus out of the sink and replaced it on the saucer by the door that led into the living room. Raoul watched Sam Chester's eyes as they followed Paula's progress through the room. He could tell that he was longing to ask Raoul about Paula's baby, but didn't dare.

Charlie read in the society pages of the Los Angeles *Times* that Sheila McCoy was writing her autobiography. Iris watched her mother's face change as she read. They were eating an early lunch of carrot salad and crab soufflé in the breakfast room. The letters from the lawyers lay on the table: there was one telling Charlie that the house was in her name and she could keep it, and another telling her that the salaries of the staff would no longer be paid by the Mullen Corporation. Charlie put down the paper. "I know exactly what I'm going to do," she announced. It was the first time in twenty days that she had been able to talk without crying.

She went to see an agent: not Szos, who had, as she knew, no power in what she called "this town." She went to see a man she had had as her guest many times, the son of one of Mike Mullen's aerospace whizzes, who was a rising young power not only in "this town" but in the thriving agency where he worked. The young man sat behind his desk dressed from head to foot in denim, his shirt open to reveal a cross, a Star of David and an ankh; he was a person who took no chances. His eyes were a deep Pacific blue behind his blue prescription aviator sunglasses. "Charlie, honey, I'm happy to be able to help you," he said as she sat down. "What's the deal?"

"My life story," she said.

"Hey, that sounds pretty interesting." He pushed a buzzer on a big wood-veneer box on his desk. "No calls until I tell you," he bayed into the box. Charlie pulled her black jacket up at the neck. She wanted to look a dignified widow, not merely a hopeful client.

"I've had a long and eventful life," she began, amending it at once to "not that long, but very eventful."

He was nodding vigorously. "Tell me," he said.

"Well"—she opened her hands to show him she had nothing to hide —"Hollywood in the great days of Harry Cohn, I was in all those really big films they made then."

"What would I have seen you in?" he asked.

"No *big* parts," she specified. "But I was there. And I knew Laszlo Glauben, and Mirisch Eckman and Laus Manheim."

"Who?" he asked.

"The composers!" she said, frowning at him. "Don't you know your Hollywood history?" He shook his head. She continued: "I roomed with

Soula Tithe, and Sheila McCoy when she was called Gertie Tamlyn; then I moved to Europe with"—she held her breath, conscious of the bombshell she was about to drop—"with Saul Hyott."

"Wow," said the boy agent.

"That's not all," said Charlie, delighted at his response. "Then I married Raoul Abime! And even before that, I was right in the center of the whole Paris expatriate community, you know, all those people who made Paris the only place to be—"

"Like Hemingway and Fitzgerald, you mean?" he asked.

"No," said Charlie quickly. "Not at all—they were way before my time, what are you thinking of?" She wanted to hit him, but knew one caught more flies with honey; her manner grew flirtatious. "You silly boy! How could you? They were in the *twenties*. I'm not yet fifty, for God's sake!"

"That's really interesting about Saul Hyott," said the agent. "I hope he won't mind. He's a big power in this town."

"How could he mind? He adores me," she said, "and if you had any idea of the kind of life we led, the parties we had, the incredible luxury and elegance of those days! I'd write all about that, and about Edith Piaf and Maurice Chevalier, and, of course, about the man I married, Raoul Abime."

"Who's Raoul Abime?" asked the boy agent.

"The director! He was Soula Tithe's husband."

"I thought you roomed with *her*," he said.

"After she died, for God's sake, what do you think I am, an adulteress?"

That was exactly the way the boy agent's father had described Charlie to him; he gave a little chuckle. "Hey man," he said. "I'm easy, you can do what you like."

"Do you think it would sell?" she asked.

"Is there any sex?" he countered.

"Sex?"

"Sex, yes." His blue glasses were steady on her. "Sheila McCoy's book is full of sex."

"I could put some in," she offered. He promised to call her.

"I've sold my life story," Charlie told Iris when she came home. "Let's go celebrate. I'll be rich, and no one will be able to take it away from me." Iris offered her mother a drink. "No, I'd better go back on my diet," said Charlie, returned to the rules of ordinary life, after the laxity of her mourning period, by the imperatives of her new career. "I have to think about looking good on the talk shows, you know."

Charlie took Iris down to spend a Sunday at the beach house of her best friend, Sally Cumberland. Sally Cumberland's husband was in real estate; Sally Cumberland's friends were actresses, beautiful wives, heiresses. It was, Charlie told Iris, a younger group than Mullen's friends. "They're people you'll really relate to," she said. The house was a little shack covered in rosewood shingles, a touch that Mr. Cumberland was most proud of. "You can't get rosewood anywhere on the West Coast," he told Iris. "I can sell this place for an extra fifty thou just for the shingles." There were shingles inside as well, and sliding glass doors opening onto a deck beyond which the Pacific inhaled deeply. It was the first time in some twenty years that Iris had seen the Pacific, and she went to look at it. "We're having lunch, come back," shouted Sally Cumberland from the house. Some seven women and five men were seated around a wide glass-topped table. Lunch itself, a spinach salad, was quickly dispatched. Occasionally one of the guests would take Charlie's hand and squeeze it gently, in an act of sympathy. "I'm okay," said Charlie. "Really I am."

"And now, what you've been waiting for!" shouted Sally. Her Mexican maid brought forth three pies: cherry, raspberry, and apple. "And there's more in the kitchen," she said. The lithe beauties sitting around the table forked off pieces from the various pies, nibbling with an affected abstraction designed to hide their voracity.

They talked about diets. Of course, thought Iris. She was on her last diet pill, and was determined to ignore the desserts. She watched the women, beautiful, all of them, with their carefully tended faces and dieted figures in tight jeans and cotton shirts, as they so willfully and deliberately undid their good work. The men retired to a corner nook upholstered in raw suede, clutching oversized brandy glasses.

"Danny'll never fuck me again if I get fat," sighed Sally. A laughing woman with long blond curls nudged her. "Better watch it, I heard you were a hot number."

"Not anymore," sighed Sally. "All I like now is food!"

Iris looked from nose to nose, all, except her mother's, marked by the same fine Beverly Hills hand. They reminded her, these women, of French ornamental gardens, snip-snip on top and prune-prune below.

"I don't care," mumbled the prettiest one as she took an entire slice of cherry pie. The eating struck Iris suddenly as a revolt against a life devoted to the prevention of age and time and fat.

"You're not eating," said Sally, looking at Iris. "What discipline."

Yes, thought Iris. Discipline, that's what I've got.

"Stretch marks are hereditary," said Sally.

"Then Iris won't get them," boasted Charlie.

Sally turned to Iris: "Are you pregnant too, or is it just Paula Abime?"

"I'm not," said Iris.

The women began discussing their bowel problems. Two were constipated, and one had a spastic colon. Charlie joined in the discussion; Iris stood up, and then, not wanting to make them feel that she despised them for what was, after all, their honesty, she gave each of them a grin. She wandered over to the men, who were discussing Hawaii. The most tanned one among them was describing the private beach he had just bought.

"Hey," said the host. "Just don't fly your plane there when you're stoned. It's a tricky place to land, believe me."

"I don't have my license yet," said the beach owner. Iris returned to the table.

"I just have this little ridge here to get rid of and then I'll be perfect," the most beautiful one was saying. Iris glanced at the men, hunched over the description of their worldly goods, and back at the women they owned. It seemed logical, after all, that these wives should clutch on to their bodily functions for security; for each of them the body was the only thing they could control in a situation where they were no more than possessions.

She went walking on the beach, having left her shoes on the rosewood deck. She tried to think of nothing, but the certainty that Kid Crane's house could not be far animated her footsteps. The waves were each a distant crash, followed by a rapid white surge along the sand. She walked left, her feet in the water, thinking of it as a pilgrimage. She gazed at the houses and rejected them one by one: too plain, too open, too bland, too athletic with dinghies and a sailboat, too prettified; the one with an American flag was definitely out. Many of them were closed for the winter; on a few she saw lunch parties in progress just like the one she had left, people standing on the decks with plastic glasses in their hands discussing, no doubt, what to do about their bulges. She turned right, and passed the Cumberland house again. Farther along she saw some people sitting beneath a rock, wrapped in sweaters, with a big dog running circles around them. She froze: that could be him and his wife, they all had dark hair. She couldn't tell; but the possibility that he could see her creeping up along the beach, spying on him, trying to ambush him, shook her. She turned back and ran toward the house.

"Chocolate icebox pie!" Sally Cumberland announced as Iris came in from the deck, rubbing the sand off her feet. The cake was set in the center of the table and the women started stealthily slivering away at it. Not one of them took a whole piece and put it on a plate.

Charlie drove her home in the Rolls-Royce, having made sure that Iris had washed her feet and put her shoes on again. "I can't have sand in the Rolls, it's not good for it," she explained.

"You know, I think I'll go to La Costa to write the book," she told Iris. "They put you on six hundred calories a day and you don't have to exercise if you don't want to."

"The book's really cheered you up," said Iris. "That's good."

"You can help me write it," said Charlie generously. Then she frowned. "La Costa's really expensive, it's about two thousand for seven days, maybe I'd better do it at home."

Iris decided to have no opinion about her mother's book; being sure that she wanted no part of it, she told Charlie that now that everything was fine, she would find a place of her own.

Before she could move out, the boy agent called. "No one's interested," he told Charlie.

"No one wants my life story?" she asked, astounded.

"I'm sorry, Charlie, but we sent out feelers to some publisher's scouts out here and no one's heard of Raoul Abime."

"What about Saul Hyott?" she asked.

The boy agent gave a little cough. "That's the main problem. He said he'd sue if you wrote a single word about him."

"Edith Piaf? Harry Cohn? Soula Tithe?" wailed Charlie.

"Sorry, Charlie, that's the bottom line. Have you thought of a novel maybe, but without Saul Hyott?"

"What do you think I am, a goddamn writer?" asked Charlie as she hung up.

Charlie took to her bed, where Iris watched over her with growing impatience. After a few days of bringing her food on trays—the Mexican staff was slowly ebbing away according to which of Mike Mullen's friends needed an extra maid, butler, gardener or seamstress—she looked Charlie squarely in the eye and said, "I have my life to live."

"You invited yourself here," said Charlie.

"You have your life to live, too. Sell the house, get an apartment with the money, simplify your life, and do something."

"What can I do? I can't change my life-style just like that, just because my Mike died."

"Sue his ex-wife. Be aggressive."

"I could sue, couldn't I?"

"Certainly," said Iris, though the only legal processes she knew had to do with libel. "You could sue and you could win."

The only car left in the garage was the Rolls-Royce: the eight others were gone, claimed by the rightful heirs and spirited away by their lawyers. Iris prevailed upon the last remaining servant, the second gardener, Juarez, to drive her down to look at apartments. The manager of the first building, a hacienda composed of units described as garden studios, shook his head at her: no young woman who got out of a silver-blue Rolls-Royce driven by a Mexican chauffeur should live in his building, he said. "You running away from home?" he asked, suspicious. The next day she took a cab, and found three rooms for $200 a month on Olive Drive, three blocks from Raoul and Paula.

She moved in with the help of the gardener, threw scarves over the lampshades, put the ficus that Paula gave her in the sink, took a cab back to Bird of Paradise Lane, and told Charlie she was beginning anew. Charlie was on the phone to the West Coast office of Ticon, Chicago, and Luzt, and waved at her. The gardener drove Iris back to her new place and she sat down to make a list. She was tired: it was her first day without the pastel pills, but she told herself she had to get through it.

The boy agent's reaction to her mother's book, which Iris had loudly dismissed as shortsighted and provincial, seemed in fact to make sense. All the billboards on Sunset were for singers Iris had never heard of; they were the coming generation, and whatever the past had given her didn't count here.

The only person who seemed to have survived to prosper was Saul, and Iris put him at the top of her list: perhaps she could become a woman executive at his studio; she had heard there was a demand for young women. Because this idea did not fit into her old structure of fame and publicity, she saw it as a reasonable option. She wrote down her list of things to do: Driving. Cooking. Washing Machine. Money. Car. Then she went to lie on her bed, newly hired from Abbey Rents.

The driving teacher was called Vince. He picked her up at eleven each morning and drove her to the top of Mulholland Drive, because, he said, it would scare her into driving well. At first her foot hesitated to touch the gas pedal, and stayed on the brake. Vince convinced her that it was safe to impel the car forward, and even safe to push it into speeds over twenty miles an hour. He was a quick and effective teacher; by the end of ten lessons, she could drive alone. He took her down to the Motor Vehicles Bureau and, on the way, drilled her with the questions she would be asked. She passed the test the first time, with only three mistakes. It was the first test she had passed since Frances Lyle; it was easy, and physical, and absolutely vital if she was to get around Los Angeles like a normal person instead of relying on stray domestics and taxicabs. She felt she had done something remarkable, although it did no more than put her on an equal plane with every seventeen-year-old in the state of California. Paula suggested that she rent a tired Mustang like her own from a firm aptly named Rent-A-Wreck, but Iris's newfound pride would not allow her to pay out money for something that advertised itself as a wreck.

She went to see Saul Hyott for a job. If she became a woman executive, she would be able to lease a car, if not buy one outright on her salary. Jill was in the outer office at Transatlantic International Pictures. She hugged Iris, who said, "Let's have lunch." Jill promised she would, if it could be near the studio. "Saul only gives me an hour," she said, and then admired Iris's craftily matched printed sweater and skirt. "Rome," said Iris.

"Oh yes, I heard all about that," said Jill.

"What did you hear?" asked Iris.

"You went shopping," said Jill, "a lot. Saul's waiting for you."

He received her in an office entirely paneled in green felt, with a sculpture made of billiard balls by the window and aerial views of Las Vegas screwed to the wall. Iris decided the green felt was evidence of great strength of character: she would have expected him to reject, or at least dissimulate, his professional origins.

Saul was just seventy; his wrinkles had settled into a niche at the base of his neck; his hair, which had long been gray, was now the color of milk chocolate, and his tanned skin had taken on the hue of the underside of a mushroom. He wore a denim suit, tailored in Rome. He apologized for not having seen more of her there; she reminded him that they had had breakfast together.

Iris asked him about the film.

"It's going to be boffo," he said. "That Elsa Verity's a hot little number, and her scenes with Kid Crane are sizzlers! When's your story coming out?"

"It isn't coming out," she said. "I quit the paper."

"Shit," said Saul. "Excuse my language, but I turned down a lot of things because you were there. I wish you coulda let me know. I blew covers on three magazines."

"I'm sorry," said Iris.

"Kid Crane was asking about it just the other day," he added.

"He was?"

"His press agent was. So, what's the story?"

"I just wanted to make contact," she said, hoping he would be touched by the sentiment. "I've moved here."

"That's nice," he growled. "So, who're you writing for out here? I'm giving a party for *Hell's Bellows* next week, you should come and do a piece on it. The whole Rome gang'll be there, Laredo, Kid and Arabella. I bet you'll be glad to see them."

"I'd love to come," said Iris. "What night?"

"Ask Jill," he said. "That's a detail."

"Isn't she great?" Iris asked.

"Who?"

"Jill."

"Jill? Sure, she's okay. So, what else can I do for you?" He crossed his hands over his chest; the pinky ring gleamed cabochons at her.

"I thought maybe you'd have a job for me," she said, staring at her shoes.

"Can you type?" he asked.

"Not that kind of a job," she said to her shoe. "An executive job."

"That's a tall order," he said. "Maybe there's something in publicity, you could help them write the handouts. Go down and see Rick in the publicity department."

Iris had a sudden vision of Grace Gregory. "I don't want to do publicity," she said. "Not that."

"Look, I have a meeting coming up," said Saul. "I'll have Jill call you when there's an opening."

"You said *Hell's Bellows* was next week," she said hopefully.

"You wanna go to premieres, or you want a job? Make up your mind, Iris."

She wrote her number on a pad on his desk and stood up. "I thought I could have both," she said softly.

"Iris, this is a tough town. Shit or get off the fence." He stood up too, and clasped her hands in his. "You're nobody here unless you work, don't forget that."

"Remember Paris?" she hazarded.

"Sure, I remember Paris, and that reminds me. Tell your mother to keep her trap shut. Good luck, Iris, good luck." He saw her out. "And let me know when you've got a job," he called after her; then he shut his door.

"He used to laugh a lot," Iris told Jill. Jill shook her head. "He only does that on holiday now."

"Lunch?" said Iris.

"I'll call you," said Jill. "He runs me off my feet."

"Any messages for Raoul and Paula?" asked Iris.

"Yes," said Jill. "You can tell him he owes me eight months' wages."

Iris walked to the gate of Transatlantic International Pictures, which had invaded the former Biotronic lot, and asked the guard to call her a taxi. "Who are you?" he asked. "A tourist?"

"No," she said. "A relation."

"I thought so," said the guard. "Real visitors have their own cars."

In the cab on the way to Raoul's house she was tempted to call Julian Sorrel and reenlist. It seemed peculiar that she would be denied access to the person of Kid Crane because she was no longer a journalist, when she had lost him because she was a journalist. She got out, full of frustration, and undertipped the driver.

Raoul listened to her abridged recital of her problems, with all references to Kid Crane edited out, and shook his head. "*La vie est dure,*" he said.

"But I thought everything was going to be wonderful," said Iris.

"No you didn't," he said. "You were always waiting for the worst."

"I could call Don Flagel," she said.

"Come to my class," said Paula, "instead of wasting your time. My breathing class."

"I know how to breathe," said Iris. She had one of her high-heeled shoes off and was massaging her toes. Paula settled herself on a cushion on the floor. "You're doing it wrong," she said. "Look at you, you're wearing full makeup, like I used to for pictures; you're all done up like for an afternoon in New York, you're wearing high heels and your arches are being deformed. This is Los Angeles. You should relax, lay back," she said, "go with the flow."

"The flow's all against me," said Iris.

"Then accept it," said Raoul from his bamboo armchair.

Paula took her to the class. The other women there had shiny intense faces and frizzy hair, and unborn babies bulging beneath their leotards. "Five of them are alone, just like me," said Paula as she changed. "Julie can't bear to live with Sam, Ed left Sarah, Judy's guy did a Hugo and ran away screaming about how was she sure it was his, and Emma isn't sure."

The women were assembling on the mat, facing the teacher, a young woman in a green bikini who was patently not pregnant.

"That's four," said Iris. "What about five?"

"Natalie's a lesbian, but she loves babies, so she went to a bar in Venice to find a guy to knock her up," said Paula. "C'mon, let's go on the mat."

Iris watched from the back row as the women breathed in and out and felt for some internal set of muscles she could neither see on them nor locate on herself, though at one point something twinged that reminded her of Kid Crane's cock deep inside her. She tried to follow what they did, and decided it was a waste of time. She lit a cigarette; the teacher shouted "Don't pollute our babies!" at her. Iris went outside; when she returned, the women were all sitting still and cross-legged, obeying the teacher's instructions to think like a flower.

"Next week she's getting Su-an Ram Dam to come to talk to us," Paula told her as she drove back to Raoul's. "She's that wonderful holy woman from Carmel."

"You're really into this," said Iris.

"I might as well be," said Paula. "There's no way I can ignore it."

Raoul took them to dinner at a restaurant where the vegetables were fried on a square searing plate in the middle of their table; Iris recognized the device from New York. "I think I'll get in touch with my father," she told them.

"That's a wonderful idea," said Paula.

Iris wanted to say something about Paris, about wanting to hold on to what they had had; she wanted to reach over to Raoul and tell him *he* was her father, but Raoul was already adding to Paula's statement. "Blood," he said. "Blood tells."

Iris would have preferred to drive down to Malibu in a car of her own and wander on the sands until she came face-to-face with Kid Crane; instead she called Tyler at the plant. "Come anytime," he said.

She took a cab to the plant, which was deep into Orange County. The ride cost forty dollars. The plant was enormous, a spread of tall silver buildings and behind them miles of groves. Workers in orange overalls milled around a catering truck; one of them directed her to her father's office. The secretary buzzed her right in.

"Iris, you sweetheart," he said. "You've come to see your old dad."

"So this is it," she said. There were prints of orange blossoms on the wall; the windows overlooked the groves that ascended a hill.

"How do you like it?" he asked.

"It's big," she said.

"There's fifteen thousand acres of oranges out there," he said. "Count 'em."

"Where are mine?" she asked, peering out the window.

"Over the hill," he said.

He asked how Charlene was, clinging to the old name. She told him Charlie was suing Mullen's ex-wife, but did not say it was her suggestion. "My lawyer's helping her," he said. "Sit down."

"You look good," he said. "Better than in New York."

She had gained weight since the last pill, but not much; her hair hung down her back like a child's, and a small scarf held it off her face, tied just below her right ear. A light winter tan remedied the incipient sallowness of her skin, and was enhanced by rouge, which she had not yet abandoned, despite Paula's entreaty to be natural.

"How long have you been here?" he asked.

"About a month; I called you at Christmas, you were away. Then all that Mullen thing happened—" She felt this was not enough, that she had to say it in a way he would understand, and found herself saying, "Mike passing away so suddenly, and I couldn't call."

"Terrible, terrible," he said.

"I'm going to stay here," she said. She smiled at him. His head was bald, wigless, undisguised. He wore an open-necked white shirt, horn-rimmed glasses, and behind them the brown eyes were kind.

"Let's look at the groves," he said.

She stumbled behind him, turning her ankles on their high heels in the banked sand, and stooped to remove her shoes. "You'll learn how to dress for oranges," he said.

I will not, she thought.

"Is your money still coming through all right?" he asked, patting the trunk of a tree and picking an orange. "Fine," she said. He gave her a segment. "They're juicy right now," he said.

They walked back out of the grove. "You need a job?" he asked her.

She shook her head; she didn't want to take anything from him, she told herself, conveniently forgetting about the money.

"It would make life easier if you worked with me," he said. "I mean that."

"You don't need me," she said. "I don't know the first thing about oranges."

"Growing them's easy, it's the marketing and promotion that's tricky."

She told him she would think about it. He invited her back to dinner in Placentia to meet Elizabeth and the twins; she declined, and asked him to call her a cab to get back to West Hollywood. "Can't you drive yet?" he asked.

"I can drive. I just don't have a car," she said.

They were in the parking lot. "Here," he said. "Take one of these. They're company cars." He pointed at a row of identical orange Pintos, parked in neat diagonal rows across the asphalt.

"I couldn't," she said.

"Why not? What's mine is yours," he said casually. "I'll have Tad find you a set of keys."

The keys were attached to a big round plastic slice of orange; Iris thought this was taking it all a little too far, and resolved to find something a little subtler at a head shop on Santa Monica Boulevard.

They kissed good-bye. "I really would love you to work here," said Tyler. "Think about it."

The freeway puzzled her, but the Pinto took it with spunky determination. She overshot exits she thought she recognized, and just before Universal City she saw a sign she knew, and turned off, heading for Mulholland Drive. She teased the car up the incline, pulling it in and letting it go, just to feel its reaction. When she reached the top and turned onto the flat winding crest, she pushed the accelerator down and opened the window. It was four o'clock, an early winter sunset. The sun was sharp over the massy relief of the San Gabriel Mountains, and the valley was a pink and indistinct bowl of cloud. The air was sharp and clear; she revved the engine and sped around the curves, conscious of control, full of an effortless joy, a torpid but nervy exaltation. She turned on the radio: it was playing *La Traviata.* Quickly she changed the channels to a rock station. The car, the mountains, the last of the sun and an infinite Los Angeles, a loud love song on the radio and the car going fast beneath her, around her.

It doesn't take much to be happy, she thought.

Epilogue

Epilogue

She learned to like simple things, and seek out what made her happy. She took to driving across the hill to the vast Hughes supermarket that nestled at the edge of the valley, where the aisles were as long as two New York blocks, the vegetables and fruits afflicted with a joyous gigantism, the checkout clerks young and blond and tanned. She found that the taste of a papaya could hold her interest longer than Paula's conversation, which was all about her child. She discovered that she liked to keep her window open at night, to hear the cicadas in her banana trees and the sirens up on Sunset; she would close it sometimes, deliberately, to check whether it made a difference, and invariably got up in the middle of the night to open it again. She became an expert on cars, and after a year with her father's company she bought her own Jeep, a solid model in which she could take off across the desert without fear of ruts.

She learned to like parking lots, the private property on public space, and the tenuous courtship that was enacted on them: the way after an evening out, she and a man each went to their own car in the big concrete park and got into their own machine, sealing their private spaces around them, and the man revved up and sped off, and she followed, twinkling the little lights on her car to show she was there. Sometimes, while following a car to a man's house, Iris would see a turning she liked the look of, and take it, leaving her swain to make his way alone up his canyon, confused and a little miffed, while she explored new streets and their trees and the fronts of their houses, and took other turnings that more often than not led nowhere, but eventually back to Olive and her own apartment, where the phone would be ringing when she got in, the man asking where the hell she'd gone.

She liked having her ignition key in her hand, her key to ignition and flight. Whenever things got a little sticky at the plant, she'd leave her office with its Renaissance Fair posters and its big white desk, and jump into her car, and drive off through Orange County, sometimes over to Laguna, where she would sit on the beach and look at the water and heave deep breaths until she felt she had cooled off.

Everything in Los Angeles was conveniently labeled, save certain freeway exits that still eluded her after four years. The avocadoes came with instructions on how to grow a plant from their seed; the Jerusalem artichokes came with instructions on how to chew them. T-shirts wore greetings. People talked in simple English, the word "space" became a verb, and under the huge bland sky all ambitions seemed tawdry. There was no one to emulate in Los Angeles, no one to look up to or be jealous of, no one whose life looked better than her own. Her month in Mike Mullen's mansion had shown her that sophistication, in Los Angeles, was a gauche and gaudy waste of time. After a few months in her apartment she had thrown out her high-heeled shoes, which were no good to drive in, put away her subtle Italian stripes, hidden her makeup. Like everyone else around her, she wore blue jeans and sneakers.

Her stepmother, Elizabeth, clucked at her sometimes for being unkempt; Elizabeth was a pink-lipstick woman with careful hair and neat nails, but a good soul. Charlie never mentioned Iris's appearance anymore; she too, in her way, had given up mundane concerns; where Iris had given up the nagging worldliness of images, Charlie had, if anything, been more thorough. She had given up everything.

When Charlie lost the lawsuit against the Mullens, she went through a period of being withdrawn and a little peculiar. To ease her over this patch, Paula introduced her to the holy woman Su-an Ram Dam, who taught Charlie meditation and exercises designed, in Su-an Ram Dam's words, to clear the inner channels. Charlie spent every day secluded at her apartment off Wilshire Boulevard, her eyes closed, her palms lifted upwards over crossed knees, as she played cassette tapes of temple bells to keep out the neighbors' vibrations. She never answered the phone until sunset.

At last she became a nun in Su-an Ram Dam's order of mendicant women, thereby prolonging the family tradition instituted by her two eldest sisters, Bridget and Caithleen.

It took Paula three years to wean her child, who, as she told anyone who would listen, gave her more satisfaction than any man ever had. The child was called, regrettably in Iris's opinion, Breeze.

Raoul was teaching at UCLA. One might have expected him to be teaching film, but he taught French.

Szos returned to New York, finding himself unable to gain a foothold in a town where his long-winded stories about whores and stallions and old Budapest amused no one. He made a wonderful deal for Vivien Legrand's autobiography; Elsa Verity played Vivien in the seven-hour TV special spun out of the book, which had been ghosted by a French novelist, a friend of Eric Castiglione's who was still trying to write a novel about New York; he was the same young man Iris had spent a night with in late 1973.

Los Angeles had humbled them all, even Tyler. A few years after Iris started working for him, a federal investigation concluded that Ezy Vite Juices owned too many groves, and Tyler was ordered to divest himself of them. This was due to faulty strategy on the part of Ticon, Chicago, and Luzt, the same lawyers who had previously blown Charlie's case. Tyler sold his groves in Orange County, and gave Iris the money from her tract; with it, Iris bought a fine house near the top of Coldwater Canyon, which rapidly appreciated in value. Tyler kept the house in Placentia, but relocated the Ezy Vite plant to City of Industry, between South El Monte and East Covina. There he applied himself to the making of orange juice by-products and research into the freeze-drying of citrus fruit.

It was Iris who invented C-Grains. Running her hands through the mush left over after the juice had been extracted from the daily thousand ton of oranges, fingering the heavy pulp and slivers of peel, she wished there were a way this could be sold to the public. The idea lay dormant during Tyler's troubles, but once they were relocated, Iris hired a chemist and bought a pair of supersonic ovens. The chemist lost a great deal of sleep, the utilities bill soared, and a year later the tiny granules of orange debris were ready, packed full of vitamins, weightless, and cheap to produce. They were launched slowly, and by the time America woke up to the fact that C-grains were as important as sunshine, Tyler had signed up the orange wastes of every plant in Orange County.

Tyler became very rich; he was a fair man, and Iris, being the inventor, was even richer. She no longer liked to hear herself described as rich; she didn't need to. Since the day she had first put her foot down on the gas pedal of Vince the teacher's car on Mulholland Drive, she had learned to trust only in the evidence of physical reality. She did not give interviews, although the Los Angeles *Times* and the women's magazines all wanted to feature the twenty-eight-year-old businesswoman who had changed the breakfast habits of the nation. She did not want to read about herself in the paper, nor have others read about her—partly from strength, but mostly from a peculiar apprehension that publicity brought bad luck. She was no longer superstitious, but this one thing clung to her. Only occasionally did she remember the Moor, and when she did, it was with relief that she had outgrown those fantasies.

At the plant, Iris was direct, forthright, tactless sometimes, but usually kind. She had three assistants and one secretary, all of whom she considered close friends. She had become used to rising early: the drive from West Hollywood to Orange County took almost an hour, and at first it had been hell, but eventually the early nights had shifted her rhythms until she could enjoy the clean air and the slow parade of cars along the freeway, their windows open, newscasts blaring.

In the evenings she went to dine with Tyler and his family (there was always more business to discuss) or she drove home by the beach, and stopped at a Santa Monica bar to pick up a beachboy and take him home. They were sweet young men, eager to please, interested in cars; but she had to give them up when she moved to her big new house: she didn't want to impress anyone with her money.

She kept her Jeep; it was a coherent blending of function and form, and never let her down. She had a brief fling with the C-Grain chemist, but he wasn't very good in bed and she turned instead to his assistant, a restrained young man who enjoyed their secret and had enormous reserves of physical energy. She varied this occasionally with young men she met at Paula's and Raoul's, male baby-sitters, the occasional UCLA student, visiting Frenchmen. Once, a Rumanian came to interview Raoul and he turned out to be a prize, a former weight lifter who combined stamina with passion. He had to return to Bucharest, but Iris didn't mind: he left a good memory and some interesting marks on her body.

She thought about Kid Crane; she couldn't help it. She did her own shopping and his face was often on the cover of the *Enquirer* at the checkout counters. Early on she had bought the magazines, and read the stories about him with dread and hope. They never said anything that she hadn't read before; the man they talked about was nothing to do with the person she had known in Rome. The *Enquirer* was of course no yardstick by which to judge the press, but it simplified the job of dismissing journalism.

Lookout gradually turned political, and endorsed Jimmy Carter for the 1976 election, after which Julian Sorrel left New York to become a Washington speechwriter.

Kid Crane in the *Enquirer* was not Kid Crane; when Iris read that he and Arabella had split up, she counted this as just another of their fabrications. Sometimes, particularly at the beach, she thought of him, and wondered at the wasted years when she could have called him and said, "Here I am, come get me." The moment had never been right, and by the time she felt happy enough within herself to have the guts to do it, she no longer wanted to see him. Sometimes one of the young men showed glimmers of his intensity; at other times, Iris's dealer came up with a particular grade of grass that almost reproduced the palpitations and hunger she had felt in Rome. Eventually the weight of his memory faded. Still, she told no one about him. To one who lives in Los Angeles and earns good money in another business, movie stars are a tawdry lot.

Paula made a comeback. Szos told her it was a comeback, a term he used to convince himself that she had once been an actress.

"Who'd want me?" Paula had asked reasonably.

"You're still young, and they make movies all the time. They need beauties. There are no more beauties," Szos said. He found her a role in a Western made in Mexico. At the last minute the star was replaced by Kid Crane. Paula phoned Iris from Durango to tell her. "It's going to be awful, I'm sure he's never forgiven me for Rome," she wailed.

"He's a nice man, really, you'll like him," said Iris. "Don't be scared. I'm sure he's forgotten all about it."

Kid Crane fell in love with Paula and she fell in love with him. He admitted that he had had profound doubts about her during the filming of *These Lustful Stones,* and that he was staggered at the change. "You're such a woman," he told her as they wandered over the arid hills of Durango.

"That's what being a mother does for a woman," said Paula.

He loved Breeze as if he were his own child. He admired Raoul: Kid Crane was a movie buff. The decline of the Rumanian director touched Kid Crane deeply; it could have happened to him if he'd stayed in Rome, he knew that. Sometimes he remembered Rome with a pang; he asked Paula about Iris.

"She's a millionaire now," said Paula, her voice full of admiration. "She runs a whole company with her father, but she does all the brainwork."

Paula and Kid Crane were married at an open-air ceremony conducted in a canyon by Su-an Ram Dam and a team of chanting Buddhist nuns, among whom was Charlie, now renamed Ahm. Raoul gave Paula away, and Breeze, his long de Vigny locks flowing over a white smock, acted as the bridesperson. Iris stood by wearing a pink dress of thin Indian cotton that clung to her body. The presence of the groom awoke a glow in her so sensual that people around her felt the hum of sex and were surprised to find themselves turned on at a wedding ceremony, especially one so spiritual. Su-an Ram Dam caught Iris's humming vibrations and offered her a private class, something she had never done before. "No thank you," said Iris. "I'm fine." Raoul brought his new son-in-law over to Iris after the ceremony was over, and introduced them. "How do you do?" said Kid Crane, offering his hand. Iris watched the fingers tremble in the air, reaching for her. She kept her hand at her side. "It's very nice to meet you," she said. "I hope you will be very happy." Then she went and hugged Paula, who whispered in her ear: "He's really very nice, and he told me he likes you."

Iris drove home to her house. It was now worth two million dollars, and when she had finished building the extra rooms it would be worth more. She found two of the carpenters still there, and helped them hone down the ridged slats for the new sun deck. After they left, Iris watching the younger one's back with its little ridge of blond hairs just above his coccyx, she went back into the house and turned on the record player. It was a heavy rock album; she considered other music sappy, having lost her patience for lyrics and lyricism long ago. She sat at her big table, hewn out of a slice of redwood and trailed south by two cowboys in a pickup truck, and looked through the mail from that morning. She saw that the cleaning woman had signed for a parcel. She got up to look for it, pulling the skirt away from her thigh; she was unused to skirts and resented the way the fabric pulled at her legs and slowed her down.

She found the package leaning by the refrigerator; it was just under five feet high, wrapped in brown paper, covered in Scotch tape applied with an inexpert hand. The kitchen clock said five o'clock. She knew that if she turned on the Merv Griffin show she could see Paula and Kid Crane, taped the day before, explaining to Merv how they had been lucky the second time they met. Raoul had gone to the taping, and told her about it when he came to have dinner with her the night before. "They treat them like cattle," he said. "The questions were stupid, the lighting was terrible, and no retakes!"

"I'm not interested," Iris had said.

Wearily she lugged the parcel into the living room; it was heavy. There was an envelope taped to the top. She opened it. "It's one of the things I have left," she read. "I thought it would make you happy. Raoul." She put the card down on the table. She hoped it wasn't a prop from one of his films; she would hate it, she thought, if he was trying to attract attention to himself on the day of his daughter's wedding. She had worked hard to eliminate folly and illusion from her life. What was Raoul doing? She turned the card over, but there was nothing else on it. She kicked off her shoes and started pulling at the Scotch tape. The package was about the height of a child. She pulled the paper off, and saw a black surface, curved, like a boy's body. She thought of the carpenter's back.

She pulled some more; the paper ripped, and the top part came away. She saw a gold turban chipped in places, speckled with little raised stars. She went on her knees and, with urgent hands, separated the last shreds of paper from the body of the statue.

It was the Moor of the Château Rose, laughing up at her insulated ceiling with unseeing ivory eyes.

ABOUT THE AUTHOR

JOAN JULIET BUCK was born in California and brought up in France and England. She now lives in Manhattan, where she is a contributing editor of *Vogue. The Only Place to Be* is her first novel.